Mrs. S. C. Hall

Sketches of Irish Character

A New Edition

Mrs. S. C. Hall

Sketches of Irish Character
A New Edition

ISBN/EAN: 9783744731546

Printed in Europe, USA, Canada, Australia, Japan

Cover: Foto ©Andreas Hilbeck / pixelio.de

More available books at **www.hansebooks.com**

SKETCHES
OF
IRISH CHARACTER

BY MRS. S. C. HALL

A New Edition

WITH 61 ILLUSTRATIONS ON STEEL AND WOOD BY MACLISE,
GILBERT, HARVEY, AND CRUIKSHANK

London
CHATTO & WINDUS, PICCADILLY
1892

DEDICATION.

My dear Sir,

The first series of these " Sketches"—then crushed into a small volume—was simply an evidence of my desire to do for my native BANNOW, what Miss Mitford had done for her "Village," and to Miss Mitford, in all the mingled anxiety and pride of young authorship, I dedicated my first fruits.

You—who have been, and are Miss Mitford's attached and zealous friend—who estimated the brightness of her nature, and the freshness of her genius, before you had witnessed her suffering and patience, and ministered to her the balm of friendship, in these—her later—yet most honoured days—must permit me to inscribe this edition to YOU, in testimony of my sincere respect and admiration of one, who blends the delicacy of the poet, with the practical wisdom of the man of business, and the benevolence of the Christian.

Your sincere friend,

ANNA MARIA HALL.

To Francis Bennoch, Esq.
&c. &c.

INTRODUCTION TO THE THIRD EDITION.

THE Public having required a third Edition of these "SKETCHES OF IRISH CHARACTER," I have been called upon to prepare it—to revise the stories originally published, and to add several new; and the publishers have given to them the advantage of very beautiful illustrations.

The "Sketches" chiefly refer to one locality—the parish of Bannow, on the sea-coast of the County of Wexford—my native place, where the earlier years of my life were passed. The world has little interest in the personal feelings of a writer; but my readers will, I hope, permit me to say that my first impressions of Ireland were derived from the very favourable circumstances under which I was placed; for, in this neighbourhood, there was, comparatively, none of the poverty, and consequent wretchedness, to be encountered, unhappily, elsewhere. I have so frequently dwelt upon its almost exclusive privileges and peculiar features in these "Sketches," as to render it unnecessary for me to preface them further than by stating they are, in general, accurate, as regards the persons and the scenery; although, no doubt, the happy associations, connected with them, have made both appear brighter, in my eyes, than they may seem to others. It is certain, however, that this district of the County of Wexford is superior to any other part of the south of Ireland. Its landlord is not an absentee; he is surrounded by an attached and prosperous tenantry; the land is naturally rich, and facilities for improving it are many.

The Baronies of Bargy and Forth, in the former of which Bannow is situated, are especially fortunate in possessing, to a very remarkable extent, all the moral, social, and natural advantages, which are to be found, although more limited, throughout the County. The inhabitants are, chiefly, descendants of the Anglo-Norman settlers, who, in the reign of the second Henry, invaded and conquered—or, rather subdued—Ireland; and, until very recently, they retained so much of their ancient customs and manners, as actually to speak a language unknown in other districts of the Kingdom.

The ruins of castles are so numerous, that, over a surface of about 40,000 acres, there stand the remains of fifty-nine; and the sites of many more can still be pointed out. The people are to this day, " a peculiar people," and retain much of their English character. This is apparent, not alone in the external aspect of the country—in the skilfully farmed fields, the comparatively comfortable cottages, the barns attached to every farmyard, the well-trimmed hedgerows, stocked with other vegetables than potatoes; the peasantry are better clad than we have seen them elsewhere, and have an air of sturdy independence, which they really feel, and to which they are justly entitled, for it is achieved by their own honest industry.

In these " Sketches" I have aimed at a higher object than mere amusement,—desiring so to picture the Irish character, as to make it more justly appreciated, more rightly estimated, and more respected, in England; at the same time, I have studied—but I trust in a kindly and affectionate spirit—so to notice the errors and faults that prevail most among my countrymen and countrywomen, as to be of some use in inducing a removal of them. There are none powerless to effect good—except those who persuade themselves that attempts to produce it are hopeless. It has been my steady purpose, and zealous wish, to do justice to the many estimable qualities of the Irish peasantry, of whom it has been truly said, " their virtues are their own ; but their vices have been forced upon them."

With these " Sketches" I was first introduced to the Public; I have since produced other works, but none into which my heart so completely entered. They gave me, I presume to say, a place in public favour ;—it has been my earnest and continued study to retain it.

CONTENTS, AND LIST OF ILLUSTRATIONS.

A RAMBLING INTRODUCTION

TO THE FIFTH EDITION OF

MY FIRST BOOK.

I AM requested to write an Introduction to the Fifth Edition of
"Sketches of Irish Character," which—although published nearly
a quarter of a century ago—still find favour with a public, from whom
I have received only indulgent kindness for so many years. Looking
clearly back upon my Childhood I seem as if I were contemplating a
handful of spring flowers—some wild, some cultivated—which have
gone on increasing and blossoming ever since. Although an Author,
I am without a grievance! I have had nothing to complain of.
The changing seasons still bring me changes of enjoyment—the
simple pleasures of my youth have not lost their zest—

> "I love the sound of waves—the first
> That woke my childhood's glee,"

as fervently as when I sat on the wild rocks of my beloved BANNOW,
or gathered sea-shells in those sandy bays—which I shall see no
more !

The flowers of my own garden are as bright and as sweet to my
senses, as those of which my grandmother was so proud; and though
the Firfield grass is not as green, as that which carpeted the meadows
of Graige—yet the buttercups of the meadow are as yellow and the
daisies as star-like as those which glittered with the cuckoo-sorrel in
our old orchard !—I feel their association of the past with the present,
and enjoy my thoughts. What a blessing it is when even sickness and
sorrow are but chronicled by gratitude that they are passed—nay, when
happiness is renewed by the remembrance. I look back with freshness
and cheerfulness upon sorrows and vexations, which though bitter and

hard to endure at the time, seem to me now, as those light clouds, that render earth more pleasant, by veiling sunshine. I can recall two of my country's proverbs which beautifully express my meaning. "The blackest thorn bears the whitest blossom." "The darkest hour is the hour before day." I relish the return to country life after some twenty "London seasons," as a renewal of my youth—yet delight as much as ever when a few days in town brings me once more among those I have long known and loved.

I am turning my introduction into a confession—but so it must be even at the risk of being an egotist. I have enjoyed so many blessings —received so much kindness from strangers as well as friends— been cheered by such sweet household love, that were I to refuse my thankfulness the right of words—I should feel self-convicted of ingratitude to my God and to my fellow creatures. The mercy of GOD has guided me all my days—and I can sing with the Psalmist, "For thou, Lord, hast made me glad through thy works : and I will rejoice in giving praise for the operations of thy hands."

So much—perhaps too much—of my present self, and now a few words of old times—to which this book has reference.

I can remember how my voice trembled when, little more than a bride, I ventured to read to my husband the sketch of "MASTER BEN,"—the very first of those "Sketches of Irish Character,"—which multiplied so rapidly, and have been so well received—more particularly in America. "The Lights and Shadows of Irish Life," "The Tales of the Irish Peasantry," even "The Whiteboy," are all akin to the "Sketches"—which, imperfect as they are as *tales*, are more true to actual life than the more varied stories which followed.

In writing the "Sketches of Irish Character," I was, as I have said elsewhere, simply anxious to make the sea-side village in which I passed my childhood favourably known to the English—I did not *then* think that I might be useful to my country by endeavouring to correct the failings of its affectionate and generous peasantry : as I have tried to do, for instance, in "We'll see about it," "Take it easy," and in others of that class. I only, as it were, copied the people whom I had known when my life was young.

My dear mother, anxious that I should become a good arithmetician, had determined that I should understand the "science of numbers" to perfection. Master Ben,—Schoolmaster of Cullinstown, being considered "grate intirely at the figures," was therefore engaged to visit twice a week the "big house," which he did, winter and summer, through fair and foul weather, for three years. Many curious specimens of shells and sea-weed—many wild birds tamed for my amusement—many strings of sea-birds' eggs, brought from the Keroe and Saltee Islands—many, many bunches of wild flowers, and curious things gathered when the waves cast back in disdain upon the shore what they had torn from hapless vessels, which they dashed against our cruel rocks—did my old master bring; and much did I learn from him quaintly and strangely of "ould ancient legends, and natural history, and botany," and superstitions and bits of garbled history which made me love my country all the more—but as to arithmetic! he certainly led me on to algebra (my mother keeps my books to this hour), but I never could, or did, comprehend any one of the four first rules, which I have often since most grievously regretted. If my improvement was doubted, MASTER BEN showed my books, where sum after sum was noted down with praiseworthy exactness, and I really believe he thought I understood all their mysteries.

I remember thinking that this quaint old schoolmaster ought to be as interesting a person as Miss Mitford's "Mole Catcher," and determined to try if I could make him so. "Master Ben" and John Williams—("The Bannow Postman")—were the first to inspire me with a literary ambition. As I have said, I well remember reading *that,* my first Sketch, to my husband, glancing from the seamed and blotted page to his young face, then unmarked by the cares and anxieties he has since often felt both for himself and me, and wondering if it were really true that I—*I* could write anything worth being printed and—paid for.

I went on from one Sketch to another, writing chiefly for those pretty Annuals now quite gone by, and grateful to him who cared for, while he corrected, all I did. When a publisher offered me a hundred pounds if I would write a new Sketch, and collect those I had written

into one little volume for publication, honestly I told him I thought it
too much, though I *did* certainly exult in the "great fact;" and then
how astonished I was to find myself "famous," in the generous pages of
the "Literary Gazette," and occupying two columns of "The Times!"
I can also remember how fearful my husband was that literature—
its cares, its claims, and its fame—would unfit me for the duties
which every woman is bound to consider only next to those
she owes her Maker. I daresay I was a little puffed up at first, but
happily for myself, and for those who had near and dear claims
upon my love and labour, I very soon held my responsibilities
as an author second to my duties as a woman; they "*dove-tailed*"
charmingly, and I have ever found the necessary change to domestic
from literary care, though sometimes laborious, not only healthful,
but pleasant.

I have said the Characters and Sketches in this volume are more
decidedly taken from "the life" than any that followed; as I became
more skilled in "author craft," I learned how I could better employ
my materials, and *combine*, as well as *copy*, grafting invention upon
facts, and facts upon invention; but the characters *here* are all
portraits, copied with fidelity and earnestness of purpose.

A buoyant yet observant child, without childish companions, I had
to seek from the animate and inanimate world interest and amusement, and of these, in and about my old home, there was an
abundance—a wild and rocky shore—bays strewn with shells—the
old Church of Bannow, with its history and legends—a cultivated
domain, gardens fruitful and beautiful—plenty of old castles and
abbeys in the neighbourhood, and but few neighbours, except in
summer, when the bays of Bannow, Cullinstown, and Graige tempted
many to put up with the accommodation of our sea-side cottages
during the bathing season; but then there was a small library of rich
and sound books, and my grandmother's Huguenot descent and extensive reading in her own language, rendered me familiar in childhood with much that was good in the literature of France. I never
remember that dear grandmother but in wretched health—her beauty
and suffering were the heroism of my childhood, while my gentle,

loving mother divided her time between the bed-room of her parent and the school-room of her child; but indeed, the whole district was my "school-room."

"Master Ben,"—"Old Frank," who had been two and forty years coachman in the family—the old bathing woman, "Nelly Parell"—my nurse, Mary Redmond—all delighted in imparting their stock of legends and fairy lore to the "darlint," who loved to listen as much as they to tell. When my poor grandmother's illness became serious, my mother was more constantly in her chamber, and I had a great deal of leisure. In the early morning returning from my sea bath, up the long walk, lingering amid the old trees, or reading, beside the stream in the domain which encircled an ornamental cottage that was covered with ivy, and formed a very city of refuge for small birds, from the golden crested wren to the overbearing starling—that cottage, with its gable, its rustling ivy, its low dark windows, its mossy seats, and grassy banks, and pure limpid stream creeping over the smooth pebbles, after escaping from a cascade, which for years was my ideal of a waterfall, its mysterious arch, composed of the jaw-bone of a whale, which I used to gaze upon with such grave astonishment—that cottage was my paradise! I could hear the ocean rolling in the distance, the refreshing sea breeze passing over fields of clover and banks of roses, was freighted with perfume; the parent birds would fearlessly pick up the crumbs at my feet. I kept my favourite books in a drawer of the rustic dresser. I had a volume of Elegant Extracts, an old edition of the Psalms of David in French, which belonged to some of my grandmother's Huguenot ancestors, and a French Testament; I had an old edition of Shakespeare and Racine, a cherished Robinson Crusoe, Watts' Logic, and Poems, odd volumes of Cowper and of Young; I knew little of Moore, and nothing of Byron, but I knew Quarles and Herbert and Shirley, and Walter Scott's Marmion, and MILTON, and often when I closed HIS volume, as the sound of the breakfast bell came through the trees slowly and deliberately, like the measured tread of the old butler Dennis, who pealed it, often have I wondered if hereafter I should meet and *know* that blind man, in heaven. I cannot account for it now, how a child so volatile as I was, so full of energy and motion, could pore for hours over grave earnest books, with as full enjoyment as over poetry, or how my even greater pleasure was to wander to the sand banks, amid which the old church of Bannow is almost entombed, and contemplate the old graves and mouldering records of humanity. I certainly never felt the time hang heavily—never felt it dreary or lonely; my mind seemed full of thoughts, and when aroused to the present, I was as joyful to bound homeward, even before tears, which gathered and fell—I knew not why—were dried. I was often reproved for my dreamy moods, but not by my gentle mother. "I trust in God," she would say, "that she thinks and feels for a purpose; she reads nothing that I do not give her; she receives all her teaching from my lips; she makes acquaintance after her own fancy with God's works by sea and land; and as to the legends, why they belong to her country, though not to mine. I know when she thinks, and I know when she dreams; every key has its minor and major, her spirits and strength would become exhausted but for these rests." A nervous terror prevented my ever wandering by moonlight; I was content to watch the moonbeams on the sea from my nursery window, and observe the light from the Hook light-house beam out upon the waters; as a child, I was afraid of the moon, and even now the less I see of it the better. I certainly was sufficiently affected by fairy and ghost lore to avoid rambling by moonlight, and to tremble at darkness. It seems to me I must have been a most happy child; I believe the only person I feared was my grandmother's second husband, the only father I ever knew; yet he it was who made me love Milton, and many winter evenings have I sat at his feet while he read aloud to my mother and grandmother grave, staid, books, and I used to look at the great birds on the window curtains, and try to listen even to that awful "Book of Martyrs," yet thinking it far pleasanter when they sang catches and trios; for even while "grandmamma" was very ill, when her pain lulled, she would sing, and I used to think it cruel to be sent to bed as they were singing—to go into that cold dark hall, all full of shadows—the moon streaming through the fanlight upon the gilt pipes of the old organ, the wind roaring round the house, and setting the old dinner bell ringing at intervals. And then we seldom passed a winter without having two or three shipwrecks on our rocky coast, and once I remember hearing the guns of a distressed vessel, and longing to arouse the house, yet perfectly unable to rush through the darkness, and bewildered by my desire to do something, in a fit of desperation ringing the wrong bell, and rousing every one, which, after all, was fortunate ; for away went my dear grandfather and the men servants to the beach. I remember thinking how beautifully the lights and lanterns shone upon the snow, and how grand and mysterious the figures and shadows were, losing all the proper feeling which ought to arise out of a shipwreck, in excitement and enthusiasm, and sitting up all night to prepare comforts for the sailors, who really were, with some few sad exceptions, housed before day-break. It seems strange to confess it, but I felt a sort of triumph in a shipwreck. I wept by the hour, and for days and nights could neither rest nor sleep ; yet a wild feeling of enjoyment mingled with my terror of a wreck. I wrote tales of shipwrecks on my slates, and set sailors' songs to music, and never but then longed to be a boy—only that I might be shipwrecked. How was it that I, who could not cross the hall in the dark without becoming paralysed by terror, had no terror of the stormiest sea that ever cast a helpless ship from the breakers to the rocks ? There was a general belief amongst the servants and the cottagers that some day or other "Miss Marie would either be drowned out of Master's boat, that she was always after, or break her neck off a horse." Yes, I certainly dearly loved a stormy sea and a wild gallop, and few little girls achieved the age of ten who had more escapes by sea and land. " It's a great blessing entirely," said Nelly Parell to my mother, "it's a wonderful blessing that Miss has a terror of the dark, and no love for the moon—if it wasn't for *that* she'd be down on the beach by night as well as by day, and there would soon be an end of her." It was simply a return of my old love for the sea that in after years forced me to write "The Buccaneer."

Perhaps some of my friends and readers, may feel an interest in seeing the foundation stone of some of my erections—hearing the key note of my small compositions.

The story of "Father Mike" originated after this fashion :

There was one guest at Graige whose knife and fork was always laid on the Sabbath day—winter and summer made little difference—there it was, and from the side window of the dining room I used to watch for the coming of the Roman Catholic priest of the parish. The good old Father Edward Murphy, had been educated in France, and was almost an ideal picture of the old abbés of past times; it would be impossible *now* to find even a *faint* copy of "Father Murphy." Mild and gracious, with all the refinement of the French school, even my stately grandmother, with all her Huguenot feeling, used to say Father Ned had but one fault—he was a Roman Catholic; but he had saved her and hers in the rebellion of '98 from destruction, and when the time of retribution came, and the priests of the county Wexford were under the ban of government, she wrote a letter to a person "having authority," representing his care of her and her daughter, and his exertions to save the property and life of her husband, and in due time the Bannow priest was told he had nothing to fear; thus they were bound to each other, and it was curious to see the good breeding with which they watched *themselves* to prevent a word escaping which might wound the religious feelings of the other. Sometimes "the Master" would indulge a sly jest at the priest's expense, but "the Mistress" invariably came with her half broken English to the rescue, and thus the Huguenot and the Roman Catholic sat at the same board as friends—fellow-labourers they certainly were for the good of the poor, and in all things appertaining to their advantage they worked together. Dear old Father Murphy was so good to me; I was his pet, and he was never tired of answering my questions, or hearing me repeat the poems I had committed to memory—but if ever those questions broached upon religious matters, he would say—"Little Marie must ask mamma that." He was never angry with me but once : and this was how I gave him displeasure. In summer he always read his Breviary for half an hour before dinner, walking round the wilderness—and in winter there was a fire in the little parlour for "Father Ned," and there he retired when the dressing bell rang. I had often seen this Breviary in his hand, a large worn book clasped with silver; it was a great mystery to me, and I longed to solve it. When done with it for the time being, he put it into the pocket of his thick blue great coat, which he wore summer and winter, and which dangled over the sides of his white horse, like a guardsman's cloak; this coat always hung in the hall, and at last I took courage, when they were deep in some political question, I crept out of the dining-room and withdrew the book from the pocket, and went into the little parlour, to examine its contents, by the blazing light of Kendal coal.

The volume was illuminated, and I became perfectly absorbed by the prayers and litanies and number of saints, until I unfortunately turned over a page where there was some consecrated wafer. I had never seen or heard of it, I thought it looked very pretty, and might be very nice; I placed a piece between my lips, when suddenly Father Ned's hand fell heavily upon my shoulder, his deep set dark eyes sparkled with indignation, and his cheeks flushed. He snatched the wafer from my lips, and called me "Heretic," I heard *that* and though he said more, I remembered nothing else. He had left the room to seek his handkerchief, and had missed the book.

I was both ashamed and indignant. I told him the truth frankly, and begged his pardon, and I clasped the book and placed it in his hands. His displeasure was short-lived, and my shame and sorrow at having displeased him were sincere, but I wept bitterly at being called "heretic," for child as I was, it taught me that between the two faiths "was a great gulph fixed."

He was a good, kind, gentle man for all that, and I loved him better than Friar Butler or Friar Doyle, of Danes Castle. They had been educated in Italy, and used to teach me Italian; and Friar Butler, I remember, kept huge greyhounds, and hunted hares, and they cultivated flowers to perfection, and I believe educated young men for the priesthood; but they only dined with us at festivals; they used to send my grandmother game, and she sent them hampers of strawberries and peaches; we were rich in peaches; our two "lions" were a peach tree which once "had been put in the newspaper," as having borne and ripened nine hundred peaches; and our myrtle was twenty feet high and fifteen broad! growing in the open air. What innocent people we all were! We were so proud of our peach tree and myrtle! There was a peach tree in the County Waterford which bore nearly as great a number, and I remember the fact made us all very uneasy and uncomfortable; but the gardener after visiting his rival, rejoiced us with the assurance that the peaches were not in any respect as fine as ours.

I wonder what Rowland Hill, that Emperor of postal arrangements, would have thought of "The Bannow Postman," poor John Williams; he was nearly, if not quite, the last of his calling. The establishment of a Post-office at Carrick hastened his death (he was not above 80, the Bannow people live to a great age), and I believe all his descendants are gone to America.

The character of Peggy the Fisher, in "Lilly O'Brien," was suggested by "Peg Dunn," a woman whose height and loud-hailing voice rendered her rather an object of terror to my childhood. She was one of the itinerant "egg women" who "travelled the country," ostensibly to purchase eggs, or wool, or butter, or whatever the cottagers or farmers' wives had to sell; and who became circulating mediums of news, and love, and smuggling—active agents during the periods of public disturbance; always a chatty, amusing class, full of anecdote and legend; enduring great bodily fatigue; a little suspected of want of good faith in their dealings, but certain of the warmest seat in the kitchen, the best bed, and a share of "whatever was going." The character was introduced in my little drama of "The Groves of Blarney;" in which Power performed with the success he always commanded, and Yates made an admirable "Peggy."

"The Bannow Boatman," whose name was not "Larry Moore," but Paddy Cahill, was, I must say, a faithful portrait. When the Sketches were first published, many persons visited the "Island of Bannow," and bore testimony to the fidelity of the sketch.

Paddy has long since slept in the church-yard, but I fear there are still many on the "Island," who, like poor Paddy, do not "think of to-morrow." I have not always given the real names to the real people, for the Irish are not like our transatlantic neighbours, fond of being "put in a book," they shrink from such exposures with peculiar sensitiveness.

"Ah, then, Ma'am, dear," said the girl who is called "Norah Clary," and who really had as many "wise thoughts," as most persons of her age and sex, "Ah, then, Ma'am, dear, knowing you all the days of your life, and loving the very ground you walked upon, wasn't it hard entirely of you *to put me in a book*—making a fair show of me all over the world!" Another instance I can call to mind—having a tolerably good Irish cook, I was provoked by her silence—a very unusual fault—I could never get her to answer a question, and when I sent for her she would hold the door in her hand, and after a brief "Yes, ma'am;" or "No, ma'am;" start off with such evident delight at her escape, that I resolved to know *why* she desired to avoid me.

"Mary," I said, one morning, "I want to know why you answer my questions so abruptly. Shut the door—there, let go the handle, and come here—have you any fault to find with your situation?"

"No, ma'am—never a fault at all with the place—Oh, no! God bless you."

"Then what is the reason that whenever I send for you I can hardly get you to answer my questions? And when I go into the kitchen, you invariably rush into the scullery?"

"It's just nothing particular, ma'am."

"But there must be a reason for such un-servant-like conduct."

"No reason in life, ma'am."

Mary had got back to the door, and regained firm possession of the handle.

"I know you can talk fast enough sometimes, and yet, as I have said before, you will not even answer my questions."

She made a sudden rush out—then returned—thrust her head through the opening, and exclaimed piteously—"Ah, then, let me alone, ma'am, dear, you know you'll be putting me in a book!"

They may have a superstition about this, as they have about being weighed and measured; but certainly the "*people*" of Ireland have no ambition to see themselves in print.

I remember, when writing those Sketches, to have been strongly imbued with a desire to do justice to the memory of the faithful old servants, whom I may rank amongst my earliest and most devoted friends. "Old Frank," the old coachman, who, I believe, loved me, because I loved horses, and often declared that "every one was born with a *ganious* for something, and Miss Marie with a ganious for horsemanship," was most devoted in his attachment to every member of the family, in which, as I have said, he had lived forty years. When my mother was yet a young girl, he was anxious for her glory as a horse-woman, as he afterwards became for mine; but she was too timid to mount fearlessly; and he always alluded to this as a misfortune, a thing to be deplored: indeed, he considered it a disgrace.

I look back at the dozen or two of old servants and old retainers who belonged to that house, and the house to them, as I do to the legends of past days—there are no such people now—here and there, when wandering amongst my friends, I see an old grey-headed "follower," or note the reverential curtsey—and hear, "God save you kindly, Ma'am;" or "You're kindly welcome to ould Ireland, madam," from an aged nurse, or housekeeper; but servants such as those my memory calls before me at this moment, are an extinct race.

Their one single devotion to their employer, and his "seed, breed, and generation,"—their earnest affection—their championship—suffering no word of disrespect to be uttered against master or mistress, family or friends—not only ready, but anxious to do battle for the glory of those, "them and all belonging to them war born under"—all this has been dying out, and the late EXODUS has swept the very ashes from the country; and no wonder—the devotion was ill-requited.—the people, some five-and-thirty years ago, looked for *no* requital—they were satisfied if not happy in their serfdom—but education and the lightning-like spread of thought and comparison, and calculation, experience, and the newly discovered power of thinking for

themselves, have combined with the Encumbered Estates Bill, to over-
throw the poetry of devotion towards the ancient families in which
they breathed, moved, and had their being. The Irish servant now
expects his *quid pro quo* quite as much as the English servant; but he
has his advantages and his disadvantages, all the same as in old
times: he is more noisy, more blundering, and untidy, than an
English footman; but though without the enthusiastic attachment
to his employer, he is more anxious, more zealous, and more physi-
cally and spiritually good-natured—he has not *much* respect for the
"honour of the family," but he has still a *little*, and would rather,
if in a tradesman's establishment, conceal the fact from his old
mother, or his pretty sweetheart, supposing her to be an Irish girl;
but the old self-denying, faithful race are gone, and my young friends
may, perhaps, fancy they never existed. Bannow was, as I have
so often joyed to repeat, a favoured spot, blessed with resident landlords, and prosperous tenants; the churchyard numbers nearly all
among its graves, whose peculiarities are chronicled in these pages;
and, except in a few instances, their children have ceased to inherit
the land—they are gone to Australia, or Canada, or New Zealand—
there are fewer cottages, and sundry new faces and new names.

> " We took no note of them,
> But by their loss ——"

The plough and the harrow have passed over the spot where Graige
House once stood, and where my happy childhood was passed.

The Master of Grange—who purchased Graige after the death of
my relatives, from the heir at law—an accomplished scholar, a
polished gentleman, and amongst the dearest friends of the poet
MOORE—he has been called "*home*," and as yet I believe his stately
residence, which took the place of the pretty clergyman's cottage,
where Henrietta and Marian and Ellen,[*] faithfully pictured in "The
Bannow Postman," lived in my time, has not since been inhabited—

> "Old times are changed—old manners gone."

---

[*] I am almost ashamed thus to chronicle the march of time, but more than *one* of
those ladies is absolutely—a grandmamma : I have this excuse to offer—*they married
very young.*

But how bewildering it is to recall the circumstances which, unobserved and imperceptible at first, have gradually revolutionized the whole aspect of Ireland. It was said, when there was no agitation the country would prosper, and as far as the bare land is concerned, there can be no doubt of the prophecy being fulfilled—the *country*, the soil, the hills and valleys, the acres—will prosper, but where are those who were " to the fore" when the prophecy was uttered ? They have taken with them beyond seas, the faith, the habits, and the *prejudices* so long cherished—parting with their native land, sooner than part with *them*.

The Encumbered Estates' Court has swept away the Castle Rackrents, and it is only in the admirable pages of Miss Edgeworth, that "Thady," and the unfortunate spendthrift on whom the old man's fidelity was lavished—find a home. Where now could Lady Morgan find an " O'Donnell," or a " Wild Irish girl ?". If Banim and Gerald Griffin were still with us, where could they find heroes and heroines ! Fortunately, Moore withdrew our melodies from amid the ruins of time, and gifted them with immortality, and Lover has wedded several of our beautiful superstitions to poetry which Moore might have acknowledged without lowering his pinions.

I could identify all my characters—but to do so—I should add a volume—not an Introduction to my " Sketches of Irish Character."

My last two visits to Ireland gave me no reading, new or old, of Irish character. What can be seen of Irish character on well-regulated railroads ? What wit can be gleaned from erect and taciturn policemen ?

It is impossible to say what may be. I should not be surprised to find an outside jaunting car driven by a London cabman. I confess to looking anxiously, and I had almost said hopefully, for even the shadow of a beggar in Sackville Street. They were too numerous at Killarney, but they were not of the " right sort"—they were beggars of the new régime ; they did not ask for " a little tester, just for the honour of auld Ireland—lady dear ;" but for " sixpence or a shilling, to help pay our passage to Amerikay—sure the sooner we can get away the better ; there's nothing here to keep us, if we want to keep flesh on our bones."

Miles, and miles, and miles we passed in 1852 without meeting one human being! Miles—up hills, down dales, over those bounding leaping rivers—and no creature to greet us with "God save you, and send you a good journey;" or, "God be praised for a fine day;" or, "Take it easy up the hill—may-be the lady would like an air of the fire within there, and the mealy potatoes are just on the boil!"

No smoke from the cottier's evening fires curling up the mountains, or climbing like incense up the blue vault of heaven, until it mingled with the atmosphere. If the deserted cottages had been fairly levelled, and the plough passed over their graves, it would have been paradise in comparison to the bleared and burnt effect of the shattered and roofless walls. More than once I saw the living skeleton of a poor cat, clinging with the instinct of its race to the abandoned dwelling, and staring, unconscious of danger, and incapable of flight, at the carriage as it passed. I daresay, nay, I am sure, the people are better away—better in another land than in the one where those they loved starved and died; but of all the wants the heart aches for, is the want of forms and voices where they once were seen and heard.

Yes! it is better for the landlords to have those people away, and better for the people to be away from the landlords. And in fifty years, or less, those who have moved off in that mighty exodus will have sunk into foreign graves, and their children have become units in the mass of a young and vigorous population—spreading their thousands and tens of thousands over the unmeasured breadths, and lengths, and depths of the new world!

Were I now to kneel upon my grandmother's square grey tomb in Bannow Church, when the moon was rising, the tide flowing gently in, the Hook light flinging its arrows of warning and guidance over the billows, I could easily, in that lonely place, fancy myself *the last woman*—the very last living creature, where once I was surrounded by young life!

Alas! I could now wander from the church, through the moor of Bannow, up the hill of Graige, past the windmill and the forge, and where the cottages stood, and not recognise a single countenance, or hear a single blessing! The children, the few left in the land, to wait until sent for to the new home of their fathers, would regard me as a stranger.

There is the Bay of Graige!—there the Keroe and Saltee Islands —there the Mountain of Forth, with its angry cloud cap—yonder I know are the houses of Grange and Kiltra, and Barristown; and the old castles of Coolhull and Danes are still mouldering away, and over the Scaur are the Seven Castles of Clonmines—and there stretches the Borough of Ballytegue and Cullinstown, and over there—

"Bag and Bun,
Where Ireland was lost and won."

And yet they are but names and memories to me now—the old people are all gone—new priests, new ministers, new people!

I look into the valley, where my own home stood so firmly against hurricane and tempest The wood has marvellously increased. I can remember when much of it was planted. Well do I know where the hospitable home was seated—the long awkward chimneys— the old gable, with its warning bell, the multitude of long narrow windows, the high-backed roof, the in-and-out quaint little courts, the myrtle hedges, the old-fashioned "flower-knot," the temple and shell house, and more than all—my darling cottage—all levelled with the earth—all a legend, a tradition—misty as a dream! And, but for ONE—my good and gentle mother—upon whose patient head the snows of eighty winters have fallen, but not pressed—I might think all Bannow a mere dream! all a mere dream—but for this dear and sweet reality beside me: still beside me, God be thanked, though five and twenty years have passed since, as an author, I first put "pen to paper!"

FIRFIELD, ADDLESTONE,
November, 1854.

LILLY O'BRIEN.

THE sweet Lilly of Bannow!—I shall never forget the morning I first saw her. Her aunt—who does not know her aunt, Mrs. Cassidy?—her aunt is positively the most delightful person in the whole parish. She is now a very old woman, but so "knowing" that she settles all debateable points that arise among good and bad housewives, from Mrs. Connor of the Hill, down to "Polly the Cadger," as to the proper mode of making mead, potato-cakes, and stirabout; and always decides who are the best spinners and knitters in the county; nay, her opinion, given after long deliberation, esta_ blished the superiority of the barrel, over the hand, churn. There is, however, one disputed matter in the neighbourhood, even to this day; Mrs. Cassidy (it is very extraordinary, but who is without some weakness?)—Mrs. Cassidy will have it that a Quern—an obsolete

hand-mill of stone, still patronised by "the ancient Irish"—grinds
wheat better than a mill, and produces finer flour; she, therefore,
abuses all mills, both of wind and water, and persists in grinding her
own corn, as well as in making her own bread. By-the-bye, this very
Quern was in great danger some time ago, when an antiquary, who
had hunted hill and dale seeking for Danish or Roman relics (I forget
which, but it is of little consequence), pounced upon it, declared it
was a stone bowl of great antiquity, and that Mrs. Cassidy's maiden
name, "Maura O'Brien," carved on it in Irish characters, proved it
to have been used, either by Dane or Roman, in some religious
ceremony, or Bacchanalian rite, I cannot take it on myself to say
which:—but this I know, that the old gentleman was obstinate; had
been accustomed to give large sums for ugly things of every description, and thought that Mrs. Cassidy could be induced to yield up her
favourite for three guineas. He never was more mistaken in his
life; nothing could have tempted Mrs. Cassidy to part with her dear
Quern; so he left the neighbourhood, almost heart-broken with
disappointment.

I respect the Quern myself, for it was the means of introducing
me to the sweet Lilly. There, that little path, bordered with oxlips,
primroses, and unobtrusive violets,—

> "Whose deep blue eyes,
> Kiss'd by the breath of heaven, seem coloured by its skies"—

that path leads to Mrs. Cassidy's dwelling. You cannot see the
cottage, it is perfectly hidden—absolutely wooded in; but it is a rare
specimen of neatness. The farm-yard is stocked with ricks of corn,
hay, and furze; with a puddle-like pond for ducks and geese, and a
sty for a little grunting animal, who thinks it a very unjust sentence
that consigns a free-born Irish pig to such confinement. How
beautiful is the hawthorn hedge!—one sheet of snowy blossom—and
such a row of beehives!—while the white walls of the cottage are
gemmed over with the delicate green, half-budded, leaves of the noble
rose-tree, that mounts even to the chimney-top; the bees will banquet
rarely there, by-and-bye. A parlour in an Irish cabin!—yes, in
good truth, and a very pretty one; the floor strewed with the ocean's
own sparkling sand; pictures of half the head saints of the calendar,
in black frames, and bright green, scarlet, and orange draperies; a
corner cupboard, displaying china and glass for use and show, the
broken parts carefully turned to the wall; the inside of the chimney
lined with square tiles of blue earthenware, and over it an ivory
crucifix, and a small white chalice full of holy water; six high-
backed chairs, like those called "education" of modern days: a well

polished round oak table, and a looking-glass of antique form, complete the furniture. The window—forget the window!—oh, that would be unpardonable! It consists of six unbroken panes of glass, and outlooks on such a scene as I have seldom witnessed. Let us open the lattice—what a gush of pure invigorating air! Behold and gaze—ay, first on the flower-bed that extends to where Mrs. Cassidy, with right good taste, has opened a view in the hawthorn hedge; then on, down that sloping meadow, dotted with sheep, and echoing the plaintive bleat of the young and tender lambs; on, on to the towering cliff, which sends, leaping over its blackened sides, a sparkling, foaming torrent, rapid as lightning, and flashing like congregated diamonds, when the sun's brightness is upon it, to the wide spreading sea, which reposes in its grandeur, like a sheet of molten silver. Yonder torrent is strangely beautiful. The rock from which it gushes is dark and frowning, not even a plant springing from its sterile bed; yet the pure water issues from it, full of light, life, and immortality, like the spirit from the Christian's clay. Dear Mrs. Cassidy loves the sea; her husband was owner and commander of a small trading vessel; and her happiest days were spent in coasting with him along the Irish, English, and Welsh shores. He died in his own comfortable home, and was quietly buried in Bannow church, leaving his widow (who, but for her rich brogue, might, from her habits, have passed for an English woman) and one son, independent of the frowns or smiles of a capricious world. They had wherewithal to make them happy in their own sphere.

Edward was, even at two years old, an embryo sailor; a careless, open-hearted boy, who loved everything ardently, but nothing long: except, indeed, his mother, who often regretted that his rambling disposition afforded her so little prospect of enjoyment in after life. She had a brother in the north of Ireland, who, dying, left an only child, our fair Lilly, lovely and desolate in a cold world; but Mrs. Cassidy would not suffer any of her kith or kin to want while she had "full and plinty;" and, accompanied by Edward, then a youth of fifteen, she journeyed to Tyrone, and returned to her cottage with the orphan girl. Soon after the circumstance (of which I was then ignorant), I paid the good lady a visit; and when the country topics, of setting hens, feeding calves, and the dearness of provisions, were exhausted, I inquired if she still used her Quern?

"Is it the Quern?—and that I do, lady; just look at this!—(producing a very nice and snowy cake)—and, sure, bad manners to me for not axing ye to taste it, and my own gooseberry, before! Look at this, there's not a mill in the counthry could turn out such bread as that; and if ye like to see it at work, I've just lifted it under the thorn yonder, to the sunny side of the ditch, and been instructing a

poor colleen, that the world 'ud be after hitting hard, because she'd
no friends, never a one, barring me, if I hadn't brought her here to
be like my own—and why not sure!—and she my brother's child?
Well, I've been tacheing her how to use the Quern, as in duty
bound; she's helpless as yet, but she shall soon know everything."

I followed Mrs. Cassidy into the garden, and, looking towards
"the sunny side of the hedge," saw the child she had mentioned.
She was then thirteen; her figure slight and bending as a willow
wand, and the deep black of her low frock finely contrasted with a
skin transparently white; her hair fell in thick curls over her neck
and shoulders, and in the sunbeams looked like burnished gold; it
was not red—oh, no!—but a pale, shining, and silky auburn. She
was occupied in turning the Quern with one hand, and letting the
grain drop from the other; when she looked towards us, and shook
back the curls from her face, I thought I had never seen so sweet a
countenance; her forehead was high and finely formed; but her soft
blue eyes seemed acquainted rather with tears than smiles : there was
something even more than polite in her address—it possessed much of
rustic dignity; and the tones of her voice were like those of a well-
tuned instrument.

The cottage now possessed for me a charm that was irresistible :
for, superior as the people of Bannow are to the general Irish com-
munity, nothing so pure as the Lilly had ever blossomed among us
before.

Even the rude peasantry seemed to look on her as something far
above them; and when, accompanied by her aunt and cousin, she
passed up Carrick-hill on the Sabbath morning, to join in the prayers
and receive the blessing of the priest, they all watched her footsteps,
and declared that she appeared "a'most like a born gentlewoman"—
no small praise from the humbler Irish, who venerate high birth.
Lilly's time was not idly spent : Mrs. Cassidy resolved that she should
know everything; and as her childish days had been occupied solely in
the business of education—as she read correctly, and wrote intel-
ligibly, it was time, the good lady thought, to teach her all useful
occupations; consequently, spinning succeeded knitting, and then
came marking, shirt-making in all its divisions, namely, felling,
stitching, button-holes, and sewing; then milking and churning;
the best practical method of hatching and bringing up chickens,
ducks, turkeys, geese, and even pea-fowl—two of the latter were,
unfortunately for poor Lilly, given to her aunt just as she arrived at
the cottage; then the never-ending boiling of eggs, and chopping of
nettle-tops for the young turkeys, that they might put forth their red
heads without danger of croup or pip; then the calf, an obstinate
orphan, had to be dosed with beaten eggs and new milk, because she

would not feed as she ought; her cousin's and aunt's stockings to be regularly mended; and, worst of all, a dirty shoeless gipsy, the maid of all work to the establishment, was given to my sweet Lilly's superintendence :—to Lilly, who had never known a mother's care, had been a foolish father's idol, and who had no more method or management than a baby of five months old; however, her patience and gentleness worked wonders; from before sunrise she toiled and thought; and at the end of six months, astonished even Mrs. Cassidy. The Quern never ground such fine flour, the poultry were never so well fatted, the needlework was never so neatly finished, and the cottage never so happy, as since Lilly had been its inmate ! when the toils of the day were comparatively ended, and the refreshing breezes of evening rambled among the sweet yet simple flowers that blossomed in the garden, Lilly loved to sit and read, and watch the blue waters; and as the night advanced, gaze on the meek moon floating in the heavens.

She had resided nearly three years at the cottage, and was, one fine summer evening, sitting under the old thorn tree ; some grief must have been heavy at her heart, for tears, in the full moonlight, were trembling on her long eyelashes : perhaps her aunt had been angry, or Edward had plagued her with too many of his never-ending errands.

" Well, cousin Lilly !" exclaimed a joyous voice, " I never saw such a queer girl as ye are ; ye've been trotting, and mending, and bothering all day, and now, instead of a race, or a dance, or any thing that way, there ye sit, with yer ould books, and yer blue eyes, that bate the world for beauty. Lilly, dear—tears !—as I stand here, you've been crying ! What ails ye, Lilly ?—what ails ye, I say ? I take it very unkind of ye, Lilly,"—and he sat down and took her hand with much affection—" I take it very unkind of ye to have any trouble unknown to me who loves ye (Lilly tried to withdraw her hand) as an own brother. Has mother vexed ye ?"

" Oh, no !"

" Well, then, cheer up ! Come, come ! James Connor has lent us his barn to-night, and I met Kelly the piper going there, and there'll be a merry spree, and you must jig it with me, and Harry too, Lilly, dear ; and mother'll be glad ye go. Come, sure ye're a blessing to the ground ye walk on. Come, put on yer pumps and white stockings. The people say ye're proud, Lilly, but ye're not; though ye might be, for there's not one in the parish like ye."

Lilly's heart fluttered like a caged bird, as she did her cousin's bidding, and accompanied him to the barn, where the piper was blowing his best for the boys and girls, who footed gaily to their favourite jigs. The Irish, old and young, rich and poor, all love dancing; and if their national dance be rude and ungraceful, there is something heart-cheering in witnessing the hilarity with which it inspires them.

While Lilly and Edward were joining in the amusements of the evening, Mrs. Cassidy was sleeping or knitting at her kitchen fire, until disturbed by the raising of the latch, and the "God save all here !" of "Peggy the Fisher."

I wish I could bring Peggy "bodily" before you, but she is almost a nondescript. Her linsey-woolsey gown, pinned up behind, fully displayed her short scarlet petticoat, sky-blue stockings, and thick brogues; a green spotted kerchief tied over her cap—then a sun-burnt, smoke-dried, flatted straw hat—while the basket of fish resting " on a wisp o' hay," completed her head gear. Whenever I met her in my rambles, her clear, loud voice was always employed either in singing the " Collen Rue," or repeating a prayer ; indeed when she was tired of the one, she always returned to the other; and, stopping short the moment she saw me, she would commence with—

" Wisha thin it's my heart bates double joy to see you this very minit. Will ye turn yer two good-looking eyes on thim beautiful fish, leaping alive out o' the basket, my jewil. Och, it's thimselves are fresh, and it's they 'ud be proud if ye'd jist tell us what ye'd like, and then we'd let ye have it a dead bargain !"

Peggy was certainly the queen of manœuvring, and thought it " no harm in life to make an honest pinny out o' thim that could afford it;" but she had strong affections, keen perceptions, and much fidelity ; her ostensible trade was selling fish, but there was often more in her basket than met the eye—French silks, rich lace, or some drops of smuggled brandy for choice customers ; when the farmers' wives could not pay her in cash, they paid her in kind—meal, feathers, chickens, and even sucking-pigs, which Peggy easily disposed of, so extensive were her connexions. Then, she was the general match-maker and match-breaker of the county. Those who could write confided to her their letters : those who could not, made her the messenger of sweet or bitter words as occasion required. But to do Peggy justice, she has even refused money, ay, solid silver and gold, rather than prate of love affairs; for she pitied (to use her own words) " she pitied the young craturs in love ; well remimbering how her own soft heart was broke, many's the day ago." Peggy lived anywhere—everywhere. There were few, married or single, who either had not needed, did not need, or might not need Peggy the Fisher's assistance; and the best bit and sup in the house were readily placed before her.

" Och, Peggy, honey !" exclaimed Mrs. Cassidy, " is that y'erself ! —sure 'tis I that's glad to see ye, agra ; and what 'll ye take ?—a drop of tay, or a trifle o' whiskey to keep the cauld out o' yer stomach ;

or may-be a bit to ate—there's lashings o' white bread, and sweet milk, and the freshest eggs ever was laid."

"Thank ye kindly, Mrs. Cassidy, ma'am; sure it's y'erself has full and plinty for a poor lone woman like myself. I'll take the laste taste in life o' whiskey—and may-be ye'd take a drop o' this, ma'am dear; a little corjial I has, to keep off the water-flash," she added, with a peculiar expression of her left eye, as she placed her basket on the table.

"Have ye got anything striking handsome under thim dirty sea-weeds and dawny shrimpeens, agra?" inquired Mrs. Cassidy.

"May-be I have so, my darlint, though it's little a poor lone cratur like me can afford to do these hard times; and the custom-officers, the thieving villains, in Waterford, Duncannon, and about there, they's grown so 'cute that there's no ho' wid em now, at all, at all. There's a thing that's fit for Saint Patrick's mother anyhow,"—displaying a green shawl with red roses on it—"there's a born beauty for ye!—and such natural flowers, the likes of it not to be met wid in a month o' Sundays—there's a beauty!"

"Sure I've the world and all o' shawls, Peggy, avourneen!—and any how that's not to my fancy. What 'ud ye be axing for that sky-blue silk handkerchief?"

"Is it that ye're after? It's the last I got o' the kind, and who 'ud I give a bargain to as soon as y'erself, Mrs. Cassidy, ma'am?—and ye shall have it for what it cost myself, and that's chape betwixt two sisters; its ra'al Frinch, the beauty!—and it's wronging myself I am to give it for any sich money—dog chape, at six thirteens."*

"Och, ye Tory," exclaimed Mrs. Cassidy: "six thirteens for that bit of a thing! Is that the way ye want to come over a poor widow, ye thief o' the world!" and she avoided looking at the tempting article by fixing her eyes on her knitting, and working with double speed.

"Well, mistress dear, I never thought ye'd be so out of all rason," and Peggy half folded up the handkerchief. Mrs. Cassidy knitted on, and never even glanced at it.

"It's for Miss Lilly, I'm thinking, ye want it; and sure there's nothing in life would look so very nate on her milk-white skin as a sky-blue handkerchief—and so, ma'am, ye won't take it, and it killing chape?"

Mrs. Cassidy shook her head.

"Well, to be sure, for you I would do——so, there! (throwing it on the table) ye shall have it for five thirteens; and that's all as one as ruination to myself."

* The English shilling was so called before the equalization of the coinage; its value being thirteen pence.

"I'll tell ye what, Peggy, a'coushla!" and Mrs. Cassidy took off her spectacles, and looked at the kerchief attentively; "I'll tell ye what; it was four thirteens ye meant; and ye meant also to give Lilly two yards o' that narrow blue riband for knots, that ye promised her long agone."

"I own to the promise, as a body may say," responded Peggy; "I own to the promise; but as to the four thirteens for such as that! —woman alive!—why——"

"Asy, asy, Peggy, honey, no harm in life!" interrupted Mrs. Cassidy, "take the blue rag, it's no consarn o' mine."

"Blue rag, indeed!—but"—after a pause—"it's no rag, Mrs. Cassidy, ma'am, and there's no one knows that betther nor you that has all the wisdom in the whole counthry to y'erself; but, howsomever, take it; sure I wouldn't disagree with an ould residenther, for the vallee of a few brass fardins."

Mrs. Cassidy extracted from the depths of an almost unfathomable pocket, a long stocking, slit like a purse in the centre seam, and tied with a portion of red tape at either end. From amid sundry crown, half-crown, "tin-pinny," and "five-pinny" pieces, the exact sum was selected, paid, and the kerchief deposited in an ancient cupboard that extended half the length of the kitchen, and frowned, in all the dignity of Jamaica mahogany, on the chairs, settle, and deal table.

"The boy and girl are out, I'm thinking," commenced Peggy, as she lit her cutty pipe, and placed herself comfortably in the chimney corner, to enjoy the bit of gossip, or, as well-bred people call it, "conversation," which the ladies, ay, and the lords of the creation, so dearly love.

"They're stept down to Connor's, to have a bit of a jig; I'm right glad to get Lilly out, she's so quiet and gentle, and cares as little for a dance, and less, by a dale, than I do!"

"Och, ma'am dear, that's wonderful, and she so young, and so perfect handsome!—and more than me thinks that same."

"Who thinks so, Peggy?" inquired Mrs. Cassidy, anxiously.

"What!—ye don't know, may be?—Why thin I'll jist hould my tongue."

"Ye'll do no such thing, Peggy; sure the colleen is as the sight o' my eye—as dear to my heart as my own child, which I hope she'll be one o' these days, plase God; and I tould ye as good as that before now—the time, d'ye mind, I bought her the green silk spencer. And why not? A'n't I rareing her up in all my own ways?—and isn't she o' my own blood? And Ned, the wild boy, that has full and plinty to keep him at home, if he'd jist mind the land a bit, and give over his sailing talk, 'ud make a fit husband for her; and thin I could make my sowl, and die aisy in yon little room, betwixt my son and daughter. And I tell ye what, Peggy the Fisher, there's no use in any boy's casting an eye at my Lilly, for Ned's wife she shall be; and I, Maura Cassidy, say it—that was never gainsaid in a thing she took in her head, by man or mortal."

"Very well, my dear, very well, why!" ejaculated Peggy, as, gathering herself over the dying embers of the turf fire, with her elbows on her knees, she jogged slowly backward and forward, like the rocking motion of a cradle. They both remained silent for some time. But Mrs. Cassidy's curiosity, that unwearying feeling of woman's heart, neither slumbered nor slept; and, after waiting in vain for Peggy to recommence the conversation, she could sustain herself no longer.

"Who was talking about Lilly's beauty, Peggy?"

"Oh, my dear, sure everybody talks of it; and why not?"

"Ay, but who in particular?"

"Och, agra!—no one to say particular—that is, very particular."

"I'll tell you what, my good woman," said Mrs. Cassidy, rising from her seat, and fixing herself opposite the Fisher: "if I find out that you've been hearing or saying anything, or what is more hiding anything from me, regarding my boy and girl, when I get you the other side o' the door (for I wouldn't say an indacent thing in my own house), I'll jist civilly tell ye my mind, and ax ye to keep yer distance, and not to be meddling and making wid what doesn't consarn ye."

Peggy knocked the ashes out of her pipe, crammed her middle finger into it to ascertain that all was safe; and, putting it into her pocket, curtsied to Mrs. Cassidy, and spoke—"As to good woman, that's what I was niver called afore; and as to not hearing—would ye have me cork my ears whin I hard Ned and Harry Connor discoorsing about the girl, and I at the other side o' the hedge? Och, och!—to think I should iver be so put upon! But good night, good night to ye, Mistress Cassidy—cork my ears, agra! And now," she continued, as she hastily stepped over the threshold, "I'm at the other side the door, so say yer say."

Mrs. Cassidy's curiosity was more excited than ever; and her short-lived anger vanished as Peggy withdrew.

"Stop, Peggy!—I don't be so hot and so hasty: sure I spoke the word out o' the face,* and meant no harm; come in, a'coushla; it's but natural I'd be fiery about thim, and they my heart's treasures."

In three minutes they were as good friends as ever, and Peggy disclosed the secret, which, notwithstanding her apparent unwillingness, she had visited the cottage to tell. "Ye mind the thorn hedge,

* Without consideration.

where the hill slopes off; well, the day was hot, and I tired with the
heat, and the basket, and one little thing or another; and so down I
sits on the shady side, thinking o' nothin' at all, only the crows—the
craturs—flying to and fro, feeding the young rawpots that kicked up
such a bobbery in their nests wid the hunger; and of what the priest
said from the altar against smuggling, as if he was in right down
arnest about it; and then it crassed my mind, to be sure, how hard
it was for a poor lone body to make an honest bit o' bread these hard
times, and the priest himself agin it; well, by an' by, who comes
shtreelin' up the hill at my back, but your Ned and young Harry
Connor; well, I was jist goin' to spake, but by grate good luck I held
my whist;* well, the first word I hears was from Ned's own mouth,
and they were a good piece off at the time, too; 'She's always the
same,' says he, 'always—sure I love her as my own sister.' 'May-be
more nor that,' says Harry, quite solid. 'Harry,' says Ned, solid
like, too, 'don't go to the fair wid a joke; look, I'd suffer this arm to
be burnt to the stump to do Lilly any good; heart friendship I have
for her, and well she desarves it, but no heart love.' Wid that, my
jewil! I thought Harry Connor 'ud have shook the hand bodily off
Ned; and thin I hard Ned say as how he'd like a more dashinger
girl for a wife nor his cousin; and thin agin he talked about travelling
into furrin parts; and thin they comaraded how Ned 'ud bring them
in company together as often as he could, and talked a dale o' the
dance, and Ned said he never see the colleen yet he'd like to marry;
and Harry's quite done over, for he swore he'd lay down his life for
one look o' love from Lilly's eyes; and they kep' on talkin' and talkin',
and I kep' creepin' an' creepin' alongside the ditch, till the road
turned:—and ye know it was my duty to find the rights of it, and
you consarned."

Mrs. Cassidy waxed very wroth as Peggy's narrative drew towards
a close; she had made up her mind that the cousins should be married,
and thought she had managed the matter admirably. She was always
praising Edward to Lilly, and Lilly to Edward; and it was quite impossible to think that two creatures so perfect (notwithstanding, it
must be confessed, that her son often occasioned her much anxiety),
and, in her opinion, so well suited to each other, should be constantly
in each other's society without falling in love. Lilly's anxiety to
promote her cousin's happiness, the perfect willingness with which
she made all her industry, all her amusements, yield to his caprice,
convinced Mrs. Cassidy that she would not oppose her wishes: and
then came another puzzling consideration—Edward had always
appeared so very fond of Lilly! The poor woman was fairly baffled;

Held my tongue—kept silence.

how she wished that Harry Connor was little, old, and withered as a
cluricawn; but, no, he was tall, handsome, and more gentle, more
polished than her son. Ned was gay and careless as ever; his raven
hair curled lightly over his finely formed head, and his hazel eyes, full
of bright laughter, accorded well with the merry smile that played
round his mouth. He was frank and generous, but he was also violent
and capricious. Had Lilly not been so much with him, nay, perhaps,
even had he not instinctively felt that his mother wished him to marry
her, he might have fallen over head and ears in love. He admired
and respected Lilly, yet her quiet virtues were a silent reproach to his
heedlessness; and at heart he longed to sail on the blue waters, and
visit other lands. Next to his mother and cousin in his regard, came
Harry Connor; and Harry well deserved it. He was a most extraordinary Irishman; cautious and prudent, even when a youth, and
gentle and constant. The second son of an opulent grazier, he had
been educated for the priesthood, and would, no doubt, have been
useful in his ministry, for he had kindly feelings towards all his
fellow-creatures, but that the death of his elder brother made it necessary for him to assist his father and family in the management of
the grass farm.

Poor Mrs. Cassidy!—do you not pity her? Mothers are the same,
I believe, all the world over; and really it is " too bad " that an out-
cry should be raised against their innocent manœuvrings, though it
must be confessed they are sometimes very annoying, and not unfrequently end in a manner little to be anticipated. Poor Mrs. Cassidy!
After a few moments' cogitation, she was about to give vent to her
anger, when the sweet voice of Lilly was heard, bidding " good night
and thank ye kindly," to—Harry Connor.

" Stay, stop, asy!" ejaculated Peggy, jumping up—"if that's
Misther Harry, may-be (calling after him) ye'd jist give me, a poor
cratur, a bit o' yer company down the lane, that I don't like to go
alone: good night to ye kindly, and the blessing be about ye." And
basket and all went off at a short trot—Peggy's peculiar gait.

" What ails ye, aunt dear?" affectionately inquired Lilly; for Mrs.
Cassidy had not spoken.

" What ails *you*, girl alive—or dead—for ye're as white as a sheet—
and where's Ned?"

" Ned went a piece of the way home with Katey Turner," replied
Lilly, blushing, and tears gathering in her eyes at the same time.

" And you came a piece with Harry Connor?"

" I could not help it, aunt, dear," said Lilly, earnestly. " Sure,
Ned ran off with Katey, and asked Harry to see me home."

" He did, did he? Why, then," cried the dame, rising in a passion,
' I'll soon tache him betther manners, the reprobate!"

"Oh, aunt, dear aunt!"—and poor Lilly threw her arms around
Mrs. Cassidy's neck—"Oh, don't say a hard word to Ned—oh, may
be he couldn't help it!" and she burst into tears. "But don't, oh,
don't, for the sake o' her that never angered ye, don't say a hard word
to Ned."

"Ye're a good girl, I'll say that for you any how, my own colleen,"
said Mrs. Cassidy, kissing her fair forehead; "there, go to bed, my
darlint; ye look very pale, a'n't ye well!"

"Yes, aunt, thank ye; but ye're not angry with Ned?"

"Well, well, go to bed, I'll not scold him much, avourneen?"

"Not at all, at all, my own dear aunt!"

"Well, there agra, you've begged him off; stay a minute, grana-
chree!"—Lilly was mounting the steps that led to her small chamber:
she returned. "I just wanted my child to tell me why she calls me
aunt, now, that used to call me mother when first she came to me.
Lilly, darlint! am I less a mother to ye now than I used to be?"

"Oh, no, no, no!—not that, dear a—mother,"—she stammered
out, and again her face and bosom were red—"not that!"

"What then, Lilly, love? I hope I'm yer frind, and ye ought to
tell me."

"Oh, nothin' at all—only Katey and the girls laughed when I called
you mother, and said——"

"What did they say?"

"Oh, all a folly!—only they said—'twas all a folly—they're very
foolish, I'm sure."

"Well, but what was it, a'coushla?"

"Why, that there could be only three sorts of mothers—born
mothers, and step-mothers—and, and—oh, it's all a folly—(poor Lilly
covered her face with her shawl)—mothers-in-law."

Mrs. Cassidy replied not, but kissed her cheek, and then Lilly flew
up the ladder—closed her door—after a pause, half opened it again,
and without showing her face, said, "Remember, you promised not
to be angry with Ned."

Lilly's feelings were both new and painful; she wept very bitterly,
as she knelt at the side of her humble couch, and pressed her face to
the coverlet; was it because her aunt was angry with Edward? No;
for her anger was like the shower in April, ardent, but passing soon.
Was she vexed at Edward's attention to Katey? She certainly thought
he danced, laughed, and jested with her more than was necessary—
but why unhappy at that?—Katey was her friend, Edward her cousin.
When Harry pressed her hand with so much tenderness, at the cottage
door, why did she shake it from him, and feel as if insulted? Lilly
knew not her own heart, and wondered why she had spoken so sharply
to poor Harry—Harry, who lent her books, and whose kindness was

proverbial all over the parish. She was bewildered; all she knew was, that she was more unhappy than ever she had been in her life. She sat long, trying to collect her senses, and at last the rushlight sunk into the socket of the white-ware candlestick; it had been her cousin's present. Then she again remembered that, although the moonbeams had long since peeped through her little window, Edward had not returned; she opened the casement, which enclosed only two small panes of glass: the glorious prospect lay before her, and the watchlight gleamed brightly, over the dark blue waters, from the distant tower of Hook. The weather had been calm and clear, and the full-blown roses, that had never felt a rough blast, or a chilling shower, imparted their sweet fragrance to the midnight air; the path by which Edward would return crossed the meadow, and her heart bounded when his figure appeared hastily striding homewards. "I hope he did not see me," thought she, as she closed the window: "yet why?—sure he's my cousin." In a moment after the latch was lifted, and she distinctly heard her aunt say:

"A purty time o'night, indeed, for you to march home, Master Edward Cassidy!—and to lave me, a poor widow, and yer own mother, alone in this desolate hut."

"It's a comfortable hut, thin," replied Edward, laughing; "and how are ye lone, whin there's Lilly, and Ruth—the dirty sowl—and Bran, to say nothin' of ould puss, sitting so snug on the hearthstone?"

"How do you know Lilly's here? It's little ye care about her, or ye'd be far from letting that long gomersal of a fellow, Harry Connor, see her home; and you flirting off with that jilting hussey, Katey Turner."

"Katey Turner's no jilt, or flirt either, but a tight, clane-skinned little girl; and Harry's no gomersal at all: but an honest fellow, that'll make a good husband for my handsome cousin, one o' these days—and not long neither. What a wedding we'll have, for sartin!"

Poor Lilly's heart sickened, and her head felt giddy, as she heard these words. She never intended listening, but her respiration was impeded in the deep anxiety with which she waited for, yet dreaded, her aunt's reply. Mrs. Cassidy was struggling for utterance: she had seldom, perhaps never, been so enraged. Ned's words, and perfect carelessness of manner, had almost maddened her.

"Look ye, Ned—Ned Cassidy!" said she, after a pause, during which Edward saw the storm gathering fiercely—"Look, I'd sooner see Lilly stretched on that table; as, I'd sooner a hundred times, and a thousand to the back of them, keen at her berrin', than see her thrown away upon that ownslugh! She's for his betthers, though little they seem to think of it."

"Whew! whew!—is that what ye're after, mother dear? Well,

then, now I'll jist tell ye the rights of it, and then we'll drop it for ever, Amin. As to Lilly, a bettther girl niver drew the breath o' life; and I regard and love her as a sister; but as to anything else, mother—I won't marry; I'll see the world. And, any how, she's not the patthern o' the wife I'd like."

Mrs. Cassidy clenched her fist, and, holding it close to her son's face, ejaculated—"Holy Mary!—ye born villain!—ye disobadient spalpeen!—ye limb o' Satan!—ye—ye—down upon yer bare knees, and ax my pardon for crassing* me; or, by the powers! I'll have father Mike himself here to-morrow mornin', and marry ye out o' hand."

"I ax pardon for contradicting ye, mother: but ye'll do no sich thing. Say two words more like that, and the dawn o' day'll see me abord the good ship 'Mary,' that's lying off Hook-head, where they'd be main glad of a boy like me, as I heard to-night, to go a few voyages, and see the world."

"And is this the thanks I get for all my love, ye scoundrel; to fly in my face after that manner? Ye may trot off as soon as ye plase; but the priest shall know yer doings, my boy. Och! ye ungrateful!—down this minit, as I tould ye; and, as God sees and hears me, ye shall be married to Lilly before to-morrow's sun sets!"

"I see, mother, ye don't mane to listen to rason: but one word for all . by the blessing o' God, I'll not marry Lilly; and I don't care that—(snapping his fingers)—for priest or minister."

"Take that, thin, for your comfort, and my heavy curse wid it!" And, enraged by her son's so wilfully destroying the hope that had latterly been the chief blessing of her life, in her fury she struck him a violent blow. Poor Lilly rushed to her door; but her powers were paralysed. She could not undo the simple fastening, but clung to the window, that was close to it, for support. Edward spoke not; and his mother's arm sank by her side. Her rage was abating, when Edward, bursting with smothered anger, which he pent up with a strong effort, deliberately took his hat, walked to the door, and out, without uttering a single word. "Ned, Ned!" exclaimed Mrs. Cassidy; but Ned returned not. Lilly, pale and wild in her appearance, in a few moments was at her aunt's side. She had seen the desperate haste with which her cousin crossed the garden, trampling the flowers in his path; and, alarmed lest his passion should lead him to some dreadful act, she rushed down the stairs.

"Oh! to think," said she, "after yer promise, that ye should be so cruel to your own child, and all for one like me! Oh, if I'd ha' thought it, sure the grass shouldn't be wet under my feet before I'd be far from this house! Oh, call him back—call him back!—and I'll fly the place for ever!"

* Contradicting.

"He'll come back fast enough, I'll engage," said the widow, "he's not sich a fool;" she opened the door, and saw in the moonlight his receding figure.

"He'll not, aunt. Oh, the blow!—the blow!—to think of your striking so high a spirit, and that 'Mary' lying off Hook-head, and the mate of her, Katey's uncle, putting his comether on Ned! Sure I saw it, only I never thought it 'ud come to this, at the weary dance to-night."

"Indeed!" responded the mother, now really alive to the danger of losing her son. "Lilly, my darlint, you can save him; fly!—you can overtake him; there, he hasn't turned the lane yet; tell him he shall do as he plases; say, that I beg his pardon; only as he valees his mother's blessing, not to desart her in her ould age."

Lilly snatch'd her cloak, drew it over her head, and ran, as fast as her strength permitted, after her wayward cousin, whose firm, quick step, as he paced towards the main road, rendered the maiden's fleetness almost ineffectual: but at length she stood panting, almost fainting, at his side. It was then that a tide of conflicting feelings deprived her of utterance; for the first time, she felt herself a rejected, despised creature, and that by the being a thousand times dearer to her heart than life itself. When he knew that she had overheard the dreadful conversation in the cottage, what must he think of her? Modesty, the sweet blossom of purity, the mild glory of woman's life, had been outraged by her pursuing, even in such a cause, one who disdained her; and, as these ideas shot like fire through her brain, she caught at a tree for support, and murmured, "Holy Mary, direct thy child!" Edward spoke not, but looked on his cousin, with more of bitterness and scorn than of any other feeling. Twice she tried to speak, but vainly she unclosed her parched lips. "Ned," she at length articulated, "you are going, I know, to lave us; her, I mane, your mother; and you know, Ned, she has no hope but you. Oh, Ned! Ned!—in her old age do not fly her: think o' the time when she carried ye in sorrow and in bitter trouble—think——"

"Of the blow she gave me!" interrupted Edward, fiercely: "by all the holy saints, if a man, ay, my own father, had dealt so with me, I'd—I'd have knocked him down, and ground him into the hard earth!" And he stamped so violently, that poor Lilly was terrified at the sudden burst of passion.

"Ned, you know you have provoked her, and——"

"And so you, Lilly," he again interrupted, "you, with all yer modesty and quietness, *you* collogued against me too: and that's the upshot of your coming among us! Och! och! I thought ye had a more dacent spirit than to follow a boy to ax him to marry ye, and he your cousin!" Lilly, roused by this unjust sarcasm, was collected in a moment; drawing her slight yet dignified figure to its full height, she shook her beautiful hair that had clustered over her mournful countenance, and stood firm and erect, with the beams of the chaste full moon beaming upon her uncovered head.

"Ye don't know me, then; and I have lived under the same roof with ye three years and more; but ye don't know me, Edward Cassidy: if, by axing the powerful king of England, who sits on his throne, to make me his queen, it could be done—the poor orphan girl would scorn it! Lilly O'Brien followed ye not for that. The grate God, that sees all hearts, knows that the words I spoke are true. Never, till this woful night, did I think that yer mother wished me to be nearer to her than I am. Ye bitterly wrong me; but that's not what I came to say. I tell ye that yer mother begs ye to come back; and not to trust to the wild sea, when every comfort in life is for ye on land. She asks ye to forget; she even begs of ye, for Christ's sake, to forgive the blow; but stop, that's not all—I, the desolate orphan, who have, innocent-like, been the cause of all this misery—I beg of you, *you* that so insulted and wronged me—and I do to you what I never did to any yet, but my heavenly comforters—on my two knees, I beg ye to return. Edward Cassidy, you shall see me no more. I have no other home, but I am young, and, for a poor girl, not ignorant, praise be to your mother for it. I will quit the house for ever; ay, before the sun rises. Do not let me feel that I have driven the fatherless boy to labour, may-be to ruin."

She raised her clasped hands as she spoke, and her eyes, filled with the pure light of virtue, met the wild gaze of her cousin.

"Lilly," he replied, raising her from the ground, and looking upon her more kindly, "things must go on as they are. What comfort would my mother—God help her!—have without you? I have been a trouble and a plague to her—but you have been like an own tender child, and smoothened every step. I'll go to sea for a while—it 'ill be long afore I can forget what she did to-night; whatever divil tempted us both to sich anger. I'll be well to do in the same ship wid Katey's uncle, and ye'll all be glad to see me, may-be, whin I come back. And Lilly, I ax yer pardon for saying the say I did of you; it wasn't from the heart, only the temper. I DO know ye betther: and my friend, Harry Connor, 'll be a happy man yet, if ye'll only jist give him that young heart that's as innocent as a new-born babe. And now, God be wid ye! The 'Mary' may sail at day-breka. God bless ye!"

The heedless youth hastened on.

"Oh, Ned, Ned!—and won't ye say a word, or even make a sign, that I may tell yer mother all is peace?" He stopped and waved his hat over his head, and the belting of many foliage trees, that enclosed Mr. Herriott's estate hid him from her sight. Tears came to her relief, and she felt happy that Edward did not suspect how dearly she loved him. She turned homeward with a sorrowing heart, and was proceeding slowly on, when Peggy the Fisher's little black dog, Coal (we beg his pardon for not mentioning the very busy, ugly little gentleman before), ran out of a break in the adjoining hedge, and renewed his acquaintance with Lilly, by jumping and whining in that peculiar tone which shows a more than friendly recognition. Lilly was astonished; but still more so when the flattened hat and round rosy face of Peggy appeared through the same opening.

"Why, then, Miss Lilly, dear, is it yer fetch?—or where are ye moving along, like a fairy queen, in the green meadows by the moonlight? Ah, gramachree!" she continued, forcing her way through the hedge, "ye look like a spirit, sure enough! My poor colleen! Sorrow soon withers the likes o' you."

Lilly felt sadly mortified, for she had little doubt that Peggy had overheard the conversation between her and Edward.

"So he's gone, the obstinate mule!—but I ax your pardon. I hard every word o' it, over the hedge, just by accident, as a body may say; for you see, mavourneen, I was waiting for a particklar frind that promised to meet me about a little bit o' business that can't just be done by daylight, on account of the law. Och! it's hard for a lone woman to get a bit o' dacent bread; and the free rovers themselves are getting so 'cute that ther's no coming up to thim at all, at all! but I'm keeping ye here, and the poor woman 'ill be half mad till she hears tidings o' Ned, the boy. I'll walk a step wid ye, and be back time enough yet. God help me; I must travel to Hook and Ballyhack too, the morrow mornin'. Och! but it's hard to 'arn an honest penny in this wicked world." And the lady smuggler crossed herself very devoutly.

"Hook! are ye going to Hook to-morrow mornin'?" inquired Lilly.

"Plase God, I'll do that same."

"Oh, Peggy, thin, it would be an act o' charity just to take Ned some o' his bits o' clothes and things; if he will go, sure he ought to go dacent: and I'll make up the bundle for him, and lave it under the black thorn, in an hour or two; for I'll try and get her to bed—the Lord console her!—and steal them out like, for I know she'll be too angry to send him any comfort yet a bit, and the ship may sail before she comes to herself."

"Why, thin, that's wise and good, the colleen 'gra—but sure you're the last that ought to grieve after the boy; it 'ill be well for you, for sartin; the old woman has all in her own power—and sure it's to the one that bides with her she'll lave it. Mind yer hits, and——"

"What d'ye mane by spakeing to me after that fashion?" said Lilly, darting a look of anger on her companion, which, if Peggy could have seen, she must have felt. "How d'ye think I could get such bitter black blood in my veins, as to plan such divil's mischief us that! Keep that sort of advice for thim that 'll put up with it; Lilly O'Brien scorns it."

"Hullabullo! there we go! Well, if ye're so wrapt up in thim that doesn't care a skreed for ye, why ye'd betther just go to the fairy woman and get a charm, and bring him back, my purty Miss."

"I'll tell ye what, Peggy—I don't meddle or make with anybody, and nobody need meddle or make with me; nobody can say agin my liking my cousin—and why not? My aunt meant all kindly to both; but the thorns are sown. and grown; and sure it's heart sorrow to think o' his flitting from his own home; but if he was willin' this minute to take me afore the priest, d'ye think I'd have the hand and not the heart? Fairy woman, indeed! I've no belief in such nonsense."

"Oh, to hear how she spakes o' the good people, and the very spot we're in, may-be—Lord save us!—full o' thim! well, there's the house—I'll take the bundle safe, agra." She stopped for a moment to watch Lilly enter the cottage, and then muttered: "I can't make her out; she's either a born natural, or something much above the common."

Lilly O'Brien found it a painful duty to administer consolation, where she herself so much needed it; but, after all, continual employment is the best balm to the sorrowing mind. Save that her cheek was somewhat paler, and her gentle smiles less frequent, six months had made little change in my sweet Lilly's appearance. Not so was it, I am sorry to say, with Mrs. Cassidy, poor woman! she felt her son's desertion, as a mother only can feel; but still more she grieved when week after week passed, and the Bannow postman brought no letter from the wandering boy. Post evenings found her at the end of the lane that led to her cottage, anxiously watching John Williams's approach. Still, no letter cheered her broken, restless spirit; though she would never confess that she wandered forth on this errand, every Monday and Friday found her on the same spot; and she was on those days more bustling and fidgetty than usual. Sometimes she would abuse the absent one in no gentle terms; but Lilly never failed to remember some kind act of her cousin's, and her low musical voice, in the soft tones of unaffected feeling, was ever ready to plead for him. At other periods the widow would weep like a child over some little circumstance that brought Ned to her recollection. The flowers he planted blossomed—the bee-hives he had watched wanted thatching—or the table he had made lost its leg—or the pig wanted ringing. Lilly never mentioned him, except when her aunt led to it; but her eyelid was often heavy with tears.

Luckily for all parties, an event occurred that fully employed, for the time, my worthy old friend's thoughts and actions.

The windmill, that, from the landlord's depending on the steward to get it repaired—from the steward's depending on the mason to see to it—from the mason's depending on the thatcher—the thatcher on the carpenter—the carpenter on somebody, or nobody, or anybody but himself (after the true Irish fashion)—the windmill, Mrs. Cassidy's particular aversion—the windmill!—that had suffered a paralysis for more than five years, although everybody said how useful it could be made—the windmill was repaired, furnished with new wings, and commenced operations within the short space of three weeks, to the astonishment of the natives, who (I must confess it, however unwillingly) are like all their countrymen and women, the most procrastinating race on the face of the earth. Mrs. Cassidy was annoyed beyond measure. The Quern was kept in constant motion, and Lilly was left at home in "pace and quietness," while her aunt sidled from house to house, exhibiting specimens of the flour ground in her own cottage, and contrasting it with what she termed "the coarse trash o' branny stuff, made up o' what not, that comes out o' that grinder a' top o' the hill."

Mrs. Cassidy was from home; Lilly had finished her allotted portion of flour, and was quietly preparing the frugal supper, when our old acquaintance, Peggy the Fisher, and Peggy's little dog, Coal, entered the cottage. Lilly had never forgotten the low cunning the Fisher had evinced on the evening, every transaction of which she so perfectly—too perfectly—remembered; and her pale cheek flushed, and a shadow passed over her brow, as she returned the greeting of the village busybody.

"I'm not for staying; may-be I'm not over welcome, Miss Lilly—but never mind agra! Whin people's angry wid people, and all for good advice, given from the heart, and wid good intintion all through—why people must only put up wid it until oder people see the rights o' it. Well, my dear young cratur, it's little ye knows o' the world yet: ah! it's a bad world for a dacent poor lone woman to get a bit o' bread in. But sure you'll not be lone in it; I seen a handsome boy not tin minutes agone, that 'ud give his best eye—(and, troth, it 'ud be hard to choose betwixt 'em) for one look of love from ye, as I hard him say, many's the day ago, with my own two ears."

"I am sorry for it, Peggy, if what you say is true; for no one in the wide world do I love, barring my own poor aunt."

"Asy, child! Sure I'm not axing ye any questions—only, it's long, may-be, since ye hard from beyant seas?"

"My aunt has never heard from Ned since he quitted," replied Lilly.

"Well, may-be, so best. No news is good news, they say."

"I hope so."

"Now, what 'ud ye say to a poor body that'ud tell ye something?"

"I'm sure I don't know," said Lilly; "it would depend on what that something was."

"Well, thin, here it is;" and Peggy drew a dirty, sailor-like letter from her bosom, and placed it in Lilly's outstretched hand. "There, my colleen 'gra!—it's from Ned, sure enough; and for yourself. One who brought it tould me, for I've no larning; how should a lone cratur like me get it! but it's little ye'll like the news that's in it; and I don't know how the ould 'ooman 'ill like it, at all, at all." Lilly stood unable to inquire, unable to open the letter she had so long wished for. Peggy, with her usual sagacity, saw the dilemma, and settling the basket on her head, departed, with "God be wid ye, mavourneen!" Lilly broke the wafer with trembling hand, and read as follows:—

"DEAR COUSIN,

"This comes hoping you and my mother is well, as I am at present—thanks be to God for the same!—and likes the sea; but the land, somehow, is a saferrer life; particular for a family man, as I am, having married out o' love, a girl I'm not ashamed of; an English born and bred, and well iddicated and mannered as need be for a boy like me. I'd have written afore, but didn't know how it'ud end, as I was terribly in love. And now I ax my mother's blessing. And, Lilly dear, it's you that can get that for me; and I know ye'll do your best to make things comfortable. I'm sorry mother and I parted in anger; but it will be all for the best in regard of the wife. And I intind bringing her home to ye, and we'll all be happy thegither agin, plase God; and I'm detarmined my child sha'n't be an Englishman, so I mean my mother to be a grandmother soon, and ax her to love Lucy—she's handsomer than her name, and had a good penny o' money too, only it's clane gone; things are dreadful dear here; and I know you'll love her, for you were always kind. And I beg you to write by return of post, and send a trifle o' money; as, for the credit o' my people, I'd like to return home dacent. Lucy joins me in love and duty; and trusting to yer good word, rests your affictionate friend and cousin till death

"E. CASSIDY."

Lilly sat long with her eyes fixed on the letter; she did not weep; but her cheek was ashy pale, and her eyes were swollen. Poor girl!—

she had used her best efforts to root love from her heart, or to calm it into that friendship which she considered duty; yet the shock she received, when the full truth was known, that Edward was actually married, and returning with his wife to Bannow, was almost too great for her to bear. She read the letter over and over again; and at last sunk on her knees, earnestly imploring God to direct and keep her in the right way. She arose, strengthened and refreshed by the pious exercise, and her pure and noble mind saw at once the course that was to be pursued. Then she reflected on her plan. Her aunt, she knew, would be terribly enraged at his marrying at all. But an Englishwoman—a Protestant, most likely—it was dreadful!

"Lilly, my darlint, what are ye in such a study about?" said the old woman, as she entered. "I've good news for ye—that vagabone mill—but save us!—why ye're like one struck!—has any thing turned contrary? It's not post-night, nor—what ails ye, child? Can't ye spake at onct?"

"Sit down, aunt, dear; there's a letter from Ned, and he's alive and well."

"Thank God for all his mercies to me and mine! Well, child?"

"And he's tired o' the sea, and coming home; and sure ye'll resave him kindly, aunt?"

"The cratur! and sure I will; why not? Sure it was only a boy's wildness after all. Resave him! after not setting my two eyes upon him for a whole tin months! Sure I will—and he'll like home all the betther! Och, I'm so happy!" The poor woman threw her arms around Lilly's neck, and kissed her affectionately. "But what makes ye look so grave, my own colleen, that'll be my raal——"

"Hush! whist! for God's sake, my dear, dear, dear aunt!" And Lilly fell on her knees: "Aunt dear, the night you and Ned had the bitter battle, ye promised me ye would not vex him; yet ye did."

"Well, agra?"

"Well, ye say the same thing now; and yet, may-be, ye'd do the same thing agin for all that!"

"Well, Lilly, darlint, there's no dread in life of it now, I am so continted; but where's the letter? read me the letter—I knew he'd come back; I——"

"Aunt, I humbly ax yer pardon; have I, since Ned left ye, ever angered ye?"

"Never, my colleen."

"Then grant me this one prayer—may-be the last I'll ever ax ye, aunt!—swear, by this blessed book, never to reproach Ned with any-thing that is gone and past; but to take him to your own fond heart, and trate him as a son for ever."

"It's a quare humour, my darlint, but I can't refuse ye anything

to-night, I'm so happy; and the letther to you and all, as fitting!'
She took the prayer-book in her hand—"To swear to forget all
that's past is it, mavourneen?—and to trate him——"

"Say, him and his—him and his," interrupted Lilly, breathlessly.

"That I will," replied Mrs. Cassidy, "and with all the veins of
my heart; to forget all that's past, and trate him and his with love
and kindness to the end of my days."

She kissed the cross on the page of the prayer-book, after the manner of her religion, and was going to do the same to Lilly's fair forehead—when she ejaculated, "Thank God!" and fainted in her aunt's
arms. She remained long insensible, and when the kind woman's
efforts succeeded in restoring her, the first words the poor girl heard
were—"that's my darlint child!—rouse up; there, lane your head
on my shoulder; no wonder, agra! he'd think o' those curls, and that
gentle face, and that sweet voice that falls upon the ear widout ever
disturbing it! Oh, sure ye'll be my raal child! I see it all: fitting
to be sure that the letther should be to you. Sure he could not but
remimber my darlint Lilly! Och, but I'm the happiest woman this
minit in the big world, let t'other be who she will!"

A loud and heavy groan, as if the last effort of a bursting heart,
which the maiden could not suppress, stayed the old woman's speech,
and fixed her attention again on Lilly's ghastly features—"Tell me
directly, this minit, my brother's own child—tell me, is there anything in that letther you've not told me, as you wish to be happy? Is
Ned coming home?" Lilly moved her head in assent. "Is he well
and happy?"

"Yes, aunt, yes."

"Then, in holy Peter's name, my lanna, what is it ails ye?
Sure I see long enough ago that ye loved him in yer heart's core;
and now—praise be to God!—whin ye'll be married, and my heart
at pace, ye're taking on as if the boy was kilt entirely! Sure, whin
ye're married——"

"Aunt, for the blessed Virgin's sake, name that last no more, for
it can't be!"

"Don't dare to tell me that, unless ye mane to start the life out o'
me at onct! Lilly, Lilly! sure, girl, ye've not been listening to
Harry, and promised unknowns't to me, out o' maidenly anger with
Ned? If ye marry Harry Connor, Lilly, ye'll sup sorrow, for it's
folly to talk, child—yer heart's not in it."

"I'll never marry either Ned or Harry, aunt, so don't mintion it."

"The girl's gone mad, clane mad," said Mrs. Cassidy, angrily.
"Why, what's to put betwixt you and Ned now?"

"His wife!" replied Lilly, solemnly, and for the first time pro-
nouncing the word which banished every lingering hope from her

heart; "his lawful wife; who," she added, "though born in a far counthry, will make ye a good daughter and a loving one when I lave ye."

It would be impossible to describe the terrific rage of Mrs. Cassidy, when informed of all the particulars; even her noble-minded niece suffered from it; for when forgetful of her oath, she declared Ned and his heretic wife should never find refuge in her house, "Remember," Lilly would say, and as she spoke, the large tears would shower down her cheeks—"you swore on the blessed book to forget the past, and to trate *him* and *his* with kindness to the end of yer days." Then Mrs. Cassidy reproached Lilly with "colloguing" against her; with "joining the whole world to make her desolate;" with "brakeing her ould heart," and "splitting it into smithereens." Then she raved about Ned, and his strange wife, and concluded with—"I'll bet my life she's no betther nor she should be."

"Oh, aunt, how can ye say such a word! D'ye think Ned 'ud be the boy to bring black shame to his mother's hearth-stone? Oh, no! Protestant she is—and English—and all that—but not bad; don't think that, any how."

"Well, any how, Lilly, if a boy sarved me as you've been sarved, I'd skiver his heart to his backbone. I wish ye had a betther spirit in ye."

Lilly replied not, but heartily rejoiced when the good lady's anger and repinings were hushed in a sound sleep. She entered her own room, and counted over her savings, for Mrs. Cassidy had ever given more than supplied her wants. She had hoarded, not from selfishness, but from a feeling of generosity, that she might have the means of assisting some of her poorer neighbours; and this she had often done. With her hands, as well as with her money, had she bestowed cleanliness and comfort to many a neighbour's cottage. Her little store only amounted to three one-pound notes, and a few shillings; the former she carefully wrapped up, and wrote as follows to her cousin:—

"DEAR NED,

"I could not ask yer mother to send you much money now, and I think she'd just as soon, when ye come, that ye didn't mention it at all having resaved it, because it's so little, on account o' Lady-day being nigh at hand, and the rent to make up, and money not plenty; and will be glad to get ye back, and the young woman that's my cousin now, too. My aunt's angry yet, but she'll soon come about. Let me know aforehand, the day we may expect ye; and, with prayers that heaven may rain down blessings on you and yours, I rest,

"Your sincere
"Well-wisher and cousin,
"LILLY O'BRIEN.

"Inside, three pounds."

D

The early grey of morning saw Lilly pattering along the sea-shore in search of Peggy the Fisher. This busy woman often lodged at a little cottage near the cliffs, that belonged to one Daniel Mc Cleary, a man of doubtful character, as regarded the revenue. Lilly thought it not unlikely that Peggy would be there; so towards it she directed her steps. The sun had not even tinged the eastern clouds with his earliest rays, and the ocean rolled in heavy masses of leaden-coloured billows towards the shore, save where, here and there, amid the mistiness of morning, a fantastic rock, rooted in the " vasty deep," raised its dark head, prouder even than the proud waves that foamed for a moment angrily at its base, and then passed on. The cabin she sought was so miserable, that its mud walls and blackened thatch, overgrown with lichens and house-leek, were hardly distinguishable from the long fern and bulrush that grew round it; it rested against (indeed, one of its sides was part of) a huge mound of mingled rock and yellow clay; and at spring-tides the sea advanced so very near, that the neighbours wondered Mc Cleary remained there. There were two paths approaching this hovel; one from the country across the marshy moor that stretched in front; the other from the cliffs which partly overshadowed it. Lilly pursued the latter, but was a good deal surprised at observing a very dark cloud of smoke issuing from an aperture in the roof which constituted a chimney. She went on, looking at the smoke, and endeavouring to guess its cause; when suddenly she felt her footing give way, and almost at the same moment discovered she had fallen into an excavation, not deep, but extensive. Before she had time to look around her, the exclamation of "Tunder and turf!—what divil brought ye here?" from the lips of Peggy herself, astonished Lilly beyond conception. Ere she could reply, three or four wild-looking men, not one of whom she recognised, gathered round her; the red, flickering light given by a peat and furze fire, and a few miserable candles, stuck without any apparent fastening against the clayey walls; the heaps of grain piled to the very roof; the blackened iron pots of all sizes; dirty tin machines, such as she had never before seen; and, above all, the smell of turf and whisky, convinced poor Lilly that she had tumbled into an illicit distillery, the existence of which, although within half-a-mile of her own home, she had never suspected.

"Peg, ye ould cat, ye've sould the pass on us!" exclaimed one of the men, whose bare sinewy arms and glaring eye told both of strength and violence.

"Look out, Jack, for God's sake!" whispered another; "who knows but the young one has a troop o' red-coats at her heels!"

"Divil drive 'em!" said a ferocious looking fellow, with a pitch-fork; "we're done up fairly now, and there's nothin' for it but to skiver the both, and then jist trate 'em to a could bath this fine mornin'."

"What's the row?" inquired Daniel Mc Cleary himself, coming forward. "Hey, powers above; ye ould traitor (turning to Peggy, who stood with her arms folded, and managed to hold her tongue for a time), is it you that brought Miss Lilly here?—we're ruinated. Och! Peggy, Peggy, to think ye'd turn informer!"

"Me—is it me?—ye lying vagabone!—Me?—ye desarve to be briled alive; to be scalded to death in yer own potteen 'ud be too dacent a death for ye. Me, an informer!—the back o' my hand to ye, Dan Mc Cleary, for ever, Amin. As for you, Mick Doole," and, as she spoke, she placed her arms a-kimbo, and advanced to the knight of the pitchfork: "you were niver good—egg nor bird—nor niver will be, plase God. And as to skivering, Mick Doole, may-be ye'll be skivered or worse, as nate as a Michaelmas goose, yerself, afore long, only I scorn to talk o' sich things. Paddy Leary! oh, it's you that's the brave man; look out for the red-coats; ah! ah! ah! fait, and it 'ud be good fun to see that innocent young cratur marching at the head of a regiment, after yer bit o' stills, that, it's my thought, she knew nothin' about till this blissid minit! Sure it's myself was struck, to see her tumbling upon a heap o' barley, through the black roof, like a snowball. Spake out, my lannan! Sure ye niver did that ye'd be ashamed to tell, and that's what none here can say but yerself."

"Ay," added the first speaker, "we'll listen to rason."

"For the first time in yer life, thin," muttered Peggy.

"You gave me a letter last night," and Lilly turned to the Fisher as she spoke.

"True for ye, it was he," pointing to Mc Cleary, "brought it from Watherford."

"It required a quick answer. I couldn't get John Williams to take it, by rason he doesn't go till to-morrow; and I thought that you, Peggy, 'ud be on the trot somewhere near a post, so I wrote it last night, and thinking ye'd put up at Dan Cleary's, 'cause ye often do, I came early to try, for fear I'd miss of ye, and ill-luck sent me the cliff path, and all of a sudden I fell into this wild place; out o' which the Lord will, I hope, deliver the poor orphan in safety."

Lilly's tall, slight figure, and flowing hair, contrasted with the stout form of the Fisher, who stood a little in front; the rosary and a cross hanging from the arm which retained its a-kimbo position; while the scarlet kerchief that confined her grizzled locks fell, like a cowl, from the back of her head, and fully exposed her large bronzed features, which showed in strong relief, as the light from the crackling fire flashed occasionally on them. Mick Doole, large and bony enough for one of the ancient inhabitants of the Giant's Causeway, leaning on his pitchfork, and looking as if the roof rested upon his huge black head, towering over both Paddy Leary and Daniel, who standing at either side of the colossus, formed another group; while some three or four beings, indescribable as to shape and features, because they were covered with dirt, and encompassed in an atmosphere of smoke and steam, filled up the back-ground.

"If ye came wid a letther, where is it?" inquired one of the party.

Lilly drew it from her bosom, and presented it to the querist. He turned it over and over, and then, observing quietly—"The smoke blinds me so, I can't read,"—handed it to Daniel Mc Cleary.

"Well, that's good enough too," said Peggy, "I niver hard tell yet of man or woman who could read widout knowing B from a bull's fut."

"It's right enough after all," observed Daniel, "for I know this is for the boy I brought the letther from; not from him straight, only from one that knows him: there's something inside it?"

The idea that Mc Cleary might extract the money crossed Lilly's mind, but only for a moment, and she replied, "Yes, three pounds."

"And I'm the one that 'll put it safe into Taghmon, my jewel, afore twelve this blissid day," exclaimed Peggy, taking possession of the letter.

"Well, ye didn't go to come here as a spy, Miss Lilly, and I ax your pardon for suspicting ye; but upon my troth it's dangerous, now ye know our sacret, to let ye go; who'll go bail for ye?"

"I will," said Peggy.

"Your bail won't do, ye cross divil," replied Paddy Leary.

"Mine will, then," said a stout, middle-sized man, coming from amid the distant group; "I've been watching ye all this tin minutes, ye cowardly set—and it's no joke to be frightening the Bannow Lilly after that fashion, ye bag of weasels! My colleen, never mind; ay, whin 'rattling Jimmy' goes bail, who grumbles?" Certainly they all appeared quite satisfied. "Sure," he continued, "only you've no gumtion, ye'd know that the kind heart is niver mane: why, look at her, d'ye think sich as she 'ud condescind to inform on yer potteen? Ah! ye don't know her as I do."

"I never saw ye before," exclaimed Lilly.

"What, not the lame bocher, that had lost the use of a leg, and was blind of an eye, all from lightning on the salt sea?" and he imitated the voice and halt of a beggar to perfection: "'twas a could night, but ye made me very comfortable, Miss Lilly; and don't ye remimber the madman that frightened ye down the park, where ye were spreading the clothes to dry, last summer? I was sorry to frighten ye, dear; but fait, I couldn't help it, for we were wanting to get a little something, that same little sthill, past the park, and couldn't for you; so I wint mad, and frightened ye; yet—God bless ye!—ye thought I looked hungry, and so ye brought out sich a dale o' foou,

nno iaid it aside the hedge; but come along, the white rose can't
blow 'mong the coarse weeds."

"Jim—Jim, ax her to promise on the book," said Paddy.

"Ax—not I: sure the honour's in her heart's blood." And so saying, "rattling Jimmy," the smuggler and the peep-o'-day-boy, lifted
Lilly kindly and respectfully out of Daniel Mc Cleary's black den.

"And now," said Peggy, "I'll finish my prayers."

A fortnight had nearly elapsed, and no letter had arrived from
Edward. Lilly most truly wished to leave the cottage, and urged
every reason she could think of to be permitted so to do. "Miss
Herriott was going for the winter to Dublin, and wanted a bettermost lady's-maid, and a little time there would do her the world and
all o' good;" or, "she had a bad cough, and it might go away if she
went more up the country;" but the entreaties and tears of her aunt,
to whose very existence she seemed as necessary as the air she
breathed, silenced her request; and she resolved to meet her relatives, however painful the meeting might be. "My aunt will get
used to Lucy after a bit," thought she, "then I can go: and, any
way, he doesn't know I ever loved him, and sure it's no sin, in the
sight o' God, to love him as I have loved." And Lilly was right;
there was no impurity in her affection. It was the feeling that seeks
the good of its object, without any reference to self. She did not
regret that Edward was happy with another; nor had she, towards
his wife, one jealous or unkind thought. "And sure I shall rejoice
to see him happy." This was her last idea, as she rested her head
on her humble pillow; and yet the morning found it wet with
tears; and then she knelt, and prayed to God to bless her aunt, and
Edward, and his wife, and to direct her in all her paths.

"There's one wants to spake a word to ye, Miss Lilly, dear, jist
down yonder," said Peggy the Fisher, as Lilly entered the garden,
after breakfast, one morning.

"Who is it, Peggy?"

"Well, thin, it's jist Harry Connor; he's had a letter from Ned,
and he wants to see ye on the strength of it." Peggy passed on
her way, and Lilly proceeded to the spot the Fisher had pointed out.
Harry Connor was there.

"I got word from yer cousin, Lilly," said Harry, "that him and
his wife are at Ballyhack, and will be here to-morrow; and they'd
have come before, but Lucy (I think he calls her) has been very ill
from sea-sickness; and he begged me to tell ye so. Dear Lilly, I was
glad of the opportunity; for there's no gettin' a sight o' ye; you're
always at home, and even on Sundays yer aunt goes on the car to
chapel, so one can't speak to ye. Oh, Lilly! Lilly! you were not
always so distant—don't you remember when I used to, sit of an
evening in that garden. between you and Edward, reading, and you

used to call me your master, and say the time passed so happily?"
Tears gathered in Lilly's eyes, as she turned away her face; for she
too, remembered those evenings. "Lilly," continued the young
man, "have you heard anything against me? Your aunt always
showed me the could shoulder; I don't blame her for that in past
times; but now she would not, if you wished. Oh, do not say you
cannot love me, Lilly! You have always shunned me when I
wanted to spake about it; but tell me now, Lilly O'Brien! I will
wait; I will do anything you wish—anything—only say, Lilly, that
you do not hate me."

"No, Harry, I do not, indeed;" and she met his eye with steady
firmness.

"Only one word more, and then," he continued, holding her
struggling hand, "you may go. I will wait any time you please, only
say that it shan't be in vain—that you will be my wife, and make one
whose heart almost bursts at the thought of losing you—happy!"

"Harry, I cannot desave ye," she replied, "nor would not, if I
could. I know I've shunned ye; because I hoped that you would
see why—to save us both all this heart-pain. I have always had
rason to respect you—and I do: but love ye I never can; and I'll
never marry the man I cannot love."

"Only one word," said Harry, earnestly—"sure you'll hear me—
you say you've a regard for me. Lilly, you go nowhere; you see
no one. I do not speak of my being well to do in the world. But
if ye were to let me near ye, to be with ye as I once was, in bygone
days, the love might come. Oh, let me only try!"

"No, Harry, no, it would be useless; my heart here tells me so.
You will find many fitter for ye, who can love ye as ye deserve.
May the Almighty bless and watch over ye, Harry! And farewell."
The young man still grasped her hand; and, as he gazed on her
beautiful face, he felt that, if it were turned from him for ever, his
sun of happiness was indeed set.

"Lilly, before ye go, hear my last resolve. If ye really cast me
off, I, who love ye more than life—I, who, to see even the glimmer
of the candle carried by this hand, have watched in rain and tempest
under yon old tree—I will leave my father's home; and, for your
sake, Lilly, I will take priest's vows, and forsake the world. Think
well, Lilly O'Brien, if from mere whim, or maiden modesty, you
would drive me to that."

"Harry, God forbid that you should ever do so! Ye would not
be fit to sarve on the altar, if for anything like that ye went there.
No, Harry, my heart must go with my hand. They're all I have to
give, but they must go together: even you would despise, ay, hate
that hand, if ye found, for lucre, it gave itself, when the betther
part was wanting."

"Lilly, may-be ye love someone else? Oh! may-be I'm proud; but surely there's not a boy all round the country could win your heart."

"I do not love any one for marriage. So, once more, God bless ye, Harry!—may ye be happy—happier," she muttered to herself, "happier than I shall ever be!"

Harry stood with his eyes fixed on the spot where Lilly had disappeared. His senses were bewildered; and it was not until a smart slap on the shoulder, and the voice of the everlasting Peggy, who appeared (one would almost believe, like Sir Boyle Roche's bird, in two places at the same time) at his elbow, with her broad platter face, shaded by the fish basket—that he became fully sensible of the reality of his interview.

"Sure I tould ye ye'd get no good of the colleen; and if ye'd ha' mintioned the matther to me afore, I'd ha' tould ye the same thing, and may-be the rason too."

"I know," said Harry, musingly, "she does not love anyone else."

"Och, ye do, do ye?—humph, agra!"

"What do you mean, woman! Sure she told me she did not; and her lips never lied, nor never will."

"Asy!—the string o' my bades broke, and I was forced to stop to mend it jist behind that big bush o' furze. A poor creature like me can't afford to be buying bades every day. So, my dear—all accident (for I scorn a listener), I hard what she said,—' *she loved no one for marriage.*' True for her; they talk a grate dale of her sinse; but it's poor sinse to go look for the snow that fell last winter. I'll tell ye what, as a dead sacret:—she loved the ground that her cousin walked on, more than all the gould that ever was in, or ever came out o' Indy. And she loves him still; ay, ye needn't look so strange; she loves him, but nothin' improper—I know that girl's heart as well as if I was inside of her—'tis of the sort that doesn't stain, or spot; and now you'll see, her delight'll be to tache his wife all the ould mistress's quare ways. And thin, whin she'll have made pace intirely among 'em she'll stale off, like the mist up the mountain; and work (and well she knows how) for his sake that doesn't know she loves him. It's mighty fine to be so romantical all for pure love. God help us, poor women, we're all tinder! It was the way wid me, when my bachelor died—rest his sowl!—and that's the rason I'm a poor lone body now. Sure I sould the pig my mother left me, to pay the clargy, to get his sowl out o' purgatory; and wasn't it well for him to have it to depind on?"

Harry, heedless of Peggy's pathetic application of the apron to her eyes, turned towards his own home, "revolving sweet and bitter thoughts." There is a delight imparted to every unsophisticated heart, by the contemplation of a noble or a virtuous action, that nothing else can give; and Harry's generous mind at once acknowledged Lilly's virtues; loving at first without knowing it; feeling it unrequited; and yet·resolved to benefit its object to the sacrifice of every personal convenience and prospect in life.

The next day Edward and his bride arrived at the cottage. Mrs. Cassidy, in compliance with her oath, received them kindly. The mother's heart yearned towards her son; but poor Lucy saw the old woman entertained a strong prejudice against her.

The "kindly welcome," that murmured from Lilly's lips, sounded sweetly on the young stranger's ear; and as fatigue compelled her to go to bed almost immediately, Lilly's kind attentions were very delightful. The kind girl had displayed much taste and care in arranging their small sleeping-room. Every article she could spare from her own chamber was added to its furniture. And when Lucy saw everything so clean and comfortable, she expressed both surprise and pleasure.

It was impossible not to love Lucy, when you looked at her; but it was somewhat doubtful if that sentiment would continue when you knew her. Her eyes were black, quick, and quite as likely to sparkle with anger as with pleasure. She was very *petite*, lively, thoughtless, and possessed precisely those acquirements that were useless in an Irish cottage. The daughter of a grocer in Plymouth, she had seen, fallen in love, ran away with, and married Edward in the short space of three weeks; and had not yet numbered sixteen years. Her youth pleaded strongly in her favour; but her extreme giddiness kept Lilly, the sweet, the patient Lilly, perpetually on the watch, lest she might do something to annoy her mother-in-law. It is true she quilled Mrs. Cassidy's caps in so new and bewitching a style that everybody said Lucy made the good lady look ten years younger. She washed her old mode cloak in some stuff, of which whiskey and beer were the principal ingredients, and made it appear, to the astonishment of the whole parish, "bran new." Then she trimmed bonnets—one yard and a half of riband, managed by her, went as far as three and a quarter ('tis an absolute fact) with any body else. She could work natural flowers upon gauze, and embroider the corners of pocket-handkerchiefs. She could even get up fine linen: but she could neither spin flax or wool, card, or milk, or churn, or cram fowl, or make butter, or a shirt or shift of any description: the worst of all was, she had said, unfortunately, that she was certain no Christian body could eat bread made from the flour that was pounded out by those dirty stones; thus bringing Mrs. Cassidy's invaluable quern into contempt. Then it was quite impossible to keep her quiet; everything excited her risibility. One day, in particular, when the turkey-cock, affronted at Mrs. Cassidy's scarlet petticoat, which outvied his own red neck, picked unmercifully at her legs, Lucy only laughed, and never went to the rescue, which induced the old lady to say, that "Ned pretended to bring home a wife, but had only brought home a doll."

Lilly might well be called her guardian angel: when, like a school-girl, she scampered over the fields, gathering flowers, or hunting every cock, hen, and chicken, over the potatoe ridges, Lilly followed to prevent her over-fatiguing herself, and to assist her home; then she would instruct her how to please her mother-in-law; and, if Mrs. Cassidy complained, Lilly had always some remark to soften down what was said. Her general apology was—"She's so young, but she'll soon be a mother, and then she'll get sense."

"I wonder Ned did not fall in love with you, Lilly," said Lucy, one day; "I'm sure you'd have made a better wife for him than ever I shall!" How poor Lilly blushed, and then turned pale; but Lucy heeded it not. "How industrious Ned grows!—well, they would not believe, in Plymouth, that he'd ever settle down into a farmer, but I'm sure he works in the fields from morning till night."

"People who are not rich must work, Lucy."

"Now, Lilly, that's a hit at me, who let you do everything; but do not look so angry with me, dearest Lilly; I beg pardon, you never hit at anybody. Oh! you are not like an Irishwoman!"

"Oh, Lucy, dear!—don't be after talking that way o' the country, afore my aunt, for it hurts her; and ye must remimber how much she's thought of in the parish."

"Well, there, I'll be as good as gold—there;" and she sat down to work at some caps for a little stranger that was expected soon.

Edward was very affectionate to his young wife, although her heedlessness often annoyed him; but when he gazed on her fairy-like beauty, he forgave it. The Protestant Church was too far for her to walk; she could not go to mass, and her husband loved her too well to permit her to be teazed on the subject. Her mother-in-law, and even Lilly, were grieved at this, and lamented that she thought so little about serious things; however, Mrs. Cassidy always reconciled it to herself, by saying, "Niver mind, she'll be all the asier brought round to the right way, by-and-by." But, of all the amusements in which the thoughtless creature delighted, nothing pleased her so much as boating; if she could even get into a boat by herself, she would paddle it round the creeks, and into the bays, which in some places are overhung by scowling rocks, where the sea-birds nestle in safety.

"The potatoes are almost done, by their bubbling, I suppose, Lilly," said she one day, "so I'll go and meet Ned as he comes from the plough, and we shall be just in time for dinner;" and away she tripped, singing as blithely as a lark.

"She has a light heart," thought Lilly; "and why not?—mine is not as heavy as it used to be: well, thank God, it does make people happy to do their duty;" and she assisted the little serving-girl in arranging all things in their kitchen—a task soon performed; the potatoes, laughing and smoking, were poured out on a clean home-bleached cloth, and the white noggins frothed with fresh buttermilk of Lilly's own churning. Something prepared with extra care, for the delicate Englishwoman, was covered between two delf plates at the fire, and Mrs. Cassidy stood watching at the door, her hand lifted to her eyes, to shade them from the noonday sun, while Lilly mixed some gooseberry wine with water and sugar for Lucy.

"Lilly, didn't ye say that Lucy went to meet Ned?"

"Yes, aunt."

"Well, here's Ned at the gate almost, and no sign o' Lucy."

"That's mighty strange," replied Lilly, advancing; "Ned, where's Lucy?"

"At her dinner, I suppose."

"Now, don't be so foolish, I'm sure she met ye."

"She did not, indeed, and I was longing to see her."

"It is some of her childish tricks," said Mrs. Cassidy.

"Her dinner 'll be stone could, though," said Lilly, looking out; "so I'll jist go see if I can meet her, and sit ye all down, or the pratees 'll not be fit to ate;" and she issued forth without further parley.

Ned did not sit down, although his mother urged him. "Her dinner has nothing to do with yours, Ned; sure Lilly has something nice under the plate for her. No sign of her yet," she continued, after a pause; "sure she wouldn't be so foolish as to go to Tim Lavery's boat, for a bit of a spree; I caught her in it reading yesterday, but it was anchored safe, sure enough."

Ned made no reply, but followed the footsteps of his cousin; the field he had been ploughing was very near the beach; he hastily gained it, and his horror and dismay can be better conceived than expressed, when, gaining the cliff, the first object he beheld was Lilly, half in and half out of the water, dragging to shore the apparently lifeless body of his wife. When Lilly left the cottage, she first looked behind the large furze and hawthorn bushes near the field and then the boat occurred to her; she sped to the sea, and saw it in shallow water, but upset, with Lucy clinging to the stern, faint and exhausted. To plunge into the water and bring her to land, was the work but of a moment, and done before Edward could descend the cliffs.

The thoughtless creature was soon conveyed home. Her nerves were quite shattered; she clung closely to Lilly's bosom, like a frightened child, and did not even return her husband's caresses. She was hardly laid on her bed, when shrieks of agony succeeded the half-murmured words and sobbings of terror; and, after long and painful suffering, the being, who, not many hours before, had bounded

in the full light and life of early youth, gave premature birth to a
living child, and then yielded up her own existence. It was very
sorrowful to mark the merry eyes closed for ever beneath their
alabaster lids, and the long black lashes resting on her colourless
cheeks.

Then came a long and loud debate between the Protestant and
Catholic priests, as to who was to perform the last rites; as if the
spirit's happiness depended on man's words repeated over inanimate
clay. The widower roused himself from the lethargy that succeeds
the first rush of impetuous grief, and said calmly but firmly—" Plase
your reverences, I'm a Catholic, and ever was and will be; but she
that's gone from me was born a Protestant—married a Protestant—
and, as she died one, so shall she be buried, and that's enough: and
what's more, I promised her, when I didn't think that death and desolation would come at this time, that if the child was a girl it should
go wid her, if a boy wid me. Now, gentlemen, I'm not a larned
man, but my mind is, that a promise to the dead or the living, is
holy and firm in its natur'; and so, as I promised, it shall be. I
couldn't look upon the babby's face for a king's ransom, nor do I
know whether it be boy or girl; mother, say what is it?"

" A girl," replied Mrs. Cassidy.

" Well, may-be more betther; may-be you'd just baptize it, Mr.
Barlow, and Lilly and my mother'll stand for it; as my notion is it
can't live—and why should it?"

But the little Lucy did live—thanks to Lilly's fostering care; and
so fragile a thing it was, that even a rough kiss might have killed it.
A nurse was immediately procured, and Lilly had the satisfaction of
seeing all Mrs. Cassidy's solicitude directed towards the infant; nay,
she almost forgot the quern, and the only danger was that the child
would be destroyed by kindness. There was, however, to Lilly's
delicate mind, something most improper in her remaining in the same
house with her cousin. He was again free; although she hoped that
he did not suspect her love, yet he knew of his mother's old plan; he
had once, in anger, reproached her as being accessory to it; and
Lilly decided on leaving our village. Edward, since sorrow had
laid her hand on him, was an altered man, and Mrs. Cassidy was enjoying a vigorous old age: so she could leave her, assured of happiness. It was a bitter trial to forsake her little godchild, yet she felt
she owed a duty to herself. Mr. Herriott's family were again about
to visit Dublin, and, without imparting her plan to any one, she offered
her services to Miss Herriott. They were joyfully accepted; not
without many expressions of wonder that "the Bannow Lilly," the
flower of the whole country side, should leave a spot where she was
so much beloved. Lilly pleaded a wish for improvement, and finally
arranged to set off with Miss Herriott in three days. As she re-

turned she heard Peggy's loud voice, singing her old favourite, " The Colleen Rue," just as she got to her favourite stanza—

> " I ranged through Asia—likewise Arabia,
> Through Penselvanie, a seeking for you ;
> Through the burning region of the siege of Paris,"—

when she espied Lilly in her decent mourning habit.

" The blessing be about ye, my precious !—and may-be ye'd tell us where ye've been.   Sorra a bit o' news going now for a poor body."

" I've been up to Mrs. Herriott's, Peggy."

" Och ! they're going to Dublin, all the way, on Tuesday.   Sure that'll be the black journey for the poor.   You needn't care, Miss Lilly ; sure you've full and plinty, and an own fireside."

" I'm going as own maid with Miss Herriott, Peggy ;—there's a small taste of news for yer comfort," continued Lilly, smiling— " and more betokens, you've the first of it, for I've not told my aunt yet."

" You going ?   Och, oh, oh !—don't be making yer fun of us after that fashion ; we know betther nor that."

" It's quite true, for all ye may think, and so God be wid ye, Peggy !   You and poor Coal will often cross my mind when I'm alone among strangers."

" Arrah, now, stop !—sure ye can't be in arnist.   Sure there's not a living soul in the parish but says you'll be married to Ned now ; and at St. Pathrick's sure I hard 'em talking about it; and how Harry Connor's priested ; sure he's Father Harry, for your sake."

" Peggy, I take shame to myself for hearkening to your palaver for a moment : dacent talk ye have, and the young grass not green on *her* grave yet !   Once more I say, God be wid ye."   I have done right, thought she, but I shall not be able to make my dear aunt think so.

Poor Mrs. Cassidy scolded and cried with might and main; and Ned remonstrated, and even said that he took it very unkind of her to leave them, and, above all, the little thing, whose life she had saved.   But Lilly was firm, and departed amid the reproaches and tears of her aunt, and the heartfelt regret of her neighbours.

How very irksome were her employments !—How did she shrink from the rude gaze of gentlemen and gentlemen's gentlemen, who, astonished at her beauty, paid homage by staring her out of countenance ; and how often did she long for the quiet of the lowly cottage in the isolated village of Bannow !   At first she imagined that city people must be very superior to country ones.   But she soon grew tired of the pert flippancy and foolish airs of the servants she met; and by Miss Herriott's permission, retired, when unoccupied, to the solitude of her kind lady's dressing-room.   She received letters once a month generally, from her cousin.   The two first, in addition to the necessary information, anxiously entreated her return, but latterly (for the stay of the family was prolonged, owing to Mrs. Herriott's illness) the subject was never mentioned; and the bitter feeling, that there no longer existed any one to love her, weighed heavily on her heart. Sixteen months had elapsed since Lucy's death; and Edward ever spoke of his child with all a father's fondness. Lilly longed to see it, but she had resolved on never again living with her aunt— and she remained firm to her resolution.

She had been dressing her young lady one morning, when, passing down stairs, the footman said, "There's one in the housekeeper's room that wants ye." She hardly entered when she was almost suffocated by the embraces of Mrs. Cassidy; and then she had to encounter the respectful but affectionate greetings of her cousin. Her aunt earnestly looked at her, would not sit down, but said, "Now, my darlint Lilly, it is much ye ought to thank me for this journey—in my ould age to take to the road agin; but ye see the rason is, that Ned is tired o' being bachelor, and he's going to change his condition, and jist wants to ax your advice and consint!"

"Mine!"

"Now, mother dear, don't be mumming," said Ned : "Lilly, I come to ax ye to accept the hand of one who is unworthy to be yer husband, but yet would die to make you happy. Lilly, don't cast me off—for my mother's sake—for my own—for this one's sake ;" and he took from the arms of our old friend, Peggy the Fisher, a smiling, black-eyed little creature, who almost instantly nestled its curly pate in Lilly's bosom. "Sure ye can make us all happy, if ye like; and we'll be all in quiet Bannow agen. Say, Lilly! Oh, don't look so could on me !"

"Will ye hould your whist, Ned!" interrupted Peggy; "if ever I see'd any body trated in this mismannerly fashion! Can't ye see wid half an eye that the cratur's as good as fainted, ye omathawn! No wonder, and ye both bellowering thegither. Ye don't know how to make a dacent proposhal; ye've frightened the grawl betwixt ye— whisht, honey, whisht! (to the child)—there's a woman !—ay—come to your own Peggy, that's hushowed ye oftin; and will agin, by the blessin' o' God."

Lilly, literally unable to stand, sank into the housekeeper's chair. Edward knelt at her side; and his mother, holding one of her hands to her heart, looked earnestly on her face, while Peggy, "hushowing" the child, was not an uninterested spectator.

"God knows," said the young woman, after a little time, "I did not expect this. Aunt, when I had no father to protect me—no mother to feel for me—you did both; you shared with me what you had; and, oh! what was more than all—while I ate o' yer bread, and drank o' yer cup, ye never made me feel that it was not my father's roof that sheltered me. Ned, we grew together, and you were to me as a born brother. But ye wronged me, Ned, that night; the first time (and God, that hears me, knows it), the first time I ever guessed my aunt wished me to be nearer to her than her brother's child: that night, when, to prevint yer laving home, I proposed to quit for ever my only frind; when I did her bidding, an' followed ye through the moonlight, to bring ye back to yer poor ould mother, ye cast a black word in my face, and ye said that I—I, Lilly O'Brien—was leagued agin ye—and that I followed ye to get a husband." She covered her face with her hands, and faintly continued "I have never forgotten it; I have prayed to do so. No one) 'er knew it, but Peggy—she overheard it. Oh! it weighed here, at the very bottom of my heart, and when I slept it was wid me; it——"

"Oh, Lilly, how can ye take on so!—sure it was the bad temper that did it, and I didn't mane it. And sure you've proved since that it's little truth was in it; sure you've been more like an angel than anything else; and sure when I ax yer pardon——"

"Stop, Ned, ye do *now*; but may be, by an' by, ye might say the same thing agen; and if ye did it, and if we were married, I could never look up after!"

"Why, Lilly," said Mrs. Cassidy, "ye're making him out a fair black villain, after all yer goodness, to think he'd do the likes o' that—after yer coming over me, to take an oath *to resave him and his, as my own*, whin a word was only wanting to make me ban him for iver."

"And after her flying at me like a mad cat," echoed Peggy, "becase I gave her a bit of advice (for I was fairly bothered) to take care of a little property for herself."

"Ay, and all her attintion to the stranger," resumed Mrs. Cassidy.

"And her sinding him her own three pounds to bring him home," said Peggy.

"How do you know that?" inquired Lilly.

"Is it how I know it? Why, thin, I'll jist tell ye. I know yer aunt hadn't a tester in the house, becase she'd given me every pinny to exchange for gould, that she might pay her rint in it—not in dirty paper—to plase the landlord."

"Yer good deeds are all known, Lilly. Oh, let me say *my* Lilly; sure ye'll forgive yer cousin. How can I admire ye as I ought?—don't shake yer head, Lilly, dear, but——"

The opening of the door prevented the conclusion of Edward's speech; and Miss Herriott entered, her face radiant with satisfaction. "So, Lilly, I am to lose you; nay, do not talk, girl, I know you love him; I knew it all along; Peggy told me all about it, at the end of the shrubbery, the night before we left Bannow; and my dress-maker has made the wedding-dress, because Edward Cassidy wrote to me, and asked my opinion and consent, which was fitting; and I assured him you had not been flirting with any one, and invited him and my old friend up to Dublin; as to you, Peggy, I never expected you, but you are not less welcome."

"Why, I thank ye, Miss, my lady; I jist came to see how ye all war, and to mind the child, and to look at the fine beautiful city, and the college, that bates the world for larning, as I have hard, and the ancient ould Parliâment-house; and then go back, and give rest to my bones among my own people; but I hope ye'll persuade Miss Lilly, my lady, for her own good; sure they love each other—and what's more wanting for happiness?"

"Ay, do, Miss, she'll do yer bidding, may-be; she's forgotten mine;" and tears rolled down the wrinkled cheeks of Mrs. Cassidy.

"Not so," replied Miss Herriott; and taking Lilly's hand, she placed it in Edward's; "and now," continued the amiable girl, "kneel for the blessing that ascends to the throne of the Almighty, like a sweet-smelling savour—the blessing of an honest parent." They dropped on their knees, and Mrs. Cassidy pressed them to her satisfied heart.

"And sure that's as good as a play," blubbered Peggy.

"Well, Peggy, you shall see a play if you please, to-morrow evening; but first I invite you to Lilly's wedding, which will take place to-morrow at four o'clock, in our great drawing-room, agreeably to the forms of the Catholic church, by a Catholic priest. Nay, Lilly, it is the last time I shall ever command you; so I bid you all farewell for the present." And the good, and kind, and generous young lady left them to their "own company," which, it is scarcely necessary to say, was not very doleful or wretched; for although the heart of one of the party was too full for words, ample amends was made for her silence by the ever talkative Peggy.

At three-quarters of an hour past three (I love to be exact in these matters), Miss Herriott inspected her company in the back drawing-room. The arrangements for the ceremony highly amused her; first, Mrs. Cassidy, in an open rose-coloured poplin dress, as stiff as buckram, with tight sleeves reaching to the elbows, where they were met by white mittens, that had been the gift of Miss Herriott's grandmother, and which the old lady prized so highly that they had only twice seen the light in twenty years; a blue satin quilted petticoat, ditto, ditto; a white muslin apron flounced all round; high-heeled shoes, with massy silver buckles; a clear kerchief, pinned in the fashion that used to be called "pigeon's craw," and a high-cauled cap, trimmed with rich lace, completed her costume. Peggy sported a large flowered chintz, whereon pink parrots, yellow goldfinches, and bunches of roses bigger than either goldfinch or parrot, clustered together in open defiance of nature and the arts; this was made after Mrs. Cassidy's pattern, and displayed to advantage a pea-green English stuff petticoat, quilted in diamonds. There was little variation from Mrs. Cassidy's fashion in the other et ceteras, except that Peggy wore a flaming yellow silk shawl, with a blue border; that, to use her own expression, "matched everything."

Lilly looked beautiful—most beautiful. Miss Herriott dressed her as she pleased; in white, pure white; would not permit her to wear a cap, but let her hair curl after its own fashion, only confining it with a wreath of lilies of the valley.

There is no use in describing Edward's dress; all bridegrooms, I believe, wear blue coats with yellow buttons and white waistcoats. The little Lucy had a clean white frock, and a lobster's claw to keep it quiet.

Oh! what a happy group of humble people were assembled in that gay drawing-room. Mrs. Cassidy—the desire of her heart gratified, the hope of years realized, the fervent and continual prayer answered —Mrs. Cassidy was, beyond doubt, the happiest of them all, as she sat, with her cheerful and grateful face, contemplating her "two children."

"Ye're both too handsome and too good for me," whispered Ned, as he conducted Lilly to the great drawing-room, closely followed by her condescending bridesmaid. Lilly courtesied as she entered, but did not look off the ground until an exclamation of surprise from the bridegroom roused her attention, and she saw—Harry Connor!— Father Harry!—ready to perform the marriage ceremony.

"It is even your old friend," said he, advancing. "Mr. Herriott, at my request, consented to my surprising you. Ned, when I give you this girl as your wife, I give you one whom no earthly feeling could tempt from the path of strict honour. She told me once that her hand should never go without her heart, and your being together proves you have it; a blessing will she be to thee, my early friend." A single tear glistened on his cheek as he pronounced the words that made them husband and wife: it was a tear of which a seraph might not have been ashamed.

Four years have passed since that happy marriage; and can you not tell who—seeking to abstract herself from household cares and blessings, only that she may render grateful homage to her Creator— sits after evening vespers, with clasped hands and downcast eyes, her national hood shading, but not obscuring, the beauty of her pensive face, near yonder cottage, that looks so joyously in the setting sun which sheds such glorious light over the ocean, that reflects every passing cloud upon its calm, clear bosom? See her again,

within the porch of her dwelling, where the flowers are blossoming;
and where she has other blossoms than the flowers give. She is
approaching the bloom of womanhood, yet grace is in all her movements. Her kerchief is carefully pinned across her bosom, and two
or three rich auburn tresses that obstinately come forth, and will
not be confined by the neat cap of snowy whiteness, move in the
passing breeze;—that dark-eyed and dark-haired little girl, buoyant
and animated, cannot be her child, yet it clings to her neck, and
calls her "mother." There—the honest farmer, returning from his
toil, is met by two almost infant prattlers; the youngest a perfect
specimen of childish helplessness and beauty; and peering from the
window is the hardly altered face of—Mrs. Cassidy.

Oh, that voice!—it is Peggy's—old Peggy—as she is still called,
"Peggy the Fisher." She has "a good penny o' money of her
own," and sometimes visits around the neighbourhood; but she is
so strongly attached to the family to whom the cottage belongs, that
she almost resides there.

"Och, ye craturs, like fairy things, come in to the tay!—sure it's
not fit for the likes o' ye to be muddling in the grass, even after yer
daddy, ye born blossoms!—ye bames o' joy!—ye comforts o' the ould
'ooman's heart!—Come, all o' ye, to your own Peggy. Och! 'tis
myself must set about, fair and asy, to make my sowl, and not be
passing my time, like the flowers in May, wid the young blossoms of
the BANNOW LILLY."

K

MARY RYAN'S DAUGHTER.

I NEVER saw any beauty in her—that's the truth"—exclaimed one of a group of females, who, lounging around a cottage door, were watching the progress of a young woman toiling slowly up a steep hill, and leading by the hand a very slight child. The cottage was in the valley—and the traveller must have passed the group— for, like most Irish dwellings, it was on the road-side.

"I had the greatest mind in the world to ask her how she had the impudence to wear a bright *goold* ring on her wedding-finger, as if she was an honest woman!" said another.

"And she asking with such mock modesty for a drink of water! I wonder how she relishes water after the fine wines she got used to," suggested a third.

"It was for all the world like a story written in a book," observed the first speaker; "how she left the Uphill farm (as good as seven years, come Easter), and no one ever knew exactly who she left it

with—only guessing that it must be one of the *sporting squireens,* that thronged the country about that time. Since the ould gentleman at the Hall died, and the place was pulled down, we have none of the kind going."

"Small loss," was the reply; "they were only good at divarshin —for themselves I mean; there was no use in them at all at all, for others."

"Did you see how white her hands were?" remarked another. "Well, I expect there will be murder of some sort done—for her father will never own her—and it's little she thinks there's a new mother to meet her. I hadn't the heart to tell her her own was dead!—bad as she is."

"Bad as who is?" exclaimed a clear but aged voice. "Who is bad, girls, agra? It's a comfort to hear of bad people, so it is; it makes one say—'Well, the saints be praised! I'm not as bad as *that* any how.'"

"Oh, Daddy Denny, is it yourself that's in it? Oh, thin, that's luck!" they exclaimed together. "Think of that now—and we never to see you coming, daddy, honey!"

"How could you see me coming," replied the stout beggarman, "when your backs were to me?"

"And that's true, Denny, dear!—but look, daddy, what do you see going up the hill?"

"Ay, wisha!—how do I know?—sure I'm sand blind any way."

"Don't bother us—your eye's as clear as a kitling's—who do you think it is?"

"A woman, dear."

"Sure we know that—what else?"

"A child, my darling."

"What news you tell us—but who's the woman, and who's the child?"

"An, then, is it a witch ye think me? How can I tell?"

"Do you know Mister Phill Ryan, of the Uphill farm?"

"Do I know my right hand?"

"Did you know his wife?"

"The Lord be good to her!—Is it know her?—the holy saints make her bed in heaven;—I never say a prayer for myself without bringing her into it. Oh, she was the darling, with the open hand: there's few like her now, by the road-side."

"Well, daddy, and you knew her daughter."

"I did, I did," replied the old man, with visible emotion: "I did —the poor darling—I did, God help me! she's heavier on my heart, this many a day, than all my sins—I often drame of her. Oh, Mary Ryan, dear, I wish you were as near all hearts as you are to mine!"

"She may be near enough to you, then, any time you like for the future," replied one of the women, "for there she goes."

"Where, where?" inquired the beggar, eagerly: "Oh, as you hope for mercy, tell me where!"

"She's out of sight now," answered the first speaker; "but you saw her going up the hill."

"And did none of you tell her that her mother was dead?" inquired Denny.

"Why, then, what's come to you, daddy?" said the eldest: "my father would go mad if he thought we spoke to her."

"He'd do no such thing—he'd go with her himself sooner than she should go alone. Ah, girls! girls! one woman should never lean heavy on another; we should lave judgment to God, my darlings, and mind mercy, for we all want it, girls." The old man grasped his stick more firmly in his bony hand, and wiping the dew from his brow, which fatigue and emotion had brought there, he proceeded rapidly up the hill.

"Stop, daddy, stop, and have something to eat:—sure, the meal father promised you is ready—and you said you'd bring us word of Ellen Mullin's wedding, and what she'd on, and all."

"The next time, the next time," answered the old man, without turning back.

"And there's a drop of something in the black bottle," shouted another.

"Well!" exclaimed Stacey, the eldest of the sisters, "that bates all; I never knew daddy refuse the bit and the sup before! Mary Ryan always had the way of bewitching the men, though to be sure, *now*, she's both old and ugly!"

"She's just your age," said Rose, the youngest girl.

"How do you know that?" was the query.

"Father said so."

"Father knows nothing about it," retorted the offended elder; but I must leave them to settle a question the most difficult to determine among either women or men, and proceed with my story. It is already known that Mary Ryan had left her father's house—but no one knew with whom—that she was returning with a child of her own, and ignorant of the fact that her mother was dead, and her father again married, and that there existed, at all events, one human being who felt interested in her fate—although he was only old Dennis, commonly called "Daddy Denny"—as notorious a beggarman as ever importuned upon the Irish highway. Daddy Denny had as many acquaintances in Waterford as Reginald's Tower, and in Wexford, as the Bridge; but he only visited towns occasionally, loving better the bye-roads, gentlemen's kitchens, and comfortable farm-houses of Wexford and Wicklow—feeling a particular interest in shipwrecks, and the waifs and strays appertaining thereunto; having an active mind and an active body, as far as walking was con-

cerned; being a devout beadsman, a good story-teller, and well read
in the domestic history of every house in what he called his three
native counties—Waterford, Wexford, and Wicklow. His bold
spirit, and reputation for sanctity, gave him an ascendancy over the
poorer class, and his quaint good-humour caused him to be more
than tolerated by the farmers and gentry.

"It's lead that's in my brogues this blessed day!" he said aloud,
as he mended his pace. "Holy Mary, speed me! Ah, yah, yah! I
never think I'm growing old, barring when I have something good to
do in a hurry—the poor girleen!—she little knows what I know;"
and on he trudged, heartily and hastily, muttering every now and
then, according to his custom, about what he thought, and praying
for what he desired. Having reached the top of the hill which had
been already climbed by Mary Ryan—for it was one of those small
perpendicular ascents that are so common in the county of Wicklow—
Daddy Denny saw at a glance (notwithstanding his being "sand
blind"), what was passing at the Uphill farm, which lay a very little
to his left; indeed, if he had not seen, his attention would have been
arrested by the voice of a woman in loud anger. A group of young
alder trees overshadowed the dwelling, which partook more of the
nature of a farm than a cabin : against one of these, which had been
planted by her father at her birth, Mary Ryan—unable to support
herself, was leaning, in hopeless anguish—uttering no word, shedding
no tear—but listening, with opened eyes and gasping lips, to the
vehement abuse poured upon her by her father's wife. Her child, a
pallid weary-looking little girl, of about six years old, was clinging
to her dress, and her own younger sister—a woman in appearance,
yet cowed into subjection by her step-mother—was standing half in
half out of the door, not knowing how to act. Mrs. Ryan was one
of a class by no means rare, who imagine that their own virtue is
best evinced by condemning, with extreme violence, every woman
who has suffered under the supposition of swerving from the right
path. She had known Mary in girlhood; she knew how beloved she
had been by the mother to whom she had succeeded; she saw her
changed, faded, and in despair; but notwithstanding all this, the
harsh tones of her voice mingled with the balmy breezes of a May
evening :—

"Go back from where you came—Father, Moyra! deed, an it's
himself that's in fine health, Lord be praised!—dacent man—and has
enough to do to provide for dacent, well-behaved children, without
having shame, and shame's daughter, to pick the potatoes God sends;
for—oh, you brazen face!—take yer brat to yer mother's grave, and
cry there!" Here Mary's sister interposed, but Daddy Denny could
not hear the words. "If you touch her, or go near her, you shan't
stay here, depend upon that!" exclaimed Mrs. Ryan. "I'll yer

father's wife, and I'll have none like her to curse our house! if we're
poor we're honest, not like other people."

"And who says she's not honest?" said the stout beggarman, in-
terposing his portly person between Mrs. Ryan and the almost unconscious Mary.—"Who *dares* to say it? Fetch yer sister a drink of
wather, to bring her to herself, Anty, this minute. I'm ashamed of
vez all, so I am; I never heard tell of the like before, in my own
three counties! Setting a case, she had been deluded—to shame I
mean—did you never see a holy picture about a prodigal's return?
Why, Mrs. Ryan, the print of it is hanging against yer own wall, the
father houlding out his arms, and the calf—red and white, and fat—
standing ready for killing; and yet ye see the crathur dying upon
these stones, and don't lift her up! Ah, yah! Mary, mavourneen,
asthore, machree! ye've supped sorrow sure enough, a lannan; but
I know my own know, a'coushla: and I tell you," he continued, while
kneeling by Mary's side, he supported her on his arm—"I tell you,
and call the Almighty, the blessed Virgin, and all the holy saints of
heaven, to witness that she who rests on me now, in a dead faint—I
tell you all—that, though foolish in what she did, she's freer from
sin than e'er one here, barring her own child—don't cry, my pet,
your mammy's only in a faint, my bird. Here!"—he continued, as
the farmer himself, unconscious of what was going on, leaped heavily
over the ditch—"here! look here, sir, if you plaze; and may the
Almighty, that stands the innocent's frind, turn yer heart to yer own
flesh and blood!"

James Ryan walked to where his daughter was still supported by
Dennis—his wife hung back, for she did not quite like to encounter
the beggarman's eloquence, which was to the full as energetic as her
own, when excited. Mary Ryan was very like her mother; and
lying pale and speechless—without sense or motion—the resemblance
to her parent on her death-bed, appealed so powerfully to his feelings,
that he raised her in his arms, calling upon Dennis to account for her
appearance.

"I wonder at you, James!" said the wife; "don't you see it's
Mary, whom you often swore should never break the daylight at your
door? I wonder at you, Denny, to be taking advantage of the poor
man's softness and innocence! Get up, James; don't be demaning
yourself be the like of *her*, before your honest wife and children."

James Ryan looked bewildered; but, as he collected his scattered
thoughts, his horror of his daughter's sin overpowered every other
feeling.

"And that's true," he said; "yet she's so like her mother—but
it's true for all that. She left us of her own accord; and the mother
that bore her could find no place but the grave to hide her sorrow

in. She broke the heart of her own mother; and, poor as I am, she was the first that ever brought shame on her name."

"Come away, come away, James," whispered her step-mother;— "come away, and don't be letting yourself down with thinking of her."

"Let me alone, woman!" he exclaimed, rudely shaking off her hand:—"let me alone, and do not turn your tongue on her—mind that. Go in, children; I swore she should never darken my door; and she never shall!" He rose up, and walked steadily towards his cottage; but before he had time to enter it, the sturdy beggar interposed.

"Look here, James Ryan," he said: "I tell you what I told her, who, I trust to the Lord, is now in glory—I said to her, when that girl left your house, that sorrow would follow her, but not shame;—I tell you, that she has never known a happy hour since; but I tell you, besides, that she'll be righted yet; and that, though the sunshine of her life be gone, you'll be proud of her—all of you— proud of her, and proud of Mary Ryan's daughter. I tell *you* this— Mrs. Ryan, ma'am—because I know you're of the sort that would give to get agin; and the time will come when you'll be glad, may-be, to pick her potatoes, and winnow her corn; and I tell it to you, Mister Ryan, because you're her father, and because the dread of her shame is just now stronger in you than your natural love— that's why I do it."

"Hear the big beggarman!" exclaimed Mrs. Ryan.

"Hearing is all one ever got by being a beggarman from you, any way!" he answered, sharply; "but it's the man of the house I'm speaking to; the father of her who lies there suffering from another's sin, and not sinning herself."

"You speak like a book, Mister Denny, but it's no good to you," said Mrs. Ryan. "Don't look back at her, James, honey, though, sure enough, I wouldn't be where I am but for her! If she hadn't broke her mother's heart, I'd never have been so happy as to be your wife." Whether or not this artful piece of feminine flattery succeeded, I cannot tell, but certainly James preceded his wife into the house, and she shut the door, pulling the latch-string inside, to prevent it being opened.

"What'll I do with her at all!" soliloquized Denny, while sur- veying Mary Ryan and her daughter—"the foolish ould nagur, to be led that way by his young slut of a wife. She may have years of trial still, God help her! And where will she shelter? Rouse yer- self, Mary, my own ould heart's darlint—rouse yerself. What's that you say?—that you murdered your mother, jewel? Faix, no, 'twas the will of God, avourneen—nothing passes His holy will—rouse, darling, and see if ould Daddy Denny can't find you a night's lodging somewhere. Oh, the hearts of some fathers—and sisters too—to see how that young clip of a sister deserted her like the rest! Where will I take her too? I know," he said, after giving his head one of those earnest scratches which seem mysteriously to revive the Irish intellect—" I know!—ould Jenny Harper, the barony Forth woman, whose husband was killed in the mines, has a sore heart still, and that makes a feeling one."

And the daddy fussed, and talked, and, at last, succeeded in rousing poor Mary into a flood of tears, while the child kept entreating her not to cry. Still the broken-hearted creature sat before her father's closed door moaning—" If he would only forgive me—only forgive me!" The night dews fell, and the moon rose; and, at last, the kind-hearted beggar persuaded her to accompany him to a cabin hard by, where she'd be sure of shelter. Silence not being one of his qualities, he muttered and jabbered all the way, like most great talkers, expecting no reply; and so busy was he with his own thoughts and opinions, that he did not hear the light foot of Anty Ryan, who flung her arms round her sister's neck, and was sobbing on her bosom. " Mary! it's your little sister that I am, and dare not speak to you before *her*—your *dawshy* Anty, agra!—don't take on too much about your mother; it was an inward complaint she had for ever so long—and sure, before the breath was out of her, she prayed for you with all her heart and soul—yes, she forgave you."

" But she thought me guilty?" inquired the poor creature, breathlessly.

" She forgave you, sister—I have no more to say; but here, don't be cast down—here's a thrifle I saved—and that saving doesn't often trouble me—but I did save a few shillings, just for something—but I'd rather give it to you, my poor Mary; it's all I have. Well, if you won't have it, the child, God help it, will! I'm your aunt, honey; and, while you're Mary Ryan's daughter, I'll love you, my poor innocent baby: there, God be with you! Daddy will tell me where you'll be. I must run back, for I pulled the loose stones from where the window's to be, to get out."

" Why, then, that's right!" exclaimed Denny; " and a good husband and soon to you, my brave hearty girl! That's the rale sort, mother's own child—success—and cross of Christ about us! that nothing may *cross* yer path worse than a beam of the May moon!"

Mary Ryan and her daughter were, within an hour from that time, established, quite to Daddy Denny's satisfaction, in the cabin of the Widow Harper, a miserable dwelling composed of turf and loose stones, and consisting only of one room, but she had not forgotten the neat habits of her childhood; and, small and poor as it was, the floor was even and well swept; the chimney did not smoke: and the bed of dried heather was raised from the floor by some long boards, and covered by a patch quilt. The old woman showed every attention to her guests, boiled them some potatoes for supper, and afterwards bathing their feet in the potato water—taking care to throw it out when done with, that it might not be converted to any improper use by the fairies, who, it is said, have a great fancy for floating boats upon bath-water, and thereby sorely bewildering the imaginations of those who sleep, either in cabin or palace.

Denny betook himself to a neighbour's barn, as was his custom; and, when he reappeared in the morning, he found poor Mary Ryan suffering from the rapid approach of fever.

"I well know the sickness that's coming over her," said the widow; "and I'll tell you what, daddy, all I have to give her is the poor bed and the shelter—she's welcome to that—and I'll take a turn among my husband's people for a couple of weeks; I'll bring her little girl with me, if she'll come; and the neighbours won't let her want a mouthful through the window, quite convaynent. I can't stay within a mile of a fever myself, on account of a promise I made my mother— and she on her death-bed—never to do so: so that's all I can say, except may the Lord forgive unnatural relations!" The widow strove to prevail on the child to accompany her, but in vain; the little creature clung to her mother, importuning her with questions of when would she go home, which she had not the power to answer.

"God be with you, Mrs. Harper, ma'am," exclaimed Denny; "you've done a Christian turn; and if there's virtue in prayers, you shall have them, dear—may-be I won't pepper away at them for your sake!" and the widow cheerfully gave up her dwelling to the outcast from her own father's house.

"The neighbours" did watch—as they always do; and the beggarman positively insisted upon having "a drop of wine, and a grain of tea," from the gentry, "for the sick woman, who had no one to look to her, only God, and the poor."

This was a common case enough; for, as I have often said, and am never tired of repeating, the Irish peasant is rich in the virtue of generosity; but the care and tenderness—the watchfulness of the child over the parent, were subjects of astonishment to all who knew it:—by day or night she never left her mother's presence—caring for her wants, and sitting quietly upon the ground in the light of day, or the darkness of night—her large lustrous eyes fixed upon the place where her mother lay. Anty Ryan, and Anty Ryan's sweetheart, had contributed largely to Mary's recovery, by bringing her those morsels of luxury which the rich do not value, and which were given to Anty by a kind lady for the purpose. The watchful child knew who approached by the step, and her thin arm, and eager hand, were immediately thrust through what the widow had pompously designated

—"the window;" and the food placed in it, and hallowed by a
blessing, was immediately conveyed to her suffering parent. Mary
recovered. Her mysterious absence—the loudly repeated declarations
of daddy (who either was, or seemed to be, deep in her secrets), that
she was innocent of shame—the harshness of her father, the benevolence of the widow, and the extraordinary conduct of the child, created
and kept alive an interest in her fate, which operated in her favour.
When she was able to creep about in the sunshine, and enjoy the
light breeze that sports amid the woods and glens of all-beautiful
Wicklow, she was assailed by numerous questions as to " Where she
had been living ?" " Who was she with ?" " Was she going back ?"
" Why did she leave ?" and so forth. To all these questions she
meekly replied, " I cannot tell ;" and though every one feared " she
had been very wicked," they felt for the poor, shadowy, worn-out
creature, in whose behalf, natural instinct seemed reversed ; for,
strangely enough, her little girl had grown into her protector ; and
the mother looked to the child for her small store of comfort. Wonders are wonders longer in the country than in the town ; Mary
Ryan continued to be regarded with sympathy long after astonishment
as to her whereabouts and position had ceased. Although three
years had elapsed since her reappearance, she still sheltered beneath
the Widow Harper's roof, knitting stockings of the finest wool, which
were sought after by the visitors to " the Meeting of the Waters,"
and the immediate neighbourhood ; and her daughter, who had none
of her mother's timidity in her composition, would offer them for
sale. She had become most useful to her mother ; and the good
widow, and Daddy Denny, were perpetually on the watch to inform
her *how* her zeal and activity might be turned to the best account.

" Darling, dear ! gather a handful of them flaggers—the blossoms,
I mean—bind them with the fairy flax, and be ready with yer courtesy
at the Avoca Hotel, and offer them to the ladies ; the quality, darling,
will be soon astir to see God's works below and above the earth ; and
sling a pair of the stockings on yer arm ; don't take any notice of me
forenint the quality ; it will do you no good to be talking with the
big beggarman—you're no begging, but selling, avourneen—so you're
above your poor daddy. Hould up yer head in the world, my girleen ;
and, above all things, don't take common charity ; if they give you
a penny, have something to give them for it :—never let any one have
to say, you was a beggar, avourneen ! mind that." Or he would
watch her going forth with a couple of baskets, into either of which
she could have almost crept herself, her abundant hair hanging over
her fawn-like eyes, when not tossed by the breeze ; her cloak, more
an incumbrance than a protection, tucked up by her arms ; and her
small bare feet, beautiful in shape and proportion, rendering her appearance a picture worthy the painter's skill. " Ye're going after eggs,

now, I'll go bail; and I heard them say at the wooden bridge, that
Mary Ryan's daughter's eggs were always fresh; and, better than
that, the farmers would trust you to market their eggs sooner than
many a grown woman: and, sure, that is a proud hearing for your
mother;" and then the poor mother's eyes would fill with tears, and
she would continue her monotonous occupation—knit, knit, knit for
ever; walking, sitting, standing, "the needles" were never out of
her hands. As the girl grew stronger, she would cut turf for their
fire, and do so with an energy and determination that astonished
every one.

"Ye're for the bog to-day, dear," the gaberlunzie said; "and, by
the blessing of God, it will not be *soft* weather; we had great
prayers intirely last Sunday against wet—the poor man's foe; but
in troth, jewel, I don't like to see you working for evermore so cruel
hard and you so young!"

"Then come and help me, daddy," laughed the child,

"Ah, darling! I own to it—I'd do anything rather than work! it
never came natural to me. Every one said I'd take to it as I grew
ould and steady; but, jewel, I suppose I never did grow steady, for
though I grow ould I like it less than ever. I used to herd sheep on
the mountains, and used to lie and think how happy the sun, moon,
and stars would be, travelling—it was their nature, you understand,
as well as mine. It does not take much to keep an Irishman; the
tongue in his head will do it, without his hands; though I don't
travel much now—no, dear, I'll advise you, and think for you, *and
watch for the time*; but as to working, it's too late in the day for me.
Bedad! the Wicklow hills would shout with wonder, if they looked
down on Daddy Denny clamping turf!"

Sometimes Mary Ryan's daughter would encounter her grandfather, and then her eye would kindle, and her cheek flush; and she
would spring out of his path with the fleetness of a wild roe. It is
quite impossible to describe the tenderness and love she bore her
mother; *she had no self but in her;* and the more feeble Mary Ryan
became, the more devoted grew her child. Daddy Denny was the
only one who knew what Mary's position really was; but he kept it
a profound secret, never hinting but once, to the priest's housekeeper,
as he was waiting to see his reverence, "that poor Mary Ryan was
like Hagar and Abraham in the picture, only much worse trated."
Denny had great Scripture knowledge, in his own estimation, and
was frequently known to argue thereon; and the poor people, not
understanding what he said, came to the invariable conclusion that,
in Denny's particular case, "the poverty had spiled a fine priest."

Days, weeks, months, and years went by; and Mary Ryan's
daughter was fast merging from the girl into the woman. She had
gleaned a little learning rom a hedge schoolmaster, one of the clever

political old fellows, who, in by-gone times, taught the "big boys" Law and Latin, Politics, and the "Read-a-made-aisy," in the same breath. He usually got up, every day, such a scene as the following:—"Spell tyrant, James Sullivan. Now, Jimmy, hould up yer head like a man, to show ye defy it." "T-i—" "Och! murder, no. What spells Ty, besides T-i?" "T-n, sir." "Och! my, ye're only fit for a slave, Jimmy; I'm sorry for ye, you poor craythur. Try *your* tongue at it, little Neddy."—"T-y-r-a-n-t!" spells out the young rogue, his bare foot placed firmly on the damp floor, and his eyes sparkling with triumph.

"There's my haro!—take the top of the class. Oh! not the Latin class, my boy; you're not up to that, Neddy, yet—but above Jimmy Sullivan. Now for the meaning: who was a tyrant?"

"Naro," replies one.—"Queen Elizabeth," says another.—"Oliver Crummel," shouts a third.—"My daddy's landlord," observed Neddy, "when he turned us to the wide world to starve!"

"That's bould spoken," said the schoolmaster; "I see you understand the word, little Neddy."

"I have good right, sir," answered the child.

"Spell mother, girls," said the schoolmaster, who gave them, as he stated, "word about," and managed to appropriate domestic phrases to the female class. "I'm not in two syllables yet, sir," said Mary Ryan's daughter, upon whom the schoolmaster's eye fell.

"M-u-d—" began one of the class.—"No, that won't do. Sure you ought all to be able to spell it; for sorra a one that does not know what it is to have a good mother, barring one or two. Mary Wright, poor child! your mother's in heaven since the day she gave you to a broken-hearted world; and, indeed yours"—and again his eye fell on Mary Ryan's daughter—"never did much for you—so I'll excuse you."

"If you please, sir," said the girl, growing very red, "I'll not be excused for that reason: my mother did the best she could for me;" and—she burst into tears—and then as suddenly checked her emotion, and spelt the cherished word correctly.

From that hour she became the old man's beloved pupil; and he suffered her to come without any payment, or at any hour she could; and often would she enter his lowly dwelling at night, with a long piece of bog-wood, or a farthing candle, and crouch at his feet—conning from borrowed and half-torn books, the lesson which he not only heard, but assisted her to learn—dismissing her with the invariable assurance that "she would be a bright girl yet."

Daddy Denny greatly encouraged this love of learning. He brought her a slate from Wexford, and books from both Arklow and Waterford—one being the "Seven Champions," and the other "Cinderella."

" Learning," he would tell her, " is better than house and land, they say ; but I'm sure it's better with the house and land than without it. Who knows what will turn up yet, if the Lord only spares poor daddy—till—the time comes ? That's all I pray for, jewel : and I take care of myself, and all for you ; though the Lord he knows it's a great loss to me—the wearing brogues I mean—to keep the could from my chest ;—for, when I attend the coaches, the vagabone beggars set the quality agin me, shouting, ' what does he want ?—look at his brogues ;' and then they call me ' brogey ;' and all because I want to live for your sake, agra !—for I'm almost kilt walking the world for divarshin, until it has turned into hard labour on me. I wish we could rouse your mother, Peggy, honey ; but she's sat under the trouble so long, that I'm thinking she'll a'most miss it, when it goes. Ah, yah ! well, it is a weary world—a long, weary road, to travel from one's birth to one's death :—an unbearable road, if a poor sinner dare say so—*only for what it leads to*—the heavenly Jerusalem. Oh ! that's great glory to think on ; and them that raise their eyes to that, won't faint with the length of the way. It raises a poor man's heart to think that a Lazarus like myself may lay in some great saint's bosom. Well, dear, you're growing to be a'most a woman, Peggy ; and don't keep company with any of the boys about the place—sorra a one of them fit for *you.* I hope you haven't got a sweetheart in your sweet head, jewel ?—it's mighty inconvanient—and—"

" Oh, daddy ! if I do get such a thing into my head, it's you that will put it there, and so I'll tell mother :—and have you seen my hen, with eleven chickens at her foot ? Mother minds them ; and the poor widow has taken over such pains at the needles, and we're going to be rich, sure enough—so I'll hold my head as high as you please, for I've got two silver testers in my pocket ; and I'll give one to you, Denny, who have been my best friend."

The old man took the little coin, and deposited it in one of his numerous pockets, muttering—" I'll fasten it on my *bades,* God bless her, for a mimorial."

" There's one thing I often want to speak about, but can't never, to *her,*" said the girl, " because it a'most kills her. Do *you* know anything of my old home and my father ?"

" Whist, a'coushla ! how should I know anything ? You never saw me there."

" No, never—I wish I could forget it, but I can't. I remember my mother catching me out of my sleep, and flying from the house like mad ;—and mind, too, the oaths and the curses that followed us. Oh ! then, I was glad to keep wandering anywhere from him."

" Whist, avourneen ! it's foolish to give sorrow a tongue. What

do I know about such things? Hould up yer head—sing at your
work—say your prayers—mind your mother—and as the schoolmaster says, Mary Ryan's daughter will be a bright girl yet."

Two months after this little scene had passed, the widow on waking
in the morning, found that Mary Ryan was up before her:—this was
something new. Peggy, indeed, was always a-foot early—the first to
rise, on the town-land; but Mary was feeble, and seldom awoke
until long after the lark had finished his matins. For a moment
the widow thought the girl had grown careless; the few sods
of turf necessary for boiling potatoes were there, and the three-legged
pot was hanging over them; but the fire, so seldom extinguished in
an Irish cabin, was out; and the kitten, singed by the turf ashes
from black to red, was seated on the stone, guiltless of pur or gambol,
and looking as sullen as possible.

"Where are they, pusheen?" said the widow, who would rather
talk to a kitten than remain silent. "Is Peggy gone after some
quality specimens for the bride and groom at the wooden bridge?—
but where's Mary Ryan? Ah! then, don't be winkin' that way,
but tell us the news."

"Pusheen" seemed as perplexed as her mistress, and said so in
her own way, uttering an abrupt mew, and then humping her back
with a dissatisfied air. The morning advanced, but no Mary returned;
no Peggy, with careful step and thoughtful face, swept the floor that
day, or fed the hens, who looked about, as if in astonishment at not
receiving their usual attention: her three books were on the poor
dresser; but her bonnet and shawl, and her mother's cloak, were
gone. Before night, Mrs. Harper had inquired of every neighbour
if they had seen her friends? No one had seen them: but a "wise
woman," who had been called in the middle of the night to attend a
farmer's wife, had met two women and a man, as she jogged double
on the farmer's horse, and was fully convinced that the youngest was
Mary Ryan's daughter. The country people were both astonished
and alarmed at this mysterious disappearance; and her father, who
had maintained his harsh conduct towards them, relented, when
it was too late, and endeavoured to trace them in every way. At one
time he thought they were in Enniscorthy;—at another, in Bray;—
but still he found them not. Some called to their remembrance that
they had seen Daddy Denny and Mary Ryan in close conversation
several times, and on several days previous to her disappearance;—
but then, as the bluff old beadsman was in the confidence of half the
women of the parish, nothing strange was thought of it at the time.

Mrs. Harper was in a state of distraction, and declared to every
one, she would travel the world until she found them. They had, in
a great degree, replaced what was lost to her; and while the helpless

nature of poor Mary worked upon her affections, the steady industry and activity of the daughter commanded her respect.

It was perfectly true that the beggarman had brought information to Mary Ryan and her daughter, by which they were induced to leave the roof that had so long sheltered them.

"All I've got to say to you, jewel, agra!" he said, when arranging how they were to "steal away" from Mrs. Harper, is "tell no news, give no information to any one;—now just mind that:—and then we can let them know about it when the end comes; there's no use in rising a talk, dear—it's just like rising a fog, which bothers all who have any call to it. Avourneen, there's a tower of strength and a rock of wisdom in a silent tongue! I blaze out a good dale, dear, myself; but one can say a power of words, without any maning, and that's the way I manage the country; and faix, many a legislature, which manes a law-maker, ma'am, would give his two born eyes for that same sacret. Ah-yah-wisha! he's a wake-minded man that can't keep his own counsel."

By the time the morning dawned, and Mrs. Harper awoke, the trio were far on their journey, and in a different direction from any it was imagined they had taken. They agreed to keep off the high road as much as possible. It was strange to observe how Denny's mendicant propensities, and his kind heart, were at variance when they reached the pretty village of Newtown-Mount Kennedy; the Wexford coach was just passing through, and it was evident the Daddy longed to prosecute his usual attack upon the pockets of the passengers, yet he was loth to forsake his companions for the purpose, and consoled himself with rejoicing that the clumsy efforts of the clamorous crew had not procured them a single penny.

"Ah!" he exclaimed, "it's wonderful hard to soften some people's hearts; they have no feelin' in them for the poor. I've heard a gentleman swear he wouldn't give a beggar-woman a farthing, barring she had some fun in her, and, at the same time, she had a matter of six soft children starving to death in the sight of her eyes—it's hard to make fun out of starving children! The insides and the outsides must have different tratement altogether. You may pass a joke with the outsides, and touch them up with a story betwixt times; but seeing that it's mostly ladies and gentlemen that's insides, they must be handled like a nest of young thrushes; no matter how ould they are—the ladies I mean—a blessing on their beauty will smoothen all the frowns away. I remember once a very stately one, and frosty-faced she was—an ould residenter upon the earth, sure enough;—well, one poor innocent young woman held up her baby to her, and bid her think of her own little grandchildren at home. Och! that turned her to hard vinegar! Another prayed the Lord

might make her bed in heaven! Well, that's foolish, for people that
are rich and ould don't like to think of their end—not a halfpenny
did they get; but, at last, 'Sweet lady,' I says, 'I'm thinking of
the little sixpence you gave me two years ago, and God bless you
for it.' 'That's a lie,' she says, 'for I never gave a beggar a sixpence in all my life.' 'Didn't ye, dear!' I says, 'well, then, it must
have been Lady Mary, the beauty of the county, and it's no wonder
I'd make the mistake, for you're as like as two peas in a pod.' I
saw the corners of her mouth move, and she gives me a penny! If
ye see a raw college boy, with a goold band to his cap, sure he wants
to be thought in the military line, and ye're safe in calling him
'handsome captain' or 'noble major.' I've known a shopboy have
the same dress outside on a week's holiday to his people; there's no
harm in mistaking every spalpeen you meet for a gentleman, though,"
added Denny, thoughtfully, "it's not pleasant to be degrading one's
self, if one could help it. When ye see a lady, with little children
about her, *praise* the children; and if they're as ugly as frogs, lay
on them all kind of angels; and if they're roaring wicked with ill-
temper, call them 'little lambs;' then, if she has any motherly feeling
about her, you're sure of a tester.* If ye see a couple mighty loving
together, ye may bless the lady's sweet face; but it's hardly sure,
for, bedad! the young men think as much of their own beauty, and
may-be it's nothing you'll get for your trouble. It's asy enough to
work the money out of any pocket if ye can understand the *nature*
of the body that carries it—that's where the knowledge is wanting.
Foreigners are mighty soft at first; and there used to be grate trade
intirely at the Pigeon-house, and about there—women with twins,
as near to match as they could get 'em—widows, deserted wives, and
fatherless children—lame men, blind men, and the falling sickness;
but that's over long ago. In the heart of the war I made a purty
penny myself as a wounded soldier, with a plate in my head and a
bad leg; anything for a bit of bread! Sure the half of us would
work if we could get it; and the Lord above knows that the lies we
tould *for variety* weren't worse than the truth;—that the plain, hard,
griping starvation was with us at home and abroad, by night and by
day; that was true, any how; but people had heard of it so often
that they did not like to be bothered with it; so, after all's said and
done, it was against that we strove. God help us and forgive us the
inventions; starvation makes one's wits bright, bedad! I was so
thin, one or two of the hard summers, that if it wasn't that I had
the wit to put stones in my wallet, I'd have been blown away."

I wish I had space to recount all Daddy Denny's stories. Some

* A fourpenny bit.

of them could not fail to make you weep; and his transitions from humour to pathos were truly characteristic of his calling. There are many who cannot fail to remember this energetic, yet lazy personage, who latterly begged from habit, rather than necessity; and who was at all times trusty, and trusted by many of his superiors, particularly in the time "of the troubles," when, I have been told, he was in the prime of life, and rendered humane assistance to whoever needed it.

The wanderers had journeyed for nearly a week, when, on the evening of the fifth day, "Do you know where you are, Peggy?" inquired Mary Ryan of her daughter. "I think I do," replied the girl. "I think I know the turn of that river; I think—yes, I do know those trees; that's just the way the crows used to be flying, with the same noise; yes, mother, though I never looked from this hill before, I know that big brick house, and the gate that I used to be climbing, but never could swing on. Och!" she added, with an involuntary shudder, "I hope we ain't going to live there again."

"Whist, honey! whist!" ejaculated the beggarman; "wishing is a mighty foolish thing for those who put their trust in God. Sure everything will turn out well to those that have faith, dear, if not well for this world, well for the next. I'll go now and hear the news, and you can sit here with yer mother till I'm back, a'coushla," and away went Denny at his own particular and professional trot.

Peggy found a "dry ditch" for her mother to rest on, and having rolled her own shawl into a "soft sate," she made her sit upon it, placing herself higher up, so that her mother's head rested in her lap. The worn-out woman did not speak a word for more than an hour, but the large tears kept rolling from her eyes, while her daughter murmured every now and then, "Mother, avourneen! don't take on so; mother, darlin', you're wearin' out my heart; mother, honey, trust in the Lord. Oh, what will I do at all! and no one near me; she'll die here with the fair trouble o' mind."

"Trouble is a long time killin', or I'd have been dead long ago," replied her mother, to whom the shedding of tears had been a relief; "but I'm easier now, God be praised; and Peggy, the time is come for me, your mother, to humble myself to tell you, my born child, the whole truth."

"Don't distress yourself, darlin' mother: don't, I know all I want to know," replied the girl, with a trembling voice; "where s the good of going it over?"

"You know nothing, Peggy—how should you?"

"Oh, bad news travels with hare's feet," she answered; "but don't, mother, I'd be happier not to hear it from your own self, because I'll be still thinking, may-be, the half was lies."

F

"Peggy, honey, in sight of his house and under the blessed canopy of heaven, and knowing the Almighty's eyes are on me, as sure as all this, so surely am I your father's wife." The girl, at first, made no reply, but clasped her hands around her parent's neck, and at last said, "An' why didn't you tell me this before? sure if it was a sacret, not to take away my shame would I own it—only just for inward satisfaction to myself."

"Why, you never let on to me you were reproached with it, my darling."

"No, mother—how could I? sure it isn't easing my own heart by chilling yours I'd be! but what does it signify? I'm able for the world now! I can look an honest woman's daughter in the face; oh, mother, jewel, and I to doubt you?"

"You must hold your tongue still, Peggy, until I give you leave to speak. Your father, dear, was above me, and I'd never have known him but for his coming about our place in the shooting season. My father and mother fixed on one in my own line of life for me, and I knew I'd be forced to marry him if I stayed at home, and all the time my heart's whole love was with your father. I tried to hide this from my father and mother, as well as from the young man I loved; but, och, hone! I blinded my parents, but not my lover. I was proud of his love, he was so above me, and he said he was proud of my beauty! Well, dear, I agreed to leave my parents, as he promised to marry me; but as he was entirely dependent on his father, he book-swore me to keep it secret from man and mortal till his father's death. I was satisfied, and went with him one Sunday evening, to return no more; he eased my heart with a marriage, but there was only us two by, and the priest, if he was a priest, who said the words. For the first few months he was very kind; and though I was under the heaviest shadow that can fall on a woman, still I was his wife, and I bowed down under it, thankful to look at him—to hear him speak; though his words became mixed with bitterness, still the voice was his. You were born, and what was such joy to me was sorrow to him; his father, he said, grew frightened for fear he should marry me; and, instead of being allowed to sit at his table, he sent me to the kitchen, there to bear the insults of an old bad woman, whose daughter had formerly filled my place. Oh, my darling child! may the Lord preserve you from the double death of finding out, bit by bit, that what you loved was beyond hate. Still I clung to him; I longed to go home, and then thought how I had no home; my mother was kind but I had a hard father. I thought may-be that, being his wife, God might turn his heart; and I told him so once. Oh! the cruelty of that laugh, when he answered that I was a fool, and dared me to find a witness for what had passed between us. As long as I thought to do him good, it was well enough; but I roused against this, and he turned us from his door with curses and blows—blows, darlin', that fell only on me. I thought to tell his father the truth, but even if I hadn't taken the oath, sure it would hurt him, and not have served you, for I wouldn't be believed. Since then, darlin', he openly married one of his own rank, for his father died."

"And why did we come here, mother, darlin'; and what has Daddy Denny to do with us?" asked Peggy.

"There's no time to tell that," interrupted the beggar, who had approached without being observed; "no time; the breath's in him still, and the use he made of it for the last twenty minutes is to rave about you: and my heart aches for the poor lady who is patient as a lamb, and begs, for God's sake, to bring any one that will ease his mind—"

"Then you were sent for, mother, dear?" inquired the poor girl, while assisting her to rise. "Yes, dear! Daddy contrived to get a friend of his own into the place, and when your father got this mortal sickness, he brought me to be near, thinking that, at the last, he might do us justice."

The three hurried to the house, which was full of lamentation—people running backward and forward, crying and howling "for the master." The priest who had administered "the last rites," was standing near the door, reproving the more noisy. Dennis advanced to his reverence, and falling on his knees to crave his blessing, which was quickly granted—told him that "the woman his honour wanted to see was come!" "Then you have a hand in this?" said the priest —"but so best, Denny: if you never do worse, the next penance I give you—(and I gave you *one*, I remember about six years ago)—I will not put you to much trouble; let the woman come in."

When Mary entered the chamber of death, the last throes of dissolving nature were convulsing the frame of the dying man! She staggered towards the bed—from which the lady he had married, had been removed—and, falling on her knees, clasped and kissed his clammy hand. He rallied, and recognised her; he felt her hand, finger by finger, and when *he touched the ring* he half rose up—stammered "Mary"—fell back—and his spirit departed. The poor woman forgot everything save the love of her early days: she uttered no complaint of his cruelty and injustice, but she wept bitterly. Not so Dennis; he had expected that wrong would have been made right —and he followed "his reverence" out of the house; when every beggar in the district crowded into it, expecting the tobacco and whisky, besides other good cheer, which in those days accompanied the funerals of all classes. Whatever his conversation with the priest may have been, it was known only to themselves, but it had the effect of sending Dennis back to the house, where he mingled among the crowd, seeking Mary Ryan, or her daughter, and hoping they might not have left the house. At last one of the servants told him, that the woman the "poor master called for," had fallen in a fit, that she had carried her to a loft, and that, for her part, she didn't think she'd live. "And the girl?" She knew nothing about her, except that she had set a strange girl in a back house to mind the boilings, or there'd be nothing for the people to eat,—the dwelling was so "throng," and would be worse as the night drew on. She locked her in, and wouldn't have thought of her for another hour or two, but for him. Dennis reconnoitred through a window, and, finding that the un-willing watcher was Mary's daughter, accomplished her liberation; and having first charged her, on no account—no matter what indignity she or her mother suffered, to leave the place until he told them they might do so—he sent her in search of Mary Ryan. After much delay and many repulses, Peggy succeeded: it was a miserable loft, in a distant part of the rambling building, where she had been carried; the slates were off in many places, and the wind rushed through the shadowy laths, tumbling, at every fresh gust, some lump of mortar, or clattering tile. As the night advanced, the voices of intoxicated persons, mingled into one great discordant noise, ascended to where the heart-broken girl was chafing her mother's hands; while she laid across her feet to impart a portion of her young warmth to her parent's weary limbs. She had arranged some old curtains that had been thrown into a corner to decay, into a tolerably comfortable bed, and moistened her lips with some milk which the servant had given her for herself; her consolation was, that *there* they were left to them-selves; and, from behind a parapet, she could see all that passed in the courtyard. The moon rose to its full height, and the shadows it threw upon the floor were, she thought, very terrible. Once a huge cat peered down upon her from a rafter, and then scampered away, while bits of the old roof tumbled on all sides. She was shivering from head to foot, and the old damp hangings she threw over her shoulders, seemed to make her still more cold; but her mother slept, breathing as gently as a sleeping child—*that*, at least, was a consola-tion; if it had not increased her loneliness the more, it would indeed have made her heart beat with thankfulness and joy. She knelt softly down by her mother's side, and, after repeating her prayers, she enumerated to herself every instance she had ever heard of God's watchful care by night, as well as by day; this strengthened and refreshed her; and yet every cloud that passed athwart the moon, and so caused a partial eclipse to the small, shivering, chilly light, which flickered through the apertures, made her repeat the words more fervently: sometimes she would fix her eyes on a bright solitary star, and then turn them on her mother, who looked, in the dim uncertain light, so deathly pale, that the girl would hold in her own breath to listen for the manifestation that she was still in life. Suddenly she was roused from a nodding sleep, by the fall of a stone, or brick, which rattled into the room, followed by a heavy grunting sort of noise, as of a person breathing hard after violent exertion. A shriek quivered on her lip, but she repressed it, and immediately felt the wisdom of having done so. "Peg—Peggy, avourneen," puffed a well-known voice, "don't be frightened, darlin'—it's me, a'coushla machree—ould Daddy Denny—wait till I catch my breath, which is flying from me like widgeon from a gun—och, hone!—I'm too ould for climbing, and couldn't have reached you at all, but for the tough bames of the stable, and a ladder, dear, that Peter Mullowny's holding. I've got the girl of the house, dear, to forget where yez are—and so keep quiet till ye're wanted, jewel; and here's more than you'll ait, I know, for the three days of the wake—or drink aither,—fresh mate, and white bread *of your own*—father's, I mane; for, poor man—God be good to him—he's to the fore still, and a fine wake as ever I was at, lashings of everything, more especially people; the lady has a fine spirit in her—an'—but, faix, dear, my head's bothered somehow, and the moon's turning round on me, so the Lord be wid yez—I needn't bid ye take care of yer mother—for sure it's Mary Ryan's daughter ye are—and pray for yer sinful soul—I mean my—hould hard and fast, Peter, dear—for somehow both myself and the ladder's mighty unsteady."

"The girl of the house" did, to all appearance, forget Mary Ryan and her daughter; but some one, every morning, placed a full measure of milk at the rough door of the loft—a measure so full, that, after both had partaken abundantly thereof, they had enough to cause the great cat, which had so frightened Mary, to pur and look as contented and cheerful as became the solidity and respectability of his ancient race. Still, these three days and nights passed in all the aching anxiety of knowing nothing—and hoping and fearing all things. At last the wild, yet solemn pageantry was over. The hearse, the mourners, the priests, the people, departed. Mary Ryan watched from the broken roof, the road it took—the same road she and her child had traversed in years long ago :—*they* had returned; but *he* who drove them to despair would return no more. Holy masses were said for the repose of his soul that day, but none prayed as fervently for his eternal repose as she whose heart he had crushed almost to bursting.

Peggy wept and prayed from sympathy with her mother, but she could hardly keep down the spirit of strong indignation that was roused by a full sense of the injustice they had sustained; and no hart ever panted for the water-brooks more than did hers for liberty.

Before the funeral was completely out of sight, the only noise that broke upon the stillness of the house was the rough shutting-to of doors, and the echo of footsteps; at last "the girl of the house" made her appearance, and beckoning them to follow down a half ladder, half stair, conducted them to a large parlour, from which the remnants of the entertainment had been hastily removed, and thrust them, with very little ceremony, and sundry mutterings of "being bothered with the like," into a sort of ante-room to which it led. The door hung loosely on its hinges, and remained unclosed. Presently, a pale, gentle looking woman entered the room, and her widow's dress made Mary's heart beat more quickly; she was followed by others, who had returned from the funeral, and, in a short time, the party were placed round the table, the priest being seated at the widow's right hand, while the attorney of the next town intimated his intention of reading the will of his "late friend."

He read and read; but all that Mary Ryan and her daughter could comprehend was, that he read the same thing over and over again. At last—was it—could it be possible—were they awake? Was it reality? Could he who had that day entered the cold and silent grave —could *he* have made such a confession? "Mary Ryan—his own lawful wife!" and such and such lands to pass to her and her child!— *"thereby hoping to make atonement for his sins."* Peggy felt her mother sinking, and clasped her in her arms; after this all was confusion: the lady who had been so greatly deceived was carried from the room insensible; her brother, roused at such indignity, declared the man must have been out of his senses, and that there was no proof; and while the attorney vowed the man's perfect sanity, the priest said that, without, of course, violating the sacredness of the confessional, there *was* proof,—and Daddy Denny was brought forward, who declared he had witnessed the marriage, by means anything but straightforward certainly; and of this fact even Mary Ryan was not aware until that moment. Daddy Denny was very unwilling to be cross-questioned on the subject, but was obliged to submit; and certainly the evidence was very clear, even according to his own showing—that he had been courting a "responsible woman"—the servant to the "couple beggar"—who performed the hasty ceremony, and that she had "put him in press," in a corner cupboard, to be out of the way, from whence he saw Mary married. After all, the woman jilted him; and, at any other time, his bitterness on the subject would have created much amusement. Mary and her daughter had come forth in the *mêlée*, and if a doubt had existed of the nobleness of Mary's nature, it would have vanished before the earnestness she evinced that nothing might be done to hurt the poor lady's feelings.

Daddy Denny always stoutly denied that he knew the contents of the will—how should he?—his anxiety to keep Mary and her daughter in the house, being (I quote his own words) "intirely from a drame he had." Be that as it may;—Peggy, or as she was called on the evening of her changed fortunes, *Miss* Margaret, is living still, and often speaks to him she loves best in all the world—her husband— of the enduring patience and virtue of her mother, who lived meekly and prosperously during the remainder of her few years, and died soon after her daughter became a wife.

What a privilege it is to know a person unspoiled by prosperity! —Mary's daughter is one of these. I have sat with her upon her mother's grave, and heard her story, of which I am the faithful chronicler; and at that time the beggerman—then hale and hearty as a frosty day—stood beside us; since then *he* has fallen asleep; but I well remember the proud expression of his bright face, as he asked me what I thought of Mary Ryan's daughter?

THE BANNOW POSTMAN.

H E'S taking his own time this evening, I'll say that; for the
sun's as good as set, and no sign of him yet. Can you spy
him out ?"

"No, colleen; how d'ye think my ould eyes could see him whin
yours can't ? But, Anty, honey, ye're mighty unasy about the postman ; d'ye expict a new riban', or a piece o' tape, or some sugar-
candy, or—a love letther, Anty ? Oh! Anty, Anty!—don't blush
after that fashion : ould as my eyes are, I can see yer rosy cheek
getting quite scarlet."

"I'll tell ye what, Grey Lambert," replied the lassie to the old
man, who was literally leaning on "the top of his staff," under the
shadow of the walls of a singularly fine and perfect castle of ancient
days; "I'll jist tell ye, it 'll be long enough afore I'll come to see ye
agin, out o' pure good-natur, in yer unchristian-like ould place, if ye

talk afther that fashion to a young cratur like me, that niver turned
to the like. Sure ye're ould enough to forget love letthers, any way."

" That's true, Anty; an ould man of three score and sixteen hasn't
much to do wid what arc called love letthers; but, may-be, there's
a differ betwixt love letthers and letthers o' love; and sure there's
one still that sinds that last to his poor grandfather; and from beyant
the salt seas too."

" Well, 'tis a comfort, sure enough; but I often wonder that ye
a'n't affeard to stay in such a place as this, without anything wid ye
but Bang, the baste, that's almost as ould as yourself—poor Bang!"
And Bang pushed his nose into Anty's hand.

There was something picturesque in the appearance of the pair,
who awaited the postman's coming—for such was really the case; the
young maiden expected a lover's letter; the aged man hoped for a
remembering token from a solitary descendant. " Grey Lambert,"
as he was called, had taken up his abode in a corner of the castle
under whose shadow they stood—the lonely castle of Coolhull—and
no entreaty could induce him to leave. He was a singular, but a fine-
looking person; wore neither hat nor cap; never cut either his beard
or hair, which were purely, perfectly white, and flowed over his
shoulders, and down his breast, even below a leather girdle that encircled his coarse frieze wrapping coat; his feet were bare; his forehead high and bald; his dress clean, betokening singularity, but not
poverty; and he had been a traveller in his youth—a sailor—a soldier
—some said a pirate; but that, I firmly assert, never could have been
the case, for Lambert was the gentlest of old men; children and
animals (who seem to have an instinctive dread of bad people) all
loved him; and on Sunday evenings the village urchins, and their
little cur dogs, visited him in his castle, or sat at his feet on the green
sward, while he recounted tales and adventures of other lands.

Anty was a merry laughing, blue-eyed lass, somewhat short, and
without one good feature in her face; yet the gipsy was esteemed
pretty. It was really very provoking—she was anything but pretty,
and yet it was absolutely impossible to look on her face and think so;
she had such coaxing smiles, and that heartfelt charm—a sweet, low
voice—" an excellent thing in woman;" with so many "ah, do's,"
and "ah, don'ts;" and a trick of blushing—and blushes, stealing
over a pure white skin, are, it must be confessed, very agreeable
things to look upon; then there was a cheerfulness, a joyousness
about her, perfectly irresistible; at wake or pattern she had all the
best boys at her command, and how she laughed at them! But I
may affirm—now that she is not before me—the little hussy was
anything but pretty.

Bang was certainly a venerable relic of canine antiquity—tall and grey, haughty and stately, of royal Danish descent, and his courtesies had an air of kingly condescension; when he noticed even the bettermost dogs of the parish, there was so much aristocratic bearing about the dignified brute, that they, one and all, shrunk from his approach. But he was faithful to his master—night and day by his side; and always paid particular attention to Anastasia McQueen, who, strange to say, was a very frequent visitor at the dilapidated castle: nay, was almost daily seen trudging towards it;—her short scarlet cloak meeting the broad hem of her blue stuff petticoat, while the hood only half covered a profusion of deep nut-brown hair (I feel it here a duty to my country peasant girls to say, that they generally have long and most luxuriant tresses, and, womanlike, are not a little proud of them); while from her well-turned, but red arm, usually hung a basket, containing such presents as a Bannow maiden could present; dried fish, fresh cockles, delicate butter, barley or oaten cakes, thin and curling, or new-laid eggs. She certainly paid very great attention to the old man, and he was very much attached to his lively visitor.

"May-be it's long since ye heard from young Pat Lambert?" she inquired, after caressing Bang.

"True, love, dear; it seems long to one like me—a poor ould, very ould, man; may-be he's forgotten his grandfather."

"No, *that* he's never done, I'm sartin sure; he's as thrue-hearted a boy as iver crossed the sea; that I know, and I take it very unkind o' ye to say he'd forget you."

"Well, Anty, whin I write agin I'll tell him that ther's some don't forget *him*, any way."

"Oh!" said Anty, blushing in good earnest, "ye need not say that; sure, in a Christian country, every body remimbers their neighbour.—How beautiful the sea looks, as if there niver was an end to it!"

"How beautiful the sea looks!" repeated Grey Lambert, smiling, and shaking his head at the same time: "Well, Anty, I see ye're an admirer o' the beauties of natur. The sea is ever beautiful to my thinking; whin the great waves foam and lash the shore, and whin they toss big ships, such as you niver saw, up and down without any trouble in life—then 'tis beautiful; and whin it sleeps under the setting sunbames, as it does now, it is beautiful. How well ye see the entrance into Watherford harbour from where ye stand!—though a score o' miles and more from ye. Well, I love this ould castle for the prospect; but it's a grand place, and now I niver could think to live anywhere else. The thickness of the walls might be one of the world's wonders; then the gometry staircase, and the curious writing on the hard stones that nobody iver understood yet; and the grate oak bames. The jewil of a castle, ye are, my darlint!—to think how bravely ye stood aginst ould Oliver, the black villain! Och! many a brave heart—many a bright eye—many a smile dancing like the sunbames on the sea, has been in ye, whin ye stood with yer high walls and turrets in the morning light; but now ye're ould, and even yer stones look withered, and the cow and the wild goat shelter where princes stood; and the owl screams where the harp sounded; and I, a poor worm of the earth, live to see it, whin their noble bones make part of the sod I stand on!"

Lambert's apostrophe to his beloved castle was lost on Anty, who eagerly exclaimed, "There he is—there he is! Now I'll run and meet him, and see if he has got a letther for you." Away she flew, swift as an arrow, to meet John Williams, postman, and. it may be truly said, carrier, to the united parishes of Bannow, Kilkaven, and Duncormuck, for above thirty years. Even in these isolated spots people cannot do without news; it is almost necessary to existence. Twice each week John Williams still journeys to the nearest post-town, and conveys "the leading journal of Europe," the Fashionable Post, the Wexford and Waterford Papers, and others, to the news-loving inhabitants. Honest John is a heedless, good-tempered fellow; but a very jewel of a postman. He had been originally engaged only as a circulating medium for letters from Wexford to Bannow; but he was either bribed, or coaxed, or both, into execu-ting commissions for everybody who had commissions to execute. John Williams's list was regularly made out; and ribands, tea, candles, sugar, books, paper, music, gowns, and even caps, garnished his Rosinante—for when his orders were many, John was obliged to take his steed; not that he ever ventured to ride the poor lame beast, whom he could out-tire at any time; but he walked in a companionable manner with it, in and out of Wexford; and, in truth, their caparisons were most extraordinary.

When Anty met him, his loose drab coat was hardly secured by a solitary button, and his leather bags dangled over his shoulders; his "cawbeen" on one side of his grey shaggy head, his scratch wig on the other, and his "doodeen" serving a double purpose—keeping his nose warm, and exhilarating his spirits; the poor horse, more fatigued than its wiry conductor, eyeing the green straggling hedgerows, and the close turf, and loitering to catch a mouthful as he passed. At either side his neck hung two blue bandboxes, filled, doubtless, with multifarious finery; while a coil of thick cable, like a huge Boa, passed over his head, and held, suspended, ten or twelve flats of cork, bespoke by the captain of a coal vessel lying at Bannow quay—three new kites, four skipping ropes, ten tops, two bags of marbles, a dozen slates (for Master Ben), a pair of pole screens (for the lady at the big house), and some blankets; all, of course, so carelessly papered, that they had more than half escaped from their confinement.

"Good even', and God save ye, Mister John!" quoth the breath-ess lass. The postman was never given to much speaking, and nodded. "May-be ye wouldn't have a bit of a letther for Grey Lambert?" John stopped, and so did the horse; while John took from his bag a long, narrow, dirty-looking letter—presented it—replaced his bag, and journeyed on. Anty stopped, and looked after him; "John, John, I want to speak to ye." John again stopped. "I wanted to ask ye, if so be that ye found—I mean met—a—a—I thought may-be, ye might have—ah, John! ye know what—for poor Anty?" John took the pipe from his mouth, and simply said:

"May-be ye'd tell a body who likes plain spaking what ye're after?"

"Well, thin, John, have ye a letther for me?"

"Yes; why didn't ye ask me that a while ago, and not give me the throuble of taking off my bag twice?"

"Why didn't you give it me, and I to the fore? Sure ye knew ye had it."

"Why, look ye, Anty Mc Queen, I have been thirty years a postman; and I have always done what the back of the letther tould me; and see, the direction on it is—'Anty Mc Queen, Hill side, Bannow, County of Wexford, Ireland—post-paid—to the care of John Williams, Bannow postman; to be kept till called for.' Sure it was no business o' mine to give it ye till ye called for it, or, what I consider the same thing, asked for it."

Anty took the letter, and, placing it in her bosom, turned towards the old castle, to give to Grey Lambert his epistle. John pursued his path, until he arrived at the village Public. There, what a crowd awaited his coming! "John, what's the news?"—"John, the paper." —"John—oh, John, don't mind 'em, but give me my cap! I hope it isn't in that bandbox that's had the dance in the mud. There—John, honey—don't 'squeege' it so!—sure no cap can bear a 'squeeging!'" —"John, is my bonnet come? Och! meal-a-murder! what made Miss Lerady put an Orange riban' in my beautiful English straw?"— "John, I hope ye didn't forget the tobaccy?"—"John, agra—the two ounces o' green tay for my granny."—"John, my twinty-four marbles."—"John, och, John! and sure it's not come to that wid ye, that ye'd forget the green silk handkerchief!"—"John," said a fine-looking fellow, pushing through the circle, "John, did ye get the thing I tould ye of?" John winked; and from his waistcoat pocket drew forth a very little parcel, wrapped up in white paper. The young man took it, smiled, and soon after there was a bustle at the far window; for the parcel contained a plain gold ring, which the saucy youth was endeavouring to try on the finger of pretty Letty, the gentle daughter of mine host of the "Public."—"John, any letthers for me?" inquired the bustling man of the big shop—"One, Darby, very like a bill."—"Humph!" said Darby.—"Did ye bring the doctor's stuff for father?" asked Minny Corish.—"Och! murder-in-Irish! sure ye're not afther forgetting the five yards o' red stuff," exclaimed no less a person than Mrs. Cassidy herself, "and I wanting to quilt it for a petticoat, to keep my ould bones from freezing!"—"John," said a village lounger, who expected nothing, and yet wanted to say something—"John, why d'ye wear yer wig over yer hair?" "Why," replied John, drily, "sure ye wouldn't have me wear my hair over my wig."—"John, I take shame that I didn't offer ye this afore," and the landlord presented a large glass of whisky to the postman, who drank it off, remarking afterwards—"thrue Parliament, to be sure," which raised a general laugh.—"Come, John, ye're enough to set a body mad," said fussy Tom Tennison, who was ever in a bustle about something or other; "Master Ben has been here more nor an hour, waiting to rade us the news, and there ye stand, taking the things out as asy as—; can't ye give us the paper?" "No—I say, no—not till it's yer turn, Mister Fussy; take the patthren o' yer manners from Mister Ben; see how quiet he stands, as the song says—'tall and straight as a popilar tree;' and two of his bran new slates cracked by that devil of a horse. Arrah, don't be bothering me, all o' ye; ye forget, so ye do, that I have five or six places to go to yet; if ye taze me afther this fashion, hang me, but ye must get another postman; the moment ye see me, ye're like a pack o' Curnel Piggot's hounds in full cry, afther a hare; can't ye larn patience? sure everybody knows it's a vartue."

John's next resting-place was the Parsonage; such a lovely spot—just what a parsonage ought to be; only look, is it not perfectly delicious? That softly swelling meadow, over which the evening mist is stealing, paled off from the mossy lawn that fays and fairies might delight to revel on; the lowly, yet elegantly thatched, cottage; the green-house, the flower borders—did you ever see such splendid flowers?—there—such balsams—such peonies—such a myrtle—such roses! roses red, white, pure white, the maiden's blush, the damask, and the many coloured Lancaster, not rivalling each other, but uniting to charm sight and smell by their combined beauty and fragrance. Ah! there is Marianne amongst the lilies, fit model for a sculptor, alike lovely in person and mind. And the eldest, Henrietta, noble and dignified, though very different from Marianne; conscious of her magnificent beauty, yet condescending and benevolent to the poorest peasant. Then, Ellen the youngest; not the handsomest, but certainly the most useful; a perfect Goody Two-shoes, with more wisdom at fifteen than most women at fifty. The postman is to them all a most welcome visitor. "Oh, John, is it you? Do give me papa's and mamma's letters." "Oh, don't, Marianne!" said the young

Ellen; "don't take them all yourself; do let me have the news-papers, at least, to give papa." "John," inquired Hetta, "the net-ting-silk, and the silver bodkin—I hope you have chosen a nice one—and the two skipping-ropes, for my sisters;—thank you." "All right I hope, Miss." "Thank you, all quite right; will you come up and take something, John?" "No, Miss, I humbly thank ye, all the same." "John, tell me—have you got a letter for poor Mrs. Clavery?" "Yes, Miss." "Ah, now I *am* happy; poor woman, she will be so delighted!"

"There," thought John to himself, as he passed on—"there, that is what I call the true breed of the gentry. Such a born beauty as that to think of a poor sorrow-struck woman! Ah, the thick blood without any puddle, for ever!—that's the sort that warms the heart."

Mrs. Clavery's story will be best told in her own words, as she herself related it to the family at the Parsonage, a few months before John brought her the letter that made Miss Henrietta so happy.

One tranquil evening in autumn, a pale delicate young woman rested her hand on the gate that opened to the green sloping lawn which fronted the Parsonage-house; uncertain whether or not she might venture to raise the latch, she gazed wistfully on the group of children who were playing on the green. Although in the veriest garb of misery, there was nothing of the common beggar in her appearance; and the two little ones, who clung to her tattered cloak, were better covered than their mother. She carried, on her back, a young sickly-looking infant, and its weak cries arrested the attention of the good pastor's youngest daughter, who bade her enter, in that gentle tone which speaks of hope and comfort to the breaking heart. How much is in a kindly voice! When the woman had partaken of food and rest, and remained a few days at the Parsonage, she thus told her tale :—

"May God reward ye!—for ye have fed the hungry, and ye have clothed the naked, and ye have spoken of hope to her that thought of it no more; and ye have looked like heaven's own angels on one who had forgot the sight o' smiles. May God's fresh blessing be about ye! —may ye never want! But a poor woman's prayer is nothing; only I am certainly sure the Almighty will grant ye a long life, and a happy death, for your kindness to one who was lone and desolate in a could world. It's little matter where one like me was born, only I came of dacent, honest people, and it could not be said that any one belonging to me or mine ever wronged man or mortal; the boys were brave and just—the girls well-looking and virtuous :—seven of us under one roof; but there was full and plinty of everything—more especially love, that sweetens all. Well, I married; and I may say a more sober, industrious boy never broke the world's bread than my

Thomas—*my Thomas!* I ask yer pardon, ladies: but my heart swells when I think that may-be he's gone to the God who gave him .o me, first for a blessing, then for a heart-trial."

The poor woman wept; and the father of the family she was addressing, adopting the figurative language which the Irish so well understand, observed, "The gardener prunes the vine even to bleeding, and suffers the bramble to grow its own way."

"That's true; thank ye, sir, for that sweet word of comfort," she replied, smiling faintly; "it's happy to think of God's care—the only care that's over the poor, though it seems ungrateful to say that to those who are so extraordinary kind to me. Well, we had a clane cabin—a milk-white cow—a trifle of poultry—two or three pigs—indeed, every comfort in life, according to our station, and thankful we were for them. Time passed as happy as heart could wish, and one babe came, and another; but the eldest now was the third then, for it pleased God to take the two first in a fever; and bad, sure enough, was the trouble, for my husband took it, and there he lay, off and on, for as good as four months; and then the rint got behind hand, and we were forced to sell the cow; one would think the baste had knowledge, for when she was going off to the fair (and by the same token it was my brother-in-law's sister's son that druv her), she turned back and mowed; ay, as natural as a child that was quitting the mother. Well; we never could rise the price of a cow agin, and that was a sore loss to us, for God sent two young ones the next time, and betwixt the both I could niver get a minit to do the bit o' spinning or knitting that the landlord's wife expected as a yearly compliment. She was not a born lady; and they're the worst to the poor. Musharoon gentry! that spring up and buy land, hand over head, from the raale sort, that are left in the long run, without cross or coin to bless themselves with; all owing to their generosity. Well, to make up for that, I was forced to give up some of my best hens, as duty fowl, to the lady, on account that she praised their handsome toppings. That wasn't all;—the pigs got the measles; and we might have sould them to advantage, but my husband says, says he, 'Mary, we have had disease and death in our own house; but don't let us be the means of unwholesome mate, upon no account —because it brings ill health, and we to answer for it, when nothin' will be to the fore but honest deeds and the roguish ones, straight aginst each other, and no one to judge them but the Almighty—the ONE who knows the rights of all;'—that was true for him. Well, we might have got up agin, for my poor Thomas worked like any negur to the full; but just after we had sowed our little field of wheat (it was almost at the corner of the landlord's park, and we depinded on it for the next gale day), nothing could sarve the landlord but he must take it out of our hands, without any notice, to plant trees upon. I went to my lady, and, to soften her like, took what was left of my poor fowls—the cock and all—as a present; she accepted them very genteelly, to be sure, and promised we should have another field and compensation money. We waited, and waited, but no sign of it; at last my husband made bould to go to the landlord himself, and tould him all that had passed between the lady and me. 'Don't bother me, man,' was the answer he made, 'compensation, indeed!—what compensation am I to have for being out of my rent so long, the time ye were sick, and ye without a lase? And I am sartain my wife never promised anything of the sort to the woman.' 'I ask yer pardon, sir,' replied Thomas, civil of course—for Thomas was always civil to rich or poor; 'but she did, for my Mary tould me.' 'She tould you a lie, then,' said the landlord; and my husband fired up. 'Sir,' said he, 'if ye were my equal you dar'n't say the likes o' that of my Mary, for though she's not of gentle blood, she's no liar!' Then the landlord called my husband an impudent blackguard; and Thomas made answer, that he, being a gentleman, might call him what he pleased; but that none should say that of his wife that she did not desarve: however, the upshot of the thing was, that we got warning to quit all of a suddent: but there was no help for it; as the neighbours said—true for them—that Thomas was by no means so strong a man as before the feaver; and the steward found out some stranger who offered money down on the nail for the land, that we had in such prime order. Every one cried shame on the landlord, but sure there's no justice for the poor! 'Twas a sorrowful parting, for somehow a body gets fond of the bits of trees, even, that grow up under their eye; and I was near my lying-in, and the troubles came all at once, and all we could get to shelter us was a damp hole of a place. My husband got plenty of work; and though it wasn't in natur not to lament by-gone comforts, yet sure the love was to the good, firm—ay, firmer than ever—and no blight was on our name, nor isn't to this day—thank God for it! —for nobody breathing can say, Thomas, or Mary, Clavery, ye owe me the value of a thraneen. Oh! but that's a fine thing and a cheering after all! Well, the change of air, and the fretting, and one thing or other, made me very weakly; and we lost the fellow twin to this one; it was happy for the darlint—but it was heart-scalding to see it peeking and peeking—wastin' and wastin' and to want the drop of wine, or the morsel of mate, that might keep it to be a blessing to its parent's grey hairs. It was then, just after my child's death, that, to drive the sorrow from his heart, Thomas took a little to the drop; and yet he wasn't like other men, that grow cross and fractious—he was always gent e to me and the young ones; but in the end it ruined us, as it does all who have any call to it—for he was as fine a young man, though I say it, as ye could see in a day's walk—standing six feet two, in his stocking vamps, and admired for his beauty; and he went to the next town to sell my little spinning, that I had done to keep the dacent stitch on the childer; and, as was fated, I suppose, who should be there but a recruiting sargent—and when the drink's in, the wit's out, and he listed—listed!—And the parting—oh! but I thought the life would lave me—sure I followed him to the place of embarkment, and there they druv me from him; and I stood on the sea-shore, and saw him on the deck of that black ship, his arms crossed over his breast like one melancholy mad; and it was long before I believed he was really gone—gone—gone; and that there was no voice to cheer me—for *these* did nothing but cry for food : it was wicked, but I wished to die, for my heart felt breaking. The little left me was soon gone; I was among strangers—I could not bear to go to my own people or place, because I was more like a shame, and my spirit was too high to be looked down on. I have travelled from parish to parish, doing a bit of work of any kind when I could get it, and trusting to good Christians to give something to the desolate children when all else failed."

" Have you never heard from your husband?"

" Oh, sir, he sends his letters to Watherford, to the care of one I know, but I cannot ofter hear, the distance is so great."

" Did he not forward you money?"

" Three pounds; but we owed thirty shillings of it, betwixt rent for the last hole we lived in, and two or three other matters. I was overjoyed to be able to send the money, for the debts lay heavy on my heart; and, to be sure, the children wanted many a little thing, and the remainder soon went."

The good pastor and his family were deeply interested in Mary Clavery's simple tale; and on further inquiry, its truth was fully established. It was also found that her husband was in a regiment then at Jamaica, commanded by the clergyman's brother, a gallant and distinguished officer. The story circulated very quickly, in a neighbourhood where every little circumstance is an event; and to the credit of my favourite Bannow, be it known that, on the very same Sabbath morning, in the Protestant church and Catholic chapel, a collection was made for the benefit of the distressed family. Another week saw Mary and her children in quiet possession of a two-roomed cabin; the parish minister and parish priest conversing at the door, as to the best manner of procuring the industrious woman continued employment; and the three young ladies busily engaged in arranging new noggins and plates, and all manner of cottage furniture, to their

G

own sweet taste. Then, Farmer Corish gave Mrs. Clavery a sack of potatoes—Master Ben engaged to "teach" the children for nothing —Mrs. Cassidy sent, as her offering, a fine fat little pig—Mrs. Corish presented a motherly, well educated goose, capable of bringing up a numerous family respectably—good Mr. Rooney, as considerate and worthy an old bachelor as ever lived (how angry I am with *good* men for being old bachelors!) sent her a sitting hen and seven eggs;—in short, the little cottage and garden were stocked so quickly, and yet so well, and the poor woman was so grateful, that she could hardly believe the reality of what had occurred. Her kind friends at the Parsonage, however, saw that something more was wanting to make their *protégé* perfectly happy. What that was, need I tell?— my lady readers have surely guessed it already, and even the gentlemen may have found it out. The clergyman, without acquainting Mrs. Clavery, had written to his brother, mentioning all the particulars, and begging Thomas's discharge; the last post had brought him a letter, stating that his request was granted.

But the three graces (as my young friends of the Parsonage were always called) denied themselves the pleasure of communicating the joyful tidings; leaving the expected letter from Thomas Clavery himself to tell the news. They could not, however, forego the gratification of witnessing the joy the cottagers would feel when the information was communicated, that the husband and the father was on the homeward journey, and they hastily followed the postman to Mary's abode.

John's next resting-place was at an old weather-beaten but spacious mansion, somewhat out of the Bannow district, and close on the beach. It belonged to a gentleman whose health obliged him to reside for a time on the continent, but who had lent his house to his relative, Sir James Horatio Banks, M.P., for the summer, as the sea-bathing is very good all along the Wexford coast: consequently, Sir James Horatio, his lady, and all his little ones and servants, were, fortunately, only birds of passage—I beg that this fact may be clearly understood, as I would on no account have the family confounded with our own dear resident gentry. Sir James Horatio Banks, M.P., was a great man in his own way, and a strange way it was. Anything but a spendthrift, in the usual acceptation of the word, and yet in perpetual embarrassments; for he was always at law;—never, to do him justice, missed an opportunity of litigation, whether for a thousand pounds or a thousand pence—an estate or an acre. Long Chancery suits were his delight, and he anticipated Term with absolute rapture. Most people complain of the law's delays. Not so, Sir James Horatio Banks. He was always anxious to retard its decisions; so much so that he was once designated, in open court, "a filthy pebble in the wheel of justice." He stood a contested election, or, rather, Lady Banks got him through it, and triumphantly *speechified* on the hustings; but the many thousands expended on that memorable occasion, would have broken his heart to a certainty—if, fortunately, three fresh law-suits had not thence arisen to console him. It was some comfort to the Irish to discover that his mother had been a native of Wales; for he was very mean in his household expenses; which they asserted, could not have been the case, had he been "raale Irish." In truth he had a miserly aspect; a thin spare body, covered with a parchment-like skin, a rattish expression of countenance, and little peering grey eyes that seemed eternally seeking for flaws in everything. He used to ride a bony black horse, and always wore overgrown jack-boots, a threadbare long coat, a flapped hat—that sometimes answered the purpose of an umbrella—and invariably fastened a pair of horse-pistols to the pommel of his saddle. One of our Bannow poets made the following rhyme on the worthy member, and contrived in a crowd, to tie them to the tail of his horse.— How he mourned that he could never discover the author!

> " The Divil Sir Jimmy to Parliament sint ;
> To plaze his master, Sir Jimmy he wint,
> On his ould black horse, that looked like a hack ;
> Success ! cried the boys ; may ye niver come back !"

Indeed, the peculiarities of the family afforded much amusement to the neighbourhood where they resided for a time. Lady Banks was the very opposite of her husband; possessed, as a brother sports-man once said of her, " blood, bone, and beauty ;" wore a scarlet riding-habit; hunted in grand style—was always in at the death; sung songs after supper—loved claret; never scrupled at an oath; called Sir James " her little man ;" always saw the horses fed; obliged her girls to stand fire—her boys to go barefoot to make them hardy; and obtained for herself, amongst the country people, the universal *sobriquet* of " Man Jack." Perhaps all these eccentricities might have been forgiven had she possessed the kindly feelings of her sex, for she was young and handsome, but she was neither an affectionate mother nor a sincere friend; she loved to dash and astonish, and left a family of beautiful children to the management of a French lady's maid and head groom.

The postman's arrival was a matter of great importance to the household, as Sir James always expected letters, and the family had many wants to be supplied. Ma'm'selle Madeline had descended to the servants' hall to await John's coming, and two or three of the younger children accompanied her; on a table, in the centre of the apartment, Miss Julia, a lovely girl of five years old, was dancing a

G 2

jig to the great amusement of two or three men servants, who sung
St. Patrick's Day to "plaze the jewil;" Carlos and Henry, two
younger urchins, were riding a magnificent Newfoundland dog; the
groom and the footman were playing cards at a small side-table near
the fire, and near it was a jug of whisky punch, to which the butler,
housekeeper, and coachman frequently resorted. Ma'm'selle Madeline looked contemptuously on them all, until roused from her reverie
by the butler's inquiring "if Miss Maddy wouldn't taste a drop of
the genuine, betther, ten to one, nor all the wine that iver sailed out
of France?" "Non, Merçie, bien, tank you, Monsieur—ver oblige,
mais—but I ha'de horreur great to your ponch. Faugh! excuse
moi—'tis von great bad shmell.—Faugh!" and the lady's maid refreshed her nose with "Eau de Luce," much to the amusement of
the servants. "Oh, John! welcome John!" "Oh, Monsieur John,
you not be come at last." "John, the rings for the pigs." John
here, John there, John everywhere, as usual. At length the papers
and letters were piled on the table, and Ma'm'selle Madeline had
received, and disappeared with, her band-boxes. "Larry," said the
butler to the footman, "take up the papers; why don't ye?" "Let
them wait till I've looked at them myself," replied Larry; "I want
to see what news from the Curragh, as my lady has a heavy bet on
Captain Lofty's sorrel coult." "Any news of the law business?"
inquired the steward. "How do I know, or what do I care?" replied Larry. "What does it signify whether law actions are gained
or not? don't we' all know what comes over the divil's back must go
under——" "Dacency!" screamed the cook. "All I know,"
observed the steward, is——"

"I'll tell ye what, boys," said John Williams, "ye'd betther
mind yer business, and take the letthers up, out of hand, for Sir
James and my lady both saw me coming down the avenue."

"Och, murder, John! why didn't ye tell me so before? by the
powers, 'Man Jack' 'll bate my brains out!" and the footman hurried
off amid the laughter of his fellow-servants.

"Any news, Sir James?" inquired the lady, as she tried on a
new velvet hunting-cap.

"Yes, my dear, I've just received the bills for my last suit in the
King's Bench."

"You lost the cause, I think."

"Yes, owing to the hurry that Counsellor Playdil was in; never
can take his time about anything."

"What's the damage?"

Poor Sir James groaned. "It will stand me in, one way or other,
eighteen hundred and thirty-seven pounds, fourteen shillings, and
threepence farthing."

" The devil it will!" exclaimed the lady, laying down the hunting-cap. " I wonder, Sir James, you don't at once take my advice; have done with the law, and the torment of it. I'll bet ten to one you'd be as happy again. Oh, if you had my spirit!"

Sir James thought, perhaps, that she had enough for both; a pause ensued, and at length the M.P. began—" My dear Lady Banks, do you know that Major McLaughlin's filly has won the cup?"

" Then I'm in for a cool hundred, that's certain, or else there's some foul play. Curse me, though," continued the lady, " but I'll find it out!—a colt like Lofty's!—such a chest—such action—such limbs! Why, McLaughlin's was no more to be compared to it—but it's all your fault, Sir James; I never have my own way: I ought to have been on the race-ground, but here you would stick and vege-tate like a cabbage; except, indeed, in Term time; you don't care what's spent on law-suits."

" 'Sdeath, Madam, were it not for the law we should be ruined, your extravagance is such—you never ask the price of anything; hadn't I to go to law with your habit-maker for his overcharges?"

" Oh, yes! and to pay three-and-thirty pounds more than the original bill."

" Well, but *still I had the law*, and I showed the fellow I could not be imposed upon. Oh, Lady Banks, Lady Banks! I wish you were less extravagant; we must retrench. Do you know, were I not a Member of Parliament I should be in a gaol; think of that, Lady Banks!—in a gaol."

" Well, and have you not to thank me for your election? Who in their senses would have sent *you*, little man, to be a representa-tive, if it hadn't been for my canvassing? The House would be half memberless if only those sat there who paid their debts!" and she laughed loudly. " Your law tells you that the M.P. is a cloak against bailiffs! *Vive le plaisir!* Why, you don't expect me to turn mourner, and spend my allowance only—like a school-girl, a woman of my spirit! *Pardonnez moi!*" She was leaving her husband surrounded by letters, all demanding money, when some idea or sensation occurred that stopped her on the threshold. " Sir James, Madeline tells me that Caroletta is ill; perhaps the child wants change of air; she grows fast—is getting quite womanly; you had better send her to your sister at Portarlington for a time; I have not a moment to attend to it, but as she is your pet I thought I would mention it." The lady went to look after horses, and the gentleman (who certainly loved his family) to inquire after his eldest child, whom he well knew not to be her mother's favourite, because she was growing so tall and handsome that the vainglorious woman dreaded a rival.

By the time our useful postman had completed his rounds, for he had much to do after he had left the Honourable Member's house, the moon was high in the heavens, and John and his steed had ensured sound slumbers by active exertion. There were many, however, who woke, and some who wept, while the stars sparkled in the blue sky, and the unruffled ocean murmured along the shore. How different is night in the country from night in town! Oh, for my native hills by moonlight! the very breeze tells of repose, and the lone and beautiful clouds, passing so silently along the heavens, that they—

> " Seem to be
> Fair islands in a dark blue sea,
> Which human eyes at eve behold ;
> But only then, unseen by day,
> Their shores and mountains all of gold."

At the Parsonage the three sisters were chattering, as only girls can chatter, arranging further plans to benefit the poor and needy; and even while their hearts were uplifted to the Giver of all good, they sank into the sweet slumbers of innocence.

A trembling light, that issued from Mrs. Clavery's window, showed she was still awake. Seated by the bed-side where her three little ones, their arms twined around each other, slept the refreshing sleep of childhood, she read, for the last time that night, the lines which her husband's hand had traced; and feeling how sweet it was to have near her anything that came from a beloved object, placed the letter under her pillow, and then, while earnest, silent tears coursed each other down her cheeks, prayed that an all-directing Providence would guide her husband in safety over the wide waste of waters.

Lady Banks had just finished her last song, after supper, which was loudly applauded by the very mixed company that sat around the board, while her husband looked gloomy enough at the foot of the table, meditating on his long debts and neglected daughter.

Our old friend, "Grey Lambert," and his faithful Bang, were soundly sleeping in the castle, while the breeze that moaned along the decaying walls was to them as a sweet and soothing lullaby.

Anty McQueen—poor Anty!—she slumbered not. Her father's cottage was on the hill side, and a very neat cabin it was; well filled, too, with children of all ages and sizes, from Anty, the eldest, who, in her own opinion, was quite old enough to be married, down to a fat rosy "lump of a boy," who, although hardly able to crawl, fought manfully with the pig for every potato it took into its mouth. The household, with the exception of Anty, were all fast asleep, and, from the nature of her dress (according to the fashionable acceptance of the word, she might have been called full dressed), it would seem she had been in bed; however, there she sat over the dying embers

of the fire, an end of candle stuck in a scooped potato, that served
as a candlestick, and an open letter in her hand, which she turned
one way, and then another, without being able to comprehend a
single word of its contents.

Poor Anty! it was only when she had received from the postman
the long expected epistle it occurred to her that she was utterly
unable to peruse it; indeed, she could hardly decipher print. But
as to writing, she never had a pen in her hand in her life. Had she
been inclined to make confidants of her father and mother she would
have been precisely in the same dilemma, for they were equally ignorant; and bitterly did she regret the obstinacy of her disposition,
which prevented her hearkening to Master Ben when he counselled
her to become a scholar. Grey Lambert, she knew, would at once
have read every word of it, "for he had grate larning," but, unfortunately, as her sweetheart was no other than his grandson, she
did not exactly wish him to have so much subject-matter to jest her
about. She had taken the letter to Mary-the-Mant, who, next to
Peggy the Fisher, perhaps knew more about the love affairs of the
neighbourhood than anybody else; but Mary-the-Mant was not at
home—gone to Waterford—would not be back for three days!
Master Ben then occurred to her. But, no! she could not bear him
to read it for her; not that he would laugh, but he would feel no
interest, and perhaps find fault, with the skill of a practised critic,
and condemn the spelling and diction of her beloved letter without
mercy. What could she do? Letty Connor—she was well educated;
but then she had been a sort of rival of hers, and she did not wish
her to know anything at all about the matter. John Williams? No;
he would make fun of her in his own quiet, sly way. What should
she do? There she sat over the fire, twisting and turning the
manuscript, that looked, to tell the truth, like a collection of strange
hieroglyphics more than anything else; and, after much consideration, Anty resolved on two things: one, even to take the letter to
Grey Lambert (for waiting three entire days for Mary-the-Mant was
out of the question), and get him to read it. The other was to offer
herself again as a pupil to Master Ben, and get herself taught writing
" out of hand"—all in a minute—and surprise her lover (who was a
wonderful scholar entirely) with her acquirements.

The next morning Anty arrived at Coolhull before Lambert had
finished his prayers; for, on peeping through a large slit in the door,
she saw the old man on his knees before a crucifix, at the farther end
of the great hall—Bang sitting by his side, while the bright red light
of morning streamed through one of the broken windows, and rested
on their heads. Her visit was immediately noticed by the faithful
dog, whose scent, or ear, soon discovered that she was outside. He

walked steadily to the time-worn door, and laying his long nose on
the ground, sniffed loudly three or four times, and moved his tail
slowly, in token of recognition, as she entered.   The young girl
busied herself in lighting the fire, and settling the few rude articles
of furniture, according to her own taste, until Grey Lambert's
orisons were finished. When he arose from his knees, she knelt and
asked his blessing.

" Well, Anty, what's come to ye, my child, to be two good miles
from your own home, and it not six o'clock yet ? ye weren't heavy
for sleep this morning, I'm sartin; is there anything the matter at
home, mavourneen, for something strange must have brought ye ?
Come, don't look so shy; what is it ails the colleen ?—have ye lost
yer tongue ?—fait, agra ! it's bad indeed wid ye, if that's gone."
Anty shook her head.   " Well, I'll sit down here, and wait till ye
choose to spake, and not spind any more o' my breath on ye; for, to
tell God's truth, I've not much to spare; only I can't think what's
over the girl."—Lambert sat down; and after a considerable pause,
during which Anty twisted and untwisted the corner of her apron
with admirable perseverance, she drew the letter from its hiding-place,
and, turning away her blushing face as she spoke, said, with considerable hesitation—

" Ye funned me about a letther last night, sure I couldn't help it
if the boy chose to write. It's no faut o' mine. I didn't put any
comether in life upon him; and more betokens, I wouldn't have
troubled ye to rade it for me if I could rade it myself; and sure,
Grey Lambert, I didn't desave ye by no manner of manes; for I
knew ye mistrusted we were almost keeping company afore Pat took
the turn for going to sea."

" So, Anty, ye mane to be Grey Lambert's grand-daughter;
whist now !—I'll rade the letther."

" MY DEAR ANTY,—I do hope that these few lines will meet
acceptance and true love from you, for ye haven't forgot the fippinny-
bit; the half of it, and the long curl, are next my bateing heart
this minnit, and sure it's in the core of it they should be, if I had
any way to get them there; but it's all the same. I'm uneasy in
my mind about two things—my poor ould ancient gran'fader, and
your little innocent flirtish ways. Ah, Anty ! sure there's all the
boys on land that you used to taze the life o' me about. And ye
think it no harm to laugh wid 'em now; but it wouldn't be the same
if we were married.—Ye'd behave yourself, thin, Anty. And that
and my ould ancient gran'fader has made up my mind.—And the
thoughts of it has prevented my spending.—And I'm coming home,
plaze God, only don't tell the ould man, nor Bang, the baste, becase

I mane every mother's sowl o' ye much joy.—And I've bought such a beautiful gown-piece for the wedding. Only to my thinking, Anty, nothing can make ye handsomer than ye are. And many charmers I have seen, but none like my Bannow girl. And Jim the boatswain has made a song upon ye, according to my telling, and every varse ends wid—

> ' Anty, the darlint of the land,
> Is still her Paddy's pride.'

Oh, it's a dale a finer song than ' Colleen das Crutheen Amo,' as you'll say whin ye hear it, which 'll be very soon afther you, and my ould ancient gran'fader, gets the letthers. And there's another boy travelling home to Bannow, by the name of Thomas Clavery, a late soldier, but discharged—an honest, dacent craythur as ever drew breath, and doating alive upon the wife and the grawls. Be faithful to him that's faithful to you, ' true as the needle to the poll.'—God's blessing be about ye, prays, my dear Anty,

"Your most affectionate lover,

"(Husband soon) till death,

"PATRICK LAMBERT."

Grey Lambert folded up the epistle, and returned it to its rightful owner; the old man did not jest upon its contents, but, rising from his seat, laid his hand on Anty's head, and, in a deep but solemn voice, said—

"So, colleen, the promise has passed betwixt ye, that in God's eye is as binding on ye as if the blessed Pope had joined yer hands in his holy temple at Rome. I knew ye had a kindness for each other, from many little things, more especially from the way Pat always mintioned ye in his letthers : but I didn't think ye were contracted, or else, Anty, who I love (and good right I have to love ye, as my own child), I would have talked more seriously to ye about the little flirting ways yer true love mintions. Anty, look up in the ould man's face, and tell him, did ye ever think—think solidly—what was required of woman in marriage ?" There was that in Grey Lambert's manner which conquered levity, and the young girl looked up with the expression of countenance which replied, "No." "Few craturs at yer age do," he continued : "and what I say to you, ye young wild flower, sweet and spotless as ye are, I will say to him ; and more too, for ye are far faithfuller in yer naturs than us. Ah, Anty ! it's asy enough to be true to the young heart's first love, whin all is full of hope ; but, in my early days I have seen affection that seemed as strong as life, and then, a breath or a word, or a look, may-be, has begun unkindness, and that has increased, until, at last, bitter scorn,

ay, and black hatred, grew, where there had been nothing but love
and smiles. And women have much to bear, Anty; for it's little men
heed an unkind word, unjustly spoken may-be, and yet to be borne
almost as if it was dear or darlint—which is the hardest word I hope
ever to hear Patrick make use of to you. But, my girl, when ye
knew of the promise it wasn't quite right of ye to skit, and laugh,
and dance, as if ye were free."

"I am sure, Grey Lambert," interrupted Anty, half crying, "ye've
no raison to turn on me, after that fashion, for I meant no harm, and
nothing in life would ever make me jilty."

"Asy, agra, till I tell ye a little story to divart ye a bit, and it's all
thrue, and I know ye'll find out my maning, for ye're 'cute enough."
And Anty listened very attentively, pulling first one and then the
other of Bang, the baste's ears, which he bore patiently, not even
increasing her perplexity by moving his head from off her lap.

"In the ancient times, when flowers, and trees, and fairies were on
spaking terms, and all friendly together; one fine summer's day the
sun shone out on a beautiful garden, where there war all sorts of
plants that ye could mintion; and a lovely but giddy fairy went
sporting about from one to the other (although no one could see her,
because of the sunlight), as gay as the morning lark; then says the
fairy to the rose—'Rose, if the sun was clouded, and the storm came
on, would ye shelter and love me still?' 'Do ye doubt me?' says
the rose, and reddened up with anger.—'Lily,' says the fairy to
another love, 'if the sun was clouded, and a storm came on, would
ye shelter and love me still?' 'Oh! do you think I could change?'
says the lily, and she grew still paler with sorrow.—'Tulip,' said the
fairy, 'if the sun was clouded, and a storm came on, would ye shelter
and love me still?' 'Upon my word!' said the tulip, making a very
gentleman-like bow, 'ye're the very first lady that doubted my constancy;' so the fairy sported on, joyful to think of her kind and
blooming friends. She revelled away for a time, and then she thought
on the pale blue violet that was almost kivered with its broad green
leaves; and, although it was an ould comrade, she might have forgotten it, had it not been for the sweet scent that came up from the
modest flower. 'Oh, violet!' said the fairy, 'if the sun was clouded,
and a storm came on, would ye shelter and love me still?' And the
violet made answer—'Ye have known me long, sweet fairy; and in
the first spring-time, when there were few other flowers, ye used to
shelter from the could blast under my leaves; now ye've almost forgotten me—but let it pass—try my truth—if ever you should meet
misfortune—I say nothing.' Well the fairy skitted at that, and clapped
her silvery wings, and whisked, singing, off on a sunbame; but she
was hardly gone, when a black cloud grew up out of the north, all in

a minit, and the light was shrouded, and the rain fell in slashings, like hail, and away flies the fairy to her friend the rose.—'Now, Rose,' says she, 'the rain is come, so shelter and love me still.' 'I can hardly shelter my own buds,' says the rose, 'but the lily has a deep cup.' Well, the poor little fairy's wings were almost wet, but she got to the lily. 'Lily,' says she, 'the storm is come, so shelter and love me still.' 'I am sorry,' says the lily, 'but if I were to open my cup, the rain would bate in like fun, and my seed would be kilt entirely—the tulip has long leaves.' Well, the fairy was down-hearted enough, but she went to the tulip, who she always thought a sweet-spoken gentleman. He certainly did not look as bright as he had done in the sun, but she waved her little wand, and 'Tulip,' said she, 'the rain and the storm are come, and I am very weary, but you will shelter and love me still.' 'Begone!' says the tulip; 'be off!' says he; 'a pretty pickle I'd be in if I let every wandering scamper come about me.'—Well, by this time, she was very tired, and her wings hung dripping at her back—wet indeed—but there was no help for it, and laneing on her pretty silver wand, she limped off to the violet; and the darlint little flower, with its blue eye, that's as clear as a kitten's, saw her coming, and never a word she spoke, but opened her broad green leaves, and took the wild wandering craythur to her bosom, and dried her wings, and breathed the sweetest parfumes over her, and sheltered her until the storm was clane gone. Then the humble violet spoke, and said—'Fairy Queen, it is bad to flirt with many, for the love of one true heart is enough for earthly woman, or fairy spirit; the ould and humble love is better than the gay compliments of a world of flowers, for *it* will last when the others pass.' And the fairy knew that it was true for the blue violet; and she contented herself ever after, and built her downy bower under the wide spreading violet leaves, that sheltered her from the rude winter's wind and the hot summer's sun; and to this very day the fairies love the violet beds."

Anty smiled, and suffered Bang's ears to escape, when the story was finished. Grey Lambert smiled also, and as she was departing, inquired if her parents knew of the contract? She frankly replied in the negative; and the old man accompanied the little gipsy to her father's cabin, where the news was joyfully received. Everybody liked Patrick; and, moreover, everybody suspected that in some sly corner the old man had wherewithal to make a plentiful wedding.

Nothing happened to prevent matters coming to a happy termination. Thomas Clavery and Patrick Lambert returned on the same day. The gown-piece was declared to be an "uncommon beauty," even by Mrs. Cassidy; and a time was fixed for the wedding:—but where do you suppose it was celebrated ?   In no other place, I assure you, than in Grey Lambert's old castle.

"It's a fancy, I know," said he, " and a strange one, but I can't help it; the bride and bridegroom can trot off to their nate little cabin, that's all ready for them, and that I defy any one to say wants a single thing; and it will make me happy to know that once more laughter and music will visit the ancient castle of Coolhull."

Such a wedding was never seen in the country from that day to this ; it was a most wonderful wedding !   More than fifty long torches of bog-wood, were stuck up and down in the walls, and the ivy and wild plants formed a singular but not unplensing contrast to the grey stones and flaring lights.—One end of the dilapidated hall was re-served for dancing; and there, on a throne of turf, sat the immortal Kelly ; a deep jug of whisky punch close to his footstool, and he " blowing away for the dear life" on his pipes.   At the other end was a long table, formed of deal spars—covered with such cloths, plates, dishes, glasses, noggins, jugs, and sundries, as the neighbour-ing farmhouses could lend—placed on stones and turfs, sufficiently elevated.   What a supper !—rounds of beef—turkey—geese—such profusion ! — the " wedding of Ballyporeen" was nothing to it ! And when the cake was fairly cut, Father Mike's perquisites were many, for Grey Lambert, whose reported wealth was no jest, laid down a golden guinea on the plate.   He had bidden many of the neighbouring gentry to the marriage, and, as the old man was much respected, and the arrangements very singular, there were few apolo-gies.   The great hall was, at an early hour, nearly filled with motley company; ladies and gentlemen, farmers and farmers' wives, " boys and girls" of all ranks, in their Sunday gear, and with happy joyous faces; some whispering so closely that Father Mike was led to believe a few more weddings would take place before Lent; then the Babelish noises !—Kelly's pipes—merry laughter—loud tongues !

Grey Lambert danced merrily with the young ladies from the Parsonage, and " bate them off the flure," at the Irish jig.   The bride looked provokingly pretty and mischievous ; and the boatswain, who came from Waterford to the ceremony, sung not only—

> " Anty, the darlint of the land,
>   Is still her Paddy's pride !"

but composed extemporaneous verses on the occasion, which were received with much applause.

Was that all ?   No; in a far corner sat Thomas and Mary Clavery !

John Williams, whose dislike to conversation disappeared in a very odd way, probably owing to his continued potations, annoyed Anty continually by calling her "Mrs. Lambert;" and the old man kept up the joke, somewhat unmercifully, by now and then reminding her of the past—"Sure I'll not come to see ye in yer unchristian-like place, if ye talk after that fashion to a young cratur like me!"

As his company departed, he conducted them with the air of a prince to the great gate; and Father Mike, after he had earnestly prayed that his full blessing might rest on them all, declared he had never been at so happy a wedding.

I am not prepared to state whether or not Anty learned writing, for she was able to prevail upon Patrick to "give up the sea," and content himself with the occasional management of a fishing boat; consequently, she was not likely, in the whole course of her life, to receive another letter. She remembered the fairy tale, and, to the credit of the sex be it spoken, left off "her flirting ways." Grey Lambert is still in possession of the old castle and extraordinary health; and John Williams may carry this tale to "mine old home," in his capacity as THE BANNOW POSTMAN.

"WE'LL SEE ABOUT IT."

W E'LL see about it!" From that simple sentence has arisen more evil to Ireland than any person, ignorant of the strange union of impetuosity and procrastination my countrymen exhibit, could well believe. They are sufficiently prompt and energetic when their feelings are concerned, but in matters of business, they almost invariably prefer *seeing about*, to DOING.

I shall not find it difficult to illustrate this observation :—from the many examples of its truth, in high and in low life, I select Philip Garraty.

Philip, and Philip's wife, and Philip's children, and all the house of Garraty, are employed from morning till night in *seeing about* everything, and, consequently, in *doing* nothing. There is Philip—a tall, handsome, good-humoured fellow, of about five-and-thirty, with broad, lazy-looking shoulders, and a smile perpetually lurking about his mouth, or in his bright hazel eyes, the picture of indolence and kindly feeling. There he is leaning over what was once a five-barred gate, and leads to the hag-yard; his blue worsted stockings full of holes, which "the suggan," twisted half-way up the well-formed leg, fails to conceal; while his brogues (to use his own words), if they do let the water in, let it out again. With what unstudied elegance does he roll that knotted twine, and then unrol it; varying his occupation by kicking the stones that once formed a wall, into the stagnant pool, scarcely big enough for full-grown ducks to sail in.

But let us take a survey of the premises.

The dwelling house is a long rambling abode, much larger than those that usually fall to the lot of small Irish farmers; for Philip rents a respectable farm, and ought to be "well to do in the world." The dwelling looks very comfortless, notwithstanding: part of the thatch is much decayed, and the rank weeds and damp moss nearly cover it; the door-posts are only united to the wall by a few scattered portions of clay and stone, and the door itself is hanging but by one hinge; the window-frames shake in the passing wind, and some of the compartments are stuffed with the crown of a hat, or a "lock of straw;" very unsightly objects. At the opposite side of the swamp is the hag-yard gate, where a broken line of alternate palings and wall betokens that it had been formerly fenced in; the commodious barn is almost roofless, and the other sheds are pretty much in the same condition; the pig-sty is deserted by the grubbing lady and her grunting progeny, who are too fond of an occasional repast in the once-cultivated garden to remain in their proper abode; the listless turkeys, and contented half-fatted geese, live at large and on the public; but the turkeys, with all their shyness and modesty, have the best of it, for they mount the ill-built stacks, and select the grain *à plaisir*.

"Give you good morrow, Mr. Philip; we have had showery weather lately."

"Och! all manner of joy to ye, my lady!—and sure ye'll walk in, and sit down; my woman will be proud to see ye. I'm sartin we'll have the rain soon agin, for it's everywhere, like bad luck; and my throat's sore with hurishing thim pigs out o' the garden—sorra a thing can I do all day for watching thim."

"Why do you not mend the door of the sty?"

"True for ye, ma'am dear; so I would if I had the nails; and I've been threat'ning to step down to Mickey Bow, the smith, to ask him to *see about it.*"

"I hear you've had a fine crop of wheat, Philip."

"Thank God for all things! You may say that; we had, my lady, a fine crop; but I have always the height of ill luck somehow; upon my sowkins (and that's the hardest oath I ever swear), the turkeys have had the most of it: but I mean to *see about* setting it up safe, to-morrow."

"But, Philip, I thought you had sold the wheat, standing."

"It was all as one as sould; only it's a bad world, ma'am dear, and I've no luck. Says the steward to me, says he, I like to do things like a man of business; so, Mister Garraty, just draw up a bit of an agreement that you deliver over the wheat field to me, on sich a day, standing as it is, for sich a sum; and I'll sign it for ye, and thin there can be no mistake—only let me have it by this day week. Well, to be sure, I came home full o' my good luck, and I tould the wife; and, on the strength of it, she must have a new gown. And sure, says she, Miss Hennessy is just come from Dublin, wid a shop-full of goods; and, on account that she's my brother's sister-in-law's first cousin, she'll let me have the first sight o' the things, and I can take my pick, and we'll have plinty of time to *see about* the 'greement to-morrow. Well, I don't know how it was, but the next day we had no paper, nor ink, nor pens in the house: I meant to send the gossoon to Miss Hennessy's for all—but forgot the pens. So, when I was *seeing about* the 'greement, I bethought of the ould gander; and while I was pulling as beautiful a pen as ever ye laid yer two eyes upon, out of his wing, he tattered my hand with his bill in such a manner that sorra a pen I could hould for three days. Well, at last I wrote it out like print, and takes it myself to the steward.—Good evening to you, Mr. Garraty, says he. Good evening kindly, sir, says I; I've got the 'greement here, sir, says I, pulling it out, as I thought—but I only cotch the paper it was wrapt in, to keep it from the dirt of the tobacco, that was loose in my pocket for want of a box; so I turned out what little bits o' things I had in it, and there was a grate hole, that ye might drive all the parish rats through, at the bottom, which the wife promised to *see about* mending, as good as six months before. Well, I saw the sneer on his ugly mouth (for he's an Englishman), and I turned it off with a laugh, and said air-holes were comfortable in hot weather, and sich-like jokes, and that I'd go home and make another 'greement. 'Greement! for what?—says he, laying down his grate outlandish pipe. Whew! may-be ye don't know, says I. Not I, says he. The wheat-field, says I. Why, says he, didn't I tell you then, that you must bring the 'greement to me by that day week?—and that was (by the same token pulling a red memorandum book out of his pocket), let me see—exactly this day three weeks. Do you think, Mr. Garraty, he goes on, that I was going to wait upon you? I don't lose my papers in the Irish fashion.

Well, that last set me up—and I had the ill luck to knock him down;
and, the coward, what does he do but takes the law o' me—and I was
cast, and lost the sale of the wheat, and was ordered to pay ever so
much money; well, I didn't care to pay it then, but gave an engagement; and I meant to *see about it*—but forgot; and, all in a jiffy,
came a thing they call an execution—and to stop the cant,* I was
forced to borrow money from the tame negur, the exciseman—and
it's a terrible case to be paying *interest* for it *still.*"

"But, Philip, you might give up or dispose of part of your farm.
I know you could get a good sum of money for that rich meadow by
the river."

"True for ye, ma'am dear, and I've been *seeing about it* for a long
time, but somehow *I have no luck.* Just as ye came up, I was thinking
to myself that the gale-day is passed, and all one as before; yarra a
pin's worth have I for the rint; and the landlord wants it as bad as I
do, though it's a shame to say that of a gintleman; for jist as he was
seeing about some old custodium, or something of the sort, that had
been hanging over the estate ever since he came to it, the sheriff's
officers put *executioners* in the house; and I am sartin he'll be racking
me for the money; indeed, the ould huntsman tould me as much:
but I must *see about it*, not indeed that it's much good, for I've no
luck."

"Let me beg of you, Philip, not to take such an idea into your
head; do not lose a moment; you will be utterly ruined if you do.
Why not apply to your father-in-law?—he is able to assist you; for
at present you only suffer from temporary embarrassment."

"True for ye, my lady; and, by the blessing of God, I'll *see about
it.*"

"Then go directly, Philip."

"Directly! I can't, ma'am dear, on account of the pigs; and sorra
a one I have but myself to keep them out of the cabbages; for I let
the woman and the grawls go to the pattern at Killaun; it's little
pleasure they see, the craturs!"

"But your wife did not hear the huntsman's story?"

"Och! ay, did she; but unless she could give me a sheaf o' bank
notes, where would be the good of her staying?—but I'll *see about
it.*"

"Immediately, then, Philip; think of the ruin that may come—nay,
that must come, if you neglect this matter: your wife, too—your
family reduced from comfort to starvation—your home desolate——"

"Asy, my lady!—don't be after breaking my heart intirely; thank
God, I have seven as fine flahulagh children as ever peeled pratee, anc

* Cant—sale.

H

all under twelve years ould; and sure I'd lay down my life tin times over for every one o' them: and to-morrow for sartin—no—to-morrow —the hurling; I can't to-morrow; but the day after, if I'm a living man, *I'll see about it.*"

Poor Philip! his kindly feelings were valueless, because of his unfortunate habit. Would that this were the only example I could produce of the ill effects of that dangerous little sentence—"*I'll see about it!*" Oh, that the sons and daughters of the fairest island that ever heaved its green bosom above the surface of the ocean, would arise and *be doing* what is to be done, and never again rest contented with "SEEING ABOUT IT!"

LINTON.   WEICALL.

THE LAST OF THE LINE.

IT was on a tranquil evening, in the sweet summer month of June,
that a lady of no ordinary appearance sat at an open casement of
many-coloured glass, and overlooked a wild, but singularly beautiful
country. From the window a flight of steep stone steps led to a narrow
terrace, that, in former times, had been carefully guarded by high
parapets of rudely-carved granite; but they had fallen to decay, and
lay in mouldering heaps on the shrubby bank, which ran almost
perpendicularly to a rapid stream that danced like a sunny spirit
through the green meadows, dotted and animated with sheep and
their sportive lambs. In the distance, rude and rugged mountains
towered in native dignity, "high in air," their grim and sterile ap-

pearance forming an extraordinary, but not unpleasing, contrast to
the pure and happy-looking valley at their base, where, however, a
few dingy peasant-cottages lay thinly scattered, injuring, rather than
enlivening, a scene that nature had done much to adorn, and man
nothing to preserve. Half way up the nearest mountain, a little
chapel, dedicated to "our Lady of Grace," hung, like a wren's nest,
on what seemed a point of rock; but even its rustic cross was invisible
from the antique casement. Often and anxiously did the lady watch
the distant figures who trod the hill-side towards the holy place, to
perform some act of penance or devotion.

It was impossible to look at that interesting woman without affection; one might have almost thought her destined—

"To come like truth, and disappear like dreams."

Though she was young, there was much of the dignity of silent sorrow
in her aspect; and it was difficult to converse with her, without feeling
her influence—not to overpower, but to soften. Her form was slight,
but rounded to the most perfect symmetry, and an extraordinary
quantity of hair, black as the raven's wing, was braided, somewhat
after the fashion of other lands, over a high and well-formed brow:
she wore no head-dress, except what nature had bestowed; yet a
golden rosary, and cross of the same metal, gemmed with many
precious jewels, hung over a harp-stand of antique workmanship; a
few of the strings of the harp were broken, and a pile of richly-bound
music gave no token of being often disturbed. Silken ottomans,
gilded vases, fresh-gathered flowers, and a long embroidered sofa, filled
up, almost to crowding, the small apartment. In a little recess,
opposite the window, a child's couch was fitted with much taste and
care; the hangings were of blue damask, curiously inwrought with
silver, such as the nuns in France and Flanders delight to emboss:
there was also a loose coverlet of the same material, and a tasseled
oblong cushion at either end. I have said that the lady was seated
at the casement: sometimes she pressed her small white fingers to
her brow, and then passed them over its rounded surface, as if to
dispel, by that simple movement, thoughts, "the unbidden guests of
anxious hours;"—but still it was only for a moment her gaze was
turned from her best treasure, her only child; her eye followed it as,
in its nurse's arms, it enjoyed the evening breeze that played amid
its light and clustering hair; the baby had blue eyes and a fair skin;
and if it sometimes, in the infantine seriousness that passed as airy
shadows over a smiling landscape, resembled its mother, now, as it
laughed and shouted, in broken accents, "Mamma! mamma!" she
thought how like its father it spoke and looked. Clavis Abbey—as
the strange mixture of ancient and modern building, inhabited by the

household of Sir John Clavis, was called—was wisely situated. The monks of old always chose happily for their monasteries; the sites of their ruined aisles tell of the good taste, as well as good sense, of their projectors. Hill, wood, and water, were ever in their neighbourhood, and the red deer and salmon were always near, to contribute to their repast.

But the fair possessions had, nearly two centuries before our tale commences, passed from the hands of "holy Mother Church." The marvellous tale of its exchange of masters is still often repeated, and always credited; it is said and believed that the stream, which runs through the valley I have described, is, every midsummer-night, of a deep red hue, in mysterious commemoration of the massacre of the priests of that abbey, which took place as late as the Elizabethan reign. Certain it is that the projector of such indiscriminate slaughter never reaped the rich harvest he anticipated; for, unable from severe illness to visit the court of the maiden queen, he despatched his son's tutor on the mission, with communications concerning the services he had rendered to the state, and a petition for a grant of the lands he had rescued from "popery." The tutor, however, made himself so agreeable to the royal lady, that she either was, or affected to be, severely angered by the unnecessary effusion of blood; and, so far from approving, testified her displeasure, and bestowed the fair lands of the murdered monks upon Oliver Clavis, the false, but handsome, accessary of the priest-slayer. But no family could take possession of consecrated ground in Ireland, without falling under the ban of both church and people; and, notwithstanding the bland and liberal conduct of the new owner of the estate, then called Clavis Abbey, Oliver lived and died unpopular. Tradition says that none of the heirs male of the family ever departed peaceably in their beds, and much learned and unlearned lore is still extant upon the subject.

Somewhat about the year 1782, Sir John Clavis entered upon his title and property, in consequence of the sudden demise of his father, Sir Henry, who was drowned on a moonshiny night, when the air and the sea were calm, and he was returning from an excursion to one of those fairy islands that at once beautify and render dangerous the Irish coast. The people who accompanied him on that last day of his existence, say that he had been in unusual health and spirits during the morning, and had fished, and sung, and drank as usual—that as the night advanced he became reserved and gloomy, and, as they neared the cost, insisted on taking the helm—that suddenly yielding the guidance of his little vessel, he sprang overboard—that immediately the crew crowded to save him, but a black cloud descended on the waters, and hid his form from their eyes, and it was not until the boat had driven an entire mile (as well as they could calculate) from the spot, they were enabled again to behold the sea and the sky. Some laughed, some surmised, but many credited the tale; for superstition had hardly, at that period, resigned any of her strong-holds; and the peasantry, to this day, believe that Sir Harry Clavis acted under the influence of a spirit-guide, that had lured him to sudden death, conformably with the old prophecy—

> " The party shall fail by Clavis led,
> And none of the name shall die in their bed."

Sir John had just completed his college course when he was called upon to support the honours of his house and name. At the University he was considered more as an amiable gentlemanly young man, than an *esprit fort*, or one likely to lead in public life. At that period the college lads were a very different set of youths from what they are at present. The rude but generous hospitality, the thoughtless daring, the angry politics, the feudal feeling, that characterized the gentry of the time, were not likely to send forth subjects submissive to college rule; and the citizens of Dublin were too often insulted and aggrieved by the insolent, aristocratic airs of unfledged boys, ripe for mischief, who, half in earnest, half in jest, sported with their comforts, and often with their lives. Party feeling, also, ran (as un-happily *there* it always does) to a dreadful height; and the young baronet, whose father had invariably drank " The Glorious Memory," and " Protestant Ascendancy," every day after dinner, was frequently called upon to defend or support his party, although he invariably declared that as yet he was of none—that he must wait to make up his mind, &c. &c. It must be confessed that this extraordinary irresolution, at such a period, was more the effect of constitutional apathy than of reflection; he had a good deal of the consciousness of birth and wealth about him, but he disliked either mental or bodily exertion. As an only child, he had suffered nothing like contradic-tion: and had he horsewhipped and abused his servants (when at the age of twelve, he sported two of his own racers at the Curragh of Kildare), instead of speaking to them as fellow-creatures in a mild and kindly voice, it would have elicited no rebuke from his father, who secretly regretted that the youth was neither likely to become a five-bottle man, a staunch Orangeman, nor a Member of Parlia-ment—the only three things he considered worth living for.

The young baronet never could have resolved upon visiting the Continent—an exploit he had long talked of—but that an anticipated general election frightened him away, as he would certainly, if at home, have been expected to offer himself as a candidate, and make speeches. He hated trouble, and of the two exertions chose the least —committed his affairs, for twelve calendar months, to the management of Denny Dacey, his nurse's son, who had acted satisfactorily, as steward, since the second childhood of the old and respected man who had for sixty years filled the situation; and left the Abbey, attended by only two servants and one travelling carriage. This was a matter of surprise and conversation to many, more particularly as Sir Henry and his neighbour, Mr. Dorncliff, a Cromwellian settler, had arranged that their children should be united, when of sufficient age. Miss Dorncliff was handsome, and an heiress, and, it was said, in no degree averse to the union; they had been companions in childhood, but the lady, it would appear, was of too unromantic a disposition to remove the young baronet's indifference. As his carriage rolled past the avenue that led to her dwelling, he merely leaned forward, and cast a fleeting glance towards the house. Where he met, and to what precise circumstance he owed the possession of so lovely a wife as the lady I have endeavoured to describe, is still a mystery; his business-letters conveyed no intelligence of his marriage; nor was it until the arrival of gay furniture, from a fashionable Dublin upholsterer, that the idea of such an event occurred to the inhabitants of Clavis.

When the baronet returned, and announced, as his lady, her who leaned upon his arm; when the domestics received her with that warm-hearted and affectionate respect for which Irish servants are so justly celebrated; and when the rumour went abroad that Sir John Clavis had married a Spanish lady, a Catholic, and "one that had little more English than a Kerry-man," great was the consternation, and many and various the conjectures. "What will become of the 'Protestant Ascendancy,' and the 'Glorious and Immortal Memory,' now that a popish mistress is come to Clavis?" said one party. "Some chance of luck and grace to the ould Abbey, now that the right sort's in it," observed the other. Not a few affirmed that the lady had absconded from a convent; others asserted that she was picked off, with a few other survivors, from a wrecked vessel in the Mediterranean; those who had not seen her whispered that she was no better than she should be; but Miss Dorncliff—who, at first, perhaps, to show she was heart-whole, and afterwards from real regard, was often Lady Clavis's guest—generously declared that she was the most charming woman she had ever met, that she was highly accomplished, and, although a Catholic and a Spaniard, anything but a bigot.

Her want of knowledge of the language, when she arrived, prevented her joining in conversation either with those who visited her, or those at whose houses she was received. Perfectly unconscious of the rules and etiquette of society in our colder regions, she was sure to commit some grievous fault in the arrangement of her guests, which invariably threw her husband into an ill temper, that, after the honeymoon was over, he seldom thought it necessary to conceal. Sir John had shaken off a good deal of his *ennui* by journeying; and when he came home he no longer stood on neutral ground, but suffered the excitement of politics to take the place of that which is the accompaniment of travelling. He had now discovered that, for the honour of the house, it was necessary he should adopt his father's side of the question; and accordingly the gardener was ordered to fill the flower beds with orange lilies, and the hangings of the spare rooms were garnished with orange bindings. Unfortunately, the members of an Orange Lodge were invited to dine at the Abbey, and Lady Clavis positively refused to wear their colour, in any way, *because* she considered it as a symbol of persecution to the Catholic religion, of which she was a devout and faithful member. When her husband after much contention gave up the point, she ordered a green velvet dress for the occasion, embroidered with golden shamrocks; she did this with a view to gratify him, never imagining that the colour which emblems the beauty and fertility of Ireland, *could* be obnoxious to any body of Irishmen. What, then, was her astonishment, when he, whom she had been so anxious to please, expressed a most angry opinion of her costume—which occasioned a flood of tears from one party and, from the other, an over-hastily expressed desire that, as she could never understand the customs of the country, she would give up trying to do so. Matrimonial disputes are dreadfully uninteresting in the recital—not entertaining as are lovers' quarrels, simply because there is no danger of a heart-breaking separation arising from them; it is only the two engaged in those unhappy differences that can understand their bitterness; the world has, for them, but little sympathy. Enough, then be it, that the innocent green velvet was the commencement of much real disagreement: the lady insisting that she had the dress made as a compliment to his party: the gentleman protesting that it could not be so, as green was always opposed to orange. This he repeated over and over again, without troubling himself to inquire whether his wife understood him or not. Many an unpleasantness grew out of this trifle, that continued silently, like the single drop of rain, to wear the rock of domestic happiness. Sir John persevered in drinking deeply of the bitter cup of politics, that universal destroyer of society and kindly feeling. He soon discovered, or imagined he had discovered, how perfectly a continental education unfits the most amiable woman in the world for the society and habits of our islands; and the very efforts Lady Clavis made to appear cheerful, were silent reproaches to him for not endeavouring to make her *so*; they had, however, still one feeling in common—affection for their child.

While the mistress of Clavis Abbey was engaged in watching every movement of her beloved daughter, as the nurse paced slowly beneath her turret-window, the baronet was sitting *tête-à-tête* with no other than Denny Dacey, who, from being what in England is termed bailiff to the estate, had risen to the rank of agent, under the title, as his correspondents set forth, of "Dionysius Dacey, Esq.," &c. &c. How this person ever acquired the influence he possessed over his patron, must now remain a mystery: it is to be supposed that he insinuated himself into his good graces, as a weasel does into a rabbit-burrow, by various twists and windings, of which nobler animals are incapable. It was no secret in the county that, although Sir John's political apathy no longer existed, he had not acquired the active habits that are so especially necessary where a gentleman's affairs are embarrassed, and where nothing but good sense and steady economy can retrieve them. During the young baronet's residence abroad, Dacey had exceedingly prospered; and though one or two shrewd landowners suspected he used means, not consistent with his employer's interests, to obtain both influence and wealth, there was so much plausibility about the man, that the most watchful could bring nothing home to him; his bearing was blunt and open; he affected honesty, but his look belied the utterance of his tongue, for his eye lacked the expression of truth, and, instead of looking forth straightly from beneath its pent-house lid, was everlastingly twisting into corners—with cat-like quickness, watching a fitting opportunity, when those with whom he conversed were busied about other matters, to scan and observe their countenances. It has been to me an entertaining, though often an unpleasing, study, to attend to the varied expressions conveyed by the mere action of the eye, almost without reference to the other features; and I would avoid, as I would a poisoned adder, the person whose eye quivers or looks down.

The two *friends* (such is the usual term given to those who eat meat at the same board) were seated at either end of a somewhat long table, on which were piled papers of various dates and dimensions: a huge bowl of punch had been nearly emptied of its contents, and the baronet did not appear particularly fit for business. He leaned listlessly on the table, as if in reverie, and it was only Dacey's voice that roused him from his reflections.

"But, my dear Sir John," he commenced, with his peculiar drawl, while his eye was fixed on the punch-ladle: "My dear Sir John, 'pon my sowl it weighs upon my conscience, so it does, to be managing here, and you to the fore, with such a fine head and so much cleverness (a sly glance to see how the flattery took); 'tis a shame you don't turn to it yourself, for by-'n-by you'll, may-be, find things worse nor you think 'em, as I have told you before, God knows——"

" And will my looking over those cursed papers make things better ?
It is positively enough to set me mad—just at a time too, when our
grand county meeting is coming on, and the general election, and so
much exertion expected from me ; and the house will be full of
English company from the castle, and Lady C. has not an idea how
English people should be entertained."

" But sure Miss Dorncliff is coming to stop with my lady while
they stay."

" Very true ; she is a capital, good-natured girl, 'faith, and much
better looking than she was eight years ago, when I left Ireland.
Oh dear ! I wonder young men of fortune marry, Dacey !"

" Sir John, it is very necessary."

" Well, well, I suppose it is, but say no more about it ; there are
enough of disagreeable subjects on the table already."   The baronet
looked upon the pile of papers, and the agent glanced keenly up,
but his eye was quickly withdrawn.

" My lady was in a convent, I believe, Sir John ?"

" Ay ; it was a fine exploit to get her out of it.   Well, poor thing,
she trusted to my honour, and was not deceived."

" Of course you were married by a priest ?"   (This was said cautiously.)

" To be sure we were, and by a jovial fellow too ; he went with me
to the convent-wall, and performed the ceremony at the foot of a
beautiful old cross, by the way-side, as the moon was sailing over our
heads, and the orange trees were showering perfume around us.
Poor Madelina," he continued almost involuntarily, " I found the
withered orange-blossoms, which that night I bound upon her maiden
brow, encased in a casket, with the hair of our child, only this
morning."

" You had the ceremony repeated on your arrival in England ?"
inquired Dacey.

Sir John Clavis fixed his eyes upon the reptile, and, in a sterner
tone of voice than was his wont, in his turn became the querist.

" Why do you ask ?"

" For no reason, only that if you had a son it would be well to see
that the marriage was firm and legal."

" Thank you," replied the baronet, drily, " there is not much
chance of that being the case ; and if there was——"

A long pause followed the last sentence, which neither seemed
inclined to disturb.   Dacey gathered the papers towards him, and,
pulling his spectacles from his forehead to his nose, occupied himself
in sorting and placing them in separate piles ; every five or ten
minutes a heavy sigh escaped from his lips, the last of which was so
audible, that Sir John exclaimed, " What the devil, man alive, do you

growl for in that manner?—one would think that you expected the ghost of your uncle, the priest, to start forth from the papers, and upbraid you with your apostacy!"

"Sorra a *ghost* at all, then, Sir John, among the papers; only the *reality* of botherin' debts, custodiums, thrown-up leases on account of the rackrent, and the Lord knows what!"

"And whose fault is it?" replied the gentleman, angrily; *did I not leave it all to your management?* The property *was* a good property, and why should it not continue so? I'm sure I can't think how the money goes; to do Lady C. justice, she spends nothing."

"There's the hounds, the hunters, and five grooms, of one sort or other, Sir John; to say nothing of town houses, and carriages, and——"

"My father always had the same establishment," interrupted Sir John, "and never kept an agent to overlook matters either."

"More's the pity!" ejaculated the manager (the exclamation might have been taken in two ways).

"There's no manner of use in my keeping *you*, if I am to be pestered with these eternal accounts—accounts—morning, noon, and night. The simple fact is," continued Sir John, rising from his seat, "the simple fact is, money I want, and money I must have. After flying to the Continent to avoid an election, I find that now, at this particular crisis, I cannot help running into the very strait I endeavoured to steer clear of. My friends say it is necessary, and would even subscribe (if I permitted) to return me free of expense; that I will never do—so money, Dacey, money I *must* have, that's certain."

"It's easy to say money," retorted the agent; "will you sell, Sir John?"

"What?" interrogated the baronet.

"There's the Corner estate, that long strip, close by Ballyraggan; your cousin Corney of the hill has long had an eye to it, and would lay down something handsome."

"You poor, pitiful scoundrel!" exclaimed Sir John; "do you think it's come to *that*, for me to sell *land*, like a huckster!—and to Corney too, a fellow that gathers inches off every estate, as a magpie picks ti'pennies!—a fellow who, basely born, and basely bred, has, nevertheless, managed to accumulate wealth, like a pawnbroker, on the miseries of others! I know he has had an eye on that property these eight years, but look—sooner than *he* should have it, I'll beg my bread—I'll sell the estate to a stranger to prevent the possibility of his ever possessing an acre of the land."

"Please yerself, sir," replied the manager, sweeping some of the papers into a wide-mouthed canvas sack which he drew from under his chair. "Here's Mr. Damask's, the upholsterer's letter—swears if he's not paid, he'll clap on an execution like lightning; it's as good as 2,500*l.* now, with costs."

"Fire and fury!" exclaimed the baronet, who, his apathy once shaken off, became terrible in his violence; "do you want to drive me mad?"

"Then I'll say nothing of Mr. Barry Mahon's little letter," continued the man of business, quietly, "who writes, that as you've decided on *standing* in opposition to him, he'll trouble you for the money he lent you as good as four years ago, to complete some purchase or another; it ends very civilly though, by saying that it's only the knowledge that a gentleman like you will be a formidable adversary, which obliges him to strain every nerve to make his own step firm."

"A blight upon him for his civility!"

"Then here is——" Mr. Dacey was prevented from finishing his sentence, by Sir John's striking the table so violently with his clenched hand, that the very punch-bowl trembled, and the agent ejaculated "Lord, save us!"

"Look here!" said the baronet, "you have, *I know*—means, somehow or other, of raising money when you like; find me the sum of ten thousand pounds by this day week, and that very estate, so coveted by my cousin Corney, shall be yours for ever, at a peppercorn rent, provided the matter be kept secret; mind, *provided it be kept secret,* and you bind yourself never to let a twig of it into Corney's possession."

"It's easy to keep secret a thing that never happens," observed Dacey, rolling the cord of the bag between his finger and thumb; "is it me get money when I like?—and I obliged to go at credit even for these brogues on my feet!"—and he put forth a topped boot, well-polished and shining, as he spoke.

"The Corner estate, as it is called," repeated Sir John.

"At a peppercorn rent," pondered Dacey; "if a body could any way make up the money, I'd do a dale to oblige you, sir; and, though I've neither cross nor coin to bless myself with, to be sure I know them that has, who, may-be, for a valuable consideration, might—though I don't know—the little estate—eh!—ten thousand—it's badly worth that, Sir John, unless indeed, you'd throw the fourteen acres of pasture by the loch into it."

"Well!" exclaimed the indolent baronet, though perfectly conscious that the land was worth double the sum; "we'll talk about that, provided you insure me the money; and now gather your parchments, and vanish; I've had enough of arithmetic to last me for some months—and, Dacey!"

"Yes, sir."

"*After* the election, I will really look into matters myself; but, at present, when the good of my country is at stake—when we are threatened with invasion from without, and rebellion from within— the man must be basely selfish who thinks of self.—Oh, Dacey! did you see the Madeira safely into the cellar ?"

"Yes, Sir John."

"Good night, Dacey!—there—good night—you won't forget— ten thousand—hard gold—none of your flimsy paper—the Corner estate."

"And the pasture."

"There, good night," repeated the baronet, as the wily agent, bowed himself out of the apartment. Sir John Clavis rose out of his seat, and threw open the window which was directly under the turret that formed the boudoir of his Spanish wife; indeed, it was the sound of her guitar that had drawn him to it: and he recognised a favourite seguidilla, to which he had written words; he remembered having taught her to repeat them; and the full rich voice that had given them so much beauty—if in that twilight hour it sounded less melodious—had never fallen upon his ear so full of tenderness; its simple burthen—

"Sweet olive-groves of Spain,"

brought the remembrance of what Madelina was to him, in the days when he playfully chid the mispronunciation of his poetry; and as the prospect of receiving the ten thousand, and not being plagued about money matters, had somewhat softened his temper (the idea that he was diminishing his property had no share whatever in his thoughts —possessing, as he did, the dangerous—nay, fatal, faculty of looking *only* on to-day), he thought, I say, of his wife, with more complacency than he had done since the affair of the green velvet. He was pleased when he heard Miss Dorncliff (of whose arrival he was unconscious) urge her to repeat the strain. She commenced, but at a line which he well remembered—

"I know no blessing like thy smile,"

Her voice faltered, and the next moment he heard her friend chiding away her tears; his first impulse was to proceed to her apartment, and inquire their cause; but then he hated scenes; and vanity or curiosity, or both, prompted him to remain; and the broken dialogue which followed, happily for the repose of his soul, roused, in his wife's cause, the best feelings of his heart. Many were the affec- tionate expressions lavished by Miss Dorncliff on her friend, and many the entreaties that she would cease to agitate herself upon what, she insisted, might be a surmise without foundation.

"You would not say so," replied Madelina, "if you had seen his attentions, his tenderness, on the Continent—or heard his repeated promises that my religion should be held sacred; the little silver shrine, that my sainted mother so often knelt to, I have been obliged to remove, even from this chamber, which it is mockery to call my own; and though I cannot understand all he says—and though his eye is bright, and his lip smiles, sometimes, yet he never looks upon me as he used; *to me his countenance is sadly changed.*"

"I'll tell you what, my dear," replied her friend, taking advantage of a pause in her complaint; "adopt the course I should have taken, if my good father's scheme had, unfortunately for me, been carried into effect. Assert your own dignity; if he looks as cold as snow, do you look as cold as ice—if he stamps, do you storm—if he orders, do you counter-order—if he says, ' I will,' do you say, ' you shan't.' My life on it! such conduct for one week would bring him sighing to your feet. Here you sit, with your baby, which if he had the common feelings of a man he would worship you for presenting to him——"

"Stop, my dear Margaret," said Lady Clavis; "do him no injustice; he loves his child as fondly as father ever loved a child; he has not changed to it——"

"*Yet,*" interrupted, in her turn, the indignant Margaret, "he has not changed *yet,* but who can tell how soon he may? The man who would change to *you* must be base indeed."

"He is not base," replied the wife, in a sweet, low tone, which penetrated into the inmost recesses of Sir John's heart, "not base, only weak; he is surrounded by a parcel of flatterers, many of whom hate me because of my religion, and others for reasons which I cannot define; but look, Margaret, were he to treat me as a dog, were he to spurn me from him, and trample me to dust, even that dust would rise to heaven's own gate to ask for blessings on his head."

"She is an angel after all," thought Sir John.

"You are a fool, my dear!" both thought and exclaimed Miss Dorncliff; "and I only wish I were big enough to throw him over the terrace of this old musty place, and I would soon choose you a husband worthy of your love!"

"Upon my word, I am much obliged to you, Miss Minx!" murmured the baronet, as he cautiously closed the window, resolving to turn over a new leaf, and station himself, for the remainder of the evening, in his wife's dressing-room. He could not avoid thinking, as he passed through the winding corridors and up the staircases, "a very pretty wife I should have had, if it had been as my worthy agent seems to think it might be even now. The fellow means well, but he is mistaken; I should not have been able to call my life my own—the termagant! Thank goodness, I have escaped her! I never valued my blessing before!"

He met his child in the lobby, and took the laughing cherub from the nurse's to his own arms. As he prepared to enter, "You may go down, Mary," he said, seeing the maid waiting to receive the child. "I will take Miss Madeline in myself."

How easily can a man make the woman who truly loves him, happy! It was enough for Lady Clavis that her husband was at her side—enough that he smiled upon her—enough that he called her "darling;" although it would have been better for them both, had she possessed the strength of mind to entitle her to the name of "friend," the most sacred, yet the most abused, of all endearing terms. Miss Dorncliff exulted in her happiness, though her more cool and delibe-rate temperament led her to believe that Sir John's "love-fit;" as she termed it in her own mind, would not be of long duration. She little knew the service she had rendered Lady Clavis by her some-what intemperate advice; nor the dread of the baronet lest any por-tion of that advice should be followed by his gentle wife.

As Mary Conway, Madelina's nurse, descended to the vestibule, she heard a voice, whose sound was familiar to her ear, repeat her name two or three times, and in various tones; she lingered for a moment, and then, as if gladly remembering that her infant charge was committed to its parent's care, turned into an abrupt passage, leading from the great hall to one of the archways, where dews and damps mouldered from day to day upon the massive walls.

"What are ye after wantin' now, Mister Benjy?" she inquired, as the outline of the figure of her lover (for there is no use in con-cealing the fact) became visible to her laughing eyes.

"Nothing particular, that is to say very particular," replied the youth, who was no other than Dacey's nephew; "only I'm going a journey to-night, and I thought I'd be all the better for your God-speed, or, may-be, a bit of prayer to the saints you think so much of."

"A journey—where to?" inquired Mary, with a palpitating heart.

"Why, thin, just to Dublin, Mary, honey. And it's glad enough I'd be to get out of this murderin' grand ould place, only just for one single thing."

"And might a body know what that is?" again inquired the maiden.

"Honour bright, Mary, because I shan't see yer sweet smilin' face for many a long day, may-be; for uncle says he's a dale o' business to transact in Dublin, and that he'll be wanting me to look after it; indeed, I'm thinkin' that he has a notion we're keeping com-pany, and don't over like it; though, Mary, darlin', it's more nor he can do to put between us."

Mary covered her face with her hand, and, though no sigh or sound escaped her lips, tears bedewed her cheeks. She was nothing more or less than a frank-hearted, good-natured girl, with only three or, perhaps, four definite ideas in her pretty round head—the first of which was decided love for her mistress, and her mistress's child—a great portion of affection for Benjamin Dacey—and no small regard for finery, in all its branches and bearings; she consequently had not a multiplicity of objects to divide her attention, which was therefore steadily devoted to the service of her three or four several propensities. The idea of her lover being sent away, and to Dublin too, overwhelmed her with grief, to which she would have given more audible vent, but that Benjamin had unwittingly observed, his "uncle didn't over like his keeping company with her," which aroused the maiden's pride; she therefore said, "that, indeed Mr. Dacey ought to remimber when he once held two or three acres of land under her father," and that, "though she was at the Abbey, she was far from being a *rale sarvant;* she took care of Miss Maddy more from pure love nor anything. else. May-be, it was Mister Benjy himself that wanted to be off the promise—if so, she was willing and ready," &c. &c. But, in fact, these lovers' quarrels are the same in all cases; I could give a recipe by which people might quarrel, *agreeably,* ten times a week on an average—only, as love would be the principal ingredient in *my* prescription, I fear the misunderstandings would be too soon understood for your genuine downright-in-earnest quarrellers. I must not tarry with those young people, during their parting scene, but only recount that "Mary," as she afterwards expressed it, "got a dale out of Benjy, which no one should be the wiser for; only her heart was fairly crushed—thinkin' what a misfortune it was to a boy like him to have such an uncle;" even this she only communicated to her particular friend and companion, Patty Grace.

When the expected company arrived from Dublin—"from the Castle," as it has been familiarly termed for ages—it was evident that Sir John had nerved his mind to some great undertaking to which he was secretly urged by Dennis Dacey. Indeed, the particular party which had once been led by his father, were anxious he should tread in the same steps, and they again regretted that his union with a Catholic was likely to cool his ardour in "the good cause!" They, however, did their best to urge him forward—and "the glorious and immortal memory" was drunk so often after dinner, that those who sacrificed to the sentiment had neither glorious nor inglorious memory left. The humble parish priest never joined in these revels; and when Dacey, in Lady Clavis's presence, hinted at this circumstance, and had, moreover the audacity to assert that his absence was a tacit acknowledgment of disloyalty, the lady roused herself in defence of her ancient friend, and told the agent that, if religion was a proof of loyalty he must be the worst of traitors, for he was a renegade from the faith of his fathers, and had changed for the love of filthy lucre. Dacey trembled and turned pale: but as he quitted the apartment he muttered a deep and bitter curse against the lady of Clavis Abbey. Not only had " the little estate" been secretly transferred to Dacey, along with the fourteen acres of pasture, and the ten thousand pounds paid for present relief, but other sums must, at this crisis, be advanced to relieve the necessities of the proprietor, and other lands sacrificed to feed the rapacity of the agent. Mr. Barry Mahon resolved to stand as the people's champion, and already were the addresses of the several candidates duly printed in the county papers. The Abbey became such a scene of interminable bustle and confusion, as the day for the commencement of the election approached, that it would be difficult to convey an idea of the strange persons and objects which crowded on each other. To Mary Conway's great delight, Benjamin unexpectedly returned; and from the manner in which his uncle received him, it might be supposed that he was not particularly pleased at the circumstance; he, however, carved out for him the task of managing (dare I say bribing?) a few refractory freeholders at some distance; but the young man did not depart until he had whispered some words of moment into his true love's ear. The same evening, when Mary was undressing the little Madeline, Lady Clavis entered the room, happy to escape from a tumult she could hardly understand.

" I'm so glad yer honourable ladyship's come in," said the girl; " I wanted so much to know what you'd have packed up to take into town to-morrow, my lady—as, in course, ye mean to go with his honour to see the election and all that?"

" Indeed, Mary," replied Lady Clavis, " I have no such intention; I shall be but too glad to escape the bustle of it here—and I should be only in the way, Sir John says."

" Och, my grief! does his honour the masther say that? but, no matter, Madam, dear; for the love o' God, as ye value yer own honour, and the honour of this sweet babby, go !—go, for God's sake !—or you'll be sorry for it—mark my words !"

Lady Clavis was astonished at the girl's vehement manner and gestures, but still she remained firm to her purpose. She was suffering acutely from mental anxiety and bodily exertion; and as Sir John had continued to treat her with great kindness, she was anxious to show how willingly she would yield to his wishes—even where they were opposed to her own. But Mary was not to be thus satisfied. She " hushowed " her little charge to sleep, and descended to the lobby that led to her master's study. She paused for a few moments at the entrance, and inclined her head so as to catch any sound that

I

might pass along, having ascertained that persons were speaking within. I cannot avoid lamenting that she was led away, by what might
be called "natural curiosity," to draw near—very near; so near that
her ear covered the key-hole—and listen—systematically listen—to
whatever conversation was going on. She might have remained some
fifteen minutes, in no very comfortable attitude, when she suddenly
started up; but had hardly receded three steps from the door, when it
was opened, and the round, vulgar face of Dacey appeared, carefully
prying into the darkness. Mary saw she could not escape unnoticed,
so, with ready wit, she inquired, "Oh, Misther Dacey, have you seen
my lady's Finny? I've been huntin' all the evenin' after the ugly
baste, and can neither get tale nor tidings of it?—Finny!—Finny!—
Finny!——"

"Can ye see in the dark, like the cats, Miss Mary, with yer fine
red top-knot?" said Dacey, earnestly.

"Troth, ye may ask that," she replied, "for my candle went out."

"And where's the candlestick, Miss Mary?" persisted the keen
querist.

"No wonder ye'd inquire, but sorra a one have we been able to
lay hands on these three weeks, for the shoals o' company, so I
just used the same candlestick my father and your father, Misther
Dacey, war best acquainted with—my fingers, why!—Finny!—
Finny!—Finny!"

She was receding, calling the dog at the same time; when Dacey,
whose ire was roused, followed her nearly to the end, and said, "You'd
better not turn yer tongue against my family, Miss Impudence, for
ye're mighty anxious to get into it, I'm thinkin'."

"Not into your family, Misther Dacey," retorted Mary, proudly.
"Anxious, indeed! I don't deny that Benjy and I have been keepin'
company, though my true belief is, he's no nevvy of yours. Ye'd
think little of *adoptin'* any man's child or property either."

"Hah!" he exclaimed, seizing her arm, and pressing it firmly, "is
that the news ye're after?—ye'd better——" but the girl prevented
his finishing his threat by screaming "Murder!" so loudly, that Sir
John Clavis rushed out, with a candle in his hand, to inquire into the
nature of the disturbance.

Dacey looked extremely foolish, while Mary lifted her apron to her
eyes, and, with well-feigned tears, declared, "It's a shame—and I'll
tell my lady, so I will, that when I was looking for little Finny, he
came out of your honour's study to kiss me, yer honour—a dacent
girl like me—I'll tell my lady, so I will. Finny!—Finny!—Finny!"
And off she marched triumphantly, leaving Dacey to explain his
equivocal situation as he best could.

The night had become dark and stormy, and when Mary put her

head from under the archway, before-mentioned, large drops of rain
were drifted on her face. She hastily folded her grey mantle round
her, and stepping from parapet to parapet of the ancient enclosure,
gained a particular elevation that overlooked the entire country.
Here she paused for a moment, and then pushed into the brushwood
that covered the slope leading to the meadows. Having reached the
stream, that partook of the agitation of the evening gale, she seemed
puzzled how to make her passage good, but her perplexity was not of
long duration, although the stepping-stones were perfectly covered
by the swollen waters. She seated herself on the wet grass, took off
her shoes and stockings, and, folding her clothes round her, prepared
to cross the river.—Having achieved her purpose, after much buffet-
ing with both wind and water, she readjusted her dress, and proceeded
on her way so intently, and with so much resolution, that I doubt if
she would have stayed her course had she even met the bogle that
frightened the good Shepherd of Ettrick—

> " Its face was black as Briant coal,
> Its nose was o' the whuustane ;
> Its mou' was like a borel-hole—
> That puffed out fire and brimstane."

Regardless of banshees, cluricauns, or any of the fairy tribe, Mary
pressed earnestly forward till she arrived opposite a small gate that
opened into an extensive park; the lock was out of repair, so that
she had but to apply her finger underneath, and push the bolt back.
She only paused to inhale a long breath, and flew onward across the
yielding grass, startling birds and herded deer from their early slumbers; this continued fleetness soon brought her opposite the gate of
a noble modern mansion, but she preferred entering through a little
postern-door, to ascending the stone steps.

" Where's her honour ?" she inquired of an old serving-man, astonished at her untimely visit.

" Lord, Mary ! you've frightened the senses out o' me."

" Why, then it's myself is glad to hear it."

" Why so, Mary ?"

" Because it's the first time I've heard of yer havin' any in—but
where's the lady ? "

" Umph," replied the old servant, evidently annoyed, " find out !"
and, turning on his heel, he was leaving the offended damsel alone,
when she snatched the candle that maintained a very equivocal
equilibrium in his hand, and ran up the back staircase.

" That one has the impudence of the ould boy in her, and makes
as free in this house as if it were her own," he observed.

" She tapped gently at the door of a small apartment; and a clear-

toned voice responded "Come in." In another moment Mary was
in Miss Dorncliff's presence. She advanced, making a courtesy at
every second step, until she stood opposite the young lady, who regarded her with much surprise.

"Why, Mary, is your mistress ill—or has anything happened to
little Madeline?"

"No, God be thanked!—nothin'—to say nothin'—yet," replied
the girl, laying her hand on the back of a chair for support, for she
had traversed nearly five Irish miles in less than an hour.

"Sit down, sit down, my good girl," said the lady, kindly; "and,
as soon as you can, tell me what has agitated you thus."

"Thank you, my lady—sure ye said that just like herself that's
the angel intirely, if ever there was one, God knows!—and God
counsel her, and you, my lady; for she won't be said or led by me,
and more's the pity!"

"You speak of your mistress, Mary, I suppose," interrupted Miss
Dorncliff, "but do come to the point at once, for I am all anxiety."

"I can't make a long story short, Madam, particular when my
heart's all in it—but as fast as I can, I'll riddle it all out, for sure my
heart's burstin' to tell it." The lady assumed the attitude of a
patient listener, and Mary, again drawing a long breath, and pulling
first one and then another of her red but taper fingers, commenced
the disclosure of her mystery.

"Ye remember, when her ladyship first came over, the boobery
and the work there was about her; and the people—the protestant
people (savin' yer favour—all but yerself) saying this, that, and t'other
about her, as if she wasn't what she ought to be. Well, to my knowledge and belief, the one who kept this stirrin' was no other than that
ould vagabond—that the beams of God's own sun and moon 'ud scorn
to rest upon (savin' yer presence, for mentionin' him before ye)—
ould Dacey; because ye're sensible he's *a turn-coat* in the first place
—and my lady is so steady to her duty, that it was ever and always
puttin' him to shame; and then to be sure my lady, seein', I suppose,
that in foreign parts the poor are all *negres*, God save us! (may-be
black bodies too) my lady was high to him—she has a high way with
her I grant, and sure so has the lilies, though they're so sweet and
gentle when you come to know them—well, for *that* he hated her;
and I'm sure it's more to get at the way of punishing her, than
even securin' the property, that he's been going on as he has
lately——"

"Securing what property?—going on how?" eagerly demanded
Miss Dorncliff.

"Let me ye tell my own way, Miss, agra! or I can't go on:
besides, how would ye get at the rights of it, if ye didn't hear it from
the beginnin'?"

Miss Dorncliff resumed her patient attitude.

" Ye see ould Dacey knows what he's afther, and Sir John has a way of his own of never seein' to anything—gentleman-like—though I can't but think it a bad fashion; and while he was away, there was a dale of plundering roguery goin' on; and when he came home, sure the agent managed to keep him employed gettin' presentments, and entertainin', an' making speeches about patriotism, and all that (I've been told he's a powerful fine speaker, though I can't say I ever heard him)—and ever divartin' him with sich things, till the right time, when he turned, my dear! as quick as a merryman, and bothered him with debts and accounts. Now the masther, bein' a scholar (as I've heard tell), didn't by coorse like the figures, which are only common larnin'; and the ould one played his cards so well, that he made him hate the sight of a bill, or a figure; till at last Sir John said, ' Manage it all yourself,' which he was glad to get the wind of the word to do, though all the time he was purtendin' he wanted the masther to look to it himself—the thief o' the world! As well as I can come at it, Madam (Miss, I ax yer pardon), Sir John agreed to let Dacey have pieces of estates, on the sly, for ready money, at half their valee—agreein' that Dacey should keep it to himself; for the pride, ye see, wouldn't let him own it; and the ould one, 'cute like, got sich another rogue as himself, in Dublin, to go somethin' in it. You're *sinsible*,* Miss, my lady ? Bein' not a well larned girl, never having got beyant my *read-a-me-daisy*, I can't understand the rights of it, only that these two was cochering together, and procurin' money—for what I know, *unlawful* money— from foreign parts, and gettin' bit by bit of the poor masther's pro- perty from him, and tyin' him down, as Benjy said."

"As who said ?" interrupted Miss Dorncliff.

" Why, Benjy said so," stammered forth the girl, confused at committing her lover's name.

"Then Benjy, as you call him, was your informant as to these pretty villanous plots, I suppose ?" interrogated the lady.

"I didn't say *that*, Miss Dorncliff: sure a body may make a remark, as the poor boy did, when they *hear* a thing, without being the one to *tell* it ?" retorted the girl, keenly looking into her face ; and the lady, wisely, seeing that Mary was now put on the *qui vive* to pre- vent her lover being suspected as the informer, merely replied, "Go on."

" Ye've put me out ever so many times ! but all I've got to say's asy said now ; it isn't enough for that ould devil's pippin that he has *eus:otied*, or some sich thing, the whole land, so as to make the noble gentleman all as one as a genteel beggar, but now that the election is come on, and Sir John goin' to stand for the county and all—what

* " You're sensible,"—you understand.

d'ye think, but he's laid a plan to get the poor gentleman into W——,
to give the word to some thraytors of vagabonds, and get him arrested
and shamed fore'nent the whole county, unless—(oh, the black
villain!)—unless—(the sneakin' ditch-hopper!)—unless—(oh, indeed,
I can't say it for the chokin' of my throat!)—unless he puts away
his darlin' wife—who can be made out not his wife, on account of the
religion, as I'm creditably informed; and that, if he doesn't give in
to this, he'll expose him in the face of the people, which I know the
masther 'ud rather die than stand.   Well, Miss, ye see, he's got Sir
John to promise intirely that he'll not take my lady with him,
because she's delicate like; and he persuaded masther she'd be in the
way.   And I want her to go—for look," continued Mary, giving full
scope to the action and energy of her country, "if she was *with* him
he couldn't desart her, and looking in her sweet patient face, and her
two darling eyes, that send the bames of true and pure love right to
his soul; he couldn't look at *that*, ma'am dear, and consent to stick
a knife in her heart, and send the blessin' of the poor, the light of
one's eyes—*the fond craythur that* trusted him, as if she was a thing
of shame abroad into the *could, could*, world!—but——" and here the
poor girl's voice sank from the highest tones of hope, to the low and
feeble ones of uncertainty—"if she's *not* with him, and that villain at
his shoulder—and the disgrace—and lose the election—and all that;
and if he agrees—plinty o' money—and the seat—and everything
smooth, and keep him more than half or whole mad, betwixt the
fame and the whisky!—it 'ill be all over with my poor lady!—Oh,
she little thinks!—this blessed night—she'll lay down her head and
die!"   Mary hid her face in her hands, and sobbed bitterly.

"My poor friend!—my dear Madelina!" exclaimed Miss Dorncliff,
as she hastily passed up and down the apartment; "how worthy of
a 'better fate!—Mary, there is no use of your denying it; Benjy *has*
given you this information, and he *must* give it publicly."

"D'ye want ruin on him too?" returned the subdued girl; "sure
he's above a trade, and has been brought up like a born gentleman
to do nothin';—and, even if he had a mind, how can he turn agin
the ould villain, his uncle, when sorra a penny he'd have in the
world, and doesn't know how to make one?"

"Look," said the lady; "if Benjamin will bring forward such
proof of trickery as can force conviction on Sir John's mind, *I* will
settle upon him a sufficiency for life; and there," she continued,
throwing her purse into Mary's lap, "is the earnest of my promise."
For a moment, the girl forgot her mistress's interest in her own, as
she eyed the glittering treasure; but soon she reverted to what, with
true Irish fidelity, was nearest to her heart.

"My lady, you'll come to her now, and persuade the masther to

take her, and make out something to oblige him to take her. Och!
my heart never warmed to ye as much as it does at this minute!—for
they said——" She stopped before the conclusion of the sentence.

"What did they say, Mary?" inquired Miss Dorncliff.

"That you, my lady—only I'm loath to repeat a lie—that, may-be,
you'd marry the masther, if he'd put away his wife."

Miss Dorncliff's face and forehead crimsoned to the deepest dye at
this villanous insinuation. "Me!" she ejaculated, as if to herself,
"Me!—the base-born churls! But I will save *her*, come what may.
Mary," she continued after a pause, "Mary, do not say a word of
your having been here—mind, not a syllable. You will see me in
the morning."

"Before masther goes?" inquired Mary.

"No, but soon—immediately after. Fear not, my good girl, your
mistress shall be safely cared for."

"May the holy Mother, whether ye've faith in her or no, preserve
ye from harm, and may heaven be yer bed at last!" replied Mary,
clasping her hands, and looking most affectionately at Miss Dorncliff;
"and a good night and a fresh blessin' to ye every mornin' that ye
see daylight!"

When Miss Dorncliff was alone again, she revolved her plans as
she paced along her chamber. For the last three years she had had
the sole management and control of her father's affairs, whose age
had, in a great degree, swallowed up his mind; and a large property
was also at her sole command, which she had already inherited from
her uncle. That night she neither slumbered nor slept; repose came
not to her body or her spirit; and from the highest window of the
dwelling, she watched until she saw Sir John's equipage, with his
troop of noisy retainers, pass the great gate on its way to W——.
She then ordered her own carriage, and in a little time was at Clavis
Abbey. The first person she inquired for was Mary, and doubtless
she derived some information from her, for they were long together.
She then proceeded to Lady Clavis's dressing-room, and found her
in tears.

"I cannot tell why," she said, "but I feel a sad anticipation of
evil hanging over me. It was so strange, John kissed me this morning when he thought I was asleep; and, do you know, he attempted
to kneel at Madelina's cradle, but he rushed, like a madman, from
the room, despite my efforts to recall him."

"We must follow him then," observed Miss Dorncliff, assuming
an air of gaiety—"we must follow him; I want most sadly to go to
the election—my presence will cheer on my own tenants to his
service; and there is no saying but that some of them, were I not on
the spot, might dare to think for themselves. Besides, I can only

go under the protection of a matron, you know. No interruption—
I must be obeyed; we will set off this afternoon, so as to hear his
maiden speech from the hustings."

Lady Clavis offered a very weak opposition to what her heart longed
to engage in, and they arrived at W—— at about half-past ten at
night. The little Madelina was left in Mary's care at the Abbey.

There was no difficulty in finding the inn, or, as it was called,
hotel, where the Orange member put up; for he had steadily refused
going to the house of either of his constituents.

The waiters immediately recognised Lady Clavis, and, with many
bows, conducted her into the passage, which was empty at the time,
though the sounds of music, singing, and loud debate, were clearly
distinguished by the ladies, even before they alighted from their
carriage.

"You can show us to a sitting-room, where we can wait till Sir
John is disengaged. We wish to surprise him," said Miss Dorncliff.

"I can't tell him ye're here just now, my lady," replied the man,
"for Mr. Dacey said they war not to be disturbed; and there's two
gentlemen, I'm thinking, from Dublin, besides two or three others,
waitin' to get speakin' with him. And it's myself don't know where to
put yer ladyships, barrin' ye'll go into a purty tidy room jist off
where his honour's settlin' a little affair of business with Mr. Dacey.
Sure, if I'd known you war comin', it's the great grand committee-
place I'd have had redied out for ye."

"Be firm and cautious now, my dear friend, for the hour of trial
is come," observed Miss Dorncliff, in French, as she pressed her
friend's arm closely to her heart;—"the men from Dublin, and all;
we have just arrived in the right time—depend upon it, all will be
well."

The waiter stared with stupid astonishment, and said, "May-be
ye'd have the goodness, my lady, not to speak out much, as Sir John's
at business in the next room, and he mightn't like to be disturbed;
it 'ill do to tell him by-'n-by, won't it, my lady? But what will you
please to take?"

"Nothing—nothing now," replied Miss Dorncliff; for Lady Clavis
appeared incapable of either mental or bodily exertion. Her friend
had revealed to her a considerable portion of her plans and anxieties
during their brief journey, and her elegant but weak mind, unable to
arrive at any conclusion, remained in a state of passive obedience.

Communicating with the next apartment was a small door, which
hung very loosely on its hinges; the cracks and chinks were many;
and through the principal one Miss Dorncliff saw Sir John sitting
at a table, his face buried in his hands; while Dacey, whose head was
approached close to his, was talking in a low, eager tone—so low that
only broken syllables reached her ear.

At last Sir John removed his hands, and, lifting his eyes slowly, while his pale and sunken features expressed the painful struggles he endured, said, "It must not be, Dacey; do you think I want to insure damnation to my soul? What possible difference can it make to you, that you thus stipulate for her destruction? Men are seldom so desperately wicked without a motive."

"Hasn't she scorned me, and ordered me out of the room as if I was a neagre?—hasn't she treated me with the contempt which a man never forgives?—hasn't she—— but the short and the long of it is, Sir John, that you know my determination: disgrace her, or disgrace yourself!—disclaim your marriage, or go to jail!—to jail, instead of to parliament!—to the jail, where Mr. Mahon can point, as he passes it, at the last of the house of Clavis! There's the pen and the ink; I don't force ye—do as ye please—it's no business of mine." The fellow pushed some parchments and papers towards the unfortunate baronet, and gathered unto himself a pile of rouleaus that were filled with gold, while his eyes gloated and glared on the agonized face of his *patron!* "Sure, there's no harm in life in keeping a foreigner like her," continued the brute; "many has done the same, and will again. Send her back to the 'olive-groves of Spain,' she's so fond of singing about, and——"

"Peace, miscreant!" roared Sir John, in a voice of thunder, quite forgetting the time and place.

"Whist!" exclaimed the coward, "never call names so loud—you know I'm yer best friend. If these sheriff's officers hear ye, it will be high mass with us all!"

The baronet sank back in a state of stupefaction, and the agent advanced towards him, pen in hand. Almost mechanically Sir John took the little instrument in his fingers—its point touched the paper —even the letter J was traced, when Miss Dorncliff pushed strongly against the door; and, in the same instant, both Sir John and Dacey were trembling in her presence. For some moments, all parties remained silent—gazing at each other with such varied expression as would be difficult to describe. With the politeness with which Nature has endowed every Irishman, from the prince to the peasant, both pushed seats towards the young heiress, which she declined; at last Sir John inquired, as the pen dropped from his fingers, "to what circumstances they were indebted for the honour of her visit?"

"I come, Sir John," she replied—and the first sentence was uttered in a trembling voice, which gained strength as she proceeded, "I come to save the HUSBAND of my friend, Lady Clavis, from destruction!"

Sir John's pride mounted, as he replied stiffly and formally, "that he was not aware to what Miss Dorncliff could allude."

"This, Sir John," she continued, heedless of the interruption, "is a bad time for compliments; you were about to sign a paper repudiating your wife, in order that that *bad* man might relieve your present necessities, and save you from arrest. I cannot now bring forward the proofs that I possess, of his villanies, and the various arts he has used to dupe your understanding, while he ruined your property. I pledge my word to do so; and to redeem all, even the *little Corner estate*, from his clutches, if, instead of signing *his* paper, you will sign *mine*—and, to relieve your present embarrassment, I will tell down guinea for guinea of the money you are to receive from that person! Need I say more?—Need I urge the love you have tried?—Need I ask if you will consign your child to shame?—Need I——"

She was interrupted by a loud and piercing shriek from Lady Clavis, as with one strong effort she rushed from the outer room, and threw herself into her husband's arms. He was so unprepared, so astonished, that he did not appear able to support her, and she sank gradually on her knees—her hands clasped—her hair falling in heavy masses over her neck and shoulders—and her eyes shining with unnatural brightness, from amid the bursting tears that flowed incessantly down her cheeks. It is impossible to describe the mingled look of hope and anxiety with which she regarded Sir John. Miss Dorncliff advanced to her side; and, as her tall, commanding figure towered over the bending form of her friend, she laid her hand on the baronet's arm, and, in a low, impressive tone, said, "*Can you look upon and crush her?*" The appeal was decisive. He pressed his wife convulsively to his bosom, and it is no disgrace to his manhood to confess that his tears mingled with hers.

"This is all mighty fine," at length exclaimed Dacey, whose vulgar perplexity was beginning to subside into assurance, "but I don't understand it."

"And who supposed that the wallowing swine comprehended the sweetness of the ringdove's note?" replied Miss Dorncliff, casting upon him a withering look of contempt and scorn.

"I don't deserve that from you, Miss," said the savage, interpreting the expression of her countenance, "for I meant to help you to a husband."

"Sir John Clavis—I call upon you to turn that man out of the room!" replied the lady; "let him and his gold vanish;—and trust for this night to the agency of your wife's friend!"

Bitter and deep were the curses he muttered, while depositing the coin in his leathern wallet; he would have formed no unapt representation of Satan preparing baits for sin—but foiled even in this effort.

"I recommend you, Dacey, to be silent," said the baronet.

"But others won't be so," growled forth the menial, as he retired. He had hardly closed the door, when he remembered the papers and parchments he had left on the table, and returned with a view of securing them. Miss Dorncliff had anticipated the movement, and, placing her hand firmly on the documents, signified so decidedly her intention of not suffering their removal, that, baffled at all points, he finally withdrew. He could hardly have reached the hall, when the officers who had been waiting outside, made their appearance, in no very gentle manner, to make good their seizure. This, however, Miss Dorncliff prevented, by paying the amount demanded, and the room was soon cleared of such graceless company.

"Now, then," said the generous girl, looking round her with a happy and cheerful countenance, "now, Sir John, *my* document must be signed. I claim *that* as my reward. My own lawyer will settle other matters at some future date, but that *must* be done before I slumber or sleep—the physician demands her fee."

The baronet seized the pen, which, a short time before, he had taken to perform a very different office, and affixed his name to the paper she presented. After placing it within her bosom, she remained some time silent, while the vacillating man was endeavouring to explain his conduct to his wife, who, loving much, forgave all.

"It is well," thought Miss Dorncliff, "that such men should be wedded to such gentle women. My affection would always expire with my esteem; but now, she loves and believes, as if he had never been about to ruin her reputation, and to stigmatize for ever their innocent child! There must be something mysterious in this love which I cannot comprehend." She could, however, comprehend the heights and depths of the noblest friendship. Her sleep that night was light and refreshing; and it was not till the morning was far advanced, that the shouts and bustle of an Irish election woke her to consciousness and activity.

It is not to be supposed that Dacey's bad but enterprising spirit would rest composedly, under detection and consequent exposure. He conjectured, truly, that Miss Dorncliff, through some means, which at present he could only suspect, had obtained information of his intentions, and was prepared to render null and void basely-earned bargains and nefarious schemes. He was aware that, until the election was over, no investigation could be systematically gone into; and he hit upon a cold and villanous design to prevent the inquiry he had so much reason to dread. He knew well the character of the opposing candidate—a fearless, careless, man—vigorous and imprudent—

> "Jealous of honour,
> Sudden and quick in quarrel;"

who had fought more duels than any man in the county; and was as often called "Bullet Mahon," as "Barry Mahon." He existed only in an atmosphere of democracy; and his hot, impatient aspect, firm tread, blustering voice, and arrogant familiarity, formed a very striking contrast to the polished, weak, but gentlemánly, bearing of Sir John Clavis. It was not at all unlikely that a quarrel would ensue, before the termination of the election, and many had even betted upon it. With the generality of Irishmen, it would have been unavoidable. But, though Sir John had never shown the white feather, he was decidedly a peaceable man—and was known to be so. Dacey, however, resolved not to trust to chance in the matter, and, on the morning of the second day, he was closeted with Mahon for nearly an hour. When the candidates appeared on the ill-con-structed hustings, to greet their respective constituents, it appeared evident that Mahon was overboiling with rage at some known or supposed injury. Sir John's address was mild, and more than usually facetious—a style better understood and appreciated in England than in the sister island; he alluded to, without exulting at, the favourable state of the poll; and, after a short and cheering exhortation to his friends, resumed his seat.

When Mahon prepared to address the crowd, he swung his body uneasily from side to side, looking, when wrapped up in his huge white coat, as the personification of those unhappy polar bears who suffer confinement in our menageries. At last, elevating his right arm, as if threatening total annihilation to all who differed from him in opinion, he began one of those inflammatory addresses that have been followed up by so many second-rate agitators in modern times; he talked of the distresses of the people, until those who had just eaten a hearty dinner imagined they were literally starving—and assured them so often that they were in a debased state of bondage, that at last they fancied they were sinking under their fetters' weight. "I would have you beware," he said, exerting to their utmost power his stentorian lungs, "I would have you *all*, green as well as orange, beware of those who would purchase your votes by bribery! If a man gives a bribe, he will take one!—and I wonder my opponent is not ashamed—*I say, ashamed*—to show his face here, after the con-duct he has practised in private!"

Sir John Clavis called upon Mr. Mahon to explain.

Mr. Barry Mahon said he did not come there to *explain*, he came to speak—and speak he would—*no descendant of an impostor* should put him down—if Sir John Clavis wished for explanation, he could seek it elsewhere—if he did not do so, he was a COWARD!

The language had grown too violent, or, as the interfering parties called it, "too warm," even for an Irish election; and the friends of both candidates endeavoured to put an end to it, or, at all events, to conclude it in another place. As Mr. Mahon refused to make any apology, or even give any explanation, it became necessary, according to the received and approved code of honour, for Sir John Clavis to send a message to the gentleman who had so grossly insulted him.

It was sent, but Clavis so worded it as to leave the matter open to apology. This, however, was not taken advantage of, and a "meeting" for the next morning was, of course, agreed upon.

Since their reconciliation, poor Lady Clavis had been suffering severely from agitation; her mind and body had received a severe shock; and though the happy arrangement, through her friend's generous sacrifice, had set her trembling heart at ease, her health had not yet mastered the struggle; she had been confined to her chamber, unceasingly attended by Miss Dorncliff.

About seven o'clock in the evening of the distressing quarrel between the candidates, Lady Clavis had just requested her friend to open the window, that she might feel the breath of heaven on her fevered cheek, even for a few moments; her fine dark eyes were fixed on the setting of a rich autumnal sun, which shed its glories over the scattered houses, and converted them into dwellings of molten gold. She was reclining on a couch formed of the high-backed chairs of the rude apartment, and, as her husband entered, she greeted him with inquiries as to the state of the poll. Miss Dorncliff thought within herself, that he looked pale and agitated, but did not allude to the circumstance. He was hardly seated, when a servant placed a note in Lady Clavis's hand; she just broke the wafer, and, glancing at the contents, burst into tears; Sir John perused it with almost the same agitation: and the intelligence it conveyed was well calculated to excite sorrow, for it said that the little Madelina had been taken dangerously ill, and Mary Conway, the writer, entreated Lady Clavis, "for God's sake, to come home, if she wished to see her child alive." The mother lost no time in her preparations; she thought not of herself; and to Sir John, under existing circumstances, her departure was a relief: he kissed and handed her into the carriage; the door was shut, and the coachman preparing to drive off, when Sir John called to him to stop. The evening sun had set, and the night wind was blowing sharply in the faces of the horses; the baronet pushed the footman away, and, unfastening the door, let the steps down, so that he could kneel upon them.

"Madelina," he said, in a low, agitated tone, and in her own dear native tongue—"Madelina, do you *from your heart* forgive me, for the unkindness I have shown—for the injury which, under the influence of a villain, I would have done you, and our innocent child."

"My soul's life," she replied, "why do you ask? I cannot think of you and injury at the same time; *from my heart*, I have forgiven you." She bent her head forward to kiss her husband, and the wind blew one of the long locks of her raven hair across his face—he seized upon it as a treasure.

"I must keep this to wear next my heart till——" " we meet, again," he would have added, but the sentence remained unfinished, while he severed the ringlet from the rest; he then extended his hand to Miss Dorncliff, and continued, even in a more broken tone, "You have been her friend, as well as my preserver—I *commit* her to your care!"

"How kind and affectionate he has grown!" observed Lady Clavis, as the carriage drove on; "when this dreadful election is over, and our darling recovered, we shall be *so* happy!—and to you, my dear, dear friend—my more than sister—I owe all this; his first love was not so sweet to me as his returning affection;" and, overcome with many contending feelings, the gentle creature sank into a troubled sleep.

The calm was but the prelude to a storm. How often, when our hopes are highest, and our certainties of happiness seem firmest, is the thunder-cloud gathering over us that will soon ruin both! Even at the very moment when the wife had the surest confidence in days of enjoyment and repose to come, and the friend was luxuriating over the consciousness of a good deed done, they were on the very brink of a precipice, from which there was, alas! no retreat. Alas! still more, that a vile hand should have had the power to force them over it. But thus it is—

> " Sorrow and guilt,
> Like two old pilgrims guised, but quick and keen
> Of vision, evermore plod round the world,
> To spy out pleasant spots, and loving hearts ;
> And never lack a villain's ready hand
> To work their purpose on them."

The roads were heavy, and the lumbering carriage and fatted horses little accustomed to hasty journeyings; they had proceeded at the rate of three miles, or three miles and a half, the hour, and were within five miles of the Abbey, when their progress was arrested by a figure on horseback seizing the reins and commanding them to stop. "God be thanked for his mercy," ejaculated a well-known voice; "by his blessin' it 'ill not be too late, and he may be saved yet."

"Who saved ?—what do you mean, Mary ?" eagerly demanded Miss Dorncliff, for Lady Clavis was not sufficiently collected to make any inquiry, and only looked wildly from the carriage-window.

"The masther ! the masther !—turn the horses' heads, Leary, as ye value salvation, or the priest's blessin' !"

'Explain first, Mary, for this is madness," replied Miss Dorncliff; " where—how is the child ?"

" Here," she replied, unfolding her cloak, and placing the smiling cherub on its mother's lap. " I knew misthress 'ud never believe it was alive and well, when I hard o' the trick just to get ye all out o' the way, my lady—and you too, Miss, who unriddled so much before, that he thought you'd be at it again—the villain ! The short an' the long of it is, that ould rascal tould some lies to the other mimber as wants to be, and, on the strengh of them lies, him, the other man, insulted masther forenent the people ; and they'd a row; and the upshot of it is that they're to fight a jewil to-morrow morning—Lord save us !—like Turks or Frenchmen ; and 'twas he wrote the note— as one let on to me, who rode a good horse to tell it—and, troth, grass didn't grow under my feet either. But turn, turn !—we'll may be get a help of horses on the road ; I'll gallop on and have 'em ready, though it's as much as we can to reach town by daylight."

The servants urged the jaded animals to their utmost speed ; and prayers mingled with the tears of Lady Clavis, shed as she pressed her child to her bosom. Miss Dorncliff endeavoured to give what she did not possess—hope. She knew that Barry Mahon's bullet was unerring ; and, from time to time, she let down the front glass to cheer forward the anxious coachman. The horses Mary procured on the road were more a hindrance than a help, so restive and ignorant were they as to carriage harness. Never did culprits who watch for, yet dread, the coming day, feel more bitterly than they did when the first thin stream of light appeared on the horizon ; the stars, one by one, faded from their gaze ; and at last the spire of the church of W—— appeared like a dark speck on the clearing sky.

" Forward, forward, my good Leary !" said Miss Dorncliff; "there's the church-steeple—hasten now, and reward shall not be wanting."

" It isn't the reward—it's the masther I'm thinking of," replied the faithful fellow. " If we had the luck to be on the Dublin road itself, there'd be some chance of help ; but here——" He groaned audibly, and by words of encouragement, and a more liberal applica- tion of the whip, forced the horses into something like a trot.

" I can see the masts of the vessels that are lying in the harbour," exclaimed Mary ; "for God's sake, hasten, Leary !"

" I may as well throw down the reins," replied Leary ; " they can only crawl; this one's sides are cut with the whip, and that one's fallen lame too !"

" I could walk faster than the horses can go now," said Miss Dorncliff.

" And so could I, and *we will* walk," replied Lady Clavis, rousing all her energies.

"Do, do, my dearest friend," retorted Miss Dorncliff, "for I see figures on the bridge that cannot be mistaken; and if we could only get there in time, all could be explained."

Lady Clavis sprung from the carriage with a promptness that astonished her friend. She folded her child closely to her bosom, and took the path, across some meadows, which led, by a nearer way than the carriage-road, to the field that, for centuries, had been the duellists' meeting-place. The agony of her mind may be imagined, but cannot be described. There was her husband—every step rendered him more visible—she pressed onward—and her child was rocked by the panting of her bosom. The ground is measured—she flew without disturbing the dew that trembled on the grass—repeatedly she raised and waved her arm, eager to arrest attention—in vain!

Man to man stood opposed—not in spirited combat, but with cold murdering designs on each other. She screamed loud and fearfully, and her scream was answered by a fiendish laugh, which seemed to proceed from the hollow of a blighted tree that stood in her pathway: as she passed it, the bad face of Dacey glared upon her with bitter exultation. She shrank involuntarily from his ken, and the report of a pistol struck upon her ear with appalling distinctness; it was followed by another, and the next minute saw her kneeling by the side of him whom she had loved with all the fervour of the glowing south, and all the fidelity of our colder climes; the innocent child crept from her arms over his bosom, and pressed her little lips to those of her dead father. Lady Clavis motioned off the people, who wished to remove the body, and, with fearful calmness, unbuttoned the bosom of his shirt, and looked intently on the wound and the oozing blood. She attempted to unfasten it still more, but started back as if some new horror had been displayed, when the tress of hair he had severed from her head the night before, appeared literally resting on his heart. Tears did not dim her eyes, which became fixed and motionless; and her whole figure assumed a frightful rigidity. The scene was even too much for Miss Dorncliff's firmness: she fainted while endeavouring to take the child from the remains of its ill-starred parent.

"It's THE LAST OF THE LINE, sure enough!" exclaimed an old keener, who had watched the melancholy proceeding; "for a girl, and such a girl, has no hoult on the land; ill-got—ill-gone!"

My tale is told, and many will recognise it as *over true.* Lady Clavis's intellect never recovered the shock it received, and some years afterwards she died in a convent in Catalonia. The property of Clavis passed into other hands; and those who obtained it were generous and honourable enough to settle upon Lady Clavis and her child a larger income than they would have been entitled to, had there even been *legal* proof of the marriage, which, it was generally supposed, could not be obtained, or Miss Dorncliff would have procured it. So perfect, however, was the evidence she had collected of Dacey's villany, that he was never suffered to enjoy his ill-gotten wealth. I remember him in extreme old age—a hated, mischievous idiot. Mary and Benjy were "as happy," to use the tale-telling phrase, "as the days were long;" and Miss Dorncliff—who was a living refutation of all the scandal ever heaped upon that most maligned class of persons called old maids—received, in her declining age, more than even a child's attention from Madelina Clavis.

THE WOOING AND WEDDING.

IT was a rich and glowing evening, in the budding and blossoming
month of May—the sun was setting with calm magnificence over
a cultivated and beautiful country, and there was nothing to obstruct
the view of his farewell glory, except the high and verdant trees,
whose leaves were hardly moved by the passing zephyr. No one
could enjoy so happy a scene more fervently than Helen Gardiner—
Helen, the most lovely lass in the whole country—purely and truly
lovely was she; so delicate, so graceful—the gracefulness of nature.
It was very strange, and I never could account for it, but Helen was
decidedly not a coquette; how she came to avoid it I know not; it

is a fault that pretty women almost universally fall into. Yet there she was, the second daughter of an opulent farmer, in her twentieth year—a belle and a beauty; and, most certainly, she never flirted one single bit in her whole life—good-tempered and affable withal—active in her domestic duties—exquisitely neat in her person (the sure index of a well regulated mind), and exact in the performance of her duty. I have said she was lovely, and it is most true; but she was very pale—it was seldom, indeed, that the faintest colour tinted her fair cheek; her hair was of a deep chestnut, plainly braided across a well-formed forehead, and confined in a large knot, or sometimes plait, at the back of her head; her eyes were decidedly beautiful, like two large dewy violets—and such eyelashes!—fancy her other features as harmonizing with her placid character—and fancy also a dignified figure, and then exert your imagination to finish the picture, and behold our rustic favourite, on such an evening as I have described, sitting at the door of a happy, well-wooded cottage in Somersetshire, sometimes looking up from her occupation (which, by the way, was trimming a neat straw bonnet with plain green ribbon), to glance at the glorious sky, or, more frequently, watching a long green lane which led to the house, and in which nothing very interesting appeared to an ordinary observer. It would seem that not many visitors came up that lonely footway, for the little path was nearly overgrown by long grass. Yet, true it is, that Helen watched it, and true, also, that when the sound of two cheerful voices rang upon her ear, she looked no more, but most assiduously pinned on the strings, arranged the simple bow, and concluded—just as two men emerged from under the overhanging trees—by running an obstinate corking-pin into her finger.

"Helen, why, Helen?" exclaimed the elder, who was her father; "here's your old friend, Mr. Connor—to be sure we are all glad to see him."

Helen extended her hand to the younger of the party, and her eyes spoke the welcome which her tongue refused. She led the way into her cottage; her father and the stranger followed. The two men were odd contrasts:—Gardiner was a perfect picture of an English yeoman, habited in a clean white "frock;" his round and florid countenance proclaiming peace, plenty, and much prudence; and his hair which, unthinned by time, fell over his moveable and wrinkled brow, was slightly touched by gone-by years. "Mr. Connor" (or, as he was called in his own land, for he was a *rale* Emeralder—"Mark, the traveller"), was a fine handsome fellow, gifted by nature with an animated, expressive countenance, and manners far above his situation in life; there was a mingling both of wildness and tenderness in his voice and address; and his garments of the blended costume of both countries, had a picturesque appearance to English eyes. He never could be reconciled to smock frocks, to which all the Irish peasantry have a decided antipathy; but he had discarded knee-breeches and woollen stockings, and wore trousers, which certainly looked better with his long blue coat; his scarlet waistcoat was "spick and span new," his yellow silk neckerchief tied loosely, so as to display his fine throat, and his smart hat so much on one side of his thickly-curling hair, that it seemed almost doubtful if it could retain its position. "Mark, the traveller," was the eldest son of a respectable cattle-dealer, and frequently visited England to dispose of live stock, whether pigs, cows, or sheep, which, of course, he could sell more cheaply than English farmers could rear them. He had long known Helen and her father, and had loved the former with fervour and constancy. She loved him, too, silently and unchangingly; the gracefulness of his manners first attracted her attention, and she saw—or what, even with a sensible girl in love, is pretty much the same thing—she fancied she saw good and noble qualities to justify her attachment. Those quiet, pensive sort of girls, have always ten times the feeling and romance of your sparkling, giddy gipsies; and, notwithstanding that Helen discharged all her duties as usual, and no common observer could have perceived any alteration, yet her heart often wandered over the salt sea, beat at the sound of the Irish brogue, and silently inquired if, indeed, the natives of the green island could be uncivilized savages? She had, moreover, a very strong passion for *green*, and it was actually whispered that she wore in her bosom, a shamrock brooch, carefully concealed by the folds of her clear white kerchief. Her elder sister had been a wife, a mother, and a widow, within twelve months, and resided with her father and Helen; they might truly be called a united, contented family: perhaps Helen was somewhat more than contented, as she prepared the simple supper for their visitor, who had been some days expected, and who sat in their neat little parlour, at the open casement, into which early roses, and the slender Persian lilac, were flinging perfume and beauty; the honest farmer puffing away at his long white pipe, as he leaned half out of the painted window-sill.

"I'm thinking, Mr. Connor, ye don't use such long pipes as these 'uns, in your country!" said the yeoman, after a pause.

"Ye may say that, sure enough;—we brake them off close to the bowl—and thin it comes hot and strong to us."

"Ye're very fond of things hot and strong in that place, Mister Connor; but I'll do you the justice to say, I never saw you in liquor all my life, though I have known you now more than six years."

"Nor never will, sir, I hope and trust. I never had a fancy for it, nor my father before me, which was a powerful blessing to the entire family, seeing it kept us out o' harm's way."

" I knew I had something particular to speak to you about," resumed the old man. " Do you remember the last lot of pigs you sold me ?"

" May-be I don't."

" That means I do, I take it, in English. Well, perhaps you recollect one with a black head—a long-bodied animal—strangely made about the shoulders."

" Ough, an' it's I remember it, the quare baste ! good rason have I ; with its wigly-wagly tail, and the skreetches of it. Sure, because ye were my friend, I warned ye to have nothing to say to her ; and you ('cause, ye mind, ye said when she was broadened out, she would make good bacon), took a great fancy to her, and so I let you have her, a dead bargain."

" Bargain, indeed ! she would eat nothing we could give her, and, knowing she was Irish, Helen picked the potatoes, mealy ones, and——"

Here Mark cast a look of indignation at his host, and exclaimed—

" Well, that bates Bannaher ! Miss Helen, who's more like an angel than a woman, pick potatoes for an unmannerly pig ; a *Connaught pig*, too, that *could* have no sort of manners ! Sure, I ought to have tould ye, sir, the Connaught chaps (the pigs, I mane) 'll never eat *boiled* potatoes—the unmannerly toads, it's just like them. Well, to make up for his ignorance, take yer pick out of the drove for nothing, and welcome, to-morrow, and I'll go bail not a Connaught pig is in the lot—not a squeak did they give, getting on board, only all quiet and civil as princes."

" Thank ye, that's honest, and more than honest," replied the farmer. " I have no objection to an abatement—that's all fair ; but to take the pig for nothing is what I won't do ; for ye see fair is fair, all the world over."

" You'll do what I say, master, because ye're an old friend ; and be in no trouble about the cost, for I have had a powerful dale of luck lately. My mother's uncle, in America, is dead, and left a dale more behind than 'ill bury him ; a good seventy a-piece to the three of us—and so, before I came this turn to England, I took a neat bit of ground on my own account ; and have as pretty a house on it as any in the county, for the size of it ; three nice rooms, with a door in the middle, and a loft ; it was built for a steward's lodge ; and a bawn at the back, with every convenience ; and when I was on the move, I left ten pounds o' the money with Matty, my youngest brother, to have the room off the kitchen boarded for a parlour, for

I mean to have it the very morral of an English cottage, as I mean—if—if—I—can—to have an English—girl for a—a—wife."

"Well done, well said, Mister Connor; but who do you think would go over with you to that unchristian country, where——"

"I ax yer pardon, sir, ye're under a mistake; there are as good Christians, and Protestant Christians, too, in Ireland as in England—(I mean no offence)—and with such as fills that purse (and he drew from his bosom a long leather bag, and flung it on the table), and such a boy as myself, an English girl may be had, Mister Gardiner; though (he added, in a subdued tone) the one my heart is set upon is not to be bought with silver or gould."

"Not bought with silver or gold, Mr. Mark! Well, hang it, that's more than I'd say to any of the sex."

"You wrong them, then, sir;—money's a powerful thing—but look, there's some of them (one that I know of in particular), so pure somehow—like a lily, for all the world—that a heavy sorrow would crush, or the least thing in life spot; and nothing could buy the love of *that* heart, because, as well as I can make it out, it has more of heaven than earth about it."

"No one can make you Irishmen out," retorted the farmer, laughing: "but may I ask *who* this lily—this delicate flower is?"

"Is it who it is?" replied Mark: "why, then, no one but yer own daughter, Helen Gardiner by name, and an angel by nature; and now the murder's out," he continued, "and my heart's a dale lighter."

The worthy yeoman put down his pipe, and looked at Mark Connor with a sort of stupid astonishment; he was a keen, sensible man, shrewd and knowing in matters concerning wheat, rye, oats, and all manner of grain; the best judge of horseflesh in the whole county; and such a cricketer! such an eye!—could get six, or, perhaps, seven notches at one hit, and was, even then, a first-rate bowler; had, moreover, an uncontaminated affection for youthful sports, marbles, balls, humming and spinning tops; and would leave his pipe at any time for a game at blind-man's-buff; yet it was certainly true that the idea of Mark Connor's aspiring to the station of his son-in-law never once entered the honest farmer's head. "My Helen! Well, Mister Connor, every father, that is, every man who has the feelings of a father, must feel as a compliment an offer—I mean such as yours—and I take it very sensible that you have mentioned the matter to me first, Mister Mark, because, of course, I must know best. As to Helen, poor girl, she has never thought about anything of the sort; and, indeed, Mister Connor, although I highly respect you and knew your father in the Bristol Market, an honest man (though an Irishman) as any in England, and know you to be a

Protestant, and all, yet I must say my girl is very dear to me, and I should not like to trust—I mean, not like her to leave Old England. '

Mark Connor was not much discomfited by these observations; he pushed his hair back from his forehead, and paused a moment or two; during the interval the farmer resumed his pipe, and puffed, and puffed.

"You were quite right, farmer," resumed the lover, after a pause, "quite right in supposing that I had never mentioned matrimony to Miss Helen, but ye see I mentioned——"

"What?"

"Why, it came quite natural like, the least taste of love; and she never gainsaid me, though she listened like any lamb."

"Indeed," said Mr. Gardiner, "you must give me leave to—almost doubt you. Now," he continued, seeing that Mark's face assumed a glowing aspect, "no anger, no getting into a passion for nothing—let us understand each other. Helen is my child; I love her more than any other living thing, and have done so ever since she, my wife, whom she is so like, was taken from this home to one she was better suited for. She was——" John Bull's heart, whatever its casket may be, retains the stamp of early affection longer than any other heart in the world, and the feelings of the honest farmer sent some big tears to his eyes, when he remembered her who had possessed his perfect love for more than thirty years. "Forgive me: if you love Helen, you can forgive me, for still mourning one my dear girl so closely resembles. It is not natural, Mister Connor, that I should like my child to leave me, particularly to go to a country of which I have been told so much evil; and, had Helen never heard of this, I certainly should not have told her: I know she regards you as a friend—but love, believe me, is out of the question; however, I will this moment speak to her, and—— but I will first speak to her on the subject."

The farmer bustled out of the room, and summoned Helen into the little apartment which she called her own; it was a neat, delicate lodgment, fit resting-place for such a maiden. The walls were of snowy whiteness; a large looking-glass, in a plain black frame, surmounted the chimney, on which were placed sundry little rural figures in variegated china. A deer, a fawn, a trim girl, with her milking-pall—(the pail, by the way, green, and the tree which over-shadowed, a bright blue, but that was of little consequence)—then a shepherd with a smart pink hat, with a purple flageolet, and two hornless goats, one minus three legs—then the pretty pictures!—the neat sampler with its border of blue strawberries, and yellow roses—"Helen Gardiner, aged ten years," in double cross-stitch at the bottom: the bed, with its white cotton hangings, its pretty

patched quilt, all diamonds, corner-pieces, and striped bordering,
harmonizing wonderfully well after all. The simple toilet with its
snowy covering—and the glistening cherry-tree wardrobe—putting
to shame French polish, and Neapolitan varnish, by its brightness.
On one of the two rush-bottomed chairs Mr. Gardiner seated himself,
and drew the other closer to him, which Helen was directed to occupy.
Helen trembled much at first, but still more, when her father somewhat
abruptly inquired, if Mr. Connor had ever asked her to marry him.

"No, father," was her immediate reply—given, nevertheless, in a
tremulous voice, while busily occupied in rolling up the end of her
band, which, by the way, was green also.

"Nor ever talked to you of love?"

"Love, father?"

"Yes, love, I suppose you call it."

"No—that is, not much, father."

"Well, I am glad he has not spoken much on the subject, Helen;
for, indeed, it would grieve me to see you married to an Irishman,
however worthy he might be. So, my dear, I will tell Connor at once
that he must give it up, as—as—it is the better way, I assure you."

"Dear father," exclaimed Helen, grasping his hand, as he rose
from his seat; "you do not, cannot mean what you say; indeed you
must not—it would—make me so—very——"

"What, child?"

"Oh, dear father, after the encouragement—indeed you must
not——"

"Here's a coil!—must not—encouragement—and all that. Why,
Mary, Mary, I say——"

Helen's widowed sister entered.

"Did you know of this pretty piece of work—your sister's listening to love-tales, and giving encouragement to a man, an Irishman
too, without my knowledge?"

"I knew, sir, certainly, that Helen was attached to Mark Connor,
and Mark Connor to her, and it was impossible to suppose that you
did not know it also; for you may remember how much they had
been together, and you never prevented it."

"How did I suppose they were to fall in love?—Helen, who was
so strict, not like other girls! Surely she refused Alexander Brownrig—a man that half the girls in the parish are after."

"I am sure," interrupted Mary, "it was Mark Connor who drove
Brownrig out of her head."

"I wish he had been driving his own pigs, then," responded the
father; "but there, Helen, there—since you choose to fall in love
without my consent, I suppose my consent is not necessary for your
marriage—there, let go my hand."

She did let go his hand, for the unkindness he expressed had such an effect on her gentle spirit that she fainted on the floor, before her sister or father could support her : the revolution in her parent's feelings was instantaneous ; he pressed his lips to her pale forehead, bestowed on her all the endearing epithets he could think of, and finally called in Mark to help to revive her : both father and lover knelt at her bed-side, while her sister chafed her temples with such refreshing stimulants as the cottage afforded.   When she opened her eyes, they rested upon the two beings she loved most, and the colour flashed over her pallid features, as words of sweet import broke upon her ear.

" I won't refuse either consent or blessing, my own Helen, but you ought to have told me you loved——"

" Hush ! dear, dear father !" cried the blushing girl, as she raised herself on the simple couch ; " do both go away, and I shall be better, quite well, in the morning."

" What piece of finery is this ?" said the father, picking off the coverlet the identical shamrock brooch which I before hinted at.

" Oh, nothing, only—a—a——"

" A little token I gave her," said Mark, smiling, " though I never knew she wore it before."

" She always wore it," observed her sister, " except when you came ; I'm sure, father, you might have seen it, confining the folds of her neckerchief."

Notwithstanding the different feelings of the little party who assembled around the plain supper-table of Farmer Gardiner on that memorable evening, they all might have been pronounced happy.   Helen and Mark were perfectly so ; the old man had resolved to make the best of the matter, and was also pleased and flattered by his intended son-in-law expressing his hopes that he would come over to them and lay out their farm upon the most approved English principles.   The youthful widow, the light of whose existence had been so dimmed by the loss of the partner her heart had chosen in all the purity of its first affection, looked upon her sister, and the smile struggled with the unbidden tear, as she pressed her own little one to her heart.

The next day it was very evident that something was going forward of a particular nature in the cottage ; a great part of the early morning was spent in consultation with Julia Malling, the little London dressmaker, who sported a French hat and French curls— " only just come up ;"—and then an adjournment to the village-shop ; and, in the afternoon, Mark Connor and Mr. Gardiner, mounted upon their trusty nags, set off to Bristol, both looking full of business, and then came a cutting and snipping of book-muslin and sundry prints, and glimpses of white satin riband, and—— but it is unnecessary

to dwell upon the preparations; my readers must know already that
nothing but a wedding is anticipated; and a wedding surely it was,
though not conducted after the bridegroom's notions of the parade
essential on such occasion. Helen, to be sure, looked most beautiful
—everybody (that is everybody who saw her) said she looked more
beautiful than any woman in the world ever looked before, but Mark
complained sadly that there were not people enough, nor dancing
enough; and then Helen did not appear to be half joyous enough;
and when, as the ceremony was concluded, he pressed her to his
bosom, and called her "wife!" he was somewhat mortified to find
her warm and glowing cheek wet with many tears; he could not
understand when he was literally half mad with joy, what could
make her sad, for he knew she loved him; and he thought to himself
that had his wedding been in Ireland, instead of in England, there
would have been more mirth, and more music, and Helen would have
been more cheerful; as it was, she would neither sing, dance, nor
speak. She sat like a beautiful marble statue between her father
and her husband; and, but for the flush that passed occasionally over
her calm face, she had little of a living being about her. Mark loved,
and, like all Irishmen, gloried in making a bustle about it; he could
not fancy a wedding without much rioting: his gentle bride loved
also; though it was not given to him to comprehend the depth or
the delicacy of her untainted affection.

But we will, if you please, leave the bride and bridegroom to make
their arrangements, and conduct their leave-taking, after the most
approved fashion, rejoining them in Ireland, on their landing in the
village of Ballyhack!—Ballyhack!—the dirtiest town—indeed, the
only dirty town—of our country; the very emporium of lean pigs,
bad butter, unclad beggars!

Helen had, therefore, an ill example of Ireland, and certainly did
think it must be a wretched country; but, when ascending the hill
that opens a view of Lord Templemore's house on one side, and the
beautiful scenery around Dunbrody Abbey on the other, she changed
her opinion, and expressed her delight at the improving prospect.
"Och! wait till we get home, Helen! and though you musn't think
to find all like in England, yet you'll soon be able to make it so."
This was easier said than done. Poor Helen!—silently and patiently
did she toil; and, to do Mark justice, he aided all her undertakings,
in open defiance of the sneers of the entire parish, with very few exceptions. Helen's calmness was called pride, and her exact neatness
was a positive reproof to the slovenly habits of the uncultivated
peasantry; and here I think it right to mention, lest there should be
any mistake about the matter, that she was not fortunate enough at
that time to be a resident exactly in Bannow. Mark had wisely

aken his cottage at a good space from his mother's dwelling, for he knew that the friendship of relatives, brought up so differently, increases with distance. They resided in the vicinity of the "Seven Castles of Clonmines"—a remarkable, and peculiarly interesting locality on the other side of "the Scar"—dim records of a gone-by history—early structures raised by the first English conquerors, to keep the possessions they had gained by the sword, and to control the "mere Irish." Matty, his younger brother, was often with them, and he improved much by the wise precepts and uniformly good example of his new sister; but Helen's greatest torment was a fault-finding, pains-taking (as far as making mischief went) old maid, the chronicle, and scandalous magazine of the county. Nobody liked her, and everybody tolerated her, for the simple reason why every gossip finds a welcome—because she was full, brimful, of news and scandal. The parish had a little occasional rest when "Judy Maggs," as she was called, pursued her vocation of carder, and wandered from county to county in search of employment; but, unfortunately, her only brother died at sea, and left her in possession of "a good penny o' money," so that, at the period to which I allude, she might be considered only as an amateur carder. She was chiefly occupied in investigating and meddling in everybody's business, within five miles of her dwelling; not that she objected to long journeys: she has gone to Waterford, a distance of seventeen miles, to find out if Katey Turner's gown really cost two shillings and eightpence per yard; and no one can deny that she was not well repaid for her trouble, when she ascertained it to be an absolute fact, that the little gipsy got it a dead bargain at two and six. She went messages for every one, from those of the squire's house, to the mud cabin of blind Peggy O'Rooney! Nothing came amiss to her in that way; she might be termed, in the exercise of walking, a most wonderful woman, a universal carrier, from a whisper to an "established fact."

"Why, then, Mrs. Connor, ma'am," said she, one morning, addressing Helen, who, as usual, was setting her house in order, "will ye be afther telling us what the young masther is ploughing the ould wheat-field for?"

"To sow flax in, Judy."

"That's English, asthore!—sure, poorer land nor that 'ud do for flax—where did ye larn to throw flax into sich rich soil?"

"In the Netherlands, I have heard, they never sow flax except in good soil; and you know the best linen comes from that country."

"I ax your pardon, civilly, Mrs. Connor, ma'am—as *if* I didn't know all relating to the seed, breed, and generation of all the flax in the world wide! Oh! wirrasthrew!—to even that to me!—the Nitherlands! what is they to the North, in regard o' linen-makin'?"

Gentle Helen Connor had enough to do to appease the angry dame, who, as a professional carder, was thought omnipotent in all flax questions; and she had at length got her into good humour, when Mark's brother, unfortunately, entered, and introduced a new subject of contention.

" Now that the reaping is over, Matty," said Helen, " I hope you will bind and stook the crop at once, not leave it on the ledge, as you did last year—I think it will rain—at all events it may; and it is better to be on the safe side."

" Bind and stook the *crap*, afore a body has time to turn round !" exclaimed Judy—" Och hone ! that's another English fashion, I suppose—or, may-be, it's from the Niverlands !—wouldn't to-morrow or the day afther, do for that ? I'll go bail for the weather—sorra a good in doing things in a hurry !"

Helen made no further remark, and Matty promised, in open defiance of Judy Maggs, to see that the corn was bound and stooked immediately. " But what I came in for, principally, Helen," said he, " was to tell you that the pig is laid out ready for burning in the barn."

" Burning in the barn !" echoed Judy, starting from her seat: " and are pigs so plinty with ye, that ye mean to burn 'em, and so many poor crathurs starving ? Och, that I should live to see such fashions ! Good mornin' !—good mornin' to ye, Mistress Mark Connor !—and God send ye better sense, and a little more Christianity !—burn a pig ! Och, my grief !"—Judy Maggs stood no further question, but trotted off, eager to communicate to her neighbours the melancholy intelligence, that Mark Connor's English wife " wint so far with her notions as to make *fire-wood* of a pig !" On her journey, it was her misfortune, or rather, considering her love of tattle, her good fortune, to encounter Mister Blaney O'Doole, the parish carpenter, who was seated on the car that, turned on end, served as a gate to stop the gap leading to the short cut to old Mrs. Connor's dwelling. Blaney was a short, thick-set man, who, all over the world, would be recognised as a real Emeralder. " Good morrow, Mr. Blaney," said she. " Good morrow to ye, kindly, ma'am," said he. " What's stopping ye, sir ?" said she. " Why thin, I'll tell ye, ma'am, dear, if ye'll give me time," said he, " but it's yerself was always the devil afther the news—though sorra a much's stirrin'— but I'm waitin' to take the stone out o' my brogue, that 'ud never ha' got there, only for the bla'gardly way they made the new road. What could the country expect from the presintment overseer, and he a Connaught man ? Didn't I see him with the sight o' my eyes, after bargaining with Tim Dacey to take tinpence a day, and a shilling allowed by the county (and paid too)—didn't I see him give poor Tim the full hire with one hand, and take back the odd pence (that weren't pence but pounds) with the other! so that, if called, he could make oath, with a *safe conscience*, that he ped the whole." That's a good story, faith!" replied Judy, laughing, and losing all feeling of the roguery of the transaction in the amusement occasioned by its cleverness,—" but hardly as smart as one that *I had the sight* of my eyes for, up in the county Kilkenny, as good as tin years agone—when a man—*a gentleman*, they called him—got a presintment to mend a piece of a road; and what does he, but lays the notes down along—along—iver so far on the bare ground of the highway, and then picks them up—claps thim into his pocket—walks off to the nixt grand jury—and makes affidavit, that 'he *laid* the money out *upon the road.*'—But is it manners to ax where 'ud ye be going wid yer bag full o' tools?"

"I'm jist stepping down to Mark Connor's, to get the *morral* of a new barrow with two wheels, that he wants made, and that he says is powerful good for all sorts and manner o' work. I wonder he didn't get it done of iron, like the cart he brought over, which cost him a good five guineas, and I could ha' made him one of wood twice as big for three."

"Of iron, agra!" repeated Judy.

"Ay, asthore!" replied the carpenter, "and so much wood in the country; wasn't it a sin? How grand he is, to be sure, as if the sort o' cars his neighbours have wasn't good enough for him!"

"Thrue for ye—that's a thrue word;—but I could tell ye more than that; pigs are so plenty with them, that his fine English madam of a wife, at this very minute, is burnin' a pig in the barn."

It was now the carpenter's turn to be astonished.

"Burnin' a pig!—Oh thin, for what?"

"For what!" said Judy, a little puzzled; "why thin it's myself that can't tell exactly," she replied; "only for sport, as I could make out, or for fire-wood, may-be!"

"Holy mother!" ejaculated the astonished man of chips, and wended on his way; while Judy called after him, "Find out for me the good o' burnin' a pig."

The evening of this day was a very pleasant and cheerful one in Mark Connor's kitchen. A neat white cloth was spread on a clean deal table; there was a small square carpet laid over the centre of the floor: and the tin and copper vessels on and under the dresser were brightly burnished; the fire certainly appeared almost as if made on the hearth, but, in fact, it was burning in a very low grate, that had both hobs and a trivet; and at each side of the capacious chimney were stuffed settles, neatly made and comfortable. On one of these, Mark was stretched at full length; the other was occupied by Matty and Blaney O'Doole; and Helen was endeavouring to convince a wild, but good-humoured looking, serving girl, that a gridiron ought to be kept clean, and was much fitter to do a pork griskin on, that was crying, like Kilkenny fowls, "Come, eat me—come, eat me," than the kitchen tongs that the lassie had extended on the fire for the purpose, although the gridiron was just as easy to get at.

The cloth, as I have said, was laid, and the supper in active preparation, when in walked old Mrs. Connor. Now, let people be ever so much inclined to find fault—let them be ever in so bad a humour, there is something almost irresistibly soothing in a group of smiling, happy faces, and a well regulated apartment. I care not whether it be in a palace or in a cottage; a wooden chair may be as well placed as one of gold and damask: and if a youth is wooingly disposed towards any damsel, as he values his happiness, let him follow my advice;—call on the lady when she leasts expects him, and take note of the appearance of all that is under her control. Observe if the shoes fit neatly—if the gloves are clean, and the hair well polished. And I would forgive a man for breaking off an engagement, if he discovered a greasy novel hid away under the cushion of a sofa, or a hole in the garniture of the prettiest foot in the world. Slovenliness will be ever avoided by a well regulated mind, as would a pestilence. A woman cannot be always what is called *dressed*, particularly one in middling or humble life, where her duty, and, it is consequently to be hoped, her pleasure, lie in superintending and assisting in all domestic matters; but she may be always neat—well appointed. And as certainly as a virtuous woman is a crown of glory to her husband, so surely is a slovenly one a crown of thorns. Now, having given what is seldom attended to, gratuitous advice, I must proceed to say, that old Mrs. Connor was never particularly sweet or gentle in her temper, and, as she entered the cottage, according to the Irish phrase, Mark wondered "what was in his mother's nose now." When, however, Helen took the great corking-pin out of her mother-in-law's cloak (which, by the way, for want of a string, had torn a large rent in the cloth), and, placing her gently on the easy settle (a luxury unknown in the generality of Irish cabins), gazed sweetly and calmly in her cranky face, and inquired affectionately after her health, the old lady softened a little, and looked around with a less dissatisfied countenance.

"Just in time, mother," said Mark, "just in time to share our supper; indeed, Helen had laid by something nice for ye, which Matty was to take over to-morrow: but make yerself comfortable; and, though it's been a busy day with us all, yet we're no ways in confusion." The old lady had not time to reply, when there was a smart knock at the door, and Mark's cheerful voice gave the usual invitation, "Come in, and kindly welcome;" our old friend Judy Maggs appeared immediately, and a sort of interchanging glance passed between the two ancient dames.

"Sure it's glad I am o' shelter," said Judy, taking off her new beaver hat, and carefully wiping it with the tail of her gown.

"Ye don't mane to say it's rainin'?" retorted Blaney O'Doole.

"Pepperin' like fun," replied Judy, "and so suddent too!"

"Och, my grief!—and all my little handful o' barley, that I had the ill-luck to rape as good as a week agone, upon the ledge."

"Ours is safe," exclaimed Matty, joyfully, "thanks to Helen for it—for Mark hasn't time to look to everything—and sure I'd ha' never heeded it, but for her." Helen smiled at her good-natured brother, and it was observed that Judy looked particularly confused.

"Mark," said Blaney, "did ye hear what a shockin' misfortune happened Mr. Clancy?—sure his crap o' flax was no crap at all, afther his takin' three years' lase of Stoney Knock, thinkin' 'twould do well enough for flax; and the agint won't let him off his bargain."

"Serve him right, I told him how 'twould be," replied Mark: "poor land never gave out a good crop yet—jist like people expecting to fatten pigs upon green food. I wish your sister Mary was over here, Helen, to teach us how to fatten them her way."

"One 'ud think yer father's son ought to know how to fatten pigs better than any one, and he bred, born, and reared, among them," observed Mrs. Connor. Poor Helen, for the life of her, could not comprehend Irish metaphor; and she repeated, with a flushed cheek, "Mark's father born and reared among pigs!—surely you mistake."

"No mistake in life, Helen; sure, there's myself and his sons to the fore, who are proud to own it." Helen looked to her husband for an explanation, but he only laughed.

"I don't understand Irish," replied Helen, smiling in her turn, "and I think I make many mistakes for that reason."

"I'll niver stand to hear any one abuse my English," said Mrs. Connor, angrily; "and, Mark, if you can stand to see me turned on afther that fashion, by yer wife, I'll not—that's all."

"Nor I, neither," added the woman of many professions.

"Helen! my Helen, abuse you, mother!—Helen!—she never abused either you or any one else; the fact is, she does not under-. stand your *Irish*, and *you* don't understand her *English*——"

"Mark," interrupted Mrs. Connor, rising hastily, and looking very angry and grand, while Judy Maggs, whose figure was little and rotund, crouched close beneath the shadow of her elbow, "Mark, I'm a plain-spoken Irishwoman, and your natural mother, and I feel it my duty to tell ye that I don't like yer goings on; I'd scorn to say a thing behind your back, for I'm neither a flea, a fly, nor a Connaught man, but I tell you to your face that I do *not* like yer outlandish ways. Now, Helen, I don't want to make ye cry, girl; and ye needn't interrupt me, Mark, for I'll say my say, and be done

wid it. In the first place, Helen, it was not manners, the day my
brother Hacket called on you, out o' civility, on his way from the
fair, for you to mix wather wid the drop o' whisky ye handed him;
and when he drank the trashy stuff, ye hadn't the dacency to fill him
another sup, but says, '*Will* you take a little more?—may-be, ye'd
rather not?'—Was that the way (I'd lave it to judge and jury) to
trate a relation?"

"Mother," said Helen, "it was not that; but indeed Mr. Hacket
had taken enough before he came here, and I didn't like——"

"That's more of it," interrupted the old lady; "I say nothin' agin
his being a little merry now and thin, but to talk of his havin' taken
enough! Oh, to think of that bein' evened to a brother o' mine!—
but wait; it's only to-day I heard that you, Mark, had sint for Jemmy
Smith, the mason, to make a back-door to yer house. What need
has any dacent quiet family like yours, of a back door? Sure, there's
no rogues among ye, that ye need a back door to escape through?"

"You don't understand, mother," said Mark.

"I don't want to understand," replied the old woman, who had
talked herself into a belief of all she uttered; "I want to spake my
mind, and to put a stop to yer *improvements,* as ye call 'em. I wonder
ye wouldn't have more pathriotism than to be bringin' foreign ways
into the counthry!—I'll say nothin' to ye about the iron car—Lord
save us!—iron! and so much wood to be had for a song—nor the
barrow with two wheels!—though my wonder is, where or how ye
can put two wheels under a barrow; nor about iron corn-stands—
and stones to be got for nothin';—but I don't see why there should
be such a set-out o' tins shinin' about the kitchen; in my time,
two or three things sarved for all—and why not?—but it's my
duty I'm doin', and——"

"Don't forget the pig," whispered the curious and impatient Judy,
raising herself on tiptoe to Mrs. Connor's ear; the old lady seized
the idea with avidity: "But, may-be, as I understand nothin'," said
she, ironically, "ye'd have the goodness to Irish me the English of
' burnin' pigs?'"

"Burning pigs!" echoed Helen.

"Burning pigs!" repeated Mark.

"Ay, burning pigs!—makin' fire-wood of them!"

"I never even heard of the like!" replied Mark, "not in all my
travels."

"Oh, the lies and wickedness of the world!" exclaimed Judy,
clasping her hands together, and turning up her eyes: "and it done
here this very day!"

"It's you that's telling lies, Miss Maggs!" exclaimed Mark, eager
to vent the anger which had been for some time accumulating; "it's

you that's telling lies, and well I know that ye're the mother of lies, and the counthry will never have rest or peace, till you, and the likes of ye, are out of it."

"Hould yer tongue, Mark!" exclaimed Mrs. Connor, "for it's the truth Judy's tellin'. Speak up, Judy, didn't ye see Matty and Helen both set fire to a live pig?"

Helen looked perfectly astonished, while Matty swore and protested that he had never done, or even thought of, such a thing in his whole life: the wind changed, and Judy, who (owing, it is to be presumed, to the imaginative organ being frequently called into action, and, consequently, acquiring considerable vigour), had certainly enlarged the report, after the fashion of all approved story-tellers; Judy found it somewhat awkward to be brought to *facts;* and, as a *dernier ressort*, denied having ever used the word "*live.*" Old Mrs. Connor continued positive in her first assertion; and, at all events, after much bitter bandying of many words, the scene closed, upon old Mrs. Connor and Judy Maggs quitting Mark's cottage, at variance with its inmates and each other; while poor Helen, leaning her head against the wall, was weeping bitterly, and even Mark appeared worried and out of temper.

Mark Connor was anything but weak; and yet, being seriously angry with his mother, and the gossiping sisterhood in general, he did not kiss the tears from Helen's cheek, his customary mode of chasing the sorrowing tokens away, but in no very gentle tone said, "Ye'd better leave off crying, Helen;—women's tongues and women's tears are always ready when not wanted."

"I seldom trouble you with my tears, Mark," replied Helen, perhaps a little, *leetle*, pettishly.

"You've seldom reason, Helen."

"I am not saying I have."

"But I say you have not."

Helen was silent—unjustly so, perhaps—but it was a slight indication of woman's temper, and Mark was in no humour to put up with it.

"I say you have not, nor never have had since you have been my wife."

The remembrance of his mother's rudeness, and Judy Maggs' vulgarity, was fresh upon her mind, and she ejaculated—

"Mark! Mark! how can you say so?"

"Oh, very well!" replied the husband, "very well! I suppose the first tale you tell your father, and he coming over next week, will be —'how ill I have used you!'"

Helen was again silent, and her calm features assumed somewhat the expression of sulkiness.

L

"Do you mean to tell your father that I have used you ill?" reiterated Mark, raising his voice at the same time.

Helen's tears flowed afresh, and she sobbed, "You never did till now."

It was very unfortunate for both Mark and Helen that others were witnesses to this first difference; for had they been alone, Mark's pride, and Helen's too, would have given way; but, as it was, neither would make the first advance towards reconciliation, and Mark swore a wicked oath, consigning all women to the care of a certain unmentionable black gentleman; and ended his pretty speech by muttering certain words; their import being that he wished he had never married an Englishwoman. This was the unkindest cut of all. Helen, now really angry with her husband, and justly hurt at his unkindness, left the kitchen with the air of an offended princess, and the cooking to the little serving maiden, who performed it most sadly. "I'll not stay supper, thankee, Mark," said Blaney O'Doole, who had wisely forborne all interference in a most *un*-Irish way, rising as he spoke, and stroking his "*cawbeen*" with the open palm of his hand, "I'll not stay supper, I thankee kindly, all the same, but I'll go home; only, Mark, if I had swore that way at Misthress Blaney O'Doole, my wife, you know, I wouldn't be in a whole skin now, that's all; good night, and God be wid ye!"

"I'll go to bed, Mark," said Matty, "I'm very tired: only, Mark, asthore! don't be hard upon Helen; sure, ye know, the English are finer-like than us, and I saw her lip shake when you swore so at her; and, indeed, I can't help thinkin' our place a dale nicer than any one else's; she does bother about it to be sure, and is horrid particklar, but she's gentle-hearted, and gave me such a beautiful green silk Barcelona for Sunday, and says she'll give me a silver watch when I'm fifteen;—don't be cruel, Mark; do you know that when I'm a man, I'll marry an Englishwoman!" And off went Matty, but not to bed; he left his brother sitting stubbornly at supper, his elbows resting on the table, and his face resting on his hands. "He's in one of his sulks," thought the good-natured boy, as he stole round the gable end of the house to his sister-in-law's bed-room window, "and, if they're long coming, they are desperate long goin'! I'll see if I can coax Helen to go and make it up with him; and I'll find some way to punish that meddlesome ould woman—for it was all of her that my mother was stirred up for a battle to-night—as if Mark hadn't a right to his own way!" These thoughts brought Matty Connor to the little window that was curtained on the outside by the leaves of some fine geraniums, Helen's own particular plants; he peeped through the foliage, and saw Helen, her eyes still red with weeping, turning over the leaves of the small Bible (it had been her father's parting gift), as she sat at the little neat dressing-table.

"Helen! Helen!" said he, softly, "Helen, avourneen! don't fret, dear, but jist make friends with Mark; the natur' of us Irish, you know, is hasty and hot; but sure, Mark loves ye (and good reason he has) more than his heart's blood, and it's proud he is to have an English wife; sure it was only this mornin' he owned so, and he guidin' the plough; when Mr. Rooney, the man with the big farm, said that this house was a pattern to the country-side, 'It's my wife I may thank for it,' made answer my brother, as well he might."

"For your mother to accuse me of burning a live pig!" said Helen, indignantly.

"Helen, dear! I know what that was owin' to; that blunderin', ould, wizen-faced, go-by-the-ground, Judy Maggs, who, whin I tould ye the pig was ready for burnin' in the barn (meanin', you know, that it was ready to have the hair singed off, the Hampshire way, for bacon, instead of bein' scalded our way), was all in a fuss to know what I was afther: I was in no way inclined to gratify her curiosity; don't you mind, I mean remimber, what a lantin' puff she set off in this very mornin' about it."

Helen sighed, and thought, as everybody else thinks who attempts to improve Ireland, that the *beginning* is difficult, if not dangerous—*c'est le premier pas qui coute!* "But you'll make it up with Mark, Helen; poor fellow! there he is sitting by himself, and the fire out, and Biddy spoilt the supper entirely—sorra a bit he's eat."

"Not eat any supper!" repeated Helen, slowly looking up.

"Not as much as 'ud fill a mite's eye!—and Helen," added the cunning rogue, "he had a hard day's work, and wasn't over well."

Helen turned over the leaves of the little book, then closed and pushed it gently from her.

"Good night, dear Matty—don't forget your prayers—good night."

Matty had an intuitive knowledge of woman's heart, which it puzzles many a philosopher to acquire, so he only murmured—a "God bless you!" and withdrew, thinking slyly to himself, "that 'ill bring her round, any way."

Soon, very soon after, a small, gentle hand lifted the latch of the kitchen door; presently, Helen's face appeared at the opening, sweet, but serious. Mark pretended to be both deaf and blind—he still retained his position—and though she advanced into the kitchen, he moved not. Helen's pride and her affection wrestled for a moment within her, *but the woman triumphed;* she threw her arms around his neck, and looked affectionately in his face;—it was enough—"there was naebody by," so Mark compromised his dignity, and the past was forgotten. I do believe this was the last, as I know it to have been the first, quarrel that followed Mark Connor's wooing and wedding. It was a long time before Judy Maggs found out the real meaning of Helen's burning the pig; and, indeed, she would never have been perfectly enlightened on the subject, but for Helen's good-nature, who sent her a portion of the "burnt" flitch, as a make-up for Mark's bluntness, he having forbidden her the house; a course that all who loved peace speedily adopted likewise. The most obstinate disciples of old customs in time saw the advantage of Mark's farming improvements; his flax was the finest in the country; his corn was always stacked in time; his bacon the best ever tasted; and even his mother confessed the superiority of the two-wheeled-barrow. The back door, I fear, was always regarded as a sad innovation, notwithstanding the proof of it's being the means of keeping the front one clean. Helen's housekeeping, even, after a long trial, received its due meed of praise, though I fear that her husband's family was the last to award it;— "the cry of the country" obliged them to do so at length, and then, as Mark himself said, "The deuce thank them for it." He was wise in suffering no interference after that night; and the greatest triumph Helen experienced was when old Mrs. Connor not only requested her receipt to make a plum-pudding, but actually begged her to go to her house to make it—a tacit acknowledgment of her superiority.

About four years after her marriage, when her father came to see her for the second time, as he walked down the garden to her little flower knot, for which he had brought some rare bulbs, and held her little boy (a rosy, "potato-faced" fellow) by the hand—who amused himself by breaking his grandfather's pipe into short pieces, an operation that was not perceived by either grandpapa or mother—the following conversation took place between them :—

"I confess, Helen, I feared you would never be as happy as you appear. I never doubted Mark's kindness—but really the people are so careless——"

"Yet good-natured," said Helen, smiling.

"So insincere."

"Not so, father; they always *mean* to perform what they promise; but they are, I confess, too apt to promise beyond their *means.*"

"So passionate."

"But so forgiving."

"So extravagant."

"So very hospitable."

"So averse to English settlers."

"About as much as we are to Irish ones."

"Averse to improvement, then."

"Not when convinced in what improvement consists."

"Helen, do you know it is very hard to convince an Irishman; be has so many quips, and cranks, and puzzling sayings, and would prefer being reduced to expedient, to attaining anything by straightforward means—provided it was not too troublesome."

"There is truth in all that," replied Helen, thoughtfully, "and no good will ever be effected by flying in the face of their prejudices; they are a people that must be led, not driven. Preconceived ideas cannot be hammered out of their heads—but they may be directed to other objects; though you cannot stop the source of a river, you may turn its course. Dear father, farewell for a little time; and, if nothing else reconciles you to Ireland, remember it was Mark's wooing, and the wedding which followed, that made your Helen happy."

JACK THE SHRIMP.

SOME ten or fifteen years ago there lived, in the neighbourhood of Bannow, a long, lean, solitary man, known by no other appellation, that ever I heard of, than that of "Jack the Shrimp." He was a wild, desolate-looking creature; black, lank hair fell over his face and shoulders, and either rested in straight lines on his pale, hollow cheeks, or waved gloomily in the passing breeze; his eyes were deep-set and dark; and there was something almost mysterious in his deportment. Some persons imagined him to be an idiot; but others, who knew Jack better, asserted that his intellects were of a superior order; however, as few enjoyed the privilege of his acquaintance, the former opinion prevailed. Jack could be found everywhere, except in a dwelling-house; he had a singular antipathy to dry or sheltered abodes, and never appeared at home except when on the rocky sea-shore, scrambling up the cliffs, or, in clear weather, looking out for the scattered vessels that passed into Waterford harbour. Nobody seemed to know how he came to our isolated neighbourhood:

his first appearance had created a good deal of village gossip, but
that had gone by, and his gentle and kindly manner endeared him to
the peasantry : the affectionate greeting of " God save ye ! "—" God
save ye kindly ! " was frequently exchanged between the solitary
shrimp-gatherer (for such was Jack's ostensible employment), and
the merry " boys and girls," who, at all seasons, collect sea-weed,
and burn it into *kelp*, on the sea shore. Often have I seen him in
the early morning, at low water, his bare, lank legs tramping over
the moist sand, or midway in the rippling wave ; his pole, some six
feet long—the net full of shrimps at one end, and the heavy hook at
the other, balancing it over one shoulder—while from the opposite
were suspended two wicker-baskets, frequently filled with lobsters, or
smaller shell fish, which he contrived to hook out of their holes with
extraordinary dexterity. The sole companion of his rambles was a
little, black—I really know not what to call it, so as to distinguish
its peculiar tribe, but it may be sufficient to state that it was a black,
ugly dog, who, by way of economy, usually walked on three legs,
partly blind, and was, like its master, lonely in its habits, and shy in
its demeanour. This animal which, appropriately enough, answered
to the name of Crab, was the means of my introduction to its taciturn
lord. Even in childhood I was devotedly attached to the sea ; somewhat amphibious—fond, when I dared, of getting off my shoes and
stockings, and dabbling in the fairy pools which the receding ocean
left in the hollow clefts of the rocks ; and fonder still of chasing the
waves as they rolled along the sloping beach. My affection for this
dangerous amusement was so well known, that I was never permitted
to go to the strand, although it was considerably within a mile of our
house, unattended by an old, steady dependent of the family, Nelly
Parrell by name, who was intrusted with the care of all the young
folk in the country on their sea-side excursions. But there was
another companion who loved to be with me—my noble favourite,
Neptune, a tall, stately, Newfoundland dog, thoughtful and sagacious.
It was not to be supposed that so high-born an animal would conde-
scend to associate with a low-bred tyke ; and no mark of recognition,
that ever I perceived, passed between him and Crab, any more than
between myself and the shrimp-gatherer, who, I dare say, thought a
noisy, laughing girl of ten, a sad disturber of his solitude. One
morning, during spring-tide, having just bathed, I had quitted the box
to take my accustomed stroll along the shore ; when, on a rock, a
considerable distance from land, and which the inflowing rapid waves
were covering fast, I saw and heard poor Crab in evident distress ;
the fact was, that part of his master's tackle wanted some alteration ;
and Jack, forgetting it was spring-tide, had placed his lobster-baskets
on a high rock, and directed his dog to watch them until his return

from the village; Crab would not desert his trust, and to save him appeared impossible, even to his master, who had just descended the cliffs, as the intermediate waters became deep and dangerous. I never saw any man in greater agony than Jack on this occasion; repeatedly did he call to the faithful animal—yet it would not quit the spot. Neptune was never particularly quick; but when he did comprehend, he was prompt in doing all things for the best; suddenly he understood the entire matter, plunged fearlessly among the waves, and soon returned, bearing Crab, between his teeth, to the shore; not content with this exploit, he twice re-entered, and brought the baskets to the feet of the grateful man of shrimps. I do believe the poor fellow would, to use his own words, at the moment, have walked "bare-foot to Jericho, to serve me or mine." He snatched the dripping animal to his bosom, and, amongst other endearing epithets, called it his only friend. Ever after, Jack and I were intimate acquaintances : not so Neptune and the black cur : the latter never forgot his obligations; but Neptune only returned the humble caresses of the little creature by a slight movement of his stately tail, or a casting down of his small dark eye, as well as to say, "I see you!"

Still there was something about "Jack the Shrimp," I, notwith-standing my most persevering curiosity, could never make out; his mornings, from the earliest dawn, in fair or bad weather, were em-ployed in catching the unwary fish; at mid-day he attended his several customers, and in the evenings he again repaired to his haunts among the wild birds, and amid the ocean spray : his general place of repose was a hollow rock, called the OTTER'S-HOLE; and there he used to eat his lonely meal, and share his straw bed, at night, with his faithful dog. I saw him one morning, as usual, poking after shrimps, and was struck by the anxiety and energy of his movements; notwithstanding his seeming employment, he was intensely watching every sail that appeared on the blue waters : when he saw me he rapidly approached.

"The top of the morning to ye, young lady, and may every sunrise increase yer happiness."

"Thank ye, Jack; have you caught many shrimps this morning?"

"Yarra no, my lannan—sorra a many.—Ye wouldn't have much company at the big house to-day?"

"I believe we expect some friends."

"Ye wouldn't know their names?" he inquired, looking at me, while his sunken eyes sparkled with feelings which I could not understand.

"Some, Jack, I know—Mr. Amble, and Mr. Cawthorne, and Father Mike, and the rector."

"Any of the red-coat officers from Duncannon, agra?"

" Not that I know of."

" Are you sure ?" he continued, peering earnestly into my face ; " ye wouldn't, sure ye wouldn't, tell a lie to poor ould Jack, Miss, darlint—you, whom he'd go tin pilgrimages to sarve, if he were to die to-morrow—you, who have so often spoke kindly to him when yer voice fell on his ear like the song of a mermaid—sure you wouldn't desave me, *mavourneen !*"

" Indeed, Jack, there is no reason to deceive you on the subject— the matter cannot concern you ; but, to make your mind perfectly easy, I will ask the housekeeper ; she knows who are expected, and I will let you know when you bring the lobsters to the house."

" God bless ye, and God help yer innocent head !—sure d'ye think I'm such an ould fool entirely as to be bothering myself about what's no business of mine ?—may-be, like the rest, ye think me a *natural ?*"

His lip curled in bitter scorn as he uttered the last sentence, and his eyes grew brightly dark under the shadows of his beetle brows. After a moment's pause, he continued, " Ax the master himself, dear —ax the master if any of the officers are to be wid ye : the house keeper won't know—that she won't ; just ax the master who's to dine wid ye to-day, particular about the officers ;—but don't, Miss, darlint, don't say I bid ye ; ye don't know what harm might come or it, if ye did—it might cost me my life ; besides, it would demean ye to turn *informer*. Now, Miss, machree,—young as ye are, ye're the only one about the big house I'd trust with that ; and so God be wid ye, I *depind* on your honour." I was ten years old, and it was a glorious thing to think that a secret (although I hardly knew in what the secret consisted), was in my keeping, and it was still more glorious to be told that my honour was depended on. Jack was, moreover, a favourite with the household, and I had never been forbidden to speak to him. Grandmamma and mamma, were, I knew, busied with the housekeeper in the preparation of jellies, and pasties, in the manu- facture of which, adhering to the fashion of the good old times, they themselves assisted, at those periods of bustle and confusion, in country-houses called company-days. I was consequently aware that I should hardly see them until dressed for the drawing-room. During my conversation with Jack, my biped attendant, Nelly Parrell, had been busily employed in packing up my bathing-dress, and lock- ing " the box ;" so she knew nothing of Jack's anxiety. I saw the old man watch me attentively, until I ascended the upper cliff on my way home, and then he returned to his occupation. I did not fail to ask my grandfather, at the breakfast table, if he expected any of the officers from Duncannon to dinner, that day ? The kind man laid down the "Waterford Chronicle," which he was perusing, and, smiling one of those sweet and playful smiles that tell, more than words can do, of peace and cheerfulness, inquired, in his turn, if "my head was beginning to think about officers already?" I was old enough to blush at this, but returned to my point, and was told that none had been invited. Soon after, I saw Jack, and little Crab, the one striding, the other trotting down the avenue; as he passed the open casement he stopped, and I told him that grandpapa did not expect any of the Duncannon officers: the old man crossed his forehead, and muttered—as he reverently bowed, and passed to the kitchen offices—"May heaven be yer bed at last, and may ye niver know either sin or sorrow."

Poor Jack! I have often thought since of his benediction. Dinner was at last over, and dessert fairly placed upon the table, when horses' feet were heard clattering into the court-yard; and, in a few seconds, the servant announced the captain of a detachment of a regiment then quartered at Duncannon; a gentleman who accompanied him, but who was not announced, entered at the same time; he was a gigantic, gloomy, harsh-looking man; and when the servant retired, the officer introduced him as Mr. Loffont, the new chief of the Fetherd and Duncannon police. This man was universally disliked in the country, and Captain Gore knew it well; he, in some measure, apologized for the intrusion of both, by stating he had been that morning called upon, by Mr. Loffont, to give assistance to the police in a rencontre with the smugglers, which was that night expected on our side the coast; this was, I believe, unwelcome intelligence to all, but to none more than myself; an undefined dread of some evil that might happen to my poor friend, the shrimp-gatherer, took possession of my mind; and, to the astonishment of my good grandmother, even my strawberries were untasted. I have since learned that, when the ladies withdrew, Captain Gore informed the company that he expected some of his men to meet them at the termination of our oak belting: and, he added, "he was convinced Mr. Herriott would render every assistance to the king's servants in such a cause." Mr. Herriott was peaceably inclined, and only agreed to go to the beach with the soldiers, because he thought it likely he might act as a mediator between the parties. Well do I remember the breathless anxiety with which I watched for his passing through the entrance-hall, for I longed to speak to him—but it was useless; he did not come out till near midnight, and then he was surrounded by gentlemen, who whispered in an under tone; at last with a palpitating heart I heard the old butler ordered to bring the long double-barrelled gun. The company departed, and I seated myself in the nursery window, which overlooked the beautiful plantations, and the distant sea that was tranquilly reposing in the beams of the full moon.

Slowly and stealthily did the party proceed to the shore; and they stole in silence, and in safety, upon the unfortunate smugglers, who were, at the time, landing their cargo at the entrance of the OTTER's-HOLE. A few peasants were waiting, with empty cars, to convey away their purchases; and the gang was, evidently, unprepared for the attack; neither party, however, wanted courage; and they fought, man to man, with desperate resolution. Loffont was foremost in the fray; youth, age, and manhood alike felt the overpowering force of his muscular arm, or the unerring ball of his pistol. Silently and darkly did he fight, more like a destroying spirit than a mortal man. At length, in the midst of a combat that had given him more than usual trouble, for he had engaged with a young and daring antagonist, he was arrested by a harsh, growling voice, like the deep but murmured anger of an African lion; and his arm was grasped by long bony fingers, that seemed the outcasts of the grave. "And you're here! —you, who crushed my brave, my eldest boy; who seduced, from her innocent home, my Kathleen—my daughter—my dear, dear girl;— you, who drove us to wandering and want! Stand back, James— drop yer hoult of my only living child, ye hell-fiend!" continued the agonized old man, as he shook the huge frame of Loffont, even as a willow-wand; "once before, when my other boy was murdered, I struggled with ye for his life, and ye cast me from ye, as an ould tree: —but now!——." His eyes glared fearfully upon his victim, and, for a moment, smugglers and soldiers remained silent and motionless. Loffont trembled in every limb; he felt as if his hour was come, and turning from the shrimp-gatherer, he said, "Pass on, John Doherty; enough of your blood is already on my head." The old man replied not, but closed upon the revenue-officer. Long and desperate was the struggle—hand to hand, foot to foot—until, as they neared the overhanging edge of the precipitous cliff, the shrimp-gatherer grappled the throat of his adversary; one step more—and both went crashing against the pointed rocks, until the deep, heavy splash in the ocean announced that the contest was over.

Speedy relief was afforded, and they were both dragged out of the water, still clasped as in the death-struggle! Loffont, his harsh and demon-like features blackened and swollen by suffocation, was indeed a corpse; and although Doherty was living, and in full possession of his faculties, it was evident his spirit was on the wing. Still did he grasp his antagonist's throat; and, even when besought by my grandfather to relax his hold, he raised himself slowly on his elbow, and turned a steady gaze upon the features of one he had hated even unto death. His son knelt by his side, his heart full, almost to bursting. In the meantime, the contest between the soldiery and the people was renewed, and every inch of cliff vigorously disputed.

"James," said the dying man, as his glazed eye followed the

bloody contest, upon which the full moon cast her bright and tranquil beams—"James—the boat—the boat—gain the ship! My murdered children now can rest in their graves—their murderer is punished."

"Jack," interrupted the kind-hearted gentleman, "for God's sake, think of the few moments you have to live—think of where you are going."

"Ay, sir, if God would spare me to make my soul, now I might think and pray to him;—but before—could I think of any but *them* who are in heaven? Now God—God have mercy upon a poor sinful man!" His hands were clenched in prayer, when a loud shout from the peasantry, which was repeated by a thousand echoes along the rocky shore, announced that they had beaten their opponents fairly off; the old man started—waved his hands wildly over his head, as in triumph—fell back—and expired on his son's bosom.

The smugglers escaped to the vessel, and the youth bore off to it the dead body of his father. The ship's crew and the peasantry disappeared, as if by magic, carrying with them as much of the brandy and tobacco as had been landed, for they knew that the police would shortly return with a reinforcement; and Mr. Herriott found himself alone with the corpse of Loffont, on the wild sea shore;—not quite alone, I should say; the dog of the shrimp-gatherer, poor Crab, came smelling to the strand where his master's body had lain, raised his little voice in weak and pitiful howlings to the receding barque, and finally laid himself down at the feet of the watchful Neptune, who had never deserted his master's side. From that hour, the noble animal became the protector of the low-born cur—never suffering him to receive either insult or injury.

The body of the wretched Loffont, who had met with so shocking a death, was conveyed to our house; it was buried—but few attended the funeral, which in Ireland is always a mark of disrespect. It was not to be wondered at, for the history of poor Jack became generally known: he had a home, and all the joys which home can give;—a wife, two sons, and one lovely daughter, the pride of her father's life, and of her native village. She was seduced by Loffont, under the promise of honourable union—but she could not survive her disgrace—her heart broke! She was found, one morning, a stiffened corpse at her father's door, with a snow-shroud for her covering, and the cold ice of December for her bed. Then it was that her mother quietly and calmly laid down and died; the fountain of her tears had dried—her heart withered within her bosom.

The husband and father, thus rendered wild and desolate, became a man of desperate fortunes, and swore that nothing but blood should wash out the memory of his daughter's shame. He joined a party of smugglers, with his eldest boy, whom, in an engagement with the

police, he saw shot and stabbed by the same hand that had brought
sin and death to his once happy dwelling. He was himself so much
injured in this engagement, as to be unable to remain at sea; so he
wandered along the sea-shore, watching the movements of the officers
stationed on the preventive service, and directing those of the smuggling vessel in which his youngest son had embarked. This will account for the great anxiety he had manifested to ascertain who was
to dine at our house on that eventful day—dreading, doubtless, that
the officers were on the look-out for the expected ship. He could
not have known that Loffont was so near his usual haunts; for he
would have stopped at nothing to shed his blood.

      *   *   *   *

This story was brought to my remembrance, many years afterwards,
when I visited the old churchyard of Bannow, in which the remains
of that "bad man" were interred. The church is of very remote
antiquity, and it overlooks a singular scene—the "Irish Herculaneum"
—a town buried beneath the sand. In the interior, among broken
walls, are the remains of several tombs, which retain abundant evidence of "long-ago magnificence"—sculptured slabs and stone coffins;
and among them are monuments to the memory of the good, and
upright, and benevolent—of, comparatively, yesterday. To me the
spot is sacred; it contains the ashes of nearly all my relatives and
many of my friends.

Alas! if in early life, we revisit the scenes of our childhood, where
shall we look for those who are dear to our hearts and memories?
In the churchyard!

The grave of Loffont, to which my story has reference—rather than
to those of characters far opposite—was pointed out to me by the
widow Parrell—my old bathing-woman—as one upon which, for a
long time, "grass would not grow." "I've seen," she said, "many a
fine funeral within these ancient walls: I remember that of the ould
Master of Graige House; and well I mind your own grandmother's
—the heavens be her bed! And the hundreds that followed her,
though an Englishwoman, to her grave—the hundreds! besides three
priests, and three ministers; and then her husband! And beautiful
are the words he had carved upon that square flat tomb, to her
memory; then the ould lady, his sister, all in the same big vault—
ah, yah!—the fine place went into other hands; and, if it was to
pass, sure, better relations and neighbours than strangers—the old
name reigns over it again—the old stock, still!—Wisha! wisha!"
she exclaimed, rubbing her finger across her sallow brow, and
then plucking tufts of maiden hair out of the ould walls;—"it
bothers one to think how often the tomb has been opened!—Well,
the Lord above grant it may not be opened for a very long time."

When I was young, I took great delight in wandering about these old tombs; and, even when Loffont was killed, I remember I'd as soon go into a graveyard, as into a flower-garden. "Death seems so so far off then, that it's no trouble to think of it—it's like the wave we see rolling between the two Keeroes; we never heed its size till it's almost at the shore; but now, I don't care if I never cross the walls—barring to look at that tomb of ould French—that's a consolation—a hundred and forty years is on the tomb—more says its a hundred and four, but I don't see why a body mayn't as well live to be the one as the other." The poor woman seemed to derive consolation from this reflection, and added, "What a pity it was that Jack the Shrimp died so soon! he'd be sure to have made ould bones, and had a fine funeral if he'd only have waited for it, as he might, and no harm." Many stories she told me of those who lie beneath that green turf; and now, she herself rests there—one of the last who, in her life-time, companioned poor Jack the Shrimp.

HOSPITALITY.

HOSPITALITY—no formality—there you'll ever see:"—so runneth the old song. Quite true—true to the very letter; and there was not a more hospitable house, in the province of Leinster, than Barrytown. "Kindly welcome" was visibly expressed by every countenance, and all things bore the stamp of—"Hospitality!" The master was large; the house was large; the trees were large; the entrance gates were large; the servants were large; all the domestic animals were large; the worthy owner's heart was large—and so was his purse. He was cheerful and happy; his house, particularly in the shooting or summer season, was always full of company, more numerous than select, but all resolved to enjoy themselves, and Mr. Barry, their worthy host, determined to promote their enjoyment. I have said his house was large—it was almost magnificent. It stood on a gentle declivity, and commanded a pleasing, though not very extensive, prospect; the entrance-hall was lofty and wide; the walls well garnished with fowling-pieces, fishing-rods, and, at the farthermost end,

the antediluvian horns of a monstrous elk, which spread even to the
ceiling's height. Of this extraordinary production of nature, Mr.
Barry was very proud, and boldly challenged the Dublin Museum to
produce its equal. The pavement of the hall was formed of beautiful
Kilkenny marble; its polish certainly had departed, yet the rich and
varied veins were distinctly visible. Dogs of varied sizes—from the
stately Dane, the graceful staghound, the shaggy Newfoundland—to
the fawning spaniel, the little rat-catching, black-muzzled terrrier, and
the sleepy, silky Blenheim—considered the hall as their own exclusive
property, yet lived on terms of perfect good fellowship with a Killarney
eagle, a Scotch raven, and a beautiful Angola cat, who shared the
same territory, the latter, indeed, looked upon a deer-skin covered
couch as dedicated to her sole use and benefit.

The great dining-room was worthy of such an entrance; it was
wainscoted with black oak, and, at the top of the apartment, the
extreme darkness of the wood threw into strong relief the massive
sideboard, with its highly-wrought, antique plate. The dining-table
rested on enormous pillars, and bore evident marks of having seen
good service in convivial times; the chairs were high-backed and
richly carved, cushioned with crimson damask; and the large wine-
coolers and plate buckets were rimmed and hooped with silver. "The
family canvas," in heavy frame-work, smiled or frowned along the
walls, just as they ought to smile or frown; and represented, to say
the truth, a grim, clumsy-looking set of personages; even the pastoral
young lady, who was playing on a pipe—the sheep (I suppose they
were sheep) looking tearfully in her face—her well-powdered hair
graced by a celestial blue riband : even she, the beauty of the party,
squinted most frightfully. But the good Mr. Barry had a profound
veneration for them all, so we will leave them without further comment.
The curtains and the carpet had seen their best days, and Mr. Barry
had been talking about purchasing new for the last ten years; nevertheless, the old remained, and certainly looked very venerable. The
withdrawing-room, or, as the "master" called it, the ladies' proper
apartment, held a motley assemblage of new and old furniture; a
splendid rosewood piano was placed next to a towering old triangular
flower-stand, with monkey heads, and scallop shells at the corners,
but which, nevertheless, served as a "what-not." Silken ottomans
reclined, in eastern luxury, near to less elegant, but more sedate, hard-
stuffed sofas; and a lumbering old arm-chair, covered with cream-
coloured embroidered satin, the cushion fringed and tasselled with
gold, stood to the right of the fire-place; a small stool, garnished
after the same antique fashion, and a little table inlaid with silver,
which appeared hardly able to support an old family Bible, with
studded clasps, were placed beside it.

The interesting occupier of the arm-chair was no less a person than Lady Florence Barry, the mother of the hospitable master. I never saw so beautiful a relic of female nobility; when I remember her, she was verging on her ninetieth birthday:—her figure delicate and much bent; her eye black as jet, small, and sparkling, fringed by brows and lashes which time had rendered perfectly white. Her features had been handsome, but at such an age were much wrinkled, and her own hair, straightly combed from under the high lappet cap, added to her venerable appearance. The dress she wore was always of the most valuable black Genoa velvet or satin, made after the olden mode, with deep ruffles of Mechlin or Brussels lace, and a small cloak of rich black silk, fastened at the breast with a diamond brooch. The old lady was very deaf, but her sight was perfect; and when she received her son's guests, she did it with so much grace, so much dignity, that it could never be forgotten. Perhaps the affectionate respect and attention manifested by Mr. Barry to his mother was the most delightful trait in his character. "She brought noble blood and a princely dower to my father," he would say, "and made him a true and loving wife to the end of his days; and when in the full bloom of womanhood, she became husbandless, for my sake she remained so. Can I honour her too much?"

Mr. Barry had nothing in particular to distinguish him from "the raale true-born gintry." He had a fair and open brow, that unerring index to a noble soul, and a manly expression of countenance; but he had more of his father's heedlessness than of his mother's penetration, and, at sixty-two, knew less of the "world" than most of our fashionables after they have been "a winter in London."

The domestics of Barrytown had grown grey in their services—in verity, all things in the house were "of a piece" except the visitors; they ruined the *harmony* of the picture, while they gave spirit and variety to the *colouring*.

The month was June, which is more like May in England, for our skies shed many tears, even in the summer time; as usual, the coach-houses and stables were crowded; the former with gigs, "suicides," and jaunting-cars, outside and in; and the latter with all manner of ponies and horses. The servants' hall, too, was full, and a "shake-down" had been ordered even in Mr. Barry's own study, a gloomy, dusty place, almost untidy enough to be the *studio* of a literary man —that odious receptacle for books and spiders; when old Mary said to old Mabby—long Mabby, as she was generally called:—

"Mabby, honey, my drame's out—for, upon my conscience, if yon, on the broken-down-looking jingle of a jaunting-car, isn't Miss Spinner and her ould trunk; and her ould maid that's as bothering a'most as her divil of a mistress. Och! it wasn't for nothing I dramed

M

of a blue-bottle fly upon master's nose, buz, buz, about, like a mill-wheel!—the jazey!—there she is, as yellow as a Yarrow blossom."

"Why, thin, it's herself sure enough," responded Mabby; "and if she had stayed in Dublin, 'mong the larned people she's always talking about, none of us would have asked what kept her. Och, it's as true as I'm standin' here, she's got a new wig!"

"New, nonsense!" said Molly, "it's only fresh grased. I'll not go look after her things;—a month won't excuse her out of this, and no mortal ever saw cross or coin afther her yet. Where'll she sleep? Sure there's two in a bed all over the house, barrin' master's. Mabby, count how many there is in now; I'll tell thim over—the best first: —Mr. Altern, his two hunters, and the groom, to say nothin' of the dogs; but he's a generous gintleman, and the groom's a hearty boy."

"That's four," said Mabby.

"Och, you born sinner!" replied Molly, "sure it's not going to count the Christians with the bastes, ye are?"

"Tell over the Christians, thin."

"Well, thin, that's two. Miss Raymond—in ranle goodness she ought to go for two, the jewil!"

"Three."

"Mrs. Croydon, Miss Lilly, Miss Livy, the footman (bad cess to that fellow!—the conceited walk of him is parfectly sickening, coming over us wid his Dublin airs), and my lady's maid, to be sure."

"You've forgot Mr. Wortley."

"Why, thin, I oughtn't to do that, for he never forgets anybody— he's both rich and kind; although he's an Englishman, I'd go from this to Bargy on my bare hands and feet to do a good turn for that gintleman—there isn't one in the house (of the visitors I mane) I'd do a civility for so soon, only Miss Raymond. What a pity it is that young lady hasn't some yellow guineas of her own! Mr. Wortley is mighty sweet upon her, I think. Och, thin, 'tis herself, the darlint, 'ud make the nice wife for him!—but the English, the poor, narrow-minded craturs, are all for the money, you know."

"Well, Mabby, any way, that's nine. Miss Spinner and her follower, sure!"

"Eleven."

"That foolish-looking clip of a boy, that looks mighty like a gauger, and his comrade that hunts among the old places for curiosities, and their outlandish man, Friday, as I hard Miss Raymond call him."

"Fourteen—and no bad increase to a family that always, when by itself, sits down twenty to dinner, counting the parlour, servants' hall, and second table, not to reckon the weeders and the gossoons; to be sure, the bit they ate is never missed; how could it, from a gintleman like our master?—the blessing be about him! My honoured mistress smiled as I passed her in the corridory to-day; well, she is very ould—and yet so cheerful; and, though she's little, there's a stateliness about her that always made me the smallest taste in life afeard; but she was wonderful good in her time, and master dotes down upon her."

After this dialogue, the two housemaids departed, mutually determining to avoid Miss Spinner, who seemed to be the terror of the establishment.

In the drawing-room, the greater part of the visitors were assembled, awaiting the ringing of the dressing-bell. Lady Florence, as usual, in her cream-coloured cushioned chair, reading her Bible; Miss Raymond sketching flowers from nature—white and blue peas, and a china rose; Mr. Wortley, neither absolutely sitting nor lounging, on one of the old-fashioned sofas, was apparently engaged in looking over a large rolled map; Mrs. Croydon, netting; Miss Livy, and Miss Letty, the one attitudinizing, and winding a skein of silk—which the other held so as to display her little white hands to advantage; when, at length, Miss Letty broke silence by asking—

"La, ma'!—who do you think is come?"

"How should I know, child?" replied her mother, looking up from her netting; "our party is so very pleasant"—and she smiled a gracious smile on all around—"that I can hardly wish it increased."

Mr. Wortley smiled also, but it was a different sort of smile.

"Guess, Livy."

"I never guess right, Mr.—Mr.——"

"It is not a Mr. at all."

"I wonder you guess at Misters," said ma', with an aside drawing-down of the brow; "I am sure, my love, *you* care so little about gentlemen—at least, so I used to hear at the Castle, where my little Olivia thought fit to be so frigid; I wonder, child, you mention *Misters.*"

The young lady, who was not as accomplished a manœuvrer as her mamma, saw she had done wrong, although she did not exactly know how to amend her error, and wisely held her tongue.

"Guess, Gertrude," recommended Miss Letitia, "Gertrude Raymond, can't you guess?—well, then, I will tell you—Miss Spinner."

"Oh, mercy!" screamed Miss Olivia and her mamma, "that blue! Oh, Miss Raymond!—Oh, Mr. Wortley!—oh! what will poor Mr. Altern say! Mr. Barry asked her once, and she makes it a general invitation!—oh, I shall be afraid to open my lips!—sha'n't you, Gertrude?"

"No," replied Gertrude, laughing.

"Oh! you are so wise, Miss Raymond," said Miss Letitia, "that you are not afraid of anybody!—I dare say you would not mind a bit being in company with Sir Walter Scott, or Lady Morgan, or Doctor Johnson!"

"Hush, my dear!" interrupted Mrs. Croydon, who, it must be confessed, had enough to do to keep the levity of one daughter, and the ignorance of the other, within bounds; "Hush!—you know Miss Raymond has had many advantages, and she is *older* than you—so she has less reason to fear clever people; but you are such a nervous little darling!"—And mamma, in patting the "little darling's" cheek, managed to give it (unperceived by the *rich* Mr. Wortley) a little pinch, which said, as plainly as pinch could say, "Hold your tongue!"

"Nobody has any reason to fear *really* clever people," said Mr. Wortley, rising from the sofa, and joining, for the first time, in the conversation, if so it might be called; "and certainly not Miss Raymond," he continued, bowing to Gertrude; who immediately bent more closely over her drawing than was at all necessary, for be it known that she had very good sight.

"There's a compliment from the sober Mr. Wortley!" laughed Olivia; "who ever heard of such a thing before?"

"It would be impossible to compliment Miss Olivia Croydon," replied the gentleman; "her beauty is so universally acknowledged that it needs not my poor commendation." The silly girl looked pleased at extorted flattery.

Mrs. Croydon was the widow of a general officer, and in twenty years' campaigning, had seen a good deal of "the world." She was a pretty and a vain woman. As her husband fell in love with her at a garrison ball, and as she calculated on a similar destiny for her daughters, she resolved on adding to their beauty every accomplishment under the sun, as they were nearly portionless. What hosts of masters! Painting on velvet, japanning, oriental tinting, music, dancing, singing, fencing, riding, French—everything in the world, except the solid usefulness of *education*. Accomplished they certainly were, but not educated.

Alas! how many lovely women shed tears of bitterness—when the flush of youth and fashion has passed, never to return—over hours spent in the acquirement of frivolous accomplishments, which, if occupied in the improvement of qualities that shed a halo, and diffuse a perfume, over home—woman's best and brightest earthly dominion—would have made them useful and beloved, even to the end of their days.

Mrs. Croydon "carried on the war," as Mr. Altern used to say, "most famously." She had good connexions; and, as her daughters' education, to use her own words, "was completed under first-rate masters," she resolved to devote herself to her friends, and let her house in Dublin, except for three months in the year, when it was absolutely indispensable that she should attend the Castle festivities, " for her daughters' sake—heigho !—she had no taste, now, for the world's pleasures !"—Nevertheless, many suspected that she wou.d not have objected to become Lady of Barrytown—a thing by no means likely, as Mr. Barry looked upon her in no other light than as the widow of his old friend.

Mr. Wortley, also, was an object of much interest to the lady. He admired beauty—so Miss Olivia was instructed to play off her best looks and best airs. He admired music—and Miss Letitia-sung, until he was tired, all the cavatinas that Mozart and Rossini ever composed. Fine girls and fine singers often go too far, and " overshoot the mark;" they are perpetually assaulting your eyes or your ears, until both ache even to weariness. Nothing unconnected with intellect can please long; we soon grow weary of scentless flowers, and senseless beauties. At all events, the ladies deserved some praise, for their perseverance in the siege—although their efforts were somewhat like those of three nautili storming Gibraltar.

Gertrude Raymond was a being of a very different order. Her figure was large—more dignified than elegant; her features when tranquil, had an expression of hauteur; her brow was lofty and expanded; her eyes, deep and well set; her skin, nearly olive; her hair rivalled the raven's wing ; her cheek was, in general, colourless, except when her feelings were excited, and then the rich blood glowed through the dark surface with the deep colouring of the damask rose, the eyes brightened, and the generally placid Gertrude Raymond burst upon you in all the magnificence of beauty ! Born of a noble but decayed family, and left an orphan at three years old, this high-minded young woman had been adopted by an elderly maiden relative, the only one who retained wealth and influence. Gertrude, of course, had numerous enemies—for no other reason than that she came between certain persons who entertained certain views on a certain property. Wherever there is a "long-tailed family" there is much grappling and intrigue to know who holds the best cards. Miss Raymond had of course observed the various schemes pursued by her cousins, but with no other emotion than that of pity. She pursued a course of undeviating rectitude, in opposition to their petty manœuvrings. Her aged friend was a woman whose temper had been soured by much early misfortune ; and Miss Raymond bore her caprices from grateful, not from interested feelings.

When Gertrude had attained her seventeenth year, Miss, or, as she was usually called, Mrs. Dorrington, resolved to leave her country house, near Barrytown, and reside for a time in Bath. The principal object of this change she declared, was her anxiety that Miss Raymond

should receive all the advantages of finishing masters, and polished
English society, as she would inherit the greater part of her fortune.
It is impossible to conceive anything like the sensation this avowal
excited! An earthquake was nothing to it! All the cousins to the
fourteenth remove, were in dreadful consternation; public and private
committees assembled; and all minor jealousies were, for a time, forgotten, in order that the common enemy—poor Gertrude!—might be
dispossessed of the stronghold she held in her rich relative's good
opinion.

"It is quite bad enough," said one, "to have her put over all our
heads, and she very little nearer the old lady than ourselves; but to
leave the country, and go off, like a duchess, to Bath, and be pampered
up, is too much entirely." "It's enough to break a heart of stone,"
said another, "to see her riding here and riding there, in the
carriage, and looking so mealy-mouthed all the time; and her kindness
to the poor—all put on to gain popularity." They plotted and
plotted, and planned and planned, but to no purpose; go the old lady
would, and go she did. In vain did the enemy declare their deep
sorrow at parting, for a time, with their beloved Mrs. Dorrington,
and their dear " Miss Gurry;" in vain did they offer, either singly, or
in a body (forty-five of them, at the very least), to accompany their
sweet friends to Bath, or all over the world, at any personal sacrifice,
rather than suffer them to go alone amongst strangers. Mrs. Dorrington thanked them for their attention, and abruptly replied, that
two thousand per annum made a home of any hotel in England, and
friends of all strangers; and that she was able to take care of Gertrude,
and Gertrude was able to take care of her. The poor of the neighbourhood sorrowed sincerely after their young benefactress. Mr.
Barry knew more of Miss Raymond's charities than any other person,
for she never failed to send him, from Bath, little sums of money, and
presents for her poor pensioners. Mrs. Dorrington was quite right
in her estimation of society; she had soon plenty of *friends* at Bath,
and Miss Raymond's attractions drew many admirers to their house.

It is a difficult thing to find an Irish agent who performs his duty
like an English one; a circumstance, perhaps, more to be attributed
to want of business-knowledge than want of inclination. Mrs. Dorrington's remittances were delayed beyond all bearing; and after
" absenteeing" for some time, she surprised Gertrude one morning by
informing her that she had made up her mind to go over to Ireland
for a fortnight or three weeks, and look into her own affairs that
wanted arranging. " It will astonish them all," she continued, " to
see the old woman looking so well; and, as you have so often promised
Mrs. Ackland to spend a little time with her at Clifton, we will separate
there; and I will not be absent more than three weeks. I shall

certainly never suffer you to revisit Ireland, until you are married in
that sphere of life which your birth, and the property *I have left you*
entitles you to."

Gertrude had not permitted any opportunity to pass, that enabled
her to say a few words in favour of her relatives; for *self* was never
uppermost in her mind. But Mrs. Dorrington's reserved, and even
austere manners to her dearest earthly tie, were seldom even so bland
as to permit such observations. Gertrude accompanied her friend to
Clifton, and saw her departure with sincere sorrow; she yearned to
behold the green hills of the country, and the dear companions of her
childhood; but Mrs. Dorrington's fiat was not to be disputed. The
first letter she received contained a long description of the bad management that had occurred during her absence, and her resolve to set all
to rights before she returned to England. The next was filled with
details of sundry arrangements; and then came a long silence. No
letters; post succeeded post; no intelligence. At length came a
letter from Mr. Barry; Mrs. Dorrington, he informed her, was
seriously ill, and begged she would come over immediately. No
packet sailed that day: the next brought another account—her friend
was dead. The shock was more than she could bear; and when she
arose from a couch of suffering and sorrow, several letters were presented to her by the lady of the house. The two principal were—one
from her old and steady friend, Mr. Barry, entreating, if she knew of
the existence of a will, to see to it at once, as the heir-at-law had
already taken possession of the property on the presumption that no
document existed leaving any provision at all for her:—the other
from the heir himself, desiring that all the letters, papers, and
personal property of "the late Miss Dorrington" (how that cold
sentence wounded!) should be forthwith delivered to Mr. Scrapthorne,
Attorney-at-law, Back Lane, Bristol; who was empowered to take
possession of the same.

"From, Madam, yours.
"Thomas Dorrington."

The very abject, who, but six months before, had requested "the
always kind interference of his friend (whom he was proud to call
relative), Miss Raymond, with that most respected lady, Mrs. Dorrington, to beg he might have forty acres of the upper farm, now out
of lease, on fair terms, and a loan of thirty pounds to help to stock it.

"From your humble servant to command,
"And most faithful cousin,
"Thomas Dorrington."

Poor Gertrude!—the ingratitude manifested by the last epistle—for
she had procured the man sixty pounds, and obtained his other request

—roused all her energies, and diligent search was made for a will; but no document, even alluding to one, could be discovered. Every body felt for " poor Miss Raymond." " Such a melancholy change !" " Pity she was not married before !" " Hard fate !" " Very distressing !" Some asked her " to spend a few days until she fixed upon her future plans ;" others extended their invitation to an entire month ; but Lady Florence Barry, albeit unused to letter-writing, adding the following postscript to her son's letter, which was despatched when all hopes of finding a will were abandoned :—" I am old, Gertrude ; my hand trembles and my eyes are dim ! but my heart is warm, warmer towards you now than in your sunnier days. Come to us—be to us as a child, and your society will bestow a blessing which we will endeavour to repay."

Gertrude's reply to this generous offer was at once simple and dignified.

" It is not," she said, " that I do not value your kindness, dear and beloved friends, above every earthly blessing, but I cannot live *dependent* even on you. I have accepted a situation as governess in Lady B——'s family, and I will endeavour to do my duty in that sphere of life unto which it hath pleased God to call me. Believe me, the change must serve ; I almost think I was too uplifted. I have now put my trust in God, who will do what seemeth best unto him. To-morrow I leave this place, its false and glittering friends, to enter on my new duties in London. I am promised a month's holiday, and, if I can summon fortitude to visit Ireland, I will see you then. I hear the new possessor has sold all off, even the ornaments of the old mansion ;—that is heartrending. But, worst of all, my poor pensioners !—however, I shall be able to spare them something out of my earnings—*my* earnings ; let me not be unthankful ; I remember, with gratitude, that my education has saved me from the bitterness of *dependence.*"

In a decent, solitary cabin, on the Dorrington estate, resided nurse Keefe, so called from having " fostered" Miss Raymond. She was considered by her neighbours "a remarkable well-bred, dacent woman ;" and, when Gertrude left Ireland, the faithful creature would have accompanied her " foster-child," had it not been that her husband was in ill-health, and demanded all her attention ; he died about six weeks before Mrs. Dorrington, but nurse had made up her mind to return with the lady to England ; her sudden death, of course, prevented it, and nurse Keefe awaited " her dear child's coming home to take possession of her own ;" mourned for the dead, and rejoiced in her young lady's prospects almost at the same moment. When she heard that the property was going into other hands, nothing could exceed her grief ; she was almost frantic, and abused the heir-at-law in no mea-

sured terms, declaring that he had made away with the will, and
all were thieves and rogues. Mr. Barry assured her he was using his
exertions to induce Miss Raymond to reside with his mother; and
that information afforded her some little comfort; but when she found
that her nursling was going as governess to a family, the poor creature's misery was truly distressing. She returned to her cottage with
a breaking heart, and did not even go to Barrytown to inquire after
" Miss Gurry" for three weeks. When she again made her appearance there, she astounded Mr. Barry with the information that she
had " canted all her bits o' things," had drawn what money she had
saved up in the bank out of it, given up her farm, and was absolutely
setting off to London to see " her child," as she generally called her.
" I'm not going to be a burthen, sir," she said to Mr. Barry, when
he pointed out to the affectionate creature the folly of her journey.
" I have as good as a hundred and twinty pounds, solid gould and
silver, that's not mine, but hers, now she happens to want it—more's
the pity! Sure it was by sarving her I got it, which makes it hers
whin she's distressed (that I should live to see it!), if not in law, any
how in justice, which is the best law, without any manner of doubt.
So I'll jist take it her myself, to save postage; and I'm stout and
strong, and able to get up fine linen, and clear starch, with any she in
the kingdom of England; and sure she'll be able to get me plinty of
work; and that trifle can lay in the London Bank for her, whin she
wants any little thing, as sure she must; and I'll be near her to keep
her from being put upon, by them English. And, God be praised!
I'm able to stand up for her still, and make her sensible of the honour
she's doing them by staying there at all. And now my blessing, and
the blessing of the poor be about yer honour! You'll not see me
until I can't be of any use to Miss Raymond—the angel!"

So nurse Keefe journeyed to London; and, at last, found herself at
Hyde Park Corner, quite bewildered by the crowd and noise, and
endeavouring to make her way to Grosvenor-place. Her quaint
appearance attracted attention, as she passed along. Short black
silk cloak—white dimity petticoat—shoes and silver buckles—small
black " mode " bonnet, hardly shading her round good-natured face,
were singular gear, even in London; and her rich brogue, whenever she inquired, " if any one could tell her, where Lady B——'s
and her young lady's house was, in Grosvenor-place," caused a
universal laugh, which she did not at all relish. She stood at the
corner opposite Hyde Park, gazing wildly about, resolved not to ask
any more questions, when a gentleman good-naturedly inquired, " if
she was looking for any particular house."

" Is it looking!—troth, and I am, sir, till I'm blind and stupid,
and can see nothing—God help me!—with the noise and the people,

skrimitching and fighting; they may hould their tongues about the
wild Irish; the English here, I'm sure, are all mad; but as ye're so
kind, and, no doubt, knowledgeable, may-be you could tell me the way
to one Lady B——'s, and my young lady's, who live somewhere here-
abouts in Grosvenor-place."

"Lady B——'s!" repeated the stranger; "I am going there,
and you may follow me, if you please." The gentleman walked on,
and the delighted nurse breathlessly addressed him:—

"Ah, then, sir, every joy in heaven to ye!—and sure ye know
my young lady?"

"I have not the pleasure."

"I ax yer pardon, but ye said ye knew Lady B——."

"I do."

"Well, yer honour, sure my young lady stops with her."

"No young lady, that I know of, lives there, except—oh, I have
heard of a young Irish lady, a governess, I believe; but, of course,
she is not seen."

"Not seen!" repeated nurse, who had no idea that Miss Raymond could be excluded from any society: "is she sick, sir?"

"Not that I know of; but I suppose she is in the nursery, or
study, or somewhere with the children."

This information could not be borne silently, and she told the
gentleman the history of her "young lady," with so much earnestness
that, although he was much interested, he heartily wished himself
housed; for nurse Keefe's eloquence attracted a crowd. As they
ascended the steps of Lady B——'s residence, Gertrude and her
pupils were descending. The poor creature sprang forward, fell on
her knees, and grasped Miss Raymond's dress, unable, fortunately,
from her violent agitation, to utter a sentence. The face of an old
friend is more delightful than sunshine in winter. Gertrude raised
the aged woman to her bosom; and, heedless of the presence of
strangers, burst into tears. When, after the lapse of an hour, nurse
Keefe and Miss Raymond were seated in the study appropriated to
Gertrude's use, the faithful creature opened her simple plan to her
foster child, and endeavoured to impress on her mind that the money
she had brought, carefully wrapped in an old stocking, belonged to
Gertrude Much did the good nurse regret that she could not make
"her darlint" understand this; and Miss Raymond, in her turn,
laboured as fruitlessly to convince her that she was perfectly happy,
and treated quite as she ought to be.

"I can't believe it—I can't believe it, Miss, machree!—How could
I, whin that fine-spoken young gentleman tould me he never set eyes
upon you, although he came often to the house? D'ye think I've
no sense?—or that I'm out an' out a fool?—Sure it's well I remim-

ber, **after yer angel** of a mother died, whin ye came to be Mrs.
Dorrington's child (who had no *born* child, on account she was an
ould maid), that I used to have to bring ye into the grand parlour as
good as tin times a day, in order that they all might admire yer
beauty; and lords and ladies, and even mimbers of Parliament,
fighting like cat an' dog for the first kiss, and I fighting to keep
them from dragging the head off o' ye. And now to be in a bit of
an English lady's family, as a sort of a—Oh! ullagone! ullagone!—
my poor ould heart 'ill split!"

Gertrude had some difficulty in pacifying her; convincing was out
of the question. "Well, may-be so, my dear.—Happy!—I can't
understand it; may-be so!"

The next thing was to provide a lodging for nurse Keefe; and, as
she soon placed what she called Miss Raymond's "trifle o' money" in
a banker's hands, she became anxious for employment. Lady B——,
who was really kind and amiable, was highly pleased with the poor
woman's generous feelings, and in less than a month, the good nurse
had more clear-starching and "fine-plaiting" than she could manage.
Thus, to use her own words, "the money powered in upon her."
She visited Gertrude once or twice a week, and never came empty-
handed; nuts, oranges, and cakes, were her general presents; but
sometimes she added pieces of gay riband, and two or three yards of
lace. The person who gave her most employment, and paid her best,
was her kind conductor when she first visited Grosvenor-place. The
gentleman knew something of the neighbourhood where Miss Raymond had resided, for Mr. Barry and his father had been college
friends at Oxford, and he often chatted with nurse Keefe when she
brought home shirts and cravats ("that would bate the snow for
whiteness") to his lodgings in St. James's-street, and highly gratified
her by the information that, as he occasionally joined Lady B——'s
family circle, he had sometimes the pleasure of seeing Miss Raymond. She was a little mortified that he did not praise her young
lady, as she thought everybody ought to do, but consoled herself by
muttering, as she went home—"Well, it's mighty quare, but these
Englishmen are afeard of wearing out their tongues; who knows,
for all that, but, may-be, he's like the countryman's goose, that
thought all the more for not spaking."

Mr. Wortley, for it was the self-same gentleman, did think much
on every subject, but, latterly, more of Gertrude than of any other;
he had not seen her often, but he had heard of her a great deal.
Lady B—— spoke of Miss Raymond in the highest terms, and the
children manifested the strongest attachment towards their "dear,
kind governess." "She is always so dignified and correct," said her
ladyship; "and is never out of temper," said little Jessica; "and

although she is sometimes melancholy," added Miss Clorinda, the
eldest of the children, "which is not to be wondered at, because once
she had almost—almost as much money as mamma, yet she smiles
away her sorrows so sweetly, and sings for us of an evening, as well
—indeed, quite as well—as Miss Stephens, and very like her, too,
the ballads that make one weep." "Dear mamma," said Charles, a
rosy boy of seven years old, "do coax Miss Raymond to drink tea in
the drawing-room with us to-night; she will never come when there's
company; but Mr. Wortley, you know, is an old friend, and nobody;
—and then she will sing for us;—do, mamma." The request was
readily granted, and he ran off with a message from mamma, begging
Miss Raymond would that evening take tea in the drawing-room.
He stopped at the door, and said playfully to Mr. Wortley, who had
been some time in the room, "Mind, I heard you say to papa, the other
day, that you wanted a wife;—now, you shan't have my Miss Raymond, for she shall be my wife, when I'm a man."

"Dignified and correct—never out of temper—with much reason
to be sorrowful, and yet chasing it away, even to the gratifying of
childhood; and singing—I never, never heard any woman sing with
half so much feeling. What an admirable wife she would make!"
So soliloquized Mr. Wortley when he left the family party one evening; and, of course, came to the resolution of knowing more of this
"very interesting and superior woman." That, however, was not
easily accomplished; the education of Lady B——'s children occupied
all Gertrude's time; and even if the duties of her situation had not
prevented it, she had so recently smarted from fashionable fickleness,
that she was not at all inclined to stake even an hour's happiness
upon it again. When Mr. Wortley met her, his very anxiety to
render himself agreeable made him awkward. He experienced, however, some alarm, when he found that Gertrude Raymond was going to
spend two entire months at Barry town, during Lady B——'s intended
tour on the Continent; and thought he would speak to her at once,
as well as he could; but a little reflection convinced him that this
would be the most effectual way to obtain a decided refusal, as he
could have yet made no progress in her affections, and he knew her
mind was too noble to calculate merely upon worldly advantages in a
matrimonial connexion. After much pro and con, he resolved to
speak to Lady B——on the subject, and without waiting for his curricle,
walked quickly towards Grosvenor-place. When he arrived, he was informed that Miss Raymond, attended by nurse Keefe and Lady B's——
own footman, had just departed for Ireland; and that Lady B——
was completing her arrangements previous to her Continental tour.
He felt at once a strong inclination to visit Ireland. "Every man of
liberal feeling should make the tour of the sister Isle—he wondered he

had never thought of it before; the Lakes of Killarney were celebrated all over the world—the Giant's Causeway, too, one of the
most wonderful works of nature—the county Wicklow—the Vale of
Avoca—(he repeated Moore's lines to the beautiful valley, with absolute enthusiasm). Besides, there was his father's old college friend
Mr. Barry; he had seen him in England during his parent's lifetime,
and knew he would be so glad to receive him—dear old gentleman!
—how delightful to talk with him of his father! It was, really,
very ungrateful not to have visited him before; and, now that London
was quite empty (the carriages were jostling at every corner), he must
go to the country—and he would go to Ireland." Accordingly he
wrote immediately to Mr. Barry, informed him of his anxiety to pay
his respects to his father's old friend, and explore the beauties of a
country of which he had heard so much; hoped he should not inconvenience Mr. B——; would await his answer at Milford; and concluded
by saying that he earnestly requested he would not mention his
intended visit to any one, except Lady Florence, as he had a particular
—very particular reason, indeed—for not wishing it mentioned, which
he would hereafter explain.

There is a sort of freemasonry in goodness, that none but the good
can understand. Mr. Barry, very soon after Mr. Wortley's arrival,
both knew and approved of his manly and disinterested attachment
to his young friend; sincerely rejoiced at the prospect of wealth and
happiness that was brightening before her; and only dreaded lest
Gertrude's high feelings would prevent her being dependent (as she
would call it) even on a husband. The manœuvrings of Mrs. C——
and Co. entertained him much; and, after dinner, on the evening of the
day the "blue lady" arrived, as the gentlemen entered the drawing-
room, Mr. Barry and Mr. Wortley paused, and whispered to each
other the same words, " How superior is she to all around her!" Certainly the contrast between Gertrude and Miss Spinner was very
ludicrous;—the real information of the one, and assumed learning of
the other, reminded one of Florian's beautiful fable, *Le Rossignol
et le Prince :*

> " Les sots savent tous se produire ;
> Le mérite se cache, il faut l'aller trouver."

One was as presuming as the sparrows; the other as retiring as the
nightingale.

" Now, re-e-ly," commenced the learned lady, " now, re-e-ly (she
was ambitious of the English accent) I am so glad you are come;
gentlemen, I contest for woman's talent, but I lowly bend to the
magnificent intellect of the creation's lords—although, it must be
confessed, you are not 'melting as a lover's prayer,' as Hughes

beautifully expresses it; and though, sometimes, 'ye are more
changeable than Proteus,' yet are ye 'glorious as Mars,' and 'lumi-
nous as stars!' There," said the lady, making a low courtesy, "is
rhyme and reason, which I consider the perfection of oratory!"

Miss Livy and Miss Letty laughed; Gertrude smiled, and the
gentlemen could scarcely keep their countenances in proper form.
Mr. Altern, the rattling foxhunter, complimented the lady on her
eloquence, which was, he said, "as good as a play;" and seated himself by her side, to draw her out;—there was little occasion for it, for
when once a woman gets a taste for display, it is like the overflowing
of the Nile, which no earthly barrier can withstand; I fear me, however, it does not fertilize like that river. When the tea equipage
was removed, Miss Spinner proposed "that they should busy themselves in some intellectual exercise. I am sure," she continued,
"Miss Raymond, who has so long enjoyed the enlightening beams of
London society, will second this motion; and, indeed, I wished
particularly to ask her, if she had seen any of the celebrated characters—the lions of the day?"

"Yes, I have, I believe, seen many of them."

"Oh, how I envy you! Perhaps you attended the celebrated Dr.
Townsend's lectures, on the use and abuse of the steam-engine;—of
course you recollect Darwin's beautiful lines :—

> 'Fresh, through a thousand pipes, the wave distils,
> And thirsty cities drink the exuberant rills.' "

Gertrude confessed she had not attended the lectures.

"What a pity! I think I saw your daughters, Mrs. Croydon, in
that sweet fellow's botanical studio, at the Rotunda—I forget his
name—Rose—Rosacynth!—do you recollect his delightful, and exquisitely touching, description of the papilionaceous tribe?—and his
hortus siccus?—so talented and classical!—to poetize the loves of
the flowers like Moore's loves of the angels!"

"Oh, yes!" replied both young ladies, "we all remember Mr.
Rosacynth; we attended his lectures, and all such things, before our
education was finished. I suppose, Gertrude, you will make Lady
B——'s daughters, *your pupils*, do so, when they are old enough?"

"Young ladies," replied Mr. Barry, quietly, "I believe Miss Raymond will soon devote her exclusive attention to one pupil—at least,
I know one who would give——"

"Dear sir," said poor Gertrude, springing up, "do, do hold—peace,
for pity's sake!"

"Bless me, what's the matter?" inquired old Lady Florence; the
Croydons exchanged glances; Mr. Wortley stooped to look for his
handkerchief, which was in his hand; and Mr. Altern gave a long

whew. The silence showed symptoms of continuance, which, never-theless, the foxhunter at length broke. "I hope you don't patronise the three B's that preside over conversazioni?"

"What are they?" laughed Mr. Barry.

"Blue stockings, blue milk, and blue looks."

"Sir—Mr. Altern," said Miss Spinner, indignantly, "I am sorry for you! You have no more taste for the beauties of literature—to think or speak so becomes a Goth, a Vandal, or—a foxhunter!"

"Whew!—dear madam, don't plunge so; a joke's a joke—though, faith, there's some truth in it. I was inveigled, once, to one of their conversazioni; what a pucker they were in!—worse than a pack of hounds in full cry, but not half the spirit or harmony, for they were all after different game; some shooting, some coursing, some angling, some (old ones too) ogling—they seemed to me to neglect no sort of business, except eating; and that was not their fault, for they had nothing to eat, save trumpery biscuits and half-starved sandwiches; my Sly would swallow plates and all, in a moment—coffee, and *eau sucrée,* and such poison!—oh, what is it to a baron of beef and a foaming tankard, or a smoking jug of whisky-punch?"

"But, sir," said Gertrude, kindly, for she saw Miss Spinner was annoyed, "surely people do not assemble merely to eat and drink; as intellectual beings, we have higher objects in society, and——"

"I'll tell you what," said the honest, but unpolished squire, "you are much too pretty for one of the sisterhood."

"Sir, I thank you," and Miss Spinner arose and courtesied low—very low—to Mr. Altern.

"Miss Olivia," said Mr. Wortley, eager to avert the coming storm, "do pray favour us with that beautiful cavatina of Rossini's—we all like music."

Miss Livy did not need a second request; and, for some time, she was listened to with much attention. At last, Miss Spinner became tired of silence, and gliding up to Mr. Barry, said, "that as Mr. —— (she forgot the name) had gone off that morning in search of Roman pavements,.and broken vessels, pipes, and interesting relics of the olden time, and had not yet returned to illumine their orbit by his brilliant discoveries, she had a few little curiosities in her bureau, up-stairs, that might afford amusement—she would bring them down while they were singing." The lady soon imported various packages, boxes, and bags, placed them on the sofa, piled up on her right hand and on her left, and looked not unlike a venerable mummy encom-passed by Egyptian relics. She exhibited her specimens of conchology; mineralogy; her little electrifying machine; her figure from the in-quisition at Goa; a snuff-box that Buonaparte had—looked at: a lock of hair, cut from the tail of Marie Antoinette's favourite lap-dog; a

bit of Pope's willow; a leaf of Shakspeare's mulberry-tree; a petrified
toe of St. Peter, which was classically labelled—"*Digit de Sancto
Pietro!*"—and many other equally valuable relics. The young people
grouped around her, and she was unusually elaborate and eloquent in
her descriptions; nay, she even repeated an extemporaneous poem
she had made upon herself on a misty morning.

Gertrude and Mr. Wortley were standing near each other, when
Miss Spinner pulled various old-fashioned boxes from a yellow silk
bag. "I purchased these very interesting relics of antiquity at a
receptacle for old furniture—vulgo, a broker's shop; it is very
obscure; I fancy there is part of this strange-looking box unopened,
it appears so thick and clumsy—perhaps the fastening is concealed by
some spring; it has hitherto baffled my utmost ingenuity, and I hardly
thought the man would sell it without examination."

"I ought to know it," said Gertrude; "it belonged, I am certain,
to my dear old friend's cabinet." She took it, and touched a spring
that was concealed by a small stud; the bottom opened, and discovered,
tightly pressed in, a folded parchment.

Mr. Barry seized it, hastily unfastened the ribbon which tied it, and
exclaimed, "Gracious Providence!—the Will—the Will—the Will!
She was neither forgetful nor unjust. Mr. Wortley, I give you joy;
—she'll have you now, because she'll be almost as rich as yourself; joy
—joy! Oh! I'm so happy!—quite right!—'all my personal and
estated property, too,'—my dear Miss Spinner, you are the sweetest
being on earth—'to Gertrude Raymond,'—just as it should be!"

"Dear—dearest Gertrude!" exclaimed Mr. Wortley; but Gertrude
had fainted on his shoulder; and salts, eau-de-luce, de Cologne, de
Millefleurs, were abundantly supplied by the young ladies, who
hardly understood the matter, but knew that all was in delightful
bustle, or, as Miss Spinner said, "soft confusion—rosy terror!"

When Gertrude had recovered, and time was afforded for delibe-
rate investigation, Mr. Barry read the will aloud. Mrs. Dorrington
had left her entire property to Miss Raymond, subject to some life
annuities, either to old and faithful servants, or poor relatives.
Amongst other paragraphs contained in it was the following:—"And
whereas, I have good and substantial reasons for believing that
Thomas Dorrington (who is, unfortunately, by the will of God, my
nearest relative) is a double-dealing craven, and a heartless man;
seeing that, like the fabled Janus, he carries two faces, I leave him
to be provided for by Gertrude Raymond, convinced that she, of her
generosity, will do more for him, in consideration of his family, than
my love of justice would permit me, knowing his duplicity as I do;—
I leave him to her mercy."

"It is singular," observed Mr. Barry, "that my old friend should so studiously have concealed all information on the subject of her will from us; to execute it with her own hand, and never mention its existence. She was a good lawyer, however, for it is duly witnessed; but where shall we find those people?—this document has been nearly four years in existence. 'Patrick Muller,' the old butler, he is dead; 'Frank Hayward,' and 'Jane Miller,' have you any idea where they are, Gertrude?"

"Frank Hayward married Jane immediately on our going to Bath, and my dear relative, you know, sir, never retained married servants; but she procured them confidential situations in Sir Thomas Harrowby's family. They have been ever since on the Continent; I believe they are now at Rome."

"How very fortunate," said Miss Spinner, "that I happened to purchase the box! My dear Miss Raymond, I give you much joy."

"Oh, so do we all!" said Mrs. Croydon; somewhat awkwardly, however, for Mr. Wortley's exclamation had convinced her that her daughters' beauty and accomplishments had been displayed in vain; and that, even when portionless, and a governess, Gertrude Raymond, notwithstanding her want of tact, advanced age (twenty-two), and what Mr. C—— always termed "very plain appearance," had conquered, what she considered, "a man worth looking after," because he had five thousand a year!

"Gertrude," said Lady Florence, who, by the assistance of her ear-trumpet, heard and understood all that had occurred—"my dear Gertrude, your old friend rejoices for you. Nearly a century has passed over this grey head, and those who number only half of my days, must experience much of joy and sorrow; yet this is one of the happiest hours I have ever known. I sorrowed, bitterly sorrowed, when you, of ancient family, and mind capable of adding lustre to the highest rank, became a labourer for independence. Yet, Gertrude, I loved you more and more; for even the pittance you worked for, you divided with the poor and the afflicted. Nay, child, I will speak; I do not often praise; but you deserve more than I can give.—Never did you utter unkindness towards those who had dashed your cup of happiness to the earth, even as it had touched your lips. Never did you suffer the breath of slander to dim *her* memory, from whom you had a right to expect so much; for you were unto her as a dear and tender child. I know the heart has ties stronger than those of kindred, but you had claims from both these sources." ·

"My dear Lady Florence," interrupted Gertrude, much affected, "you overrate—I knew my friend too well even to imagine she would forget me; I should have been base if I could for a moment have so believed!"

"Your trials are now passed," resumed the old lady; "the wind of

N

adversity separates the chaff from the wheat. You have learned to value *the world's* friendship. And when I remember the virtues that characterized your amiable and excellent parents, the words of this holy book press upon my memory—'I have been young, and now am old, yet saw I never the righteous forsaken, nor his seed begging their bread.'"

"Hang me!" said Mr. Altern, after a pause, "but it's worth riding a steeple-chase, to come in for all this."

"It would make a delightful tale if well wrought up," interrupted Miss Spinner, "quite good enough for—perhaps not for Blackwood, but for something else, particularly if it ends, as I presume, with a—a—spare my blushes!"

A sunny Sabbath morning succeeded this happy *dénoument,* and the finding of the will was noised all over the parish. The most busy agent on this occasion was nurse Keefe, who went to first mass, expressly for the purpose of telling, "how my young lady will have her right, and the bad breed 'll be forced to fly the country; and more will be happy than me—the fine English gintleman, that many was afther, the silly crathurs : as if it would be any good for them to put themselves equal to my young lady, with the raale gintleman who had sich beautiful estates, and sich a power of money, and a raale castle, built on a gould mine (as I hard tell); and whin he wants, he has nothin' to do but say to one of his men, 'James, go down and bring me up a bucket of gould;' and to another, 'Charles, my boy, go down and bring me up a bucket of silver.'"

The peasantry, who most cordially hated "the new man," rejoiced very sincerely at the intelligence. "Thos. Dorrington, Esq.," was neither fitted by nature nor education to occupy the station in society to which his wealth had raised him. He was what the poor termed "a hard man;"—let the land to the highest bidder, without any regard to the oldest tenant; and distrained for rent whenever it was not paid to the hour. Such a person was not likely to obtain popularity; and his low habits effectually prevented his associating with the gentry on equal terms.

"Well, bad as he is, Mistress Keefe," said Paddy Magin, "he didn't spirit away the Will, which for sartin I thought he did, for he always had the look of a dirty turn."

"Well, I set it down to that too, Paddy : and it's well for him he didn't. I'll stop myself, after grate mass, jist to see my young lady go to church, and pass the mock people on the road."

"Success to ye for ever, Mistress, honey!—and I'll gather the boys, and we'll have a shout for the young lady, and a groan for the by-gones, that'll shiver the mountains in no time;—it's a pity it's Sunday, or we'd have a bonfire."

"Ay, Paddy, we'll have that same whin she's set up, safe and sound in her own house; I don't think they'll have the face to dispute the will."

Paddy did "gather the boys," and a glorious shout and a deafening groan they gave.

"Thos. Dorrington, Esq.," affected at first to disbelieve the existence of the will; but he secretely procured what money he could from the tenants, and, deserting his unfortunate wife, whom he had long treated with brutal indifference, fled to America, and left them to the mercy of one who loved mercy. The reader will easily imagine that every difficulty in the way of a—a—the event, at the allusion to which Miss Spinner blushed, was by this fortunate circumstance removed; that the good Gertrude had now no scruples to overcome; and that no barrier existed to the completion of the perfect happiness to which she was so fully and so justly entitled:—

> "Heaven doth with us as we with torches do;
> Not light them for ourselves; for if her virtues
> Had not gone forth of her, 'twere all alike
> As if she had them not."

Barrytown never was so full of company as about three months after Miss Spinner's box had been found to contain so valuable a parchment; "shakedowns" in every room; open house, sheep and oxen roasted whole, barrels of ale and whisky, fiddlers and pipers; Lady Brilliant and suite; nurse Keefe, deputy mistress of kitchen ceremonies; Miss Spinner in a white satin hat, looped up with roses *à la pastorelle*, and a *real* new wig; Mrs. Croydon and her daughters (poor spite!) "so particularly engaged that they could not do themselves the honour from which they expected so much happiness —but wished the bride, and bridegroom, more than a thousand blessings." Barrytown was always noted for its hospitality; for the poor, as well as the rich, sheltered under its roof, and the generous master afforded relief to all who really wanted it. But when Gertrude Raymond was married to Alfred Wortley, everybody wondered where, even in Barrytown, such crowds could have been packed. Lady Florence Barry, who had not been outside her own avenue gate for twenty years, accompanied the bride; and Mr. Barry gave her away. More people could not have been at a priest's funeral than assembled on this memorable occasion—

> "When the wrong was made right,
> And the dark light,"

as Miss Spinner quoted it; and the "might and right" were exemplified for many years by the inhabitants of Barrytown and Mount

N 2

Gertrude (as Lady Florence called Mrs. Dorrington's old residence).

> " Hospitality,
>   No formality,"

became the motto of both houses, which were conducted on the same plan, except, indeed, that the great hall at Wortley-mount was garnished with merry, laughing children, instead of dogs, eagles, cats, and ravens.

"TAKE IT EASY."

ALL ye can do with him, Aileen, when he gets into those humours, is—to take it asy."

"Take it *asy*, indeed!" repeated the pretty bride, with a toss of her head, and a curl of her lip; "it's asy to say take it asy. I'm sure if I had thought Mark was so passionate, I'd have married Mike!"

"But Mike was mighty dark," replied old Aunt Alice; with a mysterious shake of her head.

"Well, so he was; but then I might have had Matthew."

"Ah! ah!" laughed old Alice; "he was the worst bird of the nest! Look, ye can wind Mark round yer finger, as I wind this worsted thread—if ye'll only *take it asy*."

"Oh! I wish—I wish I had known, before, that men were so ill-contrived! I'd have died sooner than have married," sobbed Aileen; who, to confess the truth, had been so much petted by the neighbours, on account of her beauty, that it would have required a large proportion of love, and a moderate allowance of wisdom, to change the village coquette into a sober wife.

" Ah, whisht! avourneen!" said Alice, " sure I tould ye all along, 'Mark,' says I, 'is all fire and tow—but it's out in a minute; Mike is *dark*, and deep as the bay of Dublin; and Matthew is all to the bad intirely.' You've got the best of the three. And ye can manage him just as the south wind that's blowing now manages the thistle-down that's floating through the air—if *ye'll take it asy*."

At first Aileen pouted, then she sat down to her wheel—was too much out of temper to do what she was doing, well—broke her thread —pushed it from her—took up her knitting—dropped the stitches— shook the needles—and, of course, dropped some more.

"*Take it asy*," said Aunt Alice, looking at her, over her spectacles.

Aileen flung the knitting away, clasped her arms round her aunt's neck, rested her head on her bosom, and wept outright.

" Let's go into the garden, sit under the ould lime tree, and watch the bees that are near swarming," observed Aunt Alice, " and we'll talk yer trouble over, avourneen. It's very sorry I am to see ye taking on so, for a thrifle, at the first going off. But you'll know better, by-'n-by, when real troubles come."

Poor Aileen, like all young people, thought her troubles were very real; observing the bees more than usually busy, she muttered, " I wonder, aunt, you don't tell the bees to take it asy."

" So I would, dear, if I saw them quarrelling : but they are too wise to quarrel among themselves, whatever they do with *furriners*. They fly together, live together, sing together, work together, and have but the one object and aim in life; ah, then, many's the good lesson we may learn from the bees, besides that which teaches us bring all that's good and useful to our own homes." The old woman paused; and then added, " Sit ye down here, my child, and listen to what I'm going to tell ye. Ye know well, avourneen, I was lawfully married, first, by ould Father John, to Richard Mulvaney—my heart's first love he was; heaven be his bed this blessed day, and grant we may meet above the world and its real troubles! Aileen, it was, in-deed, a trouble to see my brave, young, handsome husband, dragged out of the blue waters of the Shannon; to find that, when I called, he could not answer, when I wept, he could not comfort; that my cheek rested for hours on his lips, and he did not kiss it; and that never more, in this world, would I hear his sweet and loving voice!"

Fourscore years and five had passed over the head of that woman : and her age was as beautiful, according to its beauty, as had been her youth. She had been married three times; yet her eyes filled with tears at the remembrance of the love and sorrow of her early days, and it was some time before she could continue.

" Well, dear, one day, Richard and I had some little tiff, and I said more than I ought to have said. And it was by the same token, a fine midsummer morning; I strayed out to our garden, and picked up a shiny snail; and as I looked at the snail, I remembered how, the last midsummer day, I had put just such another between two plates, and sat for an hour by the rising sun, with the forefinger of my left hand crossed over the forefinger of my right hand; and then, as thrue as life, when I lifted the plate, the thing had marked as purty an R, and a piece of as beautiful an M, as the schoolmaster himself could write, upon the plate; and I cried to remember how glad I was then, and how sad now; and, at last, I cried myself to sleep. Alanna machree! I was little more than a child—not all out sixteen. Well, dear, in my drame, I suppose I must call it, I saw the beautifullest fairy (the Lord save us!)—the very handsomest of the good people that ever the eyes of woman looked upon,—a little deeshy-dawshy craythur, footing it away, all round the blossom of a snow-white lily; now twirling round upon the tip of her tiny toe; then, as if she was joining hands round, down the middle and up again, to the tune of the 'Rakes of Mallow.' "

" The 'Rakes of Mallow!' " exclaimed Aileen.

"The 'Rakes of Mallow!' " repeated Alice, solemnly; "I heard it as plain as I hear the rising march of the bees at this blessed minute. Well, of a sudden, she made a spring, and stood upright as a dart upon the green and goolden crown, in the very midst of the flower, and pushed back her ringlets, and settled her dress at a pocket looking-glass, not so big as a midge's wing; then, all in a minute she looked at me, and said, 'I don't like the sight of a wet eye;—what ails ye, young woman?'

"Well, to be sure, my heart came to my lips; but I had too much manners not to answer the great lady; and, 'Madam,' said I, 'my eyes would be as dry, though not so bright as yer honour's, if it wasn't for my husband, who wants to have a way and a will of his own.'

" ' It's the way with all the men, my own husband into the bargain,' says the queen, for she was no less; ' and there's no use fighting for the upper hand,' says the queen, ' for both the law and the prophets are against us in that; and if it comes to open war,' says the queen, ' we get the worst of it: if your husband falls into a bad temper, or a queer temper—if cross, or unkind, or odd—take it asy,' says the queen, ' even if he does not come round at once. This quiet way of yours will put you in his heart, or him at your feet (which is pretty much the same thing) at last: gentleness does wonders for us women in Fairy-land. It has great strength entirely, in the hands of a purty woman—and you are very purty for a mortal,' says she again, looking at me through the eye of a heart's-case, which she wore about her neck for a quizzing-glass.

" ' I thank you, my sweet and beautiful lady,' says I, ' for your compliment. ' Ah! ah!' and she laughed, and her laugh was full of joy and hope, like the music of the priest's own silver bell. ' It's no.

harm,' she continued, 'if now and then you give him him a taste of that
which makes your eyes so bright, and your cheeks so red, just now.'

"'What's that, Madam?' says I.

"'Flattery!' says she. 'Make a man, be he fairy, or be he mortal,
pleased with himself, and he is sure to be pleased with you.' And
then she laughed again. 'Whatever he says or does,' says her
majesty, while she was getting into a goolden saddle, a horseback on
a great dragon-fly, dressed in a beautiful jacket and gown of green
velvet, with a silver riding-whip in her hand, ' take it asy,' says she ;
and I heard her laugh and sing when she was out of sight, and her
sweet voice shook a shower of white rose-leaves, from a bush, on
my face. And when I awoke, I saw the wisdom of her words, and I
kept them close in my own bosom ; and often, when I'd be just going
to make a sharp answer to him I loved, I'd think of the fairy's word,
and the evil would pass from my heart and lips without a sound—no
one the worse for it, and I all the better. And sure Richard used to
say I was like an angel to him. Poor fellow ! he was soon to be taught
the differ, for the angels took him from me in earnest !

"After a couple of years I married again. I've no reason to fault
with the second I had ; though he was not gentle, like him who sighed
out his soul in the blue waters : he was dark, and would not tell what
offended him. Well, I'd have given the world to have had some one
to whom I could make a clean breast ; but I had none ; and, somehow, I again sat in the same spot, at the same time—again slept—and
again saw the same one of the good people. I did not think her
honour was as gay as she had been, and I wondered in my heart if
she, too, had taken a second husband; it would not have been
manners for me to spake first, but she was as free as ever.

"'Well,' she says, looking at me, 'you've tried another ; but
though you have not forgotten my advice, you do not follow it.'

"'Oh, my lady, plase yer majesty,' says I, ' the tempers of the two
do so differ !' and I thought with the words my heart would break :
for the moment poor Richard's humour was out, it was off; but
James would sulk and sulk, like a bramble under the shade of an oak :
and the fairy read my thoughts as if they were an open ballad.
'This one is dark, my lady, and gets into the sulks, and is one that I
can't manage, good or bad; not all as one as it was with my first husband, plase your majesty ; for when we had a tiff, it was soon over—
God help me, so it used to be; but this one sits in a corner, and
never speaks a word, not even to the cat.'

"'Ah,' said she, ' they are different : but the rule holds good—
gentle and simple—hot and cold—old and young—you must take
them asy, or you'll never be asy yourself. Let a passionate temper
cool; don't blow upon it—a breath may ruffle a lake, and kindle a
fire. Let a sulky temper alone, it is a standing pool; the more it is

stirred, the more it will offend.' I try to talk her fine English, Aileen, but it bothers me," continued old Alice. "Well, the end of it was, that she finished as before by telling me to *take it asy,* which after that, I did; and I must say that James's last breath was spent in blessing me. Well, dear, Miles Prendergast was rich, and I was poor; he wanted a mother for five children, and a servant for himself, and he took me. This was the worst case of the three. There was a great deal of love—young—fresh—heart-sweet love to the first; and more than is going, in general, to the second: but, oh, my grief! there was *none* to the third. Oh, but marriage to a woman without love! what is it? Where love is, it is even pleasant to bear a harsh word, or look—a satisfaction that you can show your love, by turning bitter to sweet. Service is no service then—his voice is your music—his very shadow on the ground yer brightest sunshine!"

"Aunt," said Aileen, "you did not think that with the first, at the time, or you would not have wanted the good people's advice."

"True for ye, avourneen; we never value the sunbeams so much as in the dark of the moonless night; we never value a friend's advice until he is beyond our reach; we never prize the husband's love, or the mother's care, until the grave has closed over them; and when we seek them there, the grass that we weep over is green, the mallow and the dock have covered the cross or the head-stone, and the red earth-worms we have disturbed bring us no message."

"I don't want to hear any more, aunt," said Aileen, pained by the picture her aunt had drawn; "now I'll own to the first of the quarrel, and the last word of it, if Mark will confess to the middle."

"Let a quarrel alone, when once it's over," interrupted her aunt. "A quarrel, darlint, is like buttermilk—when once it is out of the churn, the more you shake it, the more sour it grows."

"And must I say nothing when he comes home?"

"Oh, yes, say, 'Mark, my heart's delight!'"

"Oh, aunt, that would never do!"

"Well, if ye're ashamed to say what you feel, a smile and a kiss will do as well. And a smile and a kiss will work wonders, darling, if the heart goes with them; but if they are only given because they're dutiful gifts, ah! they fall like a snow-wreath upon the spring-flower, chilling and crushing, instead of warming and cheering. Not but duty's a fine thing; but it's dark and heavy to a married woman when there is no back of love to it."

"Did the fairy queen give you the same advice the third time?" said the bride, blushing like Aurora at Alice's counsel; "for I suppose you saw her the third time——"

"I must say, achora, she wasn't so civil to me the last time, as she was the first and second," answered the old dame, bridling. "She tould me I wasn't as purty as I used to be—that was true enough, to be sure, only one never likes to hear it; she tould me that, when the bloom of a woman's cheek fades, the bloom of her heart ought to increase; she talked a deal that I did not quite understand about men making laws and breaking them: and how every one has a thorn of some kind or other to bear with: she tould me how hard it was to find three roses in a garden all of the same shape, colour, and scent, and how could I expect three good husbands? She said that, as I had borne my crown, I must bear my cross; she was hard enough upon me; but the winding-up of her advice to me, in all my troubles —was to take it asy; she said she had been married herself more than five hundred years."

"The ould craythur! and to talk of your not having been so purty as you were!" said Aileen.

"Hush, avourneen! Sure they have the use of the May-dew before it falls, and the colour of the lilies and the roses before it's folded in the tender buds; and can steal the notes out of the bird's throats while they sleep."

"And still," exclaimed Aileen, half pouting, "the best advice they can give to a married woman in her trouble, is—to take it asy!"

"It's a sensible saying, if properly thought of," said old Alice, "and will bring peace, if not love, at the last. If we can't get rid of our troubles, it's wise to TAKE THEM ASY."

PETER THE PROPHET.

DON'T talk to me, Paddy Mulvany—don't talk to me!—where's the use of your talking, chitter-chatter, chitter-chatter, like a nest of magpies? Don't I know what I know?—Improvements indeed!—answer me this: am not I fifty-two years and three months old—and having a fine memory, as well as much foresight—thanks be to God for the same—don't I recollect as good as fifty years? And what then? Why this; that all the trading-boats landed on that out shore, safe and sound, whatever was wanted.—Don't tell me of the place being inconvanient, Paddy Mulvany: it's no such thing. In a peaceable village, building a quay to land coal! As if the people can't burn turf as their grandfathers did afore them! And timber! —won't wattles do for the cabins as well as ever?—but mark the up-shot of this—every potato, every grain of corn, 'll be bought up, and sent out of the country, when the English boats come in, and we shall all be starved; and neither man, woman, nor child, will be left alive to tell the story."

"Why, thin, Mister Peter, sure it's yerself that sees the sunny side of a thing: ye've a mighty cheering way wid ye, ever and always," said Paddy Mulvany, looking archly at his companion.

"Sunny side!—Why, there's no sunny side, man alive, to see. When Wellington bridge was built over the Scar—and sure they were talking of that bridge more than a hundred years before it was begun;—no good will come of it, says I, and I was right; it has now been built three years, and no road made to it yet; and, by the same token, it's cracked in the middle; I knew no good would come of it. Oh, what sarvice that money would have done the neighbours, if it had been properly laid out!"

"Troth, Master Peter, you may say that—that is, I suppose, if you had had the management of it; but, any how, the quay 'll be built in spite o' ye; for it's an English gentleman that has taken it in hand; and, bless ye, although I know ye kept a creditable shop in the town o' Ross, you have no notion how quick they get things done in England. Sure I see it all whin I used to take Mister Nick Lett's pigs to Bristol fair: ye'd hardly credit it, but I have seen an entire street of houses built up, plastered, painted, papered—great, big houses—and the people ateing, drinking, and sleeping in thim, comfortable as anything, all in one week. Bless ye, they go about things, and finish them out of hand in a jiffy!"

"So much the worse—so much the worse, Paddy Mulvany; no good can come of that; but I suppose, as you say an Englishman has taken it in hand, the quay will be built. Ye're all mad, I believe, barring myself; I see how it will end; but you mark my words, Paddy Mulvany, no good will come of it. I'll just step over to see what they're after yonder; so good-bye, Paddy—remember my words!"

"God be wid ye, Master Peter. Hulloo! I forgot to tell you that Friar Mulloy's brown nag pitched him into a ditch, and Mister Hollin's chimbly took fire on account of the new English way of sweeping; they put a goose at the top of the chimbly, and let it fly down."

"There, didn't I say so?" replied the little man, stopping, and looking as pleased as Punch at the narrative of accidents. "Sure, I told Friar Mulloy, ' that nag 'll brake yer reverence's neck,' said I—I knew it; mark my words: and as to the chimbly—sure, I guessed that, though I said nothin' about it."

"Why, thin, ye're a quare little animal of a Christian, and ye believe every word I said, ye little fool of a thing!" continued Paddy, as he looked after Master Peter Callaghan, *alias*, "Peter the Prophet," *alias*, "Peter the Croaker;" "and it's a dale more ye think of yerself than anybody thinks of ye; so much the better; one madman in the parish is enough. But yon chap's not to say clane mad, only a little touched, and mighty puffed out, thinking he's got more in his brain-box than any other body in the whole kingdom—priests and bishops into the bargain. God forgive us all our sins!"

And Paddy went off in an opposite direction from Peter the Prophet, who journeyed towards the intended quay. Peter was a slight, stiff, pertinacious, pragmatic old bachelor—sour as a crab-apple, and obstinate as a mule; he had realized a small independence, and invariably passed his summer months at Bannow, having taken it into his head that sea air did him much good; he was a source of great amusement to the peasantry, who named him "Peter the Prophet," from his habit of prognosticating; others called him "Peter the Croaker," for he always prophesied evil. Paddy Mulvany was a very different person—a cheerful, careless Irishman, whom the farmers held in constant request, as a drover. The most wealthy considered themselves fortunate in securing Paddy's services, when cattle were to be sent to England or Wales. In matters of business, Paddy's word was his bond; and, although he could neither read nor write, his accounts were always "fractionally" correct, and he made most extraordinary sales for his employers; he had not even his national fault, the love of whisky; but I confess that he sometimes indulged in most marvellous stories, and often quizzed without mercy. He took especial delight in tormenting Master Peter, and it was perfectly astonishing how "the Prophet" could ever have believed a word that Paddy Mulvany uttered. He spoke the truth, however, in saying that an English gentleman was going to build a quay in Bannow harbour; no spot could be better suited for the purpose than that so judiciously fixed upon; it was well sheltered, and beautifully situated, with sufficient water to float a thirty-ton sloop, even when the tide was out—the road which led to it was a succession of hill and dale, at one side shadowed by trees, while the view, on the other, passed over sunny fields and little cottages, and was terminated in the distance by the sea—the boundless sea, forming innumerable creeks and bays along the coast. The little island opposite was enlivened by a cheerful-looking farm-house, while a few relics of some old castles, o'er parts of which—

"The plough had passed, or weeds had grown,"

served as a relief to the sameness of the view, and afforded subject for meditation: on the land side, high hills rose above the valley in rude magnificence, their heathy hue broken by patches of cultivation; and, indeed, nowhere could a more interesting spot be found, than the one selected by the English gentleman, Mr. Townsend, for the long-projected quay. I lament, for the sake of Peter the Prophet' reputation, to be compelled to state that all things went on prospe rously at the new building; and even the gentry were astonished a the rapidity with which the work proceeded; each man had his allotted portion, and the wages were paid every Saturday evening, precisely as the clock struck six. To the quay were added stores and a salt manufactory; and before a twelvemonth had elapsed, all was finished—properly finished, plastered, and pointed; the windows were even and set—the slates regularly pegged—the tiles all of a size—and the buildings had a neat and business-like appearance.

Peter the Prophet and Paddy Mulvany met at nearly the same place where they had separated about a year before, and both turned their steps towards the new quay.

"It's a fine sunny day—God bless it!—Mister Peter, and I suppose ye're going to the new quay to see the fun; it was, I must say, very generous of Mr. Townsend to give us a let out; all the top of the gintry are to have a grand entertainment—a cold *collation* they call it—upstairs in the stores; and below there's a piper—and who knows what!—and the atin' and the drinkin' in lashins—and the two sloops, that are after comin' in with the timber and coal, have such gay streamers out as it's quite charmin' to see."

"I don't see anything charming in it, Paddy Mulvany—charming in a coloured rag flying, red and blue, like a turkey-cock!—and as to the entertainment—mark my words, no good will come of it. What are entertainments of all kinds but empty puff—'vain show,' as the poet says?—but you have no taste for poetry. No; few have; I had, however—but I gave it up—I had a turn for the grocery business, and poetry; but no man can be great in two things—so I fixed on the former."

"That was a mercy, Mister Peter; for somehow, although I am but an ignorant man, seeing I don't know B from a buttercup, yet I think yer poetry wouldn't have sold as well as yer tea and sugar."

"Humph!" replied the Prophet: "I see, Paddy, that long red house is to be let, and the owner's off to America; there—my words always come true; no good will come of that man, says I, and so it was."

"Why, I knew no good could come of him myself," replied Paddy; "who ever saw a good end come to any one that was hard to the poor?—besides being unjust, didn't he write a will, and make his dead uncle put his name on it, by houlding the corpse's hand? and then he swore he had life in him at the time—and troth so he had, for he put a live worm in the dead man's mouth—the baste!"

"That's one of your stories, Paddy; like what you tould me, long ago, about Friar Mulloy's brown nag, and Mr. Hollin's chimbly; there goes the friar; that's not a nag, but a fine hunter he's on now; I suppose that's the one Paul Doolan gave him for marrying him to that foolish widow; he's a holy man without doubt:—but mark my words, that beast will break his neck, it's so spirity!"

"As to the worm, ye may believe it or not, as you plase, Mister
Peter, but it's as true as the sun's above us; and as to Friar Mulloy,
sure all the world knows he's a holy man, and a good; never a
cratur passes his door without the bit and the sup, barring the gauger
—the blackguard!—that tuck his potteen, and kilt his ilegant little
bit of a mare. Oh! wisha! every day's bad luck to him for that
same!"

"Is it true that your niece, Alice, is going to be married to Corry
Howlan? She's a sweet pretty girl, but——"

"Now, Mister Peter, or Peter the Prophet, or whatever other
name you may have, I'll just trouble ye to hould yer tongue about
Alice and Corry; not that I care a toss-up (with all due respect)
for yer prophecies, although ye want everybody to believe ye've the
second sight, like a Highlander; but ye see, as they are to be
married, it's unlucky to have any ill laid out for them; and as to the
girl, God's blessing be about her! she's the light of my eyes, and the
joy of my heart, every day and hour of her life, the jewil."

Peter looked annoyed at hearing his prophetic powers called in
question, but he deemed it safer to hold his peace for a time; at all
events, until they came in view of the new quay.

Along a green, shady lane, which led to the centre of that day's
attraction, two people were walking, or rather strolling, very different in appearance from Paddy and Peter.—A lively, lovely girl,
with roguish, hazel eyes—not the soft sleeping eye of that bewitching colour, but a round, brilliant little orb, now twinkling, now
dazzling, now half shut, not unfrequently stealing under its pent-
house lid to "the far corner," and peeping slyly about, for fun or
mischief; the nose of this little personage was, morever, *retroussée*
—an unerring token of much spirit, and, if vexed, not a little spite.
But it was the glittering fairness of this fairy creature which, united
to the pure glow of health and cheerfulness, completed her fascination,
and made Alice Mulvany the most perfect bit of Nature's colouring
I ever had the good fortune to behold. Her companion Corry
Howlan, could not have been mistaken as belonging to any country,
principality or power, but the green little island. How often have I
been both amused and mortified at hearing my English friends exclaim, whenever a particularly miserable, dirty, round-faced person
met their view, "Oh, how like an Irishman!"—"quite impossible to
mistake that *creature* for anything but an Irishman!" Trust me, those
know little of our peasantry who judge of them from bricklayers'
labourers, superannuated watchmen, and Covent-garden basket-
women. Corry Howlan was a good specimen of our small farmers,
and I will sketch him for your amusement, gentle reader, as he loitered
down that green lane with his merry companion :—height, six feet, or
nearly so—an air of easy confidence, and every limb well propor-

tioned; face oval; teeth, white and even; nose, undefined as aquiline, Grecian, snub, or Roman, but, nevertheless, highly respec table : eyes, large, *bien foncée*, and expressive ; brow, open—shaded with rich, curling, brown hair; the dress, as usual on holiday occasions—red waistcoat, blue coat, knee-breeches, white stockings, neat, black, Spanish leather shoes—shirt-collar thrown back, *à la Byron*, loosely confined at the base by a green silk neckerchief—a " bran new beaver," placed on one side the head in a knowing position, and a stick, not dignified enough to be designated as " shilalah," nor slight enough to be called " switch." There are many likenesses which, though correct as to shape and feature, fail in expression ; and so it is in the present instance. I cannot paint the affectionate feelings portrayed in the young man's face, when his eyes rested on the careless, thoughtless girl who tripped at his side, as giddy as the gay butterfly that wavered from the perfumed meadow-sweet to the beautiful but scentless convolvulus, whose long, twirling stems were supported, at either side their path, by black thorn or greeny furze. One of the most beautiful characteristics of an Irish landscape is the quantity of small singing-birds which animate every brake and bush. As they paced along, the young folk disturbed either the soaring lark, the merry stone-chatter, the gay goldfinch, the tiny wren, the linnet, bunting, or yellow-hammer; when they approached the thicker coverts, a jetty blackbird, or timid partridge, would rustle for a moment amid the leaves, and then dart across their path, swift as an arrow.

"'The poor, harmless birdeens !" said Corry; " Alice, do you know, I never could hurt one of thim small things."

" Well, nor I, Corry," replied the lass, " particularly the robin red-breast, that has got, you know, the blessed Virgin's own Son's blood upon it; for when the Saviour was crucified, the poor bird was heart-sorry, and away it flew round the cross, and over the cross, bemoaning all the time; and whin the cruel Jew-man pierced his holy side, some of the blood flew on the cratur's breast, and then it never stopped until it nested in the holy Virgin's bosom; and, to be sure, she knew the blood, and the faithfulness of the robin, and she blessed it, and settled it so, that every red-breast has the mark of the holy blood to this very day."

" You've a good memory, Ally ; I hope you'll think of everything as clear as that; and, above all, don't forget what you more than half—indeed, as good as whole—promised me last night at yer uncle's door, and I laning against the post."

" I'm sure, Corry, I've not the laste thought of anything ;—was it about Paddy Clarey's white mare that broke into uncle's cloverfield ?" And Alice stooped to gather a wild polyanthus, whose blossomy coronal pushed its way over some cuckoo-bells and crawling " Robin-run-the-hedge."

"Ye're the devil's teazer, Ally, darling!—ye haven't yer little cocked-up nose for nothing."

"Well, if I'm the devil's teazer, you own yerself the devil; and as to my nose, there are plenty to admire it without you."

"Sure it's I that admire it, and what's more, love it, and its owner; but, Alice, last night, don't you remember, when the moonbames fell on your sweet face, and whin ye turned away, even from that weak light, to hide yer blushes—(that ye did not need, on account that ye're too handsome, even without them)—and whin I held yer hand, and did what I'm sartin no man living would dare to do but myself—kissed it with warm love, and yet with as much respect as if it had been a queen's:—do you remember—oh, I know you do;—that whin, not only I, but yer uncle, begged ye to fix the day, ye whispered—oh! it was so low, so sweet—sweeter, Alice, than ever I heard even your own sweet voice before!—'to-morrow I will tell?'—that, that was all you said; that sweet 'to-morrow.' Alice, I have thought on it ever since. You will not disappoint me. We can't fail to be happy; and all so smiling: yer uncle, who loves me next to his own; my mother, who dotes upon ye—how could she help it?—a nate farm; and this morning I've been after a milch-white cow, for the sake of the luck—such a one isn't in the whole bar'ny—and I've bought it too, and we'll look at it this evening, after a bit o' dance at the new quay. I didn't mane to tell ye yet, but somehow I can't keep anything from ye that would give ye satisfaction. And now, darlint!—Ally, my own Ally—the day, the day!" The young man took the maiden's hand within his, and was about to press it to his lips, when, instigated by a sudden fit of caprice, she jerked it from him, and averting her head, to hide the self-satisfied smile which played over her countenance, replied—

"You need not make so free, sir; I said that, jist to please uncle. I can do no such thing; and I hate white cows."

Corry had been long enough a lover to have suffered from those little whimsical tricks which poor as well as rich Misses practise for their own amusement, and their lovers' mortification. I must confess, I am often amused at the discomfiture the lords of the creation experience upon such occasions; they twist and writhe so much under their sufferings, like eels trying to get out of their skin; anxious to show off in all their native dignity, yet fearing to offend the slippery fair one, who, for all her teazing, would not lose the "tasseled gentil" for worlds. Then, after marriage, the noble Sir beginning to think it is *his* turn to show off, grows capricious; and then some old bachelor uncle, or brother, tough and crusty, and perpendicular like a church-steeple, gives the bridegroom his "word of advice, to put his feet in his shoes, keep her nose to the grinding-

o

stone, support the dignity of his sex, keep his own secrets," &c.
And the bride has her "female friends;" old maiden aunts, who hate
"male creatures," and beg their "dear niece to have a will and a way
of her own, and be mistress in her own house;" and poor relations,
anxious that the lady should have a private purse, that stumbling-
block to domestic happiness :—"so disagreeable to go to a husband
for every shilling,"—"no need to inform a man of all things,"—
"never suffer a husband to know how much you love him." And if
these counsellors are attended to, the cat-and-dog warfare commences, and the "I will," and "I won't,"—"You shall," "I shan't,"
—"Sir,"—"Madam,"—all which terminates with the mutual exclamation—"Would to heaven we had never been married!"

Now a little harmless teazing does no harm in the world : where
"bear and forbear" is moderately attended to, it gives a zest, a spirit
to existence ; and where there is much and pure affection—

> "The short *passing* anger but serves to awaken
> Fresh beauties, like flowers that are sweetest when shaken."

Not that I mean to say Alice was right in asserting "she hated white
cows," which was a decided story. No Irish girl or woman ever
hated a white cow; the thing is impossible—quite. Everybody,
who knows anything, knows that a white cow is as good as the
priest's blessing, or holy water, in the house of the early wed; and
it was much too saucy a thing to say : but her nose was up, and her
tongue went as nimbly as a greyhound's foot.

"Well, Alice," replied Corry, who, as I said before, often suffered
from his love's whimseys—"I'm perfectly astonished at yer not
liking the white cow that I bought to plase ye; but, whin ye see
her, I know ye'll admire her, beyant——"

"Ye need not have troubled yerself to buy the cow, Mr. Corry,
for *me*; for may-be I'll never own her," interrupted Alice.

"Ye're not going to be jilty after yer promise, and yer uncle to
the fore, Alice," said Corry, who loved her too well to have the
wedding jested about.

"I gave no promise to be bothered wid ye ; and whether I did or
no, I'll change my mind if I like, myself."

"Is that the pattern of yer honour, Miss Alice Mulvany ?" inquired the young man, much annoyed.

"Mind yer own business, if ye plase, Mr. Cornelius Howlan, and
I'll mind mine. I've bothered him fairly," she muttered to herself,
"I knew I'd get a rise out of him."

"May-be, Miss Alice, ye'd rather have my room than my company ?"

"There's no manner o' doubt of it."

"May-be, Miss Mulvany, ye'd wish me to take my lave ?"

"Ye have the lave, so now take yerself off," she replied, very sharply.

The young man looked earnestly in her face, and said, in his usual affectionate tone, "Dear Alice, let us be friends—dear Alice—you can't, can't really mean to quarrel with your Corry—dear——"

"Don't dear Alice me, sir, after that fashion! Don't dare to dear Alice me!—what do you mean? After callin' me jilty, and all manner o' names, to be coming ' dear Alice' over me!—no, sir; and I tell ye my mind, Mr. Cornelius Howlan, I hate you as well as the white cow, and I won't dance a step with ye, nor spake a word more to ye, this blessed day, Amen!—and if ye'll take my advice, ye'll be off with yerself!"

Alice, after this pretty piece of eloquence, tossed her little head, pressed her lips firmly together, and walked sturdily towards the main road. Corry did all he could to make her laugh or speak—but no; she was as obstinate as a mule. He gathered wild flowers, and stuck them in her hat—she flung them from her; he told his drollest stories; then he reasoned with her; then, in his fine, rich voice, he sung her favourite airs;—and the only wonder is, that she managed to hold her tongue so long—she afterwards confessed it was sore at the tip from inaction.—At last, quite wearied by her stubbornness, Corry said, as they drew near the new quay, "Now look, Alice, I'll not taze ye with spaking any more, this day; but, may-be, before night comes, you'll be sorry for this fit of the dumps."

What a cheerful, noisy assemblage! A pattern!—a pattern was nothing to it. There was the clear sea, and the small waves running little races on the firm strand; the two brigs; the largest ever seen close to the shore in that part of the world, drawn up to the quay, which was crowded by the gentry and bettermost farmers' wives and daughters, with the piper at one end, and the fiddler at the other, both playing the same tune, of which little could be heard for the shouting, the laughing, and the chattering; then the windows of the stores were all open, and such of the ladies as did not like to encounter the heat of the sun, tempered even as it was by the refreshing sea-breeze, were seated on high, enjoying the noise and bustle; while the large rooms beneath sent forth such clouds of savoury perfumes as told of roast and boiled, pickled and preserved, besides spicery and cates, that would do honour to an aldermanic assembly. Then the machines, employed to convey the company invited from various parts of the country, were amazingly curious: one or two carriages of ancient days; some few gigs; jaunting cars, under all their classifications—the double, the inside, the outside; then the common car "made comfortable," for the more homely, first filled with straw, then a feather-bed covered with that destroyer of time, calico, and taste—patch quilt. I have seen five dames, strange as it may seem, in such a conveyance; two seated next the horse's tail,

partly on the shafts of the car, two in the middle of the feather-bed
(no bad seat that), and one cross-ways at the bottom; this unfortunate is always obliged to hold fast with both hands, for a sudden
jerk would inevitably dislodge the more ponderous.   So they reached
our pretty quay of Bannow, situated in a district for which commerce
ought to do much more than it has done; although our harbour is
not a good one for large vessels, it is "elegant" for small craft. The
place is very picturesque. Directly opposite is the village of Fethard,
a corruption of "Fought-hard;" so called, it is said, because here
occurred the first battle between the Anglo-Normans and the "mere
Irish," immediately after the arrival of the former upon the soil, of
which they subsequently became possessors.   One of the earliest
castles of the invaders still exists—a picturesque ruin. A few miles
inland is "Tintern Abbey," now a modern residence, but once a
famous monastic institution where, it is reported, and universally
believed, the spirits of the murdered monks still take their solemn
walks, yearly, on the eve of the anniversary of All-Saints. Over-
looking the quay is the old church of Bannow; and still nearer to it
are the remains of one of the old square towers, of which the followers of Strongbow erected so many in all parts of our country.
The whole neighbourhood is, indeed, deeply interesting to the historian and the antiquarian.   But to my story.

The sailors mixed with the rustic groups, congregated under
several awnings that stretched along the strand, and enjoyed the
earnestness shown by the untravelled peasantry to inspect the wonders
of their barques, which were cleaned and trimmed gaily out for the
purpose of exhibition. The most interesting of all the sights, however, was a black cabin boy; scarcely any one, in Bannow, had ever
seen a negro, and the poor little fellow was subjected to all manner
of inspection; the old women were for washing and scraping him,
to see if he could be brought to a "dacent colour;" the young ones
appeared terrified; and Peter the Prophet, after much critical examination, declared "that no good could come of bringing such outlandish things among Christians."

"Ally, my dear," said Paddy Mulvany to his niece, "what ails ye,
that ye look so solid?—come, you and Corry are ilegant hands at the
jig, and ye must both put the best foot foremost to night, 'cause of
the gintry."

"I'll not dance a step this night, uncle, with Corry!" she replied,
heartily sick of her resolve, but mistaking obstinacy for firmness:
"I won't do it, because I said I wouldn't; and, for the matter of
that, he doesn't want me to—he's been flirting away this half-hour
with Ellen Muccleworth."

"He's been doing no such thing, my dear; I've been watching ye
both; you won't spake to him, and yet ye ixpict him to sit at yer

elbow, putting up with yer snouting—for what? I'll go bail ye don't know yerself. It's well, pretty Alice, I'm not yer bachelor; I'd lave ye to get rid of yer humours, as ye could, my jewel."

So saying, Paddy Mulvany turned on his heels; tears filled the fine eyes of Alice, but she remained obstinate as ever; and, when Corry danced with Ellen, she really believed herself a much injured, insulted little maiden.

"I don't care," said she to herself—"I'll not sit quiet to please him—I'll jig it with the very next boy that asks me." And so she did; throwing off her mantle; folding her gay kerchief over her head and neck; and exhibiting her pretty figure to the best advantage, in her loose "jacket," of white, bordered with muslin; while her buckled shoes marvellously set off her small feet. "The next boy that asked her," was no other than handsome Horatio Laverton, the mate of the timber vessel; and Corry had the mortification of seeing that Alice danced to perfection, and of hearing such expressions of approbation from the surrounding company, as—"Ilegantly danced!" —"Success!"—"Well, in all my time, I niver saw so sweet a couple on the flure." "Corry, ye're bate out by the English boy—clane bate—and at the jig too." "Hurra!—there's a fling; well, that *is* dancing!" Then Alice figured in a three-handed reel, with the mate and her rival, Ellen, and certainly, she had the advantage there; for Ellen was pronounced as "not fit to hould a candle to her." Yet, as the evening waned on, Alice's bad spirits increased, and even the attentions of the handsome Horatio Laverton failed to reconcile her to the reproaches of that little, silent, yet powerful, monitor within her own bosom. As the moon rose slowly over the waters, she remembered that she had been more happy at her uncle's door, with no eye upon her but her lover's, than she was at that moment, walking up and down the pier, with an almost stranger, and listening to so much praise that she began to doubt she could deserve it: still she remained obstinate.

"We will make friends to-morrow," said she to herself; and, as she stood leaning on handsome Horatio Laverton's arm, looking towards the little island of Bannow, Corry and her uncle came on the pier. She saw, in a moment, that her lover had taken too much whisky-punch, and this reminded her that he had broken a promise he had made her the preceding evening. She forgot how she had acted herself; and, when Corry good-humouredly spoke to her, turned away, curled up her nose, and replied not.

"I am glad to find, Alice," he said "that you like the smell of tar better than that of whisky." This remark was only noticed by the little nose mounting still higher; but the sailor immediately replied:

"I suppose, Mr. Irishman, the young lady may like what she chooses."

Corry, hot, hasty, and rapid, was nothing loath to answer; but Paddy Mulvany interfered immediately.

"Mister mate—that young lady, as you are so civil as to call her, is my niece, and, moreover, engaged to that young man; some tiff came betwixt them this morning, but it'll blow off, only I'm sorry my eldest brother's child should act so flirty a part. Come, you two shake hands; sure we ought all to be glad of the strangers who will bring, not only plenty, but peace, to our strand." The young men shook hands; and Paddy Mulvany placed 'his niece's arm within his, and whispered that it was time to go home.

"What do you think of our pier and harbour?" inquired Corry of the mate.

"It's nicely suited for trade," replied the sailor, "and the little island opposite, shelters it from the nor'-west wind. I'll try and swim to that spot to-morrow morning; though, if I can do it, I suppose I'm the only one in the country could; it's a long stretch."

"It's a good swim for sartin, but I'd do it as easy as kiss my hand —clothes and all, this minute, with all the ease in life."

"Well, that's good, faith!—now, do you expect me to believe that? Why, I'd bet ye a gallon of stiff grog ye'd founder before ye'd get half way."

"Done."

"Done."

"Done and done's enough betwixt us two at any time, and so here goes, clothes and all, excepting coat and shoes."

"What are ye after, Corry?" inquired Paddy Mulvany, seeing him taking off his coat.

"Going to swim to the island for a small taste of a wager; this gentleman says, though he's a seafaring man, it's impossible; so I'm jist going to show him the differ, for the honour of ould Ireland; I'm no fresh-water rat, to fear a ducking in the brine—here goes!"

Whenever a true-born Patlander meditates a dashing exploit, it is for the honour of " ould Ireland;" and many of Corry's friends, heedless of the consequence, cheered him to the undertaking. Paddy expostulated; but the voice of the thoughtless is always loud; his reasonings were not heard.

"What!—strike a bet to an Englishman?—a bet musn't be broken."

"But I say it must and shall," said Paddy; " he's not in a fit state to swim; put on your coat, Corry; here's Ally will ax you not to go."

"Will she?" exclaimed Corry; " if she does, I'll give it up—pay the grog; and that's more than I'd do for any man, woman, or child, barring herself."

"Alice," said her uncle, in an under-tone, "Alice, for the love of God, ax him not to go; as sure as ye're alive some harm 'll happen to him."

"I don't care," replied the sulky beauty.

Corry heard the words. " You don't care, Alice ;—now here goes
in earnest !" and he sprang off the pier into the ocean.   Alice flew to
the spot, and ejaculated, " Dear Corry !"—but it was too late.   " I
knew the tide would be over strong," exclaimed Mulvany ; " and so
much whisky !"

" By George, he's doing it nobly !" said the Englishman.

" Ould Ireland for ever !" shouted the peasants.   Paddy knew well
that the attempt was highly dangerous ; he had often seen Cornelius
swim, and perceived the difference now.   Without uttering a sentence, he jumped from the pier to the deck of the nearest vessel, then
dropped into a little boat that was alongside, which was quickly
unmoored, and, seizing the oars, tacked after his young friend.   This
was the work of a moment, and one of the English sailors observed—

" I say, who'd ha' thought that yon old fresh-water chap could have
slipped that craft off so nimbly ?"

It was one of the clearest evenings that ever beamed out of the
heavens ; the moon had risen up in an unclouded sky ; the waters
reflected the " night's fair queen," and the little twinkling stars, in its
clear blue bosom.   The island may be somewhat more than an Irish
mile from the pier, and the efforts Corry made to gain it were distinctly visible ; but the eddy near the shore was very strong.   As
there were many jutting crags that intercepted the even flowing of
the tide, Paddy Mulvany did not follow in the exact track, but kept to
the right of Corry ; Alice stood on the pier in breathless anxiety ;
and that feeling was increased to one of indescribable agony, when
she heard the mate exclaim, " Good God !—sure it can't be !—yes, the
current—he's struggling ! as I hope to be saved, he's gone down !"
The crowd now pressed forward to the end of the pier.   Stoutly did
Mulvany try to tack his boat so as to gain the drowning man ; but,
unfortunately she stuck upon a sand bank, and there was no time to
disengage her ; he, therefore, relinquished the oars and plunged into
the sea.   By this time Corry had risen ; but before his friend reached
him he had again disappeared.   One loud, long shriek of agony drew
the attention of the spectators for a moment, to the land ; it was
Corry's aged, widowed mother : she rushed fearfully along the quay,
exclaiming, " My boy—my boy !—my blessed boy !"   It was with
difficulty she was restrained from casting herself into the waters ; her
eyes fixed on Alice, and she said, in a tone between bitterness and
affection, " Ally, Ally !—why did ye let him go ?"

Mulvany had watched the moment for Corry's rising, and " treaded
the water," while he seized him by the collar, so as to prevent the
possibility of grappling.   Instead of the exertion he expected, he was
much horrified to find the poor fellow apparently a motionless corpse ;
and, when he placed him in the boat, no symptom of lingering life
was manifested.   A loud shout from the shore told, plainly, how

sincerely the people rejoiced in what they considered the success of
Mulvany's exertions. Alice and Corry's mother rushed into each
other's arms, tremblingly awaiting the arrival of the boat; but it is
quite impossible to describe what followed, when the wet and senseless form of the beloved of their hearts was laid on the strand.

One in the crowd tried to soothe the wild grief of Alice. " Asy,
asy, dear! sure it's God's will!" She turned towards the man who
had spoken, and pointed to the body; then, with the action of frenzy,
shook the pale hand, shrieking. "Corry, oh, Corry, dear!—why won't
ye wake? Oh, wake, wake! 'tis I that ask it!" and the unhappy
girl fell senseless on the bosom of him she had dearly loved. The
noise roused the mother, who had been wiping off the chill damp from
her son's forehead;—her sorrow " was too deep for tears." " I tell
ye, Alice, he's dead!" she murmured, when the girl's lament broke
upon her ear, " and will never wake again!" She bent over him,
while her hand rested on his ashy brow, and muttered, unconscious
of the presence of strangers, " You were a good son, agra;—the green
plant of the desert. How like his father he is now, whin I saw him
last—jist before they put him in the could grave, in the morning of
his days—dead—dead——"

" My good woman," said the captain of the vessel, pushing through
the crowd, "it is impossible that such a strong, fine fellow as that,
could be smothered in so short a time, by a mere mouthful of salt
water; come, my hearties, lend a hand, and haul him on board;
there's hot water, and stoves, and every convenience, and it won't be
the first time we brought a lad to life after a ducking!" The old
woman looked earnestly in his face, and clasping her hands, faintly
articulated, "Life—to life! God's blessing!—life—life!"—and accompanied the kind-hearted Englishman.

At any other time, the Irish would have strenuously exerted themselves to prevent the interference of the English about " death consarns;" but the captain's kind manner, and Mr. Townsend's going on
board, silenced all their scruples. Paddy Mulvany also followed,
supporting his niece, whose youthful feelings rebounded at the
prospect of Corry's recovery. As Paddy was stepping on board,
some one pulled his sleeve, and the ominous face of " Peter the
Prophet," popped over his shoulder.

"I just wanted to remind you, Paddy Mulvany, that I tould ye no
good would come of the new quay; you'll just please to remember,
Paddy Mulvany——"

Paddy turned full on him—"Ye ill-looking, croaking, money-
making, ould vagabond, if I catch yer wizen raven-face within tin
yards of me or mine, either in town or country, I'll just give ye the
finish—and here's the beginning!"

The drover made a blow at Mister Peter, which, if it had arrived at its destination, would have silenced his prognostication for a time; but he had wisely retreated, and ever afterwards kept the other side of the road when he espied Paddy's figure approaching.

The efforts of the English crew were successful; and the next morning a group of three—no—*four*, passed up the green lane, where the birds were singing, and the flowers blossoming, as sweetly as on the past evening.

An old woman could hardly be said to be in advance, so closely did she keep, and so often did she turn back to look upon the party of three, who filled up the pathway. A young man, exceedingly pale, was in the centre, and he derived support and happiness from those on whom he leaned. The girl was delicate to look upon, and the tear-drop glittered in her eye, even when the pale youth gazed upon her with looks of unspeakable affection. His hand lay, but could hardly be said to lean, upon her fairy arm; while his companion, on the other side, had enough to sustain.

Alice became a reformed flirt: and, although she never quite conquered her love for ingeniously tormenting, yet did she conquer her obstinacy, and declare unqualified approbation of the white cow.— I cannot say so much for Peter, who continues to prognosticate, after his old fashion, and bitterly complains that a prophet hath no honour in his own land.

KATE CONNOR.

TRUST me, your Lordship's opinion is unfounded," said the Lady Helen Graves; and, as the noble girl uttered the words, her eye brightened, and her cheek flushed with a better feeling than high-born "fashionables" generally deem necessary.

"Indeed!" exclaimed the Earl, looking up at the animated features of his goddaughter, "and how comes my pretty Helen to know aught of the matter?—methinks she has learned more than the mysteries of harp and lute, or the soft tones of the Italian and Spanish tongues. Come," he continued, "sit down on this soft ottoman, and prove the negative to my assertion—that the Irish act only from impulse, not from principle."

"How long can an impulse last?" inquired the lady, as she seated herself at her godfather's feet, just where he wished, playfully resting her rosy cheek on his hand, as she inquired—"tell me, first, how long an impulse can last?"

"It is only a momentary feeling, my love; although acting upon it may embitter a long life."

"But an impulse cannot last for a month, can it? Then I am quite safe; and now your Lordship must listen to a true tale, and must suffer me to tell it in my own way, *brogue* and all; and, moreover, must have patience. It is about a peasant maiden, whom I dearly love—aye, and respect, too, and whenever I think of sweet 'Kate Connor,' I bless God that the aristocracy of virtue (if I dare use such a phrase) may be found, in all its lustre, in an Irish cabin.

"It was on one of the most chilly of all November days, the streets and houses filled with fog, and the few stragglers in the square, in their dark clothes, looking like dirty demons in a smoky pantomime, that papa and myself, at that *outré* season, when everybody is out of town, arrived here, from Brighton; he had been summoned on business, and I preferred accompanying him to remaining on the coast alone. 'Not at home to any one,' were the orders issued when we sat down to dinner. The cloth had been removed, and papa was occupying himself in looking over some papers: from his occasional frown I fancied they were not of the most agreeable nature; at last I went to my harp, and played one of the airs of my country, of which I knew he was particularly fond. He soon left his seat, and, kissing my forehead with much tenderness, said, 'That strain is too melancholy for me just now, Helen, for I have received no very pleasant news from my Irish agent.' I expressed my sincere sorrow at the circumstance, and ventured to make some inquiries as to the intelligence that had arrived. 'I cannot understand it,' he said; 'when we resided there, it was only from the papers that I heard of the—dreadful murders, horrible outrages, and malicious burnings. All around us was peace and tranquillity; my rents were as punctually paid as in England; for in both countries a tenant, yes, and a good tenant too, may be sometimes in arrear. I made allowance for the national character of the people; and, while I admired the contented and happy faces that smiled as joyously over potatoes and milk as if the board had been covered with a feast of venison, I endeavoured to make them *desire* more, and then sought to attach them to me by supplying their new wants.'

"'And, dear sir, you succeeded,' I said; 'never were hearts more grateful—never were tears more sincere, than theirs, when we left them to the care of that disagreeable, ill-looking agent.'

"'Hold, Lady Mal-à-pert!' interrupted my father, sternly; *I* se-

lected Mr. O'Brien : *you* can know nothing of his qualifications.]
believe him to be an upright, but, I fear me, a stern man ; and I
apprehend he has been made the tool of a party.'

" ' Dear papa, I wish you would again visit the old castle. A winter
among my native mountains would afford me more pure gratification
than the most successful season in London.' My father smiled, and
shook his head. 'The rents are now so difficult to collect, that I fear
——' he paused, and then added abruptly, ' it is very extraordinary,
often as I mention it to O'Brien, that I can receive no information as
to the Connors. You have written frequently to your poor nurse,
and she must have received the letters—I sent them over with my
own, and *they* have been acknowledged !' He had scarcely finished
this sentence, when we heard the porter in loud remonstrance with a
female, who was endeavouring to force her way through the hall. I
half-opened the library-door, where we were sitting, to ascertain the
cause of the interruption. 'Ah, then, sure, ye wouldn't have the
heart to turn a poor crathur from the doore—that's come sich a way
jist to spake tin words to his Lordship's glory ! And don't tell me
that my Lady Hilin wouldn't see me, and she to the fore.' It was
enough ; I knew the voice of my nurse's daughter ; and would, I do
think, have kissed her with all my heart, but she fell on her knees,
and, clasping my hand firmly between hers, exclaimed, while the tears
rolled down her cheeks, and sobs almost choked her utterance—'Holy
Mary ! Thank God !—'Tis herself, sure !—though so beautiful !—and
no ways proud !—and I will have justice !' And then, in a subdued
voice, she added—' Praise to the Lord !—his care niver left me ; and
I could die content this minute—only for you, mother, dear !—yerself
only—and——' Our powdered knaves, I perceived, smiled, and
sneered, when they saw Kate Connor seated that evening by my side
—and my father (heaven bless him for it !) opposite to us in his great
arm-chair, listening to the story that Kate had to unfold.

" ' Whin ye's left us, we all said that the winter was come in arnest,
and that the summer was gone for ever. Well, my Lord, we struv
to plase the agint, why not ?—sure he was the master ye set over us !
—but it doesn't become the likes o' me, nor wouldn't be manners,
to turn my tongue agin him, and he made as good as a gintleman, to
be sure, by yer Lordship's notice—which the whole counthry knew he
was not afore, either by birth or breeding. Well, my lady—sure if
ye put a sod o' turf—saving yer presence—in a goold dish, it's only
a turf still; and he must ha' been Ould Nick's born child (Lord save
us !) when yer honour's smile couldn't brighten him ! And it's the
truth I'm telling, and no lie ;—first of all, the allowance to my mother
was stopped for damage the pig did to the new hedges ; and then we
were forced to give our best fowl as a *compliment* to Mr. O'Brien—

because the goat (and the craythur without a tooth!) they said, skinned the trees; then the priest (yer Lordship *minds* Father Lavery) and the agint quarrelled, and so—out o' spite—he set up a school, and would make all the children go to larn there; and thin the priest hindered—and to be sure we *stud* by the church—and so there was nothin' but fighting; and the boys gave over work, seeing that the tip-tops didn't care how things went—only abusing each other. But it isn't that I should be bothering yer kind honours wid. My brother, near two years agone, picked up wid the hoith of bad company—God knows how!—and got above us all—so grand-like—wearing a new coat, and a watch, and a jewil ring!—so, whin *he got the time o' day in his pocket,* he wouldn't look at the same side of the way we wint; well, dear lady, this struck to my mother's heart—yet it was only the beginning of trouble—he was found in the dead o' night—(continued poor Kate, her voice trembling)—but ye heard it all—'twas in the papers—and he was sint beyant seas. Och! many's the night we have spint crying to think of that shame—or, on our bare bended knees, praying that God might turn his heart. Well, my lady, upon that, Mr. O'Brien made no more ado, but said we were a seditious family, and that he had yer Lordship's warrant to turn us out; and that the cabin—the nate little cabin ye gave to my mother—was to go to the gauger.'

"'He did not dare to say that!' interrupted my father, proudly; 'he did not dare to use my name to a falsehood!'

"'The word—the very word I spoke!' exclaimed Kate. 'Mother, says I, 'his Lordship would niver take back for the sin of the son what he gave to the mother! Sure it was hard upon her grey hairs to see her own boy brought to shame, without being turned out of her little place, whin the snow was on the ground—in the could night, whin no one was stirring to say, God save ye. I remember it well; he would not suffer us to take so much as a blanket, because the bits o' things were to be canted next morning, to pay the rint of a field which my brother took, but never worked; my poor mother cried like a baby; and, *happing* the ould grey cat, that your ladyship gave her for a token, when it was a small kit, in her apron, we set off, as well as we could, for Mrs. Mahony's farm. It was more than two miles from us—and the snow drifted—and, och! but sorrow *wakens* a body!—and my mother foundered like, and couldn't walk; so I covered her over, to wait till she rested a bit—and sure your token, my lady—the cat ye gave her—kept her warm, for the baste had the sinse a'most of a Christian. Well, I was praying to God to direct us for the best (but, may-be, I'm tiring your honours), whin, as if from heaven, up drives Barney, and——'

"'Who is *Barney*, Kate?'

" I wish, my dear Lord, you could have seen Kate Connor when I asked that question; the way-worn girl looked absolutely beautiful; I must tell you that she had exchanged, by my desire, her tattered gown and travel-stained habiliments, for a smart dress of my waiting-maid's, which, if it were not correctly put on, looked, to my taste, all the better. Her face was pale, but her fine, dark, intelligent eyes gave it much and varied expression; her beautiful hair—even Lafont's trim cap could not keep it within proper bounds—influenced, probably, by former habits, came straying (or, as she would call it, *shtreeling*) down her neck, and her mobile mouth was garnished with teeth which many a duchess might envy; she was sitting on a low seat, her crossed hands resting on her knees, and was going through her narrative in as straightforward a manner as could be expected; but my unfortunate question as to the identity of Barney put her out;—face, forehead, neck, were crimsoned in an instant; papa turned away his head to smile, and I blushed from pure sympathy.

" ' Barney—is Barney—Mahony—my lady,' she replied at length, rolling up Lafont's flounce in lieu of her apron—' and a great true friend of—of—my mother's——'

" ' And of *yours*, also, I suspect, Kate,' said my father.

" ' We were neighbours' childer, plase your honourable Lordship, and only natural if we had a—frindly——'

" ' Love for each other,' said my lordly papa, for once condescending to banter.

" ' It would be far from the likes o' me to contradict yer honour,' she stammered forth, at length.

" ' Go on with your story,' said I, gravely.

" ' I'm thinking, my Lord, and my lady, I left off in the snow—oh, no!—*he* was come up with the car:—well, to be sure, he took us to his mother's house, and, och! my lady, but it's in the walls o' the poor cabins ye find hearts!—not that I'm down-running the gintry, who, to be sure, know better manners—but it's a great blessing to the traveller to have a warm fire, and dry lodging, and share of whatever's going—*all for the love of God*—and *cèad milc failte* with it! Well, to be sure, they never looked to our property; and Barney thought to persuade me to make my mother his mother, and never heeded the disgrace that had come to the family: and, knowing his heart was set upon me, his mother did the same, and my own mother, too—the crathur!—wanted me settled; well, they all cried, and wished it done off at once, and it was a sore trial that. Barney (says I) let go my hand; hould yer whist, all o' ye, for the Blessed Virgin's sake, and don't be making me mad intirely;—and I seemed to gain strength, though my heart was bursting. Look! (says I) bitter wrong has been done us; but no matter, I know our honourable landlord had neither art nor part in it—how could he?—and my mind misgives that my lady has often written to you, mother, for it isn't in her to forget ould frinds; but I'll tell ye what I'll do; there's nobody we know barring his riverence, and the schoolmaster, could tell the rights of it to his honour's glory upon paper: his riverence wouldn't meddle nor make in it, and the schoolmaster's a frind of the agent's; so ye see, dears, I'll jist go fair and asy off to London myself and see his Lordship, an' make him *sinsible.* And before I could say my say, they all—all but Barney—set up sich a scornful laugh at me as never was heard. She's mad! says one; she's a fool! says another; where's the money to pay your expinses? says a third; and how could ye find your way, that doesn't know a step o' the road, even to Dublin? says a fourth. Well, I waited till they were all done, and then took the thing quietly. I don't think, says I, there's either madness or folly in trying to get one's own again: as to the money, it's but little of that I want, for I've the use of my limbs and can walk, and it 'll go hard if one of ye won't lend me a pound, or, may-be, thirty shillings, and no one shall ever lose by Kate Connor, to the value of a brass farthing; and as to not knowing the road, sure I've a tongue in my head; and if I hadn't, the great God, that taches the innocent swallows their way over the salt seas, will do as much for a poor girl who puts all her trust in Him. My heart's against it, says Barney, but she's in the right;—and then he wanted to persuade me to go before the priest with him; but no, says I, I'll niver do that till I find justice; I'll niver bring both shame and poverty to an honest boy's hearth-stone. I'll not be tiring your noble honours any longer wid the sorrow, and all that, whin I left them; they'd have forced me to take more than the thirty shillings—God knows how they raised that same!—but I thought it enough; and, by the time I reached Dublin, there was eight of it gone; small way the rest lasted; and I was ill three days, from the sea, in Liverpool. Oh! when I got a good piece of the way—when my bits o' rags were all sold—my feet bare and bleeding, and the doors of the sweet white cottages shut against me, and I was tould to go to my parish—then, then I felt that I was in the land of the could-hearted stranger! Och! the English are a fine, honest people, but no ways tinder; well, my Lord, the hardest temptation I had at all (and here Lady Helen looked up into her godfather's face, with a supplicating eye, and pressed her small white hand affectionately upon his arm, as if to rivet his most earnest attention) was whin I was sitting crying by the road-side, for I was tired and hungry, and who, of all the birds in the air, drives up in a sort of a cart, but Mister O'Hay, the great pig-marchant, from a mile beyant our place; well, to be sure, it was he wasn't surprised when he seen me! Come back with me, Kate, honey!

—says he; I'm going straight home and I'll free your journey; whin
ye return, I'll let the boy, *ye know*, have a nate little cabin I've got
to let, for (he was pleased to say) you desarve it. But I thought I d
parsevere to the end, so (God bless him for it!) he had only tin shillings—seeing he was to receive the money for the pigs he had sould
at the next town—but what he had, he gave me; that brought me
the rest of the journey; and if I hadn't much comfort by the way,
sure I had hope, and that's God's own blessing to the sorrowful; and
now, here I am, asking justice, in the name of the widow and the
orphin, that have been wronged by that black-hearted man; and, sure
as there's light in heaven, in his garden the nettle and the hemlock
will soon grow, in place of the sweet roses; and whin he lies in his
bed—in his dying bed, the just and holy God——.' My father here
interposed, and in a calm, firm voice, reminded her that, before him,
she must not indulge in invective. 'I humbly ask your honour's
pardon,' said the poor girl, 'I lave it all now just to God and yer
honour; and shame upon me that forgot to power upon *you*, my lady,
the blessings that the ould mother of me sint ye—full and plinty
may ye ever know!—said she from her heart, the cratur!—may the
sun niver be too hot, or the snow too could for ye!—may ye live in
honour, and die in happiness, and, in the ind, may heaven be yer bed!'

"You may guess how happy the poor girl became, when sheltered
under our roof; for the confiding hope, so powerful with those of her
country, was strong within her, and she had succeeded in assuring
herself that at length she would obtain justice—justice which the
humbler Irish so rarely have—I may say, indeed, so rarely expect:
but which I trust to live to see extended to them as evenly and as
fully as to their brethren of England—with whom it is a right as
regularly looked for as their daily food.

"And now, my dear Lord," continued the Lady Helen, "tell me,
if a fair English maiden, with soft blue eyes, and delicate accent,
had thus suffered; if driven from her beloved home, with a helpless
parent, she had refused the hand of the man she loved, because she
would not bring poverty to his dwelling—if she had undertaken a
journey to a foreign land, suffered scorn and starvation—been
tempted to return, but, until her object was accomplished, until justice
was done to her parent, resisted that temptation—would you say
she acted from *impulse*, or from *principle?*"

"I say," replied the old gentleman, answering his god-daughter's
winning smile, "that you are a saucy gipsy to catch me in this way.
Fine times, indeed, when a pretty lass of eighteen talks down a man
of sixty! But tell me the result."

"Well, now you must hear the sequel to my story; for it is only
half finished; and I assure you the best half is to come:—

"Instead of returning to Brighton, my father, without apprizing our *worthy* agent, in three days arranged for our visiting dear Ireland! Only think, how delightful!—so romantic, and so useful, too! Kate —you cannot imagine how lovely she looked; she quite eclipsed Lafont! Then her exclamations of delight were so new, so curious —nothing so original to be met with even at the *soirées* of the literati. There you may watch for a month without hearing a single thing worth remembering; but Kate's remarks were so shrewd, so mixed with observation and simplicity, that every idea was worth noting. I was so pleased with the prospect of the meeting—the discomfiture of the agent—the joy of the lovers, and the wedding—(all stories that end properly, end in that way, you know)—that I did not even ask to spend a day in Bath. We hired a carriage in Dublin, and just on the verge of papa's estate, saw Mr. O'Brien, his hands in his pockets, his fuzzy red hair sticking out all round his dandy hat, like a burning furze-bush, and his vulgar, ugly face as dirty as if it had not been washed for a month. He was lording it over some half-naked creatures, who were breaking stones, but who, despite his presence, ceased working, as the carriage approached. 'There's himself,' muttered Kate. We stopped—and I shall never forget the appalled look of O'Brien, when my father put his head out of the window. He could not utter a single sentence. Many of the poor men, also, recognised us, and, as we nodded and spoke to some we recognised among them, they shouted so loudly, for fair joy, that the horses galloped on, not, however, before the triumphant Katherine, almost throwing herself out of the window, exclaimed, 'And I'm here, Mr. O'Brien, in the same coach wid my Lord and my Lady, and now we'll have justice!' at which my father was very angry, and I was equally delighted. Two 'weeny' children met us at the entrance to the cottage—Barney's cottage; their healthy cheeks contrasted with the wretchedness of their attire; and told my father, at once, the condition to which his negligence had reduced my poor nurse— for the children were hers. I will show them to you, one of these days, a *leetle* better dressed. It was worth a king's ransom to see the happiness of the united families of the Connors and Mahonys; the grey cat, even, purred with satisfaction :—then, such a wedding! Only fancy, my dear Lord, my being bridesmaid!—dancing an Irish jig on an earthen floor! Ye exquisites and exclusives!—how would ye receive the Lady Helen Graves, if this were known at Almacks?— From what my father saw and heard, when he used his own eyes and ears for the purpose, he resolved to reside, six months out of the twelve, at Castle Graves. You can scarcely imagine how well we get on; the people are, sometimes, a little obstinate, in the matter of smoke, and, now and then, an odd dunghill, too near the door; and

P

as they love liberty themselves, do not much like to confine their pigs. But these are only trifles. I have my own school on my own plan, which I will explain to you another time, and now will only tell you that it is visited by both clergyman and priest; and I only wish that all our *absentees* would follow our example, and then, my dear god-papa, THE IRISH WOULD HAVE GOOD IMPULSES, AND ACT UPON RIGHT PRINCIPLES."

FATHER MIKE.

HEAVEN defend us!—did ye ever hear sich a storm?—and the snow's as good as knee-deep this blessed minit, in the yard; it's hard to say whether sleet, snow, or hail, is the bittherest, for they are all drifting together, and always in a body's face. Martin, is there no sign of his reverence yet?"

Martin, who had been industriously stuffing some straw into his huge brogue, and Molly M'Clathery, who had made the inquiry, rose at the same moment, opened the window-shutter, looked forth upon the night, and listened, in hopes to hear the wonted tokens of the priest's return.

In the kitchen of old Father Mike, the usual "family circle" had assembled, of which Molly and Martin formed a principal part. The house stood on a bleak hillside, exposed to the full rush of the sea

P 2

blast, without a tree to shelter either dwelling, barn, or hayrick. On
such a night, its exterior presented anything but a comfortable appearance; it has an ill-built, slated house, flanked by thatched offices,
which formed a sort of triangle, at the smallest point of which a wide
gate stood, or rather hung, almost always open; to say the truth, it
was only supported by one hinge, the other never having been repaired since the county member's carriage frightened it to pieces,
when he visited the worthy priest, a month or two before the last
general election; although Father Mike had, a thousand times, directed Martin to get it mended, and Martin had as often replied, " Yes,
plase yer reverence, *I'll see about it.*"

At the back of the house nearly an acre of land was enclosed, as
" a garden ;" but the good priest cared little for vegetables, and less
for flowers; and it was, of course, overrun with luxuriant weeds,
insolently triumphant, in the summer time, over the fair, but dwind-
ling rose, or timid lily, that still existed, but looked as if they pined
and mourned at the waste around them. The inside of the dwelling
was rambling and inconvenient; it had a dark entrance-hall or passage, a kitchen, a parlour, a cellar, on the ground floor: while a sort
of ladder staircase led to the upper chambers. The kitchen was the
general family room, the parlour being reserved for company, and kept
in tolerable order by the priest's niece, a dark-eyed little lass of
sixteen.

Martin and Molly had resumed their seats on a black old settle,
that occupied one side of the large open chimney : Molly, of spindle-
like stiffness, her lean figure and scraggy neck supporting a face
" broad as a Munster potato," while her wide mouth, and long, sharp
teeth, betokened her passion for talking and eating : Martin, whose
shaggy elf-locks clustered thickly over a well-formed forehead, and
deep-set but bright grey eyes, resembled, very much resembled, a
cluricawn—that particularly civil, wily, sharp-sighted Irish fairy.
Martin Finchley was almost as little, quite as knowing, quite as clever,
and by trade a brogue maker, to which fraternity all cluricawns belong; yet the straw peeped forth from his brogues! Ah! but Martin
was a genius—knew more of every body and everything than any
man in the country, sung a good song, told a good story, brought
home the cows, fed the pigs, minded the horse, and performed many
domestic offices in the priest's establishment, yet found time to learn
all the news, and nurse half the children in the parish. Molly and
he had lived fifteen years with Father Mike, and had never passed a
day, during that period, without quarrelling, to the great amusement
of Dora Hay, the priest's little niece, who was now kneeling at the
other side of the fire, her wheel laid aside, while she carefully administered some warm milk to a young lamb that had suffered much
from the heavy snow. Two large dogs, a cat, and a half-grown kitten,

shared also the wide hearthstone, and enjoyed the bright, cheerful light of a turf and wood fire. On an old-fashioned table, partially covered with a half-bleached cloth, was spread the priest's supper; a large round of salted beef, a silver pint mug, with an inscription somewhat worn by time, an unbroken cake of griddle bread, with a "pat" of fresh butter on a wooden platter, and two old bottles, containing something much stronger than water. An antique arm-chair, with an embroidered but much soiled cushion, was placed opposite the massive, silver-handled knife and fork; all awaiting his reverence's coming. From the rafters of this wild looking apartment hung various portions of dried meat, fish, and pigs' heads, the latter looking ghastly enough in the flickering light. The dresser, which, as usual in Irish kitchens, extended the whole length of the room, made a display of rich china, yellow delf, wooden noggings, dim brass, and old, but chased-silver candlesticks. A long deal "losset," filled to overflowing with meal and flour, was (if I may use the expression) united to the wall by a heap of potatoes, on which a boy, or "runner," was sleeping as soundly as if he had been pillowed on down; a large herring barrel, a keg of whisky on a stand, to "be handy like," and a firkin of butter occupied the spaces along the wall of the apartment.

Still the storm continued. The fire was again heaped, and yet the master was absent.

"Miss Dora, my darlint," said Molly M'Clathery, after a very long pause, "go to bed, agra, yer eyes are heavy for sleep, and no wonder, for it's a'most elivin by the ould clock. Martin, I thought ye were to get the clock settled, but it 'll be like the gate widout the hinge, and the windy widout the glass, and the mare's leg; to say nothing of the wine last summer, that worked itself to vinegar for want of a bung. His reverence is a dale too quiet for all of ye. Whin Jacky the tinker was married—(sure, maybe, I don't remember it!)—he comes here, and talks his reverence over not to ax the money for the wedding until the nixt time he was wanting. Well, at the first christening my chap had the same story, and so on, putting his reverence off, from that to the next, and the next, and the next, and so on, till the seventh brat came. Well, that was all well, as a body may say; and at last his reverence, knowing he was getting powers of money, jist mintioned the ould score :—five shillings for the wedding, and then six christenings at a thirteen and a tester each. And, what does the spalpeen?—as keen as the north wind: ' Oh, very well,' says he, ' as yer reverence plazes, only there's Friar Kannett christens for half-price, and the Protestant minister for nothing, and one's as good as another.' And to be sure, to save the soul of the grawl, his reverence gives up intirely, and makes the thing a holy Catholic, out and out at once, for nothing."

"Will ye hould yer clack, Molly! What do I care about Jacky

the tinker ?—and as to the wine, it was as much your fault, and more, than mine. And for the mare's leg, how the plague could I hinder her breaking it if she liked, and I three mile off at the same time? But I wont be spinding my breath on ye; only—bad luck to all famales !"

"Thank you, Martin," said Miss Dora, who had really been half asleep, her small foot resting on the step of the wheel, and the thread hanging on her finger, while her head fell carelessly on her delicate shoulder.

" I humbly ax yer pardon, Miss Dory; I didn't mane you to hear that, it was only the like o' she I meant, that can never let well enough alone, but's evermore naggin', naggin', naggin' at a body like a swaddling pracher."

" Martin, I'll tell ye what it is—give us none o' yer impudence— for I haven't been Father Mike's housekeeper, or Miss Dora's nurse, for fifteen years, to stand talk from a man, much less from you, ye dawshy clodhopper !"

" Stop, Molly !" interrupted Dora, " stop; you are sometimes a little cross; and it is too late to quarrel to-night. I wish you would go to bed; and I will wait up for my uncle."

" Och, no, my dear—and lave you by yerself in this big kitchen ! Save us !—d'ye hear how that boy is snoring ? Dick ! Dick !—wake up, I say : what does his reverence give ye mate, drink, and clothing for ?—is it to lie there snoring, as comfortable, on thim illegant pratees, as the king on his throne, when yer master, a holy man like him, is out in the could snow ?"

" Sure, ye may let the boy alone, he's doin' no harm; he's not wanted till his reverence comes home, and then I'll wake him, to hould the light for the horse to the stable."

" He shall wake now; one idle body's enough in the house, Martin Finchley ;" and in her own way she proceeded to effect her purpose. Dick roared lustily at the blow which reached him, while Martin very quietly observed, " Now she's upturned everything, maybe she'll be asy herself." And so she was, for, kneeling with her face to the wall, she commenced gabbling over her prayers, " to keep her employed," as she said, till his reverence came in. Dora, to beguile the time, entered into conversation with Martin.

" Martin, was there any news stirring this morning ?"

" Nothing worth much, Miss; it's very dead for news now, on account that Mary-the-Mant's gone to Waxford, and Mrs. Murphy (oh, what a fine-spoken woman that is !) has just got two young ones that keeps her widin ;—and the poor widdy Mooney is out o' sorts. I wish ye'd jist say a kind word for her, the cratur, to his reverence, Miss, dear—may-be, the morrow, whin he's takin' his punch after dinner !—sure he spoke to her from the altar last Sunday, on account

of her havin' tasted something besides new milk in the mornin'—poor
thing! She has a wake head, and a warm heart, and a nimble tongue
(not that she's by any manner o' manes as fine-spoken a woman as
Mrs. Murphy—far from it), but, any way, she's almost ashamed to
let the bames o' day see her face; sure she can't help her wake head,
the sowl!—and she'll niver recover—barring you spake the soft word
for a poor distressed neighbour."

"Oh, Martin, you know she is always tipsy."

"Oh, no, 'pon my conscience, Miss, she niver takes more nor a
noggin afore breakfast, and, any way, she can't help it—it's the natur
o' the cratur. Oh, do spake the good word!"

"Martin, did Lavery get the saddle back?"

"Och, thin, I know I had somethin' to tell ye; ay, sure enough, it
came of itself, seemingly; sated quiet and civil at the door this mornin';
and it's Friar Donovan Jack Lavery may thank for that; for Jack
complained it to him, how he lost his beautiful saddle as good as new,
for his father bought it a little afore he died, and 'tis not much above
ten years agone, and what signifies the few times it was crossed, an'
it a Dublin saddle! So Friar Donovan, like a good Christian, didn't
wish the poor man to be at the loss of the saddle, and so, says he, an'
he preaching for Father Clancy in the chapel of Rathangan, says he
(he's a powerful man), says he—I know the boy that stole that saddle
(as well he might, for I knew him myself), and what's more, says he,
if he that has it does not return it to honest Jack Lavery afore to-
morrow night, he'll be riding upon that same saddle through——;
I ax yer pardon, it's not fit for a young lady to hear; only it's the
devil's coort he meant, and said it out plump and plain in the face of
the congregation—he'll be riding through the very hot place afore
this day week, says he, if he doesn't return it immediately; and sure
enough Jack has got the saddle, for it was sated quietly down at his
own door the next mornin' early."

"Well, Martin, I'm glad of it. Any more news?"

"Oh, nothin' particular; only ye hard, no doubt, how discontented
Father O'Shea (God be good to him!) was, at being buried in the
black North, whin his own people had sich comfortable lodging in
their own place, and how he came to his brother Mick, the farmer;
and Mick, says he, how d'ye think I can lie asy in the wet, could,
damp hole they put me in, and all my people so snug in their own
place; take me up, says he—(Och, Molly, ye need not stare, for it's
as thrue as the beads in yer hand!)—take me up, says he, and put
me in warm berring-ground; for if ye don't I'll give ye no pace, and
ye'll have no luck—to lave your brother, and he a priest, in such a
sitiation! Stale me away, says he. Now, to be sure, the brother
knew that it was far from right to take a priest from the berring-
ground of his flock, where he was placed so proper, facing his con-

gregation 'ginst the day of judgment. Nevertheless, what must be must be—so they stole him off in the dead o' the night, and settled him comfortable in the ould church-yard yonder, in the middle of his own people; it cost a power o' money—but niver mind, he's asy now.

"I dare say," continued Martin, after a long pause, "it was jist sich a night as this that the bitter desolation came upon the ancient, fine, ould town of Bannow; for, no doubt, Miss Dory, you that has such larning knows that there's an entire town under thim sand-hills. The sea rushed in one night, and all the craturs o' sinners asleep, quite innocent-like, were kilt and spilt. And when the sea went back to its own place—bad luck to it!—the storm came, and the sand heaped in mountains over the dead town; and, barring the church, that was on a high hill, every living house was kivered over, only one chimbly, that used to return a borough member, before the Union and Lord Castlereagh, and the likes o' thim, murdered ould Ireland intirely."

"But the proof, Martin, the proof!" inquired Dora, laughing.

"Is it proof ye're wanting, my darlint Miss? why, isn't the town to the fore, underground?—and isn't there, in Waxford city, the book to prove that as good as six streets, in the ould town of Bannow, paid cess, and tithe, and tolls?—and the cockle-strand, where the girleens are picking cockles?—sure that's a proof; for it's out o' that the sand come. The gintry talk of digging it up, and unkivering the sunk houses; but those that have money don't care, and those that have not—why they can't, ye know. Ye've seen the curious font inside the church; the rain water that falls in it is holy of itself— Lord save us! Father Grashby, ye know, said it was a shame to lave such a beautiful cut stone in an ould church; and so, without saying so much as 'by yer lave' to priest or minister, he claps the blessed relic in his own new chapel, tin miles off, as quiet as anything. To be sure, ye mind, whin the whole parish cried shame—and such a hulla-boo-loo as there was!—the women skreetching for the dear life, and saying (true for 'em) that the luck was gone for iver and iver from us: but the very nixt night—(now, ma'am, don't be always skitting that way: I ax yer pardon, but it's not what I'd expect from the likes o' you, to trate holy things so; and what I'm telling is as true as gospel—I'd take my bible oath of it!)—the very nixt night such a storm as you niver heard, nor any one else; and a bur-r-r, boo-ooo-b-o-o-o through the air; and the font went over the house-tops, and the trees, like a shot, whirring and bubbling, and bright as a star, and lit all along through the sky by the dazzling candles of the good people before and behind, shouting, chirming, and making such sweet music through the whirlwind—and fair and softly, they niver stopped till they placed the font in its ould place, and whir and away the charmers, to their homes in the blue-bells, and the rose-buds, and the wather-foam——"

"Lord save us!" ejaculated Molly, and muttered her prayers faster than ever. A long pause ensued, and, half asleep, Dora inquired if there had been a dance at the public that evening?

"Sorra a one," replied Martin, "whin I came away. I just looked in a minit; Phil Waddy, and yer cousin Brian, and one or two more, were there; and, by the same token, Raking Phil has a wicked look about the eyes when he's crossed."

"I never saw him look wicked," replied Dora, quickly. "He always looked so kind and good-tempered, and——"

A loud knocking prevented Dora finishing the sentence. Shag and his companion gave each one bark, and then ran wagging their tails to the door.

All were on their feet in a moment. Before Martin could hold the bridle rein, Father Mike (for it was the long expected priest) had dismounted, and with unwonted alacrity entered the kitchen, without the usual salutation of "God save all here!"

"Dear uncle," said Dora, taking his hand as he sat down, "let me take off this coat; what is the matter?—sure something has happened ye; speak, my dear uncle!" and the affectionate girl unbuttoned the collar; then, suddenly starting back, exclaimed, "Good God! here is blood, wet blood upon yer cravat!—dear, dear uncle, you are hurt—hurt!" and poor Dora, who did not possess much mental or bodily strength, nearly fainted on her uncle's arm. The old priest kissed her forehead, but it was some moments before he could reply. At length he said :—

"It is nothing, child; a mere nothing!—the bough of a tree, broken by the storm, might have scratched me here as it fell;" and he pointed to his throat, where more collected witnesses would easily have perceived a broken bough could not have harmed him; it satisfied, however, the innocent Dora, and the stupid Molly: and in a few minutes the priest was seated at the table.

"You don't eat, sir," said Dora; "you have, perhaps, supped at Mr. Heriott's, or at one of the farmers'."

"No, my dear."

"Then you do not like the beef."

"Thank God, child, it is very good."

"Well, let me make you some punch, nice whisky-punch; here's hot water, sugar—white sugar—all ye want; and, ye know, I'm a capital hand."

"I know ye're as dear to me, Dory, as ever born child was to father or mother. Make what ye please for yer old uncle. Molly, you and the boys may go to bed; I sha'n't be long, and it's Tuesday mornin' by this time."

"Hadn't Miss betther go to bed?" inquired Molly; "sure I'll sit up and do whatever's wanted wid all pleasure, as in duty bound, plase yer reverence."

"No, Molly, do you go." Molly retired, and, after a short pause, Father Mike spoke: "Dory, dear!—have ye said yer prayers to-night?"

"No, sir."

"Kneel down, then, love, at my knee, as ye've done, off and on, since my poor sister died—and that's more than fourteen years ago; ye'll be seventeen yer next birthday."

Dora smiled, and knelt as she was desired.

"Stop!—before you begin, child, take an *obligation* on yourself, to answer truly to every word I question, when ye've done; there, don't blush so; my sister's child, I know, has nothing to hide from her confessor and friend."

Dora prayed in tremulous accents, and perhaps she never looked so lovely as at that moment; her brown hair—long, thick, and some-what curled—hung over but did not conceal, the expression of her upturned face; her eyes were half closed, and the lids were beautifully fringed with dark lashes; her complexion, though somewhat em-browned, was delicate, and the lower part of her face, particularly her quivering lip, expressed feelings as yet undefined, but powerful: the priest's arms were crossed on his bosom; and when his eyes rested on the child of his adoption, his lips moved with the increased ear-nestness of heartfelt prayer.

"Now, Dora, sit down; not on that low seat—ye're always crouch-ing at my feet like a frightened hare; when Philip Waddy was here, yesterday morning, what did he say to you?—keep yer hand from yer face, and answer me!"

"Say, uncle?"

"Yes, child, say."

"Why, he said that it was a very fair morning."

"Anything else?"

"Oh, yes! he asked me if I was to be at Mary Gaharty's wedding next week, and—and—if—it was a very foolish question, uncle——"

"Well, dear, what was it?"

"Why, only—if—I'd like to be at my own wedding?"

"Well, and what did ye say?"

"I said—nothing, sir?"

"Did he not ask ye anything else?"

"Only if I loved my cousin Brian better than him."

"And what did you reply?"

"Oh," said Dora, smiling, "I said I loved Brian ten times better; and he got quite angry."

"Indeed! and is it true, Dora, that you love Brian the best?"

The girl spread her hands over her face, and even her throat coloured deeply, as she murmured—"No."

"Dora," said father Mike, "it is very unlikely that you will ever see Philip Waddy again; but if you should——" and his small grey eye, kindled by some hidden fire, as he spoke, looked dazzling bright, as it sparkled from under his dark brows,—"if you should see him, as you value my last blessing, as you value my last *curse*, shun him, fly from him, look not on him; the thunder of God will pursue, and overtake him, for he is——"

"*Remember!*" exclaimed a voice, both loud and deep.

The priest started from his seat; with one arm folded the terrified girl to his bosom, and, with the other seized the knife that lay upon the table before him. Within the apartment, all was still as the grave, except the large dog, who sprang to the half-closed shutter, but neither growled nor barked. The priest placed Dora on the chair from which he had risen, advanced to the window, with a firm step, carefully bolted it, and then returned to where his niece, the victim of many contending feelings, retained a perfect consciousness of all that passed, but was nearly deprived of reason by extreme terror.

She was, at length, roused by her uncle's affectionate kindness, and retired to her chamber, where a passionate burst of tears relieved her. Young, inexperienced, and perfectly ignorant of the world's ways, Dora Hay might have been truly called the child of nature; she had lost her mother at the moment she entered into existence, and her uncle adopted the friendless infant, (her father had died some months before,) and poured on it the affections of a heart that yearned for an object on whom it could bestow especial love. Dora, certainly, deserved all he could give, for never was child more devotedly attached to parent than she was to her uncle; when he was at home, she followed his footsteps, listened to his words, and treasured up his instruction with the greatest eagerness and attention; and, when absent, she thought only of what she could do to promote his happiness on his return. He was, indeed, her sole teacher, and, as he had received the advantages of a more polished education than falls to the lot of the priesthood generally, having resided at Paris during the old *régime*, his niece had the full benefit of all his advantages :—although, it must be confessed, he was not very competent to give lessons in the usual female acquirements. He instructed her in French; nature directed her how to sing, and that most sweetly, the wild airs of her native land; every Irish girl dances intuitively; and Martin taught her all the legends, and interested her in all the superstitions of the country. Thus, the young maiden might have been pronounced accomplished, by more fastidious judges than Father Mike's flock. Still, it must be confessed, Dora had great faults; next to her uncle's opinion, she thought her own better than any other ; and, like most girls, was vain of her beauty. The farmers' daughters she deemed too ignorant to be her companions ; and the young ladies in her immediate neighbourhood, to say the truth, were somewhat (I am sorry for it, but it is true, nevertheless) haughty, so that Dora had no friend of her own sex ; but she had what, perhaps, she thought better—two lovers—her distant cousin, Brian, and Raking Phil Waddy. Brian was a steady well-principled youth, of a slight and rather genteel appearance— gentle withal, except when influenced by the destructive spirit that has been one of the sorest curses on the land ; then he was rash and unguarded ; he had served his apprenticeship to a humble surveyor, near the priest's, and was about to commence business for himself. Any young man might have loved Dora for her own sake ; but, as she was considered " a fortune," she would no doubt be sought by many. " Raking Phil Waddy" was the third son of a half-gentleman—a noxious species, almost peculiar to Ireland ; these *half* gentry are *whole* idle, and, on the strength of their relationship to some rich family, or on the prospect of, at some future period, being rich themselves, they exist without any visible means of support, except what they " genteelly beg :" not that they are ill-dressed, or ill-fed, far from it : they go from house to house, relying upon the hospitality of the owners, and always manage to claim relationship with the opulent, who, " for the sake of the family," will not suffer them to wear a shabby appearance. The females of this species make excellent toadies, and the males, chorus laughs ; they draw corks, tell lies, smuggle occasionally, thrash bailiffs, seduce innocent girls, and end their lives generally (for the system cannot always last) either in New South Wales, or in a jail. Phil's father *as yet*, had done neither ; he dwelt some eight miles from Father Mike's with his wife, who had, at one time, possessed both money and beauty, but was now *passée*, in a tumbledown house by the wayside, where the nettle and the thistle strove for mastery, fit emblems of the bitterness and neglect that existed in the uncomfortable dwelling. Mr. and Mrs. Waddy agreed but on one subject, namely, that, as they were well connected, it was quite impossible to put their sons (fortunately, there were no daughters) to any business, and that, as they were nice-looking lads, they might visit from one house to another, until they obtained commissions either in the navy or in the army. They were received by a good many respectable families, but there was a cloud, a something, inexpressible, yet felt, that hung over their characters, more particularly that of Philip ; although he seemed a rattling lively fellow, gifted with much talent, and foremost with the jest. A relative wished him to study the law, and placed him with a very eminent solicitor in Dublin ; he returned, soon after, to his father's house—no one knew

why; but the shadow had deepened over him. In person he was not
so stout as he was muscular; his hair was light, his forehead well-
proportioned, his lip smiling, his eye, in unguarded moments, like a
cat's—fierce and prowling. Dora's fortune attracted his attention;
as to love, he knew it not; the word flew often from his lip, but it
sprung not from his heart; he had read of a new philosophy, too, and
because he was quick-sighted enough to discern the errors of Catho-
licism, he grasped at the belief that there was no religion that ought
to interfere between his passions and their gratification. The spring
budded, the summer glowed, the autumn yielded her fruit, and the
winter—the seasons' night—afforded leisure for reflection; yet Philip
heeded neither their beauty nor their usefulness, for he had said in
his heart—" There is no God!" He was too cunning to give utterance to these thoughts, and made even Father Mike believe that he
would soon settle down into a steady man; he visited frequently at
his house, as he said, to benefit by his instruction. The priest, however, perceived Dora's kindly feelings towards him, and was not inclined to encourage them: Brian, he knew, was much more likely
to make her lastingly happy, from the correctness and uniformity of
his conduct.

On the morning of the day we have just recorded, Father Mike
was pacing leisurely along the high road leading to Ross, when his
kinsman Brian, met him, with the salutation:

" I was just stepping down to ye, sir, to speak a word that's very
heavy at my heart. You know that ever since *she* was a child, you've
said, I might wear her if I could win her, when she grew up; but
there's no chance of it as long as that rattling fellow, Phil, with his
coaxing words, and his learning, and his fine clothes, is at her side;
and I just wanted to ask yer reverence if I might take upon me to
tell him to keep his distance, and then I should have some chance."

" Who are you speaking of, Brian?"

" Oh, ye know very well; who but my —— I wish ye'd marry
us out of hand, and let her be indeed, *my* dear little Dora. Sure
she could lead me with a halter o' snow."

" There are two words to that; or, indeed, I might say, but one,
and that's hers, for mine you have, and my heart along with it. As
to Philip, he is a wild, rattling boy, and a strange, but he would not
do an unhandsome turn for a king's ransom; only, to be sure, girls
do fancy odd chaps sometimes, and I'll just tell him my mind."

" For the love of God, leave me to do that, sir," said Brian,
earnestly; " don't meddle nor make with him; neither half nor
whole lawyers are good for much, and I'll speak to him myself."

" Well done, Brian, my boy!" replied Father Mike, laughing.
" So you think yourself more fit to deal with a bit of a lawyer—you,

who are only two-and-twenty—than an old, sober fellow, who has seen
summers threescore-and-two pass over his grey head. Ay, the old
story, youth and inexperience *versus* age and wisdom !" The priest
laughed again, and Brian, with a serious aspect, laid his hand on
the bridle-rein, and said :—

"Sir, there's more about that fellow than you believe. As I'm a
living soul, he meddles and makes with more than concerns him."

"There again, now !—ye think yerself sharper than me, just
because ye're a little jealous of Philip. Ah ! when I was young,
before I was priested, I was like you; but now—there's Philip, I
declare !—don't look so like a thunderstorm, Brian."

"I will see you to-night, sir, at eight, if you will be at home,"
replied the young man, hastily; "good-bye." He was going to cut
into a path which crossed some pasture-land, when Father Mike, in
an authoritative tone, ordered him to stop, and not to run as if "ould
Nick was at his heels." Accordingly, Brian met Phil with ill-
concealed dislike; while Philip smiled with gracious sweetness,
inquired kindly after Dora, and, with an unconstrained and even
careless manner, gave the "farewell kindly," and passed on.

"That fellow's a match for the 'devil and Lord Castlereagh,'"
muttered Brian ; "but for all that I'll be a match for *him*, clever as
he is. I'm just thinking, yer reverence," he commenced, after a
short pause, "that that chap's never without his fowling-piece lately ;
sure the sporting season's over."

"I'll tell ye what, Brian, I'll not listen to anything you have to
say in your present humour ; come over this evening, and we'll both
talk it out. There, don't torment me now with your nonsense ; go
your ways, and let me be at peace, though you can't be so yourself,
or I'll tell Dora what a discontented temper you possess." So
saying, the priest rode on, and, after the lapse of a few moments,
Brian proceeded homewards.

The evening advanced very slowly, in the lover's opinion ; and
when he left his office and arrived at Carrick, on his way to Father
Mike's, he found it was only five o'clock. Martin, whom he had
met, told him that Miss Dora was up the village, and he stationed
himself in the window of the publichouse, thinking she would pass
that way, and that he could walk home with her. At last a neighbour induced him to take one, only one, glass of whisky, "to keep
up his heart ;" and then, another prevailed on him to take part of a
tubler of "real Cork," that wouldn't hurt a new-born baby, and
was as mild as new milk ; and after that poor Brian needed no further
pressing. "Let the devil in, and he'll keep the castle ;" and so it
was. Glass succeeded glass, and at last, when Brian was more than
half tipsy, Philip Waddy entered. He appeared in high spirits, and
drew near the place where Brian and his friends were sitting. Brian

at first resolved to hold his peace, and keep his thoughts to himself, but some remarks that Waddy made annoyed him, and, with the restless feeling of drunkenness, he seemed anxious to engage in a quarrel. Philip, on the contrary, appeared wishful to avoid it; and their companions, Irish-like, always anxious for "a row," thought him by far too peaceable.

"Come, my boys," said Waddy, "I'll give ye something to drink upon; here goes! Oh! I bar water, it shall be the pure whisky; what, Brian!—you must drink it—fill, fill!"

"I won't," replied Brian. "I have just taken enough, and there is nothing, as Father Mike says, so much to be thought of in a young man as—sobriety."

A loud laugh followed this speech, and Philip continued:—

"Never mind—up, boys, that won't flinch from a glass, or the health of a pretty girl. Now, with three-times-three, as they used to say in our Dublin club—long life, health, and beauty for ever to Dora O'Hay!"

In an instant Brian sprang from his seat, his cheek flushing, while he hastily inquired, what right Phil Waddy had to name Dora O'Hay after that fashion?

"Now, Brian, my boy, keep cool; I suppose I've a right to name a girl I love, and one who I've positive proof doesn't hate me, when and where I please; so take it asy."

"Ye lie!" said Brian, fiercely; "ye've no proof that she loves ye—ye're a false liar!"

Phil was not brave, but he made a show of courage, advanced towards Brian with his fists clenched, and then backed, observing, "If ye weren't her cousin, by the powers I'd tear ye limb from limb!"

"I'll tell ye what, Phil Waddy, ye think yerself a gentleman; gentleman, indeed! the sweepings o' the gentry:—and ye think people are afraid of ye; but ye're mistaken; and I'll tell ye what ye are—and these honest men to the fore!—ye're no better than a well-dressed beggar; and when ye hear the dinner-bell ring at the grand houses, in ye go, and then set at the foot o' the table, and eat and drink what ye'd scorn to work for. But it's not the worst; I could say that of you, Phil Waddy, that would place ye as high as the gallows-top, if ye were as grand as Calclough, and make ye a thing that the crow and the raven would turn from, for sure natur would tell them that even yer corpse was poisoned with the badness o' yer shrivelled heart!—only mind the old vault in Dane's Castle, and who ye met there, and what ye said last Monday was a week! But never heed turning pale, I'd scorn to be an informer; only, as to Dora O'Hay, I warn ye—lave her; the vulture and the wood-quest 'ud be bad companions."

So saying, Brian strode out of the public-house, and Waddy made no attempt to follow. If Brian's threat had moved him, he concealed it effectually from his half-drunken companions, although some of them afterwards pretended to remember, when the occurrences of that evening were referred to, that Waddy's eyes glared fearfully, and that his lips quivered. Again they drank of the liquid fire, and none of the party were able to call to mind at what hour, exactly, Waddy departed; long, certainly, he did not remain. The snow was falling thickly around him, but it had not obliterated the footmarks of one who wended a somewhat unsteady pace towards the priest's dwelling on the hill. Near the village there were many prints on the whitened surface; but, as the lights twinkled more faintly in the cottage windows, there was but one track distinguishable by the light of a moon somewhat obscured by white but opaque clouds. Waddy kept on the trail like a bloodhound; his gun was slung across his shoulder, and in his right hand he carried a stout stick; the shadow of a huge blackthorn tree crossed his path; he stopped, sprang amid its branches, and bore down a thick and knotted bough; hastily, he tore off the slighter twigs, and, flinging his former staff over the hedge, firmly grasped the one he had just gathered. The next shadow he perceived was moving onwards, and his speed increased—as he thought to himself—"I was right; I knew there was some one in the under-vault; and, from its size, there could have been but *one!*"—and the murmur of a low, but fiend-like laugh mingled with the whistling wind: and then he thought, "Fool, fool, fool, not to keep his own counsel!" Brian heard not the footstep—it fell lightly—his thoughts were with Dora; they were seated, in fancy, at the priest's cheerful fire, and he almost imagined he could hear the soft music of her evening song, at the very moment when the murderous club was raised for his destruction; hard, hard it fell, and the heart was aroused from its trance, and the body was grovelling in the snow; harder, and yet more hard; and then the crackling sound of the crushed skull-bones, and the warm oozing and outpouring of the red blood on the fair white robe that covered the earth! Then, as the murderer, like a second Cain, stood over the prostrate dead, came the hasty trampling of a horse, and Father Mike issued from a grove of tall fir-trees that joined the road, and scowled on the black deed—the first within man's memory that had ever been perpetrated there. In an instant, before Waddy could move hand or foot, the priest sprang off his horse, and grappled with him; the moon shone brightly forth, as if to show the unequal struggle, for the aged man was overpowered, and his throat was pressed, for a time, almost to suffocation: the fiend, however, relaxed his hold, and spoke:

"You are there, and you see what I have done. Why ain't ye pass on, or what devil brought ye to yer own death? No—near me out; stir hand or foot, and this ends ye!" and he drew a pistol from his bosom. "Ah, ah! I'm not priest-ridden, and think as little of one sort of earth as of another. Only look ye, Father Mike, in Counsellor Finlon's desk (and a superstitious old dog he was), were the papers that, if shown would have hung you out and out, many's the day ago; you know for what—for in yer young days ye were bitter enough against government. Well, it's good to have more pocket pistols than one; so I took them, and a few others that might stand me at a pinch, and would never be missed now, as the matter's as good as forgotten; and so ye see, holy father, you tell, and hang me; and I tell, and hang you! It 'ud be easier to settle ye here, but I don't care to do that; so if you'll let me alone, I'll let you alone: there, jog off; but mark—there are those in the next barony that, if a finger is raised against me, don't care a traneen for priests, bishops, cardinals, or pope. Never mind—no nostrum of yours can make that feel again!"—and he pushed his foot against the stiffening body of poor Brian, over which Father Mike had stooped—" so much for your immortality!"

The murderer did not utter another word, but turned into the little wood that skirted the road.

Father Mike deliberately mounted his horse, and paced slowly homeward; the horrid events that pressed upon his brain almost deprived him of reason. Brian dead—Waddy, the murderer—the struggle—the papers. He writhed under the powerful coil of the serpent he had fostered and befriended. In this state of mental wretchedness, uncertain how to act, he arrived at his house.

Let us leave this fearful incident of our tale for a while, to relate a few of the circumstances that led to the dreadful occurrence which, for the first time within the memory of man, had laid an indelible stain on the parish of Bannow.

The fact was, before the Irish reign of terror of 1798, Father Mike, like many of the Romish clergy, had entered into a clandestine correspondence with foreign powers; this had been suspected, and after the rebellion he was arraigned on the charge of high treason. Proof, however, was wanting; and it was believed that Counsellor Finlon, who conducted the prosecution, had been induced to suppress the principal evidence against him; this, however, was merely suspicion. Father Mike was acquitted, returned to his parish much wiser than he had left it, and afterwards showed his good sense by never meddling with politics; and, as party feeling died away, the charge was almost forgotten.

It has been seen that poor Brian was justified in thinking so ill of

Q

Waddy; but he was most imprudent in applying his information as he did. The horror which the lower and middling class of Irish have of delivering any one up to the violated laws of their country, is a fearful source of evil; indeed, in the most civilized parts of the island, this feeling still exists. An old ruin, called Dane's Castle, was on the estate of a gentleman in the neighbourhood, and, as it was crumbling fast to decay, he wished to have it pulled down. Brian, who, in his capacity of surveyor—architect, or more properly speaking a country union of both, had been engaged to build and repair some offices about his house—was directed to examine the stones of the castle, and inform him if they could be usefully employed in the new building. The relic of olden times was far from any dwelling, and even the few cattle that used to shelter beneath its walls had lately deserted it. Some scattered brushwood grew around it, and the strong ivy might be said to repay its former support by keeping the mouldering fragments together. Evening was closing when Brian went to inspect it; he thought it almost too late to observe the ruin distinctly, but then it was a " good step to go and come ;" and, after examining the outer stones, he descended into a little cell, or cave, which, tradition said, had been the abode of a pious monk many centuries ago ; the grey twilight stole trem-blingly through the various apertures in the decayed wall and stony ceiling, and the surveyor was on the point of clambering up, when Waddy's voice struck upon his ear; he could not be said to suspect anything, yet he stood motionless, and heard him in earnest conver-sation with a stranger, one not of the province of Leinster.

"They can't have got scent of me," said Philip, " it's morally impossible; however, it 'll be a lesson to the rest not to be lettin' their land to new tenants."

"I think," replied the other, "we could have warned them off, only ye advised the burnin'; and to be sure there was nothin' else for it, when once the robbery was finished, for they all knew us. How were ye ever back in time ?"

" Oh, the mare's worth a million !—she's prime. 'Tisn't the first time, nor won't be the last, I made my neighbour's horse do the turn : and the best of it is, when Sam Cornish found her warm in the mornin', he sets off to the wise man for a charm; and there's a horse-shoe nailed to the door ; for he swears the fairies are after Black Bess !"

" Well, Phil, ye're strong and hearty. I own the job was almost too much for me : I can't bear finishing the innocent women and childer."

"Oh, I thought ye'd better sense than that ! Sure it puts 'em out of pain. But what I wanted to say most to you is, how we're to manage when this place comes down—(there 'ud be fine pickings in the house that owns it, but I'll have no hand in anything so near home); you know this is a very convenient place to stow any little thing the Roving Jenny puts in, till we send it off. Bridge's chamber's too exposed; this is far from the sea, to be sure, yet it is lonely:—however, we'll talk more about it; there's nothing hid away now, and that sop of a fellow, Brian, 'll be looking here for the sake of the stones, to-morrow, I suppose. However, you step to the Public, and hear the news—they're almost tired of talking of the burning in the county Waterford."

Even when the echo of their footsteps died away, Brian could hardly believe the reality of what he had heard, and he resolved to keep it to himself until a fit opportunity occurred of mentioning it to his father confessor, and asking his advice. His imprudence at the public-house cost him his life, for Philip was assured that he knew his secret.

When Father Mike returned to his home, after the dreadful scene he had witnessed, he was followed in the distance by the murderer, who, although he thought the priest sufficiently in his power, feared that something might induce him to deliver him up to justice. The glimmering light from the kitchen-window attracted his attention, and he carefully watched the movements within, until the moment when Father Mike was about to speak of him in the presence of Dora. He remained outside the house, like a prowling wolf, after the shutter had been fastened, and at length saw a single ray stream from Dora's window; the demoniac thought flashed across his brain that, if he could speak to the innocent and affectionate girl, he might win her to his purpose, and thus have a double hold on the priest. The window almost rested on the top of a sloping roof, and was easy of access; he crept up the thatch, and through the uncurtained lattice saw Dora sitting on the side of her small, low bed, her head resting on her hand, her whole appearance betokening much and bitter sorrow. He tapped at the window, and she looked towards it, but with a bewildered ken, as if she hardly comprehended what it meant.

"Dora, dear Dora, hush! Sure ye know me, love? I just want to speak one word to you; there, don't be frightened—why should ye?—just open the window for one little minute."

Dora moved towards it, her whole frame violently agitated; she tried to speak, but the words died on her lip, and she motioned him to begone.

"No, love, no; not till ye have heard me. Sure I'm your sweetheart, and will be your husband in spite of them all; and now every one's asleep, there's no harm in your speaking to one you love."

She drew still nearer the window, but utterance was denied her, and again she moved her hand for him to depart.

"Undo the fastening, love," he repeated; but still she motioned him away. "Then," said he, "as I must speak to you, you force me to this!" and, urged by every bad and unmanly passion, he, by one strong effort, burst open the casement. Dora gave a faint scream, and fell on the floor; he was in the act of entering, when little Martin appeared at the chamber-door, and presented to his breast a double-barrelled gun that was nearly as long as the room.

"I ax yer pardon, Mister Phil; but I can't help it; it comes quite natural-like to purtect a woman; and I'll just take lave to say that ye choose a mighty quare time for visiting, particular whin there's no one to resave ye—for Miss there looks as dead as a door-nail. Hulloo—hulloo—hulloo—oo—o! all o' ye!" and he sung out a tally-ho. "Here's housebreaking, and fire, and Miss Dory dead! —If ye stir hand or fut, Misther Phil (I'm heart-sorry for ye, but it's thrue as that I'm little Martin)—if ye stir hand or fut, ye're gone—gone, hot-trot to the devil!"

At this moment Father Mike rushed into the apartment; enraged at seeing his niece, to all appearance dead on the floor, and Waddy half in at the window, forgetful of all circumstances connected with himself, he articulated, in a voice rendered hoarse by violent feeling— "Seize—seize him, Martin!—*he is a murderer!*" By this time Dick, and another "working-boy," who lived in the house, had entered; —the wretched man made an effort to escape, by drawing back from the window. Martin, however, resolved he should not get off so easily, and discharged his gun; the fire took effect, and Philip rolled off the building over which he had climbed, but a few minutes before, in perfect strength and fiend-like vigour.

Martin looked out of the window after him, and quietly said, "He's only a taste hurt—not kilt outright: we'll step down and pick him up, and then yer reverence 'll tell us what to do wid him; there, Miss Dora's a-coming to herself, the darlint! God presarves his own!"

On examination, Philip was discovered to have been badly wounded in the shoulder; he would not suffer any dressing to be applied, but sat the picture of sullen crime and obstinacy, in the kitchen, which filled by degrees with the neighbouring peasantry. He neither spoke nor moved; when the priest addressed him he smiled—such a smile!—not like those of other days.

It may be here necessary to state that when Father Mike left his niece in her little chamber he went to the ladder-stair which led to Martin's dormitory, and called to him to arise. In a moment Martin was with his master, and the priest hastily told him that murder had

been committed in the neighbourhood—that as he was coming home
he had witnessed it, at the same time carefully concealing that
Waddy was the perpetrator of so foul a deed; he directed him to
arouse the farming boys, and bring the body to the house. Martin
obeyed, wisely thinking that he ought to take the gun, and while
in the act of loading it Dora's faint scream broke upon his ear.

When the bustle had subsided a little, the two young men, accompanied by three or four of the peasants, went to seek for the
body of poor Brian. Martin alone remained, his long gun resting
on his knees, and his eye steadily fixed on Philip.

The remains of the murdered youth were brought in. As they
passed Waddy many believed they bled afresh; he started from his
seat, and one thrill of human feeling seemed to rush through his
frame. He gazed for an instant, and then covered his face with his
hands. They laid the corpse on the long table, where, not two hours
before, the priest's supper had rested; and deep groans and bitter
sobs echoed through the humble room. The murderer sat apart, his
wound still bleeding, while all looked upon him as a being accursed.

The early morning saw the culprit in the hands of justice. When
he was led forth, manacled, to the car that was to convey him to
Wexford jail, he turned to Father Mike, and, showing his wrists,
said, in a deep under-tone, "This is the liberty you promised!"

"I—I——" replied the priest, "I promised you no liberty. I
confess I deserved what followed. You intimidated me by your
threat, at the very moment when self ought to have been a secondary
consideration; but God is wise—he would not suffer the murderer
to escape, and I am punished for my weakness. But you must have
been worse than devil, at such a moment, to think of harming that
spotless child; repent, there is yet time—repent; although there
can be no deeper hell than your own heart!"

He answered not; the car and escort pursued their way amid the
execrations of the peasantry.

The wake took place as usual, and great was the assemblage, but
the untimely death of the young man shed a gloom over it which
neither "tay, whisky, snuff, nor tobacco" could dissipate. The best
"keeners" were collected, but their hired cries were not heeded.
Many sincere tears were shed for poor Brian, and his good qualities
were amply praised. "Och, sorra o' my heart!" sobbed out Molly,
"to think the beautiful corpse he'd ha' made if he'd been let alone!"

"Is that yer trouble?" replied Martin, who was engaged in
making a "cauldron" of hot whisky-punch: "why then, Molly—
only ye haven't much mother-wit to yer own share—I think it's a
different thing to that ye ought to say."

"What 'ud you say, wise man Martin?" inquired one of the
company.

" Why, thin, I'd jist say, that it's not much matter how a corpse looks, so what was once inside was beautiful and in the thrue way."

Towards morning, when the principal number of people had departed, and only six or eight aged women remained in the apartment with the body, Dora Hay opened the chamber-door to ascertain that all was quiet, and, throwing the coverlet over her as a mantle, descended to the "wake-room." Her mind had been shaken, yet at that moment her purpose was nerved for temporary exertion, and she clearly comprehended what she was about to undertake. When she opened the door her ghastly and unexpected appearance terrified the women, and they crowded together. She advanced to the table on which the corpse lay, fully dressed, according to the custom of the country. The mangled head was covered, and she did not attempt to disturb the cloth, but took one of the hands in hers. She recoiled from the first touch, and the icy chill of death appeared to have been communicated to her. For some moments she stood motionless as chiselled marble ; again she took the hand, and, slowly bending on her knees, just touched it with her lips ; she continued keeling for about five minutes, with head elevated, and lips moving as if in prayer, but no sound escaped them. Slowly she crossed herself, and pressing the little crucifix, that was suspended from her neck, to her heart, with the same quiet step returned to her apartment.

The funeral was not only numerously but respectably attended, for rich and poor lamented Brian's untimely end; and I have before said that Father Mike was universally esteemed.

There was an old miserable-looking hag that resided over the Scar (an inlet of the sea that separates Bannow from an adjoining parish), and near the ruins of the Seven Castles of Clonmines. This wretched object, had she lived a hundred years ago, would most certainly have been burned as a witch ; as it was, she was regarded both with dislike and terror by old and young. Squalid in her appearance, her rags fluttering in every passing blast, she sat during the funeral on one of the high tombstones that "mark the lowly dead." As the crowd passed from the churchyard, she singled out Martin, and beckoned him to her. Martin was not at all flattered by the distinction, but too superstitious not to attend her command, immediately obeyed.

" God save ye kindly, Mrs. Madge !—I'm glad to see ye."

" That's a lie, Martin Finchley, and ye know it is ; there's no one glad to see me—no one cares if the earth opened and swallowed ould Madge ! But that's not what I wanted to spake about. Man alive !—if indeed ye be a man—don't stand cronauning there, but come close—closer to me !" And she stretched forth her bare, bony arm, and grasping little Martin's shoulder with her long, claw-like fingers, drew him towards her, as a cat pulls out a mouse to execution. "Ye know the Seven Castles o' Clonmines; well, the one next the wather, where there are such broad, flat stones, ye'll see one bigger nor the rest; there, under that you will find what consarns Father Mike 'bove the world, if ye'll take the trouble to find it. It's for the sake of the dark-eyed girl, that's often done me a kind turn, though she's not long for this world, for her yarn is spun. There, go yer ways; only, hark ye, mind whin ye go to the place, or, may-be, ye'll meet with more company than ye'd bargain for."

Martin loved his master too well not to risk even his life for him if it were necessary, but he felt delighted when he was fairly out of Mag's sight. Perfectly unconscious of what could "consarn Father Mike 'bove the world," he concealed himself among the ruins of Clonmines until the evening closed; he then removed the large flat stone she had described, and dug like a rabbit for some time amongst the rubbish before he discovered anything. At last he found a small bundle of papers, tied with red tape, and then a small parcel. He was proceeding in his search when he thought he heard a rustling on the pebbly shore, as if some one was approaching, and, securing what he had found, he hastily got behind a projecting buttress of one of the castles. His conjectures were right, for a man immediately turned the corner of a little bay, and proceeded direct to the flat stone, which Martin had not time to replace. The Irish dumb show is very expressive, and the gestures of the disappointed seeker were strongly indicative of rage and disappointment. The man at last went away, and Martin, who, to use his own expression, had "lain snug," proceeded home with his prize. Arrived at Father Mike's, he waited quietly in the chimney-corner until the priest was disengaged, and then went into the little parlour, and, locking the door, crept round the room, spying and peeping about, as if the wall had ears. The priest, accustomed to Martin's eccentricities, did not pay much attention to his movements, for, truth to say, he was discussing his tumbler of whisky-punch—it was not as palatable as usual, for Dora had not compounded it. Martin at last approached the great chair, and gently pulled the sleeve of his coat; Father Mike turned round, and awaited an explanation. Martin presented the packet.

Father Mike put on his spectacles, untied the fastening, and, to his no small astonishment, found various memoranda concerning circumstances long past, which at once convinced him that he had actually in his possession the papers to which the villain Waddy had alluded. The parcel contained also a few small articles of plate, and some letters that mysteriously alluded to dark and bloody deeds which either had been, or were to be, perpetrated. Martin detailed, in his own way, the manner in which he obtained them, and Father

Mike had no doubt that they were to have been made use of to his injury by some of Waddy's associates.

Every effort was made to induce Waddy to disclose his crimes, but in vain. He remained cool and collected; civil, but sarcastic, to those who approached him; and appeared to summon all his faculties for the purpose of banishing every relic of human feeling from his breast. When his mother visited his cell he received her kindly, but betrayed no emotion, although she wept upon his shoulder until the fountain of her tears seemed dried up.

As the assizes drew near rumour became more busy than ever, and crimes were imputed to the wretched man of which it is more than probable he had never been guilty. The day of trial came, and Father Mike was summoned to give evidence against the murderer, who had refused all spiritual aid, and would converse neither with priest nor minister.

The crowd assembled outside the court-house of the county town was greater than had ever been collected on any former occasion. In Ireland the feelings of the lower order of people are usually enlisted in favour of a prisoner, for they appear to think that all who come under the arm of the law are victims. But it was not so in Waddy's case; he had murdered the kinsman of a priest, and had attempted to violate the sanctity of a priest's house, which is considered as holy as the altar; the bitterest execrations were, therefore, uttered against him.

Father Mike was making his way through the motley throng, when a low murmuring growl ran along the people, and various exclamations of "Oh, the murdering reprobate!" "Oh, to think of it!" "Oh, it is impossible he could be guilty of it!" struck upon the priest's ear, and he soon learnt that Waddy had anticipated the sentence of the law, and strangled himself in prison.

*   *   *   *   *   *   *

The spring had passed, and the summer—the sunny summer—was nearly at its height, when the priest one evening entered his little parlour, and called his niece to him. She was engaged at her wheel, the only employment to which she attended; it appeared to give her occupation without the effort of thinking, and she turned it mechanically from morning until night.

"Dora," said the kind old man, as she entered, "Dora, will you take a walk to the village, or up the hill?—you have not been out since Sunday."

"Yes, uncle."

"Dora, stay one moment: do not break my heart; it is old now, and has known much sorrow—much sorrow have I known in this world, Dora; but, child, the bitterest of all my afflictions would be to

see you—you, whom my heart so joyed in—pine away, and leave me.
And oh !" continued the weeping old man, as he fell upon his knees,
"oh ! with more than enough—with plenty, plenty to my portion, of
this world's good—oh, Heavenly Father! hast thou willed that I, an
old, grey, time-worn man, should outlive all that are dear to me, and
that strangers should close my eyes ?"

Dora also knelt, calmly and deliberately, by her uncle, and looked
steadily in his face. He was much agitated; and there was something about her countenance that betokened returning feeling and
interest.

"Sure, Dora," he proceeded after a pause, "sure you can un-
burthen your mind to me ! Even your duties to God have all been
neglected—you have not been to the confessional since——"

"Stop, stop ! I well remember since when," she interrupted, hastily
—"too well ! I have been wrong, I know ; but all in this world has
appeared to me so changing, so wicked, so uncertain ! May-be, dear
uncle, my head has not been right—everything seems changed."

"Am I changed, Dory ?"

"Oh, no, no, no !"—and tears, that sweet relief to the overcharged
bosom, gushed from her eyes, as she threw her arms, with the affection of former days, round her uncle's neck. "I have not cried this
long, long time ; and now I am better—my head is not so heavy—and
I will tell you now, dear uncle, all that has passed in my mind. Brian
—poor Brian !—I did not think of him as he thought of me ; and the
black wickedness of that bad man, whose smile wiled away my thoughts!
—but when I saw Brian's corpse, I knelt, and made a vow that I
would go into a convent, and lead a holy life, for his sake whom I did
not value as I ought. Uncle dear, I am not what I was, and every
day that delays me from a holy life, adds to the sin of a broken
oath."

The poor priest was bewildered—almost distracted ; to yield up,
even to the church, the fair girl whom he had expected to be the
blessing of his old age, was a trial for which he was unprepared, and
which he had not strength to meet. It was some time before he
spoke, and his words were then scarcely articulate.

"Dear Dora, I am punished ! I gave you the love that belonged
to the Almighty ; and now you leave me in age and helplessness."

The next morning, Father Mike mounted his faithful steed, and, at
an early hour, was on the high road to his bishop's house, having
resolved to tell him the whole story, and to act according to his advice.
The bishop felt much for his old friend, and observed, that Dora could
easily be absolved from her oath, by the church. But her uncle knew
that she would persevere, with a sort of insanity, in her determination
so to devote herself. Nevertheless, the bishop thought he would

converse with her, and see if any plan could be arranged that might render Father Mike and his niece at peace in their once happy home. He accompanied the priest to his dwelling, and felt convinced, after a brief conversation with Dora, that her mind had become weak and wandering; however, he succeeded in persuading her that she could perform her vow, and still remain with her uncle, as " it was not likely he could live long."

" My dear child," said the bishop, " it would be almost killing him if you were to leave him now; but put on the dress of the holy Ursulines—the order of which you intend to become, I hope, a worthy member—perform its penances and prayers, and keep apart from the world in your uncle's house : you will make him happy; and be a blessing to that good man, whose hairs would go down with sorrow to the grave, if you deserted him in his old age."

Dora has now been some years truly a " blessing" to her uncle and the neighbouring poor; but it is difficult to determine whether or not her intellects are gaining strength, as she holds no converse with any one except Father Mike. She passes from cottage to cottage, the ministering angel of peace to the afflicted : neither joy, nor, it would seem, sorrow, have marked her pale, marble-like countenance ; and little Martin, who wears like a Turkey carpet, often observes, as she passes, with slow but noiseless step, along the old kitchen—

" To think of that banshee-looking cratur being the dancing singing fairy—light of eye—light of foot—light of heart—until that horrid night of blood and sin that brought desolation even to the house of FATHER MIKE !"

LARRY MOORE.

THINK of to-morrow!"—that is what few Irish peasants ever do, with a view of providing for it: at least few with whom I have had opportunities of being acquainted. They will think of anything—of everything, but that. There is Larry Moore, for example:—who, that has ever visited my own pastoral village of Bannow, is unacquainted with Larry, the Bannow boatman—the invaluable Larry—who, tipsy or sober, asleep or awake, rows his boat with undeviating power and precision?—He, alas! is a strong proof of the truth of my observation. Look at him on a fine sunny day in June. The cliffs that skirt the shore, where his boat is moored, are crowned with wild furze; while here and there, a tuft of white or yellow broom, sprouting a little above the bluish green of its prickly neighbour, waves its blossoms, and flings its fragrance to the passing breeze. Down to the very edge of the rippling waves is almost one unbroken bed of purple

thyme, glowing and beautiful;—and there Larry's goat, with her
two sportive kids—sly, cunning rogues !—find rich pasture—now
nibbling the broom-blossoms, now sporting amid the furze, and making
the scenery re-echo with their musical bleating.   The little island
opposite, Larry considers his own particular property; not that a
single sod of its bright greenery belongs to him—but, to use his own
words "Sure it's all as one my own—don't I see it—don't I walk
upon it—and the very water that it's set in is my own; for sorra a
one can put *foot* on it widout me and ' the coble,' that have been hand
and glove as good as forty years."   But look, I pray you, upon
Larry :—there he lies stretched in the sunlight, at full length, on the
firm sand, like a man-porpoise—sometimes on his back—then slowly
turning on his side—but his most usual attitude is a sort of reclining
position against that flat grey stone, just at high-water mark; he
selects it as his constant resting-place, because (again to use his own
words) "the tide, bad cess to it, was apt to come fast in upon a body,
and there was a dale of throuble in moving; but even if one chanced
to fall asleep, sorra a morsel of harm the salt water could do ye on
the grey stone, where a living merwoman sat every new-year's night
combing her black hair, and making beautiful music to the wild
waves, who, consequently, trated her sate wid grate respict—why
nct ?"   There, then, is Larry—his chest leaning on the mermaid's
stone, as we call it—his long, bare legs stretched out behind, kicking,
occasionally, as a gad-fly or merry-hopper skips about what it naturally
considers lawful prey :—his lower garments have evidently once been
trowsers—blue trowsers; but as Larry, when in motion, is amphibious,
they have experienced the decaying effects of salt water, and now
only descend to the knee, where they terminate in unequal fringes.
Indeed, his frieze jacket is no great things, being much rubbed at the
elbows—and no wonder; for Larry, when awake, is ever employed,
either in pelting the sea-gulls (who, to confess the truth, treat him
with very little respect), rowing his boat, or watching the circles
formed on the surface of the calm waters by the large or small pebbles
he throws into it; and as Larry, of course, rests his elbow on the
rocks, while performing these exploits, the sleeves must wear, for
frieze is not "impenetrable stuff."   His hat is a natural curiosity,
composed of sun-burned straw, banded by a misshapen sea-ribbon, and
garnished by "delisk," red and green, his "cutty pipe" stuck through
a slit in the brim, which bends it directly over the left eye, and keeps
it "quite handy widout any trouble."   His bushy, reddish hair persists in obstinately pushing its way out of every hole in his extraordinary hat, or clusters strangely over his Herculean shoulders, and
a low-furrowed brow, very unpromising to the eye of the phrenologist :
—in truth, Larry has somewhat of a dogged expression of counte-

nance, which is relieved, at times, by the humorous twinkle of his
little grey eyes, pretty much in the manner that a star or two illume
the dreary blank of a cloudy November night. The most conspicuous
part of his attire, however, is an undressed wide leather belt, that
passes over one shoulder and then under another strap of the same
material that encircles his waist; from this depends a rough wooden
case, containing his whisky bottle; a long, narrow knife; pieces of
rope, of varied length and thickness; and a pouch which contains the
money he earns at his " vocation."

Our portrait of him is sketched on the beach directly under the
old churchyard of Bannow—upon the roof of one of the houses, it
may be, for scores of them are buried beneath the sand; and the
chimney of the ancient town-hall still exists a mass of coarse mason-
work among the graves. The surrounding scenery is more interesting, perhaps, than beautiful; though, to me, there is the beauty of
association in every object within ken. But the curiosity, even of a
stranger, may be excited by the distant promontory of Bag-an-bun,
where—

> "Irelonde was lost and won,"

seen to great advantage from this particular spot. We may not
moralize, however; our intention is to converse with Larry.

" Good morrow, Larry !"

" Good morrow kindly, my lady! may-be ye're going across ?"

" No, thank ye, Larry,—but there's a silver sixpence for good luck."

" Ough! God's blessing be about ye!—I said so to my woman this
morning, and she bothering the sowl out o' me for money, as if I
could make myself into silver, let alone brass:—asy, says I, what
trouble ye take! sure we had a good dinner yesterday; and more by
tokens, the grawls were so plased wid the mate—the craturs!—sorra
a morsel o' pratee they'd put into their mouths;—and we'll have as
good a one to-day."

" The ferry is absolutely filled with fish, Larry, if you would only
take the trouble to catch it."

" Is it fish? Ough! sorra fancy I have for fasting-mate—besides,
it's mighty watery, and a dale of trouble to catch. A grate baste of
a cod lept into my boat yesterday, and I lying just here, and the boat
close up; I thought it would ha' sted asy while I hollooed to Tom,
who was near breaking his neck after the samphire for the quality,
the gomersal!—but, my jewil! it was whip and away wid it all in a
minit—back to the water.—Small loss!"

" But, Larry, it would have made an excellent dinner."

" Sure I'm after telling yer ladyship that we had a rale mate dinner,
by grate good luck, yesterday."

" But to-day, by your own confession, you had nothing."

" Sure you've just given me sixpence."

" But suppose I had not ?"

" Where's the good of thinking that, now ?"

" Oh, Larry, I'm afraid you never think of *to-morrow !*"

" There's not a man in the whole parish of Bannow thinks more of it than I do," responded Larry, raising himself up; " and, to prove it to ye, madam dear, we'll have a wet night—I see the sign of it, for all the sun's so bright, both in the air and the water."

" Then, Larry, take my advice; go home and mend the great hole that is in the thatch of your cabin."

" Is it the hole ?—where's the good of losing time about it now, when the weather's so fine ?"

" But when the rain comes ?"

" Lord bless ye, my lady ! sure I can't hinder the rain ! and sure it's fitter for me to stand under the roof in a dry spot, than to go out in the *teams* to stop up a taste of a hole. Sorra a drop comes through it in *dry weather.*"

" Larry, you truly need not waste so much time; it is ten chances to one if you get a single fare to-day;—and here you stay doing nothing. You might usefully employ yourself, by a little foresight."

" Would ye have me desert my trust ? Sure I must mind the boat. But, God bless ye, ma'am darlint! don't be so hard intirely upon me; for I get a dale o' blame I don't by no manner of means desarve. My wife turns at me as wicked as a weazel, becase I gave my consint to our Nancy's marrying Matty Keogh ; and she says they were bad to come together, on account that they hadn't enough to pay the priest; and the end of it is, that the girl and a grandchild are come back upon us; and the husband is off—God knows where !"

" I'm sorry to hear that, Larry ; but your son James, by this time, must be able to assist you."

" There it is again, my lady ! James was never very bright—and his mother was always at him, plaguing his life out to go to Mister Ben's school, and saying a dale about the time to come; but I didn't care to bother the cratur; and I'm sorry to say he's turned out rather obstinate—and even the priest says it's becase I never think of *to-morrow.*"

" I am glad to find the priest is of my opinion : but, tell me, have you fatted the pig Mr. Herriott gave you ?"

" Oh ! my bitter curse (axing yer pardon, my lady) be upon all the pigs in and out of Ireland ! That pig has been the ruin of me ; it has such a taste for eating young ducks as never was in the world ; and I always tether him by the leg when I'm going out; but he's so 'cute now, he cuts the tether."

"Why not confine him in a sty?—you are close to the quarry, and could build one in half an hour."

"Is it a sty for the likes of him! cock him up wid a sty! Och, Musha! Musha! the tether keeps him asy for the day."

"But not for the *morrow*, Larry."

"Now ye're at me agin!—you that always stood my friend. Meal-a-murder! if there isn't Rashleigh Jones making signs for the boat! Oh! ye're in a hurry, are ye?—well, ye must wait till yer hurry is over; I'm not going to hurry myself, wid sixpence in my pocket, for priest or minister."

"But the more you earn the better, Larry."

"Sure I've enough for to-day."

"But not for *to-morrow*, Larry."

"True for ye, ma'am dear; though people take a dale o' trouble, I'm thinking, when they've full and plenty at the same time; and I don't like bothering about it then. Sure, I see ye plain enough, Master Rashleigh. God help me! I broke the oar yesterday, and never thought to get it mended; and my head's splitting open with the pain—I took a drop too much last night, that makes me fit for nothing——"

"On the *morrow*, Larry."

"Faith! ma'am dear, you're too bad. Oh dear! if I had the sense to set the lobster-pots last night, what a power I'd ha' caught!—they're dancing the bays merrily down there, the cowardly black-guards! but I didn't think——"

"Of the *morrow*, Larry."

"Oh, then, let me alone, lady dear! What will I do wid the oar! Jim Connor gave me a beautiful piece of strong rope yesterday, but I didn't want it; and—I believe one of the childer got hold of it—I didn't think——"

"Of the *morrow*, Larry."

"By dad, I have it!—I can poke the coble on with this ould pitch-fork; there's not much good in it; but, never heed—it's the master's, and he's too much of a jentleman to mind trifles; though I'm thinking times a'n't as good wid him now as they used to be; for Barney Clarey tould Nelly Parrell, who tould Tom Lavrey, who tould it out forenint me, and a dale more genteel men, who were taking a drop o' comfort at St. Patrick's, as how they bottle the whisky, and salt the mate, at the big house; and if that isn't a bad sign, I don't know what is;—though we may thank the English housekeeper for it, I'm thinking—wid her beaver bonnet, and her yellow silk shawl, that my wife (who knows the differ) says, after all, is only calico-cotton."

"What do you mean by bottling the whisky and salting the meat, Larry?"

"Now, don't be coming over us after that fashion; may-be ye don't know, indeed? Sure the right way, my lady, is to have the whisky on draught! and then it's so refreshing, of a hot summer's day to take a good hearty swig; and in winter—by the powers! ma'am, honey, let me just take the liberty of advising you never to desart the whisky; it 'll always keep the could out of yer heart, and the trouble from yer eye. Sure the clargy take to it, and lawyers take to it, far before new milk; and his holiness the pope—God bless him!—to say nothing of the king, who drinks nothing but Innishown. It's next to a deadly sin to bottle whisky in a jentleman's house;—and, as to salting mate;—sure the ould ancient Irish fashion—the fashion of the good ould times—is just to kill the baste, and thin hang it by the legs in a convanient place; and every one can take a part of what they like best.'

"But do you know that the English think of *to-morrow*, Larry?"

"Ay, the tame negres! that's the way they get rich, and sniff at the world, my jewil; and they no oulder in it than Henry the Second; for sure, if there had been English before his time, it's long sorry they'd ha' been to let Ireland so long alone."

"Do you think so, indeed, Larry?"

"I'll prove it to you, my lady, if ye'll jist wait till I bring over that impatient chap, Rashleigh Jones, who's ever running after the day, as if he hadn't a bit to eat :—there, d'ye see him ?—he's dancing mad—he may just as well take it asy. It's such as him give people the feaver. There's that devil of a goat grinning at me; sorra a drop of milk can we get from her, for she won't stand quiet for a body to catch her; and my wife's not able, and I'm not willing, to go capering over the cliffs. Never mind!"

At last Larry and his boat are off, by the assistance of the pitchfork, and most certainly he does not hurry himself; but where is Rashleigh going to? As I live! he has got into Mr. Dorkin's pleasure-boat, that has just turned the corner of the island, and will be at this side before Larry gets to the other. Larry will not easily pardon this encroachment; not because of the money, but because of his privilege. I have heard it rumoured that, if Larry does not become more active, he will lose his situation; but I cannot believe it: he is, when fairly on the water, the most careful boatman in the county; and permit me to mention, in *sotto voce*, that his master could not possibly dismiss him on the charge of heedlessness, because he himself once possessed *unencumbered* property by flood and field, wooded hills, verdant vales, and pure gushing rivers. Those fair heritages are, however, passing into the hands of other proprietors; and the hair of the generous, good-natured landlord has become white, and sorrow has furrowed his brow, long before sixty summers have glowed upon his head. His children, too, do not hold that station in society to which their birth entitles them; and, latterly, he has not been so often on the grand jury, nor at the new member's dinners. The poor love him as well as ever; but the rich have neglected, in a great degree, his always hospitable board. In short, changes have come, and others still more sad are looming in the future: there are signs not to be mistaken, that "he and his" are destined to encounter much of the misery that inevitably arises from want of forethought—that terrible evil which if it be not a vice, very generally leads to it. The parish priest told me, in confidence, that all the change originated in our excellent friend's never thinking of TO-MORROW.

KELLY THE PIPER.

"JUDY—Judy Kelly—Judy!—will ye give us no breakfast to-day
—and the sun splitting the trees these two hours?—and the
pig itself—the cratur—skreetching alive wid the hunger?"

"Och, it's true for ye, Mick, honey!—true for ye—and the pratees
are almost done—and yon's Ellen. She carries the pitcher so lightly,
that it's little milk she's got from the big house, this fine harvest
morning."

And Mistress Kelly "hourisht" the pig out of the cabin—placed
three noggins on an old table that she pulled from a dark corner
(there was but one window in the room, and that was stuffed with the
piper's coat, in lieu of glass), wiped the aforesaid table with the
corner of her "praskeen," and, from another corner, lifted the kish,
that served to wash, strain, and "dish" the potatoes, feed the pig, or
rock the child, as occasion might require.

Judy Kelly was certainly one of the worst specimens of an Irish

woman I had ever the duty of inspecting. She never washed her
face except on Sundays; and then it always gave her so bad a cold in
her head—on account (to use her own words) "of the tinderness of
her skin"—that she was obliged to cure it with liberal draughts of
whisky—the effects of which rendered Judy (at other times a peaceable woman) the veriest scold in Bannow. Poor Kelly always anticipated this storm, and on Sunday evenings mounted his miserable
donkey—miscalled Dumpling (a name, however, which might have
been appropriate before he took service with his present master),
and, with pipes under arm, posted to St. Patrick—the most respectable "sheebeen shop" on the moor—and finished the night, sometimes with a comfortable nap by the road-side, or on a sand-bank.
The most delightful sleep he ever had was one night when Dumpling,
being, I suppose, tipsy, like her master, fell, ascending a nice muddy
hill, and, unable to rise, remained on her knees, until Pat Furlong
discovered them both early on Monday morning; Kelly loudly snoring,
the glorious sun casting a flood of light over a visage thin, yellow,
and ghastly—except a long, pointed, crimson nose, with a peculiar
twist at the end, which assumed a richer colouring, shading to the
very tip in deep and glowing purple; the bagpipes still tightly
grasped under the "professor's" arm.

The family of this village musician was managed like many Irish
families—that is, not managed at all; indeed the habits of the parents
precluded even the possibility of the children's improvement in any
way; they moved about, a miscellaneous mass of brown-red flesh,
white teeth, bushy elf-locks, which rarely submitted to the discipline
of a comb, and parti-coloured rags; yet were, nevertheless, cheerful,
strong, and healthy. Clooney evinced much musical talent, which
served as an excuse for idleness, uniform and premeditated. Molly
was the best jigger for ten miles round; and Ellen would have been
a pretty, roley-poley, industrious gipsy, if she had not been born to
the lazy inheritance of the Kelly household; as it was, she did more
than all the brats put together; and as her little bare feet puddled
through the extraordinary black mud, which formed a standing pool
around the stately dunghill that graced the door, she was welcomed
by her father's salutation—"The top o' the morning to my colleen!
—little to fill the noggins ye've got wid ye; well, niver mind, clane
water's wholesome, and lighter for the stomach, may-be, nor milk;
any way, the pratees are laughing, and I must make haste for once:
where's Molly?"

"She's just stept out to look after her pumps for the pathern, but
niver heed, we'll not wait," replied Mrs. Kelly, pouring the potatoes
into the kish.

"It's little use, thin, mother honey, there'll be for pumps, or pipes, or shillalahs, this harvest; for there's black news for the boys and girls, and it's myself was sorry to hear it;—there's to be no pathern."

"No pathern!" screamed Mrs. Kelly, letting half the potatoes fall on the floor to the advantage of the pig, who entered at the lucky moment, and made good use of his time; while Kelly stood with open mouth, ready to receive the one he had dexterously peeled with his thumb-nail;—poor man, he was petrified; the pattern, where, man and boy, he had played, drank, and quarrelled, in St. Mary's honour, for thirty years; the pattern, with its line of "tints," covered with blankets, quilts, and quilted petticoats, its stalls glittering with gingerbread husbands and wives for half the country: the pattern, where his seat, a whisky barrel, was placed under a noble elm, in the middle of the firm greensward, where the belles and the beaux of the neighbouring hills had footed gaily, if not gracefully, to "Moll Row," "Darby Kelly," or "St. Patrick's Day," until the morning peeped on their revellings, for more than a double century!

"It's impossible, ye little, lying hussy!—who dare stop the pathern? —the pathern, is it, in honour of the holy Vargin; for what 'ud they stop it?—there niver was even a bit of a ruction at the pathern o' Bannow, since the world was a world; ye wicked limb, tell me this moment who tould ye this news?"

Ellen looked at her father, and knowing it was a word and a blow with him when he was in a passion, meekly replied—that Pat Kenessy, the landlord of "St. Patrick," had been turned off the pattern field, when in the act of striking the tent poles, to be ready for the next day, by Mister Lamb, the 'Squire's Scotch steward; and that Mister Lamb had informed Kenessy that his master would not permit any pattern to be held on his estate, as it only drew together a parcel of vagabonds, occasioned idleness and quarrels among men and women, and flirtation and courtship among girls and boys; and that a constable was ready to take the first man to Wexford jail who pitched a tent.

Poor Kelly!—at first he would not believe it; but some of the neighbours confirmed the information, and soon a council assembled in his cabin to consider what measures ought to be adopted: the peasantry could not bear to give up quietly the only amusement they enjoyed during the year.

"That's what comes o' the 'Squire's living so long in England," said Blind Barry; "I thought little good it would end in, when he said, t'other day, that my cabin must be whitewashed every six months."

"He threatened to turn my dunghill into the ditch," cried the wrathful piper—"but if he dares to lay his finger on it——"

"Don't fear," said Mickey the tailor, who possessed great reputation, both as a wit and a sage, and who did not enter regularly into the conference, but stood leaning against the door-post—" don't fear; great men don't like to dirty their fingers with trifles."

" It's long afore his uncle would have done so; but the good ould times is past, and there's no frinds for poor Ireland now," sighed Paddy Lumley, an old, white-headed man, more than eighty years of age.

" It's hard, very hard, though," continued Kelly; " he knows well enough that the trifle I gets at the pathern, for my bits o' music, is all I have in the wide world to depind on for the rint; and sure it's little I picks up the counthry round to keep the skreeds on the woman and childer—God help thim!—to say nothin o' the 'atin and the drinkin'; but niver mind; if there's no pathern, my curse be upon him and his!—may the grass, and the nettle, and the —— "

" Asy, asy, Kelly!" cried the tailor—" asy, take it asy; can't ye think—never despair, says I; and so I said to Jim Holloway whin his wife died; never despair, says I; he took my advice, and married agin in three weeks. Why won't one field do ye instead of another? Can't ye borrow another place for the day, man alive ?"

" Did ye ever hear such gumshogue!" cried Blind Barry—" who'd gainsay the 'Squire, d'ye think ? Which of his tinants would say ay to his nay, and have a turn-out, or a double-rint, for their punishment ?"

" Barry, will ye whisht! Listen to me, Kelly, and we'll have the pathern yet. Clane yerself, and go up to the big house to Mister Herriott; he's an ould residenter, and has a heart to feel for and a hand to relieve, the poor man's sorrow; let him know the rights of it, and, I'll go bail, he'll lend you some field of his own. And as to the 'Squire, you know he does not care a brass farthin' for him, on account of the half-acre field they two went to law about; I hear say it cost them, one way or t'other, a clear seven hundred; and the field itself not worth a traneen; but that's neither here nor there.",

" Mick," said Kelly, " you have it!—by the powers, I'll go off straight; to be sure, if we have a pathern it's little matter where, excipt that it's pleasure for the girls to dance on the same sod their mothers danced afore them; but niver mind—won't some o' ye come to back me ?"

" No occasion in life for that; but we'll go wid ye to the gate, and hear the luck when ye come out."

Kelly was soon ready, and set off on the embassy in high spirits: as they journeyed, they talked over the matter more at length, suggested a variety of fields and meadows, and told the story to all they met. The Irish, careless of their time, are ever ready to " tell or hear some new thing;" and Kelly's train became almost a troop before it arrived at the hill which overlooked Mr. Herriott's small but beautiful domain.

It was indeed, very beautiful : the old mansion, with its tall white chimneys, bursting from a thick grove of many-coloured foliage that early in August, was deepening into the brown of autumn ; the long, straight line of trees that marked the avenue, and the bright blue sea at the distance, reflecting a cloudless sky ; the hill, sloping gradually down to the back of the house, which, though not exactly a common, was rendered nearly so by the kindness of its possessor, who gave grass to half the lazy cows and troublesome pigs in the parish.

"We can see the sign of the Welsh coast, the day's so clear," said Mick.

"The dickons drive it back, say I!—the Welsh and English are all foreigners alike ; and it's o' them all the bother comes," retorted Kelly.

"How dark the mountain of Forth looks! Do you remimber once when it looked bright, Jim ?" said Hurling Jack to a tall, powerful man, who strode foremost of the party.

"Do I not! The red-coats were in the hollow, and the boys on the hill ; they covered it like a swarm o' bees. Och! if we had but attacked thim as I wanted, not a mother's son would have lived to tell the story ; but they got to the whisky and the pipes, and the reinforcement came up, and it was all over. Kelly, I remimber you were blind with the drink, and yet ye kept on playing for the dear life—

'We'll down wid the orange, and up wid the green,
    Success to the croppies wherever they're seen !' "

"Whisht, Jim, whisht!" cried Kelly, looking about quite frightened ; "how do you know who's listening ?—and, as I'm a sinner, yon's the master down in the glin, looking as mild as new milk."

"How can ye tell how he looks, and his back to ye, ye natural ?" slyly inquired the tailor ; "but I'm sorry he is there, for I thought we might have taken the short cut through the round meadow."

"We may do that still," replied Kelly, "for his honour's too much the jentleman to look back whin once on the road ; and there's others know that as well as me, I'm thinking, for I see Biddy Colfer turning her two-year-ould calf in, through the gap ; well, that bates all, and she only a Kerry woman !"

Kelly and his friends were, in some measure, disappointed. They certainly took the short cut, and his honour did not look back, but he did as bad ; he seated himself deliberately on the wheel of a car that was turned upside down in the ditch-side, and answered all the purposes of gate and turnstile ; whistled two rambling spaniels to his side, to share the caresses so liberally bestowed on Neptune, a huge Newfoundland dog, who disdained frolic and fun of all description, and looked up in Mr. Herriott's face, with an owl-like gravity,

that made it doubtful whether his steadiness proceeded from sagacity
or stupidity. As the crowd advanced he drew still closer to his
master's side, and in low, sullen growls expressed much displeasure
at so ill-dressed a troop approaching the avenue.

"We are in for it," whispered Kelly, in a low voice, "so we
may as well put a bould face on it at once, and spake altogether."

In another moment Mr. Herriott was surrounded by the bare-
headed company; Kelly, and Mickey the tailor, a little in advance.

"Every blessing in life on yer honour!—and proud are we all
to see your honour looking so fresh and bravely this fine morning."

"Kelly, is it you?—and Mick?—and—why, what earthly business
brings such a gang of you here? Have I not warned you, over
and over again, not to make your confounded paths across the
clover field?—And I see half the barley is destroyed before the
sickle can be put to it, from your everlasting trespasses."

"Is it? Oh, then, more's the pity, to say nothin' o' the shame!"
exclaimed the Piper, looking very sorrowful; "but we had no intintion in life to trespass; only we saw yer honour from the top o'
the hill, and as we had a little business wid yer honour, to save
time, and not to trouble ye at the house, we thought it best to
take to the path. We've not done a taste of harm, yer honour."

"Well, Kelly, do not do so again; it sets a bad example, and
destroys the fields. (Neptune, down, sir!) But what's your business?—another disagreement with your worthy lady? or a quarrel?
or a ——"

"Nothin' at all at all, of that sort, sir; it's far worse nor that,
yer honour, long life to ye! It's all o' the pathern; a burning
sin, and a shame, and a disgrace to the whole town and counthry:
the likes of it was niver heard since the world was born!"

"Is that the way to discoorse a jentleman?" interrupted Mick;
"how can his honour understand ye?—ye're for all the world like
a born natural," and he pushed the diminished Piper back, and,
advancing one foot forward, commenced his oration, at the same
time rubbing the brim of his hat with much dexterity, "To-morrow,
as is well known to yer honour, being a raal scholar and a born
jentleman—not like some neighbours, who have a power o' money
and nothing else—will be (crossing himself) the blessed day of
our Lady, and always the pathern day of the parishes of Kilkaven
and Bannow. Now yer honour minds the little square field at the
foot o' the hill, always, in the memory o' man, called the pathern
field; well, it has plased t'other 'Squire—not that I'd iver think
of turning my tongue aginst the gintry, the raale gintry, yer
honour (bowing low to Mr. Herriott)—has thought fit to forbid
the pathern, and to threaten to sind the first man caught pitching
a tint-pole on his land by a constable to Wexford jail."

Mr. Herriott possessed a kind and benevolent temper; he loved to see the peasantry happy in their own way, and spent his fortune on his estate, anxious, both by precept and example, to instruct and serve his tenantry; but he had a decided, old-fashioned Irish hatred of jails, constables, lawyers, soldiers, &c., and often did he glory in the fact that neither soldier, constable, lawyer, physician, nor water-guard were within twelve miles of his mansion. "The rich 'Squire," as he was called, was a very good man as times went, but so fond of carrying everything with a high hand that the benefits he conferred on the poor (and they were many) were seldom received with gratitude, because he made little allowance for the customs or foibles of those among whom he dwelt. Moreover, he loved soldiers, talked of establishing a land and water-guard, and a dispensary, in the parish; all good things, but yet decidedly opposed to the views of his more gentle and amiable neighbour.

"Indeed, a constable!"

"Ay, yer honour, to a peaceable parish."

"You have been, and are, a peaceable set of men, considering you are Irish," added Mr. Herriott, smiling, "and certainly I believe no one here had anything to do with that unfortunate riot at Duncormuck, where poor Murtough was killed."

"No, no, yer honour," they loudly and unitedly replied; one, in a low voice, added, "He was only a Connaught man after all!"

"I should be sorry indeed if the Bannow boys wanted either soldiers or constables to keep them in order; but I do not see how I can interfere. I cannot oblige Mr. Desmond to lend you the field."

"No; but your honour could give us the loan of one of yer own to keep our pathern in, and long may yer honour reign over us."

"Amin!" said Kelly.

"One of my own? I do not think I could do that," replied Mr. Herriott; "the fields that join the road are surrounded by a bounds-ditch and young plantations, and as to those in the centre of the domain—impossible, quite."

"No harm would happen to the trees," replied Kelly, "but it would be very inconvanient, no doubt. So I was jist thinking, if yer honour would have no objection, the place forenent the grate gate would be quite the thing; and I'll go bail that they'll all walk as if 'twas on eggs they were threading, and neither gate nor green will resave the laste damage in life."

"Very well," said Mr. Herriott, "remember you are security for the good conduct of your friends."

"Oh! every blissing attind yer honour, and the mistress, and all the good family!—hurrah, boys! we've gained the day," cried the triumphant Piper, capering about and snapping his fingers; "we'll jig it, and peaceably too; no quieter lads in the counthry: if that ould scoundrel, Tim Mc Shane, and his fiddle, comes within a mile o' me, by the powers I'll—— "

"Stop, stop, my good fellow," said Mr. Herriott, "peace; no disturbance : the slightest fray, and, depend upon it, I will set my face against fairs and patterns for the next ten years."

"Oh! God bless yer honour! I'll take an oath against fighting and whisky, if yer honour wishes, with heart's delight."

"Never mind; if you swore against it in one parish, you would take it in another; that would be pretty much the same thing, I fancy; there, go the road way, and now no more talk this morning," continued the kind man, as he rose from his seat; "I will walk up with the ladies, and see that you are all quiet and steady, to-morrow evening."

"Long lifes," "powers o' blessings," "stores o' good luck," were bestowed upon "him and his," and the parties pursued their separate paths.

"The great gate" terminated the long straight avenue before mentioned, where, sheltered by some five or six noble beech and horse chestnut trees, and peeping from amidst a profusion of sweet-brier and wild roses, stood a little lodge, meek and lowly as a hedge primrose, with two lattice windows, and a slated roof—that unusual covering of Irish houses.

The interior of this pretty cot was more interesting even than its outward seeming; within sat an old female spinning, her white hair turned up in front, a clean kerchief pinned over her cap, and knotted under her chin, and a short red cloak, fastened by a broad black riband; her face was thickly wrinkled, perhaps by age, perhaps by sorrow. When erect her figure must have been tall and imposing; and long, bony fingers, and sinewy arms, told of strength and exertion. At her feet was sitting, on what the Irish peasantry call a "boss," a very slight girl, with a quantity of light hair, shading a face of almost unearthly paleness; she was carding flax, and laying it, in flakes, on a clean table at her side. The maiden, as she conversed with the aged crone, raised her large blue eyes to her withered face, and gazed on it with as much affection as if it possessed the most fascinating beauty; while the woman's harsh voice softened as she spoke to a being evidently so dear to the best feelings of her heart.

"Oh, blessed be the day, or rather the night, whin I saw ye first, mavourneen!—for you are the blessin' o' my life, and what was sorrow to you was joy to me."

"Joy to me, nurse, not sorrow, for, if I lost one parent, I found another in you."

"A poor parent, my darlint May, but a fond; however, God's will be done; ould Nelly Clarey's heart is not could yet."

Old Nelly Clarey, in her early days, had been a bathing woman,

ana, accustomed to the sea from infancy, had become almost amphibious; her fearless disposition induced the ladies who visited the
beautiful banks of Bannow, in summer, to rely solely on her guidance;
and, moreover, she could row a boat as well as any man in the
country. There are a pair of green islands, about three miles from
the borough of Ballytigue, called the "Keeroes," where, in summer,
a few starved sheep, or one or two goats, wander over about an acre
of moss and weeds. In spring-tides and stormy weather these rocks
are very dangerous to vessels whose pilots are not fully acquainted
with the channel; and a winter seldom passed without some shipwreck
occurring either on or near them. A dark squally morning succeeded
a fearful night of storm, about fifteen years before the period of my
story. The hovel she then lived in was so near the beach that even the
rippling of the summer surge cheered the loneliness of her dwelling;
but, on the occasion to which I refer, it was not the "soft music of the
waters" that roused her from her bed, but the often repeated boom,
sounding above the tempest, which she well knew to be the minute-
gun of distress from some perishing vessel.

The early dawn beheld her wandering among rocks, accessible
only to the sea-birds and herself. She clambered the highest point,
and extended her gaze over the ocean, which still angrily chafed
and growled along the shore. Beyond the breakers, the surface was
somewhat smooth; but little was seen to mark where the islands
rested, save the white and sparkling foam, dashing and glittering in
the early light, finely contrasted with the deep colouring of the sky
and water. Nelly still gazed, and now shaded her eyes with her
hand, for she thought she discovered something like a motionless
mast amongst the distant breakers. She was confirmed in this
opinion by observing several floating spars and casks rapidly borne
towards the main land. On descending to the beach, she found
many of the neighbours anxiously watching the approach of what
they considered lawful plunder.

"The wreck is between the Keeroes, Jack," said Nelly to a rough,
shaggy-looking man, who, half in and half out of the water, was
straining every nerve to haul in a cask, in danger of dashing against
a huge dark mass of rock, that jutted into the sea.

"And what's it to you or me, ould girl?—'twould be fitter for
you to be in your bed, than down on the wild shore, with yer whity-
brown hair streaming about yer shoulders. Ye look for all the world
like a witch!"

"It's you, and the likes of ye," she replied, "that bring disgrace
upon poor Ireland. Phil Doran's boat has passed through breakers
worse nor these, and it shall go out, or I'll know the rason why;
and so many poor strangers, may-be, dying at this blessed moment
on thim islands!"

" It's few 'll go wid ye, then," replied the man, as he grappled with the cask; and, pulling it in, added, " if it's strangers ye're thinking of, there's one come already," pointing to a heap of sea-weed—"his bed is soft enough, at any rate. The ould fool," he continued, as Nelly strided towards the spot, " she'll take more trouble about that sinseless corpse than she would to look after the bits o' Godsinds the wild waters bring us."

Nelly found the body of a youth, apparently about eighteen, nearly embedded in sea-weed. She disentangled it with speed and tender-ness, carried it up the cliffs, dripping as it was, with perfect ease, and laid it out before the turf fire in her humble hut. One of the arms was broken, and sorely mangled; and the bitten lip and extended eyelids plainly told that the youth had wrestled duringly with death.

" Ye'll no more gladden your mother's heart, or bring joy to your father's home," sighed the excellent creature, when perfectly con-vinced that restoratives were useless. " God comfort the mother that bore ye !—for ye were brave and handsome, and, may-be, the pride o' more hearts than one."

As the morning advanced, tokens of extensive shipwreck crowded the beach, and many respectable inhabitants assembled, to prevent plunder. The surf still ran so high, that Nelly's pleadings were dis-regarded. Although the mast of the lost vessel was now distinctly seen, the hardiest boatman would not venture out to the Keeroes.

" I cannot call ye Irishmen," said she, after using many fruitless arguments to urge her neighbours to attempt the passage; " vile Cromellians are ye all, wid not a drop of true Milesian blood in yer shrivelled veins !"

The evening sun had cast a deep red light over the ocean, whose waters were less disturbed than they had been at noon; and the moon rose, with calm majesty, over the subsiding waves—attended by her train of silent, but sparkling handmaids, scattering light and brilliancy over her path.

Nelly could not sleep! again she clambered the " black rock," and scared the sea-gull from its nest—anxious to ascertain, although almost beyond human ken, if any living object remained on the Keeroes, now more distinctly visible. As her eye wandered along the shore, it rested on Phil Doran's boat, which had been drawn up on the shingles; her mind was, at once, made up to a daring enter-prise. No village clock tolled the knell of the departing hours, but she knew it must be near midnight. She returned to her cabin, wrapt a long cloak around her, and secured a bottle of spirits in the hood. A few minutes found her on the strand; the oars were in the strong, but rude fishing-boat, and she soon drew it to the water. When in the act of pushing off, a head appeared, from behind one of the rocks, and a voice exclaimed—" Botheration to ye; on what fool's journey are ye now ? It's myself believes ye've doings with the ould one, for there's no rest for a body near ye, day nor night.'

"Come, Jack," replied the woman, convinced that assistance would be useful, "it's calm enough now, and ye may find something on thim islands you'd like to have. I cannot rest in pace, while I think there may be a living thing on the rocks."

The love of plunder, and the love of enterprise, the latter, perhaps, inspired by the whisky he had drank during the day, urged Jack to accompany the woman. As they approached the Keeroes, their little bark leaped lightly over the billows, and Nelly, like others of her sex, gloried in her opinion being correct, for the mast, and part of the rigging of the vessel, still adhered to the wreck, and absolutely hung over the largest island.

Jack commenced prowling for plunder; Nelly could not perceive a single body on the shore. At length she discovered, midway the mast, something like a female figure, so securely fastened, that even the waters must fail to disentangle the cords and scarfs with which the hands of affection had secured it to what appeared the last refuge.

"It's a faymale, at all events," said Jack, when Nelly succeeded in fixing his attention. "I'm sartin it's a faymale; so here goes!— bad as ye think me—bad, as may-be, I am—Jack Connor never did a bad turn to the women."

He managed to get to the mast, cut the braces, and lower the corpse (for so it was), still enveloped in many shawls, into Nelly's arms.

"She's gone, as well as the boy ye picked up this morning, Nelly," he exclaimed.

"God, in his mercy, save us all!" she exclaimed, falling on her knees, "God, in his mercy save us! Her stiff arms are locked over a living baby, and its little head is on her bare bosom!"

It was even so. The lady was dead; her weak frame had been unable to retain life amid so many horrors! and her spirit could not long have lingered behind HIS, whose last efforts were exerted to preserve the objects of his purest affections, when to others, "all earth was but one thought—and that was—death!"

Jack—croppy, smuggler, wrecker, poacher, white-boy, rogue, and rapparee, as he either was, or had been—Jack Connor (I wish to do everybody justice) placed the unfortunate lady carefully in the boat, took off his jacket, which he added as another covering to the still living infant; and, without plundering a single article, or uttering a single sentence, rowed steadily to the shore. As he carried the body up the cliffs, the morning light was stealing over the now calm ocean. "Nelly," said he, as he rested the burden on her bed— "Nelly, I'll never gainsay ye agin: if I'd done yer bidding yesterday, that cratur would be a living woman now."

Nelly's courage and humanity gained for her high approbation. The vessel was ascertained to have been a Chinese trader, on her homeward passage; but of the crew or passengers, none remained, except the infant the bathing-woman had so heroically rescued.

Mr. Herriott persuaded Nelly, for the sake of her adopted child, to take up her abode at the avenue lodge. The babe was called May, and much did Nelly complain of what she termed a "heathen name." But Mr. Herriott convinced her it was right, as the letters M.A.Y. were wrought in a bracelet found on her mother's wrist. No inquiries had ever been made about the little stranger, and her story was seldom thought of; but she was very different from the peasant children; not so fond of play, and always sweetly serious. She heard the intelligence that the pattern was to be celebrated outside the great gates, with more fear than pleasure, and could hardly understand why Miss Kelly so gloried in her father's having gained the day. Old Nelly "stood up" for Mr. Herriott's ascendancy, with true clan-like feeling; not that she cared for the pattern, but she hated soldiers, and constables, and lawyers, and water-guards, because she knew "the master" hated them; and so, in honour of the pattern victory, she told May that she should cut as good a figure as any of them—and better too, for the matter of that; there was a long, narrow scarf, that had belonged to her mother (heaven rest her soul!) and she should wear it as a sash, and she should dance, too——

"I do not care for dancing, dear nurse," observed the pale girl; "my heart's not in it: but I'll do my best to plase you; and I dare say it will be a merry pathern."

And so it was. Such a pattern!—such a sight of tents had never been seen by the oldest man in the parish, except at the fair of Bally-nasloe, which, as Kelly said, he had never seen, but only heard of! Such a "power" of people! There was the old Lord of Carrick, as he was called—the most respectable butcher for ten miles round, with his bob-wig over his grey hair, all on one side, from joy and whisky. There was Mickey the cailor, with his seven sons; such fine boys, not one of them under six feet, and the youngest only one-and-twenty. There was Pat Kenessy's tent, with a green flag flowing without, and whisky "gilloure" flowing within. There was Mary-the-Mant, in a "bran new gown;" and the five Misses Kenessy, with every earthly and heavenly colour on them, except orange. Then the Corishes—the never-ending Corishes!—Pat Corish and his childer; Jim Corish and his childer; Tom Corish and his childer; Mat Corish and his childer —not a quiet English family of three or four young ones each, but .en or fourteen romping rogues, boys and girls, with stentorian lungs, and herculean fists. And who would be cruel enough to interrupt their amusements of hurling, jumping, eating, drinking, dancing, and

fighting, in pattern time—while their parents were employed, generally speaking, pretty much in the same way?*

"The grate tint" was reserved for dancing, when the "quality"
came; and often did Kelly parade around it, to see that all was right;
and many a longing look was cast down the avenue, to watch if the
gentry were approaching.

"The great bell did not ring for dinner as early as usual," said
Nelly Clarey to her adopted, as she placed the last pin in her sash,
and arranged the flapping bows to her own peculiar taste. "I don't
want you to go amongst them yet, till the quality come; but stay,"
she continued, "let me try;" and she opened a little box, that contained a chain, three rings, and a small, but curiously wrought bracelet
—"stay; these were your poor mother's, and beautiful she looked,
and quiet, when I took them off, and swore to keep thim for you, my
darlint, and niver to let poverty part thim from me. But it's little
poverty I've known, thank God; and blessings on him and his that
presarved us from it." During this speech, Nelly had tried first one,
then the other, of the rings on May's fingers. "They're all too
small for ye; well, sure enough, *she* had the sweetest little hand I
ever saw. The fastening of the chain's not good, or ye might wear
that; but what's to hinder ye putting on the bracelet?—ye cannot
lose it. M.A.Y.—it was yer father's and mother's hair that formed
thim letters, I'll ingage." May gazed upon it, and tear-drops
gathered on her long eyelashes.

"My child—almost my own child,"—said the affectionate Nelly,
"why do ye cry?—you are always sad when others are merry. Ah,
May, May; you'd forget—look!—there's Mr. Herriott, and the mistress, and the young lady, and the strange dark gentleman—master's
ould friend they say—at the gate; and you not fit to be seen; there
—stand asy, and wash your eyes. I'll attind their honours: and in
five minutes ye'll look my queen agin."

Kelly and some of his train stood outside the gate ready to receive
"the gintry;" and way was soon made for them to pass along the
line of tents. The bustling and skirmishing instantly ceased. The
men held their hats in their hands, and the women rose and courtesied
respectfully, as Mr. Herriott and his family proceeded, while many a
heartfelt blessing followed their footsteps.

Perhaps the most perfect happiness in the world is that which a
good Irish landlord enjoys, when his tenantry are really devoted to his
service; because their devotion is manifested by those external signs,

---

* If my accomplished countryman, Mr. Maclise, met in the county of Wexford the
subject he has so admirably pictured, and which stands at the head of this story, it
must have been at Taghmon—Taghmon, cheerless, boisterous, and dirty, even in these
days of temperance and whitewash.

which can only emanate from an enthusiastic temperament. "How well his honour looks!—sure it's a blessing to see him; and the mistress so queen-like, and yet so humble, with her kind smile, and asking after the childer, so motherly."

"Who's the stranger?"

"From foreign parts, I b'lieve, by his dark skin."

"Very like: in all yer born days, did ye ever see anything like the state Kelly takes on himself? to be sure he's o' very dacent people, and the best piper in the whole barony; but there's rason in all things, and there'll be a power of gintry in the pathern before night. Mr. Cormack and the ladies, Mr. Jocelyn, and Mr. Lambton, and, may-be, they won't put up wid Kelly's talk, like the rest."

"Never heed; sure, they all know his ways; but come," and the oldest crone of the assembly rose off a seat, where four or five, "withered and wild in their attire," had been sitting, smoking their "doo-deens," and making observations on everybody, under the shadow of one of the great trees. "Come, they're crowding into the tint, and we'll be all behind, like the cow's tail, if we don't make haste."

Kelly had taken his seat, or, rather, erected his throne, on the top of one of the largest casks that could be procured in the parish; and on forms, on each side of the musician, were seated the "gentlefolk;" —a small space between—and men, women, and children, crouched or stood, as they best could manage, leaving sufficient room for the dancers; for which purpose, certainly, not much was required, as either reel or jig can be performed on a good-sized door, always taken off its hinges, and laid on "the sod" for the purpose.

The wide entrance to the tent was crowded with a mass of laughing Irish faces beaming with joy.

Paddy Madder—who but Paddy Madder was fit to open the ball? Paddy, the oldest man in the parish, and, in his youth, it was said (for none remembered it), the finest dancer ever seen in all Ireland. Paddy acquitted himself nobly, considering that he had numbered eighty and two years; and Mr. Herriott placed the old man by his side, and heard, with delight, of the youthful feats which age so dearly loves to dwell upon.

Miss Kelly next dropped her bob courtesy to young Tom Corish; who, after "covering the buckle" to admiration, and beating his partner at the "highland fling," made "a remarkable genteel bow" to poor May, heedless of the smiles and approbation pert Jane Roche bestowed on his performance. May was not at all flattered by the distinction, and clung to her nurse's side, until desired, in an authoritative tone, by Kelly, to "step out, and not look so sheepish." May danced, I must confess, very badly, but she looked very lovely; timidity and exercise gave a colour to her cheek which it seldom pos-

sessed, and her light, sylph-like form, graced by the flowing sash,
formed a strange contrast to the almost gigantic figure of her
partner.

"Who is that girl?" inquired the strange gentleman of Mr.
Herriott.

"I cannot tell you who she is, but she has been nursed by a very
deserving woman, who attends our gate lodge."

"Indeed."

The gentleman again looked at her. As May continued, she forgot
she was the object of general attention, and danced with more spirit.
The stranger rose from his seat, and appeared to watch her movements with extraordinary anxiety.

"It is strange," said he to Mr. Herriott, "but that child is singularly like one whom I loved more than any earthly being;—my sister
Anna."

"Indeed; I never saw her;—but you often mentioned her to me
when we were schoolfellows; do you remember saying how much you
would like me for a brother-in-law?"

"Boyhood's imaginings, my dear friend. She returned to her
family at Calcutta, when her education was completed, and married a
young merchant, her inferior in rank—but I knew she was happy, and
forgave it, poor Anna! She accompanied him to China, and, if their
traffic succeeded, they were to have voyaged to England. I found
they embarked on board a vessel for the purpose, but——"

"Shame upon ye!" exclaimed Tom Corish, loud enough to interrupt the narrative Mr. Herriott was so earnestly attending to; "ye
know his honour does not dance, May, but it's only manners for ye
to ax his honour's frind to take a step, now that you've bate me clane
off, lazy as you wint about it."

Poor May made her courtesy, all panting and blushing as she was,
and, without saying a word, or looking up, extended her hand to lead
him to "the floor;" but she uttered a piercing shriek, when, seizing
her arm with a powerful grasp, the stranger half dragged, half carried
her, to the entrance of the tent; there he tenderly supported the
frightened girl, but still held the arm she had extended to him with
unrelaxing firmness; while his eyes wandered from her face to the
golden bracelet which her nurse had clasped. The peasantry were
perfectly unable to comprehend the matter. Kelly descended from
his throne; and Nelly Clarey looked quite thunderstruck. She was,
however, the first to recover her surprise.

"What do you mean by glowering that way on my child?"

"Your child, woman! Herriott, you said she was not hers; you
said you could not say who she was. Speak, I entreat, for mercy
speak, and tell me how that bracelet came—who gave it her?"

"Nobody gave it her," replied Nelly, "I myself took it off her mother's arm—God rest her soul!—the very morning that Jack Connor and I picked them both out of the salt shrouds. The waves were her early cradle, poor thing!"

"How long since?"

"Oh, for the matter o' that, it will be fifteen years, come next Candlemas."

The strange gentleman let the braceleted wrist drop, and folded the trembling May to his bosom.

"She is my sister's child," said he, when he could speak, "and henceforth mine."

Mr. Herriott suggested the propriety of their going into the lodge. Poor Nelly followed the gentry, keeping close to her adopted, muttering, "I have lost her now, any how." The rings and the chains were produced; but the strongest witness was the bracelet; M. A. Y. were the united initials of May's father and mother; and a spring, under the clasp, which had escaped observation, discovered a miniature of Mr. Monnett (the strange gentleman), which he had himself given to his beloved sister, as a token of affection on her leaving Calcutta.

"So ye're a lady after all, by fortune as well as birth," said Nelly, looking affectionately at May, "and I must call ye Miss; and ye'll be no more near me; and no more shall I hear yer sweet voice in the soft summer evenings, calling to me from the wood, or reading to me whin the snow hangs the trees with white, like cherry blossoms; and the place will miss ye; and I shall be left desolate in my old age. But ye'll think of me; think of yer poor nurse, Nelly, who, on her bare knees"—and as she knelt she extended her clasped hands to heaven—"prays that the tears o' sorrow may niver dim yer eye; that the blush o' shame may niver paint yer cheek; that the blessings of the poor may strew the sweetest summer flowers in yer path; and that a long life and a happy death may be yer blessing; and after," continued she, solemnly, "in heaven—in the presence of the Father and his holy saints, may the poor Bannow woman see ye a bright angel of glory!"

May flung herself on her nurse's bosom; and Mr. Monnett assured them he hoped they would never separate; "for I think, Nelly," said he, "May looks so delicate that she will need your kind care wherever she goes; and she would be unworthy of my affection if she wished to leave you." Consequently, there was not a single sorrowful heart among the population, rich and poor, of "the united parishes of Bannow and Kilkaven."

"Anybody might see," exclaimed Kelly, half an hour afterwards, when May appeared at the gate, for a moment, to receive the con-

gratulations of her former companions, leaning on the one side on
her uncle, and on the other, on her nurse—"anybody might see that
she had always the gentle drop in her; and I tould you so, Miss
Jinny, my lady," continued he, sneeringly, to Jane Roche, who had
always treated poor May with contempt, and looked somewhat dis-
concerted at her sudden elevation; "fine feathers don't always make
fine birds." Miss Jenny, however, had one consolation; hereafter, a
powerful rival would be removed out of the way.

"Kelly," said Mr. Herriott, "but for you this discovery would not
have been made; for there would have been no pattern; therefore, my
boys, crown him king of pipers, patterns, and whisky; and plenty of
that, and good Irish roast beef, shall you have, and a glorious supper
outside these gates—peace—plenty—and whisky!"

"King Kelly for ever, and long life to the May!" cried Mickey
the tailor; and they chaired or rather shouldered, Kelly round the
green; and poured a noggin of pure whisky over his head, which
made him as good a king as the best of them (they said); and the
Piper composed a jig, extempore, that beat jig Polthouge, and all the
jigs ever made before or since, clean out of the field, and called it
the "Lady May."

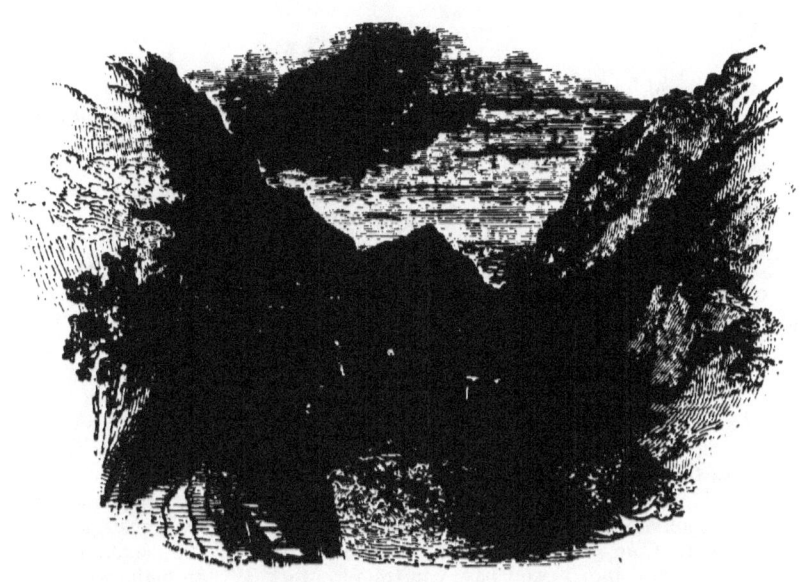

THE RAPPAREE.

TRUE for ye, ma'am dear, it is smoking up to the nines, sure
enough, but it's by no manner o' manes unwholesome, more
particularly at this season, when it's so *could;* it will clear, my lady.
in a minute—see, it's moving off now."

"Moving up, you mean," replied the young lady to whom this
speech was addressed, and whose eye followed the thick and curling
smoke that twisted and twisted, in serpent-like folds, around the
blackened rafters of "Mr. Corney Phelan's Original Inn,"—so, at
least, the dwelling was designated by the painted board that had once
graced it, but now played the part of door to a dilapidated pig-sty.
Again, another volume folded down the chimney, for so the orifice
was termed under which the good-tempered and rosy Nelly Clarey
was endeavouring to kindle a fire, with wet boughs and crumbling
turf. The maid of the inn knelt before the unmanageable combustibles, fanning the flickering flame with her apron, or puffing it with
her breath; the bellows, it is true, lay at her side, but it was bereft

of nose and handle. "Poor thing," she said, compassionately, "it wasn't in its nature to last for ever; and sure, master's grandmother bought it as good as thirty years ago, at the fair of Clonmel, as a curiosity, more nor anything else, as I heard say."

"Are you sure," interrogated the young lady, after patiently submitting to be smoke-dried for many minutes—"are you sure that the flue is clear?"

"Is it clear, my lady! Why, then, bad cess to me for not thinking of that before!—sure I've good right to remember thim devils o' crows making their nesteens in the chimbley; and it's only when the likes o' you and yer honourable father stop at the inn, that we light a fire in this place at all."

She took up the wasting candle, that was stuck in a potato in lieu of a candlestick, and placing a bare but well-formed foot on a projecting embrasure near the basement, dexterously catching the huge beam that crossed the chimney with her disengaged hand, swung herself half up the yawning cavern, without apparently experiencing any inconvenience from the dense atmosphere. After investigating for some time, "Paddy Dooley;—Paddy Dooley;" she exclaimed, "come here, like a good boy, wid the pitchfork, till we make way for the smoke."

"I can't, Nelly, honey," replied Mister Paddy, from a shed that was erected close to the "*parlour*" window, "a'n't I striving to fix a bit of a manger, that his honour's horses may eat their hay, and beautiful oats, dacently, what they're accustomed to—but Larry can go."

"Larry, avourneen!" said Nelly, in a coaxing tone, "do lend us a hand here wid the pitchfork."

"It's quare manners of ye, Nelly—a dacent girl like ye, to be asking a gentleman like me for his hand (Larry, it must be understood, was the *bocher* and wit of the establishment), and I trying for the dear life to rason wid this ould lady, and make her keep in the sty; she's nosed a hole through the beautiful sign."

"Bad luck to ye both!" ejaculated Ellen, angrily; "I'll tell the masther, so I will," she added, jumping on the clay floor, her appearance not at all improved by her ascent. "Masther, dear, here's the boys and the crows after botherin' me; will ye tell them to help me down with the nest?—the lady's shivering alive with the could, and not a sparkle of fire to keep it from her heart."

"Don't *you* be afther botherin' *me*, Nelly," replied the host; "but I ax pardon for my unmannerliness," he continued, coming into the room—his pipe stuck firmly between his teeth, and his rotund person stooping, in a bowing attitude, to Miss Dartforth—"sure I'll move it myself, with all the veins o' my heart, to pleasure the lady at any time!—Give us the loan of the pitchfork, Larry."

" To tell God's truth, master, it's broke, and the smith—bad luck
to him !—forgot to call for it, and little Paddeen forgot to lave it—
but here's the shovel 'll do as well, and better too, for it's as good as a
broom, seeing it's so nearly split at the broad end." "The master"
took the shovel, not angrily, as an English master would have done,
at such neglect; but taking for granted that a shovel would do as
well as a pitchfork, or a broom, or anything else, "when it came asy
to hand," and perfectly well satisfied with Larry's ingenuity. He
poked, and poked, up the chimney, while Ellen stood looking on at
his exertions, her head upturned, her ample mouth open, displaying
her white teeth to great advantage. Presently, down came such an
accumulation of soot, dried sticks, clay, and disagreeables, that Nelly
placed her hands on her eyes, and ran into the kitchen, exclaiming
"that she was blinded for life;" while the young lady, half suffocated, followed her example, and left "mine host of the public" to
arrange his crows' nests according to his fancy. The kitchen of an
Irish inn (not an inferior place of public accommodation—but what
would be termed in England a "posting-house"), at the period of
which I treat, would now be considered as a more befitting shelter
for a tribe of Zingari, than for Christian travellers; it was a room of
large dimensions, and high elevation, with an earthen floor worn into
many inequalities, and an enormous hole in the roof, directly over
where the fire was placed, through which the smoke escaped, after
hanging, as it were, in fantastic draperies around the discoloured
apartment. A massive bar stood out from the wall, against, or
nearly against, which the fire was lighted, and from it were suspended
sundry crooks and nondescript chains, fitting for the support of iron
pots and such cooking vessels as were put into requisition, when
"quality" stopped, either from necessity or for refreshment. in the
wild and mountainous district where resided Mr. Corney Phelan;
indeed, the house was frequented more by farmers' drovers, endeavouring to conduct wild mountain sheep to the markets of Waterford, or even Dublin (and I have now in my possession some old
family memoranda, which state the price paid for such animals, at that
time, to have been two shillings and sixpence per head), and persons
in that sphere of life, than by such gentry as Mr. Dartforth. who
travelled in his own carriage, and with a suitable number of atten-
dants; he was a rich landed proprietor, a justice of the peace, and
M.P. for the county town. It may be readily supposed that the
arrival of persons of rank was a matter of importance, and that some
preparations were made in the "parlour," as it was called, while the
worthy magistrate occupied himself in inspecting the accommodation
provided for his horses in the outhouses. The animals had undergone
much fatigue, for the gentleman and his daughter had journeyedfrom
Dublin ; and when he drew near the dwellings of some of his principal

tenants, he had called upon them, as "gale day" was passed, to collect his rents. The roads leading to those dwellings had, in many instances, been rendered heavy and nearly impassable by the rains; the horses were almost foundered; and, although within a few miles of home, it was found impossible to proceed without giving them some hours' rest. Miss Dartforth, with the cheerfulness and good-nature so charming in females of every age, accommodated herself to circumstances, took off her hat, and having in vain sought, with the ken of a laughing blue eye, for what a woman, however old and ugly, would fain see in every room—a looking glass—shook back her clustering tresses, which twined in wild luxuriance over her graceful form; then partially unclasping a silver-laced riding habit, she made her way, amid five or six barelegged "helpers," some dozens of various-sized pigs, fowl, and collies, to a three-legged seat near the fire, close to a petted white calf, that had established itself very quietly on a "lock of straw," in the most comfortable portion of the apartment. She then commenced leisurely investigating the whims and oddities of the assembly; and the smiles that occasionally separated her full rich lips, showed she was an amused spectator of the *mélange.* Everything appeared in confusion; the landlady, whose mob cap was trimmed with full and deep lace of no particularly distinguishable colour, bustled about in a loose bedgown of striped cotton, beneath which a scarlet petticoat, of Dutch dimensions, stuck forth; she was the only female in the establishment who luxuriated in shoes and stockings—the former were confined on the instep by rich silver buckles; and, though she occasionally sat with much state behind a soiled deal board, which presented a varied assortment of drinking measures, and was garnished at either end by kegs of whisky, yet did she keep a necessary, and not silent, *surveillance* over the movements of the various groups. Some idea of her conversation, or more properly speaking, her observations (for she never waited for a reply), may be gathered from the following:—

"Miss Dartforth, my lady!—(Mary Murphy, will ye never finish picking the few feathers off that bird?)—my lady, I humbly ask yer pardon on account of the smoke, and—(Nelly Clarey, Nelly Clarey, may-be it's myself won't pay you off for your villany; don't tell me of the crows; what do I give you housemaid's wages for, but to look after my best sitting-rooms?)—Miss Dartforth, ma'am, is that baste (the calf I mane) disagreeable to ye?—it's a pet ye see, on account of its being white—quite white, Miss, every hair—and lucky—Billy Thompson, ye little, dirty spalpeen! will ye have done draining the glasses into yer well of a mouth?—it's kind, father, for ye to be afther the whisky, yet I'll trouble ye to keep yer distance from my counter —Corney Phelan, it 'ud be only manners in ye to take the doodeen out o' yer teeth, and the lady to the fore; I remember when ye'd take it out before *me*—why not?—the day ye married me, dacency and dacent blood entered yer barrack of a house, and made it what it is, the most creditable inn in the country—Peggy Kelly, ye're a handy girl, jump up, astore, on the rafters, and cut a respectable piece of bacon off the best end of the flitch—asy—asy!—mind the hole in the wall, where the black hen is setting—there, just look in, for I'm thinking the chickens ought to be out to-morrow or next day— Larry, ye stricken devil! have ye nothin' to do, that ye stand chuck in the door-way?—are ye takin' pattern by yer master's idleness—he that does nothin' from mornin' till night but drink whisky, smoke, sleep—sleep, smoke, and drink whisky?—Oh! but the heart within me is breakin' fairly with the trouble—bad cess to ye all!—there's the pratees boilin' mad! and the beef!—I'll rid the place of the whole clan of ye—for it's head, hands, and eyes I am to the entire house— ye crew!" &c. &c.—And the eloquent, burly lady sprang, with the awkward velocity of a steam-carriage, towards the fire-place, over-setting everything in her way, to ascertain how culinary affairs were proceeding in two large iron vessels, round which the witches in Macbeth might have danced with perfect glee—so deep, and dark, and fitting did they seem for all the purposes of incantation.

Much amused, the young lady patted the calf, which looked into her face with the unmeaning innocence of expression that charac-terizes the animal; and, as she stooped to conceal the smiles excited by Mistress Corney Phelan's anger, the loosened tresses fell over her brow and eyes; their readjustment occupied a few moments—but when she looked up she saw a woman seated opposite to her, whom she certainly had not before noticed, and who she thought it very strange should have escaped her observation; her dress bespoke the mendicant, and she eagerly stretched her bony and muscular hands over the blazing turf fire; her frame appeared chilled by the cold of a keen October evening that was fast closing—for her cloak remained fastened, and even the hood, that perfectly concealed her features, was unremoved: Miss Dartforth could not help remarking that the cloak was much longer than is usually worn by Irish beggars, and the foot which projected from beneath its ample folds was covered by a substantial brogue. Once, and once only, the fugitive, but expressive, glance of a wild, bright eye met hers, and the idea that *somewhere* she had before encountered a similar look possessed her imagination. While she was endeavouring to remember the *where* and the *when*, her father entered, attended by one or two of his servants, and accom-panied by a relative who, according to the miserably dependant feeling that, I regret to say, is not yet banished from my country, played clerk, toady, whipper-in, understrapper, or what you please, to his patron,

who afforded him bed, board, washing, clothes, and shooting; kindly
requiring, in return, that he should act as affidavit man on all occasions (particularly when he recorded wonderful stories), and laugh
invariably at his jests;—"Time out of mind such duties wait depen-
dance." The justice was a free-hearted man, frank and violent, good-
natured and obstinate, a talker of patriotism, a practiser of tyranny,
and fonder of his pretty daughter, Norah Dartforth, than of his
hounds, his hunters, or even his landed interest. It was, however, a
well-known and accredited tale that he had broken his wife's heart
by his frequent fits of violence; or, more properly speaking, he had
frightened her out of the world while in the prime of youth, and
delicate, lily-like loveliness; he then took an oath, which, I believe,
he religiously kept, that he would never get into a rage with his
daughter. This, nevertheless, did not prevent his getting into passions with others, and, indeed, his life, as must always be the case
where anger is indulged in, was a round of sins and repentances.
The county report went to say that there was one error he more
sorrowed over than the rest:—

Some time after his marriage, disappointed in not being blessed with
an heir to his estate, he adopted a boy of singular talent and beauty,
whose parents, humble and industrious cottars, died of malignant
fever, near his avenue-gate; this boy he cherished with all a father's
love and tenderness, and even the birth of a daughter, after the lapse
of many years, did not appear to diminish the affection he entertained
for the interesting youth. Unfortunately, over-indulgence nurtured
a proud and daring spirit, which, by different management, could
have been tamed to the gentle and ennobling duties of life. The boy
grew in beauty and increased in talent; but he also became impe-
rious and overbearing: even if Mr. Dartforth and his gentle lady
were inclined to make allowances for his wayward fancies and insolent
actions, the very humblest serf on his domain was loud in complaints
of the *parvenu's* tyranny; and the worthy man, who had obstinately
persisted in a new-fangled idea, which he had imbibed from some of
the French authors of the period—that the human mind was of itself
perfection, and that there were no impulses given that needed restraint—persevered in his "system," as he called it, until the impetuous James brought himself under the strong arm of the law, by an
open act of violence, directed against one of his protector's brother
magistrates, which, but for the interposition of powerful friends,
would have banished him the country. It would have been better,
perhaps, had the law been suffered, at that time, to take its course
He returned home with an insulted, but unsubdued spirit, and the
remonstrances of his well-meaning, but ill-judging friend, were heard
with visible symptoms of impatience. The voice of reproof sounded

harshly on the ear that, for eighteen summers, had listened to nothing but the honeyed accents of praise. In an evil hour, when both were heated with that noxious spirit—of which I cannot sufficiently express my detestation, having too often witnessed its baneful and pernicious effects—words terminated in blows; Mr. Dartforth struck his *protegé*, and the other, whose tiger spirit could ill brook such an insult, hurled his almost father to the earth. It is but too probable that murder would have terminated the disgraceful scene, had not Norah, roused from her light and innocent slumbers by the fearful noise of the unnatural combat, rushed between them, and, in an instant, her soft, but energetic voice awoke the intemperate youth to a sense of his crime and ingratitude; the remembrance of the insult inflicted, was effaced by a sense of the evil he had done, and he humbled himself, even to the dust, at Mr. Dartforth's feet. Then was the moment, when his heart and feelings could have been caught on the rebound, but the wrathful and intoxicated man cursed the stripling in the madness of his rage—it was a deep, a bitter, an irrecallable curse—that made the maiden's warm blood run cold in her veins, and withered the heart of the unfortunate victim of intemperate passion. Pale, trembling with varied emotion, he crouched, for a moment, beneath the ban—then rising, as the young wolf-hound from his lair, without a word, a groan, or a tear—without even an adieu to her who had, regardless of her own interest, often palliated his faults—he left, for ever, the halls that had sheltered his childhood.

Great as James's faults certainly were, it was said that Mr. Dartforth secretly blamed himself for the result ; but even Norah was interdicted from mentioning the name of the once favoured boy, who, it was believed, had quitted the country for some far distant land. There were, however, many who asserted that, after Patrick James had left Mr. Dartforth, " his honour had never been rightly his own man ;" and, indeed, it was evident to all that his temper and habits had not improved since his *protegé* had absconded.

As the magistrate seated himself on a chair, which the bustling landlady officiously presented him, next to his gentle and affectionate child—" his heart's darling," as he termed her, in the warm language of Irish phraseology—that daughter thought she had never seen her father's cheek so pale, or his eye so rayless.

" Dear father !" she exclaimed, pressing her left cheek to his, " sit at the opposite side, I will move with you—you are chilled, but there you will be quite shielded from the draught of the door."

" Make way for yer betthers, honey !" screamed the landlady in the ear of the mendicant, who did not seem inclined to relinquish her seat to " the gentry;" a very unusual thing in Ireland, where so much outward homage is rendered to the aristocracy. " Good woman," interposed Miss Dartforth, coming up to her, and placing her hand gently on her shoulder, " will you oblige me by exchanging seats, as my father suffers by the draught from which your cloak protects you ?"

The beggar rose, and leaning, as if from excessive weakness or fatigue, on her staff, crossed over to the other side, at the same time muttering some faint words, which neither father nor daughter could comprehend.

" Is the woman deaf and dumb ?" inquired Mr. Dartforth, angry, perhaps, at her tardiness of motion.

" She's as good—just then as good as the one and t'other," replied the *bocher*, coming forward, dexterously managing so as to make his crutch supply the place of his lost leg. " She's an afflicted crathur —God presarve us !—but harmless, and's under a vow never to let the hood fall off her head, in rain or sunshine—heat or cold—night or day : and, what's more, never to lay side on a bed for the next seven years. Oh ! there's a power o' holiness about her, plaze yer honour."

" I suppose she has committed some dreadful crime, for which the religion you believe in requires such atonement ?"

" Crime ! the crathur !—bless ye, no ; she's as innocent o' crime, or passion, or anything o' that sort, as yer honour. Och ! no—the poor thing's heart aches for the sins o' the world, and she wishes to ease 'em."

" A female crying philosopher !" observed Mr. Dartforth to his daughter.

" And yet there is something that, under other circumstances, would be called philosophy about it," replied Norah ; " how often is it that situation and influence command the homage which, at first sight, appears paid to the virtue, not the person !"

" Miss Norry, you are growing too wise for me," said the male tondy, who was called, by his associates " Swallow-all-Dick ;" by his superiors, " Dick ;" and by his inferiors (meaning those who honestly worked for their living), " *Mister* Dick." He stood, with his hands in his pockets, before the fire, to the manifest inconvenience of all engaged in preparing the anticipated meal.

" What a wonder that is, to be sure !" muttered Lame Larry, " as if you were one who could shoe the goslins, catch a weasel asleep, or spit a sunbame."

" Has there been much news stirring lately—I mean during my absence ?" inquired Mr. Dartforth, addressing Larry, who certainly was the most intelligent person of " the Original Inn."

" Only a few more of Freney's tricks playing here, and there, and everywhere, plaze yer honour."

"The rascal!—has any one yet discovered who he is, or where he came from?"

"Lord, no, sir!—a body might as well hunt and catch a leprechawn as him; did yer honour hear how he sarved the judge and jury, at the ferry o' Mount Garrett? Well, ye see, there was a lot of fire-arms he wanted to get over: and the boatman tould him as how he daren't let him pass, in rason that the judge was going to cross in the coorse of the day, and his people were keepin' the boat. 'Is that all?' says Freney, says he—the blue eye dancin' out of his head wid scorn at the little wit o' the boatman; and he goes his way. Well, jist as the judge, and all the law and the justice in the country—(yer honour's glory was out of it at the same time, ye know, so it didn't take up much room)—the law and the justice all packed tight and comfortable in the boat, as need be—up comes a poor blind ould crathur of a man —seemingly as dark as dungeon, leadin' a baste, with a load o' brooms on his back. 'Och, my misery!' says the ould craythur—setting up a pulhalew that 'ud reach from this to Bantry,—'and it's I'll be too late, God help me! and miss the market.' Well, yer honour, for once a judge listened to marcy—and a poor man the pleader. 'Come, honest friend,' says he, 'we'll make room for you, and yer baste can swim over.' 'God mark ye to glory,' says the ould man, 'but what'll I do with my brooms?'—'Lay 'em in the bottom of the boat,' says the judge; and they all got over comfortable together. Well, when they reached the other side, sure as life there was a whole troop of the red-coats, waiting to cross the contrary way. 'What are ye after?' says the judge. 'Plase yer lordship,' replied the sargent, 'we've just heard that the daring rascal, Freney, is over the water, with fire-arms, and combustibles, and contrivances enough to blow up ould Ireland, and murder it entirely; and that he wants to get to this side, and waylay and destroy every mother's son at the sizes; so we're going to stop him.' 'God bless ye for that same!' said the ould crathur of a man, setting his brooms on his baste at the same time; 'it was only yesterday that the rapparee took every fardin' I had in the world—and only left me these few skreeds o' clothes; and if he's let go on that way, neither gentle nor simple will be alive in the country this day three months.' 'Could ye describe him?' says the judge. 'He's a good portly man to my seeing,' made answer the ould crathur. 'Middling-sized—middling-sized,' repeated the sargent, stepping into the boat; 'I'd know him ten miles off, if the devil himself set him a maskin.' The ould man gave a chuck of a laugh, and off wid him, after making his obadience, mannerly, to the great gentlemen—and the boat and the soldiers towed away for the other side; and the judge and grandees gathered themselves up, quite stylish-like, on the horses that were waitin' fo

them—and, by the time they were settled, from the top almost of the
hill that ye mind is so overgrown with osiers, and all kinds of creepin'
bushy herbs, came a loud, wild laugh—and they looked up, one and
all—and sure enough, there was a sight to frighten the tories !—
every plant seemed grown into a livin' man, with a musket on his
arm, by way of a shoulder-knot; and 'Freney's brooms are the
brooms that'll sweep clean !' shouted one fellow. 'Our brave little
commander for ever !' roared another : and then Freney himself
stepped upon the ancient grey rock at the top of all, and wavin' his
hat, with the air of a rank nobleman, he bowed to the company
below. 'I'll find an opportunity of returnin' yer lordship's civility ;
and you or yours shall never be harmed by me or mine,' says he;
'and I hope you won't forget Freney and the Ferry o' Mount Garrett.'
Well, before ye could say 'Cork !' there were the osiers waverin' in
the wind, so innocent-like, and the men gone, as a whiff o' smoke ;
only, as the grandees passed up the bank, wild, cheerful laughter
once or twice broke on their ear. And, may-be, the sargent and his
lobsters weren't dancin' mad in the boat with fair spite, jist over the
way ; and they forced the boatman to tow about, and, somehow or
other, as he was turnin', the vessel upset; and such scramblin' and
clawin' as they had to get safe ashore—and their ammunition all wet,
and their firelocks spoilt : and then they would have it the boatman
did it a-purpose, and swore they'd baygnot him ; the poor fellow was
frightened—why not ?—and got away out of their reach, just in time
to save his life.

"But that's nothin' to the escape he had, not long since, when he
hid in a hayrick, and seven soldiers passed him, and every one
prodded the ricks with their baygnots ; and, every time they did, it
went into him ; for all that, sorra a stir did he stir, only stud it out
like a Trojan."

"He has had a great many escapes by flood and field, papa ; I feel
quite interested for him ; he is, I have heard, brave and generous,
and particularly attentive to females," observed Norah.

"Ay, girl !—you are like the rest of your sweet sex ; give a man a
character for bravery, and, no matter whether he be brigand, or soldier,
or rapparee, you are all ready to defend his cause, and, my life on't, if
this Freney, this cut-throat, received womankind recruits, the bushes
would be covered with cast-off drapery."

"Dear papa, he is no cut-throat—no single deed of blood is regis-
tered against him ; and the instances I have heard of his charity,
taking from the rich to give to the poor, bestowing, even from his
own purse, to clothe the naked, and feed the hungry, have, I confess,
interested me in his fate ; I do not feel the least afraid of him."

"Nor never need, Miss, my lady," observed the *bocher*, bowing.

"I'll answer for it, that James Freney 'ud spill the best drop of his heart's blood for one smile from yer sweet face; sure he's every inch an Irishman."

"You know him, then?" inquired Miss Dartforth, smiling and blushing—for I dare not deny the fact, that all women like a delicately-turned compliment, even from a *bocher.*

"I can't say but I've seen him," replied the man, shifting off, at the same time, to the other end of the kitchen. It must not be imagined that this dialogue had proceeded, even thus far, without sundry interruptions from worthy Mistress Cornelius Phelan, who was all bustle and anxiety at the impropriety of such visitors dining in the kitchen; "and sure the parlour was cleared, and but little smell o' smoke in it now," &c. &c. Both gentlemen and lady, however, persevered in their determination not to enter the "crow's nest," as Norah laughingly called it; and the table was accordingly set in the centre of the kitchen, and covered, if not with elegant, certainly with substantial, fare :—boiled fowl, enormous nondescript masses of beef, "neatly boulstered up," to use Mrs. Phelan's term, with fine white cabbage and English carrots; potatoes, of course, were not wanting; and the travellers were too hungry to be fastidious. Miss Dartforth, who never forgot the wants of others, heaped a plate, after the Irish fashion, with meat and potatoes, and, before her own dinner was ended, turned to present it to the mendicant, but, to her surprise, the woman had disappeared as mysteriously as she had entered! She was about to express her surprise at this circumstance, when Nelly Clarey (who, blooming under a cap which, in some degree, confined her clustering hair, and was ostentatiously garnished with cherry-coloured ribands, stood behind her chair, to the manifest annoyance of Mr. Dartforth's old servant, who always claimed the privilege of waiting personally upon "*his young lady*"), touched her arm, whispering, at the same time, "For God's sake, never heed her."

The October evenings in Ireland are damp and dreary; nor have they the uniformly clear sunsets, or invigorating atmosphere, which characterize the farewell summer month in England. The weeping skies of Ireland have become almost proverbial; but, even while they weep, they smile—apt emblem of the happy volatile temperament of a people who have suffered much, and suffer still. I learned in early youth to love the quickly closing evenings of autumn, and, at times, delight more in rain than in sunshine. I must, however, resume the thread of my narrative, and mention that, at about the distance of a hundred or a hundred and twenty yards from the hag-yard, which flanked the inn on the north, and protected it from the cold winds, ran a long wall, intended originally as a division between the farms of two brothers who had sacrificed their property in litigation, and

died at last poor and penniless—the one in a distant land, where he
had been sent by the offended laws of his country; the other in a
jail. The wall was called, by the country people, "the brothers'
ban," and a good deal of superstitious feeling attached to it. Many
of the stones had fallen to the earth, and over them the gay green
weeds had triumphed, while others showed dimly in the moonlight,
and might have been easily converted, by the magic of imagination,
into things of living and mysterious form. A few stunted elms,
with here and there a dark poplar, waved gently in the chill evening
air; and, although the laugh and wassail sounds of the inn talkers
and revellers called to remembrance the proximity of human habitation, yet the undefinable dreariness of the spot was increased, rather
than broken, by the shadows of two persons, in earnest conversation,
the one passing rapidly backwards and forwards with a firm, undaunted
step—the other halting, or rather hopping, after the superior, endeavouring, in vain, to keep pace with him, yet bearing his rapid strides
and impatient temper with extraordinary good-humour.

"Fine times, to be sure, they must be wid ye, when ye let a good
seven hundred—I dare say goold—hard goold—slip through yer fingers as asy as kiss my hand; the boys 'll never stand it—how could
they?" observed the lame one.

"Not stand it! What the devil do you mean, Hacket—when there
is not an ounce of brains among a troop of them? Why, Breen
himself dare not—ay—I say *dare not*, dispute my will in anything."

"May-be not; but I know he looked mighty black when I tould
him ye meant that ould Huncks to get home scot-free."

"Black! did he? I wish I had seen him. I tell ye, Hacket, his
gold, if I touched it, would blister my fingers—it would kindle hell's
own fire within my heart. For fifteen years I eat of his bread—and
even his own child, that creature whose pure and spotless hand, not
two hours since, rested on my shoulder—(it was like a dove seeking
repose on a hawk's wing)—even when that child was born, the same
shelter, the same smile, was mine. Blessed Virgin!" he continued,
striking his forehead violently, "you, a poor dismembered, blighted
creature, can understand that you couldn't tear the hand that fed ye."

"It was a pity," replied the *bocher* (for my readers have doubtless
discovered that Larry and Hacket are one and the same person),
while a cold, sarcastic smile overshadowed the usually good-natured
expression of his countenance, "a murderin' pity that ye didn't
think of that when ye——ye had the little row." He would have
said, "when ye struck him to the earth;" but in the dim light he
marked James Freney's eye flashing upon him, and he finished his
sentence, modified even as it was, in a trembling voice.

The unhappy young man remained silent for a few moments, while the rapidity of his pace increased. At length Hacket ventured to observe that the gang had lately been very discontented with his liberality—particularly to Lady Duncannon, whose money he had returned, merely because her husband was not with her; and even refused to take her watch, set with diamonds, which they considered robbing them of lawful plunder. "Ay," he said, mournfully, "it is ever thus; as well might the lordly lion, that I have read of, mate with the base-born ass, that brays at the moon, as one of gentle breeding assimilate with such a set—but I am a fool to talk thus to you, Hacket—and worse than a fool to have chosen such a life; but the die is cast, and I am a dreaded, degraded outlaw, whose miserable bones will, one of these days, rattle on a gibbet, in the March winds, and scorch there in a July sun—while you—you, Hacket—my poor mother's own relation, will be the sole living thing to shed a tear in remembrance of him who, instead of his own honest name, was called James Freney."

"No such thing," replied the *bocher*, notwithstanding his habits and associations, much moved at feelings which, although he could not enter into, he could sympathize with, simply because they affected one whom he sincerely loved, not merely for the sake of kith and kin, but from mingled and undefined sensations. "No such thing, you'll live and make a fortune, and get the pardon. Sure, you never harm anything to death, and are so complaisant to the ladies, that a woman's mob 'ud save ye, if ever it came to that. Ye may be a lawyer yet; I'm sure ye understand a dale more about it than half of 'em." The compliment fell unheeded on the ear of the rapparee, who observed:

"You gave my positive instructions to Breen, that all were to pass safe?"

"I did, though I thought it mighty foolish;—for just look here now—the ould justice *owes* ye—sure it's not trusting to seven or eight hundred pounds of his money ye'd be, if ye'd remained wid him? Didn't he breed ye up for his heir? Isn't a promise a debt? —and there can be no harm in taking what's one's own."

"I tell ye what, Hacket, if all the saints, and priests, and bishops, and the blessed Virgin herself, were to absolve me the next minute, I would not—I could not!—There's the share I had out of the Waterford merchants, that troublesome job; why, half the plunder now is hid up and down the country, in bog-holes and brier-knocks; but my share they shall have of that, and of anything else going. A kind commander I have ever been, and mean to remain; but I *will* be their COMMANDER while my brain has strength to frame a resolution, or my finger power to draw a trigger."

"Well—well—yer heart's set upon it, agra! enough said; for, as I live, the ould justice is on the move. I see Nelly Clarey herself, pokin' out with the candle, lookin' for me ; and Paddy Dooley, too ; and the sarvin'-men—the overfed, poor porpoises, crawlin' about; but, Captain, dear, ye'll never be able to get your horse, Beefstakes, out of the back shed, *unknownst*, while them lazy animals are loungin', doin' nothin' at all at all."

"Too true," replied Freney, evidently much annoyed at this information. " I meant to have been off before them."

"D'ye hear that girl screaming, ' Larry,' like a skirl-a-white ? Choke ye, a'n't I going !" Larry moved several steps towards the farmyard : then, as if remembering something particular, returned, and said, "Mister Captain, I jist wanted to tell ye that I fancied, may-be, ye were throwin' a sheep's-eye after Nelly ; now, I've always had a mind to that girl myself. Ay, ye may clap a sneer on yer handsome face if ye like ; but, though I own to the loss of the limb, I'm no bad fellow to look at when the disguise is off, and a tidy bit of a wooden leg on : there's a time for all things ; and I know you'd never think of her as your wife ; but I tell ye that barefooted lass deserves honourable tratement; and it would be what *I* don't deserve, let alone *her*, to have her head turned for nothin' at all, but, may-be, to make her an open shame before the whole country : so let her alone, and for once take a fool's advice." The *bocher* swung off towards the rude stables, leaving the rapparee, captain of one of the most daring gangs that ever infested the country, in an irritated and melancholy frame of mind. He folded himself up in the long blue cloak that had served to conceal his person at the inn, and ruminated, as he reclined against the mouldering wall, on the uncertainty and waywardness of what he, in his blindness, designated FATE.

> " There is a bitterness in man's reproach,
> Even when his voice is mildest, and we deem
> That on our heaven-born freedom they encroach,
> And with their frailties are not what they seem ;
> But the soft tones in star, in flower, or stream,
> O'er the unresisting bosom gently flow,
> Like whispers which some spirit in a dream
> Brings from her heaven to him she loved below,
> To chide and win his heart from earth, and sin, and woe."

Freney, the robber and the outlaw, felt the reproving voice from " star, and flower, and stream ;" and the brief vision of one who, had he conducted himself with common propriety, might have been the cherished and respected wife of his bosom, sent many a bitter pang of self-reproach through his aching heart ;—he contrasted what he *was*, with what he could have been ; few are there who can bear so miserable a retrospect unmoved.

He had seen Norah Dartforth not an hour before, and the remembrance of her surpassing loveliness pressed upon his imagination, in gentle but firm opposition of the efforts he made to obliterate her image from his memory. Poor Nelly Clarey, whom, with Irish recklessness, he had often jested with, forgetting the impression such conduct might make upon a thoughtless, but not a heartless girl—in his present refined mood now appeared a coarse and vulgar creature! and he felt more angry with Hacket for the insinuation he had thrown out about her, than for any other portion of his remonstrance. At length, overcome with contending feelings, he rested his head against one of the huge, white stones I have before mentioned; and, even while he watched the flitting lights in the inn-yard, sleep steeped his senses in forgetfulness.

"Captain, dear, what ails ye?" were the kindly sounds which awoke him to consciousness. "Lord save us! jist at the very minute whin all the wit ye have in the world is most wantin', to find ye sleepin' in this unlucky place, in the could moonlight, and not lookin' a taste like yerself. Rouse, Captain, honey! or those ye wish well to 'll be the worse for it."

The robber eagerly and anxiously inquired what the young woman's words portended.

"Whisht—asy!" exclaimed Nelly, in a low, confidential tone; "sure they think I'm asleep—for you don't look to me *sensible* that it's close upon eleven; and the mistress's tongue itself is quite a good hour agone; and the gentry set off afore nine; and there's more hotfoot after them than you'd have a mind to, I'm thinkin'."

"Nelly, for God's sake, come to facts at once, or——"

"I will; sorra a word I ha' said that wasn't as true as gospel—but let me tell it my own way. I heard ye say to Larry (the poor, conceated crature!) that ye wanted most particular to see Breen; well, for sartain sure, the *bocher* told him so, for he has been skulking about the place all day; but, instead of coming to the fore, I noticed him hidin' and pokin', more like a *grasnoque* than a Christian. Well, ye see, I went out about the stables, jist to cool myself, after the cookin', and the flurry o' dinner, and the quality, and all; and somehow, my light (though I made a screen for it, with a cabbage-leaf), went out jist at the minute I thought o' fodderin' the cow, the craythur, that the boys don't half mind; so, knowin' she doesn't like to be 'woke of a suddent, I went asy to the door, and jist as I was goin' to pull out the kipeen (not that the door's much good, on account of the gap in the wall), I hard Breen in low discourse wid another man, that I'd no knowledge of in life; and he went on for to tell him how unreasonable ye war' in regard of takin' a turn out o' the ould gentleman's money; and how he wouldn't listen to no such

T

thing—but purtend to you, whin it was all over, that it was nothin' but a misunderstandin', and down-face the *bocher* that he said one thing, when, to the hearin' of my two ears, the poor thing said the direct contrary."

"The villain!—the double-dealing, mean-spirited villain!" ejaculated Freney.

"Ye may say that," responded Nelly, "but wait awhile till ye know all. 'I'm certain,' says t'other man, 'that the Captain 'll take to the road after them, by way of purtection, for he has a suspicion over you, when anything like this is stirring'; and ye know there's not one o' the boys 'ud disobey the Captain.' 'I'm sure he's for the road,' says Breen, 'for Hacket tould me Beefstakes was in the same cow-shed, at the back, as my Slasher; and more betokens, at the right-hand side.' 'And a noble pair o' bastes they are,' remarks t'other; 'but Beefstakes is terrible knowin', and sorra a harm it would be to put a peg to his speed for to-night.' 'What do you mean?' says Breen. 'Bathershin,' makes answer the strange man, 'you don't know—why, just run a nail up the fetlock,—sure it's only an accident, and nobody the wiser.'"

"The cold-blooded scoundrel!" muttered the Captain between his firmly-set teeth, "the noble horse that has so often saved my life!"

"Well, they coshered, and coshered, so asy, I couldn't make out the words," persisted Nelly, "only the short and the long of it was, that the stranger was to go and lame the beast at once; and, as they couldn't get the animals out while the sarvents were about the house, jist wait till they were gone; and then, takin' the short road to the black gap, wait there for the company. May-be ye think ye have it all yer own way—says I; but better than you have got into the wrong box. So I stole off asy—asy—under shelter of the wall, till I cleared the corner, and then away with me in a whisk to poor Beefstakes. And what do ye think I did? I minded well what had been said, that *your* baste was on the *right* side; so I jist made 'em change places; and, my jewil! afore you could clap yer hands—afore I could make way for myself to get out o' the scrip of a shed, the murderin' black villain comes; and sure it's myself was afeared of the horses' heels; and I *scrudged* up into a mere nothin', right under Beefstakes' legs. And, as if the baste knew the business, he never stirred all the time the fellow was lamin' his own animal. Well, when he thought his job finished, Captain, honey, he skulked off with himself like an exciseman; and, as asy as ever I could, I made the crathurs change places again, like the great parliament lords; and ye may go bail it's little I heeded fodderin' the cow, though she turned her head to me, nataral as a Christian: and, knowin' yer saddle was particular, I changed that too; and God sees I was trembling for all the world like a shakin' bog, till I got out o' the place; and the end of it was—I see

the gentry off, and Breen wasn't long behind—but he was forced to
go asy at first, on account of the road—the short cut, ye know, bein'
broke up wid the rain; but, for fear he'd suspect (for the baste must
fall lame when he puts any speed upon it), I thought it most prudent,
ye see, jist to lift Beefstakes out o' the shed entirely—and so I led
him round to the black thorn to the left, by the gap, in the corner.
And now, Captain, 'gra! ye may think as ye please—but grim as ye
look, all this blessed time, I've done a friendly turn to you and the
baste—and——"

"Grim as I look!" repeated Freney, his gallantry and his grateful
feelings both rousing to meet the accusation :—"my darling Nelly, I
never loved ye half as well as at this moment," he continued, ener-
getically, at the same time imprinting no very gentle salute on her
lips. Ellen drew the back of her hand across her mouth, as if to
efface the kiss, and then replied :

"Faigs, Captain, I'll not say that's a lie, and yet the love ye talk
of isn't deep enough to smother a kitten; I see, as plain as I see the
moon in the heavens, that I'm not the sort for you to fix honourable
love upon—and for the other sort, I'd scorn it, as men scorn the
women they bring to shame : I didn't think so *once*, may-be—(the
poor girl's voice faltered)—but I see this day the *raale* bame o' love
from under yer hood, when it *wasn't* at *me* ye looked, and I *felt* the
differ :—but never heed it, Captain, aroon!"—and she drew herself
up, and laughed a light, bravoing laugh, which any one could hear
came from the lips, not the heart, and then half said, half sung, the
old stanza :—

> "' While me you thought for to beguile,
> I cared for another all the while ;
> And knew, my boy, what ye were at :
> Och! never fear but I spied ye, Pat !
> Wid yer smiles,
> And yer wiles !
> And by the same rule,
> Ye think every girl ye meet a fool' "

Freney was too earnest, too occupied, to play the gallant on this
occasion; and contented himself with observing, as he hastened
towards the spot where his really noble animal pawed the earth, with
"proud impatience of ignoble ease :"—

"Well, Nelly, sweethearting out of the question, you have acted
the part of a true friend, which, by God's blessing, I will never forget
to you or yours. Save ye, my brave lass! The head and the heart
of an Irishwoman are always ready when wanting, and faith, that's
more than can be said of the men." He sprang lightly into his
saddle, and Beefstakes, as if conscious that his utmost speed was

required used well the freedom of the loosened bridle : horse and rider were soon out of sight.

What the feelings of Nelly Clarey were, must now for ever remain unknown, even to me, her faithful historian ; all I can record of her is, that she repeatedly wiped her eyes with the corner of her apron, and then gazing, only for a moment, upon the spot where he had disappeared, with a deep-drawn sigh retraced her steps to the miserable, almost roofless, apartment, in which her couch was spread, and where she soon sweetly and tranquilly slumbered, as if she had never known sorrow, or revelled in tears.

I know not how it is, but there is a species of—must I call it coquetry ?—(I do not mean the regular coquetting system absolutely taught to a young female on her entrance into fashionable life, and which, in nine cases out of ten, from its visible arrangement, is perfectly harmless, and not unfrequently decidedly disgusting)—but a sort of natural witchery, born, I may say, with every genuine Irishwoman, and which, in the cottages, is particularly striking and fascinating. To those who have *not* witnessed it, I fear any description would appear unnatural, simply because unknown ; those who *have*, must be heartless if they have not felt, and do not remember, its charm. I cannot think it overstrained to call it the coquetry of innocence, for in it there is neither art nor guile ; it plays most bewitchingly in their bright and beaming smiles, when they blush at the remembrance of their earnest and heartfelt laughter ; and, though a young Irish girl will seldom look at a stranger, except "out of the corner of her eye," the glance has nothing sinister or suspicious about it, but discourses at the same moment modestly yet frankly ;—it is us apart from French flippancy as from English stiffness, and yet partakes of the gaiety, but not the lightness, of the former, blended with the reserve, without the formality, of the latter.

Freney pursued his course towards the high road, and murmured within himself, in no gentle terms, at the impediments in his way : the by-path was little more than a sheep-trail, and much broken by heavy and continued rains ; and, moreover, the moon ("pale, inconstant planet") withdrew her light, just at the time when our hero required it most. Beefstakes, however, knew his road well, and Freney left him pretty nearly to his own guidance, content with now and then encouraging his speed by some kind word of approbation, or an occasional pressure of his heel against his flank. The road they had taken led almost abruptly to the top of a wild, uncultivated hill, or rather what, in England, would be denominated a mountain ; and as the animal was gaining its summit, his master heard, or fancied he heard, the report of a gun or pistol ; the horse, too, evidently gave tokens that the well-known sound of fire-arms broke upon his ear, for

he snorted, and shook his head, while pressing more eagerly onward.
Freney suddenly checked the rein, and, leaning completely over
the neck of the noble animal, seemed as if inhaling whatever sounds
the night wind bore up the hill; the pause, though momentary, was
long enough for his purpose; he muttered a deep, low curse, too fearful for repetition, and urged the impetuous animal to its utmost speed.
It was a noble steed, and cleared every impediment that obstructed
its progress, vaulted the highest enclosures, and having attained the
summit of the hill, snorted the combat afar off as he dashed in gallant
style, down the declivity, with distended nostril and fire-striking foot.
Fortunately the moon threw a full and glorious flood of light on their
path, so that, even in the distance, Freney distinctly beheld the con-
firmation of his fears, and the necessity, had it been possible, for re-
doubled exertion. The ground descended steeply, but unevenly, into
a hollow glen, one side of which was skirted by stunted and straggling
brushwood, that fringed what was called the carriage road, while the
other sloped down to a sort of shingly bottom (the black glen),
through which a mountain stream brawled angrily and restlessly on
its way. This place had been selected by Breen as the most fitting
for his purpose, and at the moment the moon shone forth, the renegade had commenced rifling the carriage of Freney's early friend.
The old gentleman's faithful servants had evidently made a desperate,
and not a bloodless, resistance; and as the captain of the gang neared
the spot, his blood boiled, and his heart throbbed, for in the dim light
he beheld Norah Dartforth, with dishevelled tresses, supporting her
father in her arms, as she half knelt, half reclined, by the way-side.
The group was one that Salvator only could have painted, nor would
it have been unworthy of his pencil. The brightness of the clear
full-moon, from which the ill-omened, scowling clouds were rapidly
receding, leaving her alone and queen-like in the purity of her own
heavens—the abrupt and frowning mountain, glowering like a gigantic
and malignant spirit over all within its influence—the wild and
tangled copsewood that partially shaded, without obscuring, the
singular and dissimilar assemblage, that had for its centre the antique
and picturesque carriage—while the richly-dressed servants, and the
beautiful and interesting attitude of the kneeling girl, finely contrasted with the demoniac appearance of the lawless plunderers.
But even my king of painters, had I power to recall him from his
repose in that warm and sunny country—

> " Where the poet's lip and the painter's hand
> Are most divine,"—

must have failed in conveying an idea of the *succession* of mingled
and warring feelings that were manifested, when Freney, fierce and

terrible as the mountain-spirit, his horse covered with foam, his eyes flashing with rage and indignation, plunged in amongst them.

"Villain!" he exclaimed, seizing the wretch Breen by the collar, as a massive pocket-book, large enough for a modern folio, dropped from the false fellow's grasp; while, with the other hand, Freney drew from his belt a large horse pistol—"you are a fit example for all who disobey orders," he continued, with a frightful coolness of tone and manner.

"Mercy and hear me!" entreated the caitiff, falling on his knees, "there is no blood spilt to signify—no harm done:" then, suddenly recollecting himself, he added, "sure I can't understand *why* ye trate me after such a fashion—judgment afore death, in this world, any way."

"Look here, boys," persevered the Captain, without loosening his hold, "my orders were given—my orders have been disobeyed, and thus I punish *all*—ay—every mother's son who dares to think and act in opposition to them!" He cocked his pistol and placed its muzzle close to the wretched man's ear, while all who breathlessly beheld the scene appeared paralysed by the energy and determination of this singular being.

"For God's sake!—as you expect mercy at your dying day!—don't send me out o' the world without cross or prayer!—one—one minute to make my soul! Oh! for the sake of the mother that bore ye, remember another woman's son!" rapidly ejaculated the unfortunate man. His entreaties had little effect, and in another moment, he would have been launched into eternity, had not a small white hand for the second time that night, rested on Freney's shoulder; and a gentle voice, trembling and faint from agitation, exclaimed, "Forbear!" By degrees, his firm grasp relaxed, the lion melted into the lamb, and the outlaw, who braved the ordinances of man, and who would not have quailed beneath the iron grasp of justice, trembled at that gentle touch..

"I know not—I dread to know," said Miss Dartforth, "by what power you command those men—but I recognise the playmate of my youth; and the child my angel mother fostered will not surely stain his hand with blood."

"Believe me," he replied, earnestly, "that though Patrick James, and James Freney, are one and the same person, I have nothing to do with this night's unfortunate affair. I have not forgotten, Norah —pardon me, Miss Dartforth, I have not forgotten what I owe to your house." He turned abruptly from her, as if afraid to trust himself under her influence. "Rise, ye poor, trembling miscreant! —to the lady you would have plundered you owe your life," he continued, after a moment's pause, addressing Breen who did not need to have the permission repeated. "And now, my men, help Mr. Dartforth's servants to replace what you would have plundered. Breen, *your* assistance is not required—you hold no communion with my free-hearted boys; not one of them, except yourself, would have dared to disobey me—you and *one other*. All share of booty, for the next three months, I disclaim; there, replace the things, my fine fellows, and I'll count scores with you afterwards."

Freney's utterance and actions were rapid and energetic; his followers did as he commanded, with the air of persons who obey more from habit than inclination. It was, nevertheless, obvious, that Freney was much agitated; not from any dread of revolt amongst his gang, but from the recurrence, at such a moment, of recollections that almost overpowered him. After issuing his brief directions, he walked to where Miss Dartforth had returned to support her father, and hardly answered the question of one of his party, who, having discovered the person I before mentioned as the family " *toady,*" coiled up, or rather squatting, like the vile reptile whose name appropriately belongs to his class, under a huge furze-bush, dragged him forth, and held him, after the fashion of a bale of cloth, at either end, while he exclaimed, "Captain, dear! what's to be done wid this parcel? Sure the jontleman 'ud be glad to get rid of it any way; though, I'm thinkin', it's little good is in it, for man or baste."

The old gentleman was evidently labouring under an aberration of mind, brought on by terror and contending feelings; his every nerve trembled, and it was with great difficulty that his daughter and his own servant supported, or rather carried him towards the carriage, by that time ready for his reception. He perfectly understood that the young man who tendered his services to assist him forward, and had saved his property, perhaps his life, was the same he had first cherished, and then abandoned; but he did not appear to understand the light in which he stood, as captain of the robbers: he seized his proffered arm with the eagerness of a drowning man, catching at aught that is even symbolic of hope, and looked long and earnestly into his face; at length his pale, dull eyes filled with unbidden tears, and with a powerful effort he threw himself on the brigand's neck, lifted up his voice, and wept most bitterly. It was a time of trial for all, and, in after years, was often thought of.

Mr. Dartforth was at length placed in the carriage, and, in broken accents, he entreated Freney to enter with him. "All shall be yours, James, as before," he murmured—"sure you've saved my life. Norah, you speak for me—he always heeded you." This was more than Freney could bear;—he rushed from his grasp, ordering the coachman to drive on, in a tone of voice not to be disobeyed.

I have heard that Mr. Dartforth never perfectly recovered from the effects of that night's adventure; the consciousness that the youth he had so loved was the rapparee chief upon whose head a price was set, and who suffered the curse of Ishmael, even in his own land, embittered every hour of his existence; but worse even than that was the consciousness that *his* mismanagement had led to such fearful consequences. Even those who suffered from Freney's plunderings, were ready to admit there was that about him which, had it been properly managed, would have rendered him the admiration, not the terror, of his country. And with this miserable knowledge the old man descended to his grave, ignorant of that, which a few years of longer life would have informed him—for Freney in process of time, repented, and became reformed, and finished his days in peace and quietness in the town of New Ross.

ANNIE LESLIE.

ANNIE LESLIE was neither a belle nor a beauty—a gentle-woman, nor yet an absolute peasant—"a fortune," nor entirely devoid of dower:—although born upon a farm that adjoined my native village of Bannow, she might almost have been called a flower of many lands; for her mother was a Scot, her father an Englishman; one set of grandparents Welsh—and it *was* said that the others were (although I never believed it, and always considered it a gos-siping story) Italians, or foreigners, "from beyant the salt sea." It was a very charming pastime to trace the different countries in Annie's sweet, expressive countenance. Ill-natured people said she had a red, Scottish head, which I declare to be an absolute story. The maiden's hair was *not* red; it was a bright chestnut, and glowing as a sunbeam—perhaps, in particular lights, it might have had a tinge—

but, nonsense! it was anything but red: the cheek-bone was, certainly, elevated; yet who ever thought of that, when gazing on the soft cheek, now delicate as the bloom on the early peach—now purely carnationed, as if the eloquent colour longed to eclipse the beauty of the black, lustrous eyes, that were shaded by long, long, eyelashes, delicately turned up at the points, as if anxious to act as conductors to my young friend's merry glances, of which, however, I must confess, she was usually chary enough? Her figure was, unfortunately, "of the Principality," being somewhat of the shortest; but her fair skin, and small, delicate mouth, told of English descent. Her father was a respectable farmer, who had been induced, by some circumstance or other, to settle in Ireland; and her mother—but what have I to do with either her father or her mother, just now?

The sun-fires had faded in the west, and Annie was leaning on the neat green gate that led to her cottage; her eyes wandering down the branching lane, then to the softening sky, and not unfrequently to a little spotted dog, Phillis by name, who sat close to her mistress's feet, looking upwards, and occasionally raising one ear, as if she expected somebody to join their party. It was the full and fragrant season of hay-making, and Annie had borne her part in the cheerful and pleasant toil.

A blue muslin kerchief was sufficiently open to display her well-formed throat; one or two wilful ringlets had escaped from under her straw hat, and twisted themselves into very picturesque, coquettish attitudes, shaded, but not hidden, by the muslin folds; her apron was of bright check; her short cotton gown, pinned in the national three-cornered fashion behind, and her petticoat of scarlet stuff, displayed her small and delicately turned ancle to much advantage. She held a bunch of mixed wild flowers in her hand, and her fingers, naturally addicted to mischief, were dexterously employed in scattering the petals to the breeze, which sported them among the long grass.

"Down, Phillis!—down, miss!" said she, at last, to the little dog, who, weary of rest, stood on its hind legs, to kiss her hand; " down, do, ye're always merry when I'm sad, and that's not kind of ye." The animal obeyed, and remained very tranquil, until its mistress unconsciously murmured to herself—" Do I really love him?" Again she looked down the lane, and then, after giving a very destructive pull to one of the blossoms of a wild rose, that clothed the hedge in beauty, repeated, somewhat louder, the words, " Do I, indeed, love him?"

"Never say the word twice—ye do, ye little rogue!" replied a voice, that sent an instantaneous gush of crimson over the maiden's cheek—while, from amid a group of fragrant elder-trees, which grew

out of the mound that encompassed the cottage, sprang a tall, graceful
youth, who advanced towards the blushing maiden.

. I am sorry for it, but it is, nevertheless, an incontrovertible fact,
that women, young and old—some more, and some less—are all
naturally perverse; they cannot, I believe, help it; but their so being,
although occasionally very amusing to themselves, is, undoubtedly
very trying to their lovers, whose remonstrances on the subject,
since the days of Adam, might as well have been given to the winds.

It so happened that James Mc Cleary was the very person Annie
Leslie was thinking about—the one of all others she wished to see;
yet the love of tormenting, assisted, perhaps, by a little maiden
coquetry, prompted her first to curl her pretty Grecian nose, and
then to bestow a hearty cuff on her lover's cheek, as he attempted to
salute her hand.

"Keep your distance, sir, and don't make so free!" said the
pettish lady.

"Keep my distance, Annie! Not make so free!" echoed James;
"an' ye, jist this minute, after talking about loving me!"

"Loving you, indeed! Mister James Mc Cleary, it was yer *betters*
I was thinking of, sir; I hope I know myself too well for that."

"My betters, Annie!—what's come over ye? Surely ye haven't
forgot that yer father has as good as given his consint; and though
yer mother is partial to Andrew Furlong—the tame negur!—jist
because he's got a bigger house (sure, it's a Public, and can't be
called his own), and a few more guineas than me, and never thinks
of his being greyer than his ould grey mare—yet she'll come round;
—let me alone to manage the women—(now, don't look angry)—and
didn't yer own sweet mouth say it, not two hours ago, down by the
loch?—and by the same token, Annie, there's the beautiful curl I
cut off with the reaping-hook—that, however ye trate me, shall stay
next my heart, as long as it bates—and, oh, Annie! as ye sat on the
mossy stone, I thought I never saw ye look so beautiful—with that
very bunch of flowers that ye've been pulling to smithereens, resting
on yer lap. And it wasn't altogether what ye said, but what ye
looked, that put the life in me; though ye did say—ye know ye did
—'James,' says you, 'I hate Andrew Furlong, that I do, and I'll
never marry him as long as grass grows or water runs, that I won't.'
Now, sure, Annie, dear, sweet Annie!—sure ye're not going aginst
yer conscience, and the word o' true love."

"Sir," interrupted Annie, "I don't like to be found fault with.
Andrew Furlong is, what my mother says, a well-to do, dacent man,
staid and steady. I'll trouble ye for my curl, Mister James—clever
as ye are at managing the women, may-be ye can't manage me."

James had been very unskilful in his last speech; he ought not to

have boasted of his managing powers, but to have put them in
practice : the fact, however, was that, though proverbially sober, the
fatigue of hay-making, and two or three "noggins" of Irish grog,
had, in some degree, bewildered his intellects since Annie's return
from the meadow.   He looked at her for a moment, drew the long
tress of hair half out of his bosom, then replaced it, buttoned his
waistcoat to the throat, as if determined nothing should tempt it from
him, and said, in a subdued voice—

"Annie, Annie Leslie !—like a darlint, don't be so fractious—for
your sake—for——"

"My sake, indeed, sir !—My sake !—I'm very much obliged to
you, very much, Mister James ; but let me tell ye, ye think a dale
too much of yerself to be speaking to me after that fashion, and ye
inside my own gate ; if ye were *outside*, I'd tell ye my mind ; but I
know better manners than to insult any one at my own door-
stone : it's little other people know about dacent breeding, or
they'd not abuse people's friends before people's faces, Mister James
Mc Cleary."

"I see how it is, Miss Leslie," replied James, really angry : "ye've
resolved to sell yerself, for yer board and lodging, to that grate cask
of London porter, Andrew Furlong by name, and a booby by nature ;
but I'll not stay in the place to witness yer parjury—I'll go to sea,
or I'll——"

"Ye may go where ye like," responded the maiden, who now
thought herself much aggrieved and injured, "and the sooner the
better !"   She threw the remains of the faded nosegay from her, and
opened the green gate at the same instant—the gate which, not ten
minutes before, she had rested on, thinking of James Mc Cleary—
thinking that he was the best wrestler, the best hurler, the best
dancer, and the most sober lad in the country ;—thinking, moreover, that he was as handsome, if not as genteel, as the young
'squire ; and wondering if he would always love her as dearly as he
did then.   Yet in her perversity, she flung back the gate for the
faithful-minded to pass from her cottage, careless of consequences,
and, at the moment, really believing that she loved him not.   So
much for a wilful woman, before she knows the value of earth's
greatest treasure—AN HONEST HEART.

"Since it's come to this," said poor James, "any how, bid me
good-bye, Annie.——What, not one ' God be wid ye,' to him who
will soon be on the salt—salt sea !"   But Annie looked more angry
than before ; thinking, while he spoke, that he would come back fast
enough to her window next morning, bringing fresh grass for her kid,
or food for her young linnets, or, perchance, flowers to deck her hair ;
or (if he luckily met Peggy the fisher) a new blue silk neckerchief as
   peace-offering.

"Well, God's blessing be about ye, Annie; and may ye never feel what I do now!" So saying, the young man rushed down the green lane, frightening the wood-pigeons from their repose, and putting to flight the timid hare and tender leveret, who sought their evening meal where the dew fell thickly, and the clover was most luxuriant. There was a fearful reality about the youth's farewell that startled the maiden, obstinate as she was;—her heart beat violently, and the demon of coquetry was overpowered by her naturally affectionate feelings. She called, faintly at first, "James, James, *dear* James;" and poor little Phillis scampered down the lane, as if she comprehended her mistress's wish. Presently, Annie was certain she heard footsteps approaching; her first movement was to spring forward, and her next (alas, for coquetry!) to retire into the parlour, and await the return of her lover;—"what she wished to be true, love bade her believe;" there she stood, her eyes freed from their tears, and turned from the open window. Presently, the gate was unlatched; in another moment a hand softly pressed her arm, and a deep-drawn sigh broke upon her ear.

"He is very sorry," thought she, "and so am I." She turned round, and beheld the good-humoured, rosy face of mine host of the Public; his yellow bog-wig evenly placed over his grey hair; his Sunday suit well brushed; and his embroidered waistcoat (pea-green ground, with blue roses and scarlet lilies) covering, by its immense lapelles, no very juvenile rotundity of figure. Poor Annie! she was absolutely dumb : had Andrew been a horned owl, she could not have shrunk with more horror from his grasp. Her silence afforded her senior lover an opportunity of uttering, or rather growling forth, his proposal. "Ye see, Miss Leslie, I see no reason why we two shouldn't be married, because I have more regard for ye, tin to one, than any young fellow could have : for I am a man of exparience, and know wrong from right, and right from wrong—which is all one. Yer father, but more especially yer mother (who has oceans of sense for a woman), are for me ; and, beautiful as ye are, and more beautiful, for sartin, than any girl in the land, yet ye can't know what's good for ye as well as they ! And ye shall have a jaunting-car—a bran new jaunting-car of yer own, to go to mass or church, as may suit yer conscience, for I'd be far from putting a chain upon ye, barring one of roses, which 'Cupid waves,' as the song says, 'for all true constant loviers.' Now, Miss, machree, it being all settled—for sure ye're too wise to refuse sich an offer!—here, on my two bare knees, in the moonbames—that Romeyo swore by, in the play I saw when I was as good as own man to an honourable member o' parliament—(it was in this service he learned to make long speeches, on which he prided himself greatly)—do I swear to be to you a kind and faithful husband —and true to you and you alone."

Mr. Andrew sank slowly on his knees, for the sake of comfort resting his elbows on the window-sill, and took forcible possession of Annie's hand, who, angry, mortified, and bewildered, hardly knew in what set terms to vent her displeasure. Just at this crisis, the garden gate opened ; and little Phillis, who, by much suppressed growling, had manifested her wrath at the clumsy courtship of the worthy host, sprang joyously out of the window. Before any alteration could take place in the attitudes of the parties, James Mc Cleary stood before them, boiling with jealousy and rage. "So, Miss Leslie—a very pretty manner you've treated me !—and it was for that *carcase* (and he pushed his foot against Andrew Furlong), that ye trampled me like the dust ; it was because *he* has a few more bits o' dirty bank notes, that he scraped by being a lick-plate to an unworthy mimber, who sould his country to the Union and Lord Castlereagh : but ye'll sup sorrow for it—ye will, Annie Leslie, for yer love is wid me, bad as ye are ; yer cheek has blushed, yer eye has brightened, yer heart has bate for me, as it never will for *you*, ye foolish, foolish ould cratur, who thinks the finest—the holiest feeling that God gives us, can be bought with gould ! But I am done ; as ye have sowed, Annie, so ye may reap. I forgive ye—though my heart—my heart—is torn— almost, almost broken ; for I thought ye faithful—I was wound up in ye—ye were the very core of my heart—and now——" The young man pressed his head against a cherry-tree, whose wide-spreading branches overshadowed the cottage. Annie, much affected, rushed into the garden, and took his hand affectionately ; he turned upon her a withering look, for the jealous fit was waxing stronger.

"What ! do ye want to make more sport of me to please your *young* and *handsome* lover ?. Oh ! that ever I should throw ye from me !" He flung back her hand, and turned to the gate ; but Andrew, the gallant Andrew, thought it behoved him to interfere when his lady-love was treated in such a disdainful manner ; and, after having, with his new green silk handkerchief, carefully dusted the knees of his scarlet plush breeches, came forward :

"I take it that that's a cowardly thing for you to do, James Mc Cleary—a cow——"

"What do you say ?" vociferated James, whose passion had now found an object to vent itself on—"did you dare call me a coward ?". He seized the old man by the throat, and, gripping him as an eagle would a land-tortoise, held him at arm's length : "Look ye, ye fat ould calf, if ye were my equal in age or strength, it isn't talking to ye I'd be ; but I'd scorn to illtrate a man of yer years—though I'd give a thousand pounds this minute that ye were young enough for a fair fight, that I might have the glory to break every bone in yer body— but there !"—He flung his weighty captive from him with so much violence, that mine host found himself extended amid a quantity of white-heart cabbages; while poor James sprang amid the elder-trees, which before had been his place of happy concealment, and rushed away.

Annie stood erect under the shadow of the cherry-tree, against which James had rested, and the rays of the clear, full moon, flickering through the foliage, showed that her face was pale and still as marble. In vain did Phillis jump and lick her hand; in vain did Andrew vociferate, in tender accents, from the cabbage-bed where he lay, trying first to turn upon one side, and then on the other—"Will no one take pity on me?"—"Will nobody help me up?" There stood Annie, wondering if the scene was real, and if all the misery she endured could possibly have originated with herself. She might have remained there much longer, had not her father and mother returned from the meadows, where they had been distributing the usual dole of spirits to their barelegged labourers. "Hey, mercy, and what's the matter noo?" exclaimed the old Scotch lady; "why, Annie, ye're clean daft for certain; and, good man Andrew! what has happened you, that ye're rubbing your clothes with your bit napkin, like a fury? Hey! mercy me, if my beautiful kail isn't perfectly ruined, as if a hail hogshead of yill had been rowed over it! Speak, ye young hizzy!"—and she shook her daughter's arm—"what is the matter?"

"Annie," said her less eloquent father; "tell me all about it, love; how pale you are!" He led his child affectionately into the little parlour, while Andrew, with doleful tone and gesture, related to the "gude-wife" the whole story as far as he was concerned. The poor girl's feelings were at length relieved by a passionate burst of tears; and, sobbing on her father's bosom, she told the truth, and confessed it was her love of tormenting that had caused all the mischief.

"I do believe," said the honest Englishman, "all you women are the same. Your mother was nearly as bad in our courting days. James is too hot and too hasty—rapid in word and action; and knowing him as you do, you were wrong to trifle with him; but there, love, I must, I suppose, go and find him, and make all right again; shall I, Annie?"

"Father!" exclaimed the girl, hiding her face in that safe resting-place, a parent's bosom.

"Send old Andrew off, and bring James back to supper—eh?"

"Dear father!"

"And you will not be perverse, but make sweet friends again?"

"Dear, *dear* father!"

The good man set off on his embassy, first warning his wife not to scold Annie; adding, somewhat sternly, he would not permit her to be *sold* to anyone. To which speech, had he waited for it, he would doubtless have received a lengthened reply.

As Mr. Leslie proceeded down the lane I have so often mentioned, he encountered a man well known in the country by the *sobriquet* of " Alick the Traveller," who, with his wearied donkey, was in search of a place of rest. Alick was a person of great importance, known to everybody, high and low, rich and poor, in the province of Leinster : he was an amusing, cunning, good-tempered fellow, who visited the gentlemen's houses as a hawker of various fish, particularly oysters, which he procured from the far-famed Wexford beds ; and, after disposing of his cargo, he was accustomed to reload his panniers from our cockle-strand of Bannow, which is equally celebrated for that delicate little fish. Neither shoes nor stockings did Alick wear ; no, he carried them in his hand, and never put them on, until he got within sight of the *genteel* houses ;—" he'd be long sorry to give dacent shoes or stockings such usage : sure his feet were well used to the stones !" His figure was tall and erect ; and the long stick of sea-weed, with which he urged poor Dapple's speed, was thrown over his shoulder with the careless air that, in a well-dressed man, would be called elegant. A weather-beaten *chapeau de paille* shaded his rough, but agreeable features ; and stuck on one side of it, in the twine which served as a hat-band, were a " cutty pipe," and a few sprigs of beautifully tinted sea-weed and delisk, forming an appropriate, but singular garniture. He was whistling loudly on his way, and cheering his weary companion, occasionally, by kind words of encouragement.

" God save ye, this fine evening, Mr. Leslie ; I was just thinking of you, and all yer good family, which I hope is hearty, as well as the woman that owns ye. And I was just saying to myself, that, may-be, ye'd let me and the baste stay in the corner to-night, for I've a power o' beautiful fish, and I want to be early among the gentry. But if the mistress likes a taste of news, or a rattling hake——"

" Alick," said Leslie, who knew, by experience, the difficulty of stopping his tongue " when once it was set a-going,"—" go to the house ; and, there's a hearty welcome—a good supper and clean straw for ye both. But tell me, have you seen James Mc Cleary this evening ?"

" Och ! is it James ye're after ? There's a beautiful lobster !—let Kenny, Paddy Kenny (may-be ye don't know Paddy, the fishmonger, wid the blue door at the corner of the ould market in Wexford), let Paddy Kenny bate that !——"

" But James Mc Cleary——"

" True for ye, he'll be glad to see ye. Now, Mister Leslie, tell us the truth, did ye ever see sich crabs as thim in England ? Where 'ud they get them, and they so far from the sea ?"

" I want——"

" I humbly ax yer pardon---I saw him jist now cutting off in that

way, as straight as a conger eel—I had one t'other day, Mister
Leslie (it's as true as that ye're standing there) it weighed——"

" What ?—did he go across the fields in that direction ?"

" Is it he ?—troth, no, I skinned him as nate——"

" Skinned who ?—James Mc Cleary ?"

" Och, no; the conger."

" Will you tell me in what direction you saw James Mc Cleary go ?
—the misfortune of all Irishmen is, that they answer one question
by asking another."

" I don't like ye to be taking the country down, after that fashion,
Mister Leslie; it's bad manners, and I can't see any misfortune about
it; and if I did, there's no good in life of making a cry about it ;—
but there's an illegant cod !—there's a whopper !—there's been no
rest or peace wid that lump of a fellow all the evening—whacking
his tail in the face of every fish in the basket; I'll let the misthress
have him a bargain if she likes, jist to get rid of him—the tory !"

Leslie at last found that his questions were useless; so he motioned " Alick the Traveller" to his dwelling, and proceeded on his
way to James's cottage ;—while Alick, gazing after him, half muttered, "There's no standing thim Englishmen ; the best of them are so
dead like—not a word have they in their head; not the least taste in
life for conversation. Catch James !—I hope it didn't turn out bad,
though," he continued, in a still lower tone : "what I said a while
agone was all out o' innocence, for a bit o' fun wid the ould one."
He turned, and, for a moment, watched the path taken by
Leslie, then proceeded on his way, muttering—"'tis very quare,
though."

At the door of James Mc Cleary's cottage, Leslie encountered the
young man's mother. " 1 was jist going to your place to ask what's
come over my boy," said she ; " I can't make him out; he came in,
in such a fluster, about tin minutes agone, and kicked up sich a bobbery in no time : flustered over his clothes in the press, cursed all
the women in the world, bid God bless me, and set off, full speed,
like a wild deer, across the country."

" Indeed !" exclaimed Leslie.

" I know, Mr. Leslie, that my boy has been keeping company wid
your girl ; and I have nothing to say agin her; she has a dale o'
the lady about her, yet is humble and modest as any lamb; but I
think, may-be, they've had a bit of a ruction about some footy thing
or other ; but men can't bear to be contradicted, though I own it's
good for them, and more especially James, who has a dale of his
father in him, who I had to manage (God rest his sowl !) like any
babby. However, James has too much sense to go far, I'm thinking
—only to his aunt's husband's daughter, by the Black-water, fancy-

U

ing, may-be, to bring Annie round; and so I was going to see her, to know the rights of it."

The kind-hearted farmer told her nearly all he knew, with fatherly feeling glossing over Annie's pettishness as much as he possibly could. Mrs. Mc Cleary remained firm in her opinion that he had only gone down to the Black-water, and would return the next day. But Leslie's mind foreboded evil. When he arrived at home, he found "Alick the Traveller" comfortably seated in the large chimney-corner—a cheerful turf-fire casting its light, sometimes in broad masses, sometimes in brilliant flashes, over the room : the neat white cloth was laid for supper; and the busy dame was seated opposite the itinerant man of fish, laughing long and loudly at his quaint jokes and merry stories. Annie was looking vacantly from the door that was shut, to the window, through which she could not see; and Phillis was stretched along the comfortable hearth, rousing herself, occasionally, to reprimand the rudeness of a small, white kitten, Annie's particular pet, which obstinately persisted in playing with the long, silky hairs of the spaniel's bushy tail. When Leslie entered, the poor girl's heart beat violently; and the colour rose and faded almost at the same moment. She busied herself about household matters, to escape observation; broke the salt-cellar in endeavouring to force it into the cruet-stand, and verified the old proverb, "spill the salt, and get a scolding," for the mother did scold, in no measured terms, at the destruction of what the careless hizzy had broken. "Did ye na ken that it had been used for twenty years and mair?" she reiterated; "and did Christian woman ever see sic folly, to force a broad salt, of thick glass, into a place that can na mair than haud a wee bottle? The girl's daft, and that's the end on't." Notwithstanding the jests of Alick, the evening passed heavily: Annie complained of illness, and went soon to bed; and as her father kissed her, at the door of her little chamber, he felt that her cheek was moist and cold. Mrs. Leslie soon followed; and the farmer replenished his long pipe, as Alick added fresh tobacco to his stumpy one. "I'm sorry to see Miss Annie so ill," said the honest hawker, in a kindly tone; "but this time all the girls get tired at the hay-making. Well, it bates all, to think how you farmers can be continted jist wid looking on the sky, and watching the crops, over and over again, in the same place! I might as well lie down and die at onst, as not keep going from place to place. One sees a dale more o' life, and one sees more o' the tricks o' the times. Och, but the world's a fine world, only for the people that's in it!—it's them *spiles* it.—I had something to say to you, Mister Leslie, very partiklar, that I came to the knowledge of quite innocent. Ye mind that Mister Mullager, Maley, as he calls himself for the sake of the *English*, has been playing the puck wid Lord Clifford's tinnants, as might be

expected; for his mother was a chimbley sweeper, that had the luck
to marry a dacent boy enough, only a little turned three-score; and
thin this beautiful scoundrel came into the world, and, betwixt the
two, they left him the power and all o' hard, yellow ginnees. Now,
he being desperate 'cute, got into my Lord's employ, being only a
slip of a boy at the time. Well, lords, to my thinking (barring the
ould ancient ones), are only foolish sort of min, any how—I could
go bail that my Lord Clifford hadn't a full knowledge box, any way;
and so, through one sly turn or other, this fellow bothered him so,
and threw dust in his eyes, and wheedled him, that, ye know, at last
he comes the gintleman over us; and tould me, t'other day, that as
fine a jacky-dorey as iver ye set yer two good-looking eyes on, was
nothing but a fluke—the ignorant baste! Fine food for sharks he'd
be; only the cratur that 'ud ate him must be hungry enough—the
thief o' the world!"

"What has all this to do with me, Alick?" inquired the Englishman, steadily, while the traveller, incensed at the remembrance of the
insult offered to his fish, scattered the burning ashes out of his cutty
pipe, to the no small consternation of the crickets—merry things!—
who had come on the hearth-stone to regale on cold potatoes. "I
know," he continued, "that the agent, or whatever he calls himself, is
no friend of mine. When my landlord came to the country, he did
me the honour to ask my opinion; I showed him the improvements,
that I, as an English farmer, thought might be profitable to the estate;
he desired me to give in an estimate of the expense; I did so; but the
honest agent, or more properly speaking, middle-man, had given one
in before. His lordship found that, by my arrangements, the expense
was lessened one half; but Maley persuaded my Lord that his plans
were best, and so——"

"Ay," interrupted Alick, "couldn't ye have been content to mind
yer farm, and not be putting English plans of improvement into an
Irish head, where it's so hard to make them fit? When the devil was
civil, and, like a jintleman, held out his paw to ye, why didn't ye make
yer bow, and take it?—sure, that had been only manners, let alone
sense—don't look so bleared! What, ye don't understand me?"
Alick advanced his body slowly forward, rested his elbows on the
small table, pressed his face almost close to Leslie's, whose turn it
was, now, to lay down his pipe, and slowly said, in a firm, audible
whisper,—"Whin Tim Mullager, the curse o' the poor—the thing in
man's shape, but widout a heart—met ye one evening, by chance as
you thought, at the far corner of the very field ye cut to day, what
tempted ye (for ye mind the time—my Lord thought a dale about yer
English notions thin), when he asked ye, as sweet as new milk, to join
him in that very estimate unknownst to my Lord, and said, ye mind,

that it might be made convanient to the both o' ye, and a dale more
to the same purpose; and, instead of seeming to come in, my jewel!
you talked something about 'tegrity and honour, which was as hard
for *him* to make out as priest's Latin; and walked off as stately as the
tower of Hook."

"But I never mentioned a syllable of his falsehood to do him
injury," exclaimed the astonished farmer; "I never breathed it, even
to Lord Clifford."

"And more fool you—I ax yer pardon, but more fool you—that
was yer time; and it was the time for more than that—it was the
time for ye to get a new laase upon the ould terms, and not to be trusting to lords' promises, which are as asy broken as anybody else's."

"You are a strange fellow, Alick; how did you know anything
about my lease? At all events, though it is expired, I am safe
enough, for I am sure that even Muley could not wish a better
tenant."

"A better tinant!" responded Alick; fairly laughing: "a better
tinant!—fait, that's not bad!—What does he care whether ye're a
good or bad tinant *to my Lord?*—doesn't he want, man alive!—to
have ye body and sowl?—the rig'lar rint, to be sure, for the master;
all fair—the little *dooshure* for himself; the saaling money, if a laase
to the fore; and a five-pound note, not amiss as a civility to his bit of
a wife; thin the duty-hens, duty-turkeys, duty-geese, duty-pigs;—
the spinning and the knitting:—sure, if my Lord or my Lady isn't
to the fore, they'll save them the trouble of looking after sich things;
and they, ye know, get the cash—that is, as much as the agent
chooses to say is their due—and spend it in foreign parts, widout
thinking o' the tears and the blood it costs at home.—Och, Mister
Leslie! it's no wonder if we'd have the black heart to sich as them!"

Leslie, for the first time of his life, felt a doubt as to the nature
of the situation in which he was placed: he looked around upon the
fair white walls, so dear, so very dear to the purest feelings of his
heart; every object had a claim on his affections,—even the long
wooden peg, upon which his great coat hung behind the door, was
as valuable to him as if it were of gold.

"I can hardly understand this," said he, at last; "you know I
have always been on good terms with my neighbours, yet I have acquired little knowledge in these matters; I have always paid my
rent to the moment; and, as my twenty-one years' lease only expired
two or three days ago, I have had little opportunity of judging how
Irish agents behave on such occasions."

"Don't be running down the country, Mr. Leslie," said Alick,
quickly, "there's a dale in the differ betwixt the raale gintry and
such *musheroons* as he; but keep a look-out, for he's after no good.

The day afore yesterday, whin he behaved so unhandsome to my
jacky-dorey—('twould ha' done yer heart good to look at that beautiful fish), he was walking with another spillogue of a fellow (the
gauger, by the same token); and so, as they seemed as thick as twa
rogues, whispering and nodding, and laying down the law, I thought
if I let the baste go on, he'd keep safe to the road; and so, as they
walked up one side of the hedge that leads to the hill, I jist streeled
up the other, to see, for the honour of ould Ireland, if I could fish
out the rogue's maning. Well, to be sure, they settled as how the
rint should be doubled on the land that fell, more especially yours,
and fines raised, and the gauger's to act as 'turney;' but he said
that he knew you'd pay anything rather than lave the house ye
settled up yerself; and then t'other said ('twas the word he spoke),
' the ould Scotch cat wouldn't let ye spind the money:' and then
t'other held to it, and said ye must go, for ye set a bad example of
indipindence to the neighbours, and a dale more: but the upshot
was, that they must get rid o' ye. And now, God be wid ye, and
do yer best; and take care of that girl o' yours, and don't let the
mistress bother her about that ould man, any more; she's full o'
little tricks—may *sense*, not *sorrow*, sober thim, say I: good night,
and thank ye kindly: Mr. Leslie, I'm the boy 'll look to ye, and
don't think bad o' my saying that to the likes o' you; for ye remimber how the swallow brought word to the eagle where the fowler
stood. God's blessing be about ye all, Amin!" And the keen,
wandering, good-natured fellow left the house to share, according to
custom, Dapple's couch of clean straw, in the neighbouring shed.

The next morning Leslie's family received a visit from the agent,
to the surprise of Annie and her mother, who welcomed him with
much civility, while the farmer's naturally independent feelings
struggled stoutly with his interests. If there be one thing more
than another to admire in the character of English yeomen, it is
their steady bearing towards their superiors; they feel that they
are free-born men, and they act as such; but an Irish farmer must
often play the spaniel to his landlord, and to all that belong to his
household, or bear his name; hardly daring to believe himself a man,
much less fancy that, from his Maker's hand, he came forth a being
gifted with quick and high intellect—with a heart to feel, and a head
to think, as well as, if not better than, the lord of the soil. But
Mind, though it may be suppressed, cannot be destroyed; with the
Irish peasant *cunning* frequently takes the place of *boldness*, and he
becomes dangerous to his oppressors. Landlords may often thank
their own wretched policy for the crimes of their tenantry, when
they cease to reside amongst, or even visit, them, but leave them to
the artful management of ignorant and debased middle-men, who

uniformly have but two principles of action—to blindfold their employers, and gain wealth at the expense of proprietor and tenant.

"Yer house is always nate and clane, Mrs. Leslie," said Maley, "and yer farm does ye credit, master; I'm sorry it's out of lase, but my duty to my employer obliges me to tell you that a new lase, if granted, must be on more advantageous terms to his Lordship. Yer present payments, arable and meadow land together, average something about two pounds five or six per acre."

"Yes," replied Leslie, "always paid to the hour."

"And if it please ye, sir," said the good dame, "when his Lordship was down here, he made us a faithful promise, on the honour of a gentleman, that he'd renew the lease on the same terms, in consideration of the money and pains my husband bestowed on the land."

The agent turned his little grey eye sharply on the honest creature, and gave a grunt, that was less a laugh than a note of preparation for one, observing, "May-be he's lost his memory; for there, Mr. Leslie, is the proposal he ordered me to make (he threw a sheet of folded foolscap on the table), so you may take it or lave it."

He was preparing to quit the cottage when his eye glanced on a basket of turkey eggs that Annie had arranged to set under a favourite hen. "What fine eggs!" he exclaimed; "I'll take two or three to show my wife." And, one after another, he deposited all the poor girl's embryo chickens in his capacious pockets.

Leslie, really aroused by the barefaced impudence of the act, was starting forward to prevent it, when his wife laid her hand on his arm; not that she did not sorrow after the spoil, but she had a point to gain.

"May-be, sir, ye'd joost tell me the Laird's present address; Annie, put it down on that bit paper."

"Tell his address!—anything ye have to say must be to me, good woman. And so ye write, pretty one; I wonder what is the use of taaching such girls as you to write : but ye're up to love-letters before this ; ay, ay, ye'll make the best of yer black eyes, my dear !" With this insulting speech the low man in power left the cottage.

Bitter was the anguish felt by that little party. The father sat, his hands supporting his head, his eyes fixed on the exorbitant demand the agent had left upon his table; large tears passed slowly down Annie's cheek ; and, if the poor mother suffered less than the others, it was because she talked more.

"Dinna be cast doon, Robert," said she, at last, to her husband; "ye hae nae reason, even if he ask sae much money as ye say, us a premium, forbye other matters ; why, there are as gude farms elsewhere, and landlords that look after their tenants themselves. Oh, that wicked, wicked wretch !—to see him pocket the eggs—and his speech to my poor Annie !"

"My darling daughter!" exclaimed the father, pressing his daughter to his bosom, where he held her long and anxiously.

It was almost impossible for Leslie to accede to the terms demanded: four pounds an acre for the farm, a heavy fine, and both duty-work, and duty provisions, required in abundance.

"Dinna think o't, Robert," repeated the dame; "we'll go elsewhere, and find better treatment. If ye keep it at that rate we shall all starve." But the farmer's heart yearned to every blade of grass that had grown beneath his eye: he hoped to frustrate the intended evil, and yet keep the land. His crops had been prosperous, his cattle healthy; then, his neighbours, when, through Alick's agency, they found how matters stood, had, with the genuine Irish feeling that shines more brightly in adversity than in prosperity, come forward, affectionately tendering their services.

"Sure, the cutting the hay need niver cost ye a brass fardin," said the kind-hearted mower; "I'm half my time idle, and I may jist as well be doing something for you as nothing for myself; so don't trouble about it, sir, dear; we like to have ye among us."

Then came "Nelly the Picker," as the spokeswoman of all her sisterhood. "Don't think of laving us, Mrs. Leslie, ma'am; sure every one of us 'll come as usual, but widout fee or reward, excipt the heart love, and do twice as much for that as for the dirty money; and I'll go bail the pratees will be as well picked, and the corn as well reaped, bound, and stacked as iver. Sure, though we didn't much like ye at first, hasn't Miss Annie grown up among us, born as she is on the sod, and a credit to it, too, God be praised!"

These were all very gratifying instances of pure and simple affection: indeed, even Andrew Furlong forgot his somerset in the cabbage-bed, and posted down to the farm with his stocking full of gold and silver coins, of ancient and modern date, which were all at Leslie's service, to pay the premium required by the agent for the renewal of the lease. This last favour, however, the worthy farmer would not even hear of; he, therefore, sold a great part of his stock, and, to the annoyance of the agent, obtained the lease. From this circumstance he might be said to triumph over the machinations of his enemy; but matters soon changed sadly: the family was as industrious as ever; the same steady perseverance on the farmer's part; the same bustle and unwearying activity on that of the good dame; and, though poor Annie's cheek was more pale, and her eyes less bright, yet did she unceasingly labour in and out of their small dwelling. Notwithstanding all these exertions, the next season was a bad one; their sheep fell off in the rot, their pigs had the measles, their chickens the pip, and two of their cows died in calf. Never did circumstances, in the little space of six months, undergo so great a change. Leslie's silence

smounted almost to sullenness; his wife talked much of their ill-fortune;
Annie said nothing, but her step had lost its elasticity, her figure its
grace, and her voice seldom trolled the joyous, or even the mournful,
songs of her native land in the elder-bower, that, before the departure
of James Mc Cleary, had rung again and again with merry laughter
and music. James never returned after that unfortunate evening;
and his mother had only twice heard from him since his absence: his
letters were brief—"He had gone," he said, "to sea, to enable him
to learn something, and to forget much." His mother and younger
brother managed the farm with much skill and attention during his
absence. No token, no word of *her* whom he had dotingly loved,
appeared in his letters. It was evident that he tried to think of her
as a heartless, jilting woman, unworthy to possess the affections of a
sensible man; but there must have been times when the remembrance of her full beauty, of her frank and generous temper, of her
many acts of charity (and in these she was never capricious), came
upon him;—then the last scene at the cottage was forgotten, and he
remembered alone her sweet voice, and sweeter look, in the hay
meadow, when he cut off the curling braid of hair, which, doubtless,
rested on his bosom in all his wanderings. And then he refreshed
his memory by gazing on it, in the clear moonlight, during the night
watches, when only the eye of heaven was upon him. Let no one
imagine such love is too refined to throb in a peasant's bosom; trust
me, it is not. The being who lives amid the beauties of nature,
although he may not express, must feel, the elevating, yet gentle
influence of herb, and flower, and tree. Many a time have I heard
the ploughman suspend his whistle to listen to that of the melodious
blackbird; and well do I remember the beautiful expression of one
of my humblest neighbours, when, resting on his hay-fork, he had
silently watched the sun as it set over a country glowing in its red
and golden ght: "It is very grand, yet hard to look upon," said
he; "one can almost think it God's holy throne!"

The last letter that reached our sailor-friend contained, amongst
others of similar import, the following passage:—"Ye'll be sorry to
hear, James (though it's nothing to ye now), that times are turned
bad with the Leslies; there has been a dale of underhand work by
my Lord's agent; and the girl's got a cold, dismal look. My heart
aches for the poor thing, for her mother is set upon her marrying
Andrew Furlong, which she has no mind in life to."

Gale-day (as the rent-day is called in Ireland) had come and gone,
and much sorrow was in the cottage of Robert Leslie. In the grey
twilight he sat in a darkened corner of his little parlour, the very
atmosphere of which appeared clouded; the dame stood at the open
casement, against which Annie reclined more like a stiffened corpse

than a breathing woman. Andrew Furlong was seated also at the
table, looking earnestly on the passing scene.

"Haven't ye seen," said the mother, "haven't ye seen, Annie, the
misery that's come upon us, entirely by my advice being no minded?
And are ye goin' tamely to see us turned out o' house and hame,
when we have na the means of getting anither? I, Annie," she
continued, "am a'maist past my labour; ah, my bonny bairn, it was
for *you* we worked—for you we toiled; your faither an' me had but
the one heart in that; and if the Lord Almighty has pleased to take
it fra us, it's na reason why you should forget how ye were still
foremost in your parents' love."

Annie answered nothing.

"Speak to her, Robert," said Mrs. Leslie, "she disna mind me noo."

Annie raised her eyes reproachfully to her mother's face. The
farmer came forward; he kissed the marble brow of his pale child,
and she rested her head on his shoulder. As he turned towards her,
she whispered, "Is all, indeed, as bad as mother says?"

"Even so," was his reply; "unless *something* be done, to-morrow
we shall have no home. Annie, it is to shield you I think of this;
my delicate, fading flower, how could *you* labour as a hired servant?
And—God in His mercy look upon us!—I should not be able to find
a roof to shelter my only child!"

"My bairn," again commenced Mrs. Leslie, "sure the mother that
gave ye birth can wish for nathing sa much as your weel-doing; and
sure sic a man as Maister Furlong could na fail to make ye happy.
All the goud your faither wants he will gi'e us noo, trusting to his
bare word; to-morrow, and it will be too late;—all these things
sauld—the sneers of that bitter man—the scorn (for poverty is aye
scorned) of a cauld warld—and, may-be, your faither in a lanely
prison; eh, child—what could ye do for him then?"

"Mother!" exclaimed the girl, starting, with convulsive motion,
from her father's shoulder; "say no more; here—a promise is all he
wants to prevent this—here is my hand—give it where you please."
She stretched out her arm to its full length—it was rigid as iron.
Furlong advanced to take it; and whether Leslie would have permitted such a troth-plight or not, cannot now be ascertained, for the
long form of Alick the Traveller stalked abruptly into the room.

"Asy, asy, for God's sake!—put up your hand, Miss Annie, dear;
keep your sate, I beg, Mr. Furlong; no rason in life for your rising;
all of you be asy. Will nobody quiet that woman, for God's sake?"
he continued, seeing that the dame was, naturally enough, angry at
this intrusion; "first let me say my say, and be off, for sorra a minute
have I to waste upon ye. Robert Leslie by name, didn't I, onst
upon a time, tell ye truth? and a sore hearing it was, sure enough.

Well then, I tell it ye again, and if it's not true, why ye may hang
me as high as Howth;—don't let your daughter mum herself away
after that fashion.   Mister Furlong, ye're a kind-hearted man, so ye
are, and many a bit an' a sup have ye bestowed upon me and the
baste—thank ye kindly for that same—but yarra a much sense ye
have, or ye wouldn't be looking after empty nuts :—what the devil
would be the good o' the hand o' that cratur, widout her heart?
and that ye'll niver have.   Mistress Leslie, ma'am, honey, don't be
after blowing me up;—now jist think—sure I know that ye left the
bonny hills and the sweet-scented broom of Scotland, to marry that
Englishman.   And ye mind the beautiful song that ye sing, far before
any one I ever heard—about loving in youth, and thin climbing the
hill, and thin sleeping at the fut of it—John Anderson ye call it:
wouldn't ye rather have yer heart's first love, though he's ould and
grey now, than a king upon his throne?   Ay, woman, that touches
ye!   And do ye think *she* hasn't some o' the mother's feel in her?
Now, Mister Leslie, don't—don't any of ye make her promise to-
night; ye'll bless me for this, even you, Mister Andrew, by to-morrow
sun-set; promise, Robert Leslie."

" You told me truth before," said the bewildered man, " and I have
no right to doubt you now, I do promise."   Alick strode out of the
cottage; Andrew followed, like an enraged turkey-cock, and the
family were left again in solitude.   The words of the fisherman had
affected Mrs. Leslie deeply : she had truly fancied she was seeking
her child's happiness; and, perhaps for the first time, she remembered
how miserable she would have been with any other husband than
" her ain gude-man."

The little family passed the night almost in the very extremity of
despair.   " Such," said Leslie, afterwards, " as I could not pass again ;
for the blood now felt as if frozen in my veins, now rushing through
them with fearful rapidity, and, as my head rested on my poor wife's
shoulder, the throbbing of my bursting temples but echoed the beating of her agitated heart."   The early light of morning found Annie
in a heavy sleep; and the mid-day sun glowed as brightly as if it
illuminated the pathway of princes, on three or four ill-looking men,
who entered the dwelling of the farmer.   Their business was soon
commenced, it was a work of heart-sickening desolation.   On Annie's
pure and simple bed sat one of the officials, noting down each article
in the apartment.   Leslie, his arms folded, his lips compressed, his
forehead gathered in heavy wrinkles over his brow, stood firmly in
the centre of the room.   Mrs. Leslie sat, her face covered with her
apron, which was soon saturated by her tears, and poor little Phillis
crouched beneath her chair; Annie clung to her father's arm ; her
energies were roused as she feelingly appealed to the heartless execu-

tors of the law. What increased the wretchedness of the scene was
the presence of Mr. Muley himself, who seemed to exult over the
misery of his victims. He was not, however, to have it all his own
way; several of the more spirited neighbours assembled, and forgot
their own interests in their anxiety for the Leslies. One young
fellow entered, waving his shilelah, and swearing, in no measured
terms, that "he'd spill the last drop of his heart's blood afore a finger
should be laid on a single scrap in the house." The agent's scowl
changed into a sneer, as he pointed to the document he held in his
hand. This, however, was no argument to satisfy our Irish champion:
and, in truth, matters would have taken a serious turn, but for the
prompt interference of an old man, who held back the arms of the
young hero. The door was crowded by the sympathizing peasantry;
some by tears, and many, by deep and awful execrations, testified
their abhorrence of the man "dressed in a little brief authority."
"Oh!" ejaculated Mrs. Leslie, "oh! that I had never lived to see
this day of ruin and disgrace! Oh! Annie, *you* let it come to——"
"Hold, woman!" exclaimed her husband; "remember what we
repeated last night to each other; remember how we prayed, when
this poor child was sleeping, as in the sleep of death; remember how
we both bethought of the fair names of our parents—how you told
me of the men of your kin who fought for their faith among your
native Scottish hills; and my own ancestors, who left their possessions and distant lands for conscience sake! Oh, woman, Janet,
remember the words, 'yet have I not seen the righteous forsaken,
nor his seed begging bread.'"
Doubtless Mrs. Leslie felt, in their full force, these sweet sounds
of consolation;—again she hid her face, and wept. It is in the time
of affliction that the words of Scripture pour balm upon the wounded
spirit; in the world's turmoil they are often unhappily forgotten;
but in sorrow they are sought for, even as the hart seeketh for the
water-brooks.
The usually placid farmer had scarcely given vent to this extraordinary burst of feeling, when there was a bustle outside the door,
which was speedily accounted for. A post-chaise! rattling down the
lane, and stopping suddenly opposite the little green gate; from off
the crazy bar, propped upon two rusty supporters, in front of the
creaking vehicle, sprang o ir old friend, Alick the traveller:—"Huzza!
huzza, boys! Ould Ireland for ever! Och! but the bones o' me are
in smithereens from the shaking! Huzza for justice! Boys, dear,
won't ye give *one* shout for justice?—*'tisn't often it troubles ye.*—
Och! stand out o' my way, for I'm dancing mad! Och! by St.
Patrick!—Stand back, ye pack o' bogtrotters, till I see the meeting.
Och! love is the life of a nate.—Och! my heart's as big as a whale!"

While honest Alick was indulging in these and many similar exclamations, capering, snapping his fingers, jumping (to use his own expression) "sky high," and shouting, singing, and swearing, with might and main, two persons had descended from the carriage. One, a tall, slight, gentlemanly man, fashionably enveloped in a fur travelling cloak; the other, a jovial sailor, whose handsome face was expressive of the deepest anxiety and feeling.

The sailor was James Mc Cleary; the gentleman—but I must carry my story decorously onwards.

Poor Annie! she had suffered too much to coquet it again. Whether she fainted or not, I do not recollect; but this I know, that she leaned her weeping face upon James's shoulder, and that the expression of his countenance varied to an almost ludicrous degree :—now beaming with love and tenderness, as he looked upon the maiden—now speaking of " death and destruction" to the crestfallen agent. The gentleman stood for a moment, wondering at everybody, and everybody wondering at him. At last, in a firm voice, he said, " I stop this proceeding; and I order you (and he fixed a withering glance upon Maley)—I do not recollect your *name*, although I am perfectly acquainted with your *nature*—I order you, sir, to leave this cottage; elsewhere you shall account for your conduct." Maley sank into his native insignificance in an instant; but then impudence, the handmaid of knavery, came to his assistance : pulling down his wig with one hand, and holding his spectacles on his ugly red snub nose with the other, he advanced to where the gentleman stood, and peering up into his face, while the other eyed him as an eagle would a vile carrion crow, inquired, with a quivering lip, that ill assorted with his words' bravery,—" And who the devil are you, sir, who interferes in what doesn't by any manner of means concern you ?"

" As you wish to know, sir," replied the gentleman, removing his hat, and looking kindly around on the peasants, " I am brother to your landlord !" Oh, for Wilkie to paint the serio-comic effect of that little minute !—the look of abashed villany—the glorious feeling that suffused the honest farmer's countenance—the uplifted hands and ejaculations of Mrs. Leslie—the joyous face of Annie, glistening all over with smiles and tears—the hearty honest shout of the villagers —and even the merry bark of little Phillis ;—then Alick, striding up to the *late* man of power, his long back curved into a humiliated bend, his hand and arm fully extended, his right foot a little advanced, while his features varied from the most contemptuous and satirical expression to one of broad and gratified humour, addressed him, with mock reverence : " Mister Maley, sir, will ye allow me (as the gintry say) the pleasure to see ye out; it's your turn now, ould boy, though ye don't know a fluke from a jacky-dorey."

"Sir—my Lord," stammered out the crestfallen villain, "I don't really know what is meant; I acted for the best—for his Lordship's interest."

"Peace, man!" interrupted the gentleman; "I do not wish to expose you; there is my brother's letter: to-morrow I will see you at his house, where his servants are now preparing for my reception." The man and his minions shrank away as well and as quietly as they could; and the Leslies had now time to wonder how all this change had been brought about; while the neighbours lingered around the door, with a pardonable curiosity, to "see the last of it."

"Ye may thank that gentleman for it all," said James; "besides being brother to the landlord, I had the honour to sarve under him, in as brave a ship as ever stept the sea; and ye mind when matters were going hard here, Alick (God for ever bless him for it!) turned to at the pen, and wrote me every particular, and all about the agent's wickedness, and (may I say it, Annie, *now?*) yer love for me: and how out o' divilment he sent the ould man to make love to you that sorrowful evening—when I went away—and then put me up to catch him; little thinking how the jealousy would drive me mad; well, his honour, the Captain, had no pride in him——"

"Stop, my brave lad, towards *you* I could have had none," exclaimed the generous officer; "where the battle raged the most, *you* were at my side; and when in boarding the Frenchman, I was almost nailed to the deck, you—you rushed forward, and, amid death and danger, bore me, sadly wounded, in your arms, back to my gallant ship." He extended his hand to the young Irishman, who pressed it respectfully to his lips.—"To see the like o' that now," said Alick; "to see him shaking hands with one that's as good as a lord!"—"I held frequent conversations with my brave friend," continued the Captain, "and, at length, he enlightened me as to the treatment my brother's tenants experienced from the agent; I am come down expressly to see justice done to all, who, I regret to find, have suffered from the ill effects of the absentee system. Miss Leslie, I am sorry to lose so good a sailor, but I only increase my number of friends when I resign James Mc Cleary to his rightful commander."

"Och! my dears," exclaimed Alick; "it's as good as a play—a beautiful play: and there's honest Andrew coming over; don't toss him in the cabbage-bed, James, honey, this time. And, James, dear, there's your ould mother running up the lane,—well, ould as she is, she bates Andrew at the step. Och! Miss Annie, don't be looking down after that fashion. And, sir, my Lord, if yer honour plases, ye won't forget the little bit o' ground for the baste."

"Everything I have promised I will perform," said the young man, as he withdrew; an example which I must follow, assuring all who

read my story that, however strange it may appear, Annie made an
excellent wife, never flirted the least bit in the world, except with
her husband; and practically remembered her father's wise and
favourite text—"*I have been young and now am old, yet have I not seen
the righteous forsaken, nor his seed begging bread.*"

MASTER BEN.

TALL, and gaunt, and stately, was "Master Ben;" with a thin sprinkling of white, mingled with the slightly-curling brown hair, that shaded a forehead high, and somewhat narrow. With all my partiality for this very respectable personage, I must confess that his physiognomy was neither handsome nor interesting: yet there was a calm and gentle expression in his pale grey eyes, that told of much kind-heartedness—even to the meanest of God's creatures. His steps were strides; his voice shrill, like a boatswain's whistle; and his learning—prodigious!—the unrivalled dominie of the country, for five miles round, was Master Ben.

Although the cabin of Master Ben was built of the blue shingle so common along the eastern coast of Ireland, and was perched, like

the nest of a pewet, on one of the highest crags in the neighbour
hood of Bannow; although the aforesaid Master Ben, or (as he was
called by the gentry) "Mister Benjamin," had worn a long black
coat for a period of fourteen years—in summer, as an open surtout,
which flapped heavily in the gay sea-breeze—and in winter, firmly
secured by a large wooden pin, round his throat—the dominie was a
person of much consideration, and more loved than feared, even by
the little urchins who often felt the effects of his "system of education." Do not, therefore, for a moment, imagine that his was one of
the paltry hedge-schools, where all the brats contribute their "sod o'
turf," or "their small trifle o' pratees," to the schoolmaster's fire or
board. No such thing;—though I confess that "Mister Benjamin"
would, occasionally, accept "a hand of pork," a kreel, or even a kish
of turf, or three or four hundred of "white eyes," or "London
ladies," if they were presented, in a proper manner, by the parents
of his favourite pupils.

In summer, indeed, he would occasionally lead his pupils into the
open air, permitting the biggest of them to bring his chair of state;
and while the fresh ocean breeze played around them, he would teach
them all he knew—and that was not a little; but, usually, he considered his lessons more effectual, when they were learned under his
roof; and it was, in truth, a pleasing sight to view his cottage assemblage, on a fresh summer morning;—such rosy, laughing, romping
things! "The juniors," with their rich curly heads, red cheeks, and
bright, dancing eyes, seated in tolerably straight lines—many on
narrow strips of blackened deal—the remnants, probably, of some
shipwrecked vessel—supported at either end by fragments of grey
rock; others on portions of the rock itself, that "Master Ben" used
to say, "though not very asy to sit upon for the gossoons, were clane,
and not much trouble." "The seniors," fine, clever-looking fellows,
intent on their sums or copies—either standing at, or leaning on, the
blotted "desks," that extended along two sides of the school-room,
kitchen, or whatever you may please to call so purely Irish an apartment: the chimney admitted a large portion of storm or sunshine, as
might chance; but the low wooden partition, which divided this useful room from the sleeping part of the cabin, at once told that Master
Ben's dwelling was of a superior order.

At four the dominie always dismissed his assembly, and heart-
cheering was the joy that succeeded. On the long summer evenings,
the merry groups would scramble down the cliffs—which, in many
places overhang the wide-spreading ocean—heedless of danger—

> "And jump, and laugh, and shout, and clap their hands
> In noisy merriment."

The seniors then commenced lobster and crab-hunting, and often showed much dexterity in hooking the gentlemen out of their rocky nests, with a long, crooked stick of elder, which they considered " lucky." The younkers were generally content with shrimping, or knocking the limpets—or, as they call them, the "branyans,"—off the rocks; while the wee-wee ones slyly watched the ascent of the razor-fish, whose deep den they easily discovered by its tiny mountain of sand.

Even during their hours of amusement, Master Ben was anxious for their welfare; and, enthroned on a high pinnacle, that commanded a boundless view of the wide-spreading sea, with its numerous creeks and bays, he would patiently sit, hour after hour—one eye fixed on some dirty, wise, old book, while the other watched the various schemes and scampings of his quondam pupils—until the fading rays of the setting sun, and the shrill screams of the sea-birds, warned master and scholar of the coming night.

Every one agreed that " Master Ben" was very learned—but how he became so, was what nobody could tell; some said (for there are scandalmongers in every village) that long ago, Master Ben's father was convicted of treasonable practices, and obliged to fly to " foreign parts" to save his life; his child was the companion of his wanderings, according to this statement. But there was another, far more probable;—that our dominie had been a poor scholar—a class of students, peculiar, I believe, to Ireland, who travel from province to province, with satchels on their backs, containing books, and whatever provisions are given them, and devote their time to study and begging. The poorest peasant will share his last potato with a wandering scholar, and there is always a couch of clean straw prepared for him in the warmest corner of an Irish cabin. Be these surmises true or false, everybody allowed that Master Ben was the most clever schoolmaster between Bannow and Dublin: he would correct even Father Sinnott, " on account o' the bog Latin his reverence used at the altar itself." " His reverence" always took this in good part, laughed at it, but never omitted adding, slyly, " the poor cratur!—he thinks he knows better than me!" I must say, that the laugh which concluded this sentence was much more joyous than that at the commencement.

The dominie's life passed very smoothly, and with apparent comfort;—strange as it may sound to English ears—comfort. A mild, half-witted sister, who might be called his shadow—so silently and calmly did she follow his steps, and do all that could be done, to make the only being she loved happy—shared his dwelling. The potatoes, she planted, dug, and picked, with her own hands; milked and tended " Nanny" and " Jenny," two pretty, merry goats, who devoured not

x

only the wild heather and fragrant thyme, which literally cover the sand-banks and hills of Bannow, but made sundry trespasses on the flower-beds at the "great house," and defied pound, tether, and fetter, with the most roguish and provoking impudence. I had almost forgotten—but she small-plaited in a superior and extraordinary manner; and—poor thing!—she was as vain of that qualification as any lady who rumbles over the keys of a grand piano, and then triumphantly informs the audience, that she has played "The Storm."

"Changeful are all the scenes of life," says somebody or other; and when I was about ten years old, "Master Ben" underwent two very severe trials—trials the poor man never anticipated; one was teaching, or trying to teach, me the multiplication table—an act no mortal man (or woman either) ever could accomplish; the other was—falling in love. As "Master Ben" was the best arithmetician in the county, he was the person fixed on to instruct me in the most puzzling science—no small compliment I assure you—and he was obliged to arrange, so as to leave his pupils twice a week for two long hours. "Master Ben" rose in estimation surprisingly when this was known; and, on the strength of it, got twopence instead of three-halfpence a week from his best scholars: he thought he should also gain credit by his new pupil's progress. How vain are man's imaginings! From the first intimation I received of the intended visits of my tutor, I felt a most lively anticipation of much fun and mischief.

"Now, Miss, dear, don't be full o' yer tricks," said pretty Peggy O'Dell, who had the especial care of my person. "Now, Miss, dear, stand asy—you wont?—well, then, I'll not tell ye the news—no, not a word! Oh, ye're asy now, are ye! Well, then—to-morrow, Frank tells me, Master Ben is to come to tache you the figures; and good rason has Frank to know, for he druv the carriage to Master Ben's own house, and hard the mistress say all about it; and that was the rason ye were left at home, mavourneen, with your own Peggy; becase the ladies wished to keep it all sacret like, till they'd tell ye their own selves. Oh, Miss, dear, asy—asy—till I tie yer sash!—there now—now you may run off; but stay one little minit—take kindly to the figures. I know you can't abide them now, but I hear they are main useful; and take to it asy—*as quiet as you can*, Master Ben has fine larning, and expicts much credit for tacheing the likes of you. And why not?"

Poor Benjamin!—he certainly did stride to the manor, and into the study, next morning; and, in due time, I worked through, that is, I wrote out the questions, and copied the sums, with surprising dexterity, in "numeration," "addition of integers," "compound subtraction," and entered the "single rule of three direct," with much *éclât*. My book was shown, divested of its blots by my kind master's enduring knife; and even my cousin (the only arithmetician in the family) was compelled to acknowledge that, if I did the sums myself, I was a very good girl indeed. That *if* destroyed my reputation. I had too much honour to tell a story.

What a passion, to be sure, the dominie got into the next day, when informed of my disgrace! I cannot bear to see a long, thin man in a passion, to this very hour; there is nothing on earth like it, except a Lombardy poplar in a storm. However, if poor Master Ben was tormented in the study by me, he was more tormented in the servants' hall by pretty Peggy.

Peggy was exactly a lively Irish coquet: such merry, twinkling, black eyes; such white teeth, which were often exposed by the loud and joyous laugh, that extended her large but well-formed mouth; and such a bounding, lissom figure, always (no small merit in an Irish lassie) neatly, if not tastefully, arrayed. She was an especial favourite with my dear grandmother, who had been her patron from early childhood; and Peggy fully and highly valued herself on this account. Then she could read and write, in her own way; wore lace caps, with pink and blue bows; and, as curls were interdicted, braided her raven locks with much care and attention.

The smartest, prettiest girl, at wake or pattern, for ten miles round, was certainly Peggy O'Dell; and many lovers had she; from Thomas Murphy of the Hill (the richest), who had a cow, six pigs, and all requisites to make a woman happy, according to his own account, to Wandering Will (the poorest), who, though not five-and-twenty, had been a jovial sailor, a brave soldier, a capital fiddler, a very excellent cobbler, a good practical surgeon (he had performed several very clever operations as a dentist and bone-setter, I assure you), and, at last, settled as universal assistant in the manor-house, cleaned the carriage and horses with Frank, waited at table with Dennis, helped Martha to carry home the milk, instructed Peter Kean how to train vines in the Portuguese fashion (which foreign treatment had so ill an effect on our poor Irish vines, that, to Wandering Will's eternal disgrace, they withered and died—a circumstance honest Peter never failed to remind him of, whenever he presumed to suggest any alteration in horticultural arrangements), had the exclusive care of the household brewing, and was even detected in assisting old Margaret hunting the round meadow for eggs, which the obstinate lady-fowl preferred hiding among brakes and bushes to depositing, in a proper manner, in the hen-house. Moreover, Will was "the jewil" of all the county during the hunting and shooting season—knew all the fox-earths, and defied the simple cunning of hare and partridge;

x 2

made love to all the pretty girls in the village; and, as he was hand-some, notwithstanding the loss of one of his beautiful eyes, everybody said that no one would refuse William, were he even as poor again as he was—an utter impossibility. The rumour spread, however, that his wandering affections were actually settled into a serious attachment for Peggy; but who Peggy was in love with was another matter. She jested with everybody, and laughed more at Master Ben than at any one else; she was always delighted when an oppor-tunity occurred of playing off droll tricks to his disadvantage; and some of her jokes were so practical, that the housekeeper frequently threatened to inform her mistress of her pranks. Master Ben was always the first to prevent this; and his constant remonstrance—"Mistress Betty, let the innocent cratur alone, she manes no harm; she knows I don't mind her youthful fun—the cratur!" saved Peggy many a reproof.

One morning I had been more than ordinarily inattentive; and my tutor, perplexed, or, as he termed it, "fairly bothered," requested to speak to my grandmother; when she granted him audience. He stammered and blundered in such a manner, that it was quite impos-sible to ascertain what he wanted to speak about; at length out it came—"He had saved a good pinny o' money, and thought it time to settle in life."

"Settle, Mister Benjamin!—why, I always thought you were a settled, sober man. What do you mean?" inquired my grandmother.

"To get married, ma'am;" rousing all his energies to pronounce the fatal sentence.

"Married?" repeated my grandmother! "married!—you, Ben-jamin Rattin, married at your time of life!—and to whom?"

"I was only eight-and-forty, madam," he replied (drawing himself up), "my last birthday; and, by your lave, I mane to marry Peggy O'Dell."

"Peggy!—you marry Peggy!" She found it impossible to main-tain the sober demeanour necessary when such declarations are made. "Mister Benjamin, Peggy is not twenty, gay and giddy as a young fawn; and, I must confess, I should not like her to marry for four or five years. Now, as you certainly cannot wait all that time, I think you ought to think of some one else."

"Your pardon, madam; she is my first, and shall be my last, love. And I know," added the dominie, looking modestly on the carpet, "that she has a tinderness for me."

"What! Peggy a tenderness for you!—poor child!—quite im-possible!" said my grandmother; "she never had the tenderness you mean for any living man, I'll answer for it," and the bell was rung to summon Miss Peggy to the presence.

She entered—blushed and simpered at the first questions put to her : at last my grandmother deliberately asked her, if she had given Mister Ben encouragement at any time, and this she most solemnly denied.

"Oh, you hard-hearted girl you!—did you ever cease laughing from the time I came in till I went out o' the house ? weren't you always smiling at me, and playing your pranks, and——"

"Stop !" said Peggy, at once assuming a grave and serious manner ; "stop; may-be I laughed too much, but I shall cry more, if—(and she fell on her knees at my grandmother's feet)—if ye don't forgive me, mistress, dear—almost the first, sartainly the last, time I shall ever offend you."

"Child, you have not angered me," replied my grandmother, who saw her emotion with astonishment.

"Oh, yes; but I know best—I have—I have—I know I have !— but I'll never do so more—never—never !" and she burst into a flood of tears. Poor Master Ben stood aghast.

"Speak," said my grandmother, almost bewildered; "speak, and at once—what have you done ?"

"Oh ! he over-persuaded me, and said ye'd never consint till it was done; and so we were married, last night, at Judy Ryan's station."

"Married ! to whom, in the name of wonder ?"

"Oh, Willy—Wandering Willy ; but he'll never wander more : he'll be tame and steady, and, to the last day of his life, he'll sarve you and yours; and only forgive me, your poor Peggy, that ye saved from want, and that'll never do the like again—no, never !" The poor girl clasped her hands imploringly, but did not dare to look her mistress in the face. My grandmother rose, and left the room ; she was much offended; nor could it be denied that Peggy's conduct was highly improper. The child of her bounty, she had acted with duplicity, and married a man whose unsteady habits promised little for her comfort.

Poor Master Ben !—lovers' sorrows furnish abundant themes for jest and jesters ; but they are not the less serious, on that account, to those immediately concerned in *les affaires du cœur*. When he heard the confession that she was truly married, he looked at her for a few minutes, and then quitted the house, determined never to enter it again. Peggy and her husband were dismissed ; but a good situation was soon procured for Will, as commander of a small vessel, that traded from Waterford to Bannow, with corn, coal, timber, "and sundries." Contrary to all expectation, he made a kind and affectionate husband.

Winter had nearly passed, and Peggy almost ceased to dread the

storms that scatter so many wrecks along our frowning coast. Her
little cabin was a neat, cheerful dwelling, in a sheltered nook; and
often, during her husband's absence, did she go forth to look out
upon the ocean-flood—

> "With not a sound beside, except when flew
> Aloft the lapwing, or the grey curlew;"

and gaze, and watch for his sail on the blue waters. On the occasion
to which I refer, he had been long expected home; and many of
the rich farmers, who used coal instead of turf, went down to the
pier to inquire if the " Pretty Peggy" (so Will called his boat) had
come in. The wind was contrary, but as the weather was fair, no
one thought of danger. Soon, the little bark hove in sight, and
soon was Peggy at the pier, watching for his figure on deck, or for
the waving of hat or handkerchief, the beloved token of recognition:
but no such token appeared. The dreadful tale was soon told.
Peggy, about to become a mother, was already a widow.

Will had fallen overboard, in endeavouring to secure a rope that
had slipped from the side of his vessel; the night was dark, and one
deep, heavy splash alone knelled the departure of poor Wandering
Willy.

Peggy, forlorn and desolate, suffered the bitter pains of child-
birth; and, in a few hours expired—her heart was broken.

About five years after this melancholy event, I was rambling
amongst the tombs and ruins of the venerable church of Bannow.
Every stone of that old pile is hallowed to my remembrance; its
bleak situation, the barren sand-hills that surround it, and—

> " The measured chime, the thundering burst,"

of the boundless ocean, always rendered it, in my earliest days, a
place of grand and overpowering interest. Even now—

> " I miss the voice of waves—the first
> That awoke my childhood's glee;"

and often think of the rocks, and cliffs, and blue sea, that first led
my thoughts " from nature up to nature's God !"

I looked through the high-arched window into the churchyard,
and observed an elderly man, kneeling on one knee, employed in
pulling up the docks and nettles that overshadowed an humble
grave, under the south wall. A pale, delicate, little girl quietly
and silently watched all he did; and when no offensive weed remained, carefully scattered over it a large nosegay of fresh flowers,

and, instructed by the aged man, knelt on the mound, and lisped a simple prayer to the memory of her mother.

It was, indeed, my old friend, " Master Ben ;" the pale child he had long called his—it was the orphan daughter of William and Peggy. His love was not the love of worldlings ; despite his outward man, it was pure and unsophisticated : it pleased God to give him the heart to be a father to the fatherless. The girl is now the blessing of his old age ; and,. as he has long since given up his school, he finds much amusement in instructing his adopted child, who, I understand, has already made great progress in his favourite science of numbers.

THE WISE THOUGHT.

SHE was sitting under the shadow of a fragrant lime tree, that overhung a very ancient well; and, as the water fell into her pitcher, she was mingling with its music the tones of her "Jew's harp,"—the only instrument upon which Norah Clary had learned to play. She was a merry maiden of "sweet seventeen;" a rustic belle, as well as a rustic beauty, and a "terrible coquette;" and, as she had what, in Scotland, they call a "tocher,"—in England, a "dowry," and in Ireland, a "pretty penny o' money," it is scarcely necessary to state, in addition, that she had—a bachelor. Whether the tune—which was certainly given *in alto*—was, or was not, de-

signed as a summons to her lover, I cannot take upon myself to say; but her lips and fingers had not been long occupied before her lover was at her side.

"We may as well give it up, Morris Donovan," she said, somewhat abruptly; "look, 'twould be as easy to twist the top off the great hill of Howth, as make father and mother agree about any one thing. They've been playing the rule of contrary these twenty years; and it's not likely they'll take a turn now."

"It's mighty hard, so it is," replied handsome Morris, "that married people can't draw together. Norah, darlint! that wouldn't be the way with us. It's *one* we'd be in heart and sowl, and an example of love and——"

"Folly," interrupted the maiden, laughing. "Morris, Morris, we've quarrelled a score o' times already; and a bit of a breeze makes life all the pleasanter. Shall I talk about the merry jig I danced with Phil Kennedy, or repeat what Mark Doolen said of me to Mary Grey?—eh, Morris?"

The long black lashes of Norah Clary's bright brown eyes almost touched her low, but delicately pencilled brows, as she looked archly up at her lover—her lip curled with a half-playful, half-malicious, smile; but the glance was soon withdrawn, and the maiden's cheek glowed with a deep and eloquent blush when the young man passed his arm round her waist, and, pushing the curls from her forehead, gazed upon her with a loving, but mournful, look.

"Leave joking, now, Norry; God only knows how I love you," he said, in a voice broken by emotion: "I'm yer equal, as far as money goes; and no young farmer in the country can tell a better stock to his share than mine; yet I don't pretend to deserve *you*, for all that; only, I can't help saying that, when we love each other (now, don't go to contradict me, Norry, because ye've as good as owned it over and over again), and yer father agreeable, and all, to think that your mother, just out of *divilment*, should be putting betwixt us, for no other reason upon earth, only to 'spite' her lawful husband, is what sets me mad entirely, and shows her to be a good-for——"

"Stop, Mister Morris," exclaimed Norah, laying her hand upon his mouth, so as effectually to prevent a sound escaping; "it's *my* mother ye're talking of, and it would be ill-blood, as well as ill-bred, to hear a word said against an own parent. Is that the pattern of yer manners, sir; or did ye ever hear me turn my tongue against one belonging to you?"

"I ask yer pardon, my own Norah," he replied, meekly, as in duty bound; "for the sake o' the lamb we spare the sheep. Why not?—and I'm not going to gainsay but yer mother——"

"The least said's the soonest mended!" again interrupted the impatient girl. "Good even, Morris, and God bless ye; they'll be after missing me within, and it's little mother thinks where I am.".

"Norah, above all the girls at wake or pattern, I've been true to you. We have grown together, and since ye were the height of a rose-bush ye have been dearer to me than anything else on earth. Do, Norah, for the sake of our young hearts' love, do think if there's no way to win yer mother over. If ye'd take me without her leave, sure it's nothing I'd care for the loss o' thousands, let alone what ye've got. Dearest Norah, think; since you'll do nothing without her consent, do think—for once be serious, and don't laugh."

It is a fact, universally known and credited in the good barony of Bargy, that Morris Donovan possessed an honest, sincere, and affectionate heart—brave as a lion, and gentle as a dove. He was, moreover, the priest's nephew,—understood Latin as well as the priest himself; and better even than that, he was the beau—the Magnus Apollo, of the parish ;—a fine, noble-looking fellow, that all the girls (from the housekeeper's lovely English niece at Lord Gort's, down to little deaf Bess Mortican, the lame dressmaker) were regularly and desperately in love with; still, I must confess, he was at times a little stupid ;—not exactly stupid either, but slow of invention,— would *fight* his way out of a thousand scrapes, but could never get *peaceably* out of one. No wonder, then, that, where fighting was out of the question, he was puzzled, and looked to the ready wit of the merry Norah for assistance. It was not very extraordinary that he loved the fairy creature—the sweetest, gayest of all Irish girls ;— light of heart, light of foot, light of eye ;—now weeping like a child over a dead chicken or a plundered nest; then dancing at the top of a hayrick, to the music of her own cheering voice ;—now coaxing her termagant mother, and anon comforting her henpecked father. Let no one suppose that I have overdrawn the sketch of my Bannow lass, for, although her native barony is that of Bargy, the two may be considered as wedded and become one. The portraits appended to this story are, at least, veritable, and "from the life." You will encounter such, and such only, in our district—neatly attired, with their white caps, when the day is too warm for bonnets—in short, altogether "well-dressed."

"I'm not going to laugh, Morris," replied the little maid, at last, after a very long pause; "I've got a wise thought in my head for once. His reverence, your uncle, you say, spoke to father, to speak to mother about it? I wonder (and he a priest) that he hadn't more sense? Sure, mother was the man; but I've got *a wise thought*. Good night, dear Morris; good night."

The lass sprang lightly over the fence into her own garden,

leaving her lover *perdu* at the other side, without possessing an idea of what her "wise thought" might be. When she entered the kitchen matters were going on as usual—her mother bustling in style, and as cross "as a bag of weasels."

"Jack Clary," said she, addressing herself to her husband, who sat quietly in the chimney-corner, smoking his *doodeen*, "it's well ye've got a wife who knows what's what! God help me, I've little good of a husband, *barring* the name. Are ye sure Black Nell's in the stable?" The sposo nodded. "The cow and the calf, had they fresh straw?" Another nod. "Bad cess to ye, can't ye use yer tongue, and answer a civil question!" continued the lady.

"My dear," he replied, "sure one like you has enough talk for ten."

This very just observation was, like most truths, so disagreeable that a severe storm would have followed had not Norah stepped up to her father and whispered in his ear, "I don't think the stable-door *is* fastened." Mrs. Clary caught the sound, and in no gentle terms ordered her husband to attend to the comforts of Black Nell. "I'll go with father myself and see," said Norah.

"That's like my own child, always careful," observed the mother, as the father and daughter closed the door.

"Dear father," began Norah, "it isn't altogether about the stable I wanted ye—but—but—the priest said something to ye to-day about—Morris Donovan."

"Yes, darling, and about yerself, my sweet Norry."

"Did ye speak to mother about it?"

"No, darlin', she's been so cross all day. Sure, I go through a dale for pace and quietness. If I was like other men, and got drunk and wasted, it might be in rason; but—— As to Morris, she was very fond of the boy till she found that *I* liked him; and then, my jewil, she turned like sour milk all in a minute—I'm afraid even the priest 'll get no good of her."

"Father, dear father," said Norah, "suppose ye were to say nothing about it, good or bad, and just pretend to take a sudden dislike to Morris, and let the priest speak to her himself, she'd come round."

"Out of opposition to me, eh?"

"Yes."

"And let her gain the day, then?—that would be cowardly," replied the farmer, drawing himself up. "No, I won't."

"Father, dear, you don't understand," said the cunning lass, "sure, ye're for Morris; and when we are—that is, if—I mean—suppose—father, you know what I mean," she continued, and luckily the twilight concealed her blushes, "If that took place, it's *you* that would have yer own way."

"True for ye, Norry, my girl, true for ye; I never thought of that before!" and pleased with the idea of "tricking" his wife, the old man fairly capered for joy. "But stay a while—stay, asy, asy!" he recommenced; "how am I to manage? Sure the priest himself will be here to-morrow morning early; and he's out upon a station now, so there's no speaking with him; he's no way quick, either—we'll be bothered entirely if he comes in on a *suddent*."

"Leave it to me, dear father—leave it all to me," exclaimed the animated girl; "only pluck up a spirit, and, whenever Morris's name is mentioned, abuse him, but not with all yer *heart*, father—only from the teeth out."

When they re-entered, the fresh-boiled potatoes sent a warm, curling steam to the very rafters of the lofty kitchen; they were poured out into a large wicker kish, and, on the top of the pile, rested a plate of coarse white salt; noggins of butter-milk were filled on the dresser; and on a small round table a cloth was spread, and some delf plates awaited the more delicate repast which the farmer's wife was herself preparing.

"What's for supper, mother?" inquired Norah, as she drew her wheel towards her, and employed her fairy foot in whirling it round.

"Plaguy *snipeens*," she replied; "bits o' bog chickens, that you've always such a fancy for; Barney Leary kilt them himself."

"So I did," said Barney, grinning; "and that stick wid a hook, of Morris Donovan's, is the finest thing in the world for knocking 'em down."

"If Morris Donovan's stick touched them they sha'n't come here," said the farmer, striking the poor little table such a blow with his clenched hand as made not only it, but Mrs. Clary, jump.

"And why so, pray?" asked the dame.

"Because nothing belonging to Morris, let alone Morris himself, shall come into this house," replied Clary; "he's not to my liking, any how, and there's no good in his bothering here after what he won't get."

"Excellent," thought Norah.

"Lord save us!" ejaculated Mrs. Clary, as she placed the grilled snipes on the table, "what's come to the man?" Without heeding his resolution, she was proceeding to distribute the savoury "birdeens," when, to her astonishment, her usually tame husband threw dish and its contents into the flames; the good woman absolutely stood, for a moment, aghast. The calm, however, was not of long duration. She soon rallied, and commenced hostilities: "How dare you, ye spalpeen, throw away any of God's mate after that fashion, and I to the fore? What do you mane, I say?"

" I mane that nothing touched by Morris Donovan shall come
under this roof; and if I catch that girl of mine looking at the same
side o' the road he walks on, I'll tear the eyes out of her head, and
send her to a nunnery !"

" You will ! And dare you to say that to my face, to a child of
mine ! You will—will ye ?—we'll see, my boy ! I'll tell ye what,
if *I* like, Morris Donovan *shall* come into this house, and, what's
more, be master of this house ; and that's what *you* never had the
heart to be yet, ye poor ould snail !" So saying Mistress Clary
endeavoured to rescue from the fire the hissing remains of the burning snipes. Norah attempted to assist her mother, but Clary, lifting
her up, somewhat after the fashion of an eagle raising a golden wren
with its claw, fairly put her out of the kitchen. This was the signal
for fresh hostilities. Mrs. Clary stormed and stamped ; and Mr.
Clary persisted in abusing, not only Morris, but Morris's uncle,
Father Donovan, until, at last, the farmer's helpmate *swore*, ay, and
roundly too, by cross and saint, that, before the next sunset, Norah
Clary should be Norah Donovan. I wish you could have seen Norry's
eye, dancing with joy and exultation, as it peeped through the latch-
hole :—it sparkled more brightly than the richest diamond in our
monarch's crown, for it was filled with hope and love.

The next morning, before the sun was fully up, he was throwing
his early beams over the glowing cheek of Norah Clary, for her
" wise thought" had prospered, and she was hastening to the tryst
ing-tree, where, " by chance," either morning or evening, she generally met Morris Donovan. I don't know how it is, but the moment
the course of true love " runs smooth" it becomes very uninteresting,
except to the parties concerned. So it is now left for me only to say
that the maiden, after a due and proper time consumed in teazing and
tantalizing her intended, told him her saucy plan, and its result.
And the lover hastened, upon the wings of love (which I beg my
readers clearly to understand are swifter and stronger in Ireland
than in any other country) to apprise the priest of the arrangement,
well knowing that his reverence loved his nephew, and niece that
was to be (to say nothing of the wedding supper, and the profits
arising therefrom), too well not to aid their merry jest.

What bustle, what preparation, what feasting, what dancing, gave
the country folk enough to talk about during the happy Christmas
holidays, I cannot now describe. The bride, of course, looked lovely
and " sheepish ;" and the bridegroom—but bridegrooms are always
uninteresting. One fact, however, is worth recording. When Father
Donovan concluded the ceremony, before the bridal kiss had passed,
Farmer Clary, without any reason that his wife could discover, most
indecorously sprang up, seized a shilelah of stout oak, and, whirling

it rapidly over his head, shouted, "Carry me out! by the powers, she's beat! we've won the day!—ould Ireland for ever! Success, boys! she's beat—she's beat!" The priest, too, seemed vastly to enjoy this extemporaneous effusion, and even the bride laughed outright. Whether the good wife discovered the plot or not I never heard; but of this I am certain, that the joyous Norah never had reason to repent her "wise thought."

MABEL O'NEIL'S CURSE.

WHERE'S the good of talking to me of a dance, or anything of the sort?" said Kathleen Ryley, raising her clear blue eyes to the good-natured countenance of Philip Murphy: "sure ye know my pumps aren't come home—nor, more betokens, won't be till Saturday night; and Saint Patrick himself couldn't cut a step in such brogues as them."

Kate was, in very truth, a frank-hearted, merry girl, with laughing blue eyes, a joyous countenance, and a sweet, love-sounding voice— one whom sorrow had shadowed, but could not cloud. Her father, a respectable farmer, had the misfortune to lose a sensible, industrious wife, when Kathleen was not more than fourteen; leaving him, besides his eldest daughter, five young, troublesome children. Everybody pitied Mark Ryley: everybody said, "he must marry again: Kate was too young and too giddy to manage such a household."— Everybody, however, was wrong. Mark Ryley did *not* marry again,

and Kate *did* manage his household. And, in sooth, it was a beau‑
tiful sight—a sight that may be often vainly sought in nobler dwell
ings, to observe the filial and sisterly tenderness of the simple Irish
lass. Kathleen was considered a pretty maiden by all who knew her,
and her mother had bestowed extraordinary pains upon her daughter's
apparel; but matters changed when the poor woman died; the fine
gingham frocks, and Sunday tippets, were cut and manufactured, by
Kate's own hands, into holiday dresses for her two little sisters: daily
did she send them to the village school, and never permit either to
remain at home, to assist her in her labours, which, certainly, were
not light. Then her three brothers occasioned her much trouble;
such clipping and shaping of jackets—which, after all, in fashionable
parlance, would have been denominated *shapeless*—such patching of
shirts, and eternal mending of Sunday stockings! It was at once her
pride and pleasure that her father's comforts should be as well cared
for as during her mother's lifetime; and, even to the public‑house
(where, it is but justice to state, his visits were seldom made), his
daughter's influence extended; for thither would she follow, and
so wile him homeward, that the neighbours declared, "of all the
girls in the world, sweet Kathleen Ryley had the most winning
way."

Kathleen did not owe any of her charms to meretricious ornament;
her everyday gear was of coarse striped linsey‑woolsey, though its
tight‑fitting body and short sleeves, it cannot be denied, set off her
fine round figure to much advantage; she was seldom guilty of the
extravagance of wearing stockings in summer, except on Sundays;
but her white muslin kerchief was always delicately clean, neatly
mended, and carefully pinned across her bosom. Her light, shining
hair—not tortured into curls, but plainly braided to the back of her
head, where it was fastened by a small tortoiseshell comb (the only
article of finery she possessed, and which, to confess the truth, had
been presented to her by no other than Philip Murphy)—she was,
perhaps, a little vain of.

Philip thought Kate very handsome in her linsey‑woolsey gown—
very handsome when washing the face of her troublesome brother,
Tom (an obstinate lad of six, lubberly and dirty as any Irish boy need
be)—very handsome, when watching to see if her father's pipe wanted
lighting, after a hard day's work—or when disrobing him of his "jock
coat," worn only on Sabbath or saints' days. Moreover he thought,
and no wonder, that she would make a very handsome bride. He had
said this, over and over again, both to her and her father; and her
father had replied, " that, as they loved each other, and as Philip was
well to do in the world, they might be married as soon as they
pleased." But the lassie's consent was wanting, although his love
was the star of her existence.

"When it pleased God (praise be to His holy name, for ever—amen!) to take my poor mother," she would say, in reply to her lover's urgent entreaties for their immediate union—" sure it was all as one as if HE said, 'Katy, machree, be an own mother to them desolate children.' Wait—wait a while, Phil: summer flowers are more plenty than spring ones; the grass will be all the longer, and the blossoms all the sweeter, for a taste o' patience; and Anty will be able to do for my father as well as me, and they'll all have their larning, and the blessing 'll be the more round our own little place, in reason of my having done my duty to the poor orphans."

Such were Kathleen's simple reasons, which, had she been a "high-born ladye," would have called down the applause of an admiring world. As it was, Kate had the approbation of her own conscience, and the increased affection of the heart she so dearly prized—for Philip could not but value more highly the girl who possessed principles so exalted and self-denying.

I must now revert to the humble dialogue with which my story commenced.

"The dickons himself carry all shoemakers, say I!" replied young Murphy: "he might have finished the pumps long enough ago, if he had a mind; to have such nate little feet as them in such vagabone brogueens, sure it's too bad intirely;—but it's always the way, you grudge yerself every dacent tack that goes on yer back, let alone yer feet;—well, 'twont be always so—for, when ye're Mistress Phil Murphy, there shan't be a better dressed girl in the parish, of a small farmer's wife. Anyway, you shan't lose the dance, Kate: for 'tisn't more than two miles across the bog to my sister's, and I'll borrow her shoes for ye—and sure she'll be proud to lend 'em. Good-bye," he continued, as he left the cottage, "God's blessing be about ye always, my own coushla!"

"He's an honest boy, and a dacent, and, by the same token, a handsome one, too," soliloquized Kathleen, as she peeped through a chink in the cottage wall; then fastening the door, by letting down the latch, and pulling in the latch string, she began arranging her dress for the dance which the borrowed slippers would enable her to attend. The snowy stockings were carefully drawn on—the white petticoat and open chintz-cotton gown neatly arranged—and her beautiful hair plaited round the tortoiseshell comb, so as to display it to the best advantage: nor will I deny (for my heroine was a true woman) that she gazed upon her own image, as reflected in the cracked looking-glass, with much self-satisfaction. Her meditations were, however, soon interrupted by a smart knock at the cottage entrance, impatiently repeated. "He can't be there yet—let alone back," she thought as she lifted the latch, where, to her no small astonishment,

Y

a very different person anxiously waited admittance. A tall, gaunt woman, whose wild and fierce appearance painfully contrasted with the mild beauty of the evening landscape, from which the last beams of the setting sun were gently departing, leaned against the door-post. Her form was partly shrouded in a tattered cloak, which, fastened by a wooden skewer to the throat, wrapped the figure to the knees; a stout leathern belt passed across one shoulder, from which a dirty canvass bag was suspended, containing the dole of meal, potatoes, grits, or whatever the kind-hearted peasantry could spare from their meagre store; her feet were bare—the scanty petticoat reached nearly to the ankles, whose masculine proportions told of extraordinary strength; her skin, eyes, and hair, almost betokened foreign origin, yet her features were remarkable for the shrewd, observant character peculiar to the inhabitants of the south of Ireland; her brow was low and projecting, and her sunken eyes appeared condensed as it were, into the expression of a deep and malignant hatred towards all the human race—but, when excited by the active passions of rage or revenge, they flashed with the rapidity, and almost the brilliancy, of lightning; her head-tire consisted simply of a kerchief knotted under the chin, which could not be said to confine her dark, matted locks, while it added much to the wildness of her appearance. The peaceable cottars considered Mabel O'Neil as a sort of wild woman, and, in truth, ceded to her the rights of hospitality more in fear than in love: for it was often whispered that, to the lawless, she was not only an adviser, but an accomplice; and many things were said of "Mad Mabel," in her absence, that it would require a good deal of courage even to think of when she was present. Kathleen, contrary to her country's usage, of opening wide the portal when a stranger seeks admittance, still held it, and almost trembled when the woman's eye rested upon her with its usual expression. Without speaking, she stretched forth her bony arm, and pushed the door so forcibly, that it swung out of Kate's hand; then she advanced her right foot inside the threshold, and, eyeing the maiden with much bitterness, said—

"And that's yer fine breeding, is it, Katy Ryley?—to stand staring at an aged woman, *outside* the door-cheek!—at one whose head is grey—whose feet are sore—whose lips are dry—whose bag is empty—who has neither kin nor friend near, to say, 'God save ye!'—nor a stick or a stone to set her mark upon—where she may lay down her bones and die!"

"Come in, Mabel O'Neil, and welcome," responded Kathleen, hesitatingly—"sure, agra, it was only the want of thought."

"Silence!" interrupted Mabel, stalking forward, "silence, girl!—it is too soon for *you* to have a lie on your lip: the time will come—

must come to you, as well as to yer betters, when it'll sit as easy there
as upon the lip of e'er a lady in the land."

She sat down upon a three-legged stool near the chimney-corner,
and Kathleen filled her a noggin of fresh milk, and presented with
it that luxury of Irish life—a piece of white bread. The woman
pushed the refreshment from her. "It's not come to that wid Mad
Mabel yet," she muttered, in a half-audible voice; "to ate the begrudged bit and drink the begrudged sup."

"Take it, Mabel," persisted the good-hearted Kate, her pity excited
by the worn-out appearance of the wild woman, conquering her fear—
"pray do; and I'll get you a *shock* of father's new tobacco, and bathe
yer feet, that I see are sore and cut—the crathurs!—Do take it."

I have often thought the music of Orpheus consisted solely in
sounds of kindness, addressed to the woodland savages; its power
over the animated world is little short of magic. Even that wayward and crime-worn creature could not resist the persuasive gentleness of Kathleen's words. She took the wooden vessel from her
hand, and, peering into her face, said, "It's a pity to look upon ye,
ye young fool, and to think that, though the lightning may spare ye,
the canker won't. I shouldn't have been angry wid yer mother's
daughter—who knew me before sin—ay, first sin, then sorrow—
black, bitter, stormy sorrow—came over me, and changed me from
the light, proud—ay, 'twas the pride that did it—but it's not asy
talking of them things."

She paused, and looked moodily on the embers of the turf fire;
then finished, at one draught, the milk which Kate had given her,
and turned her gaze upon the maiden, who endeavoured, in vain, to
arrange the remainder of her village dress under the influence of the
woman's ken.

"Did ye never hear," she said, addressing her, after a long silence,
—"did ye never hear tell of the countries beyant seas, where a
sarpent jist fixes his eye upon an innocent bird, and it trembles—
trembles—till it falls into its mouth? Kathleen Ryley, you are now,
for all the world, like that bird, and I like that other thing;—but
never heed my cronauning. Come here, to my side, and listen. You
know 'Squire Johnson—the *justice as he's called*—and ye have a sort of
a regard for the young lady, yer foster-sister—she's a fair flower; but
the curse o' the free-hearted is over them, like a thunder-cloud, and a
worse curse than *that* even over *him*, and it'll burst this very night.
And who *will* escape it, unless *you* bestir yourself, and warn them of
their danger!—and it's little time there is for that same. See," and
she pointed her finger to the glowing west, "the sun has sunk this
midsummer evening, in red, red glory—but the burning of their house
will be as bright before the clock goes twelve this blessed night!"

"Holy Father!" exclaimed the girl, crossing herself devoutly "Mabel O'Neil, for the sake o' the mercy you expect——"

"I expect mercy!" interrupted the woman, with a fearful laugh, which brought the rumour of her insanity fully to the remembrance of the young Kathleen; "I, the banned, the blighted woman!—yes —this mercy—here!" She threw off her cloak, and bent her almost fleshless figure forward. "Shall I tear away these *skreeds*, and show you the mercy of the scourgings I got in Dublin? Shall I show you the mercy of five stabs in this withered bosom, when I spread wide my arms to save my husband's life? Shall I tell ye of the mercy showed by a heretic justice to my starving childer?—to one—my brave, brave boy—to myself, when I clung by the black ship's side, that was bearing him to the land o' shame, jist to give him my last blessing—their *mercy* knocked me on the head, as if I was a thing of stone! Oh!" she continued, shrieking wildly, and pressing her hands on her temples, "I feel it now; and his last, last look, is ever before me!"

Kathleen's gentle feelings sympathized with the unfortunate creature; and when the paroxysm of her anguish abated, and she saw tears streaming between her fingers, again she spoke to her in gentle tones, mingling her soothing words with entreaties to be informed of the probable fate that awaited Mr. Johnson's house and property.

"Ay, it's for that ye care, and not for me," said the woman, at last, groaning heavily; if I warn off this burning, 'tis not for the sake o' *mercy*, but because I know the boys are so beset, by the cowardly red-coats, that, before their job 'ud be half done, they'd be powdered down upon, and kilt at once, and, after all, no good done; —and there's one, too, I wish to save from ever feeling what racks me to think upon; but that you can't understand; and moreover, I've a love for the house, that I knew but too well when the present man was nothin' but a bit of an agent to the ancient proprietor. Oh, it would destroy me intirely, to see the ruin of the place in which I spent my innocent days! And often, when my heart's full of what ye'd think could never enter into woman's bosom, I see a glimpse of the white chimleys, or, may-be, the ould turret itself, above the trees; and I cry, and the scalding tears take the venom out o' me; and then I can pray. Child! child!—there are many sorts of tears; some that come burning from the brain; others that save the heart from bursting!" She paused, and crossed her hands on her bosom; then, resting her eyes on the ground, continued in a subdued tone,— "May-be, I've other reasons, too; only, if a warning could be sent to the 'Squire, the boys would get the wind o' the word, and not attempt it, knowing that he'd be ready for them; and so both one and other 'ud be saved; for the time's past when they could ha' rid the country o' these beggarly Cromelians. And nothing can be done for a while.

any way—I tould 'em this—and more; but I'm ould now, and they never heed me."

" Why didn't ye tell it at the 'Squire's yerself?" interrupted the maiden.

" Do you indeed think me mad?" replied the woman, angrily. " D'ye think there's a big tree, or a grey stone, about the place, that, when such things are a-foot, doesn't hide a living watch? And when did ye see the descendant of Irish kings darken, as a beggar, the door of the usurping English?" She stood erect on the cottage floor, and looked around her with mingled pride and wildness.

" How am I to reach the house alive, if it's beset in that way?" said Kathleen, giving utterance to her fears: " I'll jist wait for Phil Murphy, and we'll go together."

The woman laughed a mad laugh. " For Philip Murphy is it?— why he's the ouldest united man of the set!—that's taking a lawyer to guide ye to heaven, sure enough!"

" 'Tis false!" retorted Kathleen, her eyes flashing, and her cheek crimsoning / " 'tis false! Philip Murphy would scorn to be a night-walker. He has no communion with sich ways—I know he hasn't. And I am——"

" A fool!" interrupted Mabel. " I tell you he *has*; and, if he's caught, he'll be hung—and small loss!"

" Ye're a bad woman, Mabel O'Neil, and I don't care for your wicked looks a bit now; but I'll make a liar of ye—that I will!—to slander a dacent boy after such fashion! I'll go, this minute, to 'Squire Johnson's; and, if any harm happens me—if I'm murdered outright—I'll follow ye night and day, and——"

" That's my thanks for saving the worthless lives o' yer fine friends, and, may-be, of yer bachelor! Ay, go—go; but stop, as ye hope to live and do well; take some eggs in this basket—anything, *as a cloak*; and swear never—but I needn't make you promise—none o' ye ever turned *informer*."

Poor Kathleen did as she was desired; resumed the despised brogues; and, without speaking another word, or being able even to arrange her thoughts, took the path she had, with very different feelings, watched her lover pursue, about half an hour before. The hag, who had caused so much consternation, was again re-seated, and rocking herself over the embers of the fire; in a few moments. muttering some words of unknown import, she lit her pipe, and, slowly rising, departed from the cottage in an opposite direction to that which Kathleen had taken.

It would be difficult to describe the various feelings that agitated the bosom of poor Kate, as she thought of Philip, and his uniform correctness of conduct; and, although she had not the intuitive horror of illegal meetings that an English girl of her age would have possessed, yet she feared for his safety; and the idea of danger to him was more than she could bear. Could she, by any means in her power, prevent his joining the party that night? She knew that, the alarm once given, Mr. Johnson had a sufficient number of partisans in the country to identify, at all events, some of the conspirators, and the beloved of her heart might thus be covered with shame. Should she avoid discovering the plot to the 'Squire's family? She shuddered to think of the dreadful result; and the remembrance of her delicate foster-sister—the hours they had spent together in their infancy, rambling by the silver stream—or amid the bending grain, seeking the scarlet poppy, and the blue corn-flower;—or, in riper years, the numberless times she had climbed the forked trees, to gather, for the lady-playmate, the early blossoming sloe, or the golden laburnum— the look of affectionate thankfulness with which the prize was received, came again upon her; and she hastened her steps to save one whom she had ever loved.

The ties of fosterage in Ireland are frequently stronger than those of kindred; the foster-sister or brother remains, through life, the devoted friend—the faithful ally—the obedient servant. In adversity, they shield and succour; and in prosperity, like the humble and affectionate woodbine, what they cannot aid or support, they cling to, and perfume by the odour of devoted tenderness.

"May the Holy Mother direct me!" thought Kate, as she passed into a pathway that led to a continuation of corn-fields, rich in their young greenery; and, as she looked beyond them on the solitary landscape, her eye found nought to rest upon, indicative of human habitation, save a long barn, which had been constructed as a safe place to stow corn in, during rainy weather, before it could be conveniently lodged in the hag-yard. It was a strong building, with a widely-opening gate or door; lonely in its situation, though many a harvest home had been held within its walls. On Kate journeyed, with a firmer step, but an aching heart, until, moving in the distance towards her, she saw a figure, which she instantly recognised as that of her lover.

"Kate, darling!" he exclaimed, bounding forward: "Kate, darling! what brought ye this road? Kate! What ails my colleen? Kathleen!—why do ye shrink from me, your own Philip?" He passed his arm round her waist, feeling, and almost hearing, the quick throbbings of her heart. She struggled nobly with her agitation, while conflicting ideas rushed through her brain, scorching and rapid as lightning. But soon, with the ready wit of a woman, she exclaimed, "Just lead me to that barn door, and I can sit awhile on the stone that's beside it—I'll soon come round, Phil."—He placed her on the stone: and when she looked on his kind and anxious countenance, hardly could she imagine that he was linked with those whose thirst was for blood.

"The stone is could, Phil," she said, after a pause.

"Bad manners to me, that didn't think of that afore, Katy, darling! Sure I can get ye a nice clean lock o' straw, off the hurdles inside, to sit upon, if I can only pull this great *hipeen* out of the hasp."

No sooner said than done; the "*hipeen*" was extracted; but, while Philip was making his way to the hurdles, that were at the farthermost end of the building, Kathleen rushed to the door, closed and hasped it, restoring the fastening-stick to its old situation, and hammering it down with all her might. Having ascertained that it was firmly fixed, she flew along her path, almost with the lightness and rapidity of a startled lapwing, leaving Philip Murphy in, what she considered, safe custody, for that night at least. "Thank God!" she exclaimed, as the turrets and chimneys of the old mansion, that Mabel O'Neil had so loved, appeared through the twilight: then, pausing for breath, she raised her clasped hands to heaven, and again repeated, in an earnest tone, "Thank God!" adding still more fervently, "I *will* save all."

The gable end of the house rested against the ruins of one of those castles of the Elizabethan age, so generally scattered over Ireland; and the chamber window of Caroline Johnson, set, as it were, in the castle wall, overlooked a wild and variegated scene of hill and valley; while one of the most beautiful of Irish rivers bounded, as with a band of molten silver, the distant meadows.

Caroline had often gazed upon this sweet and varying landscape; and a good deal of romance, produced, perhaps, by the surrounding scenery, mingled with her natural character, which, otherwise, would have been more regulated and reserved than that of the generality of her fair countrywomen. She might be considered alone amid the people, such as they were, with whom she associated—a garden flower blossoming unwillingly amongst wild and uncultivated weeds. She was the youngest and the only surviving child of her father's house, and many wondered how so graceful a stem could have sprung from such a root.

The long French casement of this fair girl's dwelling, with its white draperies and roseate fringe, but ill-accorded with the time-worn stones and mouldering battlements of the old castle; while the roses, which she cultivated in the deep embrasure of the walls, shed their perfume and their beauty over the gigantic ivy and many-coloured lichens. As Kate passed under this favoured window, she looked up, and saw her beloved foster-sister, as usual, busied among her plants. Placing her foot on a slight projection, she seized an overhanging branch, and, after one or two successful springs, performed with all the agility of a free-footed Irish lass, stood, eggs and all, on the rustic balcony, to the no small surprise of her young lady. When a few minutes had elapsed, and Kate's feelings had vented themselves in tears, as quickly as possible she informed her friend of the object of her mission.

"Ye see, Miss Car'line, it's what they want is to murder, burn, and destroy every mother's soul of the whole of ye—and there's no time to be lost; for look—the red flame beams from Knock Mountain, which is as bad as the devil's watchword—God save us! Whenever *that* fire lights, you may be sure mischief's going on;—and there is a long story about that same mountain, which I'll tell ye some day or other; only now, Miss Car'line, be quick, and away to the master, for there's no time to lose—and the heart within me sinks when I thing of the danger."

This sensible advice was soon followed, and arrangements were as quickly made for defence. The house, in common with many in the county Carlow, at the time to which I allude, was well prepared—the men-servants were immediately armed, and a half-witted, but cunning and faithful retainer was despatched secretly to the next police-station, to give the necessary information.

Miss Johnson would not, of course, permit Kathleen to hazard a return to her cottage that evening; and, as she often remained with "her young lady," the circumstance was not likely to excite suspicion. She, however, stayed in her foster-sister's room, and employed her fingers, almost mechanically, in telling over the beads that had been her mother's; her thoughts—uncontrollable wanderers—doubtless visiting Philip and her father; and never did Persian worshippers pray more fervently for the presence of their deity, than did both females for the speedy approach of morning.

At length, weak and nervous from watching, Miss Johnson fancied she could sleep. "Can you plait my hair, Kathleen?" she inquired, as the withdrawn band unfastened the long tresses that fell, in rich clusters over her polished shoulders.

"Sure I can; I always do my own—not that I'd be after comparing them," replied the maiden, as she slipped the rosary on her arm, and prepared to divide the silken hair.

"But I interrupt your prayers."

"Oh, no consequence in life, that, Miss! it's jist a nice employment when I've nothin' particular to do; and a comfort, somehow, to be thinking that, in the *hoight* o' trouble and dismay, the Lord's ear is always open to me, to say nothin' o' the holy saints, and others. Besides," she added, sighing deeply, "I always say my prayers best on the beads of my poor mother (God be good to her!)—when I lay my fingers to them, it's jist as if she was with me herself."

" After all, Kate, you must be a happy girl; you have nothing to trouble you—no world to please, no——"

" Oh, Miss, machree! it's little ye know if ye think that; sure there's my father to plase, and the childer to look after, and——"

" Philip Murphy to look after," added Miss Johnson, glancing at her attendant: who, it may easily be imagined, had not breathed a word, even to her lady, of the barn adventure, or her suspicions concerning Philip. Kate's fingers trembled, and she soon converted what had commenced as a three, into a five, plait; so that, at last, Miss Johnson's patience was exhausted, and she could not avoid saying, " I know you are tangling my hair, Kathleen." As she looked in the glass, that reflected the figures of both, the trifling displeasure she had felt was instantly removed on observing that large tear-drops chased each other down the poor girl's cheeks.

" No coolness between you and your bachelor, I hope, Kathleen?" she added, in her kindest voice.

" Oh, Miss, Miss!" replied Kate, clasping her hands with painful earnestness, " do not ask me; I can say nothin' about him till after the morrow—oh, do not ask me!" She then, without uttering another word, flung herself on her knees, and told over the beads with all possible rapidity, as if haste afforded relief to her overcharged heart. At this moment, the contrast between the two girls, so different in rank and appearance, would have been highly interesting to any painter of feeling and sentiment:—Miss Johnson, part of whose unbraided hair hung negligently around her, pressed her forehead to her hand; and, as her long, pencilled lashes almost rested on the soft roundness of her delicate cheek, the lustre of her clear blue eyes was intercepted by fast-coming tears, that hung like drops of dew on the gossamer webs of morning. She might have reminded one of that exquisite passage in Shelley—

> " She moved upon this earth a shape of brightness,
> A power, that from its objects scarcely drew
> One impulse of her being—in her lightness
> Most like some radiant cloud of morning dew,
> Which wanders through the waste air's pathless blue
> To nourish some far desert:
> *   *   *   *   *
> Like the bright shade of some immortal dream
> Which walks, when tempest sleeps, the wave of life's dark stream."

How frequently, in a crowded picture-gallery, do we pass, almost without notice, some exquisite gem of art, that, singly, in an unadorned chamber, we should gaze upon with rapture! Woman, to be loved, and valued as she deserves, must be seen and known in solitude—I had almost added, in sorrow. The lily's fragrance is of

more value when it blossoms and sheds its perfume in the wilderness
than when only one amid a multitude of flowers.

Another hour had passed, and her slight and graceful figure still
reclined on the arm of an old-fashioned, high-backed chair; the full
light of a painted glowing lamp fell, in all its brightness and varied
hues, upon her beautifully-shaped head; her form was the perfection
of symmetry, yet shaped in so fairy a mould that, in their youthful
days, Kathleen used to boast she could carry Miss Caroline a mile in
one hand, and never know she was there. Kate's round, red arms,
sunburnt skin, as she knelt with her back to the light—her tight,
trim figure, and rustic dress, showed strangely, combined with the
apartment and its mistress. Still she industriously told her beads;
and, as her young lady gazed upon her, she pondered many a painful
thought on what might be the destiny of both. "Poor girl!" she
ejaculated, "I thought that you at least would have been happy.
So good a daughter; so undyingly attached to one of your own
people—to one, too, of a kind and gentle character! Why is it?
(and her fair brow lowered and gloomed, as her thoughts proceeded)
—why is it—the feeling that unfolds as womanhood advances, even
as the petals of the blushing rose expand to the sun, which at first
glows and encourages, but when the fragrance is extracted, and the
canker has entered through their folded leaves, scorches, into a
loathed mass of fadedness, what its rays had first cherished—why is
it that it leads to misery, and yet we nourish it within our bosom?"
She raised her head, and shook it, as if to dispel such painful feeling;
and was again relapsing, as the working of her features plainly
showed, into the same train of thought, when a volley of musketry,
followed by a shout from the plantations, alarmed both the lady and
the peasant; instinctively they clung to each other, when a second,
from its proximity, terrified them still more. Kathleen supported
Miss Johnson to her bed, and resumed her kneeling position at its
side; again, all was silence.

The cool, grey light of morning streamed upon the pale and slum-
bering lids of the young lady; soon, however, her father's voice called
upon her to rise. "It is eight o'clock, Carry, and I am going to have
an examination of some prisoners brought in this morning; you have
now an opportunity of seeing, in safety, who these rascals are."

She descended to the long, rambling hall, where her father was
already seated in due formality; his little rotund person exalted on a
high chair of dignity, corresponding with the occasion. Mr. Johnson's
eye, in general, bore the expression of calm severity, but, when aroused,
indicated fierce and dangerous passion: his mouth was the redeeming
feature of his countenance—its formation full, and even tender—and
his smile, when it came, sweetness itself. This singular physiognomy,

perhaps, led to the following remarks from two gossiping servants. who stood at the lower end of the hall.

"Och! and it's himself that carries the oak stick between his eyes, any way."

"Hould your whisht, Nilly: sure it's his honour that bangs the world for his *crame o' sweet smiles*, when he has a mind."

"*Sour crame*, I'm thinkin'," retorted the other; "but how pale the young mistress looks, this morning!" she continued, as Caroline and her humble companion appeared on the stairs. "Well, sure the master has sweetness enough while he has that darlint; no pride in her—see how she puts her fosterer's hand under her arm, as if she was a lady!—why, Katey Ryley is as pale as herself, only her skin is another colour."

From the spot where Miss Johnson stood, when these remarks were made, a group of Irish motley was presented. "The man in authority," seated in the high-backed chair, at the foot of the staircase—a huge table before him, on which was piled a large collection of law books, in dingy covers. At his right hand, on a low chair (which, being seated thereon, prevented his chin rising much beyond a level with the table), appeared Denny, Dennis, or, *classically* speaking, Dionysius Flannery, the beetle-browed butler and clerk of the house of Johnson—employed in wiping the ink out of his pen on the cuff of his coat, previous to rendering the same fit for service. Long foolscap lay before him; nor must I forget the well-thumbed prayer-book, kissed, many a time and oft, by the false and the true. Dionysius was, or, at least, considered himself, a man of learning, having travelled, as a poor scholar, the wilds of the kingdom of Kerry, and officiated as head master in the hedge-school of Glen-Moyle. He consequently opined that Mr. Johnson had secured a perfect treasure in his person. Towards the centre, the police-sergeant—a tall, lanky fellow, with a shock-head of red, rough hair, and eyes that set at defiance all direct rules—stood a little in advance, ready to swear to the depositions that had been already taken. Farther back, some four or five policemen kept their hands on their arms, notwithstanding that two of the prisoners were firmly manacled. One of these, a slight, trembling old man, stood, so as to shield his face from the observation of "the gentry;" the other absolutely grinned with an appearance of savage good-nature on the proceedings; while the third, whom everybody recognised as "Hurling Moriarty of Ballinla," leaned, with folded arms, against a pillar, now glancing at the magistrate, and then at the crowd, which nearly filled the hall, and extended beyond the opened door to the lawn, and even the plantations in front; it consisted chiefly of men—some with coats—some without; a few females. eager to ascertain the nature of the proceedings, had left their cabins before their hair was snooded, or their cloaks fastened; but the prominent features of the accumulating assembly manifested anxiety and uneasiness, and their murmurs and surmises were, at times, more than half audible; even the countenances of the police, who were scattered amid the throng, expressed the same feeling—the same agitation. Moriarty might have. served as the model of an Hercules; his appearance bespoke strength—his bearing, fearlessness—compressed lips—dark and penetrating eyes—the *contour* evincing more than common genius, and—alas! that it should be so!—more than common vice! When his lips parted, they parted in scorn, a movement that was particularly evident as his glance rested on the rotund magistrate. His hat had not been taken off on entering the presence; but when the young lady descended, and took the seat prepared for her, a little behind her father, the covering was instantly removed, and the figure resumed a respectful position.

"Police-sergeant Smith," commenced the justice, "what is the reason that one prisoner, whom, I regret to say, has so often, I understand, appeared elsewhere, under disgraceful circumstances, should be unmanacled?"

"Plaze yer honour," replied the sapient sergeant, "we are always wishful to avoid the shedding of blood : and so, knowing that if this honest man——"

"What do you mean by calling such a scoundrel an honest man in my presence?" interrupted the magistrate, angrily.

"I ax yer honour's pardon; I didn't mean to call any one here an honest man; only ye see in regard of Hurling Morty's always being known to keep his word, either for good or bad; and, says he,—I'll give you my honour as a gentleman, says he, that I'll not stir hand or fut, only walk aisy into the hall, if ye don't offer to tie me, says he."

"That wasn't all the rason, though, ye slip o' hazel!" exclaimed the Hurler, casting a scornful look at the poor sergeant; you *couldn't* tie me—no, nor tin of ye together—though ye trapped me as if I was a fox or a weasel; but I have no fear of coming here, for you can prove nothin' agin me;—and——"

"Sure he murdered me intirely;—me, yer worship;" shouted a little policeman, in the corner, who by dint of fist and elbows, was trying to make his way through the crowd: "he *hot* me right over the head—I'll sware it, your honour."

"Put that down, my fine penman—that I *hot* him over the head," observed Moriarty, addressing the clerk; "it's down, is it?—*over* the head? Well, now, ye little, miserable, half-starved morsel, that it would be insult even to the trade, such as it is, that owns ye, to call a *tailor*—ye're parjured! He says I . *hot* him *over* the head, yer honour; I can prove that it was *on* the head—a fair, firm rap, just to see if it had any brains in it; I'd scorn to hit anything *over* the head !"

The mob enjoyed the jest—the little policeman groaned; while another of the party exclaimed, " Hould yer prate, Barney !—It's asy talking wid ye;—plaze yer worship, he made a fair riddle o' me for the moon to shine through, just with one stroak of his sledge of a fist."

"Och ! and what will I do intirely ?—and the sight of my two good-looking eyes as dark as a dungeon, wid the tratement I got from him, and he on his back at t'other side the ring-fence, after we tripped him—the grate monster !" vociferated a third.

" Ye're all a pack of false-swearing Peelers," exclaimed an old woman ; " sure it's himself that wasn't there at all at all, as I'm ready to prove, if it's truth ye're after, and *not law*, but——"

" Silence in the court, I say !" shouted Dionysius Flannery ; " were ye niver before a magistrate, till now, ye unrooly pack ? Listen, while I read the deposition to his worship."

The deposition set forth, in quaint Irish phraseology—" that, being aware that seditious organization (of course Miss Johnson had taken care that Kathleen should not be suspected as the informant), and a most horrible plan for burning and murder was meditated, Police-sergeant Smith, with collected forces, dispersed around Cairn Castle —that, skulking behind the new plantation, they discovered and took prisoner, Moriarty Sullivan——"

" That's one lie ; and the skulking's another !" exclaimed Morty, in a deep, firm voice ; " ye didn't *take* me ; ye *snared* me, as ye would a hare !"

" Mighty like a hare, ye are !" replied another policeman, whose head was bound in a stocking : "plaze yer honour's glory, he knocked us clane about like young goslings, until little Mike Corish and big Kit, and another boy (big Kit's father, by the same token), got a piece o' the road afore him, and threw a rope on the ground ; and, ye see, he was bating the boys with his pike-handle, and his baste of a gun (he hadn't time but for one volley, yer worship—backwards), whin we tripped him up, and before he could say ' Munster,' we had the half of him—his legs—axing yer pardon—safe,—seeing we twishted and twishted the cable round it——"

" Silence !" again vociferated Dionysius, while stifled expressions of " unfair !"—"beggarly Peelers !"—" cursed Orangemen !"—" fine boy !"—" more's the pity !"—and such like, murmured amid the crowd.

" Took prisoners, Moriarty Sullivan," recommenced the clerk, " Phelim Mc Gunn, and Philip Murphy——"

"'Tis false !" shrieked Kathleen, rushing from behind Miss John-son's chair (where she had hitherto leaned, a mute but most anxious spectator of the proceedings), and confronting the astonished Denny

—"I say, I know 'tis false! Philip Murphy was not—could not—have been there! I—I myself locked—" Almost stifled by agitation, she paused for a moment, and then, with firmness, added, "If you took him, where is he?"

"Here, agra!" squeaked the trembling little old man, to "my sorrow, a coushla—God break hard fortune!" Poor Kathleen staggered towards the crowd—looked for a moment, on the namesake of her lover—and a faint laugh sprang to her lip, as she fell senseless into the arms of those who were nearest to her.

"There's Kate Ryley's own Philip Murphy running like mad!" exclaimed a neighbour. On the instant, the young man entered the hall, evidently much discomposed, and unable to comprehend the proceedings; and as he stood, for a moment, in the glory of excited and youthful beauty, beside the aged person who, it was now understood, bore the same name, the contrast between the two turned instantly the quick current of Irish feeling, and a merry burst of laughter shook the oaken rafters, even while the sounds of execration lingered round the walls. The attention of the police being momentarily diverted, Philip Murphy, senior, got rid of his nervous affection, and managed also to get rid, in some unaccountable way, of the vile bonds which, it is to be suspected, too slightly restrained his motions. Swift as Robin Hood's own arrow, the *ci-devant* old man darted through the assembly, which out of pure love of what they considered "fair play," facilitated his escape. Away he flew, amid the applauding and encouraging cheers of the peasantry, and the yells of the police. "Fire! Dead or alive, bring him back!" shouted the magistrate, descending from his chair of state. "Ye'd better take heels after him yerself," said Moriarty, in a scornful tone, as he looked down upon the worthy 'Squire, who went stumping past him.

"Fetch his honour Pangandrum's boots, can't ye," observed another, "to lengthen his legs a bit?" "Look to these two fellows immediately!" interrupted the enraged justice, while his face bloated and swelled like a turkey cock angered at the sight of a scarlet cloak. "No need in life for the trouble," replied Moriarty; "I said I wouldn't run, nor I'm not going to *demane* myself. I scorn a lie, as much, and maybe more, as e'er a lord in the three kingdoms. Sorra a thing ye can prove agin me, *this* turn, that 'ill keep me in more than three months—though I'd rather it was four; for it's little I can be after these summer evenings, when the nights are so short and so light, and the sun keeps blinking about a dale longer than he ought, if he knew manners." The latter part of this speech was lost upon Mr. Johnson, who had hurried forward to the hall door, where a wild and singular scene presented itself. The rapidity with which "Phil Murphy, of Tullagh," already recognised as "Swift-footed Phil," a fearless, and, consequently, popular rapparee, proceeded, was even less wonderful than the evenness of his steps; and the sort of flying, swallow-like motion which he kept up, as he bowled along the smooth greensward, and sprang, with the lightness of a bird, over the bounds ditch that terminated the ancient lawn. While his pursuers were scrambling up and down the tangled enclosure, the culprit made rapid way, first through a clover field, then across the undulating ridges of a potato enclosure, rich in its lilac and orange blossoms. "Fire on him!" again vociferated Mr. Johnson; and the long sandy sergeant took aim, fired and wounded—not him of the swift foot, but a favourite horse of the 'Squire's, that had strayed, in search of forbidden food, into the enclosure. "Och! may ye iver have the same luck!" exclaimed several peasant-voices at once; while "swift-footed Phil," without lessening his speed, threw up his old white wig in triumph, and then the *cooleen* of dark hair, released from its confinement, fell, in abundant tresses, over his throat and shoulders. At the bottom of the potato-field ran a narrow but deep stream, a branch of the river I have before alluded to, the depth and rapidity of which had been greatly increased by recent rains. Into it, however, the daring robber plunged, swam like an otter, and, in a few moments, was on the opposite side. "The coble!—the coble!" exclaimed one of the police. They ran towards an old willow, where it was moored, although the thickness of its branches effectually concealed the little boat from their sight, as the leafy screen seemed rooted in the waters. Before they reached it, however, to their utter discomfiture, it glided from its moorings, guided by no other than our old acquaintance, Mabel O'Neil, chanting, as she waved and kissed her hand, with mock solemnity, to the "men at arms," a verse of an old ballad—

> "The boat and the water
> Were made for the free;
> The gaol and the city
> Are fitter for ye."

Those who could swim would not; those who would, could not. Some, who fancied they were competent to the undertaking, got soused and bemired, as a punishment for their temerity, and received the jests of a merciless multitude, including all the barelegged urchins —all the barking and snapping of collies—the taunting of every age and sex, who delighted in beholding the men of law and the men of war outwitted. The beldame floated slowly with the stream, still singing snatches of an old melody, waving her bony arms in wild and fearful attitudes, and intimating by her gestures, the most perfect contempt for those who failed in their attempts to arrest her progress. "Curse the hag!" muttered Johnson, enraged at all the morning's occurrences, "she's acting in concert with that fellow, and ought to smart for it. Smith, you're a famous shot; couldn't you skim the water, hit the crazy boat, and give the old devil a ducking?" "As easy as kiss my hand, sir," replied the ruffian, calmly arranging his piece for the purpose. As his finger rested on the trigger, one of the peasants struck the gun with his stick, evidently anxious to avert the shot from its intended object.

The movement was unfortunate; for the piece went off, and the old woman, uttering an agonizing scream, nearly fell over the edge of the boat. "Good God!" exclaimed Mr. Johnson, his better feelings, for a moment, triumphing, "you have struck the woman!" Urged now by their naturally kind and active feelings, the peasantry rushed into the water, and soon guided the coble and its helpless freight to the rushy margin of the water; it was sad to see the dark-red stream which trickled down its side, and left a dismal track upon the rippling wave, as they dragged it to the shore.

"I always thought it would end this way," said the dying woman, while speculation faded from her eyes, and the glaze of death appeared beneath their distended lids. "There, boys; the only thing ye can do for Mabel O'Neil now, is to carry her up to the ould castle, and let her draw her last breath within its walls."

Mr. Johnson advanced towards the party who were preparing to obey her directions, though it is impossible to know whether he intended to forbid or to command that those directions should be fulfilled.

She fixed a look of bitter remembrance and scorn on the magistrate; and, slowly elevating her withered hand, beckoned him to come nearer. He did so. She succeeded in raising herself on her elbow, and, with no gentle grasp, drew his head so down that her mouth nearly touched his ear. The word, or words (they could not have been many), that she uttered, sent a fearful shudder through his frame; his lips quivered and grew pale, his eye deadened within its socket, and a change, as extraordinary as it was sudden, passed over his whole countenance. He uttered no reply; no word escaped him, —he but motioned the people to follow to his house.

As the melancholy group approached the mansion, many who had been left in the vestibule, assembled at the portal, and amongst them, the love-beaming face of Kathleen Ryley, was easily distinguished. "I'll be even wid ye yet, Kate, for locking me up; and worse than all, doubting it's among such I'd be," said the lover, fondly: "to keep me kicking my heels, the livelong night, agin that baste of a door, where I might ha' been still, but for the good Christian who gave me my liberty at last; and the rats the crathurs, peepin' and pryin' at me from their holes—mad angry at me spoilin' their supper

Kathleen, astore, wherever there is love, there ought to be full faith—but, whisht, a lanna—och! botheration to me intirely for calling a tear to yer sweet eye, Kate; though darlint," he added, as the maiden smiled it away, "it made you look more beautiful than ever I see you afore, and that's a bould word. But wait till I catch that *gostering* ould Mabel O'Neil, and I'll pay her off, I'll——!"

"Let her alone, if ye're wise, my tight chap," interrupted the deep voice of Hurling Moriarty; for though this conversation had been carried on *sotto voce* between the two lovers, Moriarty caught the last sentence, as he joined the group that had accumulated at the door. The party bearing the wounded woman had now entered the second gate; they had been obliged to return by a longer path than they had taken during the rapparee's escape; and one of the gossiping sisterhood had only time to observe to Philip Murphy, that "he'd better not turn his tongue against Mabel O'Neil, while Morty was to the fore—as people *did* say that he was a son, somehow or other, o' Mabel's own—and it was bad talking ill o' parents under a child's breath,"—when Mr. Johnson slowly ascended the hall-steps, followed closely by some three or four who supported the unfortunate woman. Sergeant Smith had taken advantage of the confusion to disappear; he naturally feared the reaction that would take place, in the minds of the peasantry, against the murderer of the being who had so long been looked upon with either fear or sympathy by all classes, and wisely hastened to the police-barracks for a reinforcement. The eagle glance of Hurling Moriarty rested, for a moment, on the ghastly features of his reputed mother, and, in an instant, he was at her side.

With fearful energy he grasped her cold hand, and then they looked into each other's countenances, as only parent and child can look, when the tie—the first, and the dearest—is about to be broken —*and for ever.* In another moment, his ken wandered over the assembly, inquiring of her who had done the deed; and, almost unwittingly, perhaps, her look rested on the magistrate, who had entered the hall, thrown off his hat, and, having covered his burning brow with his hands, remained leaning against one of the oaken supporters of the ancient structure.

It was enough;—a bound, that, for certainty of destruction, could be likened to nothing but the fatal spring with which the young and infuriated tiger fastens on its prey, brought Moriarty to the side of the defenceless gentleman. With both hands he grasped his throat, and so appalled were even Mr. Johnson's own partisans, by the suddenness and violence of the action, that his death would have been certain, had not Mabel O'Neil with a strong and desperate effort, staggered forward, seized her son's arm, dragged him with her almost

z

to the marble floor, on which she fell, and exclaimed, in a low, but audible voice, " Morty, Morty, as you value yer mother's last *blessing* —as you fear yer mother's *dying* curse,—loose, loose yer hould, I say!—*it is yer father ye would murther!*"

He did, indeed, relax his grasp, and the swollen and discoloured features of the unfortunate Johnson plainly showed that, in a few seconds, Moriarty's forbearance would have been too late. He would have fallen, had not his daughter, attracted to the hall by the crowd and struggle, caught him in her arms, and with Kathleen's aid, supported him to a seat. If a bullet had passed through the young man's brain, he could not have appeared more subdued;—the fires of his eye were quenched, his arms hung powerless in their sockets, and he sank with a deep-drawn groan, on his knees, by his mother's side. " Morty," she said, still more faintly, " ye had no right to have any hand in sich a burning as was intended—I tould ye so, but ye wouldn't heed me; my heart warmed to the ould place, as the limb of ivy, that the lightning blasted on its walls, still clings to the same spot; moreover, I couldn't bear ye to lift a finger against him, who, perjured as he is, is still yer ——" father, she would have added, but her son's feelings burst forth. " Do not say the black word again, mother," he exclaimed furiously; "if *I* am *his* son, what must *you* be?"

" Listen, James Johnson, to that!" said the wretched woman, dragging her body—as a wounded serpent trails its envenomed length along the earth—towards the magistrate's seat : " didn't the sound o' *that* go to yer heart?—the upbraidings of a child to its own parent, when that parent is in the agonies o' death! But, though ye've murdered me, the curse is over ye still!" she continued, the bitter expression of countenance I have before mentioned, returning tenfold, and revenge lighting in her sunken eye, like the red lamp within the sepulchre : " do ye remember it! I'll tell it ye again—the whole —there's life in me yet for the whole of it. In those days, this was yer employer's house, but ye earned his gould, and then he borrowed it, and ye lent him back his own—ye may well turn pale, it's all true. I was his lady's chosen favourite—she tended me as if I had been a noble child : *you* won me to yer purposes—*you* got me to betray trust; and, when that was done, *you* turned upon *me*—*you* poisoned her heart again' me. In an hour of madness I tould o' your wickedness—I was asked for proofs—I had none—she turned me out— the snow fell—the rain poured—I deserved it all from *her*.—But, under the end wall, where the ivy is still green, and yer daughter tends her flowers—do ye mind *that* meeting, when the boy that scorns to own ye leaped within me—when the feelings of a young mother warmed about my heart? Ye met me *there—there* ye

spurned and scorned me ; and, to save myself from everlasting blight
—to save my mother's heart from breaking, I there promised, that,
as a screen to my sin, I would marry him who since turned a shame
to earth, and whose children were born both to that and sorrow.
Still they were *my* children, and God in heaven knows what I have
suffered for them. Then—then, when I clung to yer knees to bid
ye farewell, and when, like a true woman, I could ha' blessed ye,
even in my misery—for the thought of yer happiness was ever foremost in my mind—at that moment ye threw me from ye—ye called
me by the name that rings on woman's ear to everlastin', *when she
deserves it ;* then on the snow I knelt—I cursed ye from my heart's
core—my love turned to poison, both for you and myself. I knew
the people would call ye fortunate : and I prayed that the riches ye
should get, might secure to yer soul damnation—that the higher ye
rose, the more should the finger o' scorn point at ye—that ye might
be the father o' many honest childer, and that, when they were most
bright and beautiful, ye might follow them to their graves, and die
a childless man ! And didn't I"—as she spoke, the fiend seemed to
take possession of her once fine form, and deep and terrible shadows
gathered over her discoloured brow—" didn't I travel, unknownst,
many a weary mile, to hear the stones clatter on their coffin-lids ?
and when your innocent son was murthered from spite to his father,
weren't the tears, that rolled down yer cheeks like hail-drops, refreshing to *me*, us the May-dew that falls on the summer flower ?—
and sure, the young craythur that's trembling there, like the blasted
meadow-sweet, is dying fast, fast—and so am I——" Her voice
sank, and the last words were faint and murmuring, as the breath of
a fierce but expiring hurricane.

" Blessed Mary !" exclaimed Kathleen, " will nobody run for
Father Delany, that he may make her soul ?"—and the kind-hearted
girl knelt at her side, and held the crucifix to her separated and
ghastly lips. Moriarty, whose bitter feelings could find no utterance,
clasped his hands in agony to implore her blessing. Feebly she
muttered—they knew not what : then, turning her face to the
ground, and, while literally biting the dust, her erring but powerful
spirit departed from its dwelling of sin and suffering.

It might be some five or six years after this real and frightful
tragedy, that, in a cottage more comfortable than Irish cottages are
in general, an interesting peasant group were assembled round a clear
turf fire. A young and comely matron was occupied in undressing a
fine and beautiful boy, while her husband amused himself in deciphering the contents of a somewhat ancient newspaper : the wife
glanced from the babe to her husband, with that sweet expression of

proud and satisfied affection that can only rest on the countenance of a happy married woman, when she gazes on earth's greatest blessings —an affectionate husband, and a blooming child. Smilingly she pushed back the little round curls that were just beginning to cluster on her son's fair brow : and, again looking at her husband, observed, " Phil, honey, the boy grows mighty like you, I'm thinking—he's yer very *moral* just about the eyes; there, he wants to kiss his own daddy before he goes to sleep ! Philip, what ails ye, that ye don't notice the child ?—ain't ye well, astore ?" Philip Murphy deliberately laid down the paper, took the cherub-boy in his arms, hid his face on its little bosom; and while, with the sweet untutored affection of infancy, the babe played with the longer and deeper curls of his father's hair, he murmured so earnest, and even eloquent a prayer, that God would preserve it from sin and shame, that the mother's heart overflowed, and tears of tenderness rolled down her cheeks. As she took the delighted boy from his father's arms, she could not help saying, " That was a mighty fine prayer, Phil, and all out o' yer own head, I'm sure, for neither priest nor minister could make it for ye—clean up from the heart like that; it's a murdering pity, Phil, ye warn't a priest, for the sarmints would ha' come quite natural to ye."

" Then you should have been a nun, Kate," replied the husband, smilingly, yet not as cheerfully as was his wont; "and that wouldn't have been much to yer taste, would it now ?"

" I never thought o' that," said she, laughing.

" Then ye're not so quick-witted as ye were the night ye locked me up in the long barn, ye mind."

" Philip, agra !" replied she, seriously, " I can never abide the thoughts o' that night."

" Nor I, neither," sighed Philip, " only something I've just read on the paper makes me think of it."

" And what would be on the paper, Phil ?" inquired Kathleen, anxiously; at the same time rocking herself backwards and forwards, to " *hushow*" the baby to sleep.

" Two things very queer to come together then, Kate :—the death of that bad man, Mr. Johnson—a dale about him that's not thrue— and——"

" Not thrue !" repeated Kathleen; " sure I thought whatever was on a newspaper was as thrue as gospel !"

" Small is yer knowledge, then, my darlint, and so best—I hate a knowing woman; but I tell ye—and I heard it from one who under-stands it right well—that the half and more o' the papers are made up o' big lies; and sure here's a proof of it—when he that was forced to fly the country (for ye know, after the ripping up Mabel O'Neil, as they called her, made afore us all, and more especially after the death o' that sweet angel daughter, Miss Car'line, he couldn't stand it at all at all), is praised up in black and white, ' as a zealous,'— that means useful, you understand—' a zealous and good magistrate.' " Poor Kathleen threw up her eyes in silent astonishment.

"The begrudged thing never does good," she said, at last ; " and what comes over the devil's back——" " Thrue for ye, Kate," exclaimed the husband, who knew the proverb well, and, therefore, I suppose, did not permit his wife to finish it ; "but the other thing is, that Sergeant Smith, ye mind, who would have been hung for shooting that unfortunate woman, only for the power o' the party, and the bribery o' Mr. Johnson (who certainly had good right to get him off, seeing he instigated him to do it—though every one clears him of knowing, at the time, who Mabel was), was hung at Kilmainim, for murderin' some man or other out in the main ocean—so there's an end to him, any way."

"The Lord preserve us all, and keep us just and honest !" ejaculated Kathleen, crossing herself with one hand, and pressing her child more closely to her bosom with the other : adding, after a pause, " I often heard that 'Squire Johnson ought to have committed Morty to prison, though he was his son, as he was took under arms : that might be law, but there wouldn't be much nature in it."

" I don't know how it was settled," answered the husband : " sure the justices manage the law, and not the law the justices ; only Morty went clean off out o' the country, and I was glad of it ; it was the only chance he had—for he had some good in him, I've heard ; and, though the black drop couldn't but run in his veins, yet trouble and knowledge might get it out, ye know."

" Phil, I want to ask ye," observed Kathleen, after a pause, " as ye're a knowing man, if ye really think it was Mabel's curse that brought all the misery on the 'Squire's family ?"

"A curse is a bad thing, Kate, more particklar when it's desarved : but I have heard that a curse made again' the innocent is turned, by the breath of heaven, again' one's self ; however, it's ill mindin' sich things, only to keep one's own heart pure : her curse came there, for a sartinty, and it's almost a by-word now—' As bitter as Mabel O'Neil's curse.' Riches were a curse to him ; the higher he got, the more was the finger o' scorn pointed at him, for he hadn't the gentlemanly turn about him ; and, though the father o' many childer, he died childless. Temptation is bad ; so God keep us from it, or teach us how to overcome it. Howsom'ever, all he got is gone to the bad, long ago—the devil never grants long leases."

" Poor Miss Car'line !" ejaculated Kathleen, " she never rightly recovered that day—though, to be sure, it was a blessed thing that the son was saved from the sin o' the father's blood; the flowers I planted over her grave last May are in blossom again, and it crushes my heart to look at them, for she was a *raal* gentlewoman, one of God's own makin', jist let down from the holy heavens to show us what angels are; the delight of my heart you war', Miss, avourneen! only, I often think, too sweet and gentle for this world's ways. I'd ha' gone to death for you willingly any day——"

"There, darlint," said Philip, anxious to terminate so painful a reminiscence, "put the boy to bed; and, as it's fine moonlight, we'll take a walk over the field to see yer father." Kathleen passed her hand across her eyes, and prepared to fulfil her husband's wishes (which by some strange sympathy were generally her own), while he continued, "the poor man's getting ould now, darlint, yet there's none of his childer gladdens his heart like you; and, after all, *the best way to keep off a curse is not to deserve it.*"

THE FAIRY OF FORTH.

WE of Wexford, though we have the advantage of our neighbours' mountains, as terminations to our landscape, have but
one that we can call our own—the mountain of Forth. I cannot,
with all my love for it, style it handsome; though it is, certainly,
picturesque—rugged, jagged, rough, and rocky; and I remember
when not a single green field, or cultivated plot, was to be seen on
its sides. It has undergone changes.

Year after year I have watched patches of oats, potatoes, and
even barley, creeping along, and civilizing its sturdy steeps; while,
both in sheltered and unsheltered spots, cottages have sprung up—
cottages, filled with a bold race of mountain "squatters," who, I
hope, may never be dispossessed of the "estates" obtained by their
industry.

I have spent some happy, sunny hours on the rocks of my own

dear mountain, looking round and round, and climbing from crag to crag, to recognise the dwellings that shelter in the valley. There is Johnstown Castle, embedded in its own woods—the gaily-waving flag on its highest tower, intimating that those who " possess the land," are AT HOME, bestowing blessings on all around them ! I can see the curling smoke from the trim school-house, and fancy Mr. Shelly's, the good master's face, pale and anxious, lest his pupils' improvement should not keep pace with the wishes of his liberal patroness. There go the mottled deer, in the noble park, scudding right over the mound where that everlasting Oliver Cromwell is said to have reviewed his troops; there the labourers' cottages, clustered like honeycombs in the thrifty hive. All look happy and cheerful, and are what they appear. The spire of the little church of Rathaspeck is clearly defined by the blue sky; I can see the ruins in the park, and the stream, like a silver thread, where the mill's revolving wheel turns it into mimic foam——

There, and there, and there, are the dwellings of resident landlords or prosperous landowners, mingled with the venerable castles, which form so distinguished and interesting a feature in the character of the county ;—what a fine foreground they form to St. George's Channel—bearing upon its waters the produce of many lands !

Wexford harbour looks well from this noble eminence : and it is impossible not to regret that the ever-shifting sands form such a barrier to the utility of so beautiful an object.

How snugly the Barony of Forth farmers shelter in their comfortable houses !—their barns are spacious, and their hayricks and cornstacks tell of abundance. The Saltee Islands stand fearlessly amid the dashing waves—and the far-off Tower of Hook terminates the sea view.

It is a noble scene; and yet, even as the tiny bird seeks its own nest amid the varied beauties of the grove, so do I seek the white gables and green trees of my childhood's home. Well, I need look no longer; it is but to close my eyes, and now it is before me—all— I can recall the chiming dinner-bell—the dear familiar voices— passed for ever—all—even the old house-dog's bay—that roused the echoes of that wild sea shore !

My own dear home ! What home can ever feel like the sweet home of childhood ?

I love the mountain huts, and their hardy occupiers ; I love to see them descending into the valleys to their daily labour, and climbing to their homes at night, shouting to each other, or chorusing some wild Irish ditty, while their children leap from crag to crag to meet them. I do not like to hear them sneered at—as they often are— by their lowland rivals. I own they may be a little unpolished—

perhaps fond of having their own way—and I know their manners are more *brusque* than the manners of the men of the plain; they deem themselves independent freeholders—and so they are; and they receive you with warm hospitality in their cottages, if you brave their mountain air, as I have frequently done—to visit them.

Squatters, from every barony in the county, have fixed themselves upon the mountain, and do not relish people of any other county intruding among them; how they existed at first I cannot tell: a family must have made the poor man's individual labour keep them all from starving; but now, every year, I can perceive bit after bit added to their little "properties;" and the eagerness with which they send their children to school, and the interest many of them take in agriculture, lead me to hope that the next generation will be of real value to the country. I am always doubtful as to whether an improvement will be adopted if it be only practised in a gentleman's domain; the people are apt to say, "It may do for the quality, but not for us;" but the moment one cottager tries a new plan, and it succeeds, his poor neighbours are anxious to adopt it also. "I never would have believed," said John Merry,—old John Merry, who is the best dog-breaker and mountain cottier in the county,—"that the green crop plan was a good one *for the poor* if I had not seen how Mr. Pigeon, of the Red-houses, managed it." John Merry is one of the first mountain "settlers." "I'm as good as a grandfather to the mountain," says John, "for I was one of the first that sat down on it—a young man with a dark-haired wife—and every hair in her head is *white* now."

"It must have been a lonesome place then, John."

"Faix, it was mighty lonesome and quair; and shy the birds and foxes looked at us—as if they thought we'd no right to it—natural enough; and as to the snipes, when they came back after their *divarshun* abroad, ye'd think the wee black eyes would drop out of their heads at seeing the curling smoke, and smelling the burning turf on their own lands! Well, I've often thought what a wonder it was how the birds in the air found the road in the heavens to wherever they wanted to go; and I've asked every larned gentleman I ever came across how it was, and never a one of them could tell me;—it's mighty strange," added John, "but somehow, about the growing of a blade of grass, or the flying of a bird, the learned people know as little as a poor man."

John is a regular specimen of a mountaineer—fearless, free, daring, and very superstitious, as all mountaineers are: it would be utterly impossible to invent a story of fairy or spirit beyond his belief. He glories in the mountain, and wonders if the "far-off ones" look as well when you get near them as his own. He says it is a noble

thing to have the "main ocean" always before a man s eyes, rolling
away at his feet—that it makes him think of Eternity; and as for
the dogs, the mountain air and education are the best to strengthen
them in wind and limb. He will show you potatoes not larger than
walnuts, and tell you that, though they're not big of their age,
they're as dry as bread, and the wholesomest that ever grew; and a
little patch of green stunted oats will, he assures you, be prime corn
before the season's over. John, heaven bless him! makes the best
of everything, and looks so cheerful in his coat, which is composed
half of tatters, half of patches, that you feel assured the luxuries of
life would be thrown away upon him: he will wipe his face after it
has been battered by a hailstorm, and smilingly assure you it is
"no ways unwholesome." I was told that John "had" a fine
"legend" of *the* mountain, *if* he would tell it to me; but that he
feared I would laugh at it: promising to keep my countenance, and
to listen attentively, I prevailed on him to "show me the *nature* of
it." "If your honour will only just walk up some morning, and see
the grey rocks that mark the place, and prove there's no deception
in it whatever; there's the very stones over the whole, as they were
in the ancient times—and if ye remove them rocks, you may find it
yourself, though, to be sure, if ye did, you'd meet with present death."
   "Couldn't they be blown up, John?"
   "Well, there now, I knew it's laughing at me you'd be," he said,
looking seriously displeased.
   "Indeed, John, I've not laughed."
   "Sure, ma'am, it's all one, if you talk of blowing up; the
powder's not made that would blast them rocks," added John.
   "Indeed!" I said, gravely; and John, after peering very suspiciously
at me, bade me good morning. But I soon found my way to his
mountain home—no very easy undertaking, though the path he de-
clared to be both "smooth and wholesome." Seated on a fragment
of rock, a few days after, while John leaned on his staff, and every
now and then recalled to his side the half puppies, half dogs, that
constituted his retinue, John confided to me "The Legend of the
Mountain of Forth," which I give in his own language:—
   "Long ago," he began, "before that thieving villain of the world,
Oliver Cromwell, bombarded Wexford, reviewed his Ironsides in
Johnstown Park, or left his old boots behind him in the town he ill-
treated—long before all this, there lived, somewhere up here, a little
morsel of a man, with a white head, and a dale in it, by the name of
Martin Devereux. White Martin he was called, to distinguish him
from every other of the Martins; and they called him so because his
hair was white, you see. Well, White Martin was a cunning hand,
entirely, you understand, ma'am, in gathering the *mountain dew;* and

whoever wanted it in the valley used to tip the word to Martin, and
be it much, or be it little, they were sure of it—pure and fresh, the
rale sort, brewed under the moonbeam, that neither sun nor gauger
had ever winked at!"

"The gauger!" I repeated.

"Ay, just the gauger! Sure, Queen Elizabeth brought them in
first; and, for the matter of that, I've heard my mother say that
' the ould sarpent in the garden of *Aden* was nothing but a gauger
in disguise.' Well, Martin Devereux had made a bargain with the
good people, what the quality call fairies, who had their bits of
stations and divarshuns on the mountain, that he'd not only let them
alone, nor suffer mortal eye to look at them, but that he'd give them
as much of the mountain dew as they'd want for their entertainments, if they'd have an eye to his interests, you understand, and
not let any of the wrong sort come upon White Martin's bits of stills,
or little hiding-holes; and, to be sure, if the royal family of the
good people had fun before they were introduced to Martin, they
had ten times the divarshun after, because of the spirits he put into
them—the whisky. There was more fun and flirting in the fairy
court than ever was known before."

"And was there no fighting, John?" I inquired.

"See that!" exclaimed John, triumphantly, "I knew how you'd
ask that. Well, indeed, my mother said they used to kick up a
bobbery now and again, about one thrifle or another; but they were
more prudent about it than poor mortals like ourselves. Now, no
one ever did a wiser thing than make friends with the good people;
if you're churning it's no great matter to leave a drop of cream in
the keeler, or a taste of fresh butter on the churn, for the innocent
things; and, if you've nothing else to leave, why, leave a peeled
potato on the hearth-stone, that has never touched salt, and they
take the will for the deed; it's the thoughtfulness they look to, and
you'll have all the better luck for it. Now you see, ma'am (it's the
rale truth I'm telling you), the whole country was fairly riddled
with excisemen, and gaugers, and informers, and the like—every
little thing that could brew the poor Paddy's delight was seized
throughout the country, except White Martin's: he'd lay down to
sleep in the thick of stills, and everything else; the gauger would
come and walk over them—ay, maybe, into the whisky—and neither
see it nor smell it."

"Oh, John! is that possible?"

"Possible! Don't I tell your honour what my mother told me,
and sure it isn't misdoubting her or me you'd be?—it's as thrue as
that the sun is now shining on that smoky steamboat. Oh, then,
the sea has never looked the same since they came on it, dirty

things—thrue! Well, they'd walk into it, as I tell you, and the
deception the good people would put before them would blind the
sight in their ugly eyes, and they'd walk out again, and thrash the
informer for misleading them. Ever and always, after that, the
hulabaloo that would be in the poor man's place would delight your
ears!—such music!—and always they'd have the same piper; and
my own great-grandmother was up in the mountain one night,
helping White Martin and his niece, he having a great venture
entirely of *the dew*; and, trusting to the power, as well he might,
that had freed him from all trouble so long, he drew up his hogshead through a trap-door at the back of his cabin, and gathered some
blankets over it, like a tent, and filled it with poteen, ready to draw
off for the neighbours, the vale-boys, that would be up for it before
day; and the two, my great-grandmother and White Martin's niece,
got ready some ducks and chickens for the Saturday market; and
the whole of them, trusting in the good people, went peaceably to
bed, my great-grandmother sleeping with the old man's niece.

"In the thickness of the night who should knock at the door but
the gauger! 'Come in, and welcome,' says a voice, the *very moral*
of White Martin's, while he lay shaking like an ague,—'come in;
and thankful we will be to see any good creature, for we're all at
the last gasp with the small-pox.' Well, my great-grandmother
was like to die with the fright, and the *'cuteness* of the good people,
for the gauger was a *beauty*, and would as soon have put his head
into a fiery furnace as into where the small-pox was going. Well,
in his hurry to be off, he clattered down the mountain like a troop
of wild horses, and then, from behind the hogshead, came such a
hurraing and shillooing that the two girls were mad to steal out to
see who it was made the noise; and then, to tempt them more, came
the finest of music; and they forgot White Martin's bargain with
the good people, and both stole out, and, looking round the hogshead, they saw a responsible looking piper playing away for the dear
life—a little round-faced fellow, piping like mad; and they could
have looked at him all night, only that Martin Devereux pulled
them away, whispering about his agreement to let the good people
come and go without observation; but the *curiosity* of the women
had destroyed White Martin's luck, for the piper spied them, and
such a hoorishing and whirling as there was you never heard, and,
all of a suddent, a voice says—

> 'Your bond's out, White Martin—
> Your bond's out, for sartin.'

"The next night, not content with leaving the good people's
allowance, he made them some punch—hot, strong, and sweet; but

no : in the morning sorra a drop was touched, and there stood the hogshead—not one of the vale-boys but broke their appointment! The old man went and sat under his own wall, and, as he sat, who should he see toiling up the mountain but the same blackguard gauger! 'I'm done now, any way,' he says to himself; 'broke horse and foot, and I'll not stir to save all the poteen that ever was brewed,' he says ; ' I'll deliver myself peaceably to the tender mercies of the law,' he says, ' and that's present death, at the very least,' he says ; and so, like some great saint or martyr, he sticks his dudeen between his teeth with the determination of an ould Roman, and bruises down his cawbeen over his eyes, settled, as a haro, to his fate. Now the gauger, that was counted such a beauty, was no-thing, after all, but a yellow-legged Shelmalier, a sporting fellow : one that would take a bribe with one hand, and betray you with the other—a bould, daring fellow, hiding his wickedness with a brazen face, which half the world mistake for plain dealing ; his heart would fit on my thumb-nail ; and his conscience—— but, as *he* never found out that he had one, I don't see why posterity should bother about it. If the Rogue's March was played at his funeral it paid him a compliment. Now this gauger had a wife of his own at home, who was, for all the world, like a Buddaugh cow—one that goes about with a board on her forehead, to keep her from destroying the world; and, between the pair of them, the country was ruined intirely.

"Now the Shelmalier was very fond of making love to every girl that would let him ; but, above all the girls, the one that hated him most was White Martin's niece ; and, while poor ould White Martin had given himself up to his pipe and his prayers ;—' Keep up,' says a voice ; ' keep a good heart; though you can't manage the women, I can manage the men !' and, pushing his hat from over his left eye, who should he see by his side but his own niece, that frightened the piper, and she dressed up to the nines, smiling like a basket of chips, and beckoning to the Shelmalier to make haste up the mountain !

" ' Get in, you huzzy,' says the heart-broken craythur ; ' where's your modest bringing up ?—and what's come over you at all ?' and he made a blow at her with vexation.

" ' Don't offer to touch me,' she says, waving her arm above him, and, sure enough, White Martin could no more stir from where he was sitting than the Saltees could move up this ancient ould moun-tain ; ' come on,' she says to the Shelmalier gauger ; ' come on, and I'll show you every tub he has ; come on—darling.'

"Well, the tears rolled down the poor man's face, to think his sister's child should ever be so shameless, but he had no power over himself to speak or move. Well, the Shelmalier came on, grinning and smirking ; and, sure enough, she showed him every hole and

corner; while poor little White Martin sat shivering and chattering
his bits of teeth, until the dudeen he hadn't the power to remove
was crunched into forty pieces.

"'You're a beauty,' he says; 'and, upon my honour, you shall be
my second wife; but give me a kiss,' he says, 'on account.'

"'Wait till I've earned it,' makes answer the brazen slut; 'I've
only showed you the first gathering of his unlawful practices. You
think you've seen a deal; why, that's nothing; yon is his great
hiding-hole!' and with that she points to the very rocks your honour
is sitting under at this minute, only they weren't in the same place,
but standing quite silent and grand at either side of a little cave.

"'You don't mean to say,' inquires the gauger, 'that he has more
poteen there?'

"'She knows very well!' shouts White Martin, 'that I never was
in that cave in all my life, because it's a blessed——'

"'Will you hold your tongue, if you please, good man,' she inter-
rupts, 'and not disgrace your grey hairs with such lies!'

"'Oh!' thought the poor man, 'how deceitful is the world!—My
own sister's child, that I reared up as my own, and trusted with all I
had in the world,—for whom I was adding one halfpenny to another,
and who knew no other father;—to turn on me in my ould age!'
And the poor old man's tears flowed over his white beard—more for
sorrow at the girl's ingratitude, than the ruin of his little property.

"She never heeded his trouble, but walked on with the gauger,
until, just by the rocks, there were two or three geese grazing, and
they, seeing the gauger—(all living birds and beasts know them by
what's called instinct)—took to running, one, one way—another,
another, and one flew into the cave. 'Follow her! follow her!' shouts
the girl, and so he rushes on, like the March wind, after the goose.
'Well run!' she cries; 'what handsome legs you have!' and he runs
the faster. 'Look to the wild goose chase!' she says again. 'Look!
look! look!' and, while White Martin could hardly see clear for the
blinding tears that gushed from his eyes, he still saw enough to prove
that the girl stooped, and, snatching up a 'bouclawn,' that grew at her
feet, she waved it in the air, and, as she did, one rock fell over the
other, and closed up the cave, as it is closed to this day:—then,
turning to White Martin, she waved her hand to him, and he started
to his feet, and, as he did, his own *rale* niece stood beside him; and
when he looked for her, who had taken her shape, she was gone!"

"And in old times," I inquired, laying my hand upon one of the
stones, which, according to Martin, had been so miraculously removed,
"this was a cave, or a passage?"

"A passage, made by them *tarnation* thieves of the earth, the
Danes, up from Ferry Carrig Bridge, under the water; and that was

the fun of it; for, when the goose got to the end of the passage, she
swam away; but some say the gauger was drowned, others, that he
stuck fast, and is to stick fast in it, to the end of the world: and when
the *eacho* of the wind and thunder is heard from the bowels of the
earth, about here, there are people that will tell you it's the sporting
gauger, hunting the wild goose; but I don't believe that myself all
out, because,"—added John, with the air of a philosopher, who piques
himself upon his superior intelligence,—"because it's contrary to
reason."

MARY MACGOHARTY'S PETITION.

WHEN first I saw Mary, we resided near London—it may now be some ten years ago (I believe a married lady may "recollect" for a period of ten years, although it is not exactly pleasant to remember for a longer time); she was tall, flat, and bony, exceedingly clean and neat in her dress, and yet attended minutely to the *costume* of her country: her cloth petticoat was always sufficiently short to display her homely worsted stockings; her gown was not spun out to any useless extension, but was met half way by her blue check apron—the "gown-tail" being always pinned in three-corner fashion by a huge corking-pin; her cap was invariably decorated by a narrow lace border, "rale thread" (for she abhorred counterfeits), and secured on her head by a broad green riband. But Mary's dress, strange as it was, never took off the attention from the expression of her extraordinary face; it was marvellous to look upon; and, had it been formed of cast-iron, could not have been more firm or immovable. Her forehead was high, and projected over large brown eyes, that wandered about unceasingly from corner to corner; her nose—stiff, tightly cased in its parchment skin; cheek-bones—high and projecting; and such a mouth! She talked

unceasingly; but the lips moved directly up and down, like those of
an eloquent bull-frog, never relaxing into a simper, much less a smile :
even when she shed tears (for poor Mary had been acquainted with
sorrow), they did not flow like ordinary tears, but came spouting—
spouting—from under her firm-set eyelids, and made their way down
her sun-burnt cheeks, without exciting a single symptom of sympathy
from the surrounding features.   She was a good creature, notwithstanding; sincere—I was going to say, to excess.   She prided herself upon being a "blunt, honest, God-fearing, and God-serving
woman, as any in the three kingdoms, let t'other be who she might,"
and possessed a clan-like attachment to her employers.   I have been
frequently struck with the difference between Irish and English
servants in this respect; an English servant always endeavours to
erect her standard of independence, without any reference to her
master's name or fame; but Paddys and Shelahs lug in the greatness,
the ancient family, the virtues, and the wealth (when they possess
any), on all occasions.   "Sure, an' Mabby, you may hould your
whisht any way," said one servant to another ; "what dacency did
you ever see ?   Who did *you* live wid ?   A taste of an English
grocer !—who hadn't a drop of dacent blood in his veins—only
tracle, why ?—the poor spillogue !—but I can lay my hand on my
heart, and declare, in truth and honesty, that I always lived wid the
best o' good families ; and what signifies the trifle o' wages in comparison to the nobility, and the credit ?   Sure, if we must be slaves,
it's a grate comfort to have the rale gintry over us !"
    Mary performed her duty as cook in our service admirably, for some
time, and was most trustworthy ; but, in an evil hour, on a Saint
Patrick's day, she obtained leave to visit her son, a soldier in the
Guards, to make holiday, and faithfully promised to be home by ten
o'clock.   Ten, eleven—no Mary ; at last, with the awful hour of
twelve, came—no spirit from the vasty deep, I assure you, but Mary,
poor Mary, in the watchman's arms, perfectly—(and I sincerely grieve
at being obliged to tell the truth), not ill, nor nervous, nor elevated,
nor, as the Irish call it, "disguised," but absolutely, stupidly, and
irrecoverably, tipsy !   What a piece of work there was in the house ;
—cook was conveyed to bed, and, of course, dismissed the next
morning.   I was very sorry, I confessed ; but mamma was never
prone to alter her decree, and the duty was done.   Mary cried,
offered to take an oath against whisky, gin, brandy, rum,—anything
and everything—if she might only obtain pardon ; and, when all was
useless, departed in sullen silence, hardly leaving "God be wid ye ;"
although she afterwards declared, "that, barring it would be a most
cruel sin, and what no true-born Irish soul ever did, she would lave
her curse wid Saint Patrick's day for the rest of its life; for when

A A

poor innocent people met to have 'granough,' they forgot themselves, to do honour to the holy saint—why not? though it's a rale pity; and, och! if the mistress herself would just now and thin take only a thimbleful, she would not be so hard upon the poor craturs who are overtaken by the drop."

It was a long time before I heard anything more of poor Mary; summer and winter, and again summer, and again winter, passed, and, at last, I became, from a giddy, laughing girl, a staid, reflective matron with a tolerable share of cares, and a large portion of happiness of the sweetest kind, springing from a cheerful home, and beloved faces—its dearest ornaments! I had almost forgotten my old friend, her peculiarities, and her Saint Patrick's frolic, when I was, one morning, informed that an Irishwoman wanted to speak to me. In a few minutes Mary Macgoharty was ushered in—the very same as ever; even the corking-pin in the back of her gown seemed unmoved; there she stood, looking at me, with her midnight eyes, until, at last, the torrent poured down her wrinkled cheeks.

"And there ye are, God be good to ye!—looking brave and hearty, only a dale fatter; och, it seems quite heart-cheering to see a body with kivered bones these bad times! I'm worn to a 'nottomy wid grief and hardship; and I'd have been often to see ye, before now, only ye're married, and I thought, may-be, the young master wouldn't like to have a thing like me coming about the house; only, ye mind the old whisky man, the poor boy what used to bring it, ye know, from Donovan's, that fetches it over from Cork, pure as anything, only not quite so strong—*he* can't help that; well, I was strolling about, there, by Hyde Park Corner, and wondering how the people spent their money that lived in them big houses, and a cratur like me often in want of a mouthful o' pratees, let alone bread, when who should I spy coming along—just the morral of the old thing—but Paddy Dasey; his face as red as a turf fire; and his two bags, one swinging before, and one behind, to hould the whisky jars. Well, ma'am, my dear, he had always the swing, as who should say, 'the street's my own;' and, on account of his being so tall, and the eye he has left always skying—he'd ha' walked over me, only I says, says I, 'Paddy, have ye no sight for an ould countrywoman?' Well, he looks down, and after a hearty shake by the hand we walks fair and asy to a sate; and then I told him how long I'd been out o' place, and the heart trouble I had met with. Well, he wanted me to take a drop, very civil; but I told him of the obligation I had taken on myself when I left the best service, the best mistress, and the nicest young lady that ever trod English ground; and he remembered it, too; for he used to come with the whisky to the dear ould master (heaven be his bed—amin!) but, says he, why don't you go see the

young mistress? I'll go bail she'll be glad to see ye: and then he
spoke very handsome of his honour, her husband, who, he says, is
almost as good as if he was an Irishman like you!—and tould me as
how he sometimes bought whisky, and that you had the bit and the
sup, kind as ever ye had it whin ye used to taze the life out o' me, by
axing me always what o'clock it was, till that scald parrot, mistress's
pet, used to begin at four in the morning, ' Mary, what o'clock is it?
—Mary, what o'clock is it?' Ah, thin, what's come of the parrot,
Miss—ma'am—I ax your pardon?"

" It's dead, Mary."

" Och, murder!—is she dead? Well, I'll be dead myself soon;
stiff as a red-herring, and no good in me even for the worms, for sorra
a morsel o' flesh is on my bones! I thought I'd just take Paddy
Dascy's advice, and tell ye my trouble; and now I'm just come to ye,
for God's sake, knowing ye can turn yer hand to the pen at any time,
and on account of 'Squire Bromby, who is here now, making speeches
in the English Parliament, like ony Trojan as he is—though, for
sartin, his father was not that afore him; though that's neither here
nor there, as a body may say. Now, on account of the young
'Squire (who isn't the ould, because the ould one's dead—small loss!)
—seeing my father (he was a wonderful clear-spoken man, of a poor
body, and had powerful larning) lived a matter of five-and-forty years
on the 'Squire Bromby's estate (he that's dead, this boy's father)—
I being a poor, desolate, lone woman, with no one belonging to me—
barring the boy that's in the Life Guards, and had the ill luck (God
break hard fortune!) to marry a scrap of an English girl, who had
neither family nor fortune, nor a dacent tack to her back, and was
married in a dab of a borrowed white rag of a *gownd*, not worth a teaster,
and he a likely boy (and everybody knows the English girls 'ud give
their eyes—small loss it 'ud be to some of them—for an Irish boy) as
ye'd see in a day's march (ye mind, my first husband was a soldier, and
my second too; I'm a *Mac*, in earnest, as a body may say; my own
name, Mac Manus; my first's name, Macgoharty; my second's, Mac
Avoy;—though I go by poor Jim's name, Macgoharty—Mary Macgoharty, at your sarvice—because I liked him best; not but the second
was a fine boy, too; but there's nothing goes past first love)—well, I
humbly ax yer pardon, but I always like to tell a thing out of the
face at once, without any bating about the bush; so, as I was saying,
my poor father (God rest his soul!) lived five-and-forty years to the
good on his honour's father's estate, in pace, plinty, and contintment,
and no one could iver say to him, ' black is the white o' yer eye.'
May-be ye mind whin ould 'Squire Bromby was returned for Tippe-
rary—though it's as much as ye can, for ye weren't born at the time;
and who set up, too, but Jack Johnson?—'Squire Jack they called

him;—though I was but a girleen at the time, I niver could turn my tongue to say ''Squire Jack,' and he only a bit of a brewer; well, my father (oh! he was down honest) stood up for the ould gintry; and, seeing he was so main strong, 'Squire Bromby made him one of the picked men at the election; and by the same token, the shillalah he had went whirring through the air like a shuttlecock; now cracking one skull, now another, now lighting here, now there, spanking about with rale glory; from the beginning to the end, it neither gave, nor had, rest or pace. Well, there niver was such an election seen before nor since; such tearing and murdering; Jack's boys killing 'Squire Bromby's boys, and 'Squire Bromby's boys skivering 'the Jackeens' (as we called them) like curlews. Well, that wasn't all; but one night (it was either the second or third day of the election) the ould 'Squire calls my father o' one side. 'Mister Mac Manus,' says he. 'Don't Mister me,' says my father, 'if you plaze, because Mister is no part o' my name, yer honour; I'm plain James Mac Manus;' and my father (he was very proud) stood stiff as an oak of the forest. 'Well, then,' says the 'Squire, fox-like, 'honest James Mac Manus, my good friend, ye've stood firm to me for the honour of ould Ireland —a good friend, indeed, have ye been to me; and it's I won't forget it; but clap yer eye, James, my boy, upon any situation in the three kingdoms, spake but the word, and 'tis yours.' 'Thanks to yer honour—many thanks to yer honour.' My father was a well-spoken man, but innocent-like (he was no ways 'cute), took it all for gospil. Well, my jewel, the next day they fell to it again, and my father in the thick of it, to be sure, like a grate *giount*, tattering all before him, stronger nor ever; and more betokens, Jack Johnson (it's only justice to tell the truth) had powers o' money, and made no bones o' the boys aitin' and drinkin' at his expinse; he was a fine portly man, with a handsome rich nose, and deeshy-dawshy eyes, for all the world like a rat's, squinkin' and blinkin' under the dickon's own bushy, black winkers—och, so thundery! And, as the rale ancient 'Squire's tongue wasn't hung asy, and the other's went upon wires—why, he had the advantage there, too:—and a bitter ruction it was; all the boys, more or less, had smashed heads, and they tied them up with garters, or stockings, or sugans, or anything the owners came across, to keep the bones together. Why?——but the spirit and the shillalahs held out bravely! And the last day came—as it will upon the best of us some time or other; and, after all, 'Squire Bromby carried it, through thick and thin.

"Well, I'll say that for Jack Johnson—though only a brewer, he bore up like a king, not a taste out o' temper all the time, only as gay as a lark, capering about like a good one. Bromby-park was a good ten mile from the town, and nothing would do my father (for he was parfect mad with the joy), but he put up the boys to draw the new member thim ten miles, like a pack of horses (more like asses, as my mother said), and no bad load either; a heavy lump of a man, good and bad blood—though, to tell God's truth, there was more of that last. Well, away they went, huzzaing and shouting, and got him to the house in less than no time; when, fair and asy, out he steps, makes a bow, and an up-and-down taste of a speech, first swaying on one leg, then on the other, like a bothered goose; and turns into the house, without as much as offering even a drop of smalkum to a mother's son of the whole of thim. Well, after this, all the country called shame on him—the tame negre! and what made it worse, Jack Johnson gave his boys, even after, plinty of entertainment, and said that, if he did lose the election, those who voted for him could not help it, and, consequently, should not suffer for it. After it was all passed, and the people came to their senses again, father thought it was time to put him in mind of his word (mother tould him how it would be), and so he set off, making a dacent appearance, to put the 'Squire in mind of his promise. What d'ye think he said, and he o' horseback, in his scarlet jock, as grand as a Turkey-man?—'Oh, yer name is James Mac Manus. Well, James, how is the woman that owns you, and the children, all well, ay? Place, indeed, hard things to get—wish I'd a good one myself. Good morning, James—good morning:' and off he rode. Father was so stomached, that he would never go near him again: 'For,' says he, 'though he's a mimber of parliament, he's no gentleman that doesn't value his word; I'm sure I don't know how he came to be such a cankered thing (unless he was changed at nurse), for the breed of the family was always the top of the gentry.' Well, honey, dear, may-be I'm tiring ye too much intirely, but never heed, I'm a'most done; ye see, Lord help us! my father's dead, and the old 'Squire's dead. I'm in a strange country, and even my boy has no love for the sod, seeing he wasn't born on it, nor never saw the green, green grass, or the clear water, or heard the little birds sing among the beautiful woods, bright and blooming with the hawthorn, and the brier, and the wild crab-tree; it wasn't so with my Annie, my daughter, my only girl, who was born there before my husband took to soldiering; and she was so like him—his very moral; but she's gone—buried near Dunleary, they tell me, and I shall never see her soft blue eye upon me, nor hear her voice, nor—but I ax yer pardon, madam, I ought not to be troubling ye after such a fashion.

"They were pleasant woods that I sported among in my innocent morning; and ye'd hardly think, to look now upon my withered skin, and my dim eye, and my grey hair, that I was once likely, and had the pick of the boys for a husband; but they're both gone from me, and the English daughter-in-law looks could enough upon the ould Irish mother-in-law! But, you see, the young 'Squire's got a brave name, and is over here with the commoners, and, I am tould, a noble-spirited, true gentleman; so I was just thinking, as ye're handy with the pen, may-be ye'd write him (for me) a taste of a letter, just to put him in mind, ye know, that my father lived upon his father's land, and telling him how poor I am—(an' sure that's true for me! for, bad luck to the tack, I have but what I stand upright in); sure I made this petticoat (and it's a tidy one too) out of the grey cloak I got last winter (winter's a hard time on the poor) was two years, to keep me dacent, and my poor bones from freezing, and never disgraced my country, by being beholden to man or mortal—only, why the poor has a nataral claim upon estated gintlemin, ye know; and just ax him civilly to give me two or three pounds (he'll never miss it, my darling lady, never), to send me home, where there's ould people still I'd be glad to see, more partiklar my bothered sister, who lives nigh where my poor girl lies, jist by Dublin. I've had two warnings for death (they always followed my family), and I know I can't last long; only ye're sinsible, ma'am, nixt to dying in pace wid God and man, there's nothing like laving one's bones among one's own; thin, ye know, it's pleasant not to be among strangers at the resurrection; so I was thinking——"

"In one word, Mary, you want me to write a petition for you to 'Squire Bromby, as you call him?"

"Exactly—och, you've hit it now!—ye were always mighty quick that a way, may God bless ye!—but mind, lady dear, not a word of the past, ye know; it would be bad manners to be putting the dacent, noble young gintleman in mind of his ould foolish father's quare capers."

"Then, Mary, you need not have told me of them."

"Well, now, that bates all; why, how could ye get the understanding of the thing, if I did not tell ye?—sure you must know the rights of the thing, ony way, as the ould song says—

> ' I do not care for speculation—
> But tell to me the truth at onct.' "

"Well, I dare say, Mary, you were quite right; but now, as you have given me understanding, allow me to commit your ideas to paper."

Poor Mary! I saw her a few days after my scribbling, at her request, the petition she was so anxious about. She was as neat as a bride. New shawl, new bonnet, new petticoat, even a new corking-pin in the gown-tail; for, as the dress was of "stubborn stuff," it needed a strong restraint to keep the corners in proper order. She was very happy, and very grateful to "'Squire Bromby" and me; and, as she seemed only disposed to talk of "Dublin Bay herrings,"—

" Kerry cows,"—" travelling expinses," (which she had fractionally
counted up)—" turf,"—" pratees,"—and " Ould Ireland," I soon
made my adieus; faithfully promising, if I visited Erin in the ensuing
season, not to forget paying my compliments to her in her sister's
cabin; where, she assured me, " their very· hearts' blood should be
shed to do me and mine sarvice !"

I was enabled to keep my word.

* * * * * * *

Oh, but the suburbs of Dublin are miserable !—miserable !—so
miserable that, were I to attempt to describe them, your kind hearts
would sicken; you would close the page, and not accompany me on
my peregrination to the turn which opens direct on the Dunleary
road.   In the distance, the expanded Bay of Dublin, glittering like
molten silver—innumerable vessels sleeping, as it were, upon its
glorious waters, all glowing in the rich brightness of the morning
sun, formed a background worthy Turner's own gorgeous pencil.
Amongst the groups of ragged, but cheerful, peasants, I soon found
a guide to conduct me to Mary's dwelling, and gazed upon her little
cottage, hardly worthy the name; but, nevertheless, so sweetly
situated, that its extreme poverty was atoned for by its picturesque
appearance.   It was built, literally, on the side of a hill, for part
of the eminence formed the back wall of the dwelling; the roof was
covered over with lichens and moss, that mingled with the long grass,
blossoming brambles, and feathery ragweed, of the overhanging
common.   As the hill ascended, it was tufted with richly-foliaged
trees; and, below the cabin, a clear sparkling stream trickled and
murmured quietly along its channel, except where some firm-set stone
or saucy brier intercepted its way; and then it grumbled outright,
and sent forth a tiny foam, expressive of its anger !   The pig had its
own proper dwelling, hollowed out of the hill, and, whether he liked
it or not, there he was compelled to stay, by an antiquated chair-
back, that was placed across the entrance; and through its openings
he could only thrust his nose, which, from its extreme length, made
me suspect he was an uncivilized Connaught pig.   A few fowl of the
noble Dorking breed, with magnificent toppings, were wandering
about the meadows, and a noisy hen was storming, with might and
main, at her duckling progeny, who, heedless of her eloquence,
paddled in and out of the streamlet, in perfect safety : it was a calm,
and, after all, a pleasing picture.   The Irish, when suffering the
greatest privations, never lose their elastic spirits, and, even from
that lowly hut, came the merry notes of " Planxty Kelly," although
sung by a feeble voice.   I wanted to enter unperceived, but a busy
cur-dog yelped so loudly, that an aged woman came courtesying to
the door—not Mary.   I thought I had mistaken the cottage, and

was just going to inquire, when I perceived a female figure in the act of dusting the turf ashes off the hearth with her apron; her back was to me; but there was no mistaking the *corking-pin*—there it was in the self-same spot of the pinned-up gown tail!

How delighted she was to see me!—"How ashamed that she had nothing to offer me!—her sister's grand-daughter was jist gone to market with a few eggs—but, sure, Kate Kearney was on the nest, at the far corner, and she'd soon lay, and thin it would be worth atin'!—she was a beautiful hen! Or she wouldn't be a minute whipping the head off one of thim long-legged pullets, the giddy craturs!—small use it was to them!—and grill it like fun in the ashes! Or she would catch the goat for some milk—sure they had grass for a goat; Nanny gave such nice milk—only, bad cess to the cat! there was no keeping a drop in the house for her; they had nothing to kiver it, and she took the pig's share and her own; they wanted to fat him up to pay the rint, which he did regular, except last year, when he (the one that's dead) got the measles, and that was a sad loss to them."

The cabin was very poorly furnished; for the pig, the poultry, eggs, and even the little spinning and knitting the two old women could do, were insufficient to bestow upon them much comfort; and, besides that, they had an orphan relative, who had just sufficient intellect to sell the eggs, and, with true Irish feeling, they shared with her whatever they possessed. Then came the inquiries as to the "ould mistress and the young master," and every living thing she could remember as pertaining to our household. When I bade them good day, Mary hoped I'd let her show me the *short* cut; "a dale pleasanter, although, may-be, a few steps *longer*." As we wended down a narrow glen, carpeted with the short, thick, downy grass, that sheep so much delight to browse upon, I asked Mary if she was happy?

"Happy!—why, middling, God be thanked! middling so: an ould body, like me, has none, nor ought to think o' none, o' that quick joy that sets the heart dancing, and the blood mounting and tearing through the veins like mad. But the ould have the quiet and the content; the mist moves from their eyes; and they see everything past, and many things to come, as they are; they know that the heart's fresh hope will bud, and may-be bloom, but certainly fade; good luck, if it doesn't fade, or be cut off afore it bloom. Sure I'm joyous to see the young things around me dancing like the merry waters, for I know there'll be time enough for the salt, salt tears, with the best of 'em, whether they last long or short; and all I can do, I do—pray that the grate God will keep 'em from sin, and then they never can taste the worst o' sorrow; for bitter is the bed. and hard, o' the black sinner; which, thank God, no one be-

longing to me ever was; and the priest (God rest his soul!) often
said that, whin we went to make a clean breast, it's little trouble he
had with us; and the hardest pilgrimage my father ever made, was
twice to the Lady's Island, and that wasn't for much, in so long a
life. When I came over, I thought it only fitting to have a few
masses said for the rest of my poor girl's soul!—but the priest (och,
he's the good man!) tould me half as much would do as was customary
—on account she was such a God-serving girl; never missed a confession in her life. I'll show ye where she lays; and I've taken an
obligation on myself never to pass the grave without one avy.
Whin we turn this knock, we'll come right upon the poor ould
churchyard, all so quiet and lonesome by itself!—that's not the way
it 'll be at the last day! God help me!"

When we "turned the knock"—I was charmed by the old churchyard; it changed completely the style of the landscape—as it stood
at the commencement of a long marsh—a little elevated above its
level; and the prospect on that side our path was terminated by
hills above hills—some slightly wooded—others resting, as it were,
against the clear blue sky, huge masses of many-tinted rock. The
building must have been one of very ancient structure; what
remained was overgrown by ivy, and here and there a solitary tree
shadowed the mouldering walls and half-fallen arches; there were few
tomb-stones—nought but "green grass mounds," headed by small
wooden crosses—some without any inscription—others simply marked
thus—

☩
I H S

One ponderous relic of ancient days, however, stood in a corner of
the churchyard, at which a young man and woman were kneeling.

When Mary had repeated her customary prayer, she rejoined me,
observing "she would take longer next time, only she could not bear
to keep me waiting in such a dismal place."

"Mary," I inquired, "can I take any message back to your son,
in case his regiment should have returned to London?"

"Oh! God bless ye for that thought!—sure can ye—and my
heart was bustin' to ax ye, only I thought, may-be, ye'd think bad
of my making so bould. Ye see, ma'am, dear, I thought my sister
was better to do in the world; or, I'd hardly ha' troubled her, and
the times so bad; but my heart bates to see the boy—and I don't
want him here, because I know the English girl would be skitting
at the poor cabin; and, above all things, ye know, agra, I niver
bear a slut cast upon the country; I don't say but (though I'd be
long sorry to let them English hear me) there's a dale more comfort,
and eatin', and such as that, among 'em—and they're study, honest,

surly sort o' people—no variety in 'em at all—all the one way, all asy going—without much spirit, but a dale of comfort. Now seeing I got a fresh lease o' my life by breathing such air as this—though I'm ould—yet I find I can't settle myself parfect for death without once more seeing the boy—and seeing London; and so will ye tell him—God bless ye!—that, after this winter, I will have enough to carry me over, an' back, may be, on account, ye know, of laving my bones in the grey churchyard—near my poor girl; but, if I shouldn't have enough, ma'am dear, sure you'll be to the fore, and it's little ye'd think o' writing me another *petition!*—I'll engage ye're as nimble at the pen as ever. And, if ye see the boy's wife, and she axes any questions, jist put the best face upon it, ma'am, honey, for the honour of ould Ireland! So my blessing be about ye wherever ye go; and the blessing of all the saints, and St. Patrick's at the head of thim! Sure, it's a happy sight to see his beautiful head (the steeple I mean) watching above that sweet, illigint city—that the devil has no power over—the joy of my heart ye are, Dublin agra!"

I bade her adieu, and was proceeding on my way; Mary took my hand, pressed it affectionately to her heart and lips, and the tears showered on it; she could not speak her farewell blessing, but fixed her large eyes on me as I departed, with more expression of feeling than I had ever before witnessed! Poor Mary!—winters and summers have passed; but I have seen her no more!—She needs no more *petitions*.

OLD FRANK.

AS long as I can remember, Frank was called—"Old Frank." He was a little, crabbed-looking man, bent nearly double : had a healthy colouring on his cheek, and a few, very few, grey hairs straying over his bald and shrivelled forehead ; with a halt in his walk ; and was always either singing or coughing ; somewhat "cranky" in his temper, and in his capacity of coachman (which situation he had filled for a period of forty-two years in our family), exercised despotic sway over horses, dogs, and grooms. He was singularly faithful, and strongly attached to his master and mistress, his horses, and myself ; indeed, as to the two last, it was a matter of doubt which he loved best ; however "snappish" he might have been to others, he was to me, in my childish days, one of the kindest and firmest of friends ; no matter how I tormented him—no matter what pranks I played (and they were not a few), "Miss Maria" was always right, and everybody else was wrong. Having lived so long in the family, he was hardly looked upon as a servant, and neither master nor mistress disputed his dictum ; indeed, I do not know why they should, for, wherever his authority extended, matters were well managed. The coats of his carriage-horses shone like French satin, and the carriage, an old lumbering thing of the last century, could not have existed at all under the care of any other coachman. Frank, the carriage, and horses, had grown old together; they were all of a piece, and cut a remarkable appearance, whenever they walked (for that was their most rapid pace) out in the bright sunshiny summer. But it was not alone in this, his principal situation, that Frank was entitled to, and treated with, respect. All the perfect, and all the embryo, sportsmen of the neighbourhood came to consult him on every matter connected with dogs and horses; he was famed, all over the county, for educating pointers on the most approved principles, and was permitted to have three or four constantly in training for the neighbouring gentry, who always remunerated him handsomely for his trouble. He had been an excellent sportsman in his youth, and took much pride in boasting that, except his head, all the bones in his body had been broken; indeed, even his head exhibited a sufficient quantity of bumps to puzzle a phrenologist; the old man still loved sporting, and it was owing to this circumstance that Frank and I were such great friends.

I certainly was " a country child;" and to escape from study, and stroll with Frank, Frank's dogs, and Frank's daughter, " my kind and gentle nurse," was one of the greatest of my simple enjoyments. I can hardly tell why, but Bannow, in my remembrance, always seems like fairyland—its fields so green—its trees so beautiful—its inhabitants so different from any I have elsewhere met!

The aged man used to make it a constant practice to take out a steady old pointer, with a young, untaught, roving, but well-grown puppy; and I believe Joss (the old one) was as much interested in the business of educating the young dog, as Frank himself. Be that as it may, we used all to wander among the green lanes and fields, and, when I was tired, nurse would seat me on an old grey stone, or rustic stile, and Frank would lean on his gun, and tell me some of the fairy tales, or legends, with which his memory was so well stored. He had a most confirmed belief in banshees, cluricawns, fairies, and mermaids; and if Mary, who was very superior to the general order of servants, ever presumed to doubt the truth of one of her father's stories, he reproved her in no gentle terms; and no wonder,—he had a mark in his hand, which was actually given by an arrow, shot at him by a fairy queen, one evening, when he was returning home after a quiet carouse at Mr. Talbot's. He could never be prevailed upon to root up large mushrooms (fairy tables), or to pull bulrushes (fairy horses), lest he might offend the good people.

His most favourite walk was across some young plantations, admirable covers for game, to a small hill, thickly wooded at either side,

where there was a singularly fine oak, one of whose branches jutted
suddenly from the trunk, and formed a rustic seat, which, in childish
sportiveness, I used to call my throne. From thence the prospect
was very beautiful : the long, white chimneys of my old home sprung,
as it were, from amid the trees, that, from this particular point of
view, appeared to fringe the ocean's brink; while the many-coloured
foliage of the lofty poplar, dark cedar, feathery birch, or magnificent
elm, gave richness and variety to the landscape.

But in our own summer-house—a comparatively rude structure,
yet which, in those days, was, to my mind, the most perfect example
of elegance and good taste that was ever erected—how I did love to
sit, during the long evenings—nurse's arm around me, to prevent the
possibility of any irregular and restless movements terminating in an
upset, and listen with delight to Frank's fairies, about whom the good
old man so dearly loved to talk, only interrupting his narrative, now
and then, by a necessary word of caution to his dogs. Whenever I
urged him to tell me a story, he used to shake his head, and say,
" Och ! Miss, honey, ye'll, maybe, think of old Frank and his fairies,
when ye'll be far from your native land, and my poor smashed bones
at rest. But my blessing be about ye," he would add, patriotically,
" *never deny your country.*"

My favourite story was " The Stout and Strong of Heart ;" and I
believe it was Frank's favourite also; for many a time and oft has he
repeated it to me, and always have I listened with attention, pleasing
the old man, while I was myself delighted. I will give it to my
readers, although I fear it will lose much, from the absence of my
ancient friend, who, with so much earnestness and native humour,
related it.

" There was plenty of mirth, and of everything else, in the little
cabin of Jerry Mahony, for his daughter Ellen had just become a
bride, and the merry party were beguiling the time while the dinner
was in preparation. The blind piper was sitting on the hearth-stone,
making beautiful music, and now and again taking a sup of potheen,
to the long life of the wedded pair. Jerry himself was listening to
all the compliments and good wishes of the neighbours; his wife,
Biddy, busily placing all her own and the borrowed delf upon the
table, and bustling her maid Peggy with a continual ' Make haste,
hurra ! 'tis only once in a long life;' while the bride and bridegroom,
James and Ellen Deasy, sat in a corner, talking over their future
arrangements, and planning ways and means to make themselves
happy and comfortable; and, to be sure, the mother of the girl got
everything in order. And Ellen was lovely and beautiful enough
for a queen, let alone a poor man's wife. But, although she was made
much of, by rich and poor, no one thought more of her than Kit

Murtough, the blind piper; and good right had he so to do; for she
had the pity for him, the poor sightless creature:—and it was he who
made the beautiful music that night; so beautiful was it, that the
priest himself could stand it no longer, but capered like a Chinaman.
Well, the next morning, Biddy Mahony went to the foot of the
ladder that led to her daughter's room—

"'Ellen, honey,' says she, 'come down, I have some nice tay
for ye both.' She waited, and there was no answer; so she went
up a few steps, 'James, agra! won't you waken for me?' Still no
answer: well, she went into the room, and stopped, and said, 'Why
then won't either of you spake to yer own mother, that gave birth to
one, and a wife to the other? Jemmy, Nelly, dears!—get up and
look at the morning that's so smiling and happy.' Still not a word:
so she went and pulled the wisp of straw out of the window, and let
in the light. She then looked on the bed, patted her child on the
cheek, and felt that she was a cold corpse. Her bitter shrieks soon
woke the husband; and the neighbours came running in, in crowds;
and black grief was in that cabin, where, the night before, there had
been so much joy. Many suspected that James Deasy had a hand
in his wife's death, and there were some who told him so. But sobs,
from the very depth of his heart, were James's only answers. The
evening came, and the young bride was laid out for the wake. All
was got in readiness for the 'berring,' which, according to custom,
was to be on the third day. Now, nobody took the death of poor
Ellen more to heart than did Kit the piper, who wandered about the
neighbourhood of her dwelling, playing only dismal tunes, until the
night before the funeral, when he was sitting between lights, under
the cornrick that stood in the sheltered corner of Jerry Mahony's
field, while the mournful music made the place more melancholy.
Suddenly he felt a sudden gush of wind pass by him, and then all
was still; he paused for a while, and again struck up the same tune,
the tune that poor Ellen so dearly loved; then the wind came stronger
by him, and again he paused; once more he began the air, and the
wind beat furiously against him. He now crossed himself, and called
on the blessed Virgin, when he heard the voice of the dead bride
speak to him, and say, 'Kit Murtough, go to my husband, and tell
him not to weep for me, for I am a living woman, but the fairies carried me away. Bid him come here at nightfall, and bring a pail of
new milk from the cow; but tell him be careful not to spill a drop
of it, or he'll lose me for ever, but to be STOUT AND STRONG OF
HEART; and when he hears the blast rush past him, let him throw it
upon me, so that it may drench me all over, but, if he misses me, he'll
never see me more.' A joyful man was Kit that minute, and off he
posted, and told it, word for word, to the husband, who, to be sure,
put but little faith in it, yet the love to the wife made him try. So,

to make all sure, he milked the cow himself, without spilling a drop,
and off he went to the cornrick, very much troubled in his mind,
with the hope of recovering his bride, the doubts as to the piper's
story, and the fear that he should 'miss drenching her, and then lose
her for ever.' But James was a bold man, and feared nothing else.
So he waited patiently till the first blast of wind passed him. He
took up the pail, but his heart misgave him, and he laid it down again.
Once more the blast came, and more strongly, but still James Deasy
was only half a man. The third time it came furiously upon him;
then James was ready, and threw every drop upon the blast, when
all at once, he saw his wife before him, as plainly as when she stood
beside the priest; and he clasped his arms about her, while a loud
whirling tempest—full of the good people—came all round them.
But she was safe from harm, and they returned smiling to her father's
cottage.

"No one but a mother can tell Biddy Mahony's joy to see her
child come back to her again. And the evening of that day saw happiness returned to Jerry's cottage, where the piper had his old seat,
in the chimney-corner, sung many a merry song, and drank a double
portion of whisky to the health of the bridegroom and the
bride.

"But James Deasy, when he came in, went straight to the coffin,
and, in the place of the corpse, he saw a great log of wood, with the
shroud upon it. This he quickly put upon the fire, when they heard
a loud screech, and the log went up the chimney with a noise like a
thunderstorm, that almost shook the roof off the old cabin. The
neighbours came running in to know what was the matter; and there
they saw James Deasy, and Ellen his wife, sitting in the corner, as if
nothing had happened; she looking as beautiful, and he as happy, as
when Father Peter blessed them both, a few days before.

"Some months had now passed away, and Ellen was about to
become a mother, when she called her husband to her bedside, and
said, 'James, dear, happy have we been, and happy will we still be,
if you do my bidding; which is, when my little baby is born, put
three crosses on its forehead, and three on mine, and don't leave me
for a minute, however they may try to wile you away, for the fairies
will be after the both of us.' Well, James never left her bedside,
but watched her night and day, for fear the fairies should be waiting
to take off both the wife and the child; which, when it came, was
a glorious boy. But, all at once, James heard a scream outside the
door, and a small voice calling 'Ellen Deasy;' he looked round, and
saw the latch raised, and the door opening gently, then ran towards
it, and pushed it to violently, when, all in a minute, he heard a loud
laugh, as if from many persons, and when he looked on his wife's
bed, he saw that both mother and child were dead. James remem-

bered the crosses, and remembered that his wife had warned him to let nothing tempt him from her bedside. But 'twas too late, they were both gone, and James Deasy was indeed a wretched man.

"'They kept poor Ellen and her little one for a long time above the ground, and then they buried them both in the churchyard. But James could not rid himself of the idea that the bodies were not those of his wife and child, so he would not let the priest say mass or anything over them; a thing which brought much shame and scandal upon him. But he had his own reasons for it.

"Now, it happened, one morning, that James Deasy was hoeing his little garden, and thinking, as he did every day, of his poor Ellen, that he had lost nearly a twelvemonth, when his hoe struck against a sod as green as ever was spring leaf, although his spade had been into it many a time, and it had been long covered with black clay. All of a sudden he heard music under it—beautiful and sweet music, such as he had never heard before. He remembered his poor wife's warning, to 'be stout and strong of heart,' so he raised up the sod and looked down. There he saw, at a depth that seemed many miles underground, a number of little people dancing most merrily : they were all dressed in green leaves, and had fine forms and faces ; for to his great wonder, he could distinguish them plainly, although they were so far off. He thought that one of the little people resembled his dead wife ; and he knew it must be her, when he heard her say, 'to the cornrick at midnight,' while the rest of the fairies repeated her words, ' to the cornrick at midnight ;' and then the music ceased, and the ground appeared the same as it had always been ; for James could not discover the green sod he had just raised. The more he thought upon the words, 'to the cornrick at midnight,' the more he was convinced they had some meaning, and that they were addressed to him. So he waited impatiently till the night came, and went off to the appointed place.

"Now, the green island was well known over all the country as the pet of the fairies. There he waited till he heard the sound of the merry pipes, and saw a long train coming along the path. He stood quite quiet, as if he was minding nothing at all but the road-stones he pretended to be breaking, until the whole of the crowd had passed him ; when up from the ground starts James, seizes the last woman of the group, tears off the cloak from the shoulders, signs three crosses on the brow, snatches the child, and does the same to it, when, lo and behold ! his own wife, Ellen Deasy, on her knees before him, and his own beautiful little baby in her arms ! The sign of the cross had driven all the fairies away, and, safe and sound, James, and Ellen, and their little one, returned to their cottage, and never more was the life of either disturbed by the good people.

" They are still living in Dumraghodooly, and James is ever and always ready to tell his story over a glass of whisky punch ; but no inducement has yet prevailed on Ellen to give any account of her adventures in fairy-land."

" Oh, Miss, don't laugh," Old Frank would invariably add—" it's as true as I'm a sinner, and it's bad to disbelieve the fairies. Sure I was an unbeliever once myself, and this was my punishment—one of their arrows right through the flat o' my hand; I shall carry the mark to my grave. Come, Miss, it's time to go home ;—bad luck to the dog! Joss, where's Rover ?—Rover ! Oh, that young dog wants as much attindance as a Mullenavat pig !"

" How is that, Frank ?"

" Why, Miss, the Mullenavat people are Munster, ye know, and quite inferior to the Wexfordians, and depind on the pig to pay the rint, and, on that account, trate him with all the respect possible— why not ?—and so they pick out the big pratees for the pig, and ate the little ones themselves ; and they give the pig the clane straw, and sleep themselves in the dirty ; and they give the pig the candle to go to bed wid, and go to bed themselves in the dark."

" And is that true, Frank ?"

" As gospel, Miss; upon my word it is. Here, Rover !—the only way to steady that dog will be to hang him. Rover—Rover !"

Frank delighted in telling stories of the rebellion, but he left it to others to recount what true and faithful service he had rendered his master and mistress in that perilous time ; and they were nothing loth to do him ample justice. I have often heard how he buried the best old wine in the asparagus beds, to save it from falling into the hands of the rebels ; and how he concealed his favourite horses in the hen and turkey-houses ; and how, at the risk of his life, he carried a forged order to General Roche, who commanded the rebel forces in the town of Wexford ; which order purported to come from another rebel chief, and demanded the instant freedom of his master, whose life was thus preserved.

It was in the summer of 1798, that my grandfather, who had been, for a few days, in Dublin, on business of importance, embarked with his constant attendant, Frank, on board a small Wexford trading vessel. Intelligence had reached them of the disturbed state of the country ; and, as land travelling was unsafe, the " boat" was engaged to convey them direct to the Bay of Bannow.

As they passed Dalkey Isle, and coasted along the beautiful shores of Wicklow, glowing in the full richness of summer, the sea-breeze tempering the fervid heat with its invigorating freshness, my grandfather thought he had never seen the country look so tranquil or so happy ; the lowing of the cattle, the bleating of sheep, the cooing of the wood-pigeon, even the subdued warblings of the forest birds, were heard on board their light bark; but when the day passed, and the night darkened, unusual fires sparkled on the hills: and, along the shore, lights would blaze for a moment, and then suddenly disappear. The anxiety of both master and servant to arrive at home was intense, and they were much pleased to perceive, through the grey mist of the succeeding morning, the spire of Wexford Church. As the day advanced, Mr. —— distinctly saw green flags floating from the masts of the several vessels in the harbour.

"We must sport one too, sir," said Rawson, the Captain of the brig; "if we do not they will board us." He unfurled his flag immediately, after which, Frank went off deck into the cabin, and slyly took out his master's pistols from his portmanteau; he then (as he subsequently stated), poured a little water into the pans of a fowling-piece, a blunderbuss, and other fire-arms, that he had perceived lying under some coiled rope and canvas sacks. The fact was, he had ascertained, by overhearing some conversation between the Captain and one of his crew, that Rawson was a United Irishman, and one in no way to be trusted. He then crept on deck, and placed himself beside his master's elbow. My grandfather kept his eye steadily fixed on Rawson's movements; but to say the truth, if he had been tacking for the bottom of the sea, he could hardly have discovered it, being utterly ignorant of all naval tactics.

The channel into the harbour of Wexford is very narrow; nor was it until the prow of the vessel was passing between the two embankments, Mr. —— observed that Rawson, instead of steering for Carnsore Point, was making direct for the town. He instantly sprang at the Captain, who was at the helm, and seized him by the throat; while Frank, nothing loth, presented a pistol to his head, swore vehemently that, if he did not tack about, he would throw him overboard. Rawson, who was a man of great bodily strength, drew a pistol from his bosom; it missed fire: but, at the moment when my grandfather had overpowered his antagonist, he received a blow on the head from Frank; he was almost stunned, staggered a few paces forward, and fell. At that instant, two or three musket balls whizzed past, and Frank whispered,—"I humbly ax yer honour's pardon, but it was the only way I had left, to make yer honour get out of the way of three blackguards, in that boat, who took prime aim, and would have had ye down as clane as a partridge, but for my taste of a knock; the game's up now, but that bit of a blow wouldn't hurt a pointer, sir."

In another instant they were boarded by the rebels, and Mr. —— was soon bound hand and foot. He would most likely have been piked on the spot, but that the insurgents were, at this period anxious, if possible, to obtain the sanction and assistance of some of the leading gentlemen of the county. They, therefore, secured him to prevent the possibility of escape, and Frank was suffered to depart. The poor man arrived at Bannow when it was near midnight, and found my mother and grandmother marking the minutes by their tears. The whole country was in a state of open insurrection : and, although they had hitherto been treated with respect, through the kind interference of the good priest and Captain Andy, yet the uncertain fate of my grandfather, and the continued stories of death and destruction they had heard, kept them in perpetual agitation. Frank's account was not likely to soothe their misery, and they asked each other what was to be done, without receiving consolation from any plan that was suggested. Captain Andy was with his rebel regiment at the mountain of Forth. The priest had gone, it was supposed, to Ross. What plan could be adopted ?—" Frank, can you not devise any mode ?"—Frank coughed.—" Can nothing be done ?"—Frank replied to this question by asking another : " Can ye tell me, madam, if they have taken Grey Bess for the devil's sarvice yet ?"—" She was in the stable this morning, with two or three of the old horses."—" Hem ! I'm glad of that, I'll jist step out —I wonder they passed her ; she's as fine a slug of a mare as there's in the whole county."

The ladies thought Frank's attention to his quadrupeds ill-timed, but he went his way ; and, first concealing the carriage-horses in the fowl-houses, mounted Grey Bess, whose strong, well-made limbs merited the encomium he had passed on her, and without imparting his intention even to his fellow-servants, set off at a brisk trot to the mountain of Forth. Arrived at the encampment, he soon found out his friend Andy, and in a few moments, they were in close conversation at a little distance from the mass of the people, who were either sleeping, drinking, or singing, in scattered groups over the mountain, canopied by the clear, moonlit sky. " We must get him off, Frank; General Roche is in command—yet I don't know how ?" " Can you write ?"—" Is it me ?" replied Frank; " not I— can you ?" " No: an order from General Keough would do it, but he's for making a bonfire of the town."

" The baste !" exclaimed Frank; " would there be any sin in jist signing his name to a little taste of an order to General Roche, to let him go free on particular business, to be returned when called for ? If we had him safe in Bannow, 'twould be asy enough to hide him away in an ould cave, or castle, or cask, or ship him off, like a sack of pratees, to Wales. Where there's a will, there's a way; but he's clane gone if he remains in Wexford. Is Father Mike here ?" Andy bent his thumb back to intimate that he was in the camp. " I thought so—God be wid ould times ! he'll niver forget my mistress's

attintion to him, and she an Englishwoman, let alone my master's.
If ye see a man an' his bit of a wife go past in the morning on Grey
Bess, *bathershin*—God be wid ye !" and Frank went off to seek the
priest. He was easily found, and soon understood what Frank wanted.

"My simple order would be of no use, Frank, for they think me
faithless enough, because I cannot spill blood—blood of the innocent
as well as the guilty. General Keough's would do it;" the kind-
hearted man paused: "every imprisoned Protestant will, I know,
suffer before to-morrow night."

"My poor master, sir, and mistress !—I'll tell ye what, if yer
reverence will jist give me the scrapeen of an order, who'll know ye
iver wrote it ?—and sure it's I that 'ud write it in the crack of a
whip, if I knew how. Oh, sir, think of all the good they did the
poor Catholics in the hard winter !"

Father Mike hesitated no longer, drew from his pocket a little
inkhorn, and wrote the order on the top of Frank's hat, the moon
shining brightly on them at the time.

Away went Frank and Grey Bess, into Wexford, and the day had
dawned by the time he arrived at the Court-house. He unhesi-
tatingly presented his order, and my grandfather was much delighted
to find himself at liberty.

"I wonder the General wrote," said the man who let him out,
"for he'll be in Wexford himself in an hour !"

This intelligence alarmed Frank much, and he hurried his master
to a dwelling, the fidelity of whose inmates he could depend on ; it
belonged to his uncle Kit's third daughter, who was married to
Mickey Hayes, the grocer, at that time Commissary-General to the
rebel forces quartered in Wexford. There Frank equipped his master
in a good frieze suit, long coat, straw hat—mounted a bunch of
laurel at one side, and a green feather at the other, and presented to
him a sturdy pike; he then arrayed his own little person in "his
uncle Kit's daughter's" red petticoat and hooded cloak.

"And now," said he, "yer honour will remember that yer name's
Pat Kennesey, and that ye're going to the blessed priest's house, and
that I'm yer wife—that'll ride on Grey Bess behind ye."

They arrived safely at Bannow ; and my grandfather often said—
when the troublesome times were passed, and he jested at the remembrance of by-gone dangers—that, three times within forty-eight
hours, Frank saved his life—when he damped the powder—knocked
him down—and became his wife.

Honest Frank's services did not go unrewarded; he was suffered
to indulge all his little peculiarities, without let or hindrance, and to
be as cross as he pleased, without the possibility of a reprimand.
Although an ample provision was made for his latter days, he mourned
most bitterly our coming over to what he always designated "the

could-hearted English country;" and his affection was so strong,
that he would have left his children, to follow us, had he not been
(to use his own expression) "past travelling, at eighty-five."

Good old man! I well remember him when the moment of parting
arrived, and we were to take our departure for "the great metropolis
of nations." He stood foremost of a troop of weeping domestics;
his hat held reverentially in his withered hand, while the sleet of a
January morning mingled with his grey hairs; tears rolled abundantly down his wrinkled cheeks; we were seated, yet still he held
the coach-door open—"God bless you all!—shut the door, Frank,"
said my dear grandfather, almost as much affected as his faithful
servant. Frank still held it, cast a farewell look upon us, and then,
turning to a man who was close to him, exclaimed, "You do it,
James; I can't close the door that shuts me out for ever from——"
the horses went on, and I saw my kind story-teller no more.

I have said that Frank loved his horses; he also loved the old family
carriage. And when we left the country, my grandfather presented
it to him, thinking, of course he would sell it. No such thing. Frank
went to live with his daughter, my old nurse, at the village of Duncormuck; and there he erected a spacious shed, under cover of which
he deposited his favourite chariot; the poor old man's delight was to
wheel it in and out. Until within a few days of his death, he attended
to it with the most scrupulous exactness, and invariably got into a
passion whenever the propriety of selling it was hinted at.

"Who knows," he would say, "but they may come home of a
suddent?—and what a comfort it would be to them to find the ould
carriage, and ould Frank, ready for sarvice!" POOR OLD FRANK!

LUKE O'BRIAN.

I WISH, with all my heart, I could adequately describe Luke; I have often requested him to sit for his picture, and if he had done so, I think I should have had it engraved for the benefit of the English public. Luke, however, has, what he calls, "a mortal objection to his face being in print." Therefore, good reader, you can never have an accurate idea of the subject of my story. He was, when I first knew him, about two-and-twenty; in height, six feet four inches: slight, but muscular; and the too visible size of his bones renders him not unworthy of his gigantic nomenclature. His countenance is nondescript—appertaining to no particular nation, yet possessing, it may be said, the deformities of all:—an Austrian mouth, French complexion, Highland hair (of the deepest tint), small pepper-and-salt coloured eyes, that constantly regard each other with sympathetic affection, and a nose elevated and depressed in open defiance of the line of beauty, are the most striking objects in his strange physiognomy;—in common justice I must add, that his face is remarkably

long, pale, and much disfigured by a cut he received from a "hurley"
in his boyhood, which carried away his left eyebrow, and a small
portion of his cheek; this mark, Luke, who is an acknowledged wag,
terms "his beauty spot."

It was a drizzling, damp evening, in the month of November, when
the afore-mentioned Luke O'Brian, grasping his shillalah in his enormous hand, passed through the beautifully situated town of Enniscorthy;—glancing, as he could do, without inconvenience, one eye
towards Vinegar-hill, and the other towards the noble ruins of "the
Castle," he proceeded on his way, intending to reach Wexford that
night. Although Luke was a tall, stout, brave boy, he would rather
have been anywhere than just where he was: with a dreary road
before him, and no one to speak to, the huge rocks looked frowning
enough, to a lonely traveller, in the deepening twilight, on one side
of the way; and, on the other, rolled the dark blue waters of the
Slaney. Luke had been serving writs in a distant part of the country;
he was not a native of the county of Wexford, though selected for the
performance of this, by no means safe, task, by an attorney, who
shall be nameless. He had wandered away from the right road, when
he fancied he heard steps behind him; his merry whistle sank into
a kind of hiss, and his long legs trembled somewhat, as he strode
forward; he soon ascertained that his pursuers were two in number,
and, from their trot-like walk, justly concluded that they were short,
stout men; nevertheless, they soon overtook Luke; long-shanked
though he was, he had no chance of out-striding them.

"May-be you've walked far this bleak night?" they inquired.

"May-be I have," replied Luke.

"May-be ye're going far on?"

"May-be so."

"How dim the ould stones look in the grey light!" observed one
of the persevering travellers.

"So they do."

"They say they're mighty unlucky," continued one of the men.

Our hero summoned courage, and replied, firmly, "Nothing's unlucky to a stout heart."

"Say you so, my boy?" exclaimed the younger one; "then here
goes!" and the click of a pistol, that was instantly presented at
Luke's breast, sounded very disagreeably through the dark night.
His arms were instantly pinioned, with almost supernatural strength,
by the fellow-robber, and he was drawn back into a sort of fosse, or
deep dike, that skirted the path. He shouted loudly for assistance,
but was told, very coolly, to "hould his whisht." "Do ye think
that people have nothin' to do but to walk the road, to look for
young chaps in distress? Hould yer whisht, I say! By the powers!
if ye don't, I'll——"

" Stop," said the elder; " as ye value yer mother's curse or blessing!—don't ye remember what she said not two hours agone ?"

" Can't he give up what he has got ?" retorted the younger; " does
he think I'm a fool, to feel the cash in his pocket, and lave it there ?
I'll tell ye what," he continued; " give it up, and ye shall meet with
genteel tratement; it's good to have to do wid gentlemen, in our trade.
But look ye, my lad; I've a mother dying of starvation; food hasn't
crossed her lips for more than two days; and we're all hunted like
wild animals, from house and home. So, if ye've a mother of yer
own, *give* us the means of saving her life."

"In troth," replied Luke, "I never had either father or mother,
that I know of. But there,—I'm only a poor, lone boy. Sure ye
wouldn't take all I have in the world to depind on ?"

" Not *all* ye have," responded the elder of the men, with a bitter
groan; " we couldn't take *all* ye have, for ye have a good name, may-
be, and *that* is what *we* can never have again." They rifled the contents of his leather bag; which the younger was about to pocket,
when the elder interposed.

"It's only five one-pounders, and a few bits of silver. And is this
all ye have, for the many times you've been a'most kilt, sarving the
law, to be sure ? Well, the half of it will do our turn : keep the rest.
We'd be long sorry to take all he had from any fatherless boy." The
young man grumbling returned half the money; and Luke, with
that natural cheerfulness of feeling, the almost peculiar characteristic
of the Irish, felt as if he had gained, not as if he had lost anything.
Still he was sadly perplexed;—he had wandered considerably from
the main road, and, in endeavouring to regain it, grappled amid what
appeared an interminable wilderness of over-grown fern, sharp, sting-
ing furze, and low broom-wood—the most intricate thing in the world
to escape from, as the frequent cuttings it receives from the broom-
gatherers make it very spreading in its under branches; then the
turf-holes, and the various inequalities of the ground—now up; now
down; not a star twinkling in the firmament—not a light to tell of
human habitation in any direction; the rain pouring unceasingly, and
the wind blowing, as Luke afterwards declared, " in whatever direction he turned, always in his face." At length he had almost resolved
to sit down quietly upon a rock, and wait the morning dawn, when, in
what appeared a high mound of clay, at a short distance, he perceived
a little ray of light; he well knew that, in Ireland, wherever there is
a roof, there is a resting-place for the poorest traveller; and, guided
by the flickering spark, he soon arrived at what could hardly be called
a human dwelling. It was, literally speaking, a large excavation in
the earth; two boards, nailed together, closed the aperture through
which the wretched inhabitants entered, and a hole in the clayey roof

served the double purpose of chimney and window. For a moment he rested outside the threshold; and, between the intermediate blasts, the low murmurings of a female voice in earnest prayer, could be distinctly heard. He pushed aside the unprotecting door; and, stretched on the cold, wet floor, with scarcely sufficient straw to keep her wasted limbs from the earth, covered by the remains of a tattered cloak, he saw the apparently dying form of an elderly woman. The miserable rush-candle, that had guided him to the hovel, was stuck in a scooped potato, her head was supported by a bundle of rags; a broken tea-cup, and an equally mutilated plate, both without either food or liquid, were within reach of the skeleton hands that were fervently clasped together. Through the opening in the roof, the rain fell in torrents, forming sundry pools around the fireless hearth: and no article of furniture of any kind was visible in the miserable dwelling-place—the last earthly home of the departing spirit. As Luke entered, she endeavoured to turn her head towards him, but appeared unable, and barely articulated, "Is that you, Tom, honey?"

Luke returned the usual friendly salutation of "God save all here!" and advanced towards her. The look of her fast-glazing eye fixed steadily on the young man, and he has often said, "the freezing of that look will never leave his heart." I have seen him shudder at the remembrance. Slowly she pushed back the grey clustering hair from her clammy brow, and gazed on him long and fixedly. "Don't be frightened, agra!" said he, at last; "I've lost my way, and, may-be, ye'd jist let me wait here, awhile, till the storm goes by: and, may-be, also, ye'd fancy a bit of what I've got in my pocket (he pulled out the fragments of some wheaten bread); or a drop of this would bring the life to yer heart, astore." She grasped the food he offered, with all the frightful eagerness of famine: but, when she endeavoured to swallow, it almost caused suffocation. Luke took a little of the rain-water in a broken cup, and, mixing with it a small portion of whisky, knelt, and gently supporting her head, poured it down her throat. She appeared somewhat revived; and, placing her long, bony fingers on his arm, whispered:—

"God reward ye!—God reward ye!—may God keep ye from bitter sin!—there's nothin' to offer ye, nor no fire to dry ye!—but take the wet tacks off, they'll give ye yer death o' could."

Luke obeyed her bidding, and, in a few moments, the dying woman turned towards him another long and piercing look. "Can ye spare me a taste more of that cordial, honey?" she inquired. Luke again knelt, in the same position as before, and she drank with avidity of what he offered. As he was about withdrawing his arm, her eye fixed upon a mark that had been engraved upon his wrist, by a species of tattooing, which the Irish, particularly along the sea-coast, frequently use. It was of a deep blue, and he had no recollection when or how it had been impressed. She grasped his hand with fearful violence and her energies seemed at once awakened. She tried to articulate; but, although her eyes sparkled, and she sat upright on her bed of straw, yet she could not utter a single sound. "Is it the maning of that mark, ye want to make out? Why, thin, it's just myself that can't tell ye, because, ye see, I don't know: I'm sorry for it, agra! but it can't be helped; only I often think that, may-be, it will be the manes of my finding out who owns me, which, at present, I don't know from Adam. Sorra a one ever laid claim to me, only poor Peg O'Brian, of Cranaby Lane, Cork: who found me, as a new-year's gift, the first day of January, one thousand eight hundred and seven, outside——"

A scream, loud and piercing, interrupted Luke; and, at the same instant, the withered arms of the poor woman strained him, with a strong grasp, to her bosom. "I haven't an hour to live, boy!" she exclaimed, at last; "and, oh! for the sake of the mercy you expect hereafter, do not throw from ye the poor, sinful, dying mother, that bore ye;—don't, don't—for, oh! my child!—I'm still—though banned and starving—I'm still your mother!"

Luke was much affected: he had argued himself into the belief that he was a son of one of the nobles of the land; and that, some day or other, he would, according to his own phrase, "turn out a lord, or, at the laste, a gentleman;" and it would have been difficult to analyse the nature of the contending feelings that agitated him. Pity, deep and affectionate pity, for her who had just declared herself his parent, was, however, the predominant one; and he returned her embrace with warmth and sincerity.

"I must tell you all I can," she continued, in a broken voice; "but first, let me ask ye, have ye been honest in yer dealings with rich and poor? Have ye kept from the temptation of gould?—Och! but it's the yellow and the bitter curse!—that leads—but tell me, tell me!—are ye honest?"

"God knows," he replied, "I never took to the value of a traneen from man or mortal; and, what's more, many a gentleman's son would be glad to take up with the *karacter* of poor Luke."

"Heaven be thanked for these words!" ejaculated the unfortunate creature; "for, in the deep of misfortune, the best of comfort is come to me—may the Lord be praised! When I dared to strive (sinner that I am) to pray, even one word, it was, that *you* might be honest. All belonging to me are bad,—bad. My children—all, all but you, banned, cursed, but brought up as they were!—sure, the kittens of the wild cat must seek the young bird's nest!—even now, to bring me food, my husband, and my other born son, are—no, not murder! —they swore that they wouldn't take life."

The horrid truth flashed upon the young man's mind, that he had encountered his father and brother; and he explained that he had met them, and told also of their generous conduct towards him.

" Thank God!—but that man is not your father," she said : " listen for one minute. I married a man I hated, for money ; but my wild, fierce passions could not bear it—I broke his heart; you were born after his death—I loved you—but no matter—I loved also a wild and wandering man. He was handsome to look upon, and he promised to make an honest woman of me, if I got rid of you. God had a hand in ye for good, though you needn't thank me for it. So I left ye in a strange place, first setting my mark on ye ; and after, whenever I could, I found out that ye were like an own child to poor Peg. But the love of gould followed us both; and, at last, the man was transported. It is quare how my love for him held out; but it did. I followed sin, that I might be sent where he was; and, sure enough, I found him in that land which it's a shame to mintion. Still we longed to get back to ould Ireland; and, though we returned too soon, yet we meant to do well; but the informers got scent of him, and again we were forced to fly. I became a sorrowful mother to many children; and some of them I followed to the gallows-tree; and at last, my heart turned to iron, and all sins seemed one ; but, if a wretch like me can say so—I heard, and I read among some loose leaves (for I had my share of larning once), that came from a house they wracked one night, that there was a hope even for us ! And I tould *thim* of it, but they laughed at me; and, even when my heart feels burst and burning, I think upon thim, and strive to pray."

With a trembling hand she drew, from under the straw, some torn leaves of the Bible.

" I cannot see to lay them properly," she said; " but this half I give to you, and these I will leave here ; they will find them when I am dead. And God can bless them—may-be, to salvation."

Luke took the pages, while the tears flowed abundantly down his cheeks.

"And now," said she, "go. I would not have them know ye for the world; they would want ye to be like them. Go—go—I shall see them ; for they can only get food at night for me, like the wild bastes. One thing more :—in Wexford," and she accurately described the street and house, " you will find Father ——; tell him *all*, and *where* I am. Though none of us are of this country, he knows me well—he will come; and then you may know where they lay my poor bones, and, may-be, ye'd say one prayer for the soul of yer sinful mother."

The unfortunate woman had only a little ray of light afforded her to point the true path to a happy eternity; but to Luke it was granted, at a future period, to know and profit by the words of the Gospel of peace. That night he hastened to find the priest, who was a kind and benevolent man, and hastened to do his duty: his mother died before the next sunset. He has been long settled, where his early occupation is unknown; and has often rejoiced in the hope that the dead may be received, even at the eleventh hour; and prayed that he may continue in the right way!

INDEPENDENCE.

INDEPENDENCE!"—it is the word, of all others, that Irish—men, women, and children—least understand; and the calmness, or rather indifference, with which they submit to dependence, bitter and miserable as it is, must be a source of deep regret to all who " love the land," or who feel anxious to uphold the dignity of human kind. Let us select a few cases, in different grades, from a single village—such as are abundant in every neighbourhood.

Shane Thurlough, for example, " as dacent a boy," and Shane's wife, as "clune-skinned a girl," as any in the world. There is Shane, an active, handsome-looking fellow, leaning over the half-door of his cottage, kicking a hole in the wall with his brogue, and picking up all the large gravel within his reach, wherewith to pelt those useful Irish scavengers, the ducks. Let us speak to him.

"Good-morrow, Shane !"

"Och! the bright bames of heaven on ye every day!—and kindly welcome, my lady!—and won't ye step in and rest ?—it's powerful hot, and a beautiful summer, sure—the Lord be praised!"

"Thank you, Shane. I thought you were going to cut the hay-field to-day; if a heavy shower come, it will be spoiled; it has been fit for the scythe these two days."

"Sure, it's all owing to that thief o' the world, Tom Parrel, my lady. Didn't he promise me the loan of his scythe ?—and, by the same token, I was to pay him for it; and *depinding* on that, I didn't buy one—what I've been threatening to do for the last two years."

"But why don't you go to Carrick and purchase one ?"

"To Carrick ! Och, 'tis a good step to Carrick, and my toes are on the ground (saving your presence), for I *depinded* on Tim Jarvis to tell Andy Cappler, the brogue-maker, to do my shoes; and—bad luck to him, the spalpeen ;—he forgot it."

"Where's your pretty wife, Shane ?"

"She's in all the woe o' the world, ma'am, dear ; and she puts the blame of it on me, though I'm not in fault this time, any how : the child's taken the small-pock; and she *depinded* on me to tell the doctor to cut it for the cow-pock, and I *depinded* on Kitty Cackle, the limmer, to tell the doctor's own man, and thought she would not forget it, becase the boy's her bachelor—but out o' sight, out o' mind —the never a word she tould him about it, and the babby has got it nataral, and the woman's in heart trouble (to say nothing o' myself) —and it the first, and all."

"I am very sorry, indeed, for you have got a much better wife than most men."

"That's a true word, my lady—only she's fidgety-like, sometimes; and says I don't hit the nail on the head quick enough ; and she takes a dale more trouble than she need about many a thing."

"I do not think I ever saw Ellen's wheel without flax before, Shane!"

"Bad cess to the wheel !—I got it this morning about that, too— I *depinded* on John Williams to bring the flax from O'Flaharty's this day week, and he forgot it ; and she says I ought to have brought it myself, and I close to the spot : but where's the good, says I, sure he'll bring it next time."

"I suppose, Shane, you will soon move into the new cottage, at Clurn Hill. I passed it to-day, and it looked so cheerful : and, when you get there, you must take Ellen's advice, and *depend* solely on yourself."

"Och, ma'am, dear, don't mintion it!—it's that makes me so down in the mouth, this very minit. Sure I saw that born blackguard, Jack Waddy, and he comes in here, quite innocent-like—'Shane, you've an eye to 'Squire's new lodge ?' says he. 'Maybe I have,' says I. 'I'm yer man,' says he. 'How so ?' says I. 'Sure I'm as good as married to my lady's maid,' says he; 'and I'll spake to the 'Squire for you, my own self.' 'The blessing be about ye,' says I, quite grateful,—and we took a strong sup on the strength of it; and, *depinding* on him, I thought all safe ;—and what d'ye think, my lady ? Why, himself stalks into the place—talked the 'Squire over to be sure—and, without so much as by yer lave, sates himself and his new wife on the laase in the house, and I may go whistle."

"It was a great pity, Shane, that you didn't go yourself to Mr. Clurn."

"That's a true word for ye, ma'am, dear ; but it's hard if a poor man can't have a friend to DEPIND ON."

"James Doyle, General Dealer," and a neat, good-looking shop it was—double fronted—its multifarious contents, doubtless, very amusing. Mr. Doyle was a sleek, civil little man as any in the county, and much respected ; he would have been rich also, were it not that he was, unfortunately, a widower, with five daughters. If you had seen his well-stored counters and shelves, and the extraordinary crowd that assembled in his shop, you would have felt certain that everything was to be had within—pins, ribands, knives, scissors, tobacco-pipes, candles, mouse-traps, tea, soap, sugars, tape, thread, cotton, flax, wool, paper, pens, ink, snuff and snuff-boxes, beads, salt herrings, cheese, butter, muslins (such beauties), calicoes (like cambric), linens (better than lawn), twine, ropes, slates, halters, stuffs, eggs, bridles, stockings, turf, delisk, pepper, mustard, vinegar, knitting-needles, books—namely, the "Reading made Easy," "Life of Freney, and his many wonderful escapes, showing how, after his being a most famous Robber, he lived and died a good Catholic Christian in the beautiful and celebrated town of Ross, in the ancient county of Wexford," "Valentine and Orson," "Seven Champions of Christendom," and such like—which books, by the way, turn the heads of half our little girls and boys. The village shop would have vended its finery to greater advantage, if there had been no direct communication with Wexford ; for it must be confessed that some of the pretty lasses took it into their heads to be dissatisfied with the goods at the big shop, and absolutely sent for their Sunday elegancies to the county town ; but, nevertheless, James Doyle would have made a fortune, if his five daughters had been willing to assist him in his business. Had you seen them, they would not have appeared like the industrious children of an English tradesman, who invariably think it their duty to make every effort for the well-doing of their family, and exert themselves, either at home or abroad, to procure " Independence."   Could the slatternly appearance of the five Misses Doyle, or their tawdry finery, designate any beings in the world except the daughters of an ill-regulated Irish shopkeeper?   I say ill-regulated, because, truly, all are not so; very far from it.   Their mother died when they were young, and their father unadvisedly sent them to one of those hot-beds of pride and mischief, a "fifteen-pound" boarding-school in a garrison town, where they learn to work tent-stitch, and despise trade.   When they returned, honest Doyle saw he could not expect anything from them in the way of usefulness, and not possessing much of that uncommon quality, miscalled *common* sense, he was contented to support them in idleness, hoping that their pretty faces might catch the unwary.

"And sure," said Miss Sally, the first-born, to Miss Stacy, the second hope of the family, "haven't we had six months a-piece at Miss Brick's own school?—can't our father affoord us a clear hundred each, down in yellow guineas?—hasn't he got a thousand, maybe more, at the very luste pinny, in Wexford Bank?—and if he, with such a power o' money, demanes himself by keeping a paltry shop, instead of living like a gentleman upon his property, and cutting a dash to get us dacent husbands, not bog-trotters, there's no rason in life why we should attind to it.   I hope we have a better spirit, all of us, than to do the likes of that indeed!"

And so the five Misses Doyle chose the handsomest "prints" in the shop for their own especial use; loitered the mornings *en papillote* lounging up the street, or down the street, or staring out of the window, their shoes slip-shod, and the torn out strings replaced by pins, that invariably made one rent while they secured another; and, in the evenings, excited the stare of the silly, and the contempt of the wise, by their over-dressed but ill-arranged persons, parading in trumpery finery and French curls.   Then they were perpetually quarrelling, although their tastes on matrimonial points were very similar; and if a young farmer, or, more delightful still, a "boy" from Wexford or Waterford, put up at the village—mercy bless us! What a full cry!   Such a set!—five to one!

Take a specimen of the quarrels of the five rivals in love.

"Little good, Babby, there is in your trying to make anything dacent of that head of yours, as long as it's so bright a carroty." "It's no sich thing as carroty, Stacy, and, for the matter of that, look at yer own nose.   Sure no one in life would think it worth their while to be afther a pug dog."   "It's good fun to hear the pair o' ye argufying about beauty—beauty, indeed!" interrupted Miss Sally, tossing her head, and eyeing her really very pretty person in the cracked looking-glass.   "Oh, to be sure, you think yourself very wonderful handsome!" exclaimed two of the girls at once.   "I never could see any beauty in curds and whey," continued she of the elevated nose. "Ye little go-by-the-ground, keep out of my way," said the tallest sister, Johanna, to the shortest, Cicely; "ye keep as much bother about yer dress as if ye were a passable size." "Hould yer tongue, ye long gawky," retorted the little one, "there's no use in your dressing at the stranger boy—he's not a grenadier!"

Poor Doyle! Miss Sally ran off with a walking gentleman, who refused to marry her unless her portion was made three hundred pounds. "Oh," said the father, "the pride of my heart she was, but it is bad to *depind* upon beauty!" True, Doyle, or upon anything, except well-regulated industry. If he would come into partnership he might be useful, but the *gentleman* disdained trade. The poor father mortgaged part of his property, paid the money, and Sally was married; but, in less than a year, was returned on his hands, with the addition of a helpless infant, the scorn of her unfeeling sisters. Stacy was the next to heap sorrow on the old man's head; she, to use her own expression, "met with a misfortune," for she *depended* on "the boy's" honour; but her sin was too degrading to allow of her continuing in the house. Cicely married—honestly married, a daring, dashing smuggler, who, *depending* on his former good fortune, dared an exploit in the contraband trade, which would have banished him for ever from the country had not Doyle again mortgaged his property to save him; the young man's good name was gone, however, and he lived *depending* on his father-in-law, who now began to suffer seriously from pecuniary embarrassment. Johanna married what was called well, that is, the young man was a gentleman farmer, too proud to look after his own affairs; he *depended* upon "his right-hand man," or the goodness of the times, or anything but his own exertions, for his success—speculated, failed, prevailed on his unfortunate relative to bail him, and, in open defiance of truth and honesty, fled to America.

Then, indeed, the wail and the woe resounded in that house where peace, and comfort, and happiness might have dwelt; and the old man's bed was the cold gaol floor, and the family were scattered, and branded with sin and shame, and all for want of INDEPENDENT feelings.

The Honourable Mister Augustus Headerton, who once lived in yonder villa, was the youngest of eleven children, and, consequently, the junior brother of the noble Lord of Headerton, nephew of the Honourable Justice Cleaveland, nephew of Admiral Barrymore, K.C.B., &c. &c. &c., and cousin, first, second, third, fourth, fifth, sixth, or seventh remove—to half the honourables and dishonourables in the country.

When the old Earl died he left four Chancery suits, and a nominal estate, to the heir-apparent, to whom he also bequeathed his three younger brothers and sisters, who had only small annuities from their mother's fortune, being assured that (to use his own words) "he might *depend* on him, for the honour of the family, to provide for them handsomely." And so he did (in his own estimation); his lady sisters had "the run of the house," and Mr. Augustus Header-ton had the run of the stables, the use of hunters and dogs, and was universally acknowledged to possess a "proper spirit," because he spent three times more than his income. "He bates the world and all for beauty in a hunting jacket," exclaimed the groom. "He flies a gate beyant any living sowl I iver see; and his tally-ho! my jewel—'twould do yer heart good to hear his tally-ho!" said my Lord's huntsman. "He's a generous jintleman as any in the king-dom—I'll say that for him, any day in the year," echoed the coach-man. "He's admired more nor any jintleman that walks Steven's-green in a month o' Sundays, I'll go bail," continued Miss Jenny Roe, the ladies' maid.

"Choose a profession!" Oh, no! impossible! But the Honour-able Mr. Augustus Headerton chose a wife, and threw all his rela-tions, including Lord Headerton, the Honourable Justice Cleaveland, Admiral Barrymore, K.C.B., and his cousins to the fiftieth remove, into strong convulsions or little fits. She, the lady, had sixty thousand pounds; that, of course, they could not object to. She had eloped with the Honourable Mister Augustus Headerton: mere youthful indiscretion. She was little and ugly;—that only concerned her husband. She was proud and extravagant;—these were lady-like failings. She was ignorant and stupid;—her sisters-in-law would have pardoned that. She was vulgar;—that was awkward. Her father was a carcass butcher in Cole's Lane Market!—death and destruction!

It could never be forgiven!—the cut direct was unanimously agreed on, and the little lady turned up her little nose in disdain as her handsome barouche rolled past the lumbering carriage of the Right Honourable Lord Headerton. She persuaded her husband to pur-chase that beautiful villa, in view of the family domain, that she might have more frequent opportunities of bringing, as she elegantly expressed it, "the proud beggars to their trumps;—and why not?—money's money, all the world over." The Honourable Mister Augustus *depended* on his agent for the purchase, and some two thousand and odd pounds were consequently paid, or said to have been paid, for it, more than its value. And then commenced the general warfare; full purse and empty head—*versus* no purse and old nobility. They had the satisfaction of ruining each other: in due course of time the full purse was emptied by devouring duns, and the old nobility suffered by its connexion with vulgarity.

"I want to know, Honourable Mister Augustus Headerton" (the lady always gave the full name when addressing her husband; she used to say it was all she got for her money)—"I want to know, Honourable Mister Augustus Headerton, the reason why the music-master's lessons, given to the Misses Headerton (they were blessed with seven sweet pledges of affection), have not been paid for?"

"I desired the steward to see to it, and you know I *depend* on him to settle these matters."

The Honourable Mrs. Augustus Headerton rang the bell, "Send Martin up."

"Mister Martin," the lady began, "what is the reason that Mr. Langi's account has not been paid?"

"My master, ma'am, knows that I have been anxious for him to look over the accounts; the goings-out are so very great, and the comings-in, as far as I know——" the Honourable Mr. Augustus Headerton spilt some of the whisky-punch he was drinking over a splendid hearth-rug, which drew the lady's attention from what would have been an unpleasant *éclaircissement*.

"I cannot understand why difficulties should arise. I am certain I brought a fortune large enough for all extravagance," was the lady's constant remark when expenditure was mentioned. Years pass over the heads of the young, and they grow old; and over the heads of fools, but they never grow wise.

The Honourable Mister and Mistress Augustus Headerton were examples of this truth; their children grew up around them—but could derive no support from the parent root. The mother *depended* on governesses and masters for the education of her girls, and on their beauty, connexions, or accomplishments, to procure them husbands. The father did not deem the labours of study fit occupation for the sons of an ancient house:—"*Depend* upon it," he would say, "they'll all do well with my connexions—they will be able to command what they please."

The Honourable Mister Augustus Headerton died, in the forty-fifth year of his age, of inflammation, caught in an old limekiln, where he was concealed, to avoid an arrest for the sum of one hundred and eighty guineas, for Black Nell, the famous filly (who won the cup on the Curragh of Kildare)—purchased in his name, but without his knowledge, by his second son, the pride of the family—commonly called Dashing Dick.

All I know further of the Honourable Mistress Augustus Headerton is that—

"She played at cards, and died."

Miss Georgiana—the beauty, and greatest fool of the family, who *depended* on her face as a fortune, did get a husband,—an old, rich, West India planter, and eloped, six months after marriage, with an officer of dragoons.

Miss Celestina was really clever and accomplished. "Use her abilities for her own support!" Oh, no! not for worlds! Too proud to work, but not too proud to beg, she *depended* on her relations, and played toady to all who would have her.

Miss Louisa—not clever; but, in all other respects, ditto—ditto.

Miss Charlotte was always very romantic; refused a respectable banker with indignation, and married her uncle's footman—for love.

Having sketched the female part of the family, I will tell you what I remember of the gentlemen.

"The Emperor," as Mr. Augustus was called, from his stately manner and dignified deportment, aided by as much self-esteem as could well be contained in a human body, *depended*, without any "compunctious visitings of conscience," on the venison, claret, and champagne of his friends, and thought all the time he did them honour—and thus he passed his life.

"Dashing Dick" was the opposite of the Emperor; sung a good song—told a good story—and gloried in making ladies blush. He *depended* on his cousin Colonel Bloomfield's procuring him a commission in his regiment, and cheated tailors, hosiers, glovers, coachmakers, and even lawyers, with impunity. Happily for the world at large, Dashing Dick broke his neck in a steeple-chase, on a stolen horse, which he might have been hanged for purloining had he lived a day longer.

Ferdinand was the *bonne-bouche* of the family: they used to call him "the Parson!" Excellent Ferdinand!—he *depended* on his own exertions, and if ever the name of Headerton rises in the scale of moral or intellectual superiority, it will be owing to the steady and virtuous efforts of Mister Ferdinand Headerton, merchant in the good city of B——, for he possesses in perfection "the glorious privilege of being INDEPENDENT."

BLACK DENNIS.

WELL!" exclaimed Michael Leahy, as he entered his cottage,
"well! the Lord be praised!—I've seen a powerful deal of
happiness this day, one way or the other. Above, at the big house,
the mistress was giving out the medicine and food, with her own
two blessed hands, to half the parish; there she was, at the closet
window, slaving herself for the poor—that's Christianity!" He
proceeded to shake the snow from his "big coat," and hang it up.
"It's a powdering night of snow, as ever came out of the heavens;
but, any how, we have a roof to shelter us, thank God!—to say

nothin' o' the sod o' turf, and the boiling pratees; and the master gave me a good quarter o' tobaccy; so now, Norry, lay by your spinning, and let's have our bit o' supper."

"With all the joy in life, Mick—and thank God, too, that my husband comes home, when his work is done, to his wife and childer."

Mick Leahy looked affectionately at his wife—and well he might. She was clean and industrious—cheerful and contented : the mud walls of her cabin were whitewashed; a glass window, small, but unbroken, looked out on a little garden, stocked with potatoes and cabbages, and hedged with furze. No labourer in the country had thicker stockings than Mick Leahy—they were his wife's knitting; no whiter shirts were on the town-land than Mick Leahy's—and they were all of his wife's spinning. No finer children knelt to receive the priest's blessing on a summer Sunday, than Mick Leahy's; and proud were father and mother of them.

"God help all poor travellers!—it's blake and bitther weather," continued Mick, as he lit his pipe, and took his seat on the settle, under the wide chimney, after he had finished his supper; "I wish some unfortunate cratur had a share of the chimbly-corner, for there'll be neither hedge nor ditch to be seen by morning, if it snows on in this way."

"It does my heart good to see little Mary bless herself when she lays her head down for the night," said Norah, coming out of their only bedroom—which was always in neat order. "And then, Lanty has the Ave-Mary and all, so pat;—och! Mick, honey, 'tis sweet to look at childer—and very sweet to look at one's own childer; but it's bitter to think that, one day, may-be, they may come to sin and shame."

"No child of mine, Norah," said the father, proudly, "shall ever come to sin or shame."

"Whisht, Mick, whisht!" said the meek mother; "we are all born to sin, you know—but God keep away shame!—all we can do is to pray for, and show them a good patthern."

"Then, that's true, and spoken sinsible, like my own Norry," replied the father; "and the blessing o' God will always be about you and yours, at any rate. What!—agin to the wheel! Well, ye're never idle—I'll say that for ye."

Bur, bur—went the wheel, and the turf sparkled; still the storm increased, and shook the little cabin, that seemed almost beneath its vengeance.

"Was there any signs of fire-light in the place on the far moor, as ye passed it?" inquired Norah.

"None that I see," replied the husband.

"Do you know, Mick, I never could make them people out;

there's the three of 'em live upon nothin' at all—that I can think of; they never beg—they never work. Lanty met the child, this morning, picking bits o' sticks near the moor-hedge, and he tould him his daddy was dying, and his mammy not much better; so Lanty brought him home, and I gave him plenty to ate, and as many pratees as he could carry away, and a morsel o' white bread; and, to be sure, he ate, the cratur, as if he was starved; but was so shy and wild—like a young fox-cub—that I could get nothin' out of him."

"Of all the men I ever see, in my born days, that man has the black-heart look. The wicked one—Heaven bless us!—set his mark between his two eyes, or he never did it to anybody yet."

"Hush, Mick!—is that the wind shaking the windy, or a knock of the door?"

The knock was distinctly repeated, and Mick inquired who was there? A female voice requested admission, and, on his opening the door, a tall woman, enveloped in a long blue cloak, entered: when in the cottage, she threw back the hood that had quite covered her face; it might once have been handsome, but want and misery had obliterated its beauty, and given an almost maniac expression to eyes both dark and deep; the hair was partly confined by a checkered kerchief: and the outline of the figure would have been worthy the pencil of Salvator.

"Ye don't know me, and so much the betther; but I am wife to him that's dying on the far moor; and I want you, Mick Leahy, to go to Father Connor, and ask him, for the love of God, to come to the departing sinner, and—if he can—give him some comfort."

"Sit down," said Norry, kindly; shrinking, nevertheless, from her visitor. "'Tis an awful night, and a long step to his reverence's; but Mick will do a good turn for any poor sinner: yet I wonder ye didn't call to him yerself, and ye passed close by his gate coming here."

"Me call on a priest!" half screamed the woman; "me, the castaway!—the thing that's shunned as soon as seen!—Me!—but do not look so at me, Norry Leahy!—do not. Ye were kind enough, this morning, to my starving boy; ye sent food to my miserable cabin! Do not—do not! Now, when he is dying! Bad as he is, Norry, he is still my husband."

"Asy, asy," said Mick; "I do not care who he is! Sure, we're all sinners, and God is good; he may get betther."

"No, no, I do not wish him that; he has nothing to live for: the ban is on him; and, if he was known, even here, he would be torn in pieces."

Mick and Norah exchanged glances, and slowly did the former take his long coat off the peg: and wistfully did poor Norah look at her husband, for the woman's wildness had quite overpowered her; yet, co refuse going for a priest was what no Irishman ever did, and she thought it was her husband's duty; her fears, for a moment, conquered her resolution, when he was in the act of opening the door; and, laying her hand gently on the woman's cloak, she said, with a quivering lip—

"And wont ye tell us yer name; and Mick going to do yer bidding?"

"Ye will have it, Norry Leahy," replied she, almost fiercely—"Anne Dennis!—my husband was called Black Dennis, the informer!"

Norah staggered back, and Mick withdrew his hand from the latch.

"Ye will *not* go, then?" said the unfortunate creature; "and, because he's a sinner, ye think he should be left to die like a dog in a ditch; and you, Norry, you shrink from me; and what power have I to harm ye?—look!" She threw back her cloak; a worn jacket and petticoat hardly shrouded so perfectly skeleton a form; that poor Norah looked on her with pity and astonishment. "Look! —and say, if I have power to harm!—I have hardly strength enough to hold *his* dying head off the could earth."

"I'll go, in the name o' mercy," said Mick, "though it's little he deserves a good turn from any one, even on his death bed."

Norah was horrified at her husband's visiting one who had brought sorrow to so many dwellings; but he was gone, and she was left, in her cottage solitude, to brood over what she had just heard and seen. "Black Dennis" had been a United Irishman, and one of the most violent order—the projector of more burnings, murders, and robberies, than any chief of them all; and when, at last, he found that he could no longer carry on the system of rebellion and plunder, into which he had drawn so many unfortunate victims, he turned king's evidence; many were the men either transported or executed on his statements —all less guilty than himself. No wonder, then, that Black Dennis was regarded with peculiar sentiments of abhorrence, and that, whereever he went, he was a banned man! His wife had shared his plunder, and exulted in his deeds, when he was a bold rapparee; but, when he became a cold-blooded informer, she spurned both him and his wealth, and left him to his wanderings. He went abroad, but his ill-got gold wasted and wasted; and he returned to his native country, "to lave his bones," as he said, "among his own people."

His wife had been no less miserable than himself; and, when her wretched husband made his appearance at her poor door, she felt relieved at beholding the only being who could truly appreciate her varied sufferings: his money was gone—he was dying a lingering death; and her still woman's heart yearned towards its early affection. · They could not remain in the village where she and her boy

resided; because, there, Black Dennis would soon have been recognised; so she sold the few articles of furniture and clothing she
possessed, and went away with her husband, that he might die in peace
on " the far moor." Her anxiety to procure for him the rites of the
church in his last moments, overcame her repugnance to discovery;
and a sort of holy fear prevented her going to the priest herself: the
kindness shown by the Leahys to her child, induced her to confide
in them; and silently, but thankfully, she accompanied Mick to Mr.
Connor's house.

The good priest went with his guides to the hut where the informer
lay. It was, in truth, meet dwelling for such a man: " the far moor"
showed an extensive waste of snow, with but one tree to break its
white surface; and the hovel rested against its immense trunk, which
having escaped the axe and the tempest, stripped even of its bark by
time, threw far and wide its knotted and distorted limbs, as if in
mockery of the whirlwind and the storm.

The sands of life were nearly run. Black Dennis lay extended on
some straw, scarcely covered by portions of tattered clothing, and his
head rested on the knees of his boy; he moved it quickly as they
entered, and pressed a little wooden cross to his lips: the priest
poured a cordial down his throat, and, for a few moments, he revived.

" That man need not go," said he, seeing Mick about to take his
departure, in order that the sinful man might confess: " I have
nothing to tell but what all the world knows; nothing to say, except
that my heart is—hell! Oh! will your reverence tell me,"—and he
raised his head from the child's lap—" if there is hope for me, the
murderer, the burner, the rebel, the INFORMER?"—Madly his glaring
eyes watched for a reply.

" There is hope for all," replied Father Connor, " through God's
mercy."

The head feel back, the eye fixed, the lip quiveringly uttered
" Hope," and Black Dennis was no more.

The unfortunate widow shed no tears, but knelt and gazed on him
who had known so much sin, and endured so much sorrow : the child
clung around its mother's neck, and wept bitterly. Leahy endeavoured
to rouse her from her stupor, but in vain. "I cannot leave her in
this way; and the poor boy—he's innocent any way; and that's not
' Black Dennis' now, but only a lump o' dust! Yer reverence, what
am I to do?"

The priest stooped down, and endeavoured to disengage the child
from the parent : this aroused her. " My boy!—my boy!" and the
tears flowed from eyes to which they had long been strangers.
" Ye'll put him in holy ground, Father?" said she, looking at the
priest. " Ye'll not deny even an informer Christian burial? I know

'twould be a bad example to bury him by daylight; but, by night, what would hinder ?"

"Yes," replied Mr. Connor, "to-morrow night, I will see that duty properly performed; and now I can only recommend you to the mercy of God."

The grey morning dawned on Leahy and his good Norah, tracing their path to the hut on the far moor. "It would be a sin," said the latter, "to bear spite and hatred to a senseless corpse; and, bad as the woman was, she left him when he turned informer." During the day, the priest procured a rude coffin, and with the assistance of one of his own people, by the light of the waning moon, that shed her cold rays over the snow-clad country, in a corner of the old church-yard—far from any other grave—the body of Black Dennis was deposited.

No inducement could prevail on the unfortunate woman to forsake the grave: she sat on it, wrapped in her long blue cloak, and suffered her boy to be led away by the priest to his own dwelling—for the amiable man could not bear to leave a child of six years old exposed to so inclement a night.

When the morning came, the woman was not seen; the boy went crying from the churchyard to the hut, but could nowhere find his mother. He grew up in Mr. Connor's house, a solitary, but not a friendless, being—a melancholy, gentle youth, whose intellects appeared to have suffered from the recollection of early misery; he was, nevertheless, tractable and obedient, and devotedly attached to his benefactor.

It was long unknown what became of the widow. Some said she was dead—others, that she was employed in unceasing pilgrimage and penance. Although the death of Black Dennis was almost forgotten, no one cared to rebuild the hut on the far moor; and even the village children, when seeking heathbells and buttercups, avoided the shadow of the "Informer's Tree."

The youth, who was always called "Father Connor's Ned," often visited the cheerful Norah and her husband, and seemed particularly fond of every inhabitant of their happy cottage. Mick Leahy used to lament that the boy was an "innocent;" but Norry would reply, "So best, Mick, for ye see, by being weak, he escapes being wicked; and it was natural to suppose he'd be one or t'other, seeing he came from a bad stock."

Mick, and his wife and family, had been laughing over the embers of the fire, one evening, telling tales, and singing old ballads; poor Ned, who formed one of the party, was even more silent than usual, when he suddenly started up, and pointing to the window, exclaimed, "Did you see that ?"

"There, 'tis passed now," he continued, wildly. "Norry, if ever there was a banshee, that's one; and it is not the first time, nor the second either, that I've seen it, wid its large grey eyes fixed on me, so death-like; but I don't think I iver see it more than once in the same year."

"A shadow certainly passed the windy, I'll take my bible oath," said Mick. He went out, and, to his astonishment, no person was visible. "God save us all!" said he, re-entering his cabin, "it's very quare."

Soon after, the simple boy returned home; but the first news the Leahys heard, next morning, was, that, on the cold door-stone of the priest's house, an aged corpse was found—the worn and wasted corpse of Anne Dennis!

The wretched wanderer had, it was afterwards ascertained, been an occasional visitor to the neighbourhood; anxious, doubtless, to look upon her child, yet careful to avoid discovery, and feeling, most probably, that her last hour was come, she had that night laid her down at the door of the house that had sheltered the only being she loved, and expired. They buried her quietly, near her husband. The long grass, and the broad-leaved dock, wave over them in the chill blast of the winter evening; and, sometimes, poor harmless Ned is seen to stand and look, with tearful eyes, upon his parents' grave.

GERALDINE.

IT is impossible to conceive anything more beautiful, either in situation or interior, than the simple chapel of our "Lady of Grace,"
that crowns the cliffs at Honfleur, where sailors and their wives offer
their prayers, and pay their vows. I found a number of my countrymen
and women at Honfleur; and was much struck with the appearance
of one in particular, who climbed the hill leading to the chapel, every
morning, and remained there during the day. The servant who accompanied, or, rather, followed her, never revealed her surname; she spoke
of her, and to her, as "Miss Geraldine," and threw into this name of
lofty sound as great a quantity of Irish, unsophisticated brogue as the
three syllables could express. It was very pleasant to me to hear the
tones of my own country in a foreign land, and still more pleasing to
observe the attention, amounting to positive devotion, which the
good-tempered, broad-featured, woman bestowed upon the fair devotee.
"Devotee!"—I do not know exactly why I should call her so,
except from the fact of her perpetually climbing that most picturesque and winding road, leading to the chapel, and kneeling before
the pretty shrine of the Madonna, for hours together; her attitude
was one of perfect devotion; one small hand held the rosary, the
other shaded her face; the cloak appeared abandoned to its own
drapery—her hair fell, as you see, in the most *dégagé* undress; and
it was not until you approached the fair saint that you perceived her

eyes were anything but quiet—they rambled from corner to corner of their fringed pent-houses, with an observant, rather than a co-quettish, expression; certainly, with anything but the devoted one which her attitude would lead you to expect. She appeared thinking of, and expecting some one who did not come. Her step, in the morning, seemed buoyant with hope—but, in the evening, she hung her head, and descended to an obscure lodging in the town, as if weighed down by disappointment. Meeting her so frequently, and feeling deeply interested in one so beautiful, it was impossible not to evince a portion of that feeling, restrained as it must be, by the fear of offending its object; at last, however, we exchanged brief greetings; and she would, when I visited the chapel, rise from before the Madonna, and point out some particular offering for my sympathy or admiration; but our acquaintance gained no further ground: she spoke but few words, and their tone conveyed the idea that she was not in the least interested in what she said; her words were with you, but not her thoughts—they were away; but where? With her deserted country, or forsaken parents, or absent brothers, or—that is ever the uppermost thought on such occasions—a wandering lover? Her attendant seldom entered the chapel, but would sit outside, under the Cross which casts its protecting shadow over the waters.

The attendant was naturally communicative; and anxious to im-press me with a notion of Miss Geraldine's sanctity and greatness "in her own country;" but, with all her national garrulity, she guarded well her young lady's secret, whatever it was.

"It's hard, so it is," she said, one evening, just as the sun was about to set:—"it's mighty hard to have nothing to do but sit here, looking over the sea, or taking account of the *voteens* that come up to pray for the return of those that, may-be, have left their bones to the mermaids, long ago; but I don't care, it's the love and duty I owe my *fosterer;* for, although she's a lady, as any one may see, and I'm—jist what I am, and nothing more or less, we were both reared on the same milk; both slept on the same bosom—that's cold, colder than them stones, now; if it wasn't—it's in dear Ireland we'd be still;" and tears poured from her large grey eyes, but were quickly suppressed. "Oh, it's mighty grand, as I say to Miss Geraldine, to come to foreign parts;—but where's the country like our own —the country that has the nature in it—the welcome that comes from the heart,—the farewell that bursts from the eyes? Oh, my! and she in there, all day; and, when she comes out, it's more dead than alive she'll be! If you had seen her a year ago, when her beautiful face was ever in motion—like the sunbeams on the sea— and when she'd lay down, and uprise with a song upon her lips, that, like two real lovers, never parted but to meet in smiles! Oh, my! the spirit's prayed out of her—so it is."

"Not quite," I said, and I remembered the inquiring expression of her wandering eyes.

"Oh!" answered the Irishwoman—"if she prays, she watches too,—she must—though that's neither here nor there. There's fine religion in this country, and nothing to go against it; and yet I wish we were back in ould Ireland once more: but, let her go where she will, I'll never part her. I promised the dying on the death-bed, I never would—with her liking, or without it; and, as the ould verse says,

> ' By a promise to the dead,
> Through the world you may be led;'

and that's thrue, and why not?—it's a promise you can't be absolved from, only by a priest, and his reverence would not like being troubled about such a thing, at all. The sight's wore out of my eyes and the feet off my legs, and the *laugh from my heart,* just with following her; but I don't care for that;—when her vow's out, we'll have peace, may-be."

"But what is her vow to you?"

The large grey eyes dilated, until they looked half as large again as usual, while she repeated, "Is it to me, ma'am? sure I *tould* you, dear, she was Miss Geraldine, my own young lady, away from her people, and country;—and the promise! Ah, then, sure now I've just tould you of my promise to them that loved her; and little thought it's in this outlandish country she'd be, where they are so ignorant that they have no English; though it's a God-fearing country, for all that. 'What is her vow to me,' avick! Ah, were you ever in Ireland at all, to ask that, and she my fosterer—besides? 'Her vow to me,' the jewil! the heavens above knows—more than my own—ten times; may-be I wont follow her through the earth—my soul's delight!"

"But, suppose she was to become very poor," I said.

"She'd want me all the more," replied Irish fidelity. "Besides," she added, laughingly, "it is not easy to frighten any one with poverty, who has lived all her life, for seven days out of the week, upon potatoes and milk. I don't care for any hardship that would come upon myself; but I'd lay down my life to save *her,* the darling of my heart, from any harm. May the Lord put all heavy trouble past her! Sure, I pray for that on my bended knees, night and morning, as well as all day long: she's had her cross, and, in time, will have her crown. I left my country, and him I loved better than any country, to follow her; and, if she's here to-day, she may be gone to-morrow:—there she is now, as white as a snowdrop—so good evening, ma'am; and God be with you!"

About ten days after this, we had nearly achieved the summit of our favourite walk, and only paused to look back upon the town, when a gentleman passed us, with steps, it would seem, more eager

than his strength permitted; his dress was more foreign than French
—decidedly not belonging to the British Isles. We did not sée his
face, which was turned away. When we arrived on the hill—there,
in her old place, sat the faithful Irishwoman, looking over the sea;
and by some instinct, turning her head to scrutinize every one who
set foot upon the natural platform on which the chapel stands, and
the cross is planted: her recognition was a broad smile, a closing of
her hands, and a motion of her head—and then, as we approached,
she rose. We had not, however, exchanged a word, when a faint
scream sent her flying to the chapel. We followed, to see the fair
devotee weeping and sobbing, like a child, on the shoulder of the
stranger we had passed on the hill

The next morning they had quitted Honfleur—some said, in a ship
sailing for Mexico—others declared, for Sydney. The old woman of
the house protested the stranger to be Miss Geraldine's brother—
for he was so like her; and the brown-skinned, black-eyed daughter
observed, that husbands were sometimes like their wives. There was
no doubt that the servant still followed her lady's fortunes—faithful
and devoted to the last.

CAPTAIN ANDY.

GOOD day, Master Andy; you have a prosperous time of it; plenty of water to work the mill, and plenty of corn to grind. Well, Captain, after all, peace is better than war."

Andy glanced, from under his white hat, one of those undefinable looks of quiet humour, perhaps the peculiar characteristic of an Irish peasant. He made no reply, but elevated his right shoulder, and drew his left hand across the lower part of his face, as if seeking to conceal its expression; "yer honour wouldn't be going to Taghmon this fine morning?"

"No, Captain."

"Well, now, Mr. Collins, dear, may I make so bould just to beg that you'd lave off calling me Captain; and give me my own dacent name—Andy, as yer honour used afore the 'Ruction,' and sure the peaceable time has lasted long enough to make ye forget it?"

"So Captain (I beg your pardon), Andy,—the peaceable times have lasted too long, you think."

"I ax yer honour's pardon, I said no sich a thing. Maybe, if it was said, it would be nothin' but the truth; but that's neither here nor there, and no business o' mine. The government's a good government—maybe, ay—maybe, no—and the king, God bless him!"—and he lifted his hat reverently from his head—"the king's a good king!"

"Ay, ay, I remember your famous flag, made out of the green silk curtain, and garnished with real laurel leaves, mounted on the top of a sappling ash, the motto, 'God bless the king. but curse his advisers!'"

"Well, yer honour has a mighty quare way, I must say, of repating gone-by things, and tazing a person, quite useless like."

The gentleman, who had been amusing himself at the poor miller's expense, now assumed a more serious look and manner, and, placing his hand on his shoulder with kind familiarity—

"Andrew," said he, "when I speak seriously of bygone days—of times of terror and bloodshed, there is one feeling that absorbs every other—gratitude to the noble little Captain of the Bannow corps, who, when one of my own tenants declared 'it was the duty of every man in the division to spill Protestant blood, until the United men could stand in it knee-deep,' rushed forward, and, baring his bosom, as he stood before me, called to his men to strike *there*, for that not a hair of my head should fall while he had arms to use' in my defence."

The miller turned away for a moment, and then, taking off his hat, extended his broad hand to the gentleman, making sundry scrapes, and divers indescribable gestures.

"May I make so bould as to ax yer honour to walk in, and ate or drink something? and, besides, I had a little matther o' my own that I wanted to spake to ye about: and, sure, ye need never think of what ye've jist mintioned; for, if it hadn't been for yer good word, them children o' mine would have had no father. I was ready enough to die for the cause like a man, dacently; but to be hung, jist for nothing, like a dog, was another thing. It'll niver come to that wid me, now, God be praised! To be sure, we all have our own notions; but I'll not meddle nor make any more, in sich matters; for all the boys wanted

to be commanders and gentlemen at once, and wouldn't be said or led
by their betthers. But I ax pardon for talking, and ye standing
outside the mill-house, when the woman, and the fire, and all's widin,
that 'ud rejoice to see yer two feet on the hearthstone, even if it were
of pure gould."

"Oh, then, kindly welcome, sir! Jenny, set a chair for the gintleman; arrah, bother, not that one wid the three legs! (Tim, is
that the patthern o' yer manners, to stand gnawing yer thumb there;
where's yer bow? Mabby, set down the grawl, can't ye, and make
yer curtshy.)—Sure it's proud we're of the honour," continued
bustling Mrs. Andy, " and grateful; and what will yer honour take?
(Tim, have done picking the bread.)—A cruddy egg and a rasher, or
some hot cake and frish butter, yer honour, as frish as the day, made
wid my own hands. Jenny, quiet that child, will ye? Oh, Mabby,
Mabby, run, for the dear life; there's the ould pig—bad cess to her!
—and all the boneens, through the cabbages. I humbly beg yer
honour's pardon (courtesying), but, maybe, yer honour would just
taste——".

"Will ye hould yer whisht, Biddy?" interrupted the Captain,
stepping from the inner room, carrying a stone jar, and a long green
bottle; " she has a tongue in her head, sir, and likes to use it," he
continued, placing both jar and bottle on the table; "but here's
something fit for a mornin' for Saint Patrick himself, and yer honour
must taste it—raal Innishowen; or, if ye're too delicate (striking the
jar), the likes of this isn't in e'er a cellar in the county." He filled
a glass, and presented it to Mr. Collins, who looked at, tasted, and
drank it off.

"It came from foreign parts, sir, as a little testimonial from one
whose last gift it will be."

"Indeed, Andy! pity such cordials should be *last* gifts."

"True for ye, sir. Tim, make yer bow to the gintleman, and take
yer 'Voster' out under the sunny hedge, and yer slate, my man, and
do two sums in fractions, for practice. Jenny, woman, lift out your
wheel, and see that yer brother minds the sums."

"Don't ye see she's getting out the white cloth, for a snack for his
honour? I wish ye'd let the girl alone; or, any way, lave her do *my*
bidding," continued the wife; " ye've no earthly dacency in ye, or
ye'd ha' tould me his honour was coming in, and then I could have
got something proper, not trusting to rashers and eggs, and yer outlandish drops;" and the angry dame, angry because she could not pay
"his honour" sufficient attention, bustled about more than ever.

"The devil's in the woman! But—save us all!—they can't help
it," muttered Andrew; "maybe, whiles she's doing the eggs, yer
honour would walk out, and look at the new spokes in the mill-wheel,

and the little things I've been trying at; thank God, we've no middle-men in this parish, but resident landlords, who give every earthly encouragement to the improving tenant, and never rise the rint because the ground looks well; only a kind word, and every praise in life, and encourage ye wid odd presents: a wheel, a bale of flax, or a lock o' wool to the girls; a new plough or harrow, or some fine seed potatoes to the boys; and that's the true rason why the parish o' Bannow is the flower o' the country."

The neighbouring fields looked, indeed, beautiful; and the bright greenery extended, at either side, around the mill-stream; here and there a gnarled oak, or a gay thorn tree, added interest to the land-scape; while the sweet, waving willows, rooting themselves in the very depth of the rippling water, which, dancing between their trunks, and sparkling through their weeping foliage, formed a picture as calmly beautiful as even fruitful and merry England could supply. Andrew, from some cause or other, forgot the "new spokes" when he reached the mill-house with Mr. Collins, and peered behind the piled sacks, to ascertain that no one was in the small square room, which contained flour bags and piles of fresh grain, a long form, and sundry winnowing sheets, flails, and sifters.

" I have got something particular to say to yer honour, but couldn't for the woman; but I'll boult her out (fastening the door). Sure I'm king o' the castle here, any way. Oh! don't lane against thim bags, sir; there's no getting the white out o' the English cloth, at all, at all. Sure the binch—I wish yer honour was on the raale binch, (and it's then we'd have justice!)—the binch 'll do the turn." And Andy pulled off his wig, dusted with it the form, or, as he called it, "binch," replaced the powdered "bob" over his own black hair, crossed his feet, gave the wig a settling pull, folded his arms, and, leaning against the door-post, commenced the disclosure of his secret, in a confidential undertone :—

" Yer honour remimbers ould times, I'm thinking?" Mr. Collins smiled.

" And the Bannow corps?" Another smile.

" Well; I know yer honour's sinsible that, though the boys would have me head thim, yet I niver thought they'd have turned to the religion, and murdered the innocent craturs o' Protestants for nothin', or, as God's my judge, I'd have lit thim all go to Botany, afore I'd any hand in it; but that's all gone und past, and neither here nor there. Well; when once I was in, I thought it right to behave myself properly. But there were bloody sins o' both sides, as nataral; —burnings and massacres—and all bad; and time was, when I couldn't, for the life o' me, tell which was worst; only the poor Catholics had no arms, but the bits o' pikes, for the most part, to

make fight wid. Och! it was bitter bad! Well, yer honour remimbers Thomas Jarratt, the farmer, who lived on the hill-side, far
from kith or kin; a lone man, wid one son, a wild chap—yet kindly;
fierce—but gentle-like at times, and a generous boy; striking handsome, and prouder than many more rich and powerful nor himself.
Well, he always had his own way; the poor father doted down on
him; and, for many a day, he was the white-headed boy o' the whole
country.

"Now, sir, dear, call another to mind. Ould James Corish, though
suspected o' being a black Protestant (I ax pardon, but that was what
they were called), was well counted by all his neighbours; he had
seen a dale o' years, and there were not many happier; for his prosperity had lasted for more than half a hundred, and appeared sartin
to continue for the remainder o' his days. He had had a joyful fireside o' childer; but they were all gone excipt two: Mary, the eldest,
—so larned, so wise, and so charming; and James, a fine, gay boy,
rising seventeen; thoughtless—but all are thoughtless, sir, before
they mix in the world, to drink of its bitterness, or be marked by its
corruption. It used to do my heart good, of a Sunday, to see that
family passing on to their own church. The ould man, his silver
hair falling over his shoulders; his two childer, the one, wid her dark
long curls half hid under her straw hat, and her short scarlet petticoat, that set off the white stockings and slight ankles: the other
looking so cheerful, his light blue eyes jumping out of his head wid
innocent joy. Well, sir, young Thomas Jarratt cast an eye upon the
colleen, and, as he was no ways a strict Catholic, ould Corish thought,
maybe, he might answer for Mary, as he was well to do in the world;
and, though he didn't get any grate encouragement—to say grate—
yet, for all that, he went in and out, and the two boys were very
much together, and no one dare look at Mary, on account o' young
Tom. Yer honour remimbers the militia regiments; well, young
Corish was drawed to go in thim."

"I do. I remember it well," replied Mr. Collins; "I was there
the evening he went to join the Wexford militia. 'God bless you,
my only boy!' sobbed the poor father; 'it's like spilling one's own
blood, to fight against one's neighbours; but, God bless you, boy;
do your duty, as your father did before you; only remember, a Protestant soldier need not be an Orangeman.' Mary neither spoke
nor wept; but she pushed the curling locks from off her brother's
brow, and mournfully gazed upon it; and when, laughing at her fears,
he affectionately kissed her cheek, still she looked sad; and long and
anxiously did her eyes follow him, until his form was lost in the twilight mist, as he ascended the mountain of Forth."

"Poor cratur!—poor cratur!" sighed the miller; "well, sir, you know I was over-persuaded to join the boys, and we used to have little meetings in this very room, and I didn't care to let the wife know anything of it, at first; but she found it out, somehow or other (the women are very 'cute), and was all aginst it; but she comed over a bit at the thought of my being a captain, and she, to be sure, a captain's lady; well, we hid a good many pikeheads, in the grain, and sint more to the boys o' Watherford, into the very town, though it was under martial law at the time: but we hid them among brooms, and in sacks o' flour, and what not. The wife, one day, had crossed the Scar, to give a small sack o' barley male to one at the other side, and who should she meet this side, and she comin' back, but young Thomas Jarratt. 'Good morrow, Mistress Andy,' says he. 'Good morrow kindly,' says she. 'Maybe,' says he, 'ye won't tell a body where ye've been.' To be sure she up with the lie at once. 'That won't do for me,' says he; 'I know what ye're after, and good rason too, for I'm sworn in; and, by the same token, the pass-word into your own mill-house is—green boy.' Well, she was struck quite comical, for she thought of his father's white head, and of the poor lad's own rosy cheek; but, above all, of sweet Mary Corish. 'Oh, Thomas!' says she, 'sure it wasn't my man that united ye: oh! think of yer ould father, and the black-eyed girl that loves ye.' Och! the laugh he gave was heart-scalding. 'No,' says he, 'yer husband would call me a boy; and as to Mary, some one has come betwixt us, and she believes me bad, and ye know I wouldn't desave her,' and away he goes like a shot. For sartin, sorry was I whin I hard it, but it was too true: Mary soon got the wind o' the word, and it was too late—he wouldn't lade nor drive: and it was one of the *Scurroges* that drew him in, for which the same man niver had luck nor grace—for the boy was too young intirely to be brought into sich hardship. Well, I needn't tell about thim times. Thomas flourished the green flag, and did it bravely: but, in the battle of 'The Rocks,' it was his fate to cut down the brother of poor Mary. James Corish, however, wasn't much hurt, and, wid others, was carried to the barn of Scullabogue. I had little power, excipt in my own regiment, and I couldn't help the mischief. Yer honour knows, better nor me, what that cratur, Mary, wint through."

"I remember, as if it were but yesterday," said Mr. Collins; "poor old James fled with Mary to Ross, but the knowledge of her brother's danger came like a blight to her young heart, and long and eager were her inquiries as to the fate of the Wexford militia. A report reached her, that her brother was a prisoner in the barn of Scullabogue, and that the barn was to be set on fire that night or the next."

"I don't like to hear tell of that barn, at all, at all; but I should like to larn from yer honour how she made her way from Ross to Scullabogue; you were in the town at the time, so ye have a good right to know all about it."

"True, Andy; but what has that to do with your secret?"

"Och! more nor yer honour guesses, any way. I remimber her at the barn, but the cratur niver tould me how she got there."

"Poor thing!—she wrapped her blue mantle around her, and, with a blanched cheek, but a resolute eye and firm step, she passed the Ross sentries; the shades of night were thickening, yet the intrepid girl pursued her noiseless way towards the prison, or, perhaps, the grave of her brother. When some distance from Ross, she heard the trampling of horses; they drew nearer and nearer, and, for the first time, the necessity of avoiding the high road occurred to her. She concealed herself behind some furze, and, as they passed, their suppressed voices and disordered dress informed her to what party they belonged. She next trod her path across the country over the matted common, and through the swampy moor; nor did her steps fail her, until within a mile or two of Scullabogue."

"Poor colleen!" said the miller.

"The grey mist of morning had succeeded the night, and the thrush and blackbird were hailing the dawning day, as Mary sank down, exhausted on the greensward. 'Merciful heavens!' she exclaimed, 'I am near—very near, yet I cannot reach it!' and she clasped her hands in silent, yet bitter agony. At this moment she saw a horse quietly grazing upon the common, and with a desperate effort rushed towards the spot, unfastened her cloak, and girthed it round the animal, like a pillon—sprang on its back—and, having previously converted the ribands of her hat into a bridle, at a fearless and quick pace she gained the main road, encountered the rebel outposts, passed them, by naming your name, and at length, halted opposite the barn-door."

"Well, I mind it now, sir, as if but yesterday," interrupted Andy; "she looked like a banshee, in the early light; her black hair streaming over her shoulders, and her eyes darting fire, as she flung herself off the panting baste. The officer over the door was—Thomas Jarratt.

"'And you, Thomas,' said she, quite distracted like, 'you here, a commander!—you know me well! The fire blazed for ye, the roof sheltered ye, the welcome smile for ye in my father's house, since we were both childer. I have left my ould father, Thomas, and have come all alone to ask these men my brother's life, or to tell them I will die with him!'

"'You are mad, Mary,' he answered: 'neither the Captain nor I could save him if we would! you, Mary, I can save; but as for

James—there is too much Orange blood in the corps already.' That was the word he spoke. She fell on her knees, clenched her hands, and, in a deep, smothering voice, sobbed out, ' Let me see him, then; let me see James once—only once more !'

"The young man, without making answer, rushed into the barn, and, in a moment, returned, from crowds of famishing, death-doomed craturs, with James Corish. James thought they had brought him forth to the death, and he tried to draw up his fainting, bleeding, shadow-like body, to meet it as a man; but when he saw his dear sister Mary, he would have sunk to the earth, had she not sprung to his side.

" ' Now, mark me, boys !' cried she, as, half turning from her brother, she kept him up with one arm,—' now, mark me !—the man that forces him from me, shall first tear the limbs from my body. And if there be one amongst ye who denies a sister's claim to her dying brother, let him bury his pike in my heart, or burn me wid him.'

"She flung him on the nearest horse, and, mounting behind, guided the animal's bridle. The last sound of the galloping, and the last sight of her streaming black hair, were long gone, before hand or foot was moved; they stood like stocks and stones, even in the time of destruction, wondering at woman's love.* ' Fire the barn !' was the next sound I hard, and that from Thomas Jarratt's own mouth. I seized his arm. ' What do you mane ?' said I. ' Fire the barn !' he repeated, stamping, and hell's own fire flashing, like lightning, from his blood-red eyes. ' Isn't he half murdered by this hand ?' he muttered to himself; ' and isn't she whole murdered, or worse ?— for I know that in twinty-four hours, she'll be either mad or dead. United Irishmen !' he screamed out, waving his green flag, ' the soldiers are in Ross.' And, sticking his pike into a bresneugh, which some devils had lit, he rushed towards the door. I saw it was all over, so I shouted to the Bannow boys to close around their Captain ; and, sure enough, out o' my two hundred and odd, there weren't five that didn't march home that day to their own cabins. Och ! but the crackling, and the shrieks, and the yells, as we hurried on !"

The old miller covered his face with his hands, and pressed his rough fingers against his eyeballs, as if to destroy such horrid recollections.

"Poor Mary !—she gained Ross in safety," said Mr. Collins, " and her father rejoiced much. James soon recovered ; but we all know

---

* The circumstance here recorded is strictly true. I have seen my heroic country-woman, Mary Corish, often—but never without grief. The effort was too much for her mind, and her reason sank under it.

the wretched Thomas was right. When she arose from that fearful brain fever, her reason was perfectly gone. You are all kind to her, very kind. She seems more happy wandering about your mill, and gathering flowers for your children, than in her brother's farm-house. I remember well old Jarratt's funeral. His son was killed; but, I believe, his body was never found."

"He was *not* killed, sir," replied the miller, looking earnestly at Mr. Collins. "Many a night after, he slept in this very room."

"Here, Andy!—what, here?—and you knew it?"

"Yer honour may say that, when it was myself put him in it."

"But, Andy, your own life was not then safe from the king's troops. How could you commit such a very imprudent action (to call it by no harsher term), as to harbour a proscribed man, when a rich price was set upon his body, dead or alive? And such a wretch, too! I am perfectly astonished!"

"No need in life for that last, sir. As to my own head, it was but loosely on my shoulders then—sure enough;—as to the prudence, it's not the character of the counthry;—as to the price set upon his head, none o' my breed, seed, or generation, were iver informers (my curse on the black word!) or iver will be, plase the Almighty. And as to his being a wretch—we are all bad enough, and to spare. But, had he murdered my own brother, and, after, come—ay, with the very blood upon his hands—and thrown himself upon my marcy—I'm a true-born Irishman, sir, who niver refused purtection, when wanted, to saint or sinner. But the fair and beautiful boy, to see him, and he dressed like an ould woman pilgrim; his cheek hollow, his eye dead, so worn; and no life in him, but bitther sorrow, and heavy tears for sin. We kept him here, unknownst, as good as five weeks, and then shipped him off beyant seas far enough."

"But the money, Andy—how did you get money to fit him out?"

"Is it the money?—his father's land was canted; and, to be sure, he couldn't touch a pinny, and he banned: but I'll tell ye who gave some of it—young James Corish. I knew the good drop was in him, and so I tould him all about it; and, says he; 'There have been many examples made of the misfortunate, misguided people, Andy,' says he; 'and if he did hew me down, why, 'twas in battle, and I'd ha' done the same to him; but the drink and the bad company made him mad: any way, he took me out o' the barn; and, more than all, sure, *they* loved each other; and, more than all to the back o' that, doesn't the blessed word o' God tell us to love our enemies, and to do good to thim that ill use us? Sure that's the true religion, Andy; and Catholic or Protestant can't turn their tongues to betther than the words o' the gospel o' pace;' and, without more to do, he gives me twinty hard guineas, and a small Bible, and I gave Thomas the Bible on the sly; and, one way or other, we sint him clane out o' the land."

"And did you never hear of the unfortunate young man since?" inquired Mr. Collins.

"Did I not?—sure it was he sint me over the cordial ye tasted; and, more than all, sure he's come over himself, in the strange brig that's at the new quay."

"Good God!" said Mr. Collins, starting up; "he'll be hung as certainly as he lands."

"Och! no danger in life o' that," replied Andy, quietly.

"You're mad—absolutely mad!"

"I ax yer honour's pardon, I'm not mad; and sure it's nat'ral for him to wish to lave his bones in his own land."

"Leave his bones on a gibbet!" exclaimed the gentleman, greatly agitated.

"I wanted particular to spake to yer honour about it, as he is to land to-night, under the ould church, and Father Mike is to be there, and Friar Madden, and not more than one or two others, excipt the poor boy that brought him over."

"As sure as he lands," said Mr. Collins, "he will be in the body of Wexford Jail in two hours."

"Well, that's comical, too," replied Andy, quietly,—"sind a dead body to Waxford Jail!"

Mr. Collins looked perplexed.

"Yer honour's not sinsible, I see; sure it's the dead body o' what was Thomas Jarratt that's come over; and, by the same token, a letther (the priest has it), written—(he had a dale o'schooling)—jist before the breath left him; and he prays us to lay his body in Bannow Church, as near the ould windy as convanient, without disturbing any one's rest; and, on account he doesn't wish a wake, he begs us, if we want him to have pace, to put him in the ground at twelve o' the night, by the light of four torches. I can't see the use of the four, barring he took it from the little hymn—

> ' Matthew, Mark, Luke, and John,
> God bless the bed that I lie on.'

"But it's hard telling dead men's fancies; be that as it may, the letther's a fine letther—as good as a sarmint; and he sint a handsome compliment to his reverence, but nothing said about masses; and he sint forty guineas to James Corish, and remimbered Mary; and more to myself than iver he got from me; but, says he, 'I can pay the living, but what do the dead ask of me?' And the boy that came over wid him (an ould comrade) that was forced to fly, for a bit of a scrape, nothing killin' bad, only a bit of a mistake, where a chap was done for, without any malice—only all a mistake; well, he tould me, though all worldly matthers prospered, his soul troubled him night and day, but he used to read the Bible at times (sure it's the word o' God), and sob, and pray; and he wasted, while his goods increased; but where's the use o' my delaying yer honour now? I only want to ax ye if there's anything contrary to law, in landing and burying the poor ashes to-night?"

"Nothing that I know of, certainly."

"But is yer honour sartin sure about it? Becase, if there was any earthly doubt, I'd not go aginst the law now, the least bit, for the price o' the 'varsal world; and sure I'd go to the grave any time, night or day, to keep the cratur asy, only, if it's aginst the law——"

"I assure you, Andy, it is not," replied Mr. Collins; "and if you will allow me, I should like to be there myself; it is wild and singular, and Father Mike will not object, I dare say."

"Och! yer honour's kind and good."

It was agreed that they should meet at twelve that night. Mr. Collins, of course, partook of Mrs. Andy's hospitality, and exchanging kindly greetings with the honest miller's family, turned his steps homeward.

It was nearly midnight when Mr. Collins gained the cliffs that overhang the little harbour of Bannow; the moon was emerging from some light, fleecy clouds, that shaded, without obscuring her brightness, and, as she mounted higher in the heavens, her beams formed a silvery line on the calm waters, that were fleetly crossed by a small boat: at the prow stood a tall, slight figure, enveloped in a cloak, and, on the strand, four or five men were grouped, in earnest conversation. The path Mr. Collins had to descend was unusually steep, and various portions of fallen cliff made it difficult, if not dangerous. As he passed along, he thought the shadow of a human form crossed his way; but the improbability of such an event, and the flickering light, made him forget the circumstance, even before he joined the priest and Andy on the beach. No word was spoken, but hands were silently grasped in hands, and they prepared to assist in the landing of the coffin; it was large, covered with black cloth, and on the lid—"Thomas Jarratt, aged 42," was inscribed. The simple procession quickly formed. The priest and friar lighted each a torch; the young man who brought the body over, still shrouded in his cloak, supported the head of the coffin; Andy and another bore the feet; and the remaining torches, and Mr. Collins, brought up the singular procession. As they slowly ascended, the torches· threw a wild, red light over the mounds of cliff, fringed with sea moss and wild flowers, fragments of dark rock, and tangled furze, which the hardened soil appeared incapable of nourishing. When they had nearly arrived at the highest point, Mr. Collins distinctly saw the passing shadow he before imagined he had observed, fade, as it were, behind a broken mass, composed of earth and rock; at the same moment, all the party perceived it; the priest commanded a halt, and murmured an Ave Mary.

"What was it?" whispered one.

"Lord presarve us!—it's lucky they're wid us! no blight can come where the priests do be," replied Andy.

Without further hindrance, they crossed the grassy plain that extends between the ruined church and the cliffs, and entered the long aisle, where no more—

> " The pealing anthem swells the notes of praise."

If there be a solitude like unto that of the sepulchre, it is the solitude of ruins. In mountain loneliness you may image an unpeopled world, fresh from God's own hand—pure, bright, and beautiful as the new-born sun; but a moss-grown ruin speaks powerfully, in its loneliness, of gone-by days—of bleached and marrowless bones.

All was silent as the hollow grave which yawned at their feet. The innocent birds, that nestled among the wall-flowers and ivy, frightened at the unusual light, screamed and fluttered in their leafy dwellings. The moon shone brightly through the large window, as the bearers rested the coffin on the loose earth.

"He requested," said Father Mike, addressing Mr. Collins, "that his body should be placed in the ground without so much as a prayer for the repose of his soul—that was heathenish; yet his other words were those of a penitent and a Christian."

The coffin was deposited in its narrow home; and Andy held the torch over the grave, to ascertain that all had been properly managed.

The priest, the friar, and Mr. Collins, stood fixed in silent prayer, and the passing night-breeze shook the withered leaves from the dark overhanging ivy. Each individual was surrounded by the urns and tombs of his ancestors; nay, more, by those of relatives, who, in the bud or blossom of life, had passed away, and were no more seen; and it was not to be wondered at, that the silent power of death, and the everlasting doom of eternity, pressed heavily on the hearts of them all at that midnight hour. At this very moment, a dark shadow obscured the cold moonbeams that streamed from the window; a piercing shriek echoed along the broken walls; and, even while their eyes were fixed on a female, who stood, with streaming hair and extended arms, on the large window-frame—she sprang from the elevation, with unerring bound, into the open grave, and echo was again awakened by the fearful sound made by her feet upon the coffin lid.

"Heaven and earth!" exclaimed Andy, as he raised the light, "it's Mary Corish!"

She seized the torch from the astonished miller, lowered it, so as to read the inscription, which she distinctly repeated, and fell, without farther motion, on the coffin of him she had loved, even in madness. They raised her, tenderly, out of the grave, but the pulses of life were slackening, and the film of approaching death was stealing over the wild brightness of her eyes.

"She is passing," said Mr. Collins, chafing her damp temples as he spoke; "poor Mad Mary!"

"I am not mad," she murmured, and her utterance was very feeble—"not mad now; I was so, and ye all pitied me; God bless ye! I know you—and you—and you—and I know him—that's——" with a last effort she turned towards the grave, looked into it, and expired.

No one could ever discover how she was apprized of the intended funeral; but as she was always wandering about the sea-shore, it was supposed she had overheard some of the conversation that had occurred on the subject.

Poor Mary!—the innocent children who gather ocean-weed and many-tinted shells on the strand of Bannow, when they see the white sea-bird seeking its lodging in the clefted rock, after the sun has set, and the grey mist is rising, as if to shield the repose of nature, softly and fearfully whisper to each other, that it is time to return to their homes, for that Mad Mary's ghost will be flitting around the aged church of Bannow.

GOOD SPIRITS AND BAD.

WHEN I wrote the stories of which this volume is composed, in common with every other writer concerning Ireland, I had frequent occasion to notice the habitual intemperance of a people naturally excitable. This, more than all their other failings, rendered them liable to misrepresentation :—"an Irishman drunk, and an Irishman sober," were two distinct beings ; but the stranger had little time to inquire into the causes when he witnessed the effects. And though many efforts had been made to change the bad spirit for the good—though Professor Edgar, in Belfast, the Rev. George Carr, in New Ross, and some excellent men in Cork, had made strenuous exertions to establish Temperance Societies, nothing, comparatively, had been done to influence the Roman Catholic population. What the Rev. Mr. Mathew has wrought—his untiring perseverance, his disinterested efforts for the regeneration of his countrymen, his labouring unceasingly through evil report, which was, at last, silenced by the overwhelming good that became apparent throughout the country—I need not here record. During the last few years the difficulty has been, not to find an Irishman sober, but an Irishman intoxicated: the change is wonderful, and must be seen to be believed.* I trust the good may be permanent, and see every reason to think that such will be the case. A person who had not visited Ireland for some years would not know the country again; indeed, I hardly knew the people myself, some of whom I used to lecture after my own fashion; and you may lecture Paddy for ever without running the risk of an unpleasant answer: he is the most ready of all people in the world to *listen* to advice—he will agree to the letter with you in everything you state. "Bedad, ma'am, I know that, I often thought so."—"Ah, then, see that now!—Sure it was always the way, and a cruel bad habit, leaving us worse than it found us, and that's no asy matter."—"Oh, indeed, it's as clear as print, and as thrue as gospel!" but you did not carry your point a bit the sooner for all this acquiescence: the next day, the next hour, you might have chanced to meet the same Paddy in the most senseless state of intoxication. Alas! it was very, very sad! How different now! Paddy's coat, though not according to English notions of comfort, is a wonderful improvement upon my old acquaintance; his eye is clear; the yellow pallor of inebriety has given place to the colour of a healthy state of existence, and his step is firm, as of a man newly escaped from slavery. I have heard many, not conversant with the country, wonder that, in consequence of the spread of temperance, the children are not now all well clothed, and the cabins furnished. They ought to remember that the pay of an Irish labourer, at *most*, is but six shillings a week, that what he drank formerly took the absolute *food*, the potato and milk, from his children, who now are able to have sufficient of this humble fare; but a much longer period must elapse before the little that can be spared shows to the eye accustomed to the luxuries of a higher station:—a cup and saucer, a plate, a piggin, a new stool, a potato-basket, are valuable additions to the humble cottage, yet are hardly noticed by the casual visitor, who sees the misery that is, but forgets that which has been. It is not a little curious to observe how opinions alter with the times. I remember when it was considered a positive extravagance in the wife of even a decent tradesman to take a cup of tea, though the gentry who condemned her would not hesitate to

---

* Although, since the above was written, many changes have taken place, and Temperance is not altogether as entirely "natural" as it was ten years ago, it is quite certain that the beneficial effects of the "movement" have been great. Throughout Ireland, drunkenness is now not an honour but a reproach—of which the drunkard even is ashamed. I have suffered these passages to remain: for, beyond question, many of the blessings I anticipated have arisen from the introduction of Temperance.

order her husband a glass of raw alcohol when he brought home his
work. Indeed, the habit of giving *the evil spirit* to every person who
called on business was, when I was a child, so common, that neglect-
ing to do so was considered a breach of hospitality.

There was a very excellent person in Bannow, a woman whom I
never think of but with pleasure; my grandmother used to employ
her in her capacity of dressmaker and needle-woman, for, I should
think, pretty nearly six months out of the twelve. She plied her
needle in my nursery; and I have sat for hours on my little chair
by her side, looking into her beautiful face, and listening with intense
pleasure to the legends she used to tell, and the exquisite ballads she
used to sing, with the most untiring patience, for my amusement.
Poor Mrs. Bow! She little thought how she was storing my mind
with the richest treasures. She had been nearly brought up in Graige
House, and nothing could surpass her affection for all who dwelt
within its walls. Her manners and mind were superior to her station, and yet, strangely enough, she had married a man—a smith, a
good and clever workman—as remarkable for personal ugliness as
she was for personal beauty; and in proportion as her temper was
sweet, his was sour. But this was not all; Mr. Bow had a most
decided affection for whisky, raw—or whisky-punch—it was never
" too hot nor too heavy" for him; and if his temper was cranky when
sober, it was worse than cranky when, after his hard day's work, he
issued from his forge a tipsy Vulcan, overthrowing, in his homeward
progress, all who stood in his way. This was a heavy trial to his poor
wife, who, in proportion as she was proud of her husband's upright-
ness and integrity, so was she grieved at his fits of intoxication. "If,"
she would exclaim, "if he would only take to the tea I'd die happy."
Now Mrs. Bow had a dog, a very pretty black spaniel, called Diver,
a creature of extraordinary sagacity, and one of the first, as well as
firmest, advocates of Temperance: he might, had he lived long enough,
been the favourite dog of Father Mathew, and been worthy of such
a distinction. Diver hated the " bad spirit," as his mistress always
called whisky, with his entire heart. He would never accept a caress
from a hand that had the odour thereof; and the sound of drunken
revelry excited him to the bristling of hair and gnashing of teeth.
When his master returned home in the full possession of his senses
Diver would manifest the greatest joy; but when he staggered into
the room Diver would retreat under a chair, gather his lips from off
his white and glistening teeth, and looked both distressed and angry.
His master was perfectly aware of this, but did not fail to bestow on
his wife's favourite sundry epithets of dislike and contempt. Now
this antipathy to the smell of whisky could, perhaps, be accounted
for: the dog had, probably, been ill-used by persons under the
influence of intoxication; but the remarkable part of his canine cha-

racter was—his attachment to the tea-pot. Although every one declared " it was a shame for Mrs. Bow to take to the tea, every evening,
like a lady, and her husband, honest man, content with nothing
but a glass of whisky ;" still she persevered in the almost hopeless
hope of winning her spouse to partake of the exhilarating, yet harmless, beverage ; in this desire Diver apparently concurred. His mistress had only to show him the tea-pot to set him bounding and
skipping about the room with delight; he would whirl round, wag
his tail, and finally dart forward in search of his master, whom he
would endeavour, by every possible means in his power, to induce to
return with him. The smith well knew what he wanted; and, at
last, took pleasure in displaying his sagacity to his neighbours, making them accompany him home, because then, indeed, the animal's
joy knew no bounds. To see his master and mistress seated at the
tea-table was the summit of his delight; he would stretch himself
along the ground, and howl with pleasure. Poor Diver did not live
long enough to witness the triumph of " teatotalism ;" but he succeeded in making his master fond of tea. I hope this anecdote of
the first " teatotallers" of my acquaintance will not be considered
" out of place." Happily, those who sneered at the impossibility of
Irishmen becoming *sober* members of society are convinced that Irish
perseverance is worthy of respect, not ridicule. The marvel to me is,
not that some few have broken " the pledge," but that so many have
kept it. It must be remembered that it was the Irishman's *sole* luxury.

> " Surely it is my father and mother,
> My Sunday coat—I have no other ;"

was the " refrain" of one of the many songs he had heard from his
youth up. " His father liked a drop, honest man, and took it off and
on, and sure if it did harm, it was to no one but himself," was what
he had often heard. His uncles were fine, free-hearted fellows, that
"shared a drop with their neighbours." His cousins " took their glass
like men." "The piper never played up hearty till he had his eye glazed
with the whisky." " The priest was a fine man after his reverence
had the second tumbler." His landlord, the next object of his venera
tion, " was fond of his hot tumbler," and always a good hand to order it
to a poor man, wet or dry." No entertainment was given without whisky :
no bargain concluded until the libation to the evil spirit was poured
forth : no account was ever taken of the horrors produced by intoxication. " Ah, sure, he couldn't help it—he wasn't himself when he
struck the blow—bad luck to it for whisky, it does a deal of harm; but
what can a poor man do ?—sure it's the only comfort he has—the only
thing that puts the throuble past him ; it takes the feel of sorrow
from his heart, and the sight of starvation from before his eyes."

And yet—the Irishman has had the moral courage to relinquish, and the moral firmness to adhere to the determination of giving up, as I have said, his *only luxury*—and that without any of the complaining we, of a better class, should make if we abandoned one of the scores that we indulge in.

I look upon this triumph with great admiration. It is impossible not to respect those who make great sacrifices from a desire to do right; and I am sure what has been effected, in the way of self-denial, by the Irish, in this matter, proves that they have not only energy, but perseverance, for anything they undertake. *This* fact should be borne in mind by all whose duty and interest it is to see that such fine qualities are *well directed.*

I must illustrate my text of "Good Spirits and Bad" by one or two stories :—

"What I'm thinking of, Nelly, darlin'," said Roney Maher to his poor pale wife, "what I'm thinking of is—what a pity we were not bred and born in this Temperance Society, for then we could follow it, you know, as a thing of course, without any trouble."

"But——"

"Whisht, Nelly, you've one great fault, avourneen—you're always talking, dear, and won't listen to me. What I was saying is that, if we were brought up to the coffee, instead of the whisky, we'd have been natural members of the Temperance Society : as it is now, agra ! why, it's meat, drink, and clothing, as a man may say !"

He paused, and Nelly thought—though, in his present state, she had too much tenderness to tell her husband so—that whisky was a very bad paymaster.

"You're no judge, Ellen," he continued, interpreting her thoughts, "for you never took to it; and, if I had my time to begin over again, I never would either; but it's too late to change now—all—too late!"

"I've heard many a wise man say that *it's never too late* to mend," observed Ellen.

"Yah !" he exclaimed, almost fiercely, "who ever said that was a fool !"

"It was the priest himself, then, Roney, never a one else ; and sure you wouldn't call him that !"

"If I did mend," he observed, "no one would take my word for it."

"Ay, dear—but deeds, not words," and having said more than was usual for her, in the way of reproof, Ellen retreated to watch its effect.

Roney Maher was a fine, likely boy, when he married Ellen ; but when this little dialogue took place, he was sitting over the embers of a turf fire, a pale emaciated man, though in the prime of life—a torn handkerchief bound round his temples, and his favourite shillalah that he had greased and seasoned in the chimney, and tended, *with more care than his children*, lay broken by his side. He attempted to snatch it up while his wife retreated, but his arm fell powerless, and he uttered a groan so full of pain, that, in a moment, she returned, and, with tearful eyes, inquired " if it was so bad with him entirely as that?"

"It's worse," he answered, while the large drops that stood upon his brow proved how much he suffered.

"It's worse—the arm, I mean—than I thought; I'm *done* for a week, or, maybe, a fortnight—and, Nelly, the pain of my arm is nothing to the weight about my heart—now, don't be talking, for I can't stand it. If I *can't* work next week, nor this, and we without money or credit—what—what!" The unfortunate man glanced at his wife and children—he could not finish the sentence. He had only returned, the previous night, from having " been out upon a spree," as it is called; spending his money, wasting his health, losing his employment—not thinking of those innocent children whom God had given him to protect; and only returning to the abode, which his propensity had rendered one of squalid wretchedness, because he had been disabled in a disgraceful riot.

When sober, Roney's impulses were all good: but he was as easily, perhaps more easily, led away by the bad than the good; in the present instance, he continued talking, because he dared not think, and it is a fearful thing for a man to dread his own thoughts. It was a painful picture, to look upon this well-educated man—he *had* been an excellent tradesman—he *had* been respected—he *had* been comfortable; he felt lost, degraded, in pain, in sorrow, and yet he would not confess it. Once or twice he attempted to sing snatches of those foolish or bad songs which entice to intoxication, but the words " stuck in his throat;" in truth, he was too ill, either to think or act,—ashamed of the past, yet endeavouring, in vain, to convince himself that he had no right to be ashamed.

It was evening : the children crept round the fire, where their mother endeavoured to heat half-a-dozen cold potatoes for their supper—looking, with hungry eyes, upon the scanty feast. "Daddy's too bad entirely to eat to-night," whispered the second boy to his eldest brother, while his little thin blue lips trembled, half with cold, half with hunger; "*and so we'll have his share as well as our own!*" and the little shivering group devoured the potatoes, in imagination, over and over again—poking them with their lean fingers, and telling their "mammy," they were *hot* enough;—shocking that want should have taught them to calculate on their parent's illness as a source of rejoicing!

"Nelly," said her husband, at last—"Nelly, I wish I had a drop of something to warm me."

" Mrs. Kinsalla said she would give me a bowl of strong coffee for you—if you would take it."

What drunkard does not blaspheme ?

Roney swore; and, though his lips were parched with fever, and his head throbbed, he declared he must have just "one little thimbleful to raise his heart." It was in vain that Ellen remonstrated and entreated. He did not attempt violence, but he obliged his eldest boy to beg the "thimbleful;" and, before morning, the wretched man was tossing about in all the heat and irritation of decided fever. One must have witnessed what fever is, when accompanied by such misery, to understand its terrors. It was wonderful how he was supported through it—indeed his ravings, when, after a long, dreary time, the fever subsided, were more torturing to poor Nelly than the working of his delirium had been.

" If," he would exclaim—"if it wasn't *too late*, I'd take the pledge they talk about, the first minute I rise my head from the straw; but where's the good of it now ?—what can I save now ?—nothing—it's too late !"

" It's never too late," Ellen would whisper. " It's never too late," she would repeat; and, as if it were a mocking echo, her husband's voice would sigh—" Too late !—too late !"

Indeed, any who looked upon the fearful wreck of what had been the fine, manly form of Roney Maher—stretched upon a bed of straw, with hardly any covering—saw his two rooms now utterly destitute of every article of furniture—heard his children begging in the streets for a morsel of food—and observed how the utmost industry of his poor wife could hardly keep the rags together that shrouded her bent form—anyone almost, who saw these things, would be inclined to repeat the words, which have, unfortunately, but too often knelled over the grave of good feelings and good intentions—" Too late !—too late !" Many would have imagined that not only had the demon habit, which had gained so frightful an ascendancy over poor Roney, banished all chance of reformation, but that there was no escape from such intense poverty.—I wish, with all my heart, that such persons would, instead of sitting down with so helpless and dangerous a companion as despair, resolve upon two things; first of all, to trust in, and pray to God; secondly, to combat what they foolishly call fate—to fight bravely, and in a good cause; and sure am I, that those who do, will sooner or later achieve a victory.

It is never too late to abandon a bad habit, and adopt a good one. In every town of Ireland, Temperance has now its members, and these members are so thoroughly acquainted with the blessings of this admirable system, from feeling its advantages, that they are full of zeal in the cause, and, with true Irish generosity, eager to enlist

their friends and neighbours—that they, too, may partake of the
comforts which spring from temperance. The Irishman is not selfish :
he is as ready to share his cup of coffee, as he used to be to share his
glass of whisky.

One of these generous members was Mrs. Kinsalla, whose offer
of the bowl of coffee had been rejected by Roney the night his fever
commenced; she was herself a poor widow, or, according to the
touching and expressive phraseology of Ireland, "a *lone* woman ;"
and, though she had so little to bestow, that many would call it
nothing, she gave it with that goodwill which rendered it "twice
blest :" then she stirred up others to give; and often had she kept
watch with her wretched neighbour, Ellen, never omitting those
words of gentle kindness and instruction, which, perhaps, at the
time, may seem to have been spoken in vain; but not so : for we
must bear in mind that, even in the *good ground*, the seed will not
spring up the moment it is sown. Those who would effect a great
moral revolution must have patience : those who, in their families,
seek to reform a beloved object whom they love, despite his or her
errors ; or to reclaim a backslider, and teach that the ways of peace
are the ways of loving-kindness and religion, must have patience :
they must be assured that it is *never too late*, as all *do* think, whose
trust in God is founded in the belief of His mercy and forgiveness.

Roney had been an industrious and a good workman, once; and
Mrs. Kinsalla had often thought, before the establishment of the Temperance Society, what a blessing it would be if there were any means
of making him an " affidavit man ;" but, as she said, " there were so
many ways of avoiding an oath, when a man's heart was set to break
it, not to keep it, that she could hardly tell what to say about it."

Such poverty as Roney's must either die beneath its infliction, or
rise above it. He was now able to sit in the sun at his cabin-door.
His neighbour, Mrs. Kinsalla, had prevailed on a good lady to employ
Ellen, in the place of a servant who was ill ; and had lent her clothes,
that she might be able to appear decently " at the big house."
Every night she was permitted to bring her husband a little broth,
or some bread and meat; and the poor fellow was regaining his
health, though his arm still continued weak. Their dwelling, however, remained without any article of furniture : although the rain
used to pour through the roof, and the only fire was made from the
scanty "bresnaugh" the children gathered from the road-side, they
had sufficient food ; and though the lady expected all she employed
to work hard she paid them well, and caused Ellen's poor forlorn
heart to leap with joy by the gift of a blanket, and a very old suit of
clothes for her husband. And here let me observe that, wherever
man and wife continue to exist together, there is hope, amounting

almost to certainty, of better times, if one stems the torrent of vice or mismanagement. If *both* go wrong, woe, woe, to their children!—but how often is the husband rendered, as it were, the salvation of the wife, and the wife of the husband!

"I have seen yer old master to-day, Roney," said the widow Kinsalla to her neighbour, "and he was asking after you."

"I'm obliged to him," was the reply.

"And he said he was sorry to see your children in the street, Roney, honey."

"So am I——but you know he was so angry with me for that last *scrimage*, that he declared I should never do another stroke of work for him;" and he added, "that was a cruel saying for him, to lay out starvation for me and mine, because I was not worse than the rest; sure, as I said to Nelly, poor thing, and she spending her strength and striving for me—'Nelly,' says I, 'where's the good of it, bringing me out of the shades of death, to send me begging along the road?—let me die easy where I am!'"

"Well, but the master will take you back, Roney—on one condition."

The blood mounted to the poor man's face—and then he became faint, and leaned back against the wall. Three times he had been dismissed from his employment for drunkenness, and his master had never been known to receive a man back after three dismissals. Mrs. Kinsalla gave him a cup of water, and then continued—"The master told me, himself, he'd take you back, Roney, *on one condition.*"

"I'll give my oath against the whisky—barring—" he began.

"There need be no swearing—but there *must* be no *barring*. I'll tell you the rights of it—if you'll listen to me in earnest," said the widow. "The master, you see, called all his men together, and set down fair before them the state they were in from the indulgence in spirits. He drew a picture, Roney: a young man in his prime, full of life, with a fair character; his young wife by his side; his child on his knee; earning from fifteen to eighteen shillings or a pound a week; able to have his Sunday dinner in comfort; well to do, in every way; at first he drinks, maybe a glass with a friend—*and that leads to another*, and another, until work is neglected, home is abandoned, a quarrelsome spirit grows out of the high spirit which is no shame—and, in a very short time, you lose all trace of the man in the degraded drunkard. Poverty wraps her rags around him; pallid want, loathsome disease, a jail, and a bedless death, close the scene. 'But,' said the master, 'this is not all; the sneer and the reproach have gone over the world against us, and an Irishman is held up as a degraded man—as a half-civilized savage, to be spurned and laughed at—because——'"

"I know," groaned Roney—"because he makes himself a reproach. Mrs. Kinsalla, I knew you were a well-reared and a well-
learned woman, but you give that to the life; it's all true."

"He spoke," she continued, "of those amongst his own workmen,
who had fallen by intoxication; he said, if poverty had slain its
thousands, whisky had slain its tens of thousands; poverty did not
always lead to drunkenness, but drunkenness always led to poverty;
he spoke of you, my poor man, being as one whom he had respected."

"Did he say that, indeed?"

"He did——"

"God bless him for *that*, any way. I thought him a hard man;
but God bless him for remembering old times."

"And then he said how you had fallen——"

"The world knows *that*, without his telling it," interrupted Roney.

"It does, agra!—but listen! He told of *one* who was as low as
you are now, and lower, for the Lord took from him the young wife,
who died, broken-hearted, in the sight of his eyes; and yet it was not
too late for him to be restored, and able to lead others from the way
that led him to destruction.

"He touched the hearts of them all; he laid before them how, if
they looked back to what they had done when sober, and what they
had done when the contrary, they would see the *difference*; and
then, my dear, he showed them other things; he laid it down, as
plain as print, how all the badness that has been done in the country,
sprang out of the whisky—the faction-fights, flying in the face of
that God who tells us to love each other—the oaths, black and bitter,
dividing Irishmen, who ought to be united in all things that lead to
the peace and honour of their country, into parties; staining hands
with blood, that would have gone, spotless, to honourable graves,
but for its excitement.

"Then he said how the foes of Ireland would sneer and scorn, if
she became a backslider from Temperance; and how her friends would
rejoice, if the people kept true to their pledge;—how every man
could prove himself a patriot, a *rale* patriot, by showing to the world
an Irishman, steadfast, sober, and industrious, with a cooler head, and
warmer heart than ever beat in any but an Irishman's bosom!—He
showed, you see, *how Temperance was the heart's core of ould Ireland's
glory*, and said a dale more than I can repeat about her peace, and
verdure, and prosperity; and then he drew out a picture of a reformed man—his home, with all the little bits of things comfortable
about him; his smiling wife—his innocent babies; and, knowing
him so well, Roney, I made my courtesy—and, 'sir,' says I, 'if you
please, will that come about to every one who becomes a true *member*
of the Total Abstinence Society.' 'I'll go bail for it,' says he,
'though surely you don't want it; I never saw *you* overtaken, Mrs.

Kinsalla.' ' God forbid, and thank your honour,' says I ; ' but you want every one to be a member ?' says I. ' From my heart, for his own good, and the honour of old Ireland I do,' he says.

"'Then, sir,' I went on, 'there's Roney Maher, sir—and if he takes and is true to the pledge, sir—' and I watched to see if the good-humoured twist was on his mouth, 'he'll be fit for work next week, sir ; and the *evil spirit* is out of him so long now, and—' 'That's enough,' he says, ' bring him here to-morrow, when all who wish to remain in my employ will take the resolution, and I'll try him again.'"

Ellen had entered, unperceived by her husband, and flung herself on her knees by his side.

The appeal was unnecessary ; sorrow softens men's hearts ; he pressed her to his bosom, while tears coursed each other down the furrows of his pallid cheeks.

"Ellen, mavourneen ;—Ellen, aroon !" he whispered—"Nelly, agra ! a coushla machree !—you were right—' *It is never too late.*'"

* * * * * *

Nineteen months have elapsed since Roney, trusting not in his own strength, entered on a new course of life. Having learnt to distrust himself, he was certain to triumph.

You could hardly believe that the Roney Maher of the past, and the Roney Maher of the present, are the same ; the pale, shivering, sullen, and red-eyed drunkard changed by the blessing—the one blessing which every human being can make his own—the blessing of Temperance ; changed—I repeat it most joyfully—into a hale and happy, open and clear-eyed man ; his voice steady ; his step firm ; working from Monday morning until Saturday night ; the source of humble, but certain, comfort to his family ; standing before God, and his country, in the dignity of manhood, undebased by vice.

It is Sunday ; his wife has taken her two eldest children to early mass, that she may return in time to prepare his dinner ; the little lads, stout, clean, and ruddy-faced, are watching to call to their mother, so that she may know the moment he, her reformed husband, appears in sight. What there is in the cottage betokens care, and that sort of Irish comfort which is easily satisfied ; there is, moreover, a cloth on the table ; a cunning-looking dog is eying the steam of something more savoury than mere potatoes, which ascends the chimney ; and the assured calmness of Ellen's face proves that her heart is at ease. The boys are the same that, hardly two years ago, were compelled by cruel starvation, to exult—poor children ! that their father's being too ill to eat, insured them another potato.

The friends of Temperance have so great a dread of the people taking what are called, "Temperance Cordials," that I am induced to illustrate the subject by relating an incident—in the humble but fervent hope of its being useful in preventing persons from laying down *one* bad habit, only to take up another.

"Well," said Andrew Furlong to James Lacey, "that ginger cordial, of all things I ever tasted, is the nicest and warmest. It's beautiful stuff; and so cheap."

"What good does it do ye, Andrew? and what want have you of it?" inquired James Lacey.

"What good does it do me?" repeated Andrew, rubbing his forehead, in a manner that showed he was perplexed by the question, "why, no great good, to be sure, and I can't say I've any want of it; for since I became a member of the 'Total Abstinence Society,' I've lost the megrim in my head, and the weakness I used to have about my heart. I'm as strong and hearty in myself as any one can be, God be praised! And sure, James, neither of us could turn out in such a coat as *this*, this time twelvemonth."

"And that's true," replied James; "but we must remember that if leaving off whisky enables us to show a good habit, taking to 'ginger cordial,' or anything of that kind, will soon wear a hole in it."

"You are always fond of your fun. How can you prove that?"

"Easy enough," said James. "Intoxication was the worst part of a whisky-drinking habit; but it was not the only bad part—it spent TIME, and it spent what well-managed time always gives, MONEY. Now, though they do say—mind I'm not quite *sure* about it, for they *may* put things in it they don't own to, and your eyes look brighter, and your cheek more flushed, than if you had been drinking nothing stronger than milk or water—but they *do* say that ginger cordials, and all kinds of cordials, do not intoxicate. I will grant this; but you cannot deny that they waste both time and money."

"Oh, bother!" exclaimed Andrew, "I only went with two or three other boys to have a glass, and I don't think we spent more than half an hour. There's no great harm in laying out a penny that way, now and again."

"*Half* an hour even, breaks a day," said James, "and, what is worse, it unsettles the mind for work; and we ought to be very careful of any return to the *old habit*, that has destroyed many of us, body and soul, and made the name of an Irishman a bye-word and a reproach, instead of a glory and an honour. A penny, Andrew, *breaks the silver shilling into coppers;* and two-pence will buy half a stone of potatoes—that's a consideration. If we don't manage to keep things comfortable at home, the women won't have the heart to mend the coat. Not," added James, with a sly smile, "that I can deny having taken to TEMPERANCE CORDIALS myself."

"You!" shouted Andrew, "*you!* a pretty fellow you are to be blaming me, and forced to confess you have taken to them yourself; but I suppose they'll wear no hole in *your* coat? Oh, no, *you* are such a good manager!"

"Indeed," answered James, "I *was* anything but a good manager, eighteen months ago: as you well know, I was in rags, never at my work of a Monday, and seldom on a Tuesday. My poor wife, my gentle patient Mary, often bore hard words, and, though she will not own to it, I fear still harder blows, when I had driven away my senses. My children were pale, half-starved, naked creatures, disputing a potato with the pig my wife tried to keep to pay the rent, well knowing I would never do it. Now——"

"But the cordial, my boy," interrupted Andrew, "the cordial!—sure I believe every word of what you've been telling me is as true as gospel; ain't there hundreds, ay, thousands, at this moment, on Ireland's blessed ground, that can tell the same story? But the cordial!—and to think of your never owning it before; is it ginger, or aniseed, or peppermint?"

"None of these—and yet it's the *rale* thing, my boy."

"Well, then," persisted Andrew, "let's have a drop of it; you're not going, I'm sure, to drink by yourself—and as *I've broke the afternoon*——"

A heavy shadow passed over James's face, for he saw that there must have been something hotter than ginger in the *"Temperance Cordial,"* as it is falsely called, that Andrew had taken; else he would have endeavoured to redeem lost time, not to waste more; and he thought how much better the REAL Temperance Cordial was, that, instead of exciting the brain, only warms the heart.

"No," he replied, after a pause, "I must go and finish what I was about; but this evening, at seven o'clock, meet me at the end of our lane, and then I'll be very happy of your company."

Andrew was sorely puzzled to discover what James's cordial could be, and was forced to confess to himself, he hoped it would be different from what he had taken that afternoon, which certainly made him feel confused and inactive.

At the appointed hour the friends met in the lane.

"Which way do we go?" inquired Andrew.

"Home," was James's brief reply.

"Oh, you *take* it at home," said Andrew.

"I *make* it home," answered James.

"Well," observed Andrew, "that's very good of the woman *that owns ye*. Now, mine takes on so about a drop of anything, that she's as hard almost on the cordials as she used to be on the whisky."

"My Mary helps to make mine," observed James.

"And do you bottle it, or keep it on draught!" inquired Andrew, very much interested in the "cordial" question.

James laughed very heartily at this, and answered—

"Oh, I keep mine on draught—always on draught; there's nothing like having plenty of a good thing, so I keep mine always on draught:" and then James laughed again, and heartily.

James's cottage door was open, and, as they approached it, they saw a good deal of what was going forward within. A square table, placed in the centre of the little kitchen, was covered by a clean white cloth—knives, forks, and plates, for the whole family, were ranged upon it in excellent order; the teapot stood, triumphant, in the centre,—the hearth had been swept, the house was clean, the children rosy, well dressed, and all doing something. "Mary," whom her husband had characterized as "the patient," was busy and bustling, in the very act of adding to the tea, which was steaming on the table, with the substantial accompaniments of fried eggs and bacon, and a large dish of potatoes. When the children saw their father, they ran to meet him with a great shout, and clung around to tell him all they had done that day. The eldest girl declared she had achieved the heel of a stocking; one boy wanted his father to come and see how straight he had planted the cabbages; while another avowed his proficiency in addition, and volunteered to do a sum instanter upon a slate he had just cleaned. Happiness in a cottage seems always more real than its does in a gorgeous dwelling. It is not wasted in large rooms—it is concentrated—a great deal of love in a small space—a great, *great* deal of joy and hope within narrow walls, and compressed, as it were, by a low roof. Is it not a blessed thing that the most moderate means become enlarged by the affections ?— that the love of a peasant, within his sphere, is as deep, as fervent, as true, as lasting, as sweet, as the love of a prince ?—that all our best and purest affections will grow and expand in the poorest *worldly* soil ?—and that we need not be rich to be happy? James felt all this, and more, when he entered his cottage, and was thankful to God who had opened his eyes, and taught him what a number of this world's gifts were within his humble reach, to be enjoyed without sin. He stood—a poor but happy father—within the sacred temple of his home; and Andrew had the warm heart of an Irishman beating in his bosom, shared his joy.

"I told you," said James, "I had the *true Temperance Cordial* at home. Do you not see it in the simple prosperity by which, owing to the blessings of temperance, I am surrounded? Do you not see it in the rosy cheeks of my children—in the smiling eyes of my wife?' Did I not say truly that she helped to make it? Is not this a true cordial?" he continued, while his own eyes glistened with manly tears; "is not the prosperity of this cottage a *true Temperance Cordial?*—and is it not *always on draught*, flowing from an ever-filling, fountain?   Am I not right, Andrew ; and will you not forthwith take my receipt, and make it for yourself?   You will never wish for any other : it is warmer than ginger, and sweeter than aniseed.   I am sure you will agree with me, that a loving wife, in the enjoyment of the humble comforts which an industrious, *sober* husband can bestow, smiling, healthy, well-clad children, and a clean cabin, where the fear of God banishes all other fears, make

THE TRUE TEMPERANCE CORDIAL."

PRINTED BY BALLANTYNE, HANSON AND CO.
LONDON AND EDINBURGH

June, 1891.

𝔄 𝔏𝔦𝔰𝔱 𝔬𝔣 𝔅𝔬𝔬𝔨𝔰

PUBLISHED BY

CHATTO & WINDUS,

214, Piccadilly, London, W.

Sold by all Booksellers, or sent post-free for the published price by the Publishers.

ABOUT.—THE FELLAH: An Egyptian Novel. By EDMOND ABOUT. Translated by Sir RANDAL ROBERTS. Post 8vo, illustrated boards, **2s.**

ADAMS (W. DAVENPORT), WORKS BY.
A DICTIONARY OF THE DRAMA. Being a comprehensive Guide to the Plays, Playwrights, Players, and Playhouses of the United Kingdom and America. Crown 8vo, half-bound, **12s. 6d.** *[Preparing.*
QUIPS AND QUIDDITIES. Selected by W. D. ADAMS. Post 8vo. cloth limp, **2s. 6d.**

ADAMS (W. H. D.).—WITCH, WARLOCK, AND MAGICIAN: Historical Sketches of Magic and Witchcraft in England and Scotland. By W. H. DAVENPORT ADAMS. Demy 8vo, cloth extra, **12s.**

AGONY COLUMN (THE) OF "THE TIMES," from 1800 to 1870. Edited, with an Introduction, by ALICE CLAY. Post 8vo, cloth limp, **2s. 6d.**

AIDE (HAMILTON), WORKS BY. Post 8vo, illustrated boards, **2s.** each.
CARR OF CARRLYON. | CONFIDENCES.

ALBERT.—BROOKE FINCHLEY'S DAUGHTER. By MARY ALBERT. Post 8vo, picture boards, **2s.**; cloth limp, **2s. 6d.**

ALEXANDER (MRS.), NOVELS BY. Post 8vo, illustrated boards, **2s.** each.
MAID, WIFE, OR WIDOW? | VALERIE'S FATE.

ALLEN (GRANT), WORKS BY. Crown 8vo, cloth extra, **6s.** each.
THE EVOLUTIONIST AT LARGE. | COLIN CLOUT'S CALENDAR.
VIGNETTES FROM NATURE.

Crown 8vo, cloth extra, **6s.** each; post 8vo, illustrated boards, **2s.** each.
STRANGE STORIES. With a Frontispiece by GEORGE DU MAURIER.
THE BECKONING HAND. With a Frontispiece by TOWNLEY GREEN.

Crown 8vo, cloth extra, **3s. 6d.** each; post 8vo, illustrated boards, **2s.** each.
PHILISTIA. | FOR MAIMIE'S SAKE. | THIS MORTAL COIL.
BABYLON. | IN ALL SHADES. | THE TENTS OF SHEM.
| THE DEVIL'S DIE. |

THE GREAT TABOO. Crown 8vo, cloth extra, **3s. 6d.**
DUMARESQ'S DAUGHTER. Three Vols., crown 8vo. *[Shortly.*

AMERICAN LITERATURE, A LIBRARY OF, from the Earliest Settlement to the Present Time. Compiled and Edited by EDMUND CLARENCE STEDMAN and ELLEN MACKAY HUTCHINSON. Eleven Vols., royal 8vo, cloth extra. A few copies are for sale by Messrs. CHATTO & WINDUS (published in New York by C. L. WEBSTER & Co.), price **£6 12s.** the set.

ARCHITECTURAL STYLES, A HANDBOOK OF. By A. ROSENGARTEN. Translated by W. COLLETT-SANDARS. With 639 Illusts. Cr. 8vo, cl. ex., **7s. 6d.**

ART (THE) OF AMUSING: A Collection of Graceful Arts, GAMES, Tricks, Puzzles, and Charades. By FRANK BELLEW. 300 Illusts. Cr. 8vo, cl. ex., **4s. 6d.**

ARNOLD (EDWIN LESTER), WORKS BY.
THE WONDERFUL ADVENTURES OF PHRA THE PHŒNICIAN. With Introduc-
tion by Sir EDWIN ARNOLD, and 12 Illusts. by H. M. PAGET. Cr. 8vo, cl., **3s. 6d.**
BIRD LIFE IN ENGLAND. Crown 8vo, cloth extra, **6s.**

ARTEMUS WARD'S WORKS: The Works of CHARLES FARRER BROWNE,
better known as ARTEMUS WARD. With Portrait and Facsimile. Crown 8vo,
cloth extra, **7s. 6d.**—Also a POPULAR EDITION, post 8vo, picture boards, **2s.**
THE GENIAL SHOWMAN : Life and Adventures of ARTEMUS WARD. By EDWARD
P. HINGSTON. With a Frontispiece. Crown 8vo, cloth extra. **3s. 6d.**

ASHTON (JOHN), WORKS BY. Crown 8vo, cloth extra, **7s. 6d.** each.
HISTORY OF THE CHAP-BOOKS OF THE 18th CENTURY. With 334 Illusts.
SOCIAL LIFE IN THE REIGN OF QUEEN ANNE. With 85 Illustrations.
HUMOUR, WIT, AND SATIRE OF SEVENTEENTH CENTURY. With 82 Illusts.
ENGLISH CARICATURE AND SATIRE ON NAPOLEON THE FIRST. 115 Illusts.
MODERN STREET BALLADS. With 57 Illustrations.

BACTERIA.— A SYNOPSIS OF THE BACTERIA AND YEAST
FUNGI AND ALLIED SPECIES. By W. B. GROVE, B.A. With 87 Illustrations.
Crown 8vo, cloth extra, **3s. 6d.**

BARDSLEY (REV. C. W.), WORKS BY.
ENGLISH SURNAMES: Their Sources and Significations. Cr. 8vo, cloth, **7s. 6d.**
CURIOSITIES OF PURITAN NOMENCLATURE. Crown 8vo, cloth extra, **6s.**

BARING GOULD (S., Author of "John Herring," &c.), NOVELS BY.
Crown 8vo, cloth extra, **3s. 6d.** each; post 8vo, illustrated boards, **2s.** each.
RED SPIDER. | EVE.

BARRETT (FRANK, Author of "Lady Biddy Fane,") NOVELS BY.
Post 8vo, illustrated boards, **2s.** each; cloth, **2s. 6d.** each.
FETTERED FOR LIFE. | BETWEEN LIFE AND DEATH.

BEACONSFIELD, LORD : A Biography. By T. P. O'CONNOR, M.P.
Sixth Edition, with an Introduction. Crown 8vo, cloth extra, **5s.**

BEAUCHAMP.—GRANTLEY GRANGE: A Novel. By SHELSLEY
BEAUCHAMP. Post 8vo, illustrated boards, **2s.**

BEAUTIFUL PICTURES BY BRITISH ARTISTS : A Gathering of
Favourites from our Picture Galleries, beautifully engraved on Steel. With Notices
of the Artists by SYDNEY ARMYTAGE, M.A. Imperial 4to, cloth extra, gilt edges, **21s.**

BECHSTEIN.—AS PRETTY AS SEVEN, and other German Stories.
Collected by LUDWIG BECHSTEIN. With Additional Tales by the Brothers GRIMM,
and 98 Illustrations by RICHTER. Square 8vo, cloth extra, **6s. 6d.**; gilt edges. **7s. 6d.**

BEERBOHM.—WANDERINGS IN PATAGONIA ; or, Life among the
Ostrich Hunters. By JULIUS BEERBOHM. With Illusts. Cr. 8vo, cl. extra, **3s. 6d.**

BESANT (WALTER), NOVELS BY.
Cr. 8vo, cl. ex., **3s. 6d.** each; post 8vo, illust. bds., **2s.** each; cl. limp, **2s. 6d.** each.
ALL SORTS AND CONDITIONS OF MEN. With Illustrations by FRED. BARNARD.
THE CAPTAINS' ROOM, &c. With Frontispiece by E. J. WHEELER.
ALL IN A GARDEN FAIR. With 6 Illustrations by HARRY FURNISS.
DOROTHY FORSTER. With Frontispiece by CHARLES GREEN.
UNCLE JACK, and other Stories. | CHILDREN OF GIBEON.
THE WORLD WENT VERY WELL THEN. With 12 Illustrations by A. FORESTIER.
HERR PAULUS: His Rise, his Greatness, and his Fall.
FOR FAITH AND FREEDOM. With Illustrations by A. FORESTIER and F. WADDY.

Crown 8vo, cloth extra, **3s. 6d.** each.
TO CALL HER MINE, &c. With 9 Illustrations by A. FORESTIER.
THE BELL OF ST. PAUL'S.
ARMOREL OF LYONESSE: A Romance of To-day. With 12 Illusts. by F. BARNARD.
THE HOLY ROSE, &c. With Frontispiece by F. BARNARD.
ST. KATHERINE'S BY THE TOWER. With 12 full-page Illustrations by C.
GREEN. Three Vols., crown 8vo.
FIFTY YEARS AGO. With 137 Plates and Woodcuts. Demy 8vo, cloth extra, **16s.**
THE EULOGY OF RICHARD JEFFERIES. With Portrait. Cr. 8vo, cl. extra, **6s.**
THE ART OF FICTION. Demy 8vo, **1s.**

BESANT (WALTER) AND JAMES RICE, NOVELS BY.
Cr. 8vo, cl. ex., **3s. 6d.** each ; post 8vo, illust. bds., **2s.** each; cl. limp, **2s. 6d.** each.

READY-MONEY MORTIBOY.	BY CELIA'S ARBOUR.
MY LITTLE GIRL.	THE CHAPLAIN OF THE FLEET.
WITH HARP AND CROWN.	THE SEAMY SIDE.
THIS SON OF VULCAN.	THE CASE OF MR. LUCRAFT, &c.
THE GOLDEN BUTTERFLY.	'TWAS IN TRAFALGAR'S BAY, &c.
THE MONKS OF THELEMA.	THE TEN YEARS' TENANT, &c.

. There is also a LIBRARY EDITION of the above Twelve Volumes, handsomely set in new type, on a large crown 8vo page, and bound in cloth extra, **6s.** each.

BENNETT (W. C., LL.D.), WORKS BY. Post 8vo, cloth limp, **2s.** each.
A BALLAD HISTORY OF ENGLAND. | SONGS FOR SAILORS.

BEWICK (THOMAS) AND HIS PUPILS. By AUSTIN DOBSON. With 95 Illustrations. Square 8vo, cloth extra, **6s.**

BLACKBURN'S (HENRY) ART HANDBOOKS.
ACADEMY NOTES, separate years, from 1875-1887, 1889, and 1890, each **1s.**
ACADEMY NOTES, 1891. With Illustrations. **1s.**
ACADEMY NOTES, 1875-79. Complete in One Vol., with 600 Illusts. Cloth limp, **6s.**
ACADEMY NOTES, 1880-84. Complete in One Vol., with 700 Illusts. Cloth limp, **6s.**
GROSVENOR NOTES, 1877. **6d.**
GROSVENOR NOTES, separate years, from 1878 to 1890, each **1s.**
GROSVENOR NOTES, Vol. I., 1877-82. With 300 Illusts. Demy 8vo, cloth limp, **6s.**
GROSVENOR NOTES, Vol. II., 1883-87. With 300 Illusts. Demy 8vo, cloth limp, **6s.**
THE NEW GALLERY, 1888-1890. With numerous Illustrations, each **1s.**
THE NEW GALLERY, 1891. With Illustrations. **1s.**
ENGLISH PICTURES AT THE NATIONAL GALLERY. 114 Illustrations. **1s.**
OLD MASTERS AT THE NATIONAL GALLERY. 128 Illustrations. **1s. 6d.**
ILLUSTRATED CATALOGUE TO THE NATIONAL GALLERY. 242 Illusts. cl., **3s.**
THE PARIS SALON, 1891. With Facsimile Sketches. **3s.**
THE PARIS SOCIETY OF FINE ARTS, 1891. With Sketches. **3s. 6d.**

BLAKE (WILLIAM): India-proof Etchings from his Works by WILLIAM BELL SCOTT. With descriptive Text. Folio, half-bound boards, **21s.**

BLIND.—THE ASCENT OF MAN: A Poem. By MATHILDE BLIND. Crown 8vo, printed on hand-made paper. cloth extra, **5s.**

BOURNE (H. R. FOX), WORKS BY.
ENGLISH MERCHANTS: Memoirs in Illustration of the Progress of British Commerce. With numerous Illustrations. Crown 8vo, cloth extra, **7s. 6d.**
ENGLISH NEWSPAPERS: The History of Journalism. Two Vols., demy 8vo, cl., **25s.**
THE OTHER SIDE OF THE EMIN PASHA RELIEF EXPEDITION. Crown 8vo, cloth extra, **6s.**

BOWERS' (G.) HUNTING SKETCHES. Oblong 4to, hf.-bd. bds., **21s.** each.
CANTERS IN CRAMPSHIRE. | LEAVES FROM A HUNTING JOURNAL.

BOYLE (FREDERICK), WORKS BY. Post 8vo, illustrated boards, **2s.** each.
CHRONICLES OF NO-MAN'S LAND. | CAMP NOTES.
SAVAGE LIFE. Crown 8vo, cloth extra, **3s. 6d.** ; post 8vo, picture boards, **2s.**

BRAND'S OBSERVATIONS ON POPULAR ANTIQUITIES ; chiefly illustrating the Origin of our Vulgar Customs, Ceremonies, and Superstitions. With the Additions of Sir HENRY ELLIS, and Illustrations. Cr. 8vo. cloth extra, **7s. 6d.**

BREWER (REV. DR.), WORKS BY.
THE READER'S HANDBOOK OF ALLUSIONS, REFERENCES, PLOTS, AND STORIES. Fifteenth Thousand. Crown 8vo, cloth extra, **7s. 6d.**
AUTHORS AND THEIR WORKS, WITH THE DATES: Being the Appendices to "The Reader's Handbook," separately printed. Crown 8vo, cloth limp, **2s.**
A DICTIONARY OF MIRACLES. Crown 8vo, cloth extra, **7s. 6d.**

BREWSTER (SIR DAVID), WORKS BY. Post 8vo, cl. ex., **4s. 6d.** each.
MORE WORLDS THAN ONE: Creed of Philosopher and Hope of Christian. Plates.
THE MARTYRS OF SCIENCE: GALILEO, TYCHO BRAHE, and KEPLER. With Portraits.
LETTERS ON NATURAL MAGIC. With numerous Illustrations.

BRET HARTE, WORKS BY.

LIBRARY EDITION, Complete in Six Volumes, crown 8vo, cloth extra, **6s.** each.
BRET HARTE'S COLLECTED WORKS. Arranged and Revised by the Author.
Vol. I. COMPLETE POETICAL AND DRAMATIC WORKS. With Steel Portrait.
Vol. II. LUCK OF ROARING CAMP—BOHEMIAN PAPERS—AMERICAN LEGENDS.
Vol. III. TALES OF THE ARGONAUTS—EASTERN SKETCHES.
Vol. IV. GABRIEL CONROY.
Vol. V. STORIES—CONDENSED NOVELS, &c.
Vol. VI. TALES OF THE PACIFIC SLOPE.

THE SELECT WORKS OF BRET HARTE, in Prose and Poetry. With Introductory
Essay by J. M. BELLEW, Portrait of Author, and 50 Illusts. Cr. 8vo, cl. ex., **7s. 6d.**
BRET HARTE'S POETICAL WORKS. Hand-made paper & buckram. Cr. 8vo, **4s. 6d.**
THE QUEEN OF THE PIRATE ISLE. With 28 original Drawings by KATE
GREENAWAY, reproduced in Colours by EDMUND EVANS. Small 4to, cloth, **5s.**

Crown 8vo, cloth extra, **3s. 6d.** each.
A WAIF OF THE PLAINS. With 60 Illustrations by STANLEY L. WOOD.
A WARD OF THE GOLDEN GATE. With 59 Illustrations by STANLEY L. WOOD.
A SAPPHO OF GREEN SPRINGS, &c. With Two Illustrations by HUME NISBET.
COLONEL STARBOTTLE'S CLIENT, &c. With Front. by F. BARNARD. [*Preparing.*

Post 8vo, illustrated boards, **2s.** each.

GABRIEL CONROY.	THE LUCK OF ROARING CAMP, &c.
AN HEIRESS OF RED DOG, &c.	CALIFORNIAN STORIES.

Post 8vo, illustrated boards, **2s.** each; cloth limp, **2s. 6d.** each.

FLIP.	MARUJA.	A PHYLLIS OF THE SIERRAS.

Fcap. 8vo. picture cover, **1s.** each.
THE TWINS OF TABLE MOUNTAIN. | JEFF BRIGGS'S LOVE STORY.

BRILLAT-SAVARIN.—GASTRONOMY AS A FINE ART. By BRILLAT-
SAVARIN. Translated by R. E. ANDERSON, M.A. Post 8vo, half-bound. **2s.**

BRYDGES.—UNCLE SAM AT HOME. By HAROLD BRYDGES. Post
8vo, illustrated boards, **2s.**; cloth limp, **2s. 6d.**

BUCHANAN'S (ROBERT) WORKS. Crown 8vo, cloth extra, **6s.** each.
SELECTED POEMS OF ROBERT BUCHANAN. With Frontispiece by T. DALZIEL.
THE EARTHQUAKE; or, Six Days and a Sabbath.
THE CITY OF DREAM: An Epic Poem. With Two Illustrations by P. MACNAB.
THE OUTCAST: A Rhyme for the Time. With 12 Full-page Illustrations and
numerous Vignettes. Crown 8vo, cloth extra, **8s.**
ROBERT BUCHANAN'S COMPLETE POETICAL WORKS. With Steel-plate Por-
trait. Crown 8vo, cloth extra, **7s. 6d.**

Crown 8vo, cloth extra, **3s. 6d.** each; post 8vo, illustrated boards, **2s.** each.

THE SHADOW OF THE SWORD.	LOVE ME FOR EVER. Frontispiece.
A CHILD OF NATURE. Frontispiece.	ANNAN WATER. FOXGLOVE MANOR.
GOD AND THE MAN. With 11 Illus-	THE NEW ABELARD.
trations by FRED. BARNARD.	MATT: A Story of a Caravan. Front.
THE MARTYRDOM OF MADELINE.	THE MASTER OF THE MINE. Front.
With Frontispiece by A. W. COOPER.	THE HEIR OF LINNE.

BURTON (CAPTAIN).—THE BOOK OF THE SWORD: Being a
History of the Sword and its Use in all Countries, from the Earliest Times. By
RICHARD F. BURTON. With over 400 Illustrations. Square 8vo, cloth extra **32s.**

BURTON (ROBERT).
THE ANATOMY OF MELANCHOLY: A New Edition, with translations of the
Classical Extracts. Demy 8vo, cloth extra, **7s. 6d.**
MELANCHOLY ANATOMISED Being an Abridgment, for popular use, of BURTON'S
ANATOMY OF MELANCHOLY. Post 8vo, cloth limp, **2s. 6d.**

CAINE (T. HALL), NOVELS BY. Crown 8vo, cloth extra, **3s. 6d.** each
post 8vo, illustrated boards, **2s.** each; cloth limp, **2s. 6d.** each.
SHADOW OF A CRIME. | A SON OF HAGAR. | THE DEEMSTER.

CAMERON (COMMANDER).—THE CRUISE OF THE "BLACK
PRINCE" PRIVATEER. By V. LOVETT CAMERON, R.N., C.B. With Two Illustrations by P. MACNAB. Crown 8vo, cloth extra, **5s.**; post 8vo, illustrated boards, **2s.**

CAMERON (MRS. H. LOVETT), NOVELS BY.
Crown 8vo, cloth extra, **3s. 6d.** each; post 8vo, illustrated boards, **2s.** each.
JULIET'S GUARDIAN. | DECEIVERS EVER.

CARLYLE (THOMAS) ON THE CHOICE OF BOOKS. With Life by R. H. Shepherd, and Three Illustrations. Post 8vo, cloth extra, 1s. 6d.
THE CORRESPONDENCE OF THOMAS CARLYLE AND RALPH WALDO EMERSON, 1834 to 1872. Edited by Charles Eliot Norton. With Portraits. Two Vols., crown 8vo, cloth extra, 24s.

CARLYLE (JANE WELSH), LIFE OF. By Mrs. Alexander Ireland. With Portrait and Facsimile Letter. Small demy 8vo, cloth extra, 7s. 6d.

CHAPMAN'S (GEORGE) WORKS. Vol. I. contains the Plays complete, including the doubtful ones. Vol. II., the Poems and Minor Translations, with an Introductory Essay by Algernon Charles Swinburne. Vol. III., the Translations of the Iliad and Odyssey. Three Vols., crown 8vo, cloth extra, 6s. each.

CHATTO AND JACKSON.—A TREATISE ON WOOD ENGRAVING, Historical and Practical. By William Andrew Chatto and John Jackson. With an Additional Chapter by Henry G. Bohn, and 450 fine Illusts. Large 4to. hf.-bd., 28s.

CHAUCER FOR CHILDREN: A Golden Key. By Mrs. H. R. Haweis. With 8 Coloured Plates and 30 Woodcuts. Small 4to, cloth extra, 6s.
CHAUCER FOR SCHOOLS. By Mrs. H. R. Haweis. Demy 8vo, cloth limp, 2s. 6d.

CLARE.—FOR THE LOVE OF A LASS: A Tale of Tynedale. By Austin Clare. Post 8vo, picture boards, 2s.; cloth limp, 2s. 6d.

CLIVE (MRS. ARCHER), NOVELS BY. Post 8vo, illust. boards, 2s. each.
PAUL FERROLL. | WHY PAUL FERROLL KILLED HIS WIFE.

CLODD (EDW., F.R.A.S.).—MYTHS AND DREAMS. Cr. 8vo, cl. ex., 5s.

COBBAN.—THE CURE OF SOULS: A Story. By J. Maclaren Cobban. Post 8vo, illustrated boards, 2s.

COLEMAN (JOHN), WORKS BY.
PLAYERS AND PLAYWRIGHTS I HAVE KNOWN. Two Vo's, 8vo, cloth, 24s.
CURLY: An Actor's Story. With 21 Illusts. by J. C. Dollman. Cr. 8vo, cl, 1s. 6d.

COLLINS (C. ALLSTON).—THE BAR SINISTER. Post 8vo, 2s.

COLLINS (MORTIMER AND FRANCES), NOVELS BY.
Crown 8vo, cloth extra, 3s. 6d. each; post 8vo, illustrated boards, 2s. each.
SWEET ANNE PAGE. | FROM MIDNIGHT TO MIDNIGHT. | TRANSMIGRATION.
BLACKSMITH AND SCHOLAR. | YOU PLAY ME FALSE. | VILLAGE COMEDY.
Post 8vo, illustrated boards, 2s. each.
A FIGHT WITH FORTUNE. | SWEET AND TWENTY. | FRANCES.

COLLINS (WILKIE), NOVELS BY.
Cr. 8vo, cl. ex., 3s. 6d. each; post 8vo, illust. bds., 2s. each; cl. limp, 2s. 6d. each.
ANTONINA. With a Frontispiece by Sir John Gilbert, R.A.
BASIL. Illustrated by Sir John Gilbert, R.A., and J. Mahoney.
HIDE AND SEEK. Illustrated by Sir John Gilbert, R.A., and J. Mahoney.
AFTER DARK. With Illustrations by A. B. Houghton.
THE DEAD SECRET. With a Frontispiece by Sir John Gilbert, R.A.
QUEEN OF HEARTS. With a Frontispiece by Sir John Gilbert, R.A.
THE WOMAN IN WHITE. With Illusts. by Sir J. Gilbert, R.A., and F. A. Fraser.
NO NAME. With Illustrations by Sir J. E. Millais, R.A., and A. W. Cooper.
MY MISCELLANIES. With a Steel-plate Portrait of Wilkie Collins.
ARMADALE. With Illustrations by G. H. Thomas.
THE MOONSTONE. With Illustrations by G. Du Maurier and F. A. Fraser.
MAN AND WIFE. With Illustrations by William Small.
POOR MISS FINCH. Illustrated by G. Du Maurier and Edward Hughes.
MISS OR MRS.? With Illusts. by S. L. Fildes, R.A., and Henry Woods, A.R.A.
THE NEW MAGDALEN. Illustrated by G. Du Maurier and C. S. Reinhardt.
THE FROZEN DEEP. Illustrated by G. Du Maurier and J. Mahoney.
THE LAW AND THE LADY. Illusts. by S. L. Fildes, R.A., and Sydney Hall.
THE TWO DESTINIES.
THE HAUNTED HOTEL. Illustrated by Arthur Hopkins.
THE FALLEN LEAVES. | HEART AND SCIENCE. | THE EVIL GENIUS.
JEZEBEL'S DAUGHTER. | "I SAY NO." | LITTLE NOVELS.
THE BLACK ROBE. | A ROGUE'S LIFE. | THE LEGACY OF CAIN.
BLIND LOVE. With Preface by Walter Besant, and Illusts. by A. Forestier.

COLLINS (CHURTON).—A MONOGRAPH ON DEAN SWIFT. By J. Churton Collins. Crown 8vo, cloth extra, 8s. [Shortly

COLMAN'S HUMOROUS WORKS: "Broad Grins," "My Nightgown and Slippers," and other Humorous Works of GEORGE COLMAN. With Life by G. B. BUCKSTONE, and Frontispiece by HOGARTH. Crown 8vo, cloth extra, 7s. 6d.

COLQUHOUN.—EVERY INCH A SOLDIER: A Novel. By M. J. COLQUHOUN. Post 8vo, illustrated boards, 2s.

CONVALESCENT COOKERY: A Family Handbook. By CATHERINE RYAN. Crown 8vo, 1s.; cloth limp, 1s. 6d.

CONWAY (MONCURE D.), WORKS BY.
DEMONOLOGY AND DEVIL-LORE. With 65 Illustrations. Third Edition. Two Vols., demy 8vo, cloth extra, 28s.
A NECKLACE OF STORIES. 25 Illusts. by W. J. HENNESSY. Sq. 8vo, cloth, 6s.
PINE AND PALM: A Novel. Two Vols., crown 8vo, cloth extra, 21s.
GEORGE WASHINGTON'S RULES OF CIVILITY Traced to their Sources and Restored. Fcap. 8vo, Japanese vellum, 2s. 6d.

COOK (DUTTON), NOVELS BY.
PAUL FOSTER'S DAUGHTER. Cr. 8vo, cl. ex., 3s. 6d.; post 8vo, illust. boards, 2s.
LEO. Post 8vo, illustrated boards, 2s.

CORNWALL.—POPULAR ROMANCES OF THE WEST OF ENG-LAND; or, The Drolls, Traditions, and Superstitions of Old Cornwall. Collected by ROBERT HUNT, F.R.S. Two Steel-plates by GEO. CRUIKSHANK. Cr. 8vo, cl., 7s. 6d.

CRADDOCK.—THE PROPHET OF THE GREAT SMOKY MOUN-TAINS. By CHARLES EGBERT CRADDOCK. Post 8vo, Illust. bds., 2s.; cl. limp, 2s. 6d.

CRUIKSHANK'S COMIC ALMANACK. Complete in TWO SERIES: The FIRST from 1835 to 1843; the SECOND from 1844 to 1853. A Gathering of the BEST HUMOUR of THACKERAY, HOOD, MAYHEW, ALBERT SMITH, A'BECKETT, ROBERT BROUGH, &c. With numerous Steel Engravings and Woodcuts by CRUIK-SHANK, HINE, LANDELLS, &c. Two Vols., crown 8vo, cloth gilt, 7s. 6d. each.
THE LIFE OF GEORGE CRUIKSHANK. By BLANCHARD JERROLD. With 84 Illustrations and a Bibliography. Crown 8vo, cloth extra, 7s. 6d.

CUMMING (C. F. GORDON), WORKS BY. Demy 8vo, cl. ex., 8s. 6d. each.
IN THE HEBRIDES. With Autotype Facsimile and 23 Illustrations.
IN THE HIMALAYAS AND ON THE INDIAN PLAINS. With 42 Illustrations.
VIA CORNWALL TO EGYPT. With Photogravure Frontis. Demy 8vo, cl., 7s. 6d.

CUSSANS.—A HANDBOOK OF HERALDRY; with Instructions for Tracing Pedigrees and Deciphering Ancient MSS., &c. By JOHN E. CUSSANS. With 408 Woodcuts, Two Coloured and Two Plain Plates. Crown 8vo, cloth extra, 7s. 6d.

CYPLES (W.)—HEARTS of GOLD. Cr. 8vo, cl., 3s. 6d.; post 8vo, bds., 2s.

DANIEL.—MERRIE ENGLAND IN THE OLDEN TIME. By GEORGE DANIEL. With Illustrations by ROBERT CRUIKSHANK. Crown 8vo, cloth extra, 3s. 6d.

DAUDET.—THE EVANGELIST; or, Port Salvation. By ALPHONSE DAUDET. Crown 8vo, cloth extra, 3s. 6d.; post 8vo, illustrated boards, 2s.

DAVENANT.—HINTS FOR PARENTS ON THE CHOICE OF A PRO-FESSION FOR THEIR SONS. By F. DAVENANT, M.A. Post 8vo, 1s.; cl., 1s. 6d.

DAVIES (DR. N. E. YORKE-), WORKS BY.
Crown 8vo, 1s. each; cloth limp, 1s. 6d. each.
ONE THOUSAND MEDICAL MAXIMS AND SURGICAL HINTS.
NURSERY HINTS: A Mother's Guide in Health and Disease.
FOODS FOR THE FAT: A Treatise on Corpulency, and a Dietary for its Cure.
AIDS TO LONG LIFE. Crown 8vo, 2s.; cloth limp, 2s. 6d.

DAVIES' (SIR JOHN) COMPLETE POETICAL WORKS, including Psalms I. to L. in Verse, and other hitherto Unpublished MSS., for the first time Collected and Edited, with Memorial-Introduction and Notes, by the Rev. A. B. GROSART, D.D. Two Vols., crown 8vo, cloth boards, 12s.

DAWSON.—THE FOUNTAIN OF YOUTH: A Novel of Adventure. By ERASMUS DAWSON, M.B. Edited by PAUL DEVON. With Two Illustrations by HUME NISBET. Crown 8vo, cloth extra, 3s. 6d.

DE MAISTRE.—A JOURNEY ROUND MY ROOM. By Xavier de Maistre. Translated by Henry Attwell. Post 8vo, cloth limp, 2s. 6d.

DE MILLE.—A CASTLE IN SPAIN. By James De Mille. With a Frontispiece. Crown 8vo, cloth extra, 3s. 6d.; post 8vo, illustrated boards, 2s.

DERBY (THE).—THE BLUE RIBBON OF THE TURF: A Chronicle of the Race for The Derby, from Diomed to Donovan. With Notes on the Winning Horses, the Men who trained them, Jockeys who rode them, and Gentlemen to whom they belonged; also Notices of the Betting and Betting Men of the period, and Brief Accounts of The Oaks. By Louis Henry Curzon. Cr. 8vo, cloth extra, 6s.

DERWENT (LEITH), NOVELS BY. Cr. 8vo, cl., 3s. 6d. ea.; post 8vo, bds., 2s. ea.
OUR LADY OF TEARS. | CIRCE'S LOVERS.

DICKENS (CHARLES), NOVELS BY. Post 8vo, illustrated boards, 2s. each.
SKETCHES BY BOZ. | NICHOLAS NICKLEBY.
THE PICKWICK PAPERS. | OLIVER TWIST.
THE SPEECHES OF CHARLES DICKENS, 1841-1870. With a New Bibliography. Edited by Richard Herne Shepherd. Crown 8vo, cloth extra, 6s.—Also a Smaller Edition, in the *Mayfair Library*, post 8vo, cloth limp, 2s. 6d.
ABOUT ENGLAND WITH DICKENS. By Alfred Rimmer. With 57 Illustrations by C. A. Vanderhoof, Alfred Rimmer, and others. Sq. 8vo, cloth extra, 7s. 6d.

DICTIONARIES.
A DICTIONARY OF MIRACLES: Imitative, Realistic, and Dogmatic. By the Rev E. C. Brewer, LL.D. Crown 8vo, cloth extra, 7s. 6d.
THE READER'S HANDBOOK OF ALLUSIONS, REFERENCES, PLOTS, AND STORIES. By the Rev. E. C. Brewer, LL.D. With an English Bibliography. Fifteenth Thousand. Crown 8vo, cloth extra, 7s. 6d.
AUTHORS AND THEIR WORKS, WITH THE DATES. Cr. 8vo, cloth limp, 2s.
FAMILIAR SHORT SAYINGS OF GREAT MEN. With Historical and Explanatory Notes. By Samuel A. Bent, A.M. Crown 8vo, cloth extra, 7s. 6d.
SLANG DICTIONARY: Etymological, Historical, and Anecdotal. Cr. 8vo, cl., 6s. 6d.
WOMEN OF THE DAY: A Biographical Dictionary. By F. Hays. Cr. 8vo, cl., 5s.
WORDS, FACTS, AND PHRASES: A Dictionary of Curious, Quaint, and Out-of-the-Way Matters. By Eliezer Edwards. Crown 8vo, cloth extra, 7s. 6d.

DIDEROT.—THE PARADOX OF ACTING. Translated, with Annotations, from Diderot's "Le Paradoxe sur le Comédien," by Walter Herries Pollock. With a Preface by Henry Irving. Crown 8vo, parchment, 4s. 6d.

DOBSON (AUSTIN), WORKS BY.
THOMAS BEWICK & HIS PUPILS. With 95 Illustrations. Square 8vo, cloth, 6s.
FOUR FRENCHWOMEN: Mademoiselle de Corday; Madame Roland; The Princess de Lamballe; Madame de Genlis. Fcap. 8vo, hf.-roxburghe, 2s. 6d.

DOBSON (W. T.), WORKS BY. Post 8vo, cloth limp, 2s. 6d. each.
LITERARY FRIVOLITIES, FANCIES, FOLLIES, AND FROLICS.
POETICAL INGENUITIES AND ECCENTRICITIES.

DONOVAN (DICK), DETECTIVE STORIES BY.
Post 8vo, illustrated boards, 2s. each; cloth limp, 2s. 6d. each.
THE MAN-HUNTER. | TRACKED AND TAKEN.
CAUGHT AT LAST! | WHO POISONED HETTY DUNCAN?
A DETECTIVE'S TRIUMPHS. | [*Preparing.*
THE MAN FROM MANCHESTER. With 23 Illustrations. Crown 8vo, cloth, 6s.; post 8vo, illustrated boards, 2s.

DOYLE (A. CONAN, Author of "Micah Clarke"), NOVELS BY.
THE FIRM OF GIRDLESTONE. Crown 8vo, cloth extra, 6s.
STRANGE SECRETS. Told by Conan Doyle, Percy Fitzgerald, Florence Marryat, &c. Cr. 8vo, cl. ex., Eight Illusts., 6s.; post 8vo, illust. bds., 2s.

DRAMATISTS, THE OLD. With Vignette Portraits. Cr. 8vo, cl. ex., 6s. per Vol.
BEN JONSON'S WORKS. With Notes Critical and Explanatory, and a Biographical Memoir by Wm. Gifford. Edited by Col. Cunningham. Three Vols.
CHAPMAN'S WORKS. Complete in Three Vols. Vol. I. contains the Plays complete; Vol. II., Poems and Minor Translations, with an Introductory Essay by A. C. Swinburne; Vol. III., Translations of the Iliad and Odyssey.
MARLOWE'S WORKS. Edited, with Notes, by Col. Cunningham. One Vol.
MASSINGER'S PLAYS. From Gifford's Text. Edit. by Col. Cunningham. One Vol.

DUNCAN (SARA JEANNETTE), WORKS BY.
A SOCIAL DEPARTURE: How Orthodocia and I Went round the World by Ourselves. With 111 Illustrations by F. H. TOWNSEND. Crown 8vo, cloth, **7s. 6d.**
AN AMERICAN GIRL IN LONDON. With 80 Illustrations by F. H. TOWNSEND. Crown 8vo. cloth extra, **7s. 6d.**   [*Preparing.*

DYER.—THE FOLK-LORE OF PLANTS. By Rev. T. F. THISELTON
DYER, M.A. Crown 8vo, cloth extra, **6s.**

EARLY ENGLISH POETS. Edited, with Introductions and Annotations, by Rev. A. B. GROSART, D.D. Crown 8vo, cloth boards, **6s.** per Volume.
FLETCHER'S (GILES) COMPLETE POEMS. One Vol.
DAVIES' (SIR JOHN) COMPLETE POETICAL WORKS. Two Vols.
HERRICK'S (ROBERT) COMPLETE COLLECTED POEMS. Three Vols.
SIDNEY'S (SIR PHILIP) COMPLETE POETICAL WORKS. Three Vols.

EDGCUMBE.—ZEPHYRUS : A Holiday in Brazil and on the River Plate.
By E. R. PEARCE EDGCUMBE. With 41 Illustrations. Crown 8vo, cloth extra, **5s.**

EDWARDES (MRS. ANNIE), NOVELS BY:
A POINT OF HONOUR. Post 8vo, illustrated boards, **2s.**
ARCHIE LOVELL. Crown 8vo, cloth extra, **3s. 6d.** ; post 8vo, illust. boards, **2s.**

EDWARDS (ELIEZER).—WORDS, FACTS, AND PHRASES: A
Dictionary of Curious, Quaint, and Out-of-the-Way Matters. By ELIEZER EDWARDS.
Crown 8vo, cloth extra, **7s. 6d.**

EDWARDS (M. BETHAM-), NOVELS BY.
KITTY. Post 8vo, illustrated boards, **2s.** ; cloth limp, **2s. 6d.**
FELICIA. Post 8vo, illustrated boards, **2s.**

EGGLESTON (EDWARD).—ROXY : A Novel. Post 8vo, illust. bds., 2s.

EMANUEL.—ON DIAMONDS AND PRECIOUS STONES: Their
History, Value, and Properties ; with Simple Tests for ascertaining their Reality. By
HARRY EMANUEL, F.R.G.S. With Illustrations, tinted and plain. Cr. 8vo, cl. ex., **6s.**

ENGLISHMAN'S HOUSE, THE: A Practical Guide to all interested in
Selecting or Building a House ; with Estimates of Cost, Quantities, &c. By C. J.
RICHARDSON. With Coloured Frontispiece and 600 Illusts. Crown 8vo, cloth, **7s. 6d.**

EWALD (ALEX. CHARLES, F.S.A.), WORKS BY.
THE LIFE AND TIMES OF PRINCE CHARLES STUART, Count of Albany
(THE YOUNG PRETENDER). With a Portrait. Crown 8vo, cloth extra, **7s. 6d.**
STORIES FROM THE STATE PAPERS. With an Autotype. Crown 8vo, cloth, **6s.**

EYES, OUR : How to Preserve Them from Infancy to Old Age. By
JOHN BROWNING, F.R.A.S. With 70 Illusts. Eighteenth Thousand. Crown 8vo, **1s.**

FAMILIAR SHORT SAYINGS OF GREAT MEN. By SAMUEL ARTHUR
BENT, A.M. Fifth Edition, Revised and Enlarged. Crown 8vo, cloth extra, **7s. 6d.**

FARADAY (MICHAEL), WORKS BY. Post 8vo, cloth extra, **4s. 6d.** each.
THE CHEMICAL HISTORY OF A CANDLE: Lectures delivered before a Juvenile
Audience. Edited by WILLIAM CROOKES, F.C.S. With numerous Illustrations.
ON THE VARIOUS FORCES OF NATURE, AND THEIR RELATIONS TO
EACH OTHER. Edited by WILLIAM CROOKES, F.C.S. With Illustrations.

FARRER (J. ANSON), WORKS BY.
MILITARY MANNERS AND CUSTOMS. Crown 8vo, cloth extra, **6s.**
WAR: Three Essays, reprinted from "Military Manners." Cr. 8vo. **1s.** ; cl., **1s. 6d.**

FICTION.—A CATALOGUE OF NEARLY SIX HUNDRED WORKS
OF FICTION published by CHATTO & WINDUS, with a Short Critical Notice of
each (40 pages, demy 8vo), will be sent free upon application.

FIN-BEC.—THE CUPBOARD PAPERS: Observations on the Art of
Living and Dining. By FIN-BEC. Post 8vo, cloth limp, **2s. 6d.**

FIREWORKS, THE COMPLETE ART OF MAKING ; or, The Pyro-
technist's Treasury. By THOMAS KENTISH. With 267 Illustrations. Cr. 8vo, cl., **5s.**

FITZGERALD (PERCY, M.A., F.S.A.), WORKS BY.

THE WORLD BEHIND THE SCENES. Crown 8vo, cloth extra, **3s. 6d.**
LITTLE ESSAYS: Passages from Letters of CHARLES LAMB. Post 8vo, cl., **2s. 6d.**
A DAY'S TOUR: Journey through France and Belgium. With Sketches. Cr. 4to, **1s.**
FATAL ZERO. Crown 8vo, cloth extra, **3s. 6d.**; post 8vo, illustrated boards, **2s.**

Post 8vo, illustrated boards, **2s.** each.

BELLA DONNA.	**LADY OF BRANTOME.**	**THE SECOND MRS. TILLOTSON.**
POLLY.	**NEVER FORGOTTEN.**	**SEVENTY-FIVE BROOKE STREET.**

LIFE OF JAMES BOSWELL (of Auchinleck). With an Account of his Sayings, Doings, and Writings; and Four Portraits. Two Vols., demy 8vo, cloth extra. **24s.** [Preparing.

FLETCHER'S (GILES, B.D.) COMPLETE POEMS: Christ's Victorie

in Heaven, Christ's Victorie on Earth, Christ's Triumph over Death, and Minor Poems. With Notes by Rev. A. B. GROSART, D.D. Crown 8vo, cloth boards, **6s.**

FLUDYER (HARRY) AT CAMBRIDGE: A Series of Family Letters.

Post 8vo, picture cover, **1s.**; cloth limp, **1s. 6d.**

FONBLANQUE (ALBANY).—FILTHY LUCRE. Post 8vo, illust. bds., 2s.

FRANCILLON (R. E.), NOVELS BY.

Crown 8vo, cloth extra, **3s. 6d.** each; post 8vo, illustrated boards, **2s.** each.

ONE BY ONE. | **QUEEN COPHETUA.** | **A REAL QUEEN.** | **KING OR KNAVE?**
OLYMPIA. Post 8vo, illust. bds., **2s.** | **ESTHER'S GLOVE.** Fcap. 8vo, pict. cover, **1s.**
ROMANCES OF THE LAW. Crown 8vo, cloth, **6s.**; post 8vo, illust. boards, **2s.**

FREDERIC (HAROLD), NOVELS BY.

SETH'S BROTHER'S WIFE. Post 8vo, illustrated boards, **2s.**
THE LAWTON GIRL. With Frontispiece by F. BARNARD. Cr. 8vo, cloth ex., **6s.**; post 8vo, illustrated boards, **2s.**

FRENCH LITERATURE, A HISTORY OF. By HENRY VAN LAUN.

Three Vols., demy 8vo, cloth boards, **7s. 6d.** each.

FRENZENY.—FIFTY YEARS ON THE TRAIL: Adventures of JOHN

Y. NELSON, Scout, Guide, and Interpreter. By HARRINGTON O'REILLY. With 100 Illustrations by PAUL FRENZENY. Crown 8vo, cloth extra, **3s. 6d.**

FRERE.—PANDURANG HARI; or, Memoirs of a Hindoo. With Pre-

face by Sir BARTLE FRERE. Crown 8vo, cloth, **3s. 6d.**; post 8vo, illust. bds., **2s.**

FRISWELL (HAIN).—ONE OF TWO: A Novel. Post 8vo, illust. bds., 2s.

FROST (THOMAS), WORKS BY. Crown 8vo, cloth extra, 3s. 6d. each.

CIRCUS LIFE AND CIRCUS CELEBRITIES. | **LIVES OF THE CONJURERS.**
THE OLD SHOWMEN AND THE OLD LONDON FAIRS.

FRY'S (HERBERT) ROYAL GUIDE TO THE LONDON CHARITIES.

Showing their Name, Date of Foundation, Objects, Income, Officials, &c. Edited by JOHN LANE. Published Annually. Crown 8vo, cloth, **1s. 6d.**

GARDENING BOOKS. Post 8vo, 1s. each; cloth limp, 1s. 6d. each.

A YEAR'S WORK IN GARDEN AND GREENHOUSE: Practical Advice as to the Management of the Flower, Fruit, and Frame Garden. By GEORGE GLENNY.
OUR KITCHEN GARDEN: Plants, and How we Cook Them. By TOM JERROLD.
HOUSEHOLD HORTICULTURE. By TOM and JANE JERROLD. Illustrated.
THE GARDEN THAT PAID THE RENT. By TOM JERROLD.

MY GARDEN WILD, AND WHAT I GREW THERE. By FRANCIS G. HEATH. Crown 8vo, cloth extra, gilt edges, **6s.**

GARRETT.—THE CAPEL GIRLS: A Novel. By EDWARD GARRETT.

Crown 8vo, cloth extra, **3s. 6d.**; post 8vo, illustrated boards, **2s.**

GENTLEMAN'S MAGAZINE, THE. 1s. Monthly. In addition to the

Articles upon subjects in Literature, Science, and Art, for which this Magazine has so high a reputation, "TABLE TALK" by SYLVANUS URBAN appears monthly.
*** *Bound Volumes for recent years kept in stock,* **8s. 6d.** *each; Cases for binding,* **2s.**

GENTLEMAN'S ANNUAL, THE. Published Annually in November. 1s.

GERMAN POPULAR STORIES. Collected by the Brothers GRIMM and Translated by EDGAR TAYLOR. With Introduction by JOHN RUSKIN, and 22 Steel Plates by GEORGE CRUIKSHANK. Square 8vo. cloth, **6s. 6d.**; gilt edges. **7s. 6d.**

GIBBON (CHARLES), NOVELS BY. Crown 8vo, cloth extra, **3s. 6d.** each; post 8vo, illustrated boards, **2s.** each.

ROBIN GRAY. | LOVING A DREAM.	OF HIGH DEGREE.
THE FLOWER OF THE FOREST.	IN HONOUR BOUND.
THE GOLDEN SHAFT.	

Post 8vo, illustrated boards, **2s.** each.

THE DEAD HEART.	IN LOVE AND WAR.
FOR LACK OF GOLD.	A HEART'S PROBLEM.
WHAT WILL THE WORLD SAY?	BY MEAD AND STREAM.
FOR THE KING.	THE BRAES OF YARROW.
QUEEN OF THE MEADOW.	FANCY FREE. | A HARD KNOT.
IN PASTURES GREEN.	HEART'S DELIGHT. | BLOOD-MONEY.

GIBNEY (SOMERVILLE).—SENTENCED! Cr. 8vo, 1s. ; cl., 1s. 6d.

GILBERT (WILLIAM), NOVELS BY. Post 8vo, illustrated boards, **2s.** each.
DR. AUSTIN'S GUESTS. | JAMES DUKE, COSTERMONGER.
THE WIZARD OF THE MOUNTAIN.

GILBERT (W. S.), ORIGINAL PLAYS BY. In Two Series, each complete in itself, price **2s. 6d.** each.
The FIRST SERIES contains: The Wicked World—Pygmalion and Galatea—Charity—The Princess—The Palace of Truth—Trial by Jury.
The SECOND SERIES: Broken Hearts—Engaged—Sweethearts—Gretchen—Dan'l Druce—Tom Cobb—H.M.S. "Pinafore"—The Sorcerer—Pirates of Penzance.

EIGHT ORIGINAL COMIC OPERAS written by W. S. GILBERT. Containing: The Sorcerer—H.M.S. "Pinafore"—Pirates of Penzance—Iolanthe—Patience—Princess Ida—The Mikado—Trial by Jury. Demy 8vo. cloth limp, **2s. 6d.**
THE "GILBERT AND SULLIVAN" BIRTHDAY BOOK: Quotations for Every Day in the Year, Selected from Plays by W. S. GILBERT set to Music by Sir A. SULLIVAN. Compiled by ALEX. WATSON. Royal 16mo. Jap. leather, **2s. 6d.**

GLANVILLE (ERNEST), NOVELS BY.
THE LOST HEIRESS: A Tale of Love, Battle and Adventure. With 2 Illusts. by HUME NISBET. Cr. 8vo, cloth extra, **3s. 6d.**
THE FOSSICKER. With a Frontispiece. Crown 8vo, cloth extra, 3s. 6d.

GLENNY.—A YEAR'S WORK IN GARDEN AND GREENHOUSE: Practical Advice to Amateur Gardeners as to the Management of the Flower, Fruit, and Frame Garden. By GEORGE GLENNY. Post 8vo, **1s.**; cloth limp, **1s. 6d.**

GODWIN.—LIVES OF THE NECROMANCERS. By WILLIAM GODWIN. Post 8vo, cloth limp, **2s.**

GOLDEN TREASURY OF THOUGHT, THE: An Encyclopædia of QUOTATIONS. Edited by THEODORE TAYLOR. Crown 8vo. cloth gilt, **7s. 6d.**

GOWING.—FIVE THOUSAND MILES IN A SLEDGE: A Midwinter Journey Across Siberia. By LIONEL F. GOWING. With 30 Illustrations by C. J. UREN, and a Map by E. WELLER. Large crown 8vo. cloth extra, **8s.**

GRAHAM.—THE PROFESSOR'S WIFE: A Story. By LEONARD GRAHAM. Fcap. 8vo, picture cover, **1s.**

GREEKS AND ROMANS, THE LIFE OF THE, described from Antique Monuments. By ERNST GUHL and W. KONER. Edited by Dr. F. HUEFFER. With 545 Illustrations. Large crown 8vo, cloth extra, **7s. 6d.**

GREENWOOD (JAMES), WORKS BY. Cr. 8vo, cloth extra, **3s. 6d.** each.
THE WILDS OF LONDON. | LOW-LIFE DEEPS.

GREVILLE (HENRY), NOVELS BY:
NIKANOR. Translated by ELIZA E. CHASE. With 8 Illusts. Cr. 8vo, cl. extra, **6s.**
A NOBLE WOMAN. Translated by ALBERT D. VANDAM. Crown 8vo, cloth extra, **5s.**; post 8vo. illustrated boards, **2s.**

HABBERTON (JOHN), Author of "Helen's Babies"), **NOVELS BY.** Post 8vo, illustrated boards **2s.** each; cloth limp, **2s. 6d.** each.
BRUETON'S BAYOU. | COUNTRY LUCK.

HAIR, THE: Its Treatment in Health, Weakness, and Disease. Translated from the German of Dr. J. Pincus. Crown 8vo, 1s.; cloth limp, 1s. 6d.

HAKE (DR. THOMAS GORDON), POEMS BY. Cr. 8vo, cl. ex., 6s. each.
NEW SYMBOLS. | LEGENDS OF THE MORROW. | THE SERPENT PLAY.
MAIDEN ECSTASY. Small 4to, cloth extra, 8s.

HALL.—SKETCHES OF IRISH CHARACTER. By Mrs. S. C. Hall.
With numerous Illustrations on Steel and Wood by Maclise, Gilbert, Harvey, and George Cruikshank. Medium 8vo, cloth extra. 7s. 6d.

HALLIDAY (ANDR.).—EVERY-DAY PAPERS. Post 8vo, bds., 2s.

HANDWRITING, THE PHILOSOPHY OF. With over 100 Facsimiles and Explanatory Text. By Don Felix de Salamanca. Post 8vo, cloth limp. 2s. 6d.

HANKY-PANKY: A Collection of Very Easy Tricks, Very Difficult Tricks, White Magic, Sleight of Hand. &c. Edited by W. H. Cremer. With 200 Illustrations. Crown 8vo, cloth extra, 4s. 6d.

HARDY (LADY DUFFUS).— PAUL WYNTER'S SACRIFICE. By Lady Duffus Hardy. Post 8vo, illustrated boards, 2s.

HARDY (THOMAS).— UNDER THE GREENWOOD TREE. By Thomas Hardy, Author of "Far from the Madding Crowd." Post 8vo, illust. bds., 2s.

HARWOOD.—THE TENTH EARL. By J. Berwick Harwood. Post 8vo, illustrated boards, 2s.

HAWEIS (MRS. H. R.), WORKS BY. Square 8vo, cloth extra, 6s. each.
THE ART OF BEAUTY. With Coloured Frontispiece and 91 Illustrations.
THE ART OF DECORATION. With Coloured Frontispiece and 74 Illustrations.
CHAUCER FOR CHILDREN. With 8 Coloured Plates and 30 Woodcuts.
THE ART OF DRESS. With 32 Illustrations. Post 8vo, 1s.; cloth, 1s. 6d.
CHAUCER FOR SCHOOLS. Demy 8vo, cloth limp, 2s. 6d.

HAWEIS (Rev. H. R., M.A.).—AMERICAN HUMORISTS: Washington Irving, Oliver Wendell Holmes, James Russell Lowell, Artemus Ward, Mark Twain, and Bret Harte. Third Edition. Crown 8vo, cloth extra. 6s.

HAWLEY SMART.—WITHOUT LOVE OR LICENCE: A Novel. By Hawley Smart. Crown 8vo, cloth extra, 3s. 6d.

HAWTHORNE. — OUR OLD HOME. By Nathaniel Hawthorne. Annotated with Passages from the Author's Note-book, and Illustrated with 31 Photogravures. Two Vols., crown 8vo, buckram, gilt top, 15s.

HAWTHORNE (JULIAN), NOVELS BY.
Crown 8vo, cloth extra, 3s. 6d. each; post 8vo, illustrated boards, 2s. each.
GARTH. | ELLICE QUENTIN. | BEATRIX RANDOLPH. | DUST.
SEBASTIAN STROME. | DAVID POINDEXTER.
FORTUNE'S FOOL. | THE SPECTRE OF THE CAMERA.

Post 8vo, illustrated boards, 2s. each.
MISS CADOGNA. | LOVE—OR A NAME.
MRS. GAINSBOROUGH'S DIAMONDS. Fcap. 8vo, illustrated cover, 1s.
A DREAM AND A FORGETTING. Post 8vo, cloth limp, 1s. 6d.

HAYS.—WOMEN OF THE DAY: A Biographical Dictionary of Notable Contemporaries. By Frances Hays. Crown 8vo, cloth extra, 5s.

HEATH.—MY GARDEN WILD, AND WHAT I GREW THERE. By Francis George Heath. Crown 8vo, cloth extra, gilt edges. 6s.

HELPS (SIR ARTHUR), WORKS BY. Post 8vo, cloth limp, 2s. 6d. each.
ANIMALS AND THEIR MASTERS. | SOCIAL PRESSURE.

IVAN DE BIRON: A Novel. Cr. 8vo, cl. extra, 3s. 6d.; post 8vo, illust. bds., 2s.

HENDERSON.—AGATHA PAGE: A Novel. By Isaac Henderson. Crown 8vo, cloth extra, 3s. 6d.

HERMAN.—A LEADING LADY. By Henry Herman, joint-Author of "The Bishops' Bible." Post 8vo, cloth extra, 2s. 6d.

HERRICK'S (ROBERT) HESPERIDES, NOBLE NUMBERS, AND COMPLETE COLLECTED POEMS. With Memorial-Introduction and Notes by the Rev. A. B. Grosart, D.D.; Steel Portrait, &c. Three Vols., crown 8vo, cl. bds., 18s.

HERTZKA.—FREELAND: A Social Anticipation. By Dr. Theodor Hertzka. Translated by Arthur Ransom. Crown 8vo, cloth extra, 6s.

HESSE-WARTEGG.—TUNIS: The Land and the People. By Chevalier Ernst von Hesse-Wartegg. With 22 Illustrations. Cr. 8vo, cloth extra, 3s. 6d.

HINDLEY (CHARLES), WORKS BY.
TAVERN ANECDOTES AND SAYINGS: Including the Origin of Signs, and Reminiscences connected with Taverns, Coffee Houses, Clubs, &c. With Illustrations. Crown 8vo, cloth extra, 3s. 6d.
THE LIFE AND ADVENTURES OF A CHEAP JACK. By One of the Fraternity. Edited by Charles Hindley. Crown 8vo, cloth extra, 3s. 6d.

HOEY.—THE LOVER'S CREED. By Mrs. Cashel Hoey. Post 8vo, illustrated boards, 2s.

HOLLINGSHEAD (JOHN).—NIAGARA SPRAY. Crown 8vo, 1s.

HOLMES.—THE SCIENCE OF VOICE PRODUCTION AND VOICE PRESERVATION: A Popular Manual for the Use of Speakers and Singers. By Gordon Holmes, M.D. With Illustrations. Crown 8vo, 1s.; cloth, 1s. 6d.

HOLMES (OLIVER WENDELL), WORKS BY.
THE AUTOCRAT OF THE BREAKFAST-TABLE. Illustrated by J. Gordon Thomson. Post 8vo, cloth limp, 2s. 6d.—Another Edition, in smaller type, with an Introduction by G. A. Sala. Post 8vo, cloth limp, 2s.
THE PROFESSOR AT THE BREAKFAST-TABLE. Post 8vo, cloth limp, 2s.

HOOD'S (THOMAS) CHOICE WORKS, in Prose and Verse. With Life of the Author, Portrait, and 200 Illustrations. Crown 8vo, cloth extra, 7s. 6d.
HOOD'S WHIMS AND ODDITIES. With 85 Illustrations. Post 8vo, printed on laid paper and half-bound, 2s.

HOOD (TOM).—FROM NOWHERE TO THE NORTH POLE: A Noah's Arkæological Narrative. By Tom Hood. With 25 Illustrations by W. Brunton and E. C. Barnes. Square 8vo, cloth extra, gilt edges, 6s.

HOOK'S (THEODORE) CHOICE HUMOROUS WORKS; including his Ludicrous Adventures, Bons Mots, Puns, and Hoaxes. With Life of the Author, Portraits, Facsimiles, and Illustrations. Crown 8vo, cloth extra, 7s. 6d.

HOOPER.—THE HOUSE OF RABY: A Novel. By Mrs. George Hooper. Post 8vo, illustrated boards, 2s.

HOPKINS.—"'TWIXT LOVE AND DUTY:" A Novel. By Tighe Hopkins. Post 8vo, illustrated boards, 2s.

HORNE. — ORION: An Epic Poem. By Richard Hengist Horne. With Photographic Portrait by Summers. Tenth Edition. Cr. 8vo, cloth extra, 7s.

HORSE (THE) AND HIS RIDER: An Anecdotic Medley. By "Thormanby." Crown 8vo, cloth extra, 6s.

HUNT.—ESSAYS BY LEIGH HUNT: A Tale for a Chimney Corner, and other Pieces. Edited, with an Introduction, by Edmund Ollier. Post 8vo, printed on laid paper and half-bd., 2s. Also in sm. sq. 8vo, cl. extra, at same price.

HUNT (MRS. ALFRED), NOVELS BY.
Crown 8vo, cloth extra, 3s. 6d. each; post 8vo, illustrated boards, 2s. each.
THE LEADEN CASKET. | SELF-CONDEMNED. | THAT OTHER PERSON.
THORNICROFT'S MODEL. Post 8vo, illustrated boards, 2s.

HYDROPHOBIA: An Account of M. Pasteur's System. Containing a Translation of all his Communications on the Subject, the Technique of his Method, and Statistics. By Renaud Suzor, M.B. Crown 8vo, cloth extra, 6s.

INGELOW (JEAN).—FATED TO BE FREE. With 24 Illustrations by G. J. Pinwell. Cr. 8vo, cloth extra, 3s. 6d.; post 8vo, illustrated boards, 2s.

INDOOR PAUPERS. By One of Them. Crown 8vo, 1s.; cloth, 1s. 6d.

IRISH WIT AND HUMOUR, SONGS OF. Collected and Edited by
A. PERCEVAL GRAVES. Post 8vo, cloth limp, **2s. 6d.**

JAMES.—A ROMANCE OF THE QUEEN'S HOUNDS. By CHARLES
JAMES. Post 8vo, picture cover, **1s.**; cloth limp, **1s. 6d.**

JANVIER.—PRACTICAL KERAMICS FOR STUDENTS. By CATHERINE
A. JANVIER. Crown 8vo, cloth extra, **6s.**

JAY (HARRIETT), NOVELS BY. Post 8vo, illustrated boards, **2s.** each.
THE DARK COLLEEN. | THE QUEEN OF CONNAUGHT.

JEFFERIES (RICHARD), WORKS BY. Post 8vo, cloth limp, **2s. 6d.** each.
NATURE NEAR LONDON. | THE LIFE OF THE FIELDS. | THE OPEN AIR.
THE EULOGY OF RICHARD JEFFERIES. By WALTER BESANT. Second Edition. With a Photograph Portrait. Crown 8vo, cloth extra, **6s.**

JENNINGS (H. J.), WORKS BY.
CURIOSITIES OF CRITICISM. Post 8vo, cloth limp, **2s. 6d.**
LORD TENNYSON: A Biographical Sketch. With a Photograph. Cr. 8vo, cl., **6s.**

JEROME. — STAGELAND : Curious Habits and Customs of its Inhabitants. By JEROME K. JEROME. With 64 Illustrations by J. BERNARD PARTRIDGE.
Sixteenth Thousand. Fcap. 4to, cloth extra, **3s. 6d.**

JERROLD.—THE BARBER'S CHAIR; & THE HEDGEHOG LETTERS.
By DOUGLAS JERROLD. Post 8vo, printed on laid paper and half-bound. **2s.**

JERROLD (TOM), WORKS BY. Post 8vo, **1s.** each; cloth limp, **1s. 6d.** each.
THE GARDEN THAT PAID THE RENT.
HOUSEHOLD HORTICULTURE: A Gossip about Flowers. Illustrated.
OUR KITCHEN GARDEN: The Plants we Grow, and How we Cook Them.

JESSE.—SCENES AND OCCUPATIONS OF A COUNTRY LIFE. By
EDWARD JESSE. Post 8vo, cloth limp, **2s.**

JONES (WILLIAM, F.S.A.), WORKS BY. Cr. 8vo, cl. extra, **7s. 6d.** each.
FINGER-RING LORE: Historical, Legendary, and Anecdotal. With nearly 300
Illustrations. Second Edition, Revised and Enlarged.
CREDULITIES, PAST AND PRESENT. Including the Sea and Seamen, Miners,
Talismans, Word and Letter Divination, Exorcising and Blessing of Animals,
Birds, Eggs, Luck, &c. With an Etched Frontispiece.
CROWNS AND CORONATIONS: A History of Regalia. With 100 Illustrations.

JONSON'S (BEN) WORKS. With Notes Critical and Explanatory,
and a Biographical Memoir by WILLIAM GIFFORD. Edited by Colonel CUNNING-
HAM. Three Vols., crown 8vo, cloth extra, **6s.** each.

JOSEPHUS, THE COMPLETE WORKS OF. Translated by WHISTON.
Containing "The Antiquities of the Jews" and "The Wars of the Jews." With 52
Illustrations and Maps. Two Vols., demy 8vo, half-bound, **12s. 6d.**

KEMPT.—PENCIL AND PALETTE : Chapters on Art and Artists. By
ROBERT KEMPT. Post 8vo, cloth limp, **2s. 6d.**

KERSHAW. — COLONIAL FACTS AND FICTIONS : Humorous
Sketches. By MARK KERSHAW. Post 8vo, illustrated boards, **2s.**; cloth, **2s. 6d.**

KEYSER. — CUT BY THE MESS : A Novel. By ARTHUR KEYSER.
Crown 8vo, picture cover, **1s.**; cloth limp, **1s. 6d.**

KING (R. ASHE), NOVELS BY. Cr. 8vo, cl., **3s. 6d.** ea.; post 8vo, bds., **2s.** ea.
A DRAWN GAME. | "THE WEARING OF THE GREEN."
PASSION'S SLAVE. Post 8vo, illustrated boards, **2s.**
BELL BARRY. 2 vols., crown 8vo.

KINGSLEY (HENRY), NOVELS BY.
OAKSHOTT CASTLE. Post 8vo, illustrated boards, **2s.**
NUMBER SEVENTEEN. Crown 8vo, cloth extra, **3s. 6d.**

KNIGHTS (THE) OF THE LION : A Romance of the Thirteenth Century.
Edited, with an Introduction, by the MARQUESS of LORNE, K.T. Cr. 8vo, cl. ex., **6s.**

KNIGHT.—THE PATIENT'S VADE MECUM: How to Get Most Benefit from Medical Advice. By WILLIAM KNIGHT, M.R.C.S., and EDWARD KNIGHT, L.R.C.P. Crown 8vo, **1s.**; cloth limp, **1s. 6d.**

LAMB'S (CHARLES) COMPLETE WORKS, in Prose and Verse. Edited, with Notes and Introduction, by R. H. SHEPHERD. With Two Portraits and Facsimile of a page of the "Essay on Roast Pig." Cr. 8vo, cl. ex., **7s. 6d.**

THE ESSAYS OF ELIA. Post 8vo, printed on laid paper and half-bound, **2s.**

LITTLE ESSAYS: Sketches and Characters by CHARLES LAMB, selected from his Letters by PERCY FITZGERALD. Post 8vo, cloth limp, **2s. 6d.**

LANDOR.—CITATION AND EXAMINATION OF WILLIAM SHAKS-PEARE, &c., before Sir THOMAS LUCY, touching Deer-stealing, 19th September, 1582. To which is added, A CONFERENCE OF MASTER EDMUND SPENSER with the Earl of Essex, touching the State of Ireland, 1595. By WALTER SAVAGE LANDOR. Fcap. 8vo, half-Roxburghe, **2s. 6d.**

LANE.—THE THOUSAND AND ONE NIGHTS, commonly called in England THE ARABIAN NIGHTS' ENTERTAINMENTS. Translated from the Arabic, with Notes, by EDWARD WILLIAM LANE. Illustrated by many hundred Engravings from Designs by HARVEY. Edited by EDWARD STANLEY POOLE. With a Preface by STANLEY LANE-POOLE. Three Vols., demy 8vo, cloth extra, **7s. 6d.** each.

LARWOOD (JACOB), WORKS BY.
THE STORY OF THE LONDON PARKS. With Illusts. Cr. 8vo, cl. extra, **3s. 6d.**
ANECDOTES OF THE CLERGY: The Antiquities, Humours, and Eccentricities of the Cloth. Post 8vo, printed on laid paper and half-bound, **2s.**

Post 8vo, cloth limp, **2s. 6d.** each.

FORENSIC ANECDOTES.	THEATRICAL ANECDOTES.

LEIGH (HENRY S.), WORKS BY.
CAROLS OF COCKAYNE. Printed on hand-made paper, bound in buckram, **5s.**
JEUX D'ESPRIT. Edited by HENRY S. LEIGH. Post 8vo, cloth limp, **2s. 6d.**

LEYS (JOHN).—THE LINDSAYS: A Romance. Post 8vo, illust. bds., 2s.

LIFE IN LONDON; or, The History of JERRY HAWTHORN and CORINTHIAN TOM. With CRUIKSHANK'S Coloured Illustrations. Crown 8vo, cloth extra, **7s. 6d.**   [New Edition preparing.

LINSKILL.—IN EXCHANGE FOR A SOUL. By MARY LINSKILL. Post 8vo, illustrated boards, **2s.**

LINTON (E. LYNN), WORKS BY. Post 8vo, cloth limp, **2s. 6d.** each.

WITCH STORIES.	OURSELVES: ESSAYS ON WOMEN.

Crown 8vo, cloth extra, **3s. 6d.** each; post 8vo, illustrated boards, **2s.** each.

SOWING THE WIND.	UNDER WHICH LORD?
PATRICIA KEMBALL.	"MY LOVE!" | IONE.
ATONEMENT OF LEAM DUNDAS.	PASTON CAREW, Millionaire & Miser.
THE WORLD WELL LOST.	

Post 8vo, illustrated boards, **2s.** each.

THE REBEL OF THE FAMILY.	WITH A SILKEN THREAD.

LONGFELLOW'S POETICAL WORKS. With numerous Illustrations on Steel and Wood. Crown 8vo, cloth extra, **7s. 6d.**

LUCY.—GIDEON FLEYCE: A Novel. By HENRY W. LUCY. Crown 8vo, cloth extra, **3s. 6d.**; post 8vo, illustrated boards, **2s.**

LUSIAD (THE) OF CAMOENS. Translated into English Spenserian Verse by ROBERT FFRENCH DUFF. With 14 Plates. Demy 8vo, cloth boards, **18s.**

MACALPINE (AVERY), NOVELS BY.
TERESA ITASCA, and other Stories. Crown 8vo, bound in canvas, **2s. 6d.**
BROKEN WINGS. With 6 Illusts. by W. J. HENNESSY. Crown 8vo, cloth extra, **6s.**

MACCOLL (HUGH), NOVELS BY.
MR. STRANGER'S SEALED PACKET. Second Edition. Crown 8vo, cl. extra, **5s.**
EDNOR WHITLOCK. Crown 8vo, cloth extra, **6s.**

McCARTHY (JUSTIN, M.P.), WORKS BY.

A HISTORY OF OUR OWN TIMES, from the Accession of Queen Victoria to the General Election of 1880. Four Vols. demy 8vo, cloth extra, **12s.** each.—Also a POPULAR EDITION, in Four Vols., crown 8vo, cloth extra, **6s.** each.—And a JUBILEE EDITION, with an Appendix of Events to the end of 1886, in Two Vols., large crown 8vo, cloth extra, **7s. 6d.** each.

A SHORT HISTORY OF OUR OWN TIMES. One Vol., crown 8vo, cloth extra, **6s.** —Also a CHEAP POPULAR EDITION, post 8vo, cloth limp, **2s. 6d.**

A HISTORY OF THE FOUR GEORGES. Four Vols. demy 8vo, cloth extra, **12s.** each. [Vols. I. & II. *ready*

Crown 8vo, cloth extra, **3s. 6d.** each; post 8vo, illustrated boards, **2s.** each.

THE WATERDALE NEIGHBOURS.	**MISS MISANTHROPE.**
MY ENEMY'S DAUGHTER.	**DONNA QUIXOTE.**
A FAIR SAXON.	**THE COMET OF A SEASON.**
LINLEY ROCHFORD.	**MAID OF ATHENS.**
DEAR LADY DISDAIN.	**CAMIOLA:** A Girl with a Fortune.

"THE RIGHT HONOURABLE." By JUSTIN McCARTHY, M.P., and Mrs. CAMPBELL-PRAED. Fourth Edition. Crown 8vo, cloth extra, **6s.**

McCARTHY (JUSTIN H., M.P.), WORKS BY.

THE FRENCH REVOLUTION. Four Vols., 8vo, **12s.** each. [Vols. I. & II. *ready.*
AN OUTLINE OF THE HISTORY OF IRELAND. Crown 8vo, **1s.**; cloth, **1s. 6d.**
IRELAND SINCE THE UNION: Irish History, 1798-1886. Crown 8vo, cloth, **6s.**
ENGLAND UNDER GLADSTONE, 1880-85. Crown 8vo, cloth extra, **6s.**
HAFIZ IN LONDON: Poems. Small 8vo, gold cloth, **3s. 6d.**
HARLEQUINADE: Poems. Small 4to, Japanese vellum, **8s.**
OUR SENSATION NOVEL. Crown 8vo, picture cover, **1s.**; cloth limp, **1s. 6d.**
DOOM! An Atlantic Episode. Crown 8vo, picture cover, **1s.**
DOLLY: A Sketch. Crown 8vo, picture cover, **1s.**; cloth limp, **1s. 6d.**
LILY LASS: A Romance. Crown 8vo, picture cover, **1s.**; cloth limp, **1s. 6d.**

MACDONALD (GEORGE, LL.D.), WORKS BY.

WORKS OF FANCY AND IMAGINATION. Ten Vols., cl. extra, gilt edges, in cloth case, **21s.** Or the Vols. may be had separately, in grolier cl., at **2s. 6d.** each.

Vol. I. WITHIN AND WITHOUT.—THE HIDDEN LIFE.
,, II. THE DISCIPLE.—THE GOSPEL WOMEN.—BOOK OF SONNETS.—ORGAN SONGS.
,, III. VIOLIN SONGS.—SONGS OF THE DAYS AND NIGHTS.—A BOOK OF DREAMS.—ROADSIDE POEMS.—POEMS FOR CHILDREN.
,, IV. PARABLES.—BALLADS.—SCOTCH SONGS.
,, V. & VI. PHANTASTES: A Faerie Romance. | Vol. VII. THE PORTENT.
,, VIII. THE LIGHT PRINCESS.—THE GIANT'S HEART.—SHADOWS.
,, IX. CROSS PURPOSES.—THE GOLDEN KEY.—THE CARASOYN.—LITTLE DAYLIGHT.
,, X. THE CRUEL PAINTER.—THE WOW O' RIVVEN.—THE CASTLE.—THE BROKEN SWORDS.—THE GRAY WOLF.—UNCLE CORNELIUS.

THE COMPLETE POETICAL WORKS OF DR. GEORGE MACDONALD. Collected and arranged by the Author. Crown 8vo, buckram, **6s.** [*Shortly.*

MACDONELL.—QUAKER COUSINS: A Novel. By AGNES MACDONELL.

Crown 8vo, cloth extra, **3s. 6d.**; post 8vo, illustrated boards, **2s.**

MACGREGOR. — PASTIMES AND PLAYERS: Notes on Popular

Games. By ROBERT MACGREGOR. Post 8vo, cloth limp, **2s. 6d.**

MACKAY.—INTERLUDES AND UNDERTONES; or, Music at Twilight.

By CHARLES MACKAY, LL.D. Crown 8vo, cloth extra, **6s.**

MACLISE PORTRAIT GALLERY (THE) OF ILLUSTRIOUS LITER-

ARY CHARACTERS: **85 PORTRAITS;** with Memoirs — Biographical, Critical, Bibliographical, and Anecdotal—illustrative of the Literature of the former half of the Present Century, by WILLIAM BATES, B.A. Crown 8vo, cloth extra, **7s. 6d.**

MACQUOID (MRS.), WORKS BY. Square 8vo, cloth extra, **7s. 6d.** each.

IN THE ARDENNES. With 50 Illustrations by THOMAS R. MACQUOID.
PICTURES AND LEGENDS FROM NORMANDY AND BRITTANY. With 34 Illustrations by THOMAS R. MACQUOID.
THROUGH NORMANDY. With 92 Illustrations by T. R. MACQUOID, and a Map.
THROUGH BRITTANY. With 35 Illustrations by T. R. MACQUOID, and a Map.
ABOUT YORKSHIRE. With 67 Illustrations by T. R. MACQUOID.

Post 8vo, illustrated boards, **2s.** each.
THE EVIL EYE, and other Stories. | **LOST ROSE.**

MAGIC LANTERN, THE, and its Management: including full Practical Directions for producing the Limelight, making Oxygen Gas, and preparing Lantern Slides. By T. C. Hepworth. With 10 Illustrations. Cr. 8vo. 1s.; cloth, 1s. 6d.

MAGICIAN'S OWN BOOK, THE: Performances with Cups and Balls, Eggs, Hats, Handkerchiefs, &c. All from actual Experience. Edited by W. H. Cremer. With 200 Illustrations. Crown 8vo, cloth extra, 4s. 6d.

MAGNA CHARTA: An Exact Facsimile of the Original in the British Museum, 3 feet by 2 feet, with Arms and Seals emblazoned in Gold and Colours, 5s.

MALLOCK (W. H.), WORKS BY.
THE NEW REPUBLIC. Post 8vo, picture cover, 2s.; cloth limp, 2s. 6d.
THE NEW PAUL & VIRGINIA: Positivism on an Island. Post 8vo, cloth, 2s. 6d.
POEMS. Small 4to, parchment, 8s.
IS LIFE WORTH LIVING? Crown 8vo, cloth extra, 6s.

MALLORY'S (SIR THOMAS) MORT D'ARTHUR: The Stories of King Arthur and of the Knights of the Round Table. (A Selection.) Edited by B. Montgomerie Ranking. Post 8vo, cloth limp, 2s.

MARK TWAIN, WORKS BY. Crown 8vo, cloth extra, 7s. 6d. each.
THE CHOICE WORKS OF MARK TWAIN. Revised and Corrected throughout by the Author. With Life, Portrait, and numerous Illustrations.
ROUGHING IT, and INNOCENTS AT HOME. With 200 Illusts. by F. A. Fraser.
THE GILDED AGE. By Mark Twain and C. D. Warner. With 212 Illustrations.
MARK TWAIN'S LIBRARY OF HUMOUR. With 197 Illustrations.
A YANKEE AT THE COURT OF KING ARTHUR. With 220 Illusts. by Beard.

Crown 8vo, cloth extra (illustrated), 7s. 6d. each; post 8vo, illust. boards, 2s. each.
THE INNOCENTS ABROAD; or New Pilgrim's Progress. With 234 Illustrations. (The Two-Shilling Edition is entitled MARK TWAIN'S PLEASURE TRIP.)
THE ADVENTURES OF TOM SAWYER. With 111 Illustrations.
A TRAMP ABROAD. With 314 Illustrations.
THE PRINCE AND THE PAUPER. With 190 Illustrations.
LIFE ON THE MISSISSIPPI. With 300 Illustrations.
ADVENTURES OF HUCKLEBERRY FINN. With 174 Illusts. by E. W. Kemble.

THE STOLEN WHITE ELEPHANT, &c. Cr. 8vo. cl., 6s.; post 8vo, illust. bds., 2s,

MARLOWE'S WORKS. Including his Translations. Edited, with Notes and Introductions, by Col. Cunningham. Crown 8vo, cloth extra, 6s.

MARRYAT (FLORENCE), NOVELS BY. Post 8vo, illust. boards, 2s. each.
A HARVEST OF WILD OATS. | WRITTEN IN FIRE. | FIGHTING THE AIR.
OPEN! SESAME! Crown 8vo, cloth extra, 3s. 6d.; post 8vo, picture boards, 2s.

MASSINGER'S PLAYS. From the Text of William Gifford. Edited by Col. Cunningham. Crown 8vo, cloth extra, 6s.

MASTERMAN.—HALF-A-DOZEN DAUGHTERS: A Novel. By J. Masterman. Post 8vo, illustrated boards, 2s.

MATTHEWS.—A SECRET OF THE SEA, &c. By Brander Matthews. Post 8vo, illustrated boards, 2s.; cloth limp, 2s. 6d.

MAYHEW.—LONDON CHARACTERS AND THE HUMOROUS SIDE OF LONDON LIFE. By Henry Mayhew. With Illusts. Crown 8vo, cloth, 3s. 6d.

MENKEN.—INFELICIA: Poems by Adah Isaacs Menken. With Biographical Preface, Illustrations by F. E. Lummis and F. O. C. Darley, and Facsimile of a Letter from Charles Dickens. Small 4to, cloth extra, 7s. 6d.

MEXICAN MUSTANG (ON A), through Texas to the Rio Grande. By A. E. Sweet and J. Armoy Knox. With 265 Illusts. Cr. 8vo, cloth extra, 7s. 6d.

MIDDLEMASS (JEAN), NOVELS BY. Post 8vo, illust. boards, 2s. each.
TOUCH AND GO. | MR. DORILLION.

MILLER.—PHYSIOLOGY FOR THE YOUNG; or, The House of Life: Human Physiology, with its application to the Preservation of Health. By Mrs. F. Fenwick Miller. With numerous Illustrations. Post 8vo, cloth limp, 2s. 6d.

MILTON (J. L.), WORKS BY. Post 8vo, 1s. each; cloth, 1s. 6d. each.
THE HYGIENE OF THE SKIN. With Directions for Diet, Soaps, Baths, &c.
THE BATH IN DISEASES OF THE SKIN.
THE LAWS OF LIFE, AND THEIR RELATION TO DISEASES OF THE SKIN.
THE SUCCESSFUL TREATMENT OF LEPROSY. Demy 8vo, 1s.

MINTO (WM.)—WAS SHE GOOD OR BAD? Cr. 8vo, 1s.; cloth, 1s. 6d.

MOLESWORTH (MRS.), NOVELS BY.
HATHERCOURT RECTORY. Post 8vo, illustrated boards, 2s.
THAT GIRL IN BLACK. Crown 8vo, picture cover, 1s.; cloth, 1s. 6d.

MOORE (THOMAS), WORKS BY.
THE EPICUREAN; and ALCIPHRON. Post 8vo, half-bound, 2s.
PROSE AND VERSE, Humorous, Satirical, and Sentimental, by THOMAS MOORE;
with Suppressed Passages from the MEMOIRS OF LORD BYRON. Edited by R.
HERNE SHEPHERD. With Portrait. Crown 8vo, cloth extra, 7s. 6d.

MUDDOCK (J. E.), STORIES BY.
STORIES WEIRD AND WONDERFUL. Post 8vo, illust. boards, 2s.; cloth, 2s. 6d.
THE DEAD MAN'S SECRET; or, The Valley of Gold: A Narrative of Strange
Adventure. With a Frontispiece by F. BARNARD. Crown 8vo, cloth extra, 5s.;
post 8vo, illustrated boards, 2s.

MURRAY (D. CHRISTIE), NOVELS BY.
Crown 8vo, cloth extra, 3s. 6d. each; post 8vo, illustrated boards, 2s. each.

A LIFE'S ATONEMENT.	A MODEL FATHER.	A BIT OF HUMAN NATURE.
JOSEPH'S COAT.	HEARTS.	FIRST PERSON SINGULAR.
COALS OF FIRE.	THE WAY OF THE	CYNIC FORTUNE.
VAL STRANGE.	WORLD.	

BY THE GATE OF THE SEA. Post 8vo, picture boards, 2s.
OLD BLAZER'S HERO. With Three Illustrations by A. McCORMICK. Crown 8vo,
cloth extra, 6s.; post 8vo, illustrated boards, 2s.

MURRAY (D. CHRISTIE) & HENRY HERMAN, WORKS BY.
Crown 8vo, cloth extra, 6s. each; post 8vo, illustrated boards, 2s. each.
ONE TRAVELLER RETURNS.
PAUL JONES'S ALIAS. With 13 Illustrations by A. FORESTIER and G. NICOLET.
THE BISHOPS' BIBLE. Crown 8vo, cloth extra, 3s. 6d.

MURRAY.—A GAME OF BLUFF: A Novel. By HENRY MURRAY.
Post 8vo, picture boards, 2s.; cloth limp, 2s. 6d.

NISBET (HUME), BOOKS BY.
"BAIL UP!" A Romance of BUSHRANGERS AND BLACKS. Cr. 8vo, cl. ex., 3s. 6d.
LESSONS IN ART. With 21 Illustrations. Crown 8vo, cloth extra, 2s. 6d.

NOVELISTS.—HALF-HOURS WITH THE BEST NOVELISTS OF
THE CENTURY. Edit. by H. T. MACKENZIE BELL. Cr. 8vo, cl., 3s. 6d. [Preparing.

O'CONNOR. — LORD BEACONSFIELD: A Biography. By T. P.
O'CONNOR, M.P. Sixth Edition, with an Introduction. Crown 8vo, cloth extra, 5s.

O'HANLON (ALICE), NOVELS BY. Post 8vo, illustrated boards, 2s. each.
THE UNFORESEEN. | CHANCE? OR FATE?

OHNET (GEORGES), NOVELS BY.
DOCTOR RAMEAU. Translated by Mrs. CASHEL HOEY. With 9 Illustrations by
E. BAYARD. Crown 8vo, cloth extra, 6s.; post 8vo, illustrated boards, 2s.
A LAST LOVE. Translated by ALBERT D. VANDAM. Crown 8vo, cloth extra, 5s.;
post 8vo, illustrated boards, 2s.
A WEIRD GIFT. Translated by ALBERT D. VANDAM. Crown 8vo, cloth, 3s. 6d.

OLIPHANT (MRS.), NOVELS BY. Post 8vo, illustrated boards, 2s. each.
THE PRIMROSE PATH. | THE GREATEST HEIRESS IN ENGLAND.
WHITELADIES. With Illustrations by ARTHUR HOPKINS and HENRY WOODS,
A.R.A. Crown 8vo, cloth extra, 3s. 6d.; post 8vo, illustrated boards, 2s.

O'REILLY (MRS.).—PHŒBE'S FORTUNES. Post 8vo, illust. bds., 2s.

O'SHAUGHNESSY (ARTHUR), POEMS BY.
LAYS OF FRANCE. Crown 8vo, cloth extra, 10s. 6d.
MUSIC AND MOONLIGHT. Fcap. 8vo, cloth extra, 7s. 6d.
SONGS OF A WORKER. Fcap. 8vo, cloth extra, 7s. 6d.

OUIDA, NOVELS BY. Cr. 8vo, cl., **3s. 6d.** each; post 8vo, illust. bds., **2s.** each.

HELD IN BONDAGE.	FOLLE-FARINE.	MOTHS.
TRICOTRIN.	A DOG OF FLANDERS.	PIPISTRELLO.
STRATHMORE.	PASCAREL.	A VILLAGE COMMUNE.
CHANDOS.	TWO LITTLE WOODEN	IN MAREMMA.
CECIL CASTLEMAINE'S	SHOES.	BIMBI.
GAGE.	SIGNA.	WANDA.
IDALIA.	IN A WINTER CITY.	FRESCOES.
UNDER TWO FLAGS.	ARIADNE.	PRINCESS NAPRAXINE.
PUCK.	FRIENDSHIP.	OTHMAR. | GUILDEROY.

Crown 8vo, cloth extra, **3s. 6d.** each.

SYRLIN.   RUFFINO.

WISDOM, WIT, AND PATHOS, selected from the Works of OUIDA by F. SYDNEY MORRIS. Post 8vo, cloth extra, **5s.** – CHEAP EDITION, illustrated boards, **2s.**

PAGE (H. A.), WORKS BY.
THOREAU: His Life and Aims. With Portrait. Post 8vo, cloth limp, **2s. 6d.**
ANIMAL ANECDOTES. Arranged on a New Principle. Crown 8vo, cloth extra, **5s.**

PASCAL'S PROVINCIAL LETTERS. A New Translation, with Historical Introduction and Notes by T. M'CRIE, D.D. Post 8vo, cloth limp, **2s.**

PAUL.—GENTLE AND SIMPLE. By MARGARET A. PAUL. With Frontispiece by HELEN PATERSON. Crown 8vo, cloth, **3s. 6d.**; post 8vo, illust. boards, **2s.**

PAYN (JAMES), NOVELS BY.
Crown 8vo, cloth extra, **3s. 6d.** each; post 8vo, illustrated boards, **2s.** each.

LOST SIR MASSINGBERD.	A GRAPE FROM A THORN.
WALTER'S WORD.	FROM EXILE.
LESS BLACK THAN WE'RE	SOME PRIVATE VIEWS.
PAINTED.	THE CANON'S WARD.
BY PROXY.	THE TALK OF THE TOWN.
HIGH SPIRITS.	HOLIDAY TASKS.
UNDER ONE ROOF.	GLOW-WORM TALES.
A CONFIDENTIAL AGENT.	THE MYSTERY OF MIRBRIDGE.

Post 8vo, illustrated boards, **2s.** each.

HUMOROUS STORIES.	THE CLYFFARDS OF CLYFFE.
THE FOSTER BROTHERS.	FOUND DEAD.
THE FAMILY SCAPEGRACE.	GWENDOLINE'S HARVEST.
MARRIED BENEATH HIM.	A MARINE RESIDENCE.
BENTINCK'S TUTOR.	MIRK ABBEY.
A PERFECT TREASURE.	NOT WOOED, BUT WON.
A COUNTY FAMILY.	TWO HUNDRED POUNDS REWARD.
LIKE FATHER, LIKE SON.	THE BEST OF HUSBANDS.
A WOMAN'S VENGEANCE.	HALVES.
CARLYON'S YEAR. | CECIL'S TRYST.	FALLEN FORTUNES.
MURPHY'S MASTER.	WHAT HE COST HER.
AT HER MERCY.	KIT: A MEMORY. | FOR CASH ONLY.

Crown 8vo, cloth extra, **3s. 6d.** each.

IN PERIL AND PRIVATION: Stories of MARINE ADVENTURE Re-told. With 17 Illustrations.
THE BURNT MILLION. | THE WORD AND THE WILL.
SUNNY STORIES, and some SHADY ONES. With a Frontispiece by FRED. BARNARD.

NOTES FROM THE "NEWS." Crown 8vo, portrait cover. **1s.**; cloth, **1s. 6d.**

PENNELL (H. CHOLMONDELEY), WORKS BY. Post 8vo, cl., **2s. 6d.** each.
PUCK ON PEGASUS. With Illustrations.
PEGASUS RE-SADDLED. With Ten full-page Illustrations by G. DU MAURIER.
THE MUSES OF MAYFAIR. Vers de Société, Selected by H. C. PENNELL.

PHELPS (E. STUART), WORKS BY. Post 8vo, **1s.** each; cloth, **1s. 6d.** each.
BEYOND THE GATES. By the Author | AN OLD MAID'S PARADISE.
  of "The Gates Ajar." | BURGLARS IN PARADISE.
JACK THE FISHERMAN. Illustrated by C. W. REED. Cr. 8vo, **1s.**; cloth, **1s. 6d.**

PIRKIS (C. L.), NOVELS BY.
TROOPING WITH CROWS. Fcap. 8vo, picture cover, **1s.**
LADY LOVELACE. Post 8vo, illustrated boards, **2s.**

PLANCHE (J. R.), WORKS BY.
THE PURSUIVANT OF ARMS; or, Heraldry Founded upon Facts. With Coloured Frontispiece, Five Plates, and 209 Illusts. Crown 8vo, cloth, 7s. 6d.
SONGS AND POEMS, 1819-1879. Introduction by Mrs. MACKARNESS. Cr. 8vo, cl., 6s.

PLUTARCH'S LIVES OF ILLUSTRIOUS MEN. Translated from the Greek, with Notes Critical and Historical, and a Life of Plutarch, by JOHN and WILLIAM LANGHORNE. With Portraits. Two Vols., demy 8vo, half-bound, 10s. 6d.

POE'S (EDGAR ALLAN) CHOICE WORKS, in Prose and Poetry. Introduction by CHAS. BAUDELAIRE, Portrait, and Facsimiles. Cr. 8vo, cloth, 7s. 6d.
THE MYSTERY OF MARIE ROGET, &c. Post 8vo, illustrated boards, 2s.

POPE'S POETICAL WORKS. Post 8vo, cloth limp, 2s.

PRICE (E. C.), NOVELS BY.
Crown 8vo, cloth extra, 3s. 6d. each ; post 8vo, illustrated boards, 2s. each.
VALENTINA. | THE FOREIGNERS. | MRS. LANCASTER'S RIVAL.
GERALD. Post 8vo, illustrated boards, 2s.

PRINCESS OLGA.—RADNA ; or, The Great Conspiracy of 1881. By the Princess OLGA. Crown 8vo, cloth extra. 6s.

PROCTOR (RICHARD A., B.A.), WORKS BY.
FLOWERS OF THE SKY. With 55 Illusts. Small crown 8vo, cloth extra, 3s. 6d.
EASY STAR LESSONS. With Star Maps for Every Night in the Year, Drawings of the Constellations. &c. Crown 8vo, cloth extra, 6s.
FAMILIAR SCIENCE STUDIES. Crown 8vo, cloth extra, 6s.
SATURN AND ITS SYSTEM. With 13 Steel Plates. Demy 8vo, cloth ex., 10s. 6d.
MYSTERIES OF TIME AND SPACE. With Illustrations. Cr. 8vo, cloth extra, 6s.
THE UNIVERSE OF SUNS. With numerous Illustrations. Cr. 8vo, cloth ex., 6s.
WAGES AND WANTS OF SCIENCE WORKERS. Crown 8vo, 1s. 6d.

PRYCE.—MISS MAXWELL'S AFFECTIONS. By RICHARD PRYCE, Author of "The Ugly Story of Miss Wetherby," &c. 2 vols., crown 8vo. [Shortly.

RAMBOSSON.—POPULAR ASTRONOMY. By J. RAMBOSSON, Laureate of the Institute of France. With numerous Illusts. Crown 8vo, cloth extra, 7s. 6d.

RANDOLPH.—AUNT ABIGAIL DYKES: A Novel. By Lt.-Colonel GEORGE RANDOLPH, U.S.A. Crown 8vo, cloth extra, 7s. 6d.

READE (CHARLES), NOVELS BY.
Crown 8vo, cloth extra, illustrated, 3s. 6d. each ; post 8vo, illust. bds., 2s. each.
PEG WOFFINGTON. Illustrated by S. L. FILDES, R.A.—Also a POCKET EDITION, set in New Type, in Elzevir style, fcap. 8vo, half-leather, 2s. 6d.
CHRISTIE JOHNSTONE. Illustrated by WILLIAM SMALL.—Also a POCKET EDITION, set in New Type, in Elzevir style, fcap. 8vo, half-leather, 2s. 6d.
IT IS NEVER TOO LATE TO MEND. Illustrated by G. J. PINWELL.
THE COURSE OF TRUE LOVE NEVER DID RUN SMOOTH. Illustrated by HELEN PATERSON.
THE AUTOBIOGRAPHY OF A THIEF, &c. Illustrated by MATT STRETCH.
LOVE ME LITTLE, LOVE ME LONG. Illustrated by M. ELLEN EDWARDS.
THE DOUBLE MARRIAGE. Illusts. by Sir JOHN GILBERT, R.A., and C. KEENE.
THE CLOISTER AND THE HEARTH. Illustrated by CHARLES KEENE.
HARD CASH. Illustrated by F. W. LAWSON.
GRIFFITH GAUNT. Illustrated by S. L. FILDES, R.A., and WILLIAM SMALL.
FOUL PLAY. Illustrated by GEORGE DU MAURIER.
PUT YOURSELF IN HIS PLACE. Illustrated by ROBERT BARNES.
A TERRIBLE TEMPTATION. Illustrated by EDWARD HUGHES and A. W. COOPER.
A SIMPLETON. Illustrated by KATE CRAUFURD.
THE WANDERING HEIR. Illustrated by HELEN PATERSON, S. L. FILDES, R.A., C. GREEN, and HENRY WOODS, A.R.A.
A WOMAN-HATER. Illustrated by THOMAS COULDERY.
SINGLEHEART AND DOUBLEFACE. Illustrated by P. MACNAB.
GOOD STORIES OF MEN AND OTHER ANIMALS. Illustrated E. A. ABBEY, PERCY MACQUOID, R.W.S., and JOSEPH NASH.
THE JILT, and other Stories. Illustrated by JOSEPH NASH.
READIANA. With a Steel-plate Portrait of CHARLES READE.
BIBLE CHARACTERS: Studies of David, Paul, &c. Fcap. 8vo, leatherette, 1s.
SELECTIONS FROM THE WORKS OF CHARLES READE. With an Introduction by Mrs. ALEX. IRELAND, and a Steel-Plate Portrait. Crown 8vo, buckram, 6s.

RIDDELL (MRS. J. H.), NOVELS BY.
Crown 8vo, cloth extra, **3s. 6d.** each; post 8vo, illustrated boards, **2s.** each.
HER MOTHER'S DARLING. | **WEIRD STORIES.**
THE PRINCE OF WALES'S GARDEN PARTY.
Post 8vo, illustrated boards, **2s.** each.
UNINHABITED HOUSE. | **FAIRY WATER.** | **MYSTERY IN PALACE GARDENS.**

RIMMER (ALFRED), WORKS BY. Square 8vo, cloth gilt, **7s. 6d.** each.
OUR OLD COUNTRY TOWNS. With 55 Illustrations.
RAMBLES ROUND ETON AND HARROW. With 50 Illustrations.
ABOUT ENGLAND WITH DICKENS. With 58 Illusts. by C. A. VANDERHOOF, &c.

ROBINSON CRUSOE. By DANIEL DEFOE. (MAJOR'S EDITION.) With
37 Illustrations by GEORGE CRUIKSHANK. Post 8vo, half-bound, **2s.**

ROBINSON (F. W.), NOVELS BY.
Crown 8vo, cloth extra, **3s. 6d.** each; post 8vo, illustrated boards, **2s.** each.
WOMEN ARE STRANGE. | **THE HANDS OF JUSTICE.**

ROBINSON (PHIL), WORKS BY. Crown 8vo, cloth extra, **7s. 6d.** each.
THE POETS' BIRDS. | **THE POETS' BEASTS.**
THE POETS AND NATURE: REPTILES, FISHES, INSECTS. [Preparing.

ROCHEFOUCAULD'S MAXIMS AND MORAL REFLECTIONS. With
Notes, and an Introductory Essay by SAINTE-BEUVE. Post 8vo, cloth limp, **2s.**

ROLL OF BATTLE ABBEY, THE : A List of the Principal Warriors
who came from Normandy with William the Conqueror, and Settled in this Country,
A.D. 1066-7. With Arms emblazoned in Gold and Colours. Handsomely printed. **5s.**

ROWLEY (HON. HUGH), WORKS BY. Post 8vo, cloth, **3s. 6d.** each.
PUNIANA: RIDDLES AND JOKES. With numerous Illustrations.
MORE PUNIANA. Profusely Illustrated.

RUNCIMAN (JAMES), STORIES BY.
Post 8vo, illustrated boards, **2s.** each; cloth limp, **2s. 6d.** each.
SKIPPERS AND SHELLBACKS. | **GRACE BALMAIGN'S SWEETHEART.**
SCHOOLS AND SCHOLARS.

RUSSELL (W. CLARK), BOOKS AND NOVELS BY :
Crown 8vo, cloth extra, **6s.** each; post 8vo, illustrated boards, **2s.** each.
ROUND THE GALLEY-FIRE. | **A BOOK FOR THE HAMMOCK.**
IN THE MIDDLE WATCH. | **MYSTERY OF THE "OCEAN STAR."**
A VOYAGE TO THE CAPE. | **THE ROMANCE OF JENNY HARLOWE.**
ON THE FO'K'SLE HEAD. Post 8vo, illustrated boards, **2s.**
AN OCEAN TRAGEDY. Cr. 8vo, cloth extra, **3s. 6d.** ; post 8vo, illust. bds., **2s.**
MY SHIPMATE LOUISE. Crown 8vo, cloth extra, **3s. 6d.**

SAINT AUBYN (ALAN), NOVELS BY.
A FELLOW OF TRINITY. With a Note by OLIVER WENDELL HOLMES and a
Frontispiece. Crown 8vo, cloth extra, **3s. 6d.** ; post 8vo, illust. boards, **2s.**
THE JUNIOR DEAN. 3 vols., crown 8vo. [Shortly.

SALA.—GASLIGHT AND DAYLIGHT. By GEORGE AUGUSTUS SALA.
Post 8vo, illustrated boards. **2s.**

SANSON.—SEVEN GENERATIONS OF EXECUTIONERS : Memoirs
of the Sanson Family (1688 to 1847). Crown 8vo, cloth extra, **3s. 6d.**

SAUNDERS (JOHN), NOVELS BY.
Crown 8vo, cloth extra, **3s. 6d.** each; post 8vo, illustrated boards, **2s.** each.
GUY WATERMAN. | **THE LION IN THE PATH.** | **THE TWO DREAMERS.**
BOUND TO THE WHEEL. Crown 8vo, cloth extra, **3s. 6d.**

SAUNDERS (KATHARINE), NOVELS BY.
Crown 8vo, cloth extra, **3s. 6d.** each; post 8vo, illustrated boards, **2s.** each.
MARGARET AND ELIZABETH. | **HEART SALVAGE.**
THE HIGH MILLS. | **SEBASTIAN.**
JOAN MERRYWEATHER. Post 8vo, illustrated boards, **2s.**
GIDEON'S ROCK. Crown 8vo, cloth extra, **3s. 6d.**

SCIENCE-GOSSIP : An Illustrated Medium of Interchange for Students
and Lovers of Nature. Edited by Dr. J. E. TAYLOR, F.L.S., &c. Devoted to Geology,
Botany, Physiology, Chemistry, Zoology, Microscopy, Telescopy, Physiography
Photography, &c. Price 4d. Monthly ; or **5s.** per year, post-free. Vols. I. to XIX.
may be had, **7s. 6d.** each ; Vols. XX. to date, **5s.** each. Cases for Binding, **1s. 6d.**

SECRET OUT, THE: One Thousand Tricks with Cards; with Entertaining Experiments in Drawing-room or "White Magic." By W. H. CREMER. With 300 Illustrations. Crown 8vo, cloth extra, **4s. 6d.**

SEGUIN (L. G.), WORKS BY.
THE COUNTRY OF THE PASSION PLAY (OBERAMMERGAU) and the Highlands of Bavaria. With Map and 37 Illustrations. Crown 8vo, cloth extra, **3s. 6d.**
WALKS IN ALGIERS. With 2 Maps and 16 Illusts. Crown 8vo, cloth extra, **6s.**

SENIOR (WM.).—BY STREAM AND SEA. Post 8vo, cloth, **2s. 6d.**

SHAKESPEARE, THE FIRST FOLIO.—Mr. WILLIAM SHAKESPEARE'S COMEDIES, HISTORIES, AND TRAGEDIES. Published according to the true Originall Copies. London, Printed by ISAAC IAGGARD and ED. BLOUNT. 1623.— A reduced Photographic Reproduction. Small 8vo, half-Roxburghe. **7s. 6d.**
SHAKESPEARE FOR CHILDREN: LAMB'S TALES FROM SHAKESPEARE. With Illustrations, coloured and plain, by J. MOYR SMITH. Crown 4to, cloth, **6s.**

SHARP.—CHILDREN OF TO-MORROW: A Novel. By WILLIAM SHARP. Crown 8vo, cloth extra, **6s.**

SHELLEY.—THE COMPLETE WORKS IN VERSE AND PROSE OF PERCY BYSSHE SHELLEY. Edited, Prefaced, and Annotated by R. HERNE SHEPHERD. Five Vols., crown 8vo, cloth boards, **3s. 6d.** each.
POETICAL WORKS, in Three Vols.:
Vol. I. Introduction by the Editor; Posthumous Fragments of Margaret Nicholson; Shelley's Correspondence with Stockdale; The Wandering Jew; Queen Mab, with the Notes; Alastor, and other Poems; Rosalind and Helen; Prometheus Unbound; Adonaïs, &c.
Vol. II. Laon and Cythna; The Cenci; Julian and Maddalo; Swellfoot the Tyrant; The Witch of Atlas; Epipsychidion; Hellas.
Vol. III. Posthumous Poems; The Masque of Anarchy; and other Pieces.
PROSE WORKS, in Two Vols.:
Vol. I. The Two Romances of Zastrozzi and St. Irvyne; the Dublin and Marlow Pamphlets; A Refutation of Deism; Letters to Leigh Hunt, and some Minor Writings and Fragments.
Vol. II. The Essays; Letters from Abroad; Translations and Fragments, Edited by Mrs. SHELLEY. With a Bibliography of Shelley, and an Index of the Prose Works.

SHERARD.—ROGUES: A Novel. By R. H. SHERARD. Crown 8vo, picture cover, **1s.**; cloth, **1s. 6d.**

SHERIDAN (GENERAL). — PERSONAL MEMOIRS OF GENERAL P. H. SHERIDAN. With Portraits and Facsimiles. Two Vols., demy 8vo, cloth, **24s.**

SHERIDAN'S (RICHARD BRINSLEY) COMPLETE WORKS. With Lie and Anecdotes. Including his Dramatic Writings, his Works in Prose and Poetry, Translations, Speeches, Jokes, &c. With 10 Illusts. Cr. 8vo, cl., **7s. 6d.**
THE RIVALS, THE SCHOOL FOR SCANDAL, and other Plays. Post 8vo, printed on laid paper and half-bound. **2s.**
SHERIDAN'S COMEDIES: THE RIVALS and THE SCHOOL FOR SCANDAL. Edited, with an Introduction and Notes to each Play, and a Biographical Sketch, by BRANDER MATTHEWS. With Illustrations. Demy 8vo, half-parchment, **12s. 6d.**

SIDNEY'S (SIR PHILIP) COMPLETE POETICAL WORKS, including all those in "Arcadia." With Portrait, Memorial-Introduction, Notes, &c. by the Rev. A. B. GROSART, D.D. Three Vols., crown 8vo, cloth boards, **18s.**

SIGNBOARDS: Their History. With Anecdotes of Famous Taverns and Remarkable Characters. By JACOB LARWOOD and JOHN CAMDEN HOTTEN. With Coloured Frontispiece and 94 Illustrations. Crown 8vo, cloth extra, **7s. 6d.**

SIMS (GEORGE R.), WORKS BY.
Post 8vo, illustrated boards, **2s.** each; cloth limp, **2s. 6d.** each.
ROGUES AND VAGABONDS. | MARY JANE MARRIED.
THE RING O' BELLS. | TALES OF TO-DAY.
MARY JANE'S MEMOIRS. | DRAMAS OF LIFE. With 60 Illustrations.
TINKLETOP'S CRIME. With a Frontispiece by MAURICE GREIFFENHAGEN.
Crown 8vo, picture cover, **1s.** each; cloth, **1s. 6d.** each.
HOW THE POOR LIVE; and HORRIBLE LONDON.
THE DAGONET RECITER AND READER: being Readings and Recitations in Prose and Verse, selected from his own Works by GEORGE R. SIMS.
DAGONET DITTIES. From the *Referee*.
THE CASE OF GEORGE CANDLEMAS.

SISTER DORA: A Biography. By MARGARET LONSDALE. With Four Illustrations. Demy 8vo, picture cover, **4d.**; cloth, **6d.**

SKETCHLEY.—A MATCH IN THE DARK. By ARTHUR SKETCHLEY.
Post 8vo, illustrated boards, 2s.

SLANG DICTIONARY (THE): Etymological, Historical, and Anecdotal. Crown 8vo, cloth extra, 6s. 6d.

SMITH (J. MOYR), WORKS BY.
THE PRINCE OF ARGOLIS. With 130 Illusts. Post 8vo, cloth extra, 3s. 6d.
TALES OF OLD THULE. With numerous Illustrations. Crown 8vo, cloth gilt, 6s.
THE WOOING OF THE WATER WITCH. Illustrated. Post 8vo, cloth, 6s.

SOCIETY IN LONDON. By A FOREIGN RESIDENT. Crown 8vo,
1s.; cloth, 1s. 6d.

SOCIETY IN PARIS: The Upper Ten Thousand. A Series of Letters
from Count PAUL VASILI to a Young French Diplomat. Crown 8vo. cloth, 6s.

SOMERSET. — SONGS OF ADIEU. By Lord HENRY SOMERSET.
Small 4to, Japanese vellum. 6s.

SPALDING.—ELIZABETHAN DEMONOLOGY: An Essay on the Belief
in the Existence of Devils. By T. A. SPALDING, LL.B. Crown 8vo, cloth extra, 5s.

SPEIGHT (T. W.), NOVELS BY.
Post 8vo, illustrated boards, 2s. each.
THE MYSTERIES OF HERON DYKE. | THE GOLDEN HOOP.
BY DEVIOUS WAYS, and A BARREN | HOODWINKED; and THE SANDY-
TITLE. | CROFT MYSTERY.

Post 8vo, cloth limp, 1s. 6d. each.
A BARREN TITLE. | WIFE OR NO WIFE?

THE SANDYCROFT MYSTERY. Crown 8vo, picture cover, 1s.

SPENSER FOR CHILDREN. By M. H. TOWRY. With Illustrations
by WALTER J. MORGAN. Crown 4to, cloth gilt, 6s.

STARRY HEAVENS (THE): A POETICAL BIRTHDAY BOOK. Royal
16mo, cloth extra, 2s. 6d.

STAUNTON.—THE LAWS AND PRACTICE OF CHESS. With an
Analysis of the Openings. By HOWARD STAUNTON. Edited by ROBERT B. WORMALD.
Crown 8vo, cloth extra, 5s.

STEDMAN (E. C.), WORKS BY.
VICTORIAN POETS. Thirteenth Edition. Crown 8vo, cloth extra, 9s.
THE POETS OF AMERICA. Crown 8vo, cloth extra, 9s.

STERNDALE. — THE AFGHAN KNIFE: A Novel. By ROBERT
ARMITAGE STERNDALE. Cr. 8vo, cloth extra, 3s. 6d.; post 8vo, illust. boards, 2s.

STEVENSON (R. LOUIS), WORKS BY. Post 8vo, cl. limp, 2s. 6d. each.
TRAVELS WITH A DONKEY. Eighth Edit. With a Frontis. by WALTER CRANE.
AN INLAND VOYAGE. Fourth Edition. With a Frontispiece by WALTER CRANE.

Crown 8vo, buckram, gilt top, 6s. each.
FAMILIAR STUDIES OF MEN AND BOOKS. Fifth Edition.
THE SILVERADO SQUATTERS. With a Frontispiece. Third Edition.
THE MERRY MEN. Second Edition. | UNDERWOODS: Poems. Fifth Edition.
MEMORIES AND PORTRAITS. Third Edition.
VIRGINIBUS PUERISQUE, and other Papers. Fifth Edition. | BALLADS.

NEW ARABIAN NIGHTS. Eleventh Edition. Crown 8vo, buckram, gilt top, 6s.;
post 8vo, illustrated boards, 2s.
PRINCE OTTO. Post 8vo, illustrated boards, 2s.
FATHER DAMIEN: An Open Letter to the Rev. Dr. Hyde. Second Edition.
Crown 8vo, hand-made and brown paper, 1s.

STODDARD. — SUMMER CRUISING IN THE SOUTH SEAS. By
C. WARREN STODDARD. Illustrated by WALLIS MACKAY. Cr. 8vo, cl. extra, 3s. 6d.

STORIES FROM FOREIGN NOVELISTS. With Notices by HELEN and
ALICE ZIMMERN. Crown 8vo, cloth extra, 3s. 6d.; post 8vo, illustrated boards, 2s.

STRANGE MANUSCRIPT (A) FOUND IN A COPPER CYLINDER. With 19 Illustrations by GILBERT GAUL. Third Edition. Crown 8vo, cloth extra, **5s.**

STRUTT'S SPORTS AND PASTIMES OF THE PEOPLE OF ENGLAND; including the Rural and Domestic Recreations, May Games, Mummeries, Shows, &c., from the Earliest Period to the Present Time. Edited by WILLIAM HONE. With 140 Illustrations. Crown 8vo, cloth extra, **7s. 6d.**

SUBURBAN HOMES (THE) OF LONDON : A Residential Guide. With a Map, and Notes on Rental, Rates, and Accommodation Crown 8vo, cloth, **7s. 6d.**

SWIFT'S (DEAN) CHOICE WORKS, in Prose and Verse. With Memoir, Portrait, and Facsimiles of the Maps in "Gulliver's Travels." Cr. 8vo, cl., **7s. 6d.**
GULLIVER'S TRAVELS, and A TALE OF A TUB. Post 8vo, printed on laid paper and half-bound, **2s.**
A MONOGRAPH ON SWIFT. By J. CHURTON COLLINS. Cr. 8vo, cloth, **8s.** [*Shortly.*

SWINBURNE (ALGERNON C.), WORKS BY.

SELECTIONS FROM POETICAL WORKS OF A. C. SWINBURNE. Fcap. 8vo, **6s.**
ATALANTA IN CALYDON. Cr. 8vo, **6s.**
CHASTELARD: A Tragedy. Cr. 8vo, **7s.**
NOTES ON POEMS AND REVIEWS. Demy 8vo, **1s.**
POEMS AND BALLADS. FIRST SERIES. Crown 8vo or fcap. 8vo, **9s.**
POEMS AND BALLADS. SECOND SERIES. Crown 8vo or fcap. 8vo, **9s.**
POEMS AND BALLADS. THIRD SERIES. Crown 8vo, **7s.**
SONGS BEFORE SUNRISE. Crown 8vo, **10s. 6d.**
BOTHWELL: A Tragedy. Crown 8vo, **12s. 6d.**
SONGS OF TWO NATIONS. Cr. 8vo, **6s.**

GEORGE CHAPMAN. (*See* Vol. II. of G. CHAPMAN's Works.) Crown 8vo, **6s.**
ESSAYS AND STUDIES. Cr. 8vo, **12s.**
ERECHTHEUS: A Tragedy. Cr. 8vo, **6s.**
SONGS OF THE SPRINGTIDES. Crown 8vo, **6s.**
STUDIES IN SONG. Crown 8vo, **7s.**
MARY STUART: A Tragedy. Cr. 8vo **8s**
TRISTRAM OF LYONESSE. Cr. 8vo, **9s.**
A CENTURY OF ROUNDELS. Sm. 4to, **8s.**
A MIDSUMMER HOLIDAY. Cr. 8vo, **7s.**
MARINO FALIERO: A Tragedy. Crown 8vo, **6s.**
A STUDY OF VICTOR HUGO. Cr. 8vo, **6s.**
MISCELLANIES. Crown 8vo, **12s.**
LOCRINE: A Tragedy. Cr. 8vo, **6s.**
A STUDY OF BEN JONSON. Cr. 8vo, **7s.**

SYMONDS.—WINE, WOMEN, AND SONG : Mediæval Latin Students' Songs. With Essay and Trans. by J. ADDINGTON SYMONDS. Fcap. 8vo, parchment, **6s.**

SYNTAX'S (DR.) THREE TOURS : In Search of the Picturesque, in Search of Consolation, and in Search of a Wife. With ROWLANDSON's Coloured Illustrations, and Life of the Author by J. C. HOTTEN. Crown 8vo, cloth extra, **7s. 6d.**

TAINE'S HISTORY OF ENGLISH LITERATURE. Translated by HENRY VAN LAUN. Four Vols., medium 8vo, cloth boards, **30s.**—POPULAR EDITION, Two Vols., large crown 8vo, cloth extra, **15s.**

TAYLOR'S (BAYARD) DIVERSIONS OF THE ECHO CLUB : Burlesques of Modern Writers. Post 8vo, cloth limp, **2s.**

TAYLOR (DR. J. E., F.L.S.), WORKS BY. Cr. 8vo, cl. ex., **7s. 6d.** each.
THE SAGACITY AND MORALITY OF PLANTS : A Sketch of the Life and Conduct of the Vegetable Kingdom. With a Coloured Frontispiece and 100 Illustrations.
OUR COMMON BRITISH FOSSILS, and Where to Find Them. 331 Illustrations.
THE PLAYTIME NATURALIST. With 366 Illustrations. Crown 8vo, cloth, **5s.**

TAYLOR'S (TOM) HISTORICAL DRAMAS. Containing "Clancarty," "Jeanne Darc," "'Twixt Axe and Crown," "The Fool's Revenge," "Arkwright's Wife," "Anne Boleyn," "Plot and Passion." Crown 8vo, cloth extra, **7s. 6d.**
⁎⁎ The Plays may also be had separately, at **1s.** each.

TENNYSON (LORD) : A Biographical Sketch. By H. J. JENNINGS. With a Photograph-Portrait. Crown 8vo, cloth extra, **6s.**

THACKERAYANA : Notes and Anecdotes. Illustrated by Hundreds of Sketches by WILLIAM MAKEPEACE THACKERAY, depicting Humorous Incidents in his School-life, and Favourite Characters in the Books of his Every-day Reading. With a Coloured Frontispiece. Crown 8vo, cloth extra, **7s. 6d.**

THAMES. — A NEW PICTORIAL HISTORY OF THE THAMES. By A. S. KRAUSSE. With 340 Illustrations Post 8vo, **1s. ;** cloth, **1s. 6d.**

THOMAS (BERTHA), NOVELS BY. Cr. 8vo, cl., 3s. 6d. ea.: post 8vo, 2s. ea.
CRESSIDA. | THE VIOLIN-PLAYER. | PROUD MAISIE.

THOMSON'S SEASONS, and CASTLE OF INDOLENCE. Introduction
by ALLAN CUNNINGHAM, and Illustrations on Steel and Wood. Cr. 8vo. cl., 7s. 6d.

THORNBURY (WALTER), WORKS BY. Cr. 8vo, cl. extra, 7s. 6d. each.
THE LIFE AND CORRESPONDENCE OF J. M. W. TURNER. Founded upon
Letters and Papers furnished by his Friends. With Illustrations in Colours.
HAUNTED LONDON. Edit. by E. WALFORD, M.A. Illusts. by F. W. FAIRHOLT, F.S.A.

Post 8vo, illustrated boards, 2s. each.
OLD STORIES RE-TOLD. | TALES FOR THE MARINES.

TIMBS (JOHN), WORKS BY. Crown 8vo, cloth extra, 7s. 6d. each.
THE HISTORY OF CLUBS AND CLUB LIFE IN LONDON: Anecdotes of its
Famous Coffee-houses, Hostelries, and Taverns. With 42 Illustrations.
ENGLISH ECCENTRICS AND ECCENTRICITIES: Stories of Wealth and Fashion,
Delusions, Impostures, and Fanatic Missions, Sporting Scenes, Eccentric Artists,
Theatrical Folk, Men of Letters, &c. With 48 Illustrations.

TROLLOPE (ANTHONY), NOVELS BY.
Crown 8vo, cloth extra, 3s. 6d. each; post 8vo, illustrated boards, 2s. each.
THE WAY WE LIVE NOW.   MARION FAY.
KEPT IN THE DARK.   MR. SCARBOROUGH'S FAMILY.
FRAU FROHMANN.   THE LAND-LEAGUERS.

Post 8vo, illustrated boards, 2s. each.
GOLDEN LION OF GRANPERE. | JOHN CALDIGATE. | AMERICAN SENATOR.

TROLLOPE (FRANCES E.), NOVELS BY.
Crown 8vo, cloth extra, 3s. 6d. each; post 8vo, illustrated boards, 2s. each.
LIKE SHIPS UPON THE SEA. | MABEL'S PROGRESS. | ANNE FURNESS.

TROLLOPE (T. A.).—DIAMOND CUT DIAMOND. Post 8vo, illust. bds., 2s.

TROWBRIDGE.—FARNELL'S FOLLY: A Novel. By J. T. TROW-
BRIDGE. Post 8vo, illustrated boards, 2s.

TYTLER (C. C. FRASER-).—MISTRESS JUDITH: A Novel. By
C. C. FRASER-TYTLER. Crown 8vo, cloth extra, 3s. 6d.; post 8vo, illust. boards, 2s.

TYTLER (SARAH), NOVELS BY.
Crown 8vo, cloth extra, 3s. 6d. each; post 8vo, illustrated boards, 2s. each.
THE BRIDE'S PASS.   BURIED DIAMONDS.
NOBLESSE OBLIGE.   THE BLACKHALL GHOSTS.
LADY BELL.

Post 8vo, illustrated boards, 2s. each.
WHAT SHE CAME THROUGH.   BEAUTY AND THE BEAST.
CITOYENNE JACQUELINE.   DISAPPEARED.
SAINT MUNGO'S CITY.   THE HUGUENOT FAMILY.

VILLARI.—A DOUBLE BOND. By LINDA VILLARI. Fcap. 8vo, picture
cover. 1s.

WALT WHITMAN, POEMS BY. Edited, with Introduction, by
WILLIAM M. ROSSETTI. With Portrait. Cr. 8vo, hand-made paper and buckram, 6s.

WALTON AND COTTON'S COMPLETE ANGLER; or, The Con-
templative Man's Recreation, by IZAAK WALTON; and Instructions how to Angle for a
Trout or Grayling in a clear Stream, by CHARLES COTTON. With Memoirs and Notes
by Sir HARRIS NICOLAS, and 61 Illustrations. Crown 8vo, cloth antique, 7s. 6d.

WARD (HERBERT), WORKS BY.
FIVE YEARS WITH THE CONGO CANNIBALS. With 92 Illustrations by the
Author, VICTOR PERARD, and W. B. DAVIS. Third ed. Roy. 8vo, cloth ex., 14s.
MY LIFE WITH STANLEY'S REAR GUARD. With a Map by F. S. WELLER,
F.R.G.S. Post 8vo, 1s.; cloth, 1s. 6d.

WARNER.—A ROUNDABOUT JOURNEY. By CHARLES DUDLEY
WARNER. Crown 8vo, cloth extra, 6s.

WALFORD (EDWARD, M.A.), WORKS BY.
WALFORD'S COUNTY FAMILIES OF THE UNITED KINGDOM (1891). Containing the Descent, Birth, Marriage, Education, &c., ot 12,000 Heads of Families, their Heirs, Offices, Addresses, Clubs, &c. Royal 8vo, cloth gilt, **50s.**
WALFORD'S SHILLING PEERAGE (1891). Containing a List of the House of Lords, Scotch and Irish Peers, &c. 32mo, cloth, **1s.**
WALFORD'S SHILLING BARONETAGE (1891). Containing a List of the Baronets of the United Kingdom, Biographical Notices, Addresses, &c. 32mo, cloth, **1s.**
WALFORD'S SHILLING KNIGHTAGE (1891). Containing a List of the Knights of the United Kingdom, Biographical Notices, Addresses, &c. 32mo, cloth, **1s.**
WALFORD'S SHILLING HOUSE OF COMMONS (1891). Containing a List of all Members of Parliament, their Addresses, Clubs, &c. 32mo, cloth, **1s.**
WALFORD'S COMPLETE PEERAGE, BARONETAGE, KNIGHTAGE, AND HOUSE OF COMMONS (1891). Royal 32mo, cloth extra, gilt edges **5s.**
WALFORD'S WINDSOR PEERAGE, BARONETAGE, AND KNIGHTAGE (1891). Crown 8vo, cloth extra, **12s. 6d.**
TALES OF OUR GREAT FAMILIES. Crown 8vo, cloth extra, **3s. 6d.**
WILLIAM PITT: A Biography. Post 8vo, cloth extra, **5s.**

WARRANT TO EXECUTE CHARLES I. A Facsimile, with the 59 Signatures and Seals. Printed on paper 22 in. by 14 in. **2s.**
WARRANT TO EXECUTE MARY QUEEN OF SCOTS. A Facsimile, including Queen Elizabeth's Signature and the Great Seal. **2s.**

WEATHER, HOW TO FORETELL THE, WITH POCKET SPEC-TROSCOPE. By F. W. CORY. With 10 Illustrations. Cr. 8vo, **1s.**; cloth, **1s. 6d.**

WESTROPP.—HANDBOOK OF POTTERY AND PORCELAIN. By HODDER M. WESTROPP. With Illusts. and List of Marks. Cr. 8vo, cloth, **4s. 6d.**

WHIST.—HOW TO PLAY SOLO WHIST. By ABRAHAM S. WILKS and CHARLES F. PARDON. Crown 8vo, cloth extra, **3s. 6d.**

WHISTLER'S (MR.) TEN O'CLOCK. Cr. 8vo, hand-made paper, **1s.**

WHITE.—THE NATURAL HISTORY OF SELBORNE. By GILBERT WHITE, M.A. Post 8vo, printed on laid paper and half-bound, **2s.**

WILLIAMS (W. MATTIEU, F.R.A.S.), WORKS BY.
SCIENCE IN SHORT CHAPTERS. Crown 8vo, cloth extra, **7s. 6d.**
A SIMPLE TREATISE ON HEAT. With Illusts. Cr. 8vo, cloth limp, **2s. 6d.**
THE CHEMISTRY OF COOKERY. Crown 8vo, cloth extra, **6s.**
THE CHEMISTRY OF IRON AND STEEL MAKING. Crown 8vo, cloth extra, **9s.**

WILLIAMSON.—A CHILD WIDOW. By Mrs. F. H. WILLIAMSON. Three Vols., crown 8vo.

WILSON (DR. ANDREW, F.R.S.E.), WORKS BY.
CHAPTERS ON EVOLUTION. With 259 Illustrations. Cr. 8vo, cloth extra, **7s. 6d.**
LEAVES FROM A NATURALIST'S NOTE-BOOK. Post 8vo, cloth limp, **2s. 6d.**
LEISURE-TIME STUDIES. With Illustrations. Crown 8vo, cloth extra, **6s.**
STUDIES IN LIFE AND SENSE. With numerous Illusts. Cr. 8vo, cl. ex., **6s.**
COMMON ACCIDENTS: HOW TO TREAT THEM. Illusts. Cr. 8vo, **1s.**; cl., **1s. 6d.**
GLIMPSES OF NATURE. With 35 Illustrations. Crown 8vo, cloth extra, **3s. 6d.**

WINTER (J. S.), STORIES BY. Post 8vo, illustrated boards, **2s.** each.
CAVALRY LIFE. | REGIMENTAL LEGENDS.

WISSMANN.—MY SECOND JOURNEY THROUGH EQUATORIAL AFRICA, from the Congo to the Zambesi, in 1886, 1887. By HERMANN VON WISS-MANN. With a Map and 92 Illustrations. Demy 8vo, cloth extra, **16s.**

WOOD.—SABINA: A Novel. By Lady WOOD. Post 8vo, boards, **2s.**

WOOD (H. F.), DETECTIVE STORIES BY.
Crown 8vo, cloth extra, **6s.** each; post 8vo, illustrated boards, **2s.** each.
PASSENGER FROM SCOTLAND YARD. | ENGLISHMAN OF THE RUE CAIN.

WOOLLEY.—RACHEL ARMSTRONG; or, Love and Theology. By CELIA PARKER WOOLLEY. Post 8vo, illustrated boards, **2s.**; cloth, **2s. 6d.**

WRIGHT (THOMAS), WORKS BY. Crown 8vo, cloth extra, **7s. 6d.** each.
CARICATURE HISTORY OF THE GEORGES. With 400 Pictures, Caricatures, Squibs, Broadsides, Window Pictures, &c.
HISTORY OF CARICATURE AND OF THE GROTESQUE IN ART, LITERA-TURE, SCULPTURE, AND PAINTING. Illustrated by F. W. FAIRHOLT, F.S.A.

YATES (EDMUND), NOVELS BY. Post 8vo, illustrated boards, **2s.** each.
LAND AT LAST. | THE FORLORN HOPE. | CASTAWAY.

LISTS OF BOOKS CLASSIFIED IN SERIES.

, *For full cataloguing, see alphabetical arrangement, pp. 1-25.*

THE MAYFAIR LIBRARY.   Post 8vo, cloth limp, 2s. 6d. per Volume.

A Journey Round My Room. By XAVIER DE MAISTRE.
Quips and Quiddities. By W. D. ADAMS.
The Agony Column of "The Times."
Melancholy Anatomised: Abridgment of "Burton's Anatomy of Melancholy."
The Speeches of Charles Dickens.
Literary Frivolities, Fancies, Follies, and Frolics. By W. T. DOBSON.
Poetical Ingenuities. By W. T. DOBSON.
The Cupboard Papers. By FIN-BEC.
W. S. Gilbert's Plays. FIRST SERIES.
W. S. Gilbert's Plays. SECOND SERIES.
Songs of Irish Wit and Humour.
Animals and Masters. By Sir A. HELPS.
Social Pressure. By Sir A. HELPS.
Curiosities of Criticism. H. J. JENNINGS.
Holmes's Autocrat of Breakfast-Table.
Pencil and Palette. By R. KEMPT.

Little Essays: from LAMB's Letters.
Forensic Anecdotes. By JACOB LARWOOD
Theatrical Anecdotes. JACOB LARWOOD.
Jeux d'Esprit. Edited by HENRY S. LEIGH.
Witch Stories. By E. LYNN LINTON.
Ourselves. By E. LYNN LINTON.
Pastimes & Players. By R. MACGREGOR.
New Paul and Virginia. W. H. MALLOCK.
New Republic. By W. H. MALLOCK.
Puck on Pegasus. By H. C. PENNELL.
Pegasus Re-Saddled. By H. C. PENNELL.
Muses of Mayfair. Ed. H. C. PENNELL.
Thoreau: His Life & Aims. By H. A. PAGE.
Puniana. By Hon. HUGH ROWLEY.
More Puniana. By Hon. HUGH ROWLEY.
The Philosophy of Handwriting.
By Stream and Sea. By WM. SENIOR.
Leaves from a Naturalist's Note-Book. By Dr. ANDREW WILSON.

THE GOLDEN LIBRARY.   Post 8vo, cloth limp, 2s. per Volume.

Bayard Taylor's Diversions of the Echo Club.
Bennett's Ballad History of England.
Bennett's Songs for Sailors.
Godwin's Lives of the Necromancers.
Pope's Poetical Works.
Holmes's Autocrat of Breakfast Table.

Holmes's Professor at Breakfast Table.
Jesse's Scenes of Country Life.
Leigh Hunt's Tale for a Chimney Corner.
Mallory's Mort d'Arthur: Selections.
Pascal's Provincial Letters.
Rochefoucauld's Maxims & Reflections.

THE WANDERER'S LIBRARY.   Crown 8vo, cloth extra, 3s. 6d. each.

Wanderings in Patagonia. By JULIUS BEERBOHM. Illustrated.
Camp Notes. By FREDERICK BOYLE.
Savage Life. By FREDERICK BOYLE.
Merrie England in the Olden Time. By G. DANIEL. Illustrated by CRUIKSHANK.
Circus Life. By THOMAS FROST.
Lives of the Conjurers. THOMAS FROST.
The Old Showmen and the Old London Fairs. By THOMAS FROST.
Low-Life Deeps. By JAMES GREENWOOD.

Wilds of London. JAMES GREENWOOD.
Tunis. Chev. HESSE-WARTEGG. 22 Illusts.
Life and Adventures of a Cheap Jack.
World Behind the Scenes. P. FITZGERALD.
Tavern Anecdotes and Sayings.
The Genial Showman. By E. P. HINGSTON
Story of London Parks. JACOB LARWOOD.
London Characters. By HENRY MAYHEW.
Seven Generations of Executioners.
Summer Cruising in the South Seas. By C. WARREN STODDARD. Illustrated.

POPULAR SHILLING BOOKS.

Harry Fludyer at Cambridge.
Jeff Briggs's Love Story. BRET HARTE.
Twins of Table Mountain. BRET HARTE.
A Day's Tour. By PERCY FITZGERALD.
Esther's Glove. By R. E. FRANCILLON.
Sentenced! By SOMERVILLE GIBNEY.
The Professor's Wife. By L. GRAHAM.
Mrs. Gainsborough's Diamonds. By JULIAN HAWTHORNE.
Niagara Spray. By J. HOLLINGSHEAD.
A Romance of the Queen's Hounds. By CHARLES JAMES.
The Garden that Paid the Rent. By TOM JERROLD.
Cut by the Mess. By ARTHUR KEYSER.
Our Sensation Novel. J. H. MCCARTHY.
Doom! By JUSTIN H. MCCARTHY, M.P.
Dolly. By JUSTIN H. MCCARTHY, M.P.
Lily Lass. JUSTIN H. MCCARTHY, M.P.

Was She Good or Bad? By W. MINTO.
That Girl in Black. Mrs. MOLESWORTH.
Notes from the "News." By JAS. PAYN.
Beyond the Gates. By E. S. PHELPS.
Old Maid's Paradise. By E. S. PHELPS.
Burglars in Paradise. By E. S. PHELPS.
Jack the Fisherman. By E. S. PHELPS.
Trooping with Crows. By C. L. PIRKIS.
Bible Characters. By CHARLES READE.
Rogues. By R. H. SHERARD.
The Dagonet Reciter. By G. R. SIMS.
How the Poor Live. By G. R. SIMS.
Case of George Candlemas. G. R. SIMS.
Sandycroft Mystery. T. W. SPEIGHT.
Hoodwinked. By T. W. SPEIGHT.
Father Damien. By R. L. STEVENSON.
A Double Bond. By LINDA VILLARI.
My Life with Stanley's Rear Guard. By HERBERT WARD.

THE PICCADILLY (3/6) NOVELS—*continued.*

By CHARLES GIBBON.

Robin Gray. | The Golden Shaft.
In Honour Bound. | Of High Degree.
Loving a Dream.
The Flower of the Forest.

By JULIAN HAWTHORNE.

Garth. | Dust.
Ellice Quentin. | Fortune's Fool.
Sebastian Strome. | Beatrix Randolph.
David Poindexter's Disappearance.
The Spectre of the Camera.

By Sir A. HELPS.

Ivan de Biron.

By ISAAC HENDERSON.

Agatha Page.

By Mrs. ALFRED HUNT.

The Leaden Casket. | Self-Condemned.
That other Person.

By JEAN INGELOW.

Fated to be Free.

By R. ASHE KING.

A Drawn Game.
"The Wearing of the Green."

By HENRY KINGSLEY.

Number Seventeen.

By E. LYNN LINTON.

Patricia Kemball. | Ione.
Under which Lord? | Paston Carew.
"My Love!" | Sowing the Wind.
The Atonement of Leam Dundas.
The World Well Lost.

By HENRY W. LUCY.

Gideon Fleyce.

By JUSTIN McCARTHY.

A Fair Saxon. | Donna Quixote.
Linley Rochford. | Maid of Athens.
Miss Misanthrope. | Camiola.
The Waterdale Neighbours.
My Enemy's Daughter.
Dear Lady Disdain.
The Comet of a Season.

By AGNES MACDONELL.

Quaker Cousins.

By FLORENCE MARRYAT.

Open! Sesame!

By D. CHRISTIE MURRAY.

Life's Atonement. | Coals of Fire.
Joseph's Coat. | Val Strange.
A Model Father. | Hearts.
A Bit of Human Nature.
First Person Singular.
Cynic Fortune.
The Way of the World.

By MURRAY & HERMAN.

The Bishops' Bible.

By GEORGES OHNET.

A Weird Gift.

THE PICCADILLY (3/6) NOVELS—*continued.*

By Mrs. OLIPHANT.

Whiteladies.

By OUIDA.

Held in Bondage. | Two Little Wooden
Strathmore. | Shoes.
Chandos. | In a Winter City.
Under Two Flags. | Ariadne.
Idalia. | Friendship.
CecilCastlemaine's | Moths. | Ruffino.
Gage. | Pipistrello.
Tricotrin. | Puck. | A Village Commune
Folle Farine. | Bimbi. | Wanda.
A Dog of Flanders. | Frescoes.
Pascarel. | Signa. | In Maremma.
Princess Naprax- | Othmar. | Syrlin.
ine. | Guilderoy.

By MARGARET A. PAUL.

Gentle and Simple.

By JAMES PAYN.

Lost Sir Massingberd.
Less Black than We're Painted.
A Confidential Agent.
A Grape from a Thorn.
Some Private Views.
In Peril and Privation.
The Mystery of Mirbridge.
The Canon's Ward.
Walter's Word. | Talk of the Town.
By Proxy. | Holiday Tasks.
High Spirits. | The Burnt Million.
Under One Roof. | The Word and the
From Exile. | Will.
Glow-worm Tales. | Sunny Stories.

By E. C. PRICE.

Valentina. | The Foreigners.
Mrs. Lancaster's Rival.

By CHARLES READE.

It is Never Too Late to Mend.
The Double Marriage.
Love Me Little, Love Me Long.
The Cloister and the Hearth.
The Course of True Love.
The Autobiography of a Thief.
Put Yourself in his Place.
A Terrible Temptation.
Singleheart and Doubleface.
Good Stories of Men and other Animals.
Hard Cash. | Wandering Heir.
Peg Woffington. | A Woman-Hater.
ChristieJohnstone. | A Simpleton.
Griffith Gaunt. | Readiana.
Foul Play. | The Jilt.

By Mrs. J. H. RIDDELL.

Her Mother's Darling.
Prince of Wales's Garden Party.
Weird Stories.

By F. W. ROBINSON.

Women are Strange.
The Hands of Justice.

By W. CLARK RUSSELL.

An Ocean Tragedy.
My Shipmate Louise.

By JOHN SAUNDERS.

Guy Waterman. | Two Dreamers.
Bound to the Wheel.
The Lion in the Path.

THE PICCADILLY (3/6) NOVELS—*continued.*

By KATHARINE SAUNDERS.

Margaret and Elizabeth.
Gideon's Rock. | Heart Salvage.
The High Mills. | Sebastian.

By HAWLEY SMART.
Without Love or Licence.

By R. A. STERNDALE.
The Afghan Knife.

By BERTHA THOMAS.
Proud Maisie. | Cressida.
The Violin-player.

By FRANCES E. TROLLOPE.
Like Ships upon the Sea.
Anne Furness. | Mabel's Progress.

THE PICCADILLY (3/6) NOVELS—*continued.*

By ANTHONY TROLLOPE.
Frau Frohmann. | Kept in the Dark.
Marion Fay. | Land-Leaguers.
The Way We Live Now.
Mr. Scarborough's Family.

By IVAN TURGENIEFF, &c.
Stories from Foreign Novelists.

By C. C. FRASER-TYTLER.
Mistress Judith.

By SARAH TYTLER.
The Bride's Pass. | Lady Bell.
Noblesse Oblige. | Buried Diamonds.
The Blackhall Ghosts.

CHEAP EDITIONS OF POPULAR NOVELS.

Post 8vo, illustrated boards, 2s. each.

By ARTEMUS WARD.
Artemus Ward Complete.

By EDMOND ABOUT.
The Fellah.

By HAMILTON AIDE.
Carr of Carrlyon. | Confidences.

By MARY ALBERT.
Brooke Finchley's Daughter.

By Mrs. ALEXANDER.
Maid, Wife, or Widow ? | Valerie's Fate.

By GRANT ALLEN.
Strange Stories. | The Devil's Die.
Philistia. | This Mortal Coil.
Babylon. | In all Shades.
The Beckoning Hand.
For Maimie's Sake. | Tents of Shem.

By ALAN ST. AUBYN.
A Fellow of Trinity.

By Rev. S. BARING GOULD.
Red Spider. | Eve.

By FRANK BARRETT.
Fettered for Life.
Between Life and Death.

By SHELSLEY BEAUCHAMP.
Grantley Grange.

By W. BESANT & J. RICE.
This Son of Vulcan. | By Celia's Arbour.
My Little Girl. | Monks of Thelema.
Case of Mr.Lucraft. | The Seamy Side.
Golden Butterfly. | Ten Years' Tenant.
Ready-Money Mortiboy.
With Harp and Crown.
'Twas in Trafalgar's Bay.
The Chaplain of the Fleet.

By WALTER BESANT.
Dorothy Forster. | Uncle Jack.
Children of Gibeon. | Herr Paulus.
All Sorts and Conditions of Men.
The Captains' Room.
All in a Garden Fair.
The World Went Very Well Then.
For Faith and Freedom.

By FREDERICK BOYLE.
Camp Notes. | Savage Life.
Chronicles of No-man's Land.

By BRET HARTE.
Flip. | Californian Stories
Maruja. | Gabriel Conroy.
An Heiress of Red Dog.
The Luck of Roaring Camp.
A Phyllis of the Sierras.

By HAROLD BRYDGES.
Uncle Sam at Home.

By ROBERT BUCHANAN.
The Shadow of the | The Martyrdom of
Sword. | Madeline.
A Child of Nature. | Annan Water.
God and the Man. | The New Abelard.
Love Me for Ever. | Matt.
Foxglove Manor. | The Heir of Linne.
The Master of the Mine.

By HALL CAINE.
The Shadow of a Crime.
A Son of Hagar. | The Deemster.

By Commander CAMERON.
The Cruise of the "Black Prince."

By Mrs. LOVETT CAMERON.
Deceivers Ever. | Juliet's Guardian.

By AUSTIN CLARE.
For the Love of a Lass.

By Mrs. ARCHER CLIVE.
Paul Ferroll.
Why Paul Ferroll Killed his Wife.

By MACLAREN COBBAN.
The Cure of Souls.

By C. ALLSTON COLLINS.
The Bar Sinister.

MORT. & FRANCES COLLINS.
Sweet Anne Page. | Transmigration.
From Midnight to Midnight.
A Fight with Fortune.
Sweet and Twenty. | Village Comedy.
Frances. | You Play me False.
Blacksmith and Scholar.

Two-Shilling Novels—*continued.*

By WILKIE COLLINS.

Armadale.	My Miscellanies.
After Dark.	Woman in White.
No Name.	The Moonstone.
Antonina. | Basil.	Man and Wife.
Hide and Seek.	Poor Miss Finch.
The Dead Secret.	The Fallen Leaves.
Queen of Hearts.	Jezebel's Daughter
Miss or Mrs?	The Black Robe.
New Magdalen.	Heart and Science.
The Frozen Deep.	"I Say No."
Law and the Lady.	The Evil Genius.
The Two Destinies.	Little Novels.
Haunted Hotel.	Legacy of Cain.
A Rogue's Life.	Blind Love.

By M. J. COLQUHOUN.
Every Inch a Soldier.

By DUTTON COOK.
Leo. | Paul Foster's Daughter.

By C. EGBERT CRADDOCK.
Prophet of the Great Smoky Mountains.

By WILLIAM CYPLES.
Hearts of Gold.

By ALPHONSE DAUDET.
The Evangelist; or, Port Salvation.

By JAMES DE MILLE.
A Castle in Spain.

By J. LEITH DERWENT.
Our Lady of Tears. | Circe's Lovers.

By CHARLES DICKENS.

Sketches by Boz.	Oliver Twist.
Pickwick Papers.	Nicholas Nickleby.

By DICK DONOVAN.
The Man-Hunter. | Caught at Last!
Tracked and Taken.
Who Poisoned Hetty Duncan?
The Man from Manchester.
A Detective's Triumphs.

By CONAN DOYLE, &c.
Strange Secrets.

By Mrs. ANNIE EDWARDES.
A Point of Honour. | Archie Lovell.

By M. BETHAM-EDWARDS.
Felicia. | Kitty.

By EDWARD EGGLESTON.
Roxy.

By PERCY FITZGERALD.

Bella Donna.	Polly.
Never Forgotten.	Fatal Zero.
The Second Mrs. Tillotson.	
Seventy-five Brooke Street.	
The Lady of Brantome.	

ALBANY DE FONBLANQUE.
Filthy Lucre.

By R. E. FRANCILLON.

Olympia.	Queen Cophetua.
One by One.	King or Knave?
A Real Queen.	Romances of Law.

By HAROLD FREDERIC.
Seth's Brother's Wife.
The Lawton Girl.

Pref. by Sir BARTLE FRERE.
Pandurang Hari.

Two-Shilling Novels—*continued,*

By HAIN FRISWELL.
One of Two.

By EDWARD GARRETT.
The Capel Girls.

By CHARLES GIBBON.

Robin Gray.	In Honour Bound.
Fancy Free.	Flower of Forest.
For Lack of Gold.	Braes of Yarrow.
What will the	The Golden Shaft.
World Say?	Of High Degree.
In Love and War.	Mead and Stream.
For the King.	Loving a Dream.
In Pastures Green.	A Hard Knot.
Queen of Meadow.	Heart's Delight.
A Heart's Problem.	Blood-Money.
The Dead Heart.	

By WILLIAM GILBERT.
Dr. Austin's Guests. | James Duke.
The Wizard of the Mountain.

By HENRY GREVILLE.
A Noble Woman.

By JOHN HABBERTON.
Brueton's Bayou. | Country Luck.

By ANDREW HALLIDAY.
Every-Day Papers.

By Lady DUFFUS HARDY.
Paul Wynter's Sacrifice.

By THOMAS HARDY.
Under the Greenwood Tree.

By J. BERWICK HARWOOD.
The Tenth Earl.

By JULIAN HAWTHORNE.

Garth.	Sebastian Strome.
Ellice Quentin.	Dust.
Fortune's Fool.	Beatrix Randolph.
Miss Cadogna.	Love—or a Name.
David Poindexter's Disappearance.	
The Spectre of the Camera.	

By Sir ARTHUR HELPS.
Ivan de Biron.

By Mrs. CASHEL HOEY.
The Lover's Creed.

By Mrs. GEORGE HOOPER.
The House of Raby.

By TIGHE HOPKINS.
'Twixt Love and Duty.

By Mrs. ALFRED HUNT.
Thornicroft's Model. | Self-Condemned.
That Other Person. | Leaden Casket.

By JEAN INGELOW.
Fated to be Free.

By HARRIETT JAY.
The Dark Colleen.
The Queen of Connaught.

By MARK KERSHAW.
Colonial Facts and Fictions.

By R. ASHE KING.
A Drawn Game. | Passion's Slave.
"The Wearing of the Green."

Two-Shilling Novels—*continued.*

By HENRY KINGSLEY.
Oakshott Castle.

By JOHN LEYS.
The Lindsays.

By MARY LINSKILL.
In Exchange for a Soul.

By E. LYNN LINTON.
Patricia Kemball. | Paston Carew.
World Well Lost. | "My Love!"
Under which Lord? | Ione.
The Atonement of Leam Dundas.
With a Silken Thread.
The Rebel of the Family.
Sowing the Wind.

By HENRY W. LUCY.
Gideon Fleyce.

By JUSTIN McCARTHY.
A Fair Saxon. | Donna Quixote.
Linley Rochford. | Maid of Athens.
Miss Misanthrope. | Camiola.
Dear Lady Disdain.
The Waterdale Neighbours.
My Enemy's Daughter.
The Comet of a Season.

By AGNES MACDONELL.
Quaker Cousins.

KATHARINE S. MACQUOID.
The Evil Eye. | Lost Rose.

By W. H. MALLOCK.
The New Republic.

By FLORENCE MARRYAT.
Open! Sesame! | Fighting the Air.
A Harvest of Wild Oats.
Written in Fire.

By J. MASTERMAN.
Half-a-dozen Daughters.

By BRANDER MATTHEWS.
A Secret of the Sea.

By JEAN MIDDLEMASS.
Touch and Go. | Mr. Dorillion.

By Mrs. MOLESWORTH.
Hathercourt Rectory.

By J. E. MUDDOCK.
Stories Weird and Wonderful.
The Dead Man's Secret.

By D. CHRISTIE MURRAY.
A Model Father. | Old Blazer's Hero.
Joseph's Coat. | Hearts.
Coals of Fire. | Way of the World.
Val Strange. | Cynic Fortune.
A Life's Atonement.
By the Gate of the Sea.
A Bit of Human Nature.
First Person Singular.

By MURRAY and HERMAN.
One Traveller Returns.
Paul Jones's Alias.

By HENRY MURRAY.
A Game of Bluff.

By ALICE O'HANLON.
The Unforeseen. | Chance? or Fate?

Two-Shilling Novels—*continued.*

By GEORGES OHNET.
Doctor Rameau. | A Last Love.

By Mrs. OLIPHANT.
Whiteladies. | The Primrose Path.
The Greatest Heiress in England.

By Mrs. ROBERT O'REILLY.
Phœbe's Fortunes.

By OUIDA.
Held in Bondage. | Two Little Wooden
Strathmore. | Shoes.
Chandos. | Ariadne.
Under Two Flags. | Friendship.
Idalia. | Moths.
CecilCastlemaine's | Pipistrello.
Gage. | A Village Com-
Tricotrin. | mune.
Puck. | Bimbi.
Folle Farine. | Wanda.
A Dog of Flanders. | Frescoes.
Pascarel. | In Maremma.
Signa. | Othmar.
Princess Naprax- | Guilderoy.
ine. | Ouida's Wisdom,
In a Winter City. | Wit, and Pathos.

MARGARET AGNES PAUL.
Gentle and Simple.

By JAMES PAYN.
Bentinck's Tutor. | £200 Reward.
Murphy's Master. | Marine Residence.
A County Family. | Mirk Abbey.
At Her Mercy. | By Proxy.
Cecil's Tryst. | Under One Roof.
Clyffards of Clyffe. | High Spirits.
Foster Brothers. | Carlyon's Year.
Found Dead. | From Exile.
Best of Husbands. | For Cash Only.
Walter's Word. | Kit.
Halves. | The Canon's Ward
Fallen Fortunes. | Talk of the Town.
Humorous Stories. | Holiday Tasks.
Lost Sir Massingberd.
A Perfect Treasure.
A Woman's Vengeance.
The Family Scapegrace.
What He Cost Her.
Gwendoline's Harvest.
Like Father, Like Son.
Married Beneath Him.
Not Wooed, but Won.
Less Black than We're Painted.
A Confidential Agent.
Some Private Views.
A Grape from a Thorn.
Glow-worm Tales.
The Mystery of Mirbridge.

By C. L. PIRKIS.
Lady Lovelace.

By EDGAR A. POE.
The Mystery of Marie Roget.

By E. C. PRICE.
Valentina. | The Foreigners.
Mrs. Lancaster's Rival.
Gerald.

Two-Shilling Novels—*continued.*

By CHARLES READE.
It is Never Too Late to Mend.
Christie Johnstone.
Put Yourself in His Place.
The Double Marriage.
Love Me Little, Love Me Long.
The Cloister and the Hearth.
The Course of True Love.
Autobiography of a Thief.
A Terrible Temptation.
The Wandering Heir.
Singleheart and Doubleface.
Good Stories of Men and other Animals.

Hard Cash.	A Simpleton.
Peg Woffington.	Readiana.
Griffith Gaunt.	A Woman-Hater.
Foul Play.	The Jilt.

By Mrs. J. H. RIDDELL.
Weird Stories. | Fairy Water.
Her Mother's Darling.
Prince of Wales's Garden Party.
The Uninhabited House.
The Mystery in Palace Gardens.

By F. W. ROBINSON.
Women are Strange.
The Hands of Justice.

By JAMES RUNCIMAN.
Skippers and Shellbacks.
Grace Balmaign's Sweetheart.
Schools and Scholars.

By W. CLARK RUSSELL.
Round the Galley Fire.
On the Fo'k'sle Head.
In the Middle Watch.
A Voyage to the Cape.
A Book for the Hammock.
The Mystery of the "Ocean Star."
The Romance of Jenny Harlowe.
An Ocean Tragedy.

GEORGE AUGUSTUS SALA.
Gaslight and Daylight.

By JOHN SAUNDERS.
Guy Waterman. | Two Dreamers.
The Lion in the Path.

By KATHARINE SAUNDERS.
Joan Merryweather. | Heart Salvage.
The High Mills. | Sebastian.
Margaret and Elizabeth.

By GEORGE R. SIMS.
Rogues and Vagabonds.
The Ring o' Bells.
Mary Jane's Memoirs.
Mary Jane Married.
Tales of To-day. | Dramas of Life.
Tinkletop's Crime.

By ARTHUR SKETCHLEY.
A Match in the Dark.

By T. W. SPEIGHT.
The Mysteries of Heron Dyke.
The Golden Hoop. | By Devious Ways.
Hoodwinked, &c.

Two-Shilling Novels—*continued.*

By R. A. STERNDALE.
The Afghan Knife.

By R. LOUIS STEVENSON.
New Arabian Nights. | Prince Otto.

BY BERTHA THOMAS.
Cressida. | Proud Maisie.
The Violin-player.

By WALTER THORNBURY.
Tales for the Marines.
Old Stories Re-told.

T. ADOLPHUS TROLLOPE.
Diamond Cut Diamond.

By F. ELEANOR TROLLOPE.
Like Ships upon the Sea.
Anne Furness. | Mabel's Progress.

By ANTHONY TROLLOPE.
Frau Frohmann. | Kept in the Dark.
Marion Fay. | John Caldigate.
The Way We Live Now.
The American Senator.
Mr. Scarborough's Family.
The Land-Leaguers.
The Golden Lion of Granpere.

By J. T. TROWBRIDGE.
Farnell's Folly.

By IVAN TURGENIEFF, &c.
Stories from Foreign Novelists.

By MARK TWAIN.
Tom Sawyer. | A Tramp Abroad.
The Stolen White Elephant.
A Pleasure Trip on the Continent.
Huckleberry Finn.
Life on the Mississippi.
The Prince and the Pauper.

By C. C. FRASER-TYTLER.
Mistress Judith.

By SARAH TYTLER.
The Bride's Pass. | Noblesse Oblige.
Buried Diamonds. | Disappeared.
Saint Mungo's City. | Huguenot Family.
Lady Bell. | Blackhall Ghosts.
What She Came Through.
Beauty and the Beast.
Citoyenne Jaqueline.

By J. S. WINTER.
Cavalry Life. | Regimental Legends.

By H. F. WOOD.
The Passenger from Scotland Yard.
The Englishman of the Rue Cain.

By Lady WOOD.
Sabina.

CELIA PARKER WOOLLEY.
Rachel Armstrong; or, Love & Theology

By EDMUND YATES.
The Forlorn Hope. | Land at Last.
Castaway.

$$\frac{R}{200}$$

14 DAY USE
RETURN TO DESK FROM WHICH BORROWED

LOAN DEPT.

This book is due on the last date stamped below, or
on the date to which renewed.
Renewed books are subject to immediate recall.